FRANCIS BRETT YOUNG
(1884–1954)

Born at Halesowen, Worcestershire, the son of
a doctor. Educated at Epsom College, he
studied medicine at Birmingham University and
practised at Brixham from 1907 until 1914.
Married Jessie Hankinson, a singer, in 1907.
During World War One he served with the
Royal Army Medical Corps in East Africa.
Invalided out, he settled with his wife in Capri
but returned to England in 1932. His first novel,
Deep Sea, was published in 1914, but his
great success was *Portrait of Clare* (1927)
which was awarded the Tait Black Memorial
Prize. Ill health forced him to leave his
Worcestershire home in 1945 for the sunnier
climes of South Africa – where several of his
books were set. He died in Capetown in 1954.

The City of Gold is the result of many years
of research and describes a country that he
knew personally and loved. It is part of an
incomplete trilogy of which the first book was
They Seek a Country.

By the same author
in Mayflower Books

MY BROTHER JONATHAN

The City of Gold
Francis Brett Young

A Mayflower Paperback

THE CITY OF GOLD
Francis Brett Young

This edition Copyright © C. Combridge Ltd.
1966

First published in 1939

Published as a Mayflower Paperback 1971

*Mayflower Paperbacks are published
by Mayflower Books,
3 Upper James Street, London, W.1.
Made and printed in Great Britain by
Cox & Wyman Ltd., London, Reading and Fakenham*

for
Florence Phillips
and to the memory of
Lionel Phillips

AUTHOR'S NOTE

THE historical sources of this novel are so many and so various, comprising the research and reading of more than twenty years, that it would be irksome to compile a full list of 'authorities'; but, as in the case of *They Seek a Country*, I wish to record my major indebtedness. For the period of Burgers' Presidency I have relied on Carter (the historian of the First Boer War) and Aylward, the picturesque ex-Fenian journalist who wrote *The Transvaal of Today*, 1878. Early Kimberley emerges most vividly from the suppressed Reminiscences of Mr. L. Cohen. Cecil Rhodes – a heavily documented figure – derives not only from the biographies of Michell and Sarah Millin and Colvin's *Life of Jameson*, but also – and even more clearly – from the record of his speeches edited by 'Vindex'. For the contentious subject of the Jameson Raid I have balanced the claims of Fitzpatrick's *Transvaal from Within* against the Blue Books of the British and Cape Governments and the Green Book of the South African Republic in which the sworn evidence of the protagonists is set down. In my account of early Johannesburg I am indebted to a lively book *Out of the Crucible* by Hedley Chilvers and a mass of contemporary newspapers; while the incident of the 'diggers for treasure' was suggested to me by a passage in a letter sent to me by an Eastern Lady. As a final court of appeal in matters of historical fact I have accepted the Cambridge History of the British Empire and Professor Eric Walker's admirable *History of South Africa*. Many valuable details have come to me by word of mouth, and in twenty years of study I have actually read more than a hundred printed works which bear on the subject; my personal contribution, indeed, is limited to the descriptions of the country which I have known and loved. My friend Sir Edward Marsh has dealt patiently with nearly nine hundred pages of proof-correcting, and Mrs. A. E. Coppard has kept a jealous eye on my Afrikaans.

Book One

CHAPTER ONE

(1)

LISBET sat on the stoep at Wonderfontein and waited for her husband, John Grafton – or 'Jan', as everyone called him – to come home from the lands. It was late in the afternoon of a day in early winter: the hour and the season in which the High Veld reveals itself in the height of its loveliness. Lisbet Grafton knew every aspect of Wonderfontein; she had loved the place and belonged to it now for thirty-two years, ever since the day when, trekking over the Drakensberg out of Natal, her young husband and she had out-spanned their wagon-team and encamped by the spring of clear water from which they had taken its name. It was here, on the southern slope of the Witwatersrand, that in lonely travail she had borne her eldest son, Adrian. It was here that she and John had built their first house of sun-dried brick thatched with grass, and broken the soil to plant their first patch of mealies. It was here that the rest of their long family of ten had been born. She had seen the farm and her children grow side by side, in a life so fully occupied that she rarely had leisure to notice the changes time wrought in either, or even the change in herself. Yet, however Wonderfontein itself and the folk who inhabited it might change, the great prospect that lay before it and had captured her heart more than thirty years since, still had power to enthral and strengthen it – never more than on such an afternoon as this, never more than in this precise moment.

She knew such moments well. They came, in the earlier days of the High Veld winter, at the hour when the sun would seem to have reached the culmination of its trajectory; when the force which had hurled it into the zenith at dawn began, as it seemed, to wane; when it appeared, for a moment, to falter on the verge of its majestic decline towards the horizons of molten earth and fiery vapour its heat had kindled – that mysterious distance into which before long its red-hot plummet would plunge and be extinguished. This final transfiguration had always moved her

9

more poignantly than the paler fire of dawn, proclaiming day, or the full splendour of noontide; for dawn may be shrewd, intimidating in its uncertainties, and the heat of noon may be cruel; while this latter hour of gold, preceding brief twilight and star-frosted night, bred a sense of tranquillity in which the heart seemed to expand – and more especially the hearts of those like herself, who were no longer young, and with whose sober mood this moment seemed consonant.

At such times the life of mankind, as that of all nature, became lulled and suspended. The eyes were no longer dazzled with light, but caressed by it. There was no influence against which mind or body had need to oppose unconscious resistance. The tissues of brain and muscle quietly relaxed; one absorbed, through the pores of one's skin as it were, an essence that made human beings feel themselves one (as the light made their bodies one) with earth, air, and their numberless denizens: with the still, scattered thorns and grey brushwood twigs tipped with fire, the veld-grass, in its motionless dips and billows of pallid gold; the sparse birds awakening to drowsy song; the myriad floating specks of insect life newly made visible, each vibrant wing imprisoning light in its gauzy nets; with those immeasurable flawless depths of the upper air, which sight can hardly sound, where, in regions of thin and glacial purity, vultures wheel and float like motes in a sunbeam.

There were vultures wheeling now in the upper air. Lisbet Grafton, watching them idly, wondered what marvels were seen by their tawny, gluttonous eyes; for those eyes were keener, their sight reached farther, than hers. They could see on the veld, it was said (for it was sight, not scent, John told her, that dragged them down, visibly swooping earthward on tattered pinions) – they could see from a height of thousands of feet their choice carrion: the bloated hulk of a foundered trex-ox, a wounded buck, a sick lamb, or the mangled kill that lions had left at sunrise on the edge of their dongas. (There were no lions near Wonderfontein now, thank goodness, though in the year when their first house was built John had shot half a dozen!) They could see, she told herself, from those dizzy stations, a hundred thousand square miles of this country called the Transvaal – not the still sea of winter-stricken grass which her eyes now beheld, but one vast spread of golden carpet drenched with light, unrolled between two steely tracks of Vaal and Limpopo – the whole sweep of the High Veld, its surface unbroken by any

10

flaw but here and there irregular slow-moving shapes which resembled shadows of cloud, but in fact were herds of game that grazed as they strayed.

They could see, Lisbet Grafton thought, the northern mountain massifs, Magaliesberg, Waterberg, Zoutpansberg, not as the mighty monsters they were, but dwarfed and fore-shortened, their deep kloofs clogged with the moss of tiger-haunted forests – and the thought of the distant Zoutpansberg suddenly troubled her, bringing into her mind the face of her second son Andries, who, more adventurous than the rest (save her poor Dirk and Sarel, who had fallen in the Basuto war), had broken away with his wife – a girl in whom, for the life of her, she could see nothing – and trekked northwards to settle near Schoemansdal more than three years ago. They had never heard a word from Andries since then, and she knew that no white man's life was secure on that smouldering frontier: she had heard, though her husband and sons tried to keep the tale from her, of the sack of the Schoemansdal settlement and the almost too late relief of the starving laager at Marabastad. But now men spoke of a new insurgent chief in the North – Sekukuni. John said that no news was good news. Perhaps he was right. His mind was more solid and reasonable than hers, she admitted. It was like him, too, to realize what she, alas, found it so hard to accept: that the unknown was always beset with unreasoning terror. And what could she do for Andries, in any case? The boy's nature had always been fierce and turbulent, like her brother Barend's, their neighbour, who never spoke to them. It came, she supposed, from the Bezuidenhout strain in their race. Andries had made his own life and his ways were no longer theirs – if indeed they had ever been theirs. When she thought of him now it was usually as she remembered him when he was a baby – protectively. That was why she had felt that quick shiver of anxiety for him now, far away in the mountainous savagery of the Zoutpansberg – though, heaven knew, her Andries (or this strange young woman's Andries) could look after himself better than most!

Still, these endless Kaffir wars, Lisbet thought, were real and terrible enough for those who had known them – even though the men of her family hadn't actually fought in one since the day when John (with her boys Dirk and Sarel, who had not come back) had ridden away to join the Free State commandos against Moshesh and the Basutos. Yes, life was full of reminders that would never let her forget the horrors of the Blauwkrans massacre, from which she and John had escaped in the year before they were married. Why, the very wagon-bench on which she now sat on the stoep, looking up to the pellucid winter sky and the wheeling vultures, still carried the scars cut by Zulu assegais, and traces of charring by fire which not even thirty-four years of waxing and polishing had erased. She could feel the smoothed clefts in the hard wood now as her hand strayed over them. And her memory, too, carried scars that no lapse of time could obliterate.

Such reminders were better disregarded, she told herself, picking up the thread of thought she had dropped, compelling herself to renew her fanciful speculations on what the vultures' eyes saw. They must see, she thought, the long ridge of the Witwatersrand – a mere crinkle or crease such as a careless ironer might have left in the cloth of gold. They must see, looking down, the string of farms scattered along its southern declivity, each named from its fountain: Sterkfontein, her brother Barend's farm a few miles to eastward, hardly separable by sight from the unclaimed veld around it – for Barend, like generations of Prinsloos before him, was herd rather than husbandman – and deserted now, since in winter he took to his wagon and drove his cattle north-east to graze in the Low Veld; next, Wonderfontein itself, the pride of her heart and her husband's, with its trim, whitewashed steading, its fruitful garth, its red tilth and its paddocks – which even now, when winter had nipped them, lay emerald green in the network of water furrows which John had planned.

Then, westward again, they would see Witfontein, the farm of her third son Janse, so named after his father and her kinsman, Janse van Rensburg, a poor place indeed by comparison with Wonderfontein, though its poverty was surely excusable when one considered that Janse was lame, poor boy, and lived there alone with no more than one Hottentot and a couple of Kaffirs to help him. She was always ready to make excuses for Janse when John or her other sons showed their impatience with him. Quite apart from his lameness – a misfortune that would never have happened if there had been a skilled doctor within reach at the time when the charging buffalo smashed his thigh-bone – he was different from the others in looks as well as in temperament: a failure, by common standards, no doubt, yet in some ways more like herself than the other boys, having a

12

larger share of the French Huguenot blood which had come to her through her mother Jacoba Celliers. That was why she had been glad in her heart when he had left them and taken up Witfontein, bad farmer though he might be, for, although she missed him, she knew he had inward resources that made him happy in solitude, his private dreams undisturbed.

Nor need Janse be really so lonely, she thought; for there, on his western boundary, in a fold of the veld which the vultures could see though she couldn't, stood the fourth and perhaps the richest of all those farms – Brakfontein, the home of a middle-aged Englishman – or half-Irishman – from the diamond-fields named Haskard, who had settled there some years since with his wife and two children (how small English families were!) in the hope of healing a sick lung with the pure High Veld air. She was happy to think that Janse had the Haskards for neighbours and friends. Though she hardly knew them at all – her husband though born in England himself, was always restive and ill at ease in English company – she was aware (and a trifle envious, too) of the fact that the Haskards' life was richer and easier and wider in its interests than their own life at Wonderfontein. The Haskards were sojourners in the land; they did not even pretend to belong to it. The perils – even the catastrophes – of a farmer's lot – drought, locusts, cattle-diseases – did not shadow their lives. If disaster came, Major Haskard could cut his losses, write a cheque and begin all over again. Brakfontein was always in touch with the outer world, an open house of call for officials and travellers and officers from the Cape garrison out on a hunting-trip. The Haskards had monthly parcels of English books and music and newspapers; they knew, and took trouble to know, what civilized folk were thinking and writing and saying. The children had both been well educated at the Cape: Lavinia Haskard even possessed a piano and played it, as Janse said, brilliantly. When he spoke of Lavinia, who was only a few years younger than himself, Lisbet thought she had detected in Janse a tone of controlled excitement. But this rather amused her than made her jealous. She felt it was lucky for all of them that it was Janse and not one of her other sons who had taken up Witfontein; Janse, she knew, was the only member of her family who could appreciate the advantages conferred on him by his neighbours' culture and wealth.

It was their wealth, of course, that made their more gracious life and their children's culture possible – the money that

13

poured unceasingly into the bank at Kimberley while James Haskard played at farming on the Witwatersrand and healed his lung; and the thought of this gushing source of an unearned prosperity, so prodigious compared with the minute hoard which she and her husband, starting with nothing but their portion of the wagons and herds they had driven up from Natal, had scraped together from the face of their niggardly veld, turned her thoughts and her eyes towards the southern horizon, where the golden air thickened above the River Vaal, beyond which the new town of Kimberley, only three years ago undreamt-of and still incredible, now lay hot with the ant-like seething of over ten thousand inhabitants.

She had never seen Kimberley, and doubted if she ever would see it. When the miraculous stories of the first diamond finds at Hopetown had reached the Transvaal (it was Mr. Meninsky, the little Jew trader, who brought the news to Wonderfontein) the farming folk who met in the quarterly gossip-exchange of Natchmaal made light of them. The damned English, they said, were always eager to drop honest work and chase some new hare. Gold, diamonds, this new-fangled truck over which they lost their heads, were too easily come-by to last. In a year or two the excitement would be forgotten; the diggers, men sadder if not wiser, would slink back to their ruined farms or come begging charity. But the search for diamonds, the finding of diamonds went on. From Hopetown to the Vaal River diggings and back to the dry diggings; and then, of a sudden, at Vooruitsicht, the richest find of all, on which the hungry myriads swarmed and settled and burrowed like ants that pick the bones of a carcase.

So Kimberley came: a pitted camp of tents and tin shanties set up in a treeless desert and girt by leagues of knee-deep sand, where a man could earn more in a week by bossing-up natives than the shrewdest of farmers could drag out of the land in half a lifetime. Old farmers scratched their heads and muttered still of Achan the son of Carmi the son of Zabdi the son of Zerah, saying that no good would come of touching the accursed thing; but their sons, more quick-witted and more adventurous, saw that, even without touching the accursed thing, money could be had for the asking by any man who possessed a bullock-wagon and cared to go transport-riding, dragging fuel and farm-produce and goods through the sand-belt to Kimberley, coming home light, with wagons empty and pockets full.

John Grafton, poor though he was, would have none of it. There were too many English in Kimberley, he said, for his liking – and indeed he was right, for within two years the diggings had been annexed and the English law, of which he was frightened (and how could she blame him?), ran there – if any law ran! Now would Adrian, farmer all through like his forbears, forsake his lands. But Piet, her youngest, her darling, would give them no peace till they let him go transport-riding with one of the rickety wagons that had survived the Great Trek.

Lisbet Grafton had let him go reluctantly. In some ways these mild journeys of his to Kimberley seemed to her more perilous than Andries' migration to the turbulent Zoutpansberg. The predikant, her old friend Mr. Blair, had warned them all from the pulpit what this Kimberley was: a new City of the Plain wherein God was neither heard nor worshipped, a new Babel of tongues, resort and refuge of the froward – men of Belial, whose whoredoms and drunkenness and violence cried aloud to heaven for punishment. And her Piet was so young, so guileless, so innocent! When he first rode transport to Kimberley a year ago, in the days when it was still called New Rush, he had been barely seventeen, in her eyes a mere child, though the males of her race reached maturity early; and indeed, up till now, his manners had seemed none the worse for these evil communications, while the money he brought back from Babel had helped them to face the results of the last year of drought, which had broken others. There was, moreover, a certain hardness in Piet, an appropriately diamond-like hardness that had shown itself even when he was a child, in the steadfastness of his eyes, the firm lines of his mouth. Though he wasn't so 'fine' a man as her first-born Adrian, who stood six foot three and appeared fantastically large for the fruit of so small a body as hers, Piet's brain was clearer than Adrian's, his nature stronger. He was as bold and self-reliant as Andries, but not so reckless. He had as much imagination as Janse, though its kind – and the way in which he used it – was different. Piet had always known what he wanted, and not only got it far sooner than anyone expected, but also was wise enough to refrain from saying 'I told you so' – though sometimes the shape of his firm young mouth (which she knew so well) implied that challenge. Yes, Piet could look after himself, Lisbet Grafton decided, as well as any of them.

Even so, she was always relieved when the empty wagons came back from Kimberley. It was so easy for an adventurous young man, however virtuous, to find himself caught up innocently in one of the brawls which made the place a scandal that cried to heaven, to be waylaid and robbed – or even murdered – outside it by some gang of the desperate foreign adventurers who lived by their wits – more particularly because transport-riders habitually travelled in darkness. Ever since noon that day – by which time she had expected him home – she had felt a trifle uneasy about Piet. Now, focusing her dreamy eyes more sharply, she searched the southern plain for the reassuring sight of the rising dust-clouds which, even at a distance, betrayed the wagon's approach.

There was no dust rising in the south-west from the track to Kimberley – only the blank sweep of golden veld which had now darkened to apricot and in a few moments more would turn blood-red; but farther west, where her eyes idly moved to mark how the sun was sinking, there was not only a cloud of dust but also a single-horse cape-cart, a long shadow moving before it and the shape of its tilt defined like a cut silhouette of black paper against the flaming sky; and when Lisbet Grafton saw this familiar shape her grave and tired but still rather sweet lips smiled. She rose from the war-scarred wagon bench and crossed the stoep to call through the door of the *voorhuis* to Maria, her youngest daughter, the family's baby.

'Heat some coffee, my little heart,' she said. 'The predikant's coming.'

(2)

Lisbet, standing on the stoep, watched the slow approach of Mr. Blair's cape-cart over the darkening land. When it reached the block of chocolate-coloured outbuildings, which had been the original dwelling-house at Wonderfontein, she saw Klass, the old Hottentot servant, run out to meet him. Deliberately, Mr. Blair's tall black figure dismounted. Between them they unharnessed the bony horse, let him roll for a moment, then set him straying, knee-haltered, to feed on the grass that tufted the arid soil. From the back of the shadowed stoep, unseen Lisbet saw Blair turn and move stiffly, slowly up the steep garden path.

16

Once he paused and threw back his head to take breath. She watched him compassionately. When she saw him stop for breath she was moved by a maternal solicitude (not so strange, after all, in one who had been the mother of eight sons) for the helplessness of an old man.

Now that the gold had gone out of the sky Mr. Blair's upturned face, with the heavily-furrowed skin that clothed its bones as loosely as the skirted frock-coat of his calling hung from his shoulders, was almost as white as his wispy beard. Of course he was old – at least seventy-six, she reckoned – and older in arduous experience even than in years. She had thought of Mr. Blair as elderly when first she had known him, herself a child at Welgelegen in the Assegai Bush; yet it came to her now as a shock when she remembered how thirty-five years ago (and it seemed but a day) he had asked her to marry him in the laagered camp at Winburg. Supposing she had married him, she thought – as but for her being in love with John she might easily have done! It would have been strange for a woman who felt as young as she felt now to be tied to this tired, old man, so frosty and brittle, for whom, in spite of her relative youth, she could not but have felt protective and motherly. Yet her heart warmed towards Mr. Blair as she saw him approach, and he greeted her too with a smile of friendliness that brought life into his sagging features and the firm, kindly eyes beneath their prodigious thicket of eyebrow. He was her oldest friend and John's too. If John's children had been his own he could not have been more concerned for them.

'This is a happy surprise,' she said. 'It's so long since we have seen you.'

'A long time. Too long. Since last Nachtmaal, when you came to the dorp. But my ears are open and my eyes are not bad: I know all is well with you.'

'Well enough. Sit down now: the air is still warm and pleasant on the stoep. Maria is making the coffee. Let us drink it here before the air grows cold. You look tired, my friend.'

'No, not tired ... not tired. I grow older: that is all, Lisbet. And life doesn't grow more easy, that is the trouble. My garden is full of tares and the labour grows harder.'

'Your garden?'

'My spiritual garden, I mean.' He laughed softly. 'God's rule is so simple. Just three words: Love one another. And yet they

17

won't. Was there ever such a people for quarrelling as yours, Lisbet?'

'How should I know?'

'Or I, for that matter. Perhaps human beings are much the same the world over. We've no means of knowing. But sometimes, you know, I wonder if there may not be something in the air of this country of ours: too high, too exciting, too restless. It's a blessing sometimes to get away from the dorp and find oneself among people like John and you, who don't spend all their time in talking and, when they talk, don't talk dogma or politics.'

Lisbet smiled. 'Don't make any mistake; we have plenty of politics here – particularly now that Adrian's a member of the Raad and comes back from Pretoria boiling with all the latest grievances.'

'Is Adrian at home? That's a good lad, your Adrian. I wish there were more of his kind.'

'Yes, Adrian's at home. He came back from Pretoria last night. The Raad has dismissed Pretorius. Have you heard? John and he will be in before dark. And here comes Maria with your coffee. Set it down on the bench between us, my child.'

The predikant turned with a smile. 'Let me have a good look at you, my dear. Gracious, how your baby grows! How old are you, Maria?'

'Fourteen,' the child said. Her voice had a deep melodious quality, by no means childish, which reminded the predikant instantly of that of Lisbet's mother, Jacoba Prinsloo. She was tall for her age, in shape already a woman, with a sweet but rather solemn face, her grey eyes wide apart and shadowed by brows which were not only too straightly set for beauty, in a manner which gave her a look of grave concentration beyond her years, but also jet-black, as though drawn by one determined sweep of a brush dipped in Indian ink, in strange contrast to the thick plaits of her hair, the colour of dark honey, which hung down on either side of a face that still was childish – and now, beneath the scrutiny of the predikant's critical gaze, a trifle embarrassed.

'She is like you, Lisbet,' he said, 'as you were at Welgelegen.'

'No, no, not like me,' her mother protested, smiling. 'If the light were less dim you'd see that her eyes are almost blue, not hazel, and her hair is not dark, as mine used to be before it

18

turned grey, though she's blessed with what John always called my self-willed eyebrows.'

'Yes, perhaps I am wrong. At my age one tends to see ghosts. But her mouth is determined, like yours, you know.'

'Let's say no more about it or we shall make the child shy.' She went on in Dutch: 'Does Sarie know that the predikant's come for the night, my little one? He must have the best bed.'

'*Ja, mamma,* she knows: I told her as soon as you called; she is making ready.'

'Go and help her, then, Maria – and you, my friend, drink your coffee or it will go cold. It is not such good coffee as I should have wished to give you, and yet, do you know, Piet paid four shillings a pound for it in Kimberley! The diamond-fields send up the price of everything.'

Mr. Blair shook his head. 'That is not the worst thing the diamond-fields have done for us. There are times when I wish they had never been discovered. Our people begin to think too much about money.'

Lisbet laughed. 'We may well do that nowadays, when you think that all the blue-black paper-money we've saved and put by for our children is worth less than a quarter of what is printed on it!'

'Yes, yes, that is bad, I know. But it's not what I meant. Thirty years ago when the people first came to the High Veld, our life was so clean and simple. It seemed as if we had come out of the wilderness of tribulation into the Land of Promise. We worked hard and lived soberly, as men should, and God gave us increase. Nobody was rich, and nobody had need to starve. It seemed almost too good to last, this peace, this un-troubled living . . .'

'There were always Kaffir wars.'

'Ay, but those hardly touched us here, Lisbet.'

'They touched *me*, my friend.'

'I know. I spoke too hastily. Of course you have suffered. Yet our life as a whole was peaceful and sweet and contented: one felt there could be no reason why it should change. But of late it has changed, mark my word. The diamond-fields have changed it. Those holes in the ground have released some kind of poison that has found its way into men's brains. They see the ungodly grow rich and their minds are troubled by greed and restless envy, and out of these two spring hatred and violence and bit-terness. The hand of the devil is in it.'

Lisbet smiled. 'You are not the only one who feels that. The old men are with you. Do you remember the fuss they made about that poor Mr. Baines who was Mr. Livingstone's friend, because he carried some instrument – a sextant I think they called it – and the surveyor in Potchefstroom who was mobbed because he measured land with some other sort of instrument, instead of pacing it out like the old veld-valkt master? And the Volksraad itself with their new law last year: a fine of six hundred dollars for anyone finding metals or diamonds and letting anyone else know where he's found them? My own Adrian voted for it! Would you believe it?'

Mr. Blair shook his head: 'I know well how he felt.'

'But you don't maintain he was right? Must we for ever and remain the same? We can't shut ourselves up here for ever and pretend that the world outside isn't changing. It surely wouldn't change if God didn't want it to. If new knowledge and power or even wealth come to us through our faculties or other men's faculties, shouldn't we use them?'

'That depends on how we're going to use them. I don't think the wealth that has flowed out of Kimberley has done anybody much good.'

'Poor Major Haskard!' She teased him, as thirty years ago she would not have dared.

'Ah, you've caught me out. No, I've nothing to say against Haskard. He's a kindly man, though I never liked the Irish, and I fear that the thing of the spirit don't mean much to him. I'm in his debt for the books that he lends me: they've made a great difference to me since he came here – though, mind you, I cannot say I always approve of his choice or his taste. Of course I'm old-fashioned, my dear, but these writers on Science, Darwin and Huxley, in whom he delights, appear to me dangerous and superficial influences. I called in for a moment at Brakfontein on my way here today. Your Janse was there. By the way, I ought to have given you a message. He asked me to say he was riding over tonight.'

'I'm glad. We don't see him often in these days. I'm afraid the attractions of Brakfontein are rather too strong.'

'Of Brakfontein?'

'Well ... of Lavinia if you prefer it. Poor Janse. ... You know he doesn't quite fit in here. Neither John nor Adrian – nor even Piet, for that matter – has ever understood him. His mind works so differently from theirs that they won't even try.'

'And do you?'

'Understand him? Of course. He's part of me, isn't he? Not the part that you know, my dear, and John, bless him, knows, but the part that was left behind when I finished my schooling in Capetown, the romantic part of me which I had to forget when I became a farmer's daughter at Welgelegen. But Janse is much more sensitive and alive than I ever was, and his thoughts are – what shall I say? – bolder than mine – they fly much farther. He sees beauty in things that aren't useful, only think of it! How could any of them understand that? He's bored by politics, and says so. Adrian thinks that a disgrace. He cares nothing whatever for money . . .'

'At least let's thank God for that.'

'Piet doesn't. That makes poor Janse no better than a fool in his eyes. I suppose the poor boy should really have been a poet, or a painter, or perhaps a musician. He's hungry for books and music which we can't give him. I think it is partly Lavinia's music that draws him to Brakfontein.'

'Yet you always call him "poor" Janse. Why do that if he's found what he wants and is happy?'

Lisbet Grafton hesitated: 'I'm not so sure that he is. Not that he'd ever admit it: he's much too proud. And too shy – yes, even with me. I think he is conscious most of the time of his lameness – this is no life for a man who is maimed as well as sensitive. He forgets it sometimes, of course, and then, when it comes back to him, his mind turns harsh and bitter inside. And that harshness and bitterness, you know, people feel it, most of all when he smiles as he does at those times. It shocks them and scares them away from him, and he can't think why. He sees that there's something that makes them shrink from him, so he shrinks back too, like a tortoise that draws in its head – or sometimes bristles with quills like a porcupine. They're sharp, too, Janse's quills! Ach, and he's restless, restless . . .'

'We're all restless in these days. There's unrest in the air. I tell you something is happening or going to happen. It's a fey sensation. You know, all the years we've been here I have felt as if God had rewarded our people for all their past sufferings and faithfulness by giving them as their portion this wide sunlit veld (do you mind how your father called Natal the land that had shadows?) with a blue sky above and a surface of solid ground under their feet. Now I feel – you may laugh at me, but it's true – that the earth is no longer solid. The surface is like a volcanic

21

crust, a thin crust maybe, with something hot and terrible seething beneath it. There's evil under the earth, Lisbet. Perhaps yon deep pits at Kimberley have stirred it, like the cracks in the bed of the sea which they say stir up the volcanoes, and some day, in God's time, we shall find ourselves standing on the edge of a chasm, as when the ground clave asunder and the earth opened her mouth and swallowed up all the congregation of Korah and Dathan and Abiram, their house and their goods and their wives and their little children. I feel it, my dear, I feel it and I'm afraid, though I may not live to see it, please God. I grow old and weary.' His gaunt shoulders shivered.

Lisbet laid her hand on his. 'Yes, yes, you are tired, and it's already too cold to stay here. Come in now with me and sit down in peace by the fire till the others come home.'

She took his cold bony hand and led him into the *voorhuis*. This submissiveness in one whom she had known as an iron-like man touched her deeply, yet warmed her heart. Another man to be mothered, she thought. That, it seemed, was her part in life. She had room and strength for all of them.

(3)

The moon was up by the time Janse left Brakfontein. He excused himself from the bland, lamp-lit family circle brusquely; but for the message he had sent to his mother by Mr. Blair he would gladly have accepted Mrs. Haskard's gentle persuasions to stay to supper; yet, in another way, he was glad to find a pretext for escaping. In his divided mind his increasing intimacy with the Haskards was vitiated by an under-flow of doubt and suspicion. Though nothing could have been more natural or candid than the way in which they had accepted him and welcomed him to their home, though their company and the atmosphere in which they lived had been an inexpressible boon, revealing to him in tangible shape, a world of new thoughts and new interests which miraculously (and so easily) fulfilled the vague, unexpressed aspirations which had troubled him and separated him from his own folk since he was a child, though he greedily accepted a share in so much that had been denied him, he distrusted and sometimes, in fits of exasperated pride or humiliation, almost hated his benefactors.

It was not easy – even for him – to hate the Haskards. They

were, in fact, simple people. Their culture, which alternately fascinated and intimidated Janse, was little more than the customary veneer of moderately intelligent, well-educated folk in easy circumstances. Yet the contrasts between their standards of life, their manner of thought, and those of Wonderfontein, which were perpetually engrossed in the problem of mere subsistence and stripped bare of any pretensions to ease or graciousness, aroused in him a recurrent grudging which – particularly when he felt himself most in their debt, as on this evening – he could not suppress.

At such times he rebelled against accepting his new friends at their face value. Major Haskard's bluff good-nature, his wife's gentle kindliness, were equally suspect. Both were exercised, he suspected, with the deliberate purpose of putting at his ease an outsider, who, because he happened to be their nearest neighbour (and half-English at that), must be kept on good terms, and again, because he was lame – poor fellow! – and uncouth, must be treated with a nicely-adjusted excess of consideration. *Noblesse oblige*: the virtue of the conscious superior.

Nor could he be sure of Edward, the Haskards' son, though Edward, too, seemed natural enough in all conscience and anything but patronizing. In all practical aspects of African life, in the things that really mattered, this smooth-voiced, smooth-featured young man was a child compared with him. Edward's mind moved more slowly than his – it had never known and would never know the need to move faster, having been adapted to the usage of a world in which manners (and his were delightful) were apparently the only quality essential to success. Yet though Edward's faculties were so much less awake and alive than his, because he had never had occasion to use them, Janse knew that in its actual content Edward's boyish brain was in other ways better equipped than his own – not by any deliberate effort or even will, but by a process of passive absorption, like that of a sponge that has been submerged in a solution of common knowledge, which enabled him to take for granted things that Janse had never heard of. Whenever they talked together there would come humiliating moments in which some chance phrase or allusion which had no connotation for Janse would drop clean through one of the gaping lacunae in his mind. Even the English the Haskards spoke was different from the English habitually spoken at Wonderfontein; and the fact that in Dutch, which none of the Haskards had taken the

23

trouble to acquire, they would have been equally at sea, was a small consolation: for the *taal*, at best, was no more than a local dialect, adapted to the concrete needs of a pastoral life, incapable of expressing abstractions, while English – the Haskards English – was the language in which books were written, the vehicle of the knowledge which Janse coveted and the power that sprang from it.

As for Lavinia Haskard – that was a different matter. In some ways she seemed nearer to Janse, in others more unapproachable. For though he could find in her eyes (they were dusky blue, like a hyacinth) not even that hint of contempt for himself which he suspected rather than saw in the eyes of the others, he could find little else; her thoughts were more secret than theirs, he felt that they moved in a mysterious, exquisite sphere of their own, nearer music than words, a rarefied element which he despaired of sharing or even penetrating. Yet, in spite of this unattainable spiritual aloofness, he believed she had more in common with him, the stranger, than with her own kin, and hoped, against hope, that she knew it. When she played or sang or sometimes, to please him, read poetry, there seemed to exist between them a complete understanding which had no need of speech to confirm it, a sympathy, recognized by both, that transported them to a plane on which their differences of race, of culture, of breeding, were of no account. He knew, and rejoiced in knowing, that in such things he, the uncouth barbarian, was more sensitive, more like her, understood her better than the others. He believed that she understood him, that she took count of his devastating shyness and of the humility which compelled him at times to make himself seem harsher and clumsier and bitterer than he actually was; but his very consciousness of the way in which her understanding pierced these reflex defences, gave him a sense of nakedness and vulnerability which made him take fright and withdraw himself – for he felt that, already knowing so much of his heart, she might go even farther and discover the inmost secret of all: that he was in love with her, and that his knowledge would lay him open to the risk of a humiliation he dreaded far more than contempt or condescension: her pity for his maimed limb, his poverty, his shy, proud soul. Even if she mingled love with her pity he would reject it. He was taking no qualified favours from any man or woman alive – not even from her, Lavinia, whom he already

24

loved with an aching that made the sight of her or her absence an equal torment.

A torment – yet also an exaltation transcending all other experience in its glory. When he made his abrupt and clumsy farewells to the Haskards that evening and captured his horse which had been grazing, knee-haltered, within the circle of light that streamed from the windows of Brakfontein, his brain was still dizzy with the ecstasy he had taken such pains to dissimulate. He mounted and set out eastward along the ridge. The sudden spectacle of the moonlit winter veld took his breath away. It lay blanched and immense as far as his eyes could see, the moving shadow of himself and his horse etched black upon its dull silver. There was frost in the air: the horse's breath made small clouds of moonlit vapour, and about him lay a silence so vast that it seemed to be that of all Africa. As it smote him, this sudden beauty exasperated him. How was it, he asked himself, that an emotion which he distrusted should have power to enrich the visible earth and vex his heart with new strangeness, new loveliness? He touched the horse into a tripple, and then to a canter, and then, out of need for release in some violence, to a break-neck gallop.

They went thundering over the moon-silvered veld, through the icy air. He knew there was danger in this; that at any moment an ant-bear's hole might bring down the horse and himself spinning; yet in this furious progress there was an exhilaration of pride as well as the glow that the rushing icy air whipped into his cheeks. Astride a horse he forgot his shortened thigh-bone, he was the physical equal of any man he knew, and better than most – a centaur, and were not the centaurs more than men, with the blood of a god in their veins? Here, at least, was a physical mastery and glory that life could not deny to him.

He strode straight as an arrow, without pause till he saw on the outskirts of Wonderfontein the glow-worm light of fires the natives had kindled. There were several – which meant that visitors had arrived, and this guess was confirmed, when he drew nearer, by the sight of three wagons outspanned, their trek-touws and empty yokes stretched out in front of them, as well as the predikant's cape-cart. Two of the wagons he recognized as belonging to Wonderfontein; it was evident that Piet had come home; but the ownership of the third was unknown to him, though he marked that the well-greased axles were plastered, as were those of Piet's, with the Vaal's yellow sand.

For a moment he hesitated. In his present mood of unrest he was in no humour for the company of strangers. He was more of a mind to turn back unseen to Witfontein. But the memory of his promise to his mother and the obvious fact that his horse, unused to such violent proceedings, was thoroughly blown, decided him to remain. He yelled for the old Hottentot, Klaas, who came running towards him through the firelight, and told him to fasten a blanket round the beast's belly and tie him up under cover as soon as he had rolled. He asked whose the strange wagon was. Klaas could not tell him. There were two *base*, one young and one older, though even he was not very old, whom his brother Piet had picked up with a broken disselboom and helped on the way from Kimberley. He thought by their speech they were Englishmen, and one of them wore a beard. Their servant, a Griqua, said they were on the way to Baas Haskard's at Brakfontein, but the *ou baas* (the head of the house, in other words) had told them it was too late to go on with tired oxen and said they must eat in the house before going to sleep in their wagon.

Janse grunted and left him, repeating his orders for the care of his horse. He was not sorry to hear that the strangers had failed to reach Brakfontein. The fewer young men from Kimberley there, the better he was pleased. He made his way between his mother's rose hedgerows and mounted the stoep.

(4)

Janse opened the upper half of the double door and looked inside. He saw the whole length of the high-roofed *voorhuis* misted with the reek of rope-tobacco, which, wreathing upward through candlelight, like wisps of mare's-tail cloud in a windy sky, became lost amid the smoke-blackened beams and in the dark recesses, cluttered with stores and lumber, beneath the thatch.

At the head of the table, facing him, he saw his father, John Grafton, a vigorous man in the early fifties, spare and sinewy, with a dark beard, carefully trimmed, but streaked with grey. On his father's right, in the place of honour, sat the predikant, to whose rugged features, set in their mane of silver, the smoke-wreathed atmosphere gave an aspect fierce and prophetic.

Facing Mr. Blair, with the narrow table between them, sat the eldest son Adrian, a golden-bearded giant whose massive frame made his father, well-built as he was, appear almost frail, and the predikant, for all his prophetic fire, fragile, and mortally old. Adrian looked precisely what he was: a back-veld farmer, begotten and born and bred under the tilt of a wagon. His sun-tanned, heavy-featured face, less intelligent and less sensitive than his father's, gave an impression of straightness and resolution. His pale blue eyes appeared to see life simply without half-tones and to confront it without fear.

None of these three noticed Janse standing framed in the doorway, or heard his step on the ant-heap floor when he entered. Nor yet did his brother Piet, a fair, broad-shouldered young man with keen, lively eyes, a humorous mouth, and a slight, well-knit figure which, even as he sat at ease, expressed the tension of an eager, inquisitive mind unwilling to let the least word of practical importance escape it. They were all, as were his two sisters, Sarie and little Maria, intently listening to the elder of the two Englishmen, a tall man, with a pleasant, unaffected voice and a friendly enthusiasm, who, sitting on Lisbet's right, at the nearer end of the table, was recounting with expansive gestures, between heroic puffs of smoke from a meerschaum pipe, a story that seemed to entertain the whole company. He, too, was enjoying himself far too much to notice Janse.

But Lisbet, his mother, was instantly aware of his presence. She turned her head quickly, smiling: and Janse, seeing her, thought how sensitive and vivid she was – this grey-haired woman with the slight shape of a girl, whose face, softened by candlelight, amused and gently excited, now seemed to him so radiantly young and alive. No other woman – not even Lavinia, – could match that gay tenderness.

'Ah, Janse,' she said. 'So you've come at last! Have you eaten? Yes? That is good.' She turned to the guest apologetically. 'I'm sorry I interrupted you. The world is so far from us here that we want to hear everything. This is Janse, my third son, who lives at Witfontein.'

The Englishman smiled and nodded, with a casual 'How d'e do?' He knitted his brows: 'Where was I?'

Lisbet laughed. 'Sugar-planting in Natal.'

'Ah, yes. Of course. I assure you the job was no joke. The steamy heat and the mosquitoes alone made it intolerable – quite apart from bore-worm. No money in sugar either. So Charles Rudd, the fellow I spoke of, and three others from the Twentieth, and I and my young brother here, decided to cut away and have a shot at the Diggings – I'm a bit of a rolling stone, I'm afraid at the best of times, and the idea of a change just suited my book. So off we went, and fetched up at Klipfontein, and then on to Vooruitzicht: extremely odd – wasn't it? – that the old chap who owned the farm should have given it that name. Means "Foresight", they tell me. It was round about there that I first saw your son. When he helped us out with that broken disselboom today, I tried to speak Dutch to him. You could have knocked me down when he came back in English, I give you my word.'

'My husband, of course, is English,' Lisbet explained. 'But I am pure Dutch – a regular Boer *vrou*.'

'Well, I should never have believed it, ma'am – and I can't even now.'

Lisbet smiled. Glancing swiftly along the table, she saw that Janse was smiling too. They usually smiled at the same things. But there was no smile on Adrian's face. It darkened; his big hands lay clenched on the table in front of him. 'Dear, dear. Now for politics!' she thought.

'And you liked Kimberley better than Natal, I hope?' she said nervously.

'If we'd turned up earlier we should have made a sight more money – although, mind you, we've not done so badly. And we missed the almighty muddle and disorder the place was in under the Free State Government and poor Stafford Parker's ridiculous Diggers' Republic. We got there just in time to see the good old flag go up for the Annexation.'

'For the theft, you mean, sir.' The deep voice was Adrian's.

The stranger jumped as though he had sat down on a wasps' nest. Janse smiled at the pained surprise or hurt innocence on his good-humoured (and really rather charming) face.

'I beg your pardon?'

'The theft, sir,' Adrian repeated. 'You may call it an Annexation if you like, but barefaced theft it was. The Diggings belong by right to the two republics. Until diamonds were found, not a soul ever questioned their right. The Diggings were stolen, by fraud. Can I put it more plainly?'

'Well ... hardly.' The stranger stroked his beard meditatively. 'No, I really don't think you can.'

Janse saw him shoot a swift glance, that was half-humorous protest and half an appeal, towards his younger companion, whom he had described as his brother. Up till now he had hardly noticed the second visitor, so unobtrusively had he established himself in a leather-thonged chair by the angle of the fire, where the candlelight scarcely reached him. He had sat there completely silent and out of the picture: a lanky, overgrown youth, inappropriately dressed in shrunken white flannel trousers and a brown jacket, much too small for him, both its pockets bulging with the shapes of what might have been books. He sat there with his left hand on his crossed knee, the right firmly clutching the arm of his chair. Protruding from his unbuttoned flannel shirt was a short neck supporting a square, sun-blistered face, hook-nosed like an owl's, and surmounted again by a vigorous tousle of fair, curly hair. As he examined that face, with its large, heavy-lidded eyes and flushed cheeks, it occurred to Adrian that the silence of this ungainly, slovenly youth actually carried more weight than his brother's loquacity. The mute appeal which had been launched at him passed unheeded. His lips, which drooped slightly at the corners, did not move. He took one of the books from his bulging coat-pocket, and opened it, though he could not see to read. The other, embarrassed by the silence, went floundering on:

'Well, of course, you know, I'm no politician,' he said; 'but I thought the award, or whatever they call it, was made by a referee accepted by both sides, Mr. Keate of Natal, and – well, generally accepted as all for the best. It certainly rescued the Diamond Fields from chaos. I've heard nothing against it in Kimberley.'

'In Kimberley? Of course you wouldn't. The riff-raff of Kimberley have only one thought – to make money quickly. And they're none too particular how they make it, I'm told. But if you think Keate's award is accepted in the Free State or here in the Transvaal, you're much mistaken, sir. It was a fraud, based on falsified evidence. Jan Brand, the Free State president, didn't know it was false. But the English lawyers knew it and laughed up their sleeves. I wish to God those accursed diamonds had never been found!'

'Well, well. .... You can't say the Republics haven't gained

29

by them, anyway. The Free State, which was damn near broke –
if you'll excuse my saying so – got ninety thousand pounds
sterling to save their bacon. The fellows who go transport-
riding, like your brother here, pick up money for jam. Kimberley pays through the nose for what it buys from you, too. Eggs
six shillings a dozen and butter five shillings a pound, and two
shillings a bundle for oat-hay. That's not so dusty. And, after
all, if you want to go and dig for diamonds yourself there's
nothing to stop you. Lots of young fellows from the Free State
have picked up enough in a month to buy themselves farms.
Wagon-builders, too, have made fortunes. This money flows
everywhere. It's saved the whole of South Africa.'

'Money ... money ... always money!' Adrian growled savagely. 'That's the only thing you Kimberley folk ever think of.
We've gained money, yes; but money means little north of the
Vaal. And what have we lost? We've lost labour. We've lost
security. The diamond-fields have tempted away all our Kaffir
labourers. We can't pay them the wages they earn in the mines:
we haven't the money. The town has corrupted them, too: no
Englishman ever yet knew how to handle a Kaffir. Kimberley's
ruined our natives with drink; it's taught them to steal, it's
made them despise the white man – and who can blame them?
More than that: it takes back the money they've earned and
supplies them with firearms and ammunition. The guns that are
sold in Kimberley are flooding the country: they go east in a
steady stream to Basutoland, and north to the Zoutpansberg to
Sekukuni. Kimberley's arming our enemies – understand that –
in defiance, in absolute defiance of the two conventions. What
do the English care, so long as they get back their money? It's
we folk of the two republics, not they, who'll have to fight them.
Then, to crown all, they partition our country; they bite off as
much as they want – the richest part – and call it West Griqualand! And you say we have gained by the diamond-fields!' He
threw back his great bearded head contemptuously.

'Ah, but listen,' the Englishman said, his good humour unbroken. 'What did you fellows *do* with West Griqualand before
you lost it? The country was never settled: it wasn't worth
settling. I'm ready to bet you yourself wouldn't want to live in
that waste of sand and stones.'

'And yet it was our land they annexed,' Adrian answered
more calmly. 'The Government was allowed to annex it, not
because it was in the right but because it was strong.'

'I'm bound to say that comes oddly from you, an Englishman.'

'An Englishman? God forbid!'

'In that case there's no more to be said.'

John Grafton smiled. Throughout this passage of arms he had sat with folded hands, his eyes watching either speaker, grave and tolerant. Now he spoke in a voice that still kept its West-Midlands burr.

'There is more behind this than you see, my friend,' he said. 'You are new to the country. I've dwelt here for thirty-five years, and my old friend here even longer; so it's easier for us to see the Dutchmen's point of view, while my sons, who have grown up among them, see it even more easily. They don't like the sound of that word annexation. Neither do I. It's too familiar. Years ago – before you or your brother were born, I suppose – we trekked down with the emigrant farmers into Natal, which Piet Retief had been given by Dingaan, the Zulu. Then Dingaan fell on Retief and we had to fight him.'

'Yes, yes, I've heard tell of that', the stranger said. 'A great exploit, sir. If I remember rightly, I think the English helped you?' he added, a little mischievously.

'Indeed they did. Their safety was at stake as much as ours, and they were fewer in number. When that trouble was over we built a town of thanksgiving, called Pietermaritzburg. The English hauled down their flag and sailed from the port; they gave our little republic their blessing and permission to live its own life in peace on the lands Retief had received from Dingaan before he was butchered. But in five years – only five years, mark you! – the English went back on their word: they landed again, in force, and their flag went up again. Natal was annexed. Our people were in the right, as my son has said, but the English were stronger; so the folk from Natal were driven back over the Drakensberg to join their kin in the Orange Free State and Transvaal. Their coming bound us together: our leaders settled the quarrels that had divided them. We grew stronger; the English signed two conventions with us which set down our boundaries for ever. We've kept them, in peace, for just on twenty years. But the Diamond Diggings were inside those boundaries; and now what happened in Natal has happened again: they have been annexed, just as Basutoland was annexed five years ago. The habit of annexation is becoming too

31

common for our liking. I think my son is wondering, a little uneasily, whose turn will come next.'

The stranger nodded. 'Of course you know more of these things than I do, sir; but didn't both the republics agree to the Keate award?'

'I say they did nothing of the sort,' Adrian broke in angrily. 'The two presidents were unprepared, expecting fair treatment, and that slim *verneuker* lawyer Arnot played each of them off against the other and tricked them out of their claims. Jan Brand may slink back to Bloemfontein with his ninety-thousand-pound bribe; but we, in the Transvaal, have known how to deal with Marthinus Pretorius: we've sent him packing and found a new president, Thomas Burgers, who'll be up to all their tricks, thank God!'

The predikant raised his head. Until the mention of the new President's name he had appeared to be sunk in a tired stupor. The words 'Thomas Burgers' stabbed him wide-awake.

'You may thank God for Burgers too soon, nephew,' he said. 'The man may be clever enough – I'll not be denying it – but he's no man for us: a branded heretic, condemned – ay, suspended too – by the synod of our own Reformed Church for the deadly errors of Rationalism; a man who scoffs at the literal inspiration of the Holy Scriptures. Is yon the type of man we should trust to lead us?'

Adrian waved the question aside. 'We've heard all those stories: they've run like a grass-fire all over the veld. What his enemies never say is that Burgers was proved innocent and reinstated when he took his case to the Privy Council in England, and that he made the presbytery of Graaf Reinet eat their words.'

'Ay, he's up to all their tricks, as you say.'

'He's a strong, determined man, and that's what we need.'

'The Lord giveth strength, and by his own strength shall no man prevail. I misdoubt if the Lord is with him, my son ... I gravely misdoubt it.'

Adrian gave an impatient gesture. 'Must we always be torn by these wretched religious controversies and spend our time smelling out heresy while our land is taken from us? Isn't it better to realize what this annexation of the Diamond Fields means? It's a new jumping-off place. That's their game. The next step is Northward, along the old missionary road as far as the Limpopo. They'll bring out their old hypocritical excuse

32

and say they're "protecting" the natives. But they know there's gold in the North, and that's what they're after. They want to encircle our land and then annex it. They want to cut us off from the sea and strangle us. Thomas Burgers is clever enough to know that, and he'll see that it's stopped.'

Mr. Blair shook his head: 'A house that is divided against itself, my son, cannot stand. I am an old man now, but my heart is full of sorrow when I hear the young talking. God has given this great wide land to two kindred races. Isn't Africa big enough for both our races to live without enmity?'

'Federation. . . . The only solution is federation.'

The young man by the fire had spoken at last, surprisingly, for all the rest had forgotten him. He spoke in a high-pitched squeaky voice which sounded almost ridiculous issuing from that lanky frame. Adrian turned on him savagely.

'Federation? We've heard that word too, young man. It sounds well enough, but it's only another snare for us. Since this annexation we know where we are. It would mean the same thing in the end. Federation is dead. You may take it from me.'

'And yet it will come,' the boy said. 'In our time it will come.' He closed the volume, which lay open on his knees, with a snap.

Lisbet signalled to Maria.

'Go and fetch the books, little heart,' she said quietly. 'It is late, and time for prayers; the predikant's tired and so, I'm sure, are our guests. Will you choose the portion, old friend?'

(5)

It froze hard that night. When the moon had set, the veld still glimmered white with rime in starlight. Janse, riding his tired horse home to Witfontein in a dream, saw the nibbling hares that scattered fan-wise before him, with, here and there, a small antelope – duiker or steenbok – which heard him and cowered with crouched haunches, ready to spring – and once the silver ghost of a solitary jackal, which stood with one forefoot uplifted and stared at him, then went loping away. His mind had been deeply stirred by the talk at Wonderfontein, which aggravated its unrest. He resented and dreaded this atmosphere of tension and controversy which menaced the only things he desired: spiritual tranquillity in whch to indulge his aspirations; racial peace, without threat to his friendship with the Haskards. If zealots like Adrian had their way, he told himself, the Haskards might find the Transvaal too hot to be comfortable, and leave Brakfontein. His heart echoed old Mr. Blair's despairing cry: 'Isn't Africa big enough for our two races to live without enmity?' His mind was too sorely troubled and vexed for sleep that night.

Maria, too, found sleep difficult. The visits of strangers to Wonderfontein were so rare that they always excited her. The night was bitterly cold, and the bed in which she and Sarie slept had been robbed of its blankets to chafe Mr. Blair's old bones. She snuggled her thin body close to Sarie's, which was warm and dark and comfortable. It was so still outside that she could hear the oxen stamping in the kraal and, from far away, the excited whining of jackals. In the room beyond, Adrian shook the wall with his snoring. It was long past midnight before she got to sleep.

When she woke the sun had risen triumphantly. Her father and Adrian had already ridden out to their work, and the *voorhuis* was full of the aroma of steaming coffee which her mother had made to send out to the visitors' wagon.

'Can't I take it down to them, Mamma?' she said.

Lisbet looked at her eager face and smiled.

'Yes, if you like you can take it down. But don't climb into the wagon if they're not awake, and mind you don't spill the coffee.'

Maria ran down the garden path between the quince hedges. It was a peerless morning: not a breath of wind stirred the cold crisp air which enveloped the scene in a matrix of ice or crystal. She ran for sheer joy, like a young colt frisking, over the dry veld from which the last spangles of rime had vanished. Only one of the strangers was visible, the silent youth who had lurked in the chimney corner. He sat now, as he had sat overnight, with knees crossed, on a canvas chair – one book open in his hands and another on the ground beside him. As Maria came skipping towards him, he looked up with a solemn smile.

'Good morning, madam,' he said.

'I've brought you some coffee,' she panted. 'Where's your brother?'

'He isn't up yet. He was always a lazy beggar, and doesn't have to shave, either.'

'It's not very good coffee,' she said, 'but it's hot, and there's plenty of sugar.'

She poured out a cup of the black, sweet concoction from the jug and watched his face as he tasted it. In the light of day the young man did not look so owlish. The sun sparkled in his fine blue eyes and his curly hair; and his small mouth, apart from its downward drooping corners, had a childlike sweetness.

'My word, but it's hot!' he said. 'You must have run.'

'I felt like running this morning,' she said. 'I couldn't help it. Don't you feel like that?'

'It's a change after the dust of Kimberley; but I don't feel exactly like running; I'm not running much just now. I've had a bad heart.'

She looked at him with awed eyes, wondering what she ought to say next. She saw the patches of red upon his high cheek-bones and noticed that when he drank he seemed out of breath. It seemed to her more tactful to change the subject.

'What a funny book!' she said.

He gave a high, squeaky laugh. 'Want to have a look at it?'

'Yes, please.' She examined the print with puzzled eyes. 'I've never seen anything like this. They aren't proper letters. At least some of them are and some aren't.'

'They're all right. It's Greek.'

'That must be what my brother Janse means when he says a thing's Greek to him. Can you really read it?'

'Not very well. I'm trying to.'

'Why?'

'Because when this trip to the goldfields is over I'm going to Oxford.'

'Where's that? In the Colony?'

'No, over the sea, in England.'

'Do they talk Greek there?'

'They have to be able to understand it.'

For a moment Maria contemplated the page in silence.

'Isn't it rather a waste of time?' she said at last.

He laughed. 'Perhaps it is. But it's got to be done.'

'Are you going to stay there . . . always, I mean?'

'Oh no, I shall come back to Kimberley and go on digging diamonds.'

'I've never seen a diamond,' she said.

'Well, here you are. Have a look at them.'

He had thrust his short fingers into the pocket of his soiled flannel trousers and produced a handful of tiny pebbles. He spread them out on the page of the open book. Maria regarded them sceptically.

'Are these stones really diamonds?' she said.

'Yes. ... There's what your brother calls your country's ruin.'

He poked them here and there with a thick – and not too clean – forefinger, and began to explain.

'This one here is a typical alluvial stone from the river-diggings – you can see how the water's worn it. It's a smoky stone, too.' He held it up to the sun. 'And this is a mine-stone. I should say it comes from de Beers': the surface is oily and it's a dodecahedron.'

'What does that mean?'

'It's Greek. It just means it's got twelve sides. Then this diamond here – it's too small to pick up without tweezers – is a Bulfontein stone – pure white. Many Kimberley stones are white, too. This yellow fellow comes from Du Toit's Pan: they run larger there.'

'Are they really worth all that money?'

'Enough to take me to Oxford.'

'It seems silly to me. They're nothing, really – are they?'

'No. Just carbon. But women all over the world will sell their souls for them. You will, when you grow up.'

Maria shook her head, pursing her lips.

'I'm quite certain I shan't,' she declared.

The young man laughed. 'Then you'll be unique. I'll tell you what you shall do. You shall choose a stone for yourself, and when you're engaged to be married – if you still want to keep it mind – I'll have it cut and made into a ring for you. Now, take your choice, madam.'

She picked out what she thought was the biggest.

'No, I shouldn't have that, if I were you,' he said seriously. 'It's a bit of what we call rubbish. It's yellow bort. This one isn't so large, but it won't need much cutting. It's a Kimberley Mine octahedron without a flaw in it. Be careful not to lose it.'

'Can I really have this?'

'I told you you could.'

'But ... but how shall I send it to you when ... you know what you said? I don't even know your name.'

'You'll find my name inside the book, on the fly-leaf. The address doesn't count; but Kimberley will find me all right, I expect. Hadn't you better write it down? You'll never remember it. Here's a pencil.'

'I shan't forget it,' Maria said. She read the name and address to herself with slow emphasis: *C. J. Rhodes. The Vicarage. Bishop's Stortford. Herts.*

CHAPTER TWO

(1)

NEXT day the Rhodes Brothers trekked north on their way to the Lydenburg Goldfields. Mr. Blair, too, harnessed his bony horse and went jolting back to his flock at Potchefstroom in his cape-cart. Piet set out on his transport-riding again. Lisbet was thankful to know that, this time, he was going to Natal. At this time of the year tracks were dry, the Drakenberg passes were open: the trek-path, which Retief and his followers had scraped and hewn out of the face of the precipice below Van Reenen, was by now so well worn with the going and coming of wagons that the descent was no longer the perilous venture which Lisbet remembered; the rivers, crashing down from the Berg, ran so low that the passage of drifts was not threatened by freshets, and the danger of lightning, which she always dreaded, was less. Every year, at this season, the men of the family (or such of them as had not driven the cattle herds to the low country) were wont to trek down with the durable produce they had accumulated in the summer – not the wheat: the greedy bellies of Kimberley had absorbed as much as they could grow and more – but the leather goods which John Grafton, brought up as a cobbler, was so apt in shaping: ox-reins, whips and sjamboks, bales of tanned leather, sun-dried biltong and fruit and honey. Piet would bring back little money – this trade was conducted by barter – though for the extra span of red oxen he drove down with him and the shaggy Basuto ponies he picked up on the way he usually pocketed forty or fifty pounds; but always, in these days, the agents in Pietermaritzburg were thankful to pay handsomely for the transport of mining-implements, canned goods and imported liquor, and Piet, with his shrewd business head, could be trusted to make a good bargain. The only thing that irked her in Piet's departure was the fact that she would not see him again till the spring. And that would not be long in coming. Time passed so swiftly in these days – almost too swiftly.

Adrian, too, rode away to Pretoria for the sittings of the

Volksraad. He was full of high hopes for the Burgers administration. Whether the new President, as Mr. Blair had declared, were a heretic or no, he was the man for this moment. Though his advanced religious views might not suit the Doppers, who still lived in the seventeenth century, they were in keeping with the character of a man of the world who had travelled in Europe and fitted himself to deal in their own language with the subtleties of the lawyers who had outwitted the slow brains and tongues of Brand and Pretorius. Not merely an orator but a man of action. Already he was persuading the Republic to put its finances in order. He was raising a loan of sixty thousand pounds on the security of the government lands, as yet unappropriated. He was shocking the eyes of back-veld burgers by a holocaust of the depreciated blue-back paper currency, which would be replaced by a coinage of gold – gold dug and minted in the Transvaal, the gold they had despised! – worth as much as Queen Victoria's sovereigns. He had seen through the English designs of confederation and their strategy of encirclement. He would find the way to the sea which the English denied them, and free the Transvaal from its helpless dependence on their ports. A road from Lydenburg to the Portuguese boundary was already surveyed and begun. Within a few years a railway would have been built to Lorenço Marques, when the English could do their worst and be damned. It was merely a matter of money.

Lisbet smiled at her son's enthusiasms, half sharing them. She had always recognized the dual character of his nature: half stubborn and retrograde, after the manner of her ancestors, Prinsloos, Celliers and Bezuidenhouts; half progressive and open to new ideas, like his father's. Throughout all his life, she supposed, his mind would be cleft by the struggle between these two tendencies; and now, as it seemed, they had achieved an unusual harmony – his dislike and distrust of the English domination persuading him to imitate the methods by which they had achieved it. The situation was faintly comical: yet what did that matter, so long as Adrian were happy?

Yet she could not help wishing that his politics absorbed less of his time and did not take him so far from home. Now that Andries was lost in the North, Janse established at Witfontein, and Piet wandering over the face of the earth as a transport-rider, the whole weight of the six-thousand-acre farm was thrown on her husband's shoulders. In their earlier days, when there had seemed to be no end to his resources of faith and energy, he could have borne it easily; but John Grafton, though still a man of exceptional force and initiative compared with most of his neighbours, was no longer young. If he had consented to admit what he felt (and she saw), matters might have been easier; but in this he was stubborn; he refused to recognize any limit to his powers – with the result that by the end of the day he showed signs of exhaustion. In thirty-three years of experience he was still incapable of realizing what their neighbours, men of her own race, appeared to know instinctively from the day of their birth: that nature – above all the natural inertia of this vast, brooding land – cannot be hurried or mastered by the will of man; that man must adapt himself to the vagaries of season and climate in which he lives, and that the earth, which at last will hold his bones, has its way with him. But that was against John Grafton's nature. He could not spare himself. From the day on which he had ridden out the marches of his farm, he had never relaxed.

Nor did there seem to be any hope of his ever relaxing. In the days when they first settled at Wonderfontein there had been an abundance of native labour: the remnants of those tribes which the hordes of the Matabele had savaged and eaten up on their fierce progress northward. When their tribal organization was disintegrated, these unwarlike natives were only too thankful to earn their living under the protection of the Boers who had broken Moselikatse and driven him away. They were a happy folk who asked little of life but security from their persecutors and food to fill their bellies. But now, in the dust and swelter of Kimberley, they could earn English money as well as food – as much as ten shillings a week! – and buy with that money all the 'truck' for which their hearts lusted: bead-necklaces for their women and gay printed calicoes, as well as clothes for themselves, knives of Sheffield steel, tin cups and pannikins. And here, on the Diamond Fields, was a different kind of white man, who sold them drink that would numb fatigue or pain, and *dagga* which sent them mad with exaltation. These white men were not remote and severe like the masters they knew, but ready to treat them as equals and ready to give them more money and drink and *dagga* in return for the stones they secreted about them while they worked; while some of these men would sell gas-pipe muskets, the possession of which, if they could smuggle them back to their kraals, made them great

40

among their people. Every day, as they toiled on the farm, the Wonderfontein Kaffirs would see black men like themselves, who had worked in the mines at Kimberley, stalking past on their homeward journey with coin in their new trouser-pockets and boxes crammed with treasures poised on their heads. They would sit on the ground and mock them as they worked, and tell stories of the wonders of the mines where black men and white were equal. So the young men drifted away from Wonderfontein until only the old and the decrepit were left, and John Grafton was glad to avail himself of half-caste Hottentots, who had half of the Kaffir's strength and none of his pride or his virtues, a degenerate race who settled on the farm like fleas on a sick dog and, like fleas, proliferated, only doing work when his eye was on them, and scamping that.

All the farms on the Witwatersrand suffered from this draining away of their strength, but none so much as Wonderfontein, which had most to lose – since John Grafton was not – though his herds were half his living – primarily a herdsman or flockmaster, but a born tiller of the soil, which Boer and Kaffir were not. It was this innate love for tilled soil and for things growing, which he had learnt at his grandfather's home in Worcestershire, that had distinguished the green lands of Wonderfontein from their neighbours' veld. Now that the new market of Kimberley was ready to absorb every bag of meal or truss of oat-hay he could produce, it began to look as if this unusual policy were about to be justified, as if easier days lay ahead of him. But the Diamond Fields, which swallowed his produce, removed simultaneously his power of supplying it. He had been forced at last to see his tilled fields revert to wind-sown pasture, and to build up his head of stock as a compensation.

All promised well. That autumn, in May, the lambing had been good. In the previous summer abundant rains had fallen and the coats of his Afrikander cattle were glossy with the rich feed of a fruitful grass-harvest. He doubted if his brother-in-law Barend Prinsloo's herds would look any kinder than his when they came up from the Low Country to graze on the grass which began to shoot through the cindered veld he had set on fire as he drove them away.

Barend Prinsloo drove home his cattle in mid-September by way of his sister Anna Kruger's farm beneath the Magaliesberg: he was still friendly with Anna, though he had not spoken to Lisbet for thirty years. As he trekked back from

41

Paardekraal over the ridge, his way took him across the northernmost portion of John Grafton's land. There was no fencing set to prevent their feeding as they went, and it pleased him to think that they were having a little free grazing at his enemy's expense while he outspanned at noon. Nor yet did it trouble him when, reaching Sterkfontein just before sunset, he heard that three yellow heifers were missing. They were only a few miles from home and would follow the spoor of the others without any difficulty. He told the herdsman to kraal them as soon as they arrived, and set himself to off-loading his wagons and opening the house which had been shut up all winter.

But at nightfall the missing cattle had still not returned, nor by next morning. The Kaffir herd brought Barend Prinsloo the news as he stood, drinking coffee on the primitive stoep, in his stockinged feet and the clothes in which he had slept. His swarthy black-bearded face grew red beneath the tan; his mouth went ugly. He bawled to his wife: 'My shoes, and bring me my gun!' While she laced up the thongs of his veldschoens, the Kaffir led round the horse which he had been told to saddle: a valuable schimmelblauw grey that had been salted by recovery from horse-sickness. Barend Prinsloo loaded the gun and slipped the strap over his shoulders. He mounted and sat there, long-stirruped, a lean, dark man, with a skin of crinkled leather and the amber eyes of a falcon, smouldering with rage.

'Where are you going, *ou baas*?' his wife called after him anxiously.

'That is no business of yours. I go to Wonderfontein.'

'To Wonderfontein? Almighty! What next?'

'Jan Grafton or Grafton's men have stolen my cattle. I am going to fetch them.'

He rode straight to Wonderfontein, never urging his horse beyond a walk or a tripple. The Kaffir padded behind him on pink-soled feet: he was armed with a Swazi assegai brought from the Low Country. Barend did not speak. By middle age he had become a man of few words and brooding thought. He walked his horse up to the stoep at Wonderfontein, where Maria sat sewing. The winter season had treated her kindly too. Since the Rhodes brothers went North she had shot up prodigiously, she was turned fifteen and a woman as tall as her mother. When she heard the horse's steps she looked up from her work over the new-green veld that lay bathed in warm spring sunshine. She shaded her eyes and watched the strange

42

rider advance, with the native trotting behind. There was something menacing and purposeful in his deliberate approach. She believed she knew him as the uncle her mother had pointed out to her once at Nachtmaal. She dropped her sewing and scuttled into the house.

'Mamma ... Mamma ...', she called excitedly 'A man is coming. I think it is Uncle Barend.'

'Uncle Barend!' her sister Sarie scoffed, in her low, dark voice. 'You must be mad, child. He'd sooner be dead than set foot in this house, your Uncle Barend.'

Lisbet appeared, and Maria repeated what she had said. The smile left her mother's lips; her face was troubled.

'If you are right this means something bad,' she said. 'But you cannot be right.'

She hurried through to the door to meet the strange horseman. The two girls stood inside the house listening. They heard her gasp.

'Barend ...' she cried. She spoke swiftly in Dutch. 'What has happened? What do you want? Is it death, brother?'

'I want no word with you,' he answered, 'I want your Englishman or one of your mongrel sons.'

'Tell me what it is, Barend.'

'It is theft. Your men have stolen my cattle: three yellow cows.'

'You know that cannot be true.'

'I shall see for myself. Where are they?'

'John and Adrian set out at sunrise. They went that way.' She pointed northwards.

'Then I go to find them.'

He pulled round his horse's head viciously and rode off without another word. Lisbet stood with a set face and watched him. Maria and Sarie came out to besiege her with excited questions, but she neither listened nor answered them. She turned of a sudden and pushed past them, hurrying straight to the rack where the guns were hung at the back of the *voorhuis*. They were all there: a great elephant *roer*, two old-fashioned muskets and a new Westley-Richards rifle. She shuddered to see them all in their places; for she had noticed that Barend was armed, and knew that her own men were not. From a child she had known that hot look in her brother's eyes and dreaded it. When Barend's eyes smouldered like that there was no knowing what he would do. If there had been time, she would have

43

saddled a horse and ridden to warn them; but already Barend had broken into a canter and was moving rapidly up the slope. It would be wrong, she told herself, to frighten the girls, so she left them still anxiously wondering and bolted herself in the bedroom, where she fell on her knees beside the great bed and prayed desperately.

Barend Prinsloo rode straight to the top of the ridge which commanded the whole extent of Wonderfontein. In the distance, towards his own beacons, he saw a slow-moving mass of cattle and two mounted men following them, side by side. He made a wide swerve eastward, to cut them off. The Kaffir, running, could not keep pace with him. The two horsemen paused when they saw his wild figure circling the skyline, and the cattle stopped too. Barend checked and rode slowly towards them, his eyes searching the stationary herd for his missing cattle. When he came within earshot he shouted:

'You damned Englishman, what have you done with my yellow heifers?'

John Grafton looked at his son in questioning surprise. Adrian shrugged his huge shoulders.

'We don't know what your meaning is, uncle,' he shouted back. 'We have none of your cattle. Look, you can see for yourself.'

'I want nothing of you, young half-breed,' Barend cried angrily. 'You are one of the skelms who have thrown out Pretorious and elected the heretic Burgers. Let the Englishman answer.'

He unslung his gun from his shoulders and advanced with it in his hands. His aspect was threatening.

John Grafton spoke quietly: 'Put away your gun, brother, and tell us what you want. I understand nothing of this.'

Barend rode up close to them, his finger still on the trigger, and spluttered out his complaint. John Grafton and Adrian shook their heads. Adrian was watching his uncle closely: at the first hostile movement he was prepared to vault from his horse and overpower him. With one anxious eye he saw Barend's Kaffir panting up and the assegais in his hand; he did not like that.

'You outspanned on my land, then,' John Grafton was saying. 'That was friendly, brother: in another mile your cattle could have grazed your own veld. But let that be. We will go to the place where you left your yellow heifers. They may be there still. So you lead the way.'

Adrian nodded approvingly: he would rather the loaded gun were in front of them than behind them. Barend sullenly acquiesced and walked his horse on before them, over the green rise scattered with marigolds, climbing the ridge. As the three horsemen neared the crest there was a flurry of creaking wings: a flock of vultures rose clumsily, circling above them, from the edge of a patch of rushes fringing a pan of rain-water by which the three heifers lay. The Kaffir ran forward shouting at them and lashed at one with his assegai, but the beast did not attempt to rise. He stabbed at its haunches: it floundered on to its knees and rolled over again. Barend Prinsloo roared at him to leave them alone. The three white men rode up together.

'Well, here are your heifers, brother,' John Grafton said calmly. 'But I doubt if they'll be of much use to you now.'

Barend turned on him, snarling. 'They are poisoned. Your veld is foul. I shall have compensation.'

'You brought them here yourself, and my veld's clean enough – or was before you fouled it. Look at the froth on their mouths and the way they fight for breath. This is no poison. This is the lung-sickness. Where they caught it from I do not know; but you have done me and my land an injury.'

'I say it is poison, and you shall pay for it.'

'You know it is lung-sickness. We shall all of us pay for it. This is a bad day for Witwatersrand: up till now it has been clean. You're the only one of us with a gun, so you'd better use it. Put these poor brutes out of their misery and then take yourself off my veld and look to the rest of your herd. We will burn their carcasses and bury them. Pray God it may go no farther.'

Barend Prinsloo sullenly levelled his gun and fired. The sick heifer kicked and lay still. Once more there was a sudden flurry and a creaking of wings as the vultures, a hundred or more of them, which had floated down from the sky to sit round in a noisome circle, rose into the air. Prinsloo loaded his gun and reloaded it and fired two more shots. Then, without any word or salutation, he turned and cantered away.

So that pestilence came to Wonderfontein for the first time. And not only to Wonderfontein: the infection smote every farm on the Witwatersrand over which Barend Prinsloo's herd had passed on the way home from Paardekraal. On some few, such as the Haskards (who, ironically, could bear it most easily), it fell lightly. Others, including Lisbet's old comrades in the Great Trek, the Oosthuizens of Langlaagte, lost nine-tenths of the cattle which were their sole wealth, and Janse – 'poor Janse' as usual! – was hit almost as heavily. Not three beasts in every ten infected survived the disease. When the short cough, which every ear recognized, once began, they might just as well have been shot; but in such a catastrophe even the faintest hope of recovery was enough to save them from slaughter. Some died within fourteen days; a few others hung on for two months, till the fever had burnt them away to mere skeletons in bags of hide.

By the end of that spring, John Grafton, and even more Janse, were faced with the need for an immediate change in policy. If they wanted to make up their leeway and earn money to replenish their head of stock they must plough more land at once and sow mealies and Kaffir corn for the Kimberley market. But before the ploughing was finished much time had been lost, and in October, when liberal rains should have broken, the earth was still bone-dry. It was sad to watch these late-sown seedlings languish. At Wonderfontein John Grafton could keep them at least alive by bringing to their roots a trickle from his water-furrows; but Janse, who had to rely on the bounty of nature, saw his thin-stalked corn turn yellow before its tassels were out. By the time the widow-birds put on their funereal tails in November the whole crop had withered.

For him this year had been well-nigh ruinous. By the end of it, he had neither cattle nor corn. What was more, he had worked himself out: not a soul (save, perhaps, his mother) ever realized the double labour imposed on him by his useless leg whose weight he must drag along with him wherever he went on foot. He felt so worn (and knew that he looked it) that he had little heart to visit the Haskards. Though he longed for the sight of Lavinia and the sound of her voice, his pride would not bear to let her see him as a broken man.

46

Now he rarely left the stoep of his house at Witfontein where he sat brooding or reading and listening to the twitter of the red-breasted swallows that built their nests in the scaffolding-holes in the wall. Only once did he venture afield – and then for his mother's sake – to drive with his family into the dorp for the quarterly Nachtmaal. It should have been a festal occasion, for Maria had now been confirmed and become an 'accepted member' of the Dutch Reformed Church, and marriageable. They were all amused by the child's suppressed excitement at appearing in church with her hair up, in the new white silk dress which Lisbet had made out of scraps of material stored in her mother's ancient wagon-chest. But though Maria enjoyed her triumph there was little joy to be seen among the gathered community who outspanned their wagons in the market square. All had suffered more or less from the drought and the lung-sickness.

Nor did Mr. Blair improve matters when, on the great day, he mounted the pulpit and preached a three-hour sermon, with twelve distinct headings which exhausted his congregation even more than himself. The predikant had reasons (if not con-solations) to give for all their ills. Both the drought and the lung-sickness were divine visitations, he said; both were fore-shadowed and paralleled in the Book of Exodus. They had deserved the anger of God for two main reasons: first by their trafficking with the heathen of Kimberley, that new City of the Plain, where men worshipped the calf of gold and broke the Sabbath – and as he spoke he glared down from the pulpit at Piet with all the fierceness of an Old Testament prophet in his accusing eyes. Secondly, they had tempted God's wrath, as had Dathan and Abiram, by deposing that godly man Marthinus Pretorius and setting up over them the known heretic, Burgers – this was one for Adrian! – a man who confessedly questioned the verbal inspiration of Holy Scripture. How could they look for the mercy and protection of a jealous God if they wantonly rebelled against Him and flouted His will? Let them not ima-gine, he warned them, that, unless their hearts were changed, the Almighty would content Himself with such modest inflictions. There were ten plagues with which He had vexed the Egyptians, and of these they had only suffered the dust and the murrain. Let them repent and return to God's ways, or, of a certainty, the rest would fall on them.

Janse returned to Witfontein in a mood of hot resentment. It infuriated him to see that the rest of the family (save Piet, who secretly treated the sermon as a joke, and Maria, still bubbling with the excitement of her new frock) were deeply impressed by Mr. Blair's fulminations. Only the Haskards, he told himself, could understand how he felt and give his indignation the sympathy it needed. He rode over to Brakfontein the same evening and told them his story.

'But, of course,' Major Haskard said, 'the old fool was talking pure balderdash. The trouble with your parsons is that they're still living in the seventeenth century and this is the nineteenth. Divine vengeance, my eye! The lung-sickness was partly bad luck and partly criminal ignorance of the nature of the disease. It's due to a transmissible germ. Read this article in *The Times*. All diseases are due to germs, whatever they are, according to this chap Lister. As for drought: we know perfectly well that this country is subject to droughts. Like everything else it's a matter of cause and effect. Unfortunately nobody has time to find out the causes. If you worked it out you'd probably find that they obey some law of periodicity. As it is, we just have to bank on the law of averages. This year was a dry one. Therefore, in all probability, next year will be wet, or wetter than this. At any rate that's the principle I mean to go on. But, you know, my boy,' he went on, 'I often wonder if this is really a country for farming. It's a violent, capricious land: you never know the next trick it's going to play on you. If I weren't a man of some means, not dependent on the land for my living, I should feel as depressed as yourself. And yet nothing could ever drive me away from South Africa. It's got hold of me, and I love it as much as you do. Only . . . Somehow I think its real future lies not on the top of the soil, but under it. In its diamonds – possibly in its gold: in the tremendous hidden mineral wealth of all sorts that lies here for the asking. What would your good Mr. Blair say to that?'

He laughed in his jolly boisterous way; but a moment later his face was serious.

'You know,' he went on, 'I'm not at all sure you're cut out for a farmer!' (Janse winced. Though his eyes were lowered he could have sworn that Haskard was looking at his leg.) 'You're not made like the rest of your people. If you were, we shouldn't be talking together like this. As things are, the men of your race seem blind – unless it's sheer obstinacy – to their opportunities. They're the same today as they were two hundred years ago. They bought this land with their blood – but what have they done with it?'

Janse shook his head. 'They found peace and freedom,' he said.

'To a certain extent that's true. But how long will they keep them? They'll have to bear the pressure of evolution. You've read Darwin, I know. The world can't stand still, my dear fellow, nor yet can its species. The only man in the country who seems to realize that is your new President, Burgers – and you've heard what the Church thinks of him! If I were a chap of your age and your intelligence, d'you know what I'd do? I'd cut my losses and make a new start in more promising circumstances. What's more, I'm ready to help you. Though my damned lungs compel me to live here – and I can't say I'm sorry – I have interests and influence in Kimberley. If you'll say the word, I'll write to my friends and ask them to give you a job. I'll buy Witfontein, too, if you like. How big is it? Six thousand acres? I can certainly afford to hold it much better than you. Why not go, while there's time?'

Janse raised his eyes and looked at Lavinia. 'If I go,' he thought, 'she'll forget me. Out of sight, out of mind.' While her father was speaking, her grave, lovely face had betrayed no emotion, nor even now, when Janse looked at her, did it change. It seemed to him just as exquisite and just (alas!) as remote as ever. 'She doesn't care a button,' he told himself, 'whether I go right out of her life or stay at Witfontein. And why should she? Who am I? What am I? Less than nothing.'

Yet while he searched that perfect mask in vain for the least flicker of regret or encouragement, his mind was at work. 'If I go to Kimberley,' he thought rapidly, 'I shall probably make my fortune. It's brains that count there, not strength, and God knows, though I may be uncouth and ignorant, I'm sharp enough. I shall make myself money and a name. If I come back rich and famous, she'll have to look at me.' And again he thought: 'If I accept this man's charity – for that's what it comes to – I shall be confessing weakness, failure, defeat; I shall be giving her an excuse for despising me; she'll be right if she takes it.' And again: 'Why should I, who am just as good as they are, accept this patronage? What right has this Englishman, kindly though he may be, to speak of my folks as if they were an inferior, stupid race, already condemned to go under in the struggle for survival? Are we so blind as he says, after all?

49

Isn't there something rather magnificent in the way which we Afrikanders have kept our character? Isn't there dignity in our isolation, in our instinctive refusal to compete or join this mob that scrambles for money?'

With an effort he mastered these divided thoughts and spoke calmly, always watching the effect of his words.

'That is kind, sir,' he said, 'very kind of you. Don't think me ungrateful. There are things – and people – in these parts dearer to me than all the money in Kimberley . . . yes, dearer than life. I must stay on at Witfontein and make what I can of it, encouraged' (he smiled) 'by what you said about the law of averages. I'm sorry I talked so excitedly and so long. It's time I was going.'

'Well, you may be unwise, young man,' Major Haskard said slowly. 'But I can't say you haven't got courage: I'll give you that. And, look here: if you're short of money to make a new start don't hesitate to ask for a loan.' He laughed, as though excusing himself for an impropriety. 'I've always been a bit of a gambler, you know, and backed my fancies.'

Janse shook his head: 'No, I couldn't. I want to do this by myself.'

'All right. Just as you wish.'

As he shook hands with all of them, departing, in the formal manner of the veld, it seemed to him that Lavinia's soft handclasp was warmer and more positive than ever before, transcending mere formality. There was a confident smile on her lips. He dared not look at her eyes. . . .

As he rode home through the dark under the vast vault of African indigo, in which the stars seem nearer to earth and more brilliant than in any other sky, he felt his stature and power increased, his spirit refreshed, heroic, invincible. He was conscious of a triumphant integrity; of having wrestled with an enemy and felled him; of being enriched and fortified by the very strength he had subdued.

(3)

Janse had something more definite now, he felt, to live and to work for. In spite of the 'law of averages' he was taking no risks. Though this was a season of almost intolerable heat, he set to work building and puddling a new dam, so that, if

50

drought came again, there might be some reserves of water. He worked all day in the sun and lay down at nightfall exhausted, but full of proud satisfaction, to sleep, to a dreamless sleep that lasted till dawn.

At Wonderfontein they were working equally hard extending their acreage of tilth. Adrian lent his vast strength to this labour as often as he could. He was less wrapped up in politics now. The Burgers regime, for better or worse, appeared to be firmly established and no longer in urgent need of support in the Volksraad. Even Paul Kruger and Joubert, the bitterest of irreconcilables, who equally distrusted the new President's policy and abhorred his religious views, had consented to take office under him – somewhat cynically, Adrian thought: for he knew they submitted under protest and only clung to their posts for the sake of the money and influence that office gave them. And in spite of these men's doubtful loyalty Burgers' programme was going through. The loan had been raised (there was no grumbling about that, for the treasury was leaky) and work begun on the new Delagoa Railway.

Only Piet took no part in the family's struggle for survival. The scourge of lung-sickness had not touched him. As soon as he heard of it, that astute young man had decided to keep his teams clear of the infected areas. The destruction of bullocks by the disease had pushed up transport-rates, so that a single journey of five hundred miles from the coast to Kimberley brought more than a hundred pounds to the transport-rider's pocket. He was accumulating money rapidly and had bought a third wagon. Once in every three months he rode home, leaving his wagons behind him, and deposited his earnings, British paper and gold, in a box which Lisbet kept hidden at the bottom of a wagon-chest. She never knew how much he brought home: he was secretive as well as shrewd. When she begged him to stay for a week or two and give his father and Adrian a hand with their heart-breaking labours, he smiled at her quizzically.

'Why should I be such a fool as to throw away my time and my energy,' he asked, 'in work that is only a gamble against the weather, when I know I can earn a definite sum by transport-riding: five shillings a mile for certain, without any risk?'

'They need your help, Piet,' she said, 'and so does poor Janse.'

'Then why don't they ask for it?'

She shook her head. She knew that her husband would never do that: it wasn't his way to ask favours of anyone – not even of his sons – and no more was it Adrian's. Between him and Piet there had always been a lack of sympathy: each, in his heart, despised the other, she knew, though they never quarrelled openly.

'As for helping Janse: that's just throwing time away. And don't forget, Mother,' he told her, 'there may come a day when the money I've made will be wanted to save the lot of you.'

Lisbet smiled to herself. Though she admitted his capability and self-confidence and loved him no less – perhaps, secretly, more – than his brothers, for he was still, in her eyes, the baby of the family, she couldn't see Piet readily parting with his savings out of sheer filial piety. There was an alien vein of adamant in Piet's nature, a tenacity which perhaps made for greatness, and certainly for success; yet she wished he would sometimes soften a little – if only to please her.

So John Grafton and Adrian and Janse worked the land without ceasing that winter, and on into the spring. Their mealies and corn were sown early, for the weather was mild, with early sprinklings of rain to soften the soil and no threat of late frosts. When the veld encircling the two farms still wore the pale gold of winter, flawed here and there by patches of black where the grass had been fired, the tawny tilth of their fields was already fledged with a green so faint that it seemed more like vapour than substance. Then the summer rains broke with less than their accustomed violence, but with no less relief to the parched air or the aching sky overcharged with electricity. All day thunder rolled and cloud gathered, with storms sullenly prowling about the sky; from the blackness of night the veld leapt out livid in flickers of lightning; the horizon lay girt by friezes of cloud that hung in inky tatters or slanted to earth in columns of solid water. Yet the rain that drenched the Witwatersrand was no such thunderous deluge. Janse heard it beat on his galvanized roof at night with a sound that was like a long roll and throbbing of distant kettledrums; but when daylight came, the sky was usually of a limpid blue, and the rain-washed atmosphere so diamond-clear, that the rays of the sun, as it climbed, seemed to pierce it without impediment – or even to be concentrated by it as though passed through a burning-glass. The heat they gave was more tolerable to cobras and puffadders basking on the rocks than to men; but the springing maize-plants gloried in it; their pale green stalks shot up like a forest of lances set with reflected pennons of leaf, and Janse gloried too in the spectacle of a growth so prodigious of a sudden released from so small a seed – and he the ploughman and sower – that they soon overtopped him. One could almost see them growing from hour to hour, he thought; when a wind moved they swayed stiffly with a gentle sound of dry rustling that was like a whisper of content.

Janse, too, was contented. Such a crop had never been seen before at Witfontein. In spite of the heat he limped, sedulously hoeing, among them, rejoicing to see how soon the sheathed cobs swelled in the axils, tipped with silk, and the male flowers flaunted their panicles overhead. When the day was done he would sit on the stoep and watch his mealie-fields rippling beneath him or moving in waves of silver under the moon. There was only one flaw for him in this proud fruition: that he could not show it to Lavinia. As soon as the great rains broke and the high-veld grew steamy, Major Haskard had begun to wheeze and had packed-off himself and his family to the Cape where the air was cooled by sea-breezes and the summer was rainless. And of course, besides this, there was always the lurking dread of some unforeseen disaster before the crop ripened.

'Pray God we may have no hail!' John Grafton said.

They did pray for protection from hail as they stood in the *voorhuis* at Wonderfontein for their evening devotions. Even Janse himself, though his rationalist reading had shaken his faith in a Providence as minutely concerned in particular human destinies, was half tempted to add his prayers to theirs, until his pride of spirit accused him of truckling to a primitive superstition and laughed him out of the temptation, assuring him, also, that the falling of hail – that thunder-born scourge of the High Veld – was a strictly local phenomenon and just as fortuitous as that of the tower of Siloam – at which, as an instrument of divine vengeance, Jesus himself had scoffed. And, though he declined to join in their prayers, no hailstorm in fact smote Witfontein. Only kindly rains watered his mealies, and the cobs continued to swell.

Yet while Janse smoked his pipe on the stoep and gloated over his crop, invisible distance forces were moving. Far away to the west in the thirst-land of Kalahari also rain had fallen,

53

moistening into activity cylindrical masses of millions upon millions of eggs that had lain buried in the sand till their shells were cracked and the surface of the earth began to seethe with hungry life. The brown locusts swelled without sustenance and grew themselves rudimentary wings; but long before they could fly they were on the march. The desert was grey with these hordes of *voetgangers* crawling south-eastward with one acord. They crawled on their way, unchecked but not unharassed; for all other living things were their enemies. First, out of an empty sky, flocks of locust-birds gathered in myriads and shadowed them; they were ashen-grey, like the locusts themselves, and their wheeling cohorts darkened the sky as the locusts darkened the earth, converging on their victims in dense clouds from every quarter.

When the bushmen who camped by the water-holes of the Kalahari sighted these living clouds, they leapt in the air for joy and chattered excitedly; for they knew from these signs in the sky that the locusts had come and that their time of privation was over. They picked up their tiny bows and their quivers of poison-tipped arrows and ran: naked groups of yellow-skinned pigmy men, with thin bow-legs and protuberant bellies, and their womenfolk, even more dwarfed than they, with concave loins and grotesquely bulging haunches. All ran and leapt as they went like klip-springers, bounding from rock to rock, until they came to the edge of the moving locust-stream and fell on it greedily, competing with the hungry birds that beat in their faces. They crammed their monkey-mouths with the living insects, cracked brittle bodies and wings with their teeth and swallowed them whole, while the children sat on the ground and picked them to pieces and sucked. When they had gorged themselves, the bushmen lay prostrate and slept under the vertical sun, knowing well that when they awakened they would see new multitudes of *voetgangers* hopping and crawling – or that, if they had passed, they would surely find them again when they halted at nightfall, clustered densely like swarms of bees on the hills of the termite-ants, encrusting every visible bush and twig with their motionless masses.

Not only the locust-eaters and bushmen preyed on them. Every four-footed creature that roamed those dry plains took its toll as they passed. Herds of springbok and sassaby and oribi stood fetlock deep in the slow-moving current. They stamped in it with their hooves and licked up crushed locusts with their tongues, while from the trampled mash there arose a nauseous odour, faintly sweet and foetid. Even the timid dik-diks, small grass-nibbling antelopes no bigger than a hare, turned carnivore, and ostriches came striding down-wind to gobble their share. All these shy beasts grew bold and tame in this orgy of gluttony. They knew they had nothing to fear from the bushmen's arrows so long as a food more delicate than the warm flesh torn from their quivering flanks lay there for the taking and going to waste.

Mile after mile and day after day the carnival went on – until, of a sudden, it seemed that the locusts became conscious of the wings they had grown. They stirred and stretched them. And then, with a sound of dry rustling that was like a sigh, with one accord they rose and took to the air, swirling up like a dust-devil, spreading a curtain so thick that the midday sun could not pierce it and the land beneath them went dark, so high that only the birds could now attack them – as they did, one black cloud falling on the other and slashing it into holes that were no sooner made than closed.

When once they had tried their wings, the winged locusts flew south-east, as the *voetgangers* had trekked south-east, not so very high in the air. Here and there, where a pitiful patch of green marked the labour of man, the moving cloud would dip downward and smother it momently, then rise, and no green was left. They flew over the sources of great rivers – the Notwani and the Marico, which join to form the Limpopo; they passed from the wastes of bush and sand to the grassy highveld, and stripped the new farms that sheltered beneath the Magaliesberg. They reached the Witwatersrand at the very moment when the Graftons' mealie-fields had attained their prime – when the grains in the cobs had swollen to their full fatness, but were still milky and sweet.

Janse saw them coming in the ultimate distance: a tiny cloud that puzzled him – for it seemed, somehow, too solid for vapour. He watched the cloud grow in size, but it did not lessen in density. It must surely be dust, he thought, sucked up by some fierce whirl of wind in the upper air. But the cloud did not rotate as a dust-devil would, and he had never seen a sandstorm so huge as this or one whose size increased so rapidly. For, as it approached, this strange cloud seemed to be spreading in every direction, until, soon, it veiled half the sky – just as though a dark curtain were being drawn over the vault by a slow, deliberate hand.

Even now, though the strangeness of the sight had an element of terror in it, he was perplexed rather than frightened. It was only when the advancing blackness reached the level of the Haskards' farm, Brakfontein, and the sharp edge of the curtain appeared to curl under itself and drop downwards, blotting out the horizon, that he guessed what it was. Then true horror seized him. He jumped to his feet and shouted for Cobus, his Hottentot herdsman. The old man came hobbling up to the stoep, his slant eyes narrowed by sleep, and stared stupidly in the direction where Janse pointed.

'Ja, sprinkane, baas. The locusts have come to Baas Haskard's. It's ten years since the sprinkane came.' He chuckled and nodded and licked his lips. The bushman blood in him quickened at the thought of this delicacy.

'I know they're sprinkane, fool,' Janse shouted. 'But what can we do?' The old man only laughed. The question needed no answer.

Janse turned away, cursing him. There were several vague thoughts in his mind. He had heard that sometimes, when locusts approached, men would beat tin cans to scare them, or light fires of pungent herbs in the midst of their crops to drive them higher with smoke; but no sooner had these ideas entered his mind than he saw their futility. The locusts were too many, too many. ... The flight that had fallen on Brakfontein and blotted it out had left the advancing curtain apparently undiminished. Every second it seemed to draw nearer and to gather speed as it came.

Another wild impulse struck him. Should he jump on his horse and gallop to Wonderfontein to warn his father and Adrian? That would be equally futile. Already the sun had gone out and three-parts of the landscape lay shadowed. And there was no time to give warning in any case. Even as he stood there irresolute, gloom fell on him; the air seemed to thicken; and now it was full of rasping wings and flying bodies that beat in his face and eyes and clawed at his clothes as though they hoped to devour them. They beat on the galvanized roof like flurries of hail and stunned themselves; they silted up on the stoep like drifts of dead leaves and lay there seething.

Janse beat the air with his hands to keep them away from his face. This was only the fringe of the locust cloud, but soon, hardly knowing how, he found himself in the thick of it. He had plunged like a madman down-hill to the mealie-fields, with his hat in one hand and a stiff *sjambok* in the other. He was stamping and kicking and wading through locusts ankle-deep, and lashing the air with his hat and his *sjambok* in an impotent lust to kill. Hundreds must have been crushed by his feet: his *veldskoene* were clotted with them; and the stercorous stink of the pulped mass rose and sickened him.

Then suddenly, as he stood stamping, and beating the half-solid air, it came to him that all this fury was useless. These myriads would have their way whatever he did. He stood, gasping and panting, the sweat rolling down his face, and watched them at work. There was even an awful fascination in seeing the mechanical thoroughness with which they set about their destruction, beginning at the feathery crown of the mealies and working downwards – stripping every fragment of leaf that still had sap in it, tearing away with their vicious jaws at the envelope that sheathed the cob, devouring the cob itself, grain by grain, from its tapered tip to its base. He gazed at this miracle of destructive energy till he could bear it no longer. Then he found himself sobbing in spite of himself, hot tears mingling with the sweat on his cheeks. He turned slowly and limped back to the house, no longer trying to protect himself from the hail-flurries of flying insects that lashed his face. He flung himself on his bed and lay there motionless till the senseless sobbing that shook him had ceased. When he opened his eyes, the darkness that covered the earth had vanished, the sun shone brilliantly. A few locusts still struggled or fluttered with damaged wings or floundered with broken legs on the stoep. But the sky was clear; the visitation had vanished. Only, before his eyes, where a few hours since the mealies had stood and shimmered in their pride, lay a waste of bare red earth set with naked stalks.

(4)

Janse pulled himself together. If he stood there much longer brooding over that desolate scene, he told himself, he would surely lose his senses. He forced his thoughts deliberately in the direction of Wonderfontein: it was less dangerous to the emotions to pity others than to pity one's self. His father's loss

57

would be not merely greater materially but graver than his own; for he, after all, was still young, responsible for nobody but himself, possessed of the power and the will, if needs were, to 'cut his losses' as Major Haskard's prophetic wisdom had advised him; whereas his father was a middle-aged man who had lived a hard life and had put more than thirty years of toil and devotion into the making of Wonderfontein, only to see it smitten by three crushing blows, of which this last was the heaviest. It could not be easy, Janse felt, to start life all over again at fifty-three.

He thought of his mother, too. Though he respected his father's courage and tenacity of purpose, it was she, he knew well, who in adversity such as this was the stronger of the two, and, for that reason, ready to bear the double burden on her slight shoulders. Yet what affected him even more deeply than his concern for these demands on her readily-accepted love and courage, was a vision that suddenly came to him not of herself but of the little garden in front of the stoep at Wonderfontein which, ever since he could remember, had been her particular pride and care. That small green plot was so much hers as to seem almost a part of her: its reserved graciousness, set in the open veld, a symbol of her inner life; its order a reflection of her devotion and patience. There was little chance of its having escaped destruction; and when he thought of the havoc wrought on her shady trees of orange and loquat, of her peaches and quinces pillaged of their ripening fruit, of her beloved roses stripped naked of leaf and her new seedlings nipped off close to the ground, an anger fiercer and bitterer than any he had felt in his own misfortune seized him and whipped him out of his stupor. It seemed more bearable that his father or Adrian or himself should be ruined than that she, so gentle and innocent, should be hurt. When he thought of his mother having been hurt, he wanted to be near her.

He mounted his horse and rode straight across the ravaged mealie-fields, plunging ruthlessly through the bare stalks, breaking and trampling them as he went. Masses of gorged insects, too heavy to rise, still cluttered the ground, and stragglers of the flocks of locust-birds, which still preyed on them, fluttered up from the horse's feet. His mad, personal fury against the obscene creatures had passed. They had done their mischief; he no longer wished to destroy them; yet, as he neared the crest that looked down on Wonderfontein, he was awed by anticipation of what he would see, and steeled himself consciously to meet it.

He topped the rise and halted and gazed. Below him, seen through air that quivered with heat, the fields of Wonderfontein stretched, unbelievably green – though whether this sight were mirage or miracle he could not at first decide. It was no mirage. They stood there, so proud and rich in their splendid growth – Kaffir corn and mealies, and oats ripened ready for reaping – that he found it difficult to believe that his own nightmare experience had been real. And then, comparing the direction in which he had ridden with the line on which the locusts had been travelling when they settled on Witfontein, he saw that his old home, in fact, lay well to the north of its course, and realized that its escape was not surprising.

At Wonderfontein they had had their share of anxiety, holding their breath as they saw the dark cloud approach, thanking heaven when they saw it pass at a merciful distance. It was Lisbet whose thoughts, in that moment of relief, had first turned to Janse.

'Mount quickly, Adrian,' she had said, 'and ride over to Witfontein and see what has happened.'

The brothers met midway down the falling slope. When he saw Janse's dishevelled figure and wild eyes Adrian knew the worst, and his stolid face grew grave with concern.

'So they hit you?' he said. 'My poor fellow, we feared as much. Mamma sent me to see.'

Janse laughed. It was as much as he could do to stop himself breaking down again.

'There's nothing to see at Witfontein – not so much as a blade of grass. The brutes did their job thoroughly.'

Adrian nodded in sympathy, but made no reply. He turned his horse and they rode down, side by side, in silence. Suddenly Janse laughed again: he was more sure of himself now.

'Mr. Blair will blame you and your Burgers for this,' he said.

'No doubt. And our father will blame you, Janse, because he knows you smiled when he prayed against hail.'

'What, in God's name, has hail got to do with it?' Janse cried. 'Well, anyway, I'm past praying for now.'

When she saw him, Lisbet's heart bled for him. She knew better than the rest the meaning of the air of bravado which he assumed to hide the bitterness of his defeat.

'Stay with us for a little while, Janse,' she pleaded. 'There's no need for you to go back to Witfontein. It will only depress you, my son, and you know there is nothing to be done.'

Janse shook his head. 'There is much to be done, mother,' he told her. 'I have got to pull myself together and decide what I'm going to do. I shall have to think hard – and, when one is thinking, it's better to be alone.'

'Let us make a plan, Janse. There's no need to be in a hurry. Wait till Piet comes home and talk matters over with him. He's young, but he's full of wisdom – in such matters wiser than any of us.'

'Piet's thoughts are not my thoughts, mother, and never will be,' he told her. 'I must make a plan for myself.' ('He's jealous of Piet,' she thought. 'They're all jealous of Piet.') She said:

'If you're lonely, you'll come to me, Janse? Promise me that.'

He smiled. 'Never fear. I'm used to loneliness, mother. On the whole, I think it suits me.'

She let him go, reluctantly.

(5)

But it was not so easy, he found, to think at Witfontein – or was it, perhaps, too easy? – though even the wildest, the most contradictory of speculations on his future were more tolerable than the present desolation of which he became aware as soon as he ceased from thinking. One fact, at least, emerged clearly. It would be useless as well as unreasonable for him to attempt to drag out an idle existence at Witfontein. As a farmer he had to confess he was ruined beyond recovery.

There remained a number of alternatives. He might abandon his farm and join the family at Wonderfontein, lending a hand with the harvest and helping his father when Adrian was away, settling down, as did many younger sons, on the outskirts of the farm, an unpaid *bywoner*, dependent on Wonderfontein for his sustenance: a man without a future. Though this was the path of least resistance he could not accept the humiliation of such a parasitic manner of life.

Again, he might fall back on Major Haskard's offer and take up some small salaried post in the mines at Kimberley. His pride rebelled against claiming the help he had already refused

– it stood even more stiffly against being beholden to the Haskards: a circumstance that would certainly lower him in Lavinia's eyes. It was his nature, he felt, to stand on his own feet; he could not easily take orders or adapt himself to being a mere cog in a machine that made money for others; and these temperamental defects would prevent him from being a success and rising to a position in which he might make money for himself. No . . . he told himself: that wouldn't do.

As a last resort, indeed, he might induce Piet to let him 'go in' with him in his profitable business of transport-riding; but unless he could join Piet on equal terms (which was impossible without capital) he would still be subordinate – and that to a younger brother – and even if he could scrape together enough money to take a share (which seemed most unlikely) he doubted if he and Piet could ever agree. He was fond of Piet and even, in some ways, admired him; but Piet's thoughts, as he had said, were not his; sooner or later, there would be quarrels, and these would give pain to his mother. That was a risk he refused to take. All these possible ways of escape seemed equally dangerous, their destinations equally dark.

The first ray to illuminate his future broke through unexpectedly one evening when Isaac Meninsky, the little Jew *smous*, arrived in his donkey-wagon at Witfontein. Among Dutch-speaking Afrikanders Meninsky was usually known as 'the Peruvian' – by heaven knows what odd confusion of ideas, for he had come to South Africa from Poland by way of Whitechapel. Every farmer and farmer's wife on that part of the highveld knew 'the Peruvian' and welcomed him. He was not merely their main source of information (to say nothing of gossip) as to what was taking place in the outer world, but he set the fashion as the sole purveyor of imported luxuries and cheap European merchandise, which he brought to their doors in his donkey-wagon and bartered for the less perishable kinds of country produce – ostrich feathers and ivory and beeswax or honeycombs.

Janse had always liked little Meninsky, in spite of himself and in spite of the Peruvian's unprepossessing exterior. He was a shrimp of a man, with a short body and relatively long bowlegs whose thinness, enhanced by the tightness of the trousers he wore, suggested those of an insect. His face, too, was against him. Though he shaved himself regularly, his cheeks and chin were always dull blue-black, prolonging the shadow of coarse, close-cropped black hair as stiff as a dog's, which grew low on his forehead above large brown eyes, superficially lustrous yet oddly opaque. It was in some ways an animal – and also an aged – face. Though the smoothness of those blue-black cheeks suggested that he was still young, harsh experience had given it a look of cunning and wariness. Yet the ugliness of the upper part of it was discounted and counteracted by a mobile, humorous mouth which displayed quite admirable teeth. The curve of that mouth in repose had a certain melancholy sweetness when he spoke and smiled (and he rarely spoke without smiling) its liveliness made one forget his expressionless eyes.

In spite of its meagre proportions Meninsky's body was not only wiry but also remarkably agile. His mind, too, was quicker in its reactions than the minds of most of his customers; his Cockney intelligence divined what they thought or wanted almost sooner than they knew it for themselves; but though this agility made many fear his shrewdness, Meninsky was not, as were many of his kind, rapacious. He could even be, on occasion, bewilderingly generous – not so much for his customers' sake as for his own, since the lavish gesture heightened his sense of his own importance and – whatever it might cost – was well worth the money to a man whose appearance, as he knew, invited distrust.

This tendency to 'show off' to his own disadvantage, was one of the reasons, perhaps, why the Peruvian had not shared in the rewards of the scramble for money from which many men of his race had profited at the expense of Kimberley. On his arrival in South Africa as a penniless immigrant, his first thought had been to restore the self-respect which had been crushed out of him in a humiliating childhood. If he dreamed of money, he had been less anxious to make it than to be regarded as a human being, and this rather pathetic ambition he had managed to achieve by establishing a reputation for honesty, rare among vagrant foreigners, in his dealings among the simple, unprejudiced folk of the high-veld, who had found him a man of his word who gave value for money and not one of those *Boerverneukers* who lived on his sharper wits and exploited their ignorance.

In this way, during the last four years, Meninsky had made himself welcome and familiar among the scattered farms of the Northern Free State and Southern Transvaal. Having none of the Englishman's self-consciousness, and a helpful knowledge of Yiddish, he had picked up the local Dutch dialect without difficulty and spoke it fluently. The men tolerated him as a harmless oddity; the women liked him – not merely for the exciting merchandise (and the gossip) he brought, but because he never took liberties and had no 'designs' on them. The approach of his rickety wagon with its team of fourteen donkeys, in which he wandered over the roadless veld from farm to farm, unarmed and inoffensive, became in their empty lives the signal for a festal evening. When he had told them the news and given them the messages he carried from distant relations or friends, he would repair to his outspanned wagon and bring back his concertina; and then there would be singing of hymns and of the old Cape songs (not always too decorous) and sometimes – though Mr. Blair would have frowned on this – the earth floors, blackened with cow-manure and smelling of sour milk, would be cleared for dancing that went on far into the night.

But it was not these elementary qualities of gaiety and good nature, by which Meninsky had endeared himself to the simple folk of the back-veld farms, nor even his radiant vitality, that attracted Janse to him. He had long suspected that there was more behind the Peruvian's opaque eyes than he liked to reveal to people of whose sympathy he was uncertain. He had guessed that this odd little Cockney Jew was, like himself, a dreamer of dreams – a suppressed (and even more strictly suppressed) romantic. Again and again, in Meninsky's talk of small things, the romantic vein revealed itself. He was still, Janse saw, overwhelmed and yet exalted by the vastness of this new continent over which he wandered. When he spoke casually, almost excusing himself for mentioning them, of his more remote adventures on the Basutoland border or in the mountainous parts of the Transvaal, Meninsky's voice warmed, as it were, with an inward rapture. He spoke with a tinge of awe, the attitude of a man who had found beatuy and terror there as well as the laughable misadventures out of which he concocted such good stories against himself; and this note in his talk had made Janse curious to know more of him – not only because it seemed odd to associate this mean little pedlar with such perceptions, but also because, so far as he knew, none other of his acquaintance (and certainly none of his own family) had ever considered South Africa from any point of view but that of the practical farmer whose intereest in it was to know whether the veld of a district was sweet or sour, healthy or poisonous, and whether the natives were friendly or hostile to white men. He welcomed Meninsky also because he was bored. Having chewed his thoughts over and over again and eaten his heart out through nearly three weeks of savage loneliness, he was glad of the diversion of meeting anybody.

When he saw the donkeys come trotting up with their quick little feet and Meninsky jumping down from the wagon-seat, Janse opened a bottle of his mother's peach-brandy and brought glasses out on to the stoep.

'Come along, Peruvian,' he shouted. 'Just in time for a sopie.'

Meninsky pursed his thick lips and shook his head. 'No drink for me, Janse,' he said. 'That's not in my line. Used to wait for my mother outside a gin-palace in the Whitechapel Road, and saw too much of it. It's not any too good for you either, my lad, I should say. My God, but you don't half look nervy! Took a bit of a knock with those damned locusts: is that it?'

'Knocked flat. Down and out.'

'Well, you're not the only one, if that's any comfort to you. Farm after farm – all the way from the Magaliesberg into Basutoland.'

'I've been floored three years running. This time I'm going to stay down. I've had enough.'

'I can see you've taken it pretty hard, but you ought to know better, having been born in the country and knowing no different. That's Africa, that is, Cocky. You never know where you are with this blessed country. As for trusting it. . . . Look: it's like making a pet of a leopard. One day you're scratching its stomach and the next it tears your throat out. I often ask myself: Why the hell do we live here?'

'God knows.'

'So do I, my son. Because it's worth it. South Africa's the best country on earth.'

'You're not broke, Meninsky.'

The little man laughed: 'I have been. I know all about it. Before you come teaching me, just you try being broke in Warsaw or London on a wet night in February! Well, all right: you're broke. Half the people in this country are broke if they only knew it. What are you going to *do*? That's the point.'

'Oh, let's talk about something more cheerful.'

But the little Jew had his way. Janse told him of the three solutions that had presented themselves. Meninsky listened, nodding occasionally, but made no comment until he had finished.

'And so none of these ideas suit you,' he said. 'Well, you're perfectly right. They certainly wouldn't suit me. First: staying at Wonderfontein. That wouldn't take you anywhere. At the end of five years you'd probably be just a bit better off than you are now; but you'd have lost those five years, and, what's more, you wouldn't have lived them. As for taking a job in an office in Kimberley: the answer to that is just that you'd break your heart there. You'd find it a prison, as I did. All the time you'd be chafing to escape; and you wouldn't escape till they had no use for you – and then it'd be too late. As for going in with your brother: that wouldn't do either. To begin with, you're chalk and cheese or oil and water; you'd never get on. And I'll tell you something else. Transport-riding's seen its best days. They're pushing on the railway from Capetown to Beaufort West. Where will your ox-wagons be then? And I'll ask you another question that's come to my mind. How long will Kimberley last?'

'As long as they go on getting diamonds.'

'I'm not putting my shirt on that either. There's diamonds all over Africa: I've bought one myself that was found here, on the Witwatersrand. Suppose you or me discovered another diamond-field bigger than Kimberley – and why the hell shouldn't we? Suppose we went and gave them a glut of diamonds? There'd be a lot of burnt fingers in Kimberley, I can tell you that! And why? Because, when you come to think of it, diamonds ain't *worth* anything, not in themselves. They fetch money because there ain't enough to go round the women who want them.'

'There's more money in them than in farming, anyway,' Janse said ruefully.

'Well, I'll give you that. But there's surer money in gold.'

'I don't see any difference. Is gold in itself worth any more than diamonds? Supposing you and I discovered a gold-field . . .'

Meninsky's eyes almost grew bright. 'Supposing we did. Go on . . .'

'The same thing would happen. That's all.'

'Give me the chance to try! The same thing wouldn't happen, Janse, and I'll tell you why. All the business in the world is based upon gold. It's the currency of all civilized nations, and always will be, because, first of all, its quality doesn't vary: pure gold is pure gold; you can divide it up as you like and say that one piece is exactly as valuable as another of the same weight. Another thing: you can't destroy it and it don't deteriorate. Another: it's easily tested and can't be faked. Sum it up: gold's the only uniform metal of which there's enough to go round, and that's rare enough, at the same time, to give a high value in a small compass. The more gold you find, the more gold is going to be wanted. I've gone into this, mind. When the last big strikes were made in Australia and California, did the value of gold go down? Not a bit of it! That's twenty-five years ago, and the price today is as high as it was before those discoveries that trebled the output. You may keep your diamonds! Gold's the only thing about which you can prophesy safely. And that's why I've been after it, mate, for the last three years.'

'After gold, Meninsky?'

The Peruvian screwed up his eyes and chuckled silently. 'You must think I'm a lot softer than I am if you imagine I want to spend the rest of my life in a donkey-wagon selling ribbons and tooth-combs. Not me! Look here, mate, when I came up to Kimberley, and had a look round, I saw all the bright boys from Whitechapel, Barney and Cohen and Co., had shoved in on the ground-floor and didn't want any new company. I was too late by a year. That's when I began to think about gold. Why did I think of it? Because I was a good boy, mate, and always read my Bible. Where did Solomon get the gold for his temple? From Africa. Not a doubt of it. Wherever you go among the natives, like I do, you'll hear about gold. But you have to go easy. These old Boers, you know, they're terrified of anyone finding it. If they think there's gold on a farm they'd just as soon hide it. "Where shall we get grazing or cornland or garden-land," they say, "if a lot of damned *rooinekke* come digging on our land?" And Kaffirs are just the same: they're afraid of the white man turning them out of their villages. If you mention gold, the game's up. But supposing you're only a poor bloody Jew in a donkey-cart, who's not a *Boer-verneuker* come to skin them but a harmless bloke that can tootle a song and play the concertina? That's a different matter: you can go wherever you like and nobody will mind. Well, I've been where I liked, and nobody did. I've driven my donkeys over pretty near every square mile of the High Veld. I've kept my eyes open, likewise my ears, and I've picked every brain, black and white, I've come across. And one thing I know for certain now: there's no gold here, mate. You can keep the Witwatersrand! I've finished with it. But farther north? Now you're talking! Nothing big as yet. Nothing noisy enough to make the swine in Kimberley prick up their ears and stop guzzling diamonds. But we're getting hot, as they say. Last year I was having a look round Lydenburg where they're picking up bits of alluvial in the creeks. That's all right as far as it goes, but it's not enough yet. What I want to know is where that alluvial gold's been washed down from. What *I* want is a reef, and by Gad, I'm going to find it before I've finished. Look here, now, I'm talking serious. I'm going up to the Low Veld tomorrow. So what about it?'

'What about what?'

'What about coming along with me, mate? You've nothing to lose by it and a hell of a lot to gain if it pans out right. I believe in luck, and I believe in first thoughts – intuitions, or whatever you call 'em. I landed up here by luck. I'd intended to outspan tonight at Oosthuizen's place, Langlaagte. But I lost a wheel in a donga and here I am. When I saw you sitting on the stoep here, looking like death, I said to myself: "God of Abraham, Isaac Meninsky, this is the very chap you've been looking for: a right Afrikander with brains in his head who can speak Dutch as easy as English and won't be suspected." If you want to try your luck, here's your chance, mate. Half and half: that's the terms. I can't say fairer than that.'

'What could I do with my farm here?'

'Your farm? Look at it! What's it worth, anyway?'

Janse laughed: 'Not much, I'm afraid.'

'It won't be worth any less if you leave it. I reckon. You've got a good wagon, haven't you?'

'Yes, the wagon's all right; but I've got no oxen. The lung-sickness took my best. What's wrong with your own wagon?'

'What's right with it? Just you try! That wagon's no more than a faggot of firewood tied up with reins. It's got to be patched up day by day even here on the High Veld where the going's easy. In the Low Country I give it three days – and that's with good luck. Not that that would stop me – but it

67

would be asking for trouble, mind you. Can't you raise a team out of your dad?'

Janse shook his head. 'The lung-sickness hit him too. I know he has no oxen to spare.'

'What about Piet, then?'

'Well. . . . You know him.'

'Yes, I know him. That kid, Piet, is the smartest of the bunch. I won't say he has better brains than you, mate; but he's got 'em better in hand and knows how to use 'em. He must have made a good bit; but I don't think he's one to take risks. You may do something bigger than Piet before you've finished; but if I were playing for safety Piet's the one I'd back. He's honest, too. In a crooked hole like Kimberley it don't take long to find out who's straight, and young Piet's straight. He's a man of his word. When he says a thing he means it. With trade slackening off as it is, I reckon he ought to be able to spare you a team.'

'Well, I'll ask him. Piet's fond of money, you know.'

'Damn it, man – after all, you're his brother. He ought to trust you.'

They sat talking – or rather Janse was listening – far into the night. He was astonished to find how thoroughly the Peruvian, whom he had always regarded as amiable and comic, had mastered his subject. This little gnome had a prodigious memory. His brain was crammed, like some vast lumber-room, with a disorderly welter of facts about gold over which his romantic imagination fluttered continually, darting to and fro like an imprisoned bird. He knew all about the Portuguese legends of Ophir and Monomotapa; he had gleaned all there was to be known of Carl Mauch who, feigning madness, had journeyed on foot to Tati beyond the Limpopo and seen the great ruined city of Queen Sheba, Zimbabwe, in Lobengula's country. He had talked with Australians who had washed for gold at Todd's creek and then abandoned it. He knew of the quartz reefs discovered at Eersteling and near Marabastad; but all these were small things, very different from the great gold-field that still lay hidden, far away in the North, the gold core of the backbone of Africa which he knew he was destined to discover. He had even bought books and tried to master the elements of geology. He talked on and on, with his quick, apeish gestures, never losing the heat of his argument, until Janse reached a point at which he could keep his eyes open no longer.

'Will you doss down here, Meninsky, or sleep in your wagon?' he said.

'In the wagon, I reckon. I don't need much sleep. I shall be off before you're awake. But, mind you, we meet in Pretoria in a month's time. In the Church Square outspan at Pretoria. Is that a bargain?'

Janse smiled. 'Perhaps. We'll see. If I'm there, I'm there, Meninsky.'

The Peruvian laughed out loud. 'You'll be there all right, mate,' he said. 'You'll be there: otherwise I should have been sleeping at Langlaagte this night.'

He was as good as his word. When Janse woke next morning the donkey-wagon had vanished. His mind was still so confused by the torrent of Meninsky's talk that he might have been excused if he had wondered if it had actually ever been there. But that talk had already infected his imagination and made him restless. Looking out over the wintry high-veld that morning he felt himself imprisoned, as never before, by its vast monotony, and reproached himself for never having tried to escape – for not having even realized that escape was possible. Beyond those horizons there lay the beauty and mystery of a whole continent of which this odd little man, who had only landed at Capetown four years ago, already knew more than he who had lived all his life within reach of it. No doubt one explanation for this physical unadventurousness was his lameness. A maimed man, and a shy one at that, was hardly cut out for the heroic. Yet this challenge to adventure, coming from a man of Meninsky's mettle, had put him to shame. If only to justify his relatively high opinion of himself he felt he ought to accept it; while it was clear that if he continued to go on brooding and dreaming at Witfontein he would never be any nearer to his ambitions – including his desire of shining in Lavinia's eyes. Supposing that, having gone North with Meninsky, he did make his fortune? Then – for such was human nature – not only his brothers but also the Haskards would be compelled to respect him. And supposing he failed? Even then he would not be any worse off than he was at this moment and at least could congratulate himself on having put up a fight.

He still doubted Meninsky. Though he had allowed himself for a while to be carried away and was still intoxicated by his effervescence, there was a solid strain in Janse that recoiled from the oriental opulence of the Peruvian's ideas and distrusted their volatility. Even so, they continued to haunt him with such persistence that in the afternoon he rode over to Wonderfontein and sought out Piet.

'I want a good span of oxen, Piet,' he told him.

'They're none too easy to come by just now, and prices are high. What do you want them for, anyway?'

'I'm thinking of going up North to the gold-fields to try my luck.'

'You'll find more coming back than going up in these days. Whom are you thinking of going with?'

'Meninsky.'

'That little rat? He's a Kimberley *smous*. What d'you think he knows about gold?'

'Rather more than you might imagine. He's sharp, you know.'

'Oh, he's sharp enough. A bit too sharp for you, Janse, I should say.'

'There are more than a thousand diggers round Lydenburg.'

'Yes. . . . Loafers who wouldn't work hard enough to earn a living in Kimberley. I know.'

'If I took up a load of stuff to Lydenburg I could be certain of selling it.'

'If it was a square-face gin you could. But you'd be a darned sight less certain of getting paid for it.'

'Will you lend me a team of oxen, Piet, and help me to have a shot at it?'

'Lend you oxen to take into the North? Why, half of it's fly-country. You might lose the lot in a week. I wouldn't go through that part myself without a good guide. If you're fool enough to want to take such a chance I can make up a team of sorts and sell it you cheap.'

'You know I'm more or less broke. Will you trust me till I come back, then?'

Piet looked him square in the face with his open blue eyes.

'No, I'm damned if I will, Janse. We're good friends and all the rest of it, but that's asking a bit too much.'

'Ah, well, if you won't, there's an end to it. Never mind.'

Piet stood and looked at him in silence. His eyes were narrowed. It was impossible to guess what thoughts were taking shape behind that firmly critical but not unkindly face. He liked Janse, and Janse knew it.

'Look here, Janse,' he said, with that pleasant slow smile of his, 'I'm not going to sell you a team of oxen on credit, and I won't lend you money either. We've always been pretty good friends, you and I, and the quickest way of breaking up any friendship is lending or borrowing money. But I tell you what I will do, if you like: I'll buy Witfontein.'

'Buy Witfontein?'

'Well, you're going to leave it, anyway, on this wild-goose chase of yours, aren't you? I won't say it will come to a lot of harm – when all's said and done, you haven't put much into it – but whatever you have done is certainly bound to go back unless somebody holds it together. That'd be waste, and I can't bear waste. I'm not mad keen on buying it, mind you; but I'm not going to go on transport-riding for the rest of my life. I shall have to settle down sooner or later, I suppose, and if I buy land I'd sooner it were near Wonderfontein for mother's sake. Adrian's so much away from home, and neither she nor father are as young as they were. The only other farm that's available, so far as I can see, is Grobler's place, to the east of Uncle Barend's – and I naturally don't want *him* for a neighbour: who would? And the Haskards are decent folk. What do you think of that, Janse?'

He had been thinking desperately hard as he listened to the measured flow of Piet's voice. As soon as Piet spoke of 'settling down' he had remembered Meninksy's warning that the railway, slowly approaching Kimberley, would kill transport-riding. In spite of his brother's casual, unemotional tone, he was conscious of a guarded undercurrent of eagerness; but when he told himself this he had despised himself for being suspicious and ungenerous – particularly when Piet spoke of his concern for their mother and their father. And while the idea of parting with Witfontein – the background of many exalted dreams and hopes no less than of his misfortunes – came to him as a shock, wasn't it just as well, he asked himself, now that he had decided to throw in his lot with Meninsky, to make a clean sweep, an irreparable break with the unlucky past, and set out on this new adventure unhampered by any ties of possession or sentiment?

'What will you give me for Witfontein, Piet?' he asked.

Piet hesitated. 'It's not worth a lot, Janse. It's poor veld –

much more rocky than Wonderfontein – and the spring, as you found to your cost, fails badly in times of drought. It needs money and labour to make anything of it, and the house isn't up to much either.'

'Well, what will you give me, anyway?'

'I'll give you eight yoke of oxen and guarantee they're all sound in hoof and limb and salted for lung-sickness. They'll be worth seven pounds apiece: a hundred and twelve in all – and considering I could buy Grobler's place for sixty, you can't say that's not fair.'

'Very well: we'll call it a bargain,' Janse said.

When they had shaken hands, he was not so sure of himself. He was free, indeed, and lighter for the shedding of his only responsibility; yet the loss of Witfontein – not so much of its lands as of the mean mud-built house which had been a protection and refuge for his sensitiveness for so long that it had become part of his natural covering – gave him an odd feeling of nakedness and vulnerability: he felt like a snail that has ventured out of its shell.

There were other emotional embarrassments that he found hard to face, such as the moment when he was forced to break the news to his mother. Lisbet was less disturbed by it than he had expected.

'We shall miss you, Janse, my darling,' she said, 'but that doesn't matter so long as this change makes you happy. And you haven't been really happy at Witfontein, have you? You've done your best, I know, but the luck's been against you. You've fought against it so long, my son, and you've worn yourself out, though you may not know it. And I've sometimes thought—' she hesitated as though she were not quite sure the words might not wound him – 'I've sometimes wondered whether your being so near the Haskards, whose life is so much easier than ours and so different in every way, may not possibly have been disturbing and made you more restless. Of course, I know you like them and they've been kind to you. But even so . . .'

'They've been down at the Cape all summer, mother. I've almost forgotten them.'

Lisbet smiled and shook her head.

'I'm not so sure of that, Janse. Perhaps you might be happier if you did forget them.'

He laughed and kissed her, but made no answer. After a moment of silence she said:

'It will be nice for me to have Piet at Witfontein, won't it? He's the sort of boy who ought really to settle down.' And again, after another long pause: 'If you go as far North as the Zouspansberg, you may see your brother Andries. You'll be able to tell us all about him when you come home.'

Book Two

CHAPTER ONE

---

(1)

JANSE crossed the crown of the Witwatersrand where the waters of Africa are divided, flowing westward by Vaal and Orange, to the Atlantic, and eastward, by Crocodile and Limpopo, to the Indian Ocean. His wagon jarred and jolted over outcrops of quartz that protruded from the thin soil like the spines or ribs of monsters that had been stranded and sunken in silt.

It was a meagre veld, he reflected, as Piet had said. Piet had been honest enough in his bargaining; the sixteen trek-oxen with which he had paid him for Witfontein were of good value too: sleek-skinned beasts and powerful-shouldered – as needs they must have been to have ploughed, hauling heavy loads, through the ten-mile belt of bottomless sand that surrounded Kimberley. Piet's bullocks were well-broken and wise; each knew his place in the span (even better than Janse did) and most of them answered to their names – those old-fashioned Dutch names, Holland, Blauwberg, Slingveld, Creishmann, Blesmann, Weinberg, which oxen had borne since the pioneers' wagons first went rolling over the Cape flats towards the dark interior. Janse had taken only one servant with him, the decrepit Hottentot Cobus, who knew well how to handle oxen, and trotted beside his team wielding a whip with a thirty-foot lash of giraffe-hide. But though Cobus could flick a fly from the leader's ears and cracked his lash in the air with the sound of a pistol-shot, he had no need to use his whip; for in this part of their trek the great road northward lay deeply scored on the veld, and the oxen followed the spoor without persuasion or guidance. Three miles an hour they could move at a walk, and five at a trot when the wagon was light; but for Janse there was no hurry. Allowing three days for the thirty-odd miles from Witfontein to Pretoria, he would still be well ahead of the time Meninsky had appointed; and the going was not only easy but also downhill, falling more than a thousand feet over the open veld that sloped from the watershed to the capital.

By the morning of the third day, Janse was already aware of the change in altitude. At this level the lungs breathed less deeply; the air grew sensibly warmer. It was small wonder, he thought, that members of the Volksraad, sitting in Pretoria, were accused of taking life more easily than their brethren on the stark High Veld. The town itself which he had never seen before, appeared half asleep in its deep-sunken, watery hollow, with the protective foot-hills of the Magaliesberg rising behind it. Yet, for all its apparent drowsiness, the capital had more pretensions to grace and dignity than the High Veld dorps which he knew. One entered it through a long avenue of magnificent blue-gums which gave the approach a ceremonial air. Though the one-storeyed houses of unburnt brick were no larger than those of Potchefstroom or Paardekraal, they were surrounded by ample gardens and orchards of flowers and sub-tropical fruit which gave them an air of ease and opulence, each set in its matrix of living green. As he advanced towards the church square over a wagon-track that meandered through the wide, grassy street beside a rippling water-course, Janse became aware of the pervasive fragrance of roses. Roses grew everywhere – standing stiffly in the hedges that bounded the gardens and orchards, trailing rampantly over every house-wall and stoep. The whole village (for it was no more) lay wrapped in a heavy sweetness that, to nostrils accustomed to the air of the High Veld, which is well-nigh odourless, seemed vaguely enervating.

Janse drove his team to the square where several other wagons were already stranded; when the Raad was in session, as now, its members usually slept in their own. There was no sign of Meninsky's donkey-wagon, so he told Cobus to outspan and drive the oxen away to graze on the town-lands. He himself accosted a tradesman, who sat solemnly smoking on the rose-wreathed stoep in front of his shop, and inquired the way to the Raadsaal, where he hoped to find Adrian, who had left Wonderfontein before the momentous decision had been made. The man did not answer but spat and jerked his pipe nonchalantly in the direction of a low thatched shed, which looked like a stable, on the opposite side of the street. Janse waded through the rank grass that bordered the wagon-track, jumped the water-course, and approached it. A shallow verandah ran the whole length of the building, and to its posts were tethered three patient donkeys which had long since cropped every blade of grass within reach. All three looked so downcast that Janse scratched the velvety ear of the one nearest to him. It accepted the caress unresponsively. He crossed the stoep on tiptoe and entered the House of Assembly.

It was an oblong barn, perhaps sixty feet long and twenty in width, with a high ceiling of canvas nailed to the cross-beams, and whitewashed walls girt by a dado of garish blue. Three-quarters of it were occupied by two horse-shoe-shaped tables, joined together and covered with green baize, at which the forty-two deputies of the Volksraad were sitting. Near the head of this, supported by the four members of his Executive Council, sat the President of the Republic, Thomas Burgers, distinguished from the rest not only by the chair of state which he occupied, but also by a green sash of office embroidered with gold slung across his breast, and by his clothes, which were of finer material and more elegant cut than the other members' short black jackets of broadcloth. He was a tallish man, Janse judged, middle-aged, but still vigorous. He had a tawny beard, fine eyes, and a high intellectual forehead, oddly pale in contrast with the sun-tanned faces of the rest. When he rose it appeared that he was not so tall as he seemed, yet he made an imposing figure: in the confidence of his poise, in his measured speech, which was that of a practised preacher or orator, and in the calculated gestures of his sensitive hands, it was easy to divine the qualities that separated him from the bulk of his audience. He was a man conscious of his culture. There was a suggestion of impatience – even of condescension – in the smile that lurked in the corners of his lively eyes – as though he were aware of their ignorance and obstinacy yet confident of his powers of persuasion. And the Raad members, Janse saw – more clearly, perhaps, than did this enthusiast – suspected, and even resented, his masterful mood.

They were most of them Boers, Afrikander farmers of the old-fashioned type, slow of thought, unpractised in speech, yet quick in instinct: a set of dour, heavily-bearded men whose big bodies were ill at ease in their ceremonial dress of badly-fitting black broadcloth and folded white handkerchief – to say nothing of the top-hats, swathed in crêpe, upturned on the floor beside them. Their brawny hands, which from time to time moved instinctively in search of forbidden pipes and tobacco-bags – looked oddly large and gnarled and out of place on the

77

green baize table-top littered with papers in front of them. They sat with lowered eyes and sullen faces, wrapped in their own thoughts. When the President spoke few of them looked at him. Though they sat there patiently enough, they would have been happier, Janse thought, on their feet, among the small group of farmers in corduroy and moleskin, reeking of tobacco and cattle, among whom, at the back of the hall, he found himself wedged.

From among the Raad members two figures immediately forced themselves on Janse's attention. The first was that of his brother Adrian, gigantic and golden-bearded, half-way down the table on the President's right. His blue eyes were alight. Though his honest face wore a slightly puzzled expression, he was clearly concentrating on every word Burgers spoke, so deeply engrossed in the search for its meaning that he remained unaware of his brother's arrival.

The other predominant figure was that of a clumsy, middle-aged man whose sturdy build and superb breadth of shoulder made his stature appear less than it actually was. He had massive craggy features framed in a fringe of whiskers and beard already touched with grey; but the force of the low-browed face appeared in its shrewd, steady eyes, in the coarse, dogmatic nose and in the heavily-moulded mouth whose projecting lower lip expressed an unusual degree of resolution if not pugnacity. His vast hands, too, lay on the table in front of him, with fists clenched. Janse noticed that from one of them, the right, the thumb was missing, and by this mutilation he recognized a man whom he had often heard tell of but never yet seen: Paul Kruger, the senior member for Rustenburg.

As he surveyed him sitting there still as a figure rough-hewn out of rock, he was immediately aware of Paul Kruger's physical and spiritual prepotence. This was no ordinary man. Though his brooding eyes were fixed as intently as Adrian's on the President's mobile face, though he, too, marked every syllable Burgers uttered, his air was judicial and wary and non-committal. Janse felt that, compared with this heavy, saturnine man, the President, for all his erudition and eloquence, looked oddly unsubstantial.

So far Bergers had been dealing with a number of *besluites* or resolutions affecting only matters of administrative routine, which the Raad approved perfunctorily with gruff rumblings of '*Hoor! Hoor!*' though the little group in the midst of which

78

Janse was standing appeared to be dissatisfied by the speed with which they were taken. Behind him, he heard a low, muttering voice:

'How can we know what new laws these fellows are putting over on us? Why can't this damned dominie speak a tongue we can understand instead of this finicking Hollands, or whatever it is? Why doesn't Paul Kruger stop him, instead of sitting there watching him like a sleepy buffalo in the grass?'

Janse turned his head. The speaker was a dark, stormy-eyed man of sixty or more whose face seemed familiar, though, for a moment, he could not place it. At last he remembered. The man was called Piet Bezuidenhout. He came from the Potchefstroom district and was actually, through the Bothmas, a distant connection of his own. An unruly race, these Bezuidenhouts: this man's father, in fact, had been the first cause and victim of the tragedy of Slachter's Nek. As he went on muttering behind Janse, a younger man's voice reproved him.

'Quiet, quiet, Oom Piet,' it whispered, 'or you'll have us turned out.'

'Turned out?' Bezuidenhout answered angrily. 'What? Can't a burgher speak his mind in the Volksraad that he's elected? What is this outlandish speech that nobody can understand?'

'It's good High Dutch, Bible Dutch,' another voice said. 'You forget that the President's a predikant.'

'A fine predikant from what I've heard,' Bezuidenhout growled.

'Before long, Oom Piet, you'll have to learn to speak Hollands yourself,' the other chuckled, 'or the collectors of taxes won't understand you. They're half of them Hollanders. The President has a fancy for foreigners.'

'What? More taxes? Is that what they're after?'

Piet Bezuidenhout spoke so loudly that the President stopped in the middle of a sentence and a burgher who acted as Serjeant-at-Arms called for silence. The President smiled and went on.

'Well, honourable gentlemen,' he said, 'now that our routine business is over, there is a matter affecting the prosperity of the whole state and all its citizens, which has been exercising my mind ever since our last great affliction: the visitation of locusts from which a large area of the Republic has suffered recently. To this end I have caused inquiries to be made from the most learned entomologists . . .'

79

('What's that his honour is saying?')

'. . . the most learned entomologists – authorities on insect life – in the University of Leyden.' ('What do Hollanders know about locusts?') 'As a result the Government has been supplied with exhaustive particulars as to the insect's life-history and a number of recommendations as to the best way of dealing with this scourge. Honourable gentlemen will have the opportunity of perusing these important documents; but I think I may as well explain that, according to these authorities, the locust's main breeding-ground is probably in the Kalahari desert, beyond our boundaries.' ('Who says we have any boundaries on the west? He talks like an Englishman!') 'In a series of dry years, the eggs accumulate. When rain comes, a number of generations of eggs may hatch out. Then the *voetgangers* start on their journey. My point is this: it is at this stage of the insect's life that it can be most easily destroyed. Therefore, gentlemen, in the next session of the Volksraad it is my intention to introduce a decree, compelling every burgher, as soon as he is cognizant of the presence of *voetgangers* on his lands – no matter how small the number may be – to communicate at once with the landdrost of his district, who, in his turn will communicate with the government, with the purpose of concerting measures for the destruction of this pest in its earliest stages. The text of the resolution will be issued immediately.' He paused, surveying the assembly with a confident smile. 'And now for another matter . . .'

'Mr. State President!'

On Adrian's right hand an old man had risen: a lean old man, of enormous height, with a flowing, snow-white beard stained yellow in streaks with tobacco-juice. He wore the traditional short jacket of the Dopper community.

'Your honour,' he said, in an ancient, quavering voice, 'you know I have done my best to prevent your election. Principally because of your religious views, which appear to me to be mistaken. As you have been elected by the majority, I submit as a good republican to this vote of the people, trusting that you are a more earnest believer than I thought.'

The President bowed and smiled.

'Burgher, you who voted against me for conscience' sake, you are as dear to me as those who voted for me.'

The old man waved the compliment aside: 'But now that I

hear you speak such things,' he said, 'my doubts are renewed, and even renewed more strongly. What is this resolution you would make but a flouting of God's will and word? For now, President, you would remove a visitation of God that is sent upon the people for their sins, even as the Lord, in His wisdom, sent locusts upon the Egyptians when His servant Moses stretched forth his rod over the land of Egypt, and the Lord brought an east wind upon the land all the day and all that night, and when it was morning the east wind brought the locusts that covered the face of the whole earth, so that the land was darkened. Even Pharaoh, the heathen, knew that those locusts were sent by the Lord. Even Pharaoh did not destroy them. Instead of that he called upon Moses and Aaron in haste and said he had sinned, and Moses went out from Pharaoh and entreated the Lord; and the Lord turned a mighty strong west wind which took away the locusts and cast them into the Red Sea, so that there remained not one locust in all the coasts of Egypt. It is true, honourable sir, that these locusts which have smitten our people came from the west, from the Kalahari maybe; but if the people had humbled themselves even as Pharaoh humbled himself, and prayed, who knows that the Lord might not have turned the wind to the east, and taken away the locusts and cast them into the ocean? I say it is by the help of the Lord, by appeasing His wrath with prayers for mercy and by humbling ourselves for those sins of false doctrine which you, Mr. President, are said to have harboured, that we should seek deliverance from the punishment we have deserved – not by acting on the advice of these men in Holland, of whom we know nothing but that they set themselves up as being more wise than their Maker. I say this without fear, and I know that Mr. Kruger shares my thoughts.' The patriarch sat down with a sigh.

Paul Kruger might possibly have shared his thoughts, but he made no sign of approval or disapproval. He sat there, stock-still and impassive, his heavy-lidded eyes half-closed, his stubborn lips motionless. Piet Bezuidenhout's image was right, Janse thought: a buffalo-bull in the long grass, sleepily biding his time.

President Burgers was up again, thoughtfully fingering his tawny beard. His tone was conciliatory.

'Honourable member,' he said, 'it is right that you should

have spoken your thoughts on this matter and I welcome them. But this is no time for discussion. When the resolution is introduced in the coming session, I assure you that it will be fully debated. At least you will be prepared. But there is one other matter that I want to mention before we adjourn. I have something to show you. It is a small thing in itself, but I think you, honourable gentlemen, will agree with me that it is a thing of great significance.' He searched in his trousers-pocket and jingled a handful of coins. 'Some time ago, I was authorized by the executive to mint a new coinage of gold. It is new in every way, for this gold was actually dug in the Republic's territory and paid for, in part, by the receipts from mining-licences. It comes, of course, from the diggings at Lydenburg. We have minted a thousand pieces. Here are some of them. I will pass them round for honourable members to examine. We need not be ashamed of their appearance, I think, for they were designed for us by a prominent artist in Holland.'

'What did I tell you, Oom Piet?' the young man behind Janse whispered mischievously: 'Holland again!'

'But what I want the Volksraad to realize,' Burgers went on, 'is that these small coins are bigger and mightier than they seem. If gold exists in large quantities, as we have reason to believe, this first minting marks a new era in the history of the Republic. That is the one thing we have always lacked, the thing the lack of which has kept us at the mercy of jealous neighbours: a negotiable currency of stable value and of our own. We have been oppressed and threatened with encirclement because we are poor. They call gold the sinews of war: it is also a guarantee of security, gentlemen. As you know, when you elected me as your President, I took every step in my power to increase our security. I raised with much difficulty, in Holland, a loan of sixty thousand pounds sterling to pay for the railway that will give us an outlet to the coast and free us from our dependence on our southern neighbours. Now, if things develop as they should, that loan and the railway that carries our gold will be paid for by the gold our railway carries. This first minting is only an earnest of what is to come. I think, honourable members, that this is a moment for modest but not unappropriate self-congratulation.'

He sat down. Adrian called *'Hoor, Hoor!'* and many of the others nodded approval; but one small group of members, clustered round the old man who had denounced the measures proposed for fighting locusts, were already on their feet, gesticulating and talking excitedly. One of them was waving in the air the new sovereign that Burgers had passed round: a small, swart, thick-set man, with what was either a closely-cropped beard or a thicket of unshaven stubble.

'A question ... a question!' he shouted. 'A question, Mr. State President!'

Burgers bowed. 'Let the honourable gentleman put his question.'

'Your Honour,' the old man began ...

'One must speak at a time, burgher.'

'I speak first,' the small dark man broke in, 'and here is my question.' He held up the coin. 'Whose image and superscription is this?'

'On one side you see the arms of the South African Republic: on the other the head of its President. That is the usual design for coinage in European countries.'

'I say it is against the commandment of God. Who is the President of the Republic that his likeness should be made in gold? Thou shalt not make thee any graven image or any likeness of anything that is in heaven above or in the earth beneath or that is in the waters beneath the earth. So it is written. If the rulers of a people set themselves up in this proud fashion, I say: "Woe unto that people!" '

'And *I* say, right honourable President ...' The old man could not keep silence; he rose up like a wild-haired prophet, his lips trembling with passion and one accusatory finger outstretched towards Burgers ... 'I say that this stiff-necked flouting of God's word in your wicked pride is only part of the sin that you have committed and for which the people will suffer. Your sin is the sin with which the people corrupted themselves when Moses received the commandments, when Aaron told the people to break off the golden ear-rings which were in the ears of their wives and their daughters and bring them unto him, and he received the ear-rings at their hands and fashioned them with a graving tool and made of them a god of gold. You are making a god of this gold, Mr. President – you; who should have learned in the scriptures. We have lived well enough without gold, which is the cause of all evil and envy, since God brought us up out of Egypt and the house of bondage into a strange country. Let this gold which the foreigners – and you, Mr. President – lust after, remain in the rocks where the Lord saw fit to hide it; though perhaps you will say,' he added bitterly, 'as Aaron said when Moses returned from the mountain of Sinai: "They gave it me; then I cast it into the fire – and there came out this golden image of Thomas Burgers!" '

Burgers shook his head. 'You put it hardly, old friend. We are a small state, trying to live our own lives in conditions that change, as you yourself know they are changing.'

'The commandments of the Lord do not change.'

'This people, burgher, has elected me as its President. By the grace of God I shall endeavour to keep my trust and do what is best for them. The issue of coinage was authorized by a large majority of the Volksraad. Its form was a matter for the Executive Council to decide. *Ik heb gezegd*. I have spoken.'

'You, Paul Kruger . . .' the old man pleaded.

The member for Rustenburg sat with his heavy eyes lowered, his thumbless fist clenched on the table. He did not speak.

(2)

'That is how we waste half our time,' Adrian told Janse indignantly. 'I myself am a religious man, and so is the President, but we can't govern a new country, a little country, that's fighting for its life, as he says, by settling every matter we have to deal with by biblical precedent and referring every detail to the Book of Exodus. Wherever Burgers turns, the poor fellow spends all his energy in fighting prejudice. He has very few friends, I'm afraid; but those he has are loyal, and generally more intelligent than his open enemies.'

'And Paul Kruger?'

'Ah, there's a man I don't understand. When we forced Pretorius to resign after he had thrown away the Diamond Fields, Paul Kruger could easily have made himself President if he'd wished. But he didn't. Instead of that, he and his Dopper friends put up a man of no weight to fight against Burgers, and when Burgers won, see what happens: here's Paul Kruger serving under him on the Executive Council!'

'Is it simply that he likes money?'

'How can it be that? As President he could have had all the money he wanted – and power as well.'

But if Burgers fails, as he may, Paul Kruger will be able to say: "My friends, I opposed this man from the first on grounds of conscience; but when the people elected him, I accepted their decision and consented to work under him, hoping for the best and always trying to influence him in the right direction. Now that he's failed, in spite of my influence, those who followed him as I did can see I was right and accept my leadership, while those who opposed him, as I did originally, must thank me for having saved the Republic from even greater disasters. If I gave Burgers a rope to hang himself with, don't forget that I never let go the end of it!" That is making the best of two worlds. A dangerous game, Adrian.'

'Nobody can say that Paul Kruger's frightened of danger. He's known as a man without fear.'

'Old Piet Bezuidenhout, who was standing behind me in the Raadsaal, said he looked like an old buffalo-bull lying down in long grass.'

Adrian laughed. 'That was good, very good. There's another thing, don't forget. When once you've wounded a buffalo, it's your life or his. He may take his time, but sooner or later he'll get you.'

They sat by the fire in the outspan under the lee of Janse's wagon, talking and eating. Janse was glad to discuss his new plans with Adrian, not because he expected much guidance, but because of the comforting solidity of the mind that matched his great body: he was far cleverer and more complicated than Adrian, he knew, but probably less wise. It encouraged him to find that, on the whole, his brother approved of his plans.

'I doubt if you'd ever have made a success of Witfontein, Janse,' he said. 'The veld's thin and rocky to begin with, and luck's been against you. Your heart's never been in farming either, as mine is; and more than heart is needed to put such a place in order: one must be a strong man.' (Janse felt himself blushing as he saw that Adrian's kindly eyes were fixed on his leg.) 'What do you say Piet paid you for Witfontein?'

'Eight span of good oxen.'

'I think that was fair – more than fair. You have not done badly: such places go cheap. It will be a comfort to mamma to have Piet so near home, and I believe Piet will prosper. He's a hard one, our Piet; his brains are sharp, and he sees only one thing at a time. What's more, he has behind him the money he's earned won't have to wait for a fortunate year, as you would, before he starts putting the place in order. Yes, I think this is all for the best.'

Janse sighed: 'Well, I hope it may be. I'm taking a chance.'

'You're the kind of fellow who ought to take chances. You're different from Piet and myself: it's our nature to play for safety. And it's because, as a race, we refuse to take chances that we're where we are. This country of ours is full of riches, as Burgers says, and we leave it to foreigners to find them. Not that I've any use for foreigners! But he's right – I say it again and again: what this country needs is money. Things change, but we won't admit it. The consequence is we've wasted the best part of half a century. The only thing that can save our folk is this gold which they hate.'

A couple of hours after sundown Meninsky's donkeys came pattering into the outspan. He was tired and powdered with red dust from head to foot, but bubbling with jubilant energy. As he squatted down and fell voraciously on the remains of the meal, he hardly ever stopped talking and fluttering his hands. No two human beings, Janse thought, could have shown a more amusing contrast than the ponderous Adrian, his blue eyes wide open with surprise and the firelight playing on his golden beard, and this agile, quick-witted little gnome whose hands and tongue were never for a moment still. Yet even Adrian was forced to laugh, as he was intended to do, at the Peruvian's recital of his latest misfortunes: how one night he had lost a donkey and after scouring the veld in terror of lions for over five hours, had returned to find it standing in its own place in the team and licking a new-born foal that stood trembling beside it. There was another story of how he had spent the night at a farm called Wonderboomspruit. He had been worried about that name because there wasn't so much as a stick of a tree in sight, and no spruit either; but the farmer explained that there had been a camel-thorn tree near-by in his father's time, until a traveller whose wagon had broken down in the spruit which no longer existed had felled it to make a temporary disselboom.

This same farmer, Meninsky said, had refused to take any payment for food or lodging: 'So I said to him, "Oom, you have been a good friend to me, and I like to meet a man who cares nothing for money. You know how my great-great-great-grandfather Abraham entertained three angels unawares in the plain

86

of Mamre? Well, that's what you've done, old cock, and I'm going to prove it!'

' "What? D'you mean to tell me you're father Abraham's great-great-great-grandson?" he says. "If you'd said that before I'd have given you a bed to sleep in!"

' "Never mind about that," I told him. "Do you see this gold watch? It's worth forty pounds, and is guaranteed by the Astronomer Royal in Whitechapel, where he lives and I come from, not to lose a second in fifty years. Well, I'm going to make you a present of it. For friendship. See?" '

The Peruvian chuckled: 'It was one of them Brummagem things, you know, that cheap-jacks sell for half a crown and make two bob profit. The old chap had a look at it. "Don't drop it, for God's sake," I says, "or it may stop for the first time in fifty years." I could see his eyes goggling.

' "Nay, nephew," he said. "I can't take such a valuable gift; it would not be right."

' "Well, have it your own way," I said, "but remember you're not likely to be visited by an angel again. It only happened to my great-great-great-grandfather two or three times!"

' "See now what we will do, nephew," he says: "I will give you ten pounds for the watch." '

'And you let this old man give you that for a worthless watch?' Adrian broke in, his blue eyes blazing.

'Wait a bit, wait a bit. Give a fellow a chance,' Meninsky protested. 'You darned Afrikanders are always in such a hurry. I said: "Now, look here, uncle, this isn't a forty-pound watch and it isn't gold, and what's more, the Astronomer Royal don't live in Whitechapel, leastways, *I* never saw him there. This watch loses ten minutes an hour when it's going – which isn't often – and it's not worth a rix-dollar. So when next a stranger comes round and offers you bargains, just tell him to go to hell, see? And thank God on your bended knees this night," I told him, "that this stranger happened to be a Jew. Remember *that*," I told him: "the seed of old father Abraham never tell lies" – though that was a good one to start with!'

'That was good, that was good,' Adrian laughed. 'You taught the old man a lesson.'

'Well, I doubt it,' Meninsky said. 'I don't think he believed me, anyway. He'd have given me ten pounds for the damned thing even after that. And I could have done with ten pounds,' he added reflectively, 'for apart from the stuff I've got in the wagon, I'm ruddy well broke to the wide. Have you got some good oxen, Janse?'

'Good enough. Eight span.'

'Well, we'd better off-load my wagon. It's broke down three times between here and Kimberley, and I won't trust it any farther. If you want any firewood, baas,' – he winked at Adrian – 'you're welcome to what's left of it. Come on, Janse. Let's get at it. We don't want to lose any time. We're off tomorrow morning.'

There was no damping his energy. Though it was dark and late, he insisted on transferring the contents of his wagon into Janse's.

'Now you can see why I'm broke,' he said. 'Every ruddy penny I possessed and some I've borrowed have gone into this.'

Adrian lent them a hand off-loading. It was not surprising that the rickety donkey-wagon had broken down. It was crammed to the tilt, not only with tinned and dry provisions and cases of liquor, but also with every imaginable kind of junk: spades, shovels and pickaxes, with sheaves of spare handles of various lengths to fit them; bales of dirty blankets for lining a water-race, and yellow-wood planks for flumes and sluice-boxes; a number of iron prospecting-pans of various sizes; a rusty portable forge, with bellows blown by a foot-treadle; a square Egyptian tent, tarpaulins, coils of rope and hanks of wire; grass mats, sheets of copper and tin; rolls of printed calico, boxes of Kaffir truck; filled cartridges, powder, two shot-guns and a single rifle, an old Westley-Richards carbine; saws, hammers, horse-shoes, rod-iron, nails and tin-tacks. There were few emergencies, indeed, which the Peruvian's agile intelligence had not apparently prepared itself to meet. It was hard to imagine how the donkeys had managed to pull such a weight from Kimberley to Pretoria.

Though he proposed to drive the poor beasts along with him 'in case they might come in useful', as he remarked – though whether they were to be sold or eaten he did not say – Meninsky's conscience was rather tender about the donkey-mare that had foaled. She stood apart from the rest, with tired eyes, occasionally nuzzling her offspring – a timid toy-animal with long legs and a skin like crumpled velvet.

'We can't take the mother without her,' he said, 'though her milk would come in handy. I reckon your brother had better take the two of them home with him.'

'Yes, Adrian, take them along with you,' Janse said, 'and give the foal to Maria as a present from me.'

'And now,' Meninsky declared, 'I'm going to doss down – and I can tell you I shan't half sleep! We'll be off at dawn, lad.'

(3)

And at dawn next morning they were off. For ten days the course which Meninsky had set carried them over the High Veld, those vast plains of grass-land, now shimmering in the cold wind from the south, which were the Africa in which Janse has been bred, the only Africa he knew. Meninsky had preferred this circuitous approach to the Lydenburg gold-fields because of the weight of the over-burdened wagon.

'It may take us a week or two more, mate,' he said, 'but the longest way round, as they say, is the shortest way home. What I've done' – he wrinkled his simian brows and tapped his nose with his finger – 'what I've done is to take a leaf out of Moodie's book and stick to the line he's mapped out for the railway to Delagoa. Now it stands to reason, don't it? that a railway line must follow the easiest gradients. Farther north you'd have to cross the head-waters of the Olifants River, which means one damned spruit and donga after another. They'll be dry as a bone at this season, I know; but your wagon, to say the least of it, has seen better days, and I don't want no breakdowns.'

Janse laughed. 'You're right. This old wagon went over the Drakensberg with Piet Retief: it belonged to my grandfather.'

'Well, now it's got to slide down the face of the Berg, and that's not much better. There's another point, too. On the northern route, from what I have heard, you're liable to run into fly-belts, and I don't fancy the idea of us finding ourselves in the soup without any oxen. Here we're safe from fly for a matter of a hundred miles, though I'm told that the Low Veld is full of red-water. We must take our chance on that. If the oxen pass out we can always fall back on the donkeys. Them beasts are that

89

thick-skinned and obstinate, Janse, that nothing on earth can kill them short of a lion; and not even a lion fancies a moke so long as he can get his teeth into anything tenderer. You and me, for instance.'

Even so, though the course he had chosen made going comparatively easy, they found they could cover no more than twelve miles a day in six hours of steady trekking. There was grazing enough for the oxen turned loose in the midday outspans; but water was scarce, and because of the lack of it the game on which the Peruvian had counted to fill the pot was scarce too. This was his only miscalculation. When he had travelled that way six months earlier the veld had been populous with wandering herds of springbok and blesbok and wildebeeste. Now, through all the day's trek, hardly a head of game could be seen; and though the oxen, apart from occasional spells of thirst, fared well enough, and the donkeys appeared to thrive on the grass they cropped as they strayed, Meninsky and Janse were glad to husband their stock of provisions by outspanning at night, whenever they could, in the neighbourhood of the isolated farms of *vee-boere* (or ranchers) with which, at long, dreary intervals, the veld was scattered.

Many of these they found empty, their owners, cunning as the game, having already dropped down to lower levels, seeking winter pasturage for their herds and easy shooting for themselves; but in those that were occupied the travellers always found an abundance of food and a ready welcome. It astonished Janse to see in how many of them Meninsky and his concertina were already familiar. The Peruvian had cultivated a prodigious memory, not only for names and faces, but also for details of family history. In four years of wandering he had made himself a universal friend, as well as a universal provider; he was more at home, indeed, with these back-veld folk than Janse; and if the squat hovels of sun-dried brick in which they lived were primitive, frowsty, and sometimes not over-clean, the inhabitants were simple and kindly, and the warmth of their acrid-smelling cow-dung fires seemed preferable to the bitterness of the night air outside.

Only once during their ten days' trek to the brim of the High Veld did they encounter anything approaching suspicion or hostility. This was at the farm of a man named Trichard, a kinsman of the pioneer who had made the first disastrous expedition to the Zoutpansberg. As their wagon approached it at sundown the owner rode out to meet them: a spare, swart, middle-aged man with bony features and close-set eyes, to which a bristling beard and a tangle of uncropped hair gave an aspect of sullen ferocity like that of a dangerous bull. He was so tall that the pony he rode appeared by contrast no bigger than one of Meninsky's donkeys, and his long-stirruped legs swept the grass through which he rode. He pulled up and stood waiting for them, monstrous against the skyline; the barrel of a long gun peaked over his shoulder. When they came within ear-shot he hailed them:

'Who are you, and what do you want?'

'Leave this beggar to me,' Meninsky said, 'I'll soon get round him.'

Janse watched the Peruvian's insect-like shape skipping forward. He could see him laughing, gesticulating, waving his arms, while the mounted giant towered over him, still and mute as a statue. Then the *vee-boer* turned his horse's head and rode slowly away.

Meninsky trotted back to the wagon.

'It's all right, mate,' he panted. 'Would you believe it? The poor cove thought we was something to do with the railway. He's got a bloody great bee in his bonnet about that, so you'd better be careful.'

The house was meaner than any that Janse had yet encountered, swarming with children (he counted thirteen) and even more embarrassing forms of life. Yet the welcome Gert Trichard grudgingly gave them had a patriarchal dignity. They were given water with which to wash their feet, and a bellyful of a highly-seasoned stew of mutton swimming in grease. When the lengthy prayer that ended the meal was over and they had touched hands formally with every member of the family, Gert Trichard lit his pipe and sat listening in silence to their answers to the catechism with which his wife plied them: what were their names and where had they come from, and were they married, where were they bound for and what was their business and where were their horses?

When Janse had done his best to satisfy this far-reaching curiosity, her husband too shot forth a volley of inquiries. He was still apparently unconvinced that they had nothing to do with the railroad, and set himself out to catch them with cunning cross-questioning.

'You speak like one of our own folk, nephew,' he said at last, 'though this little man who goes with you is clearly a foreigner.

Yet one thing I tell you: if I had been certain that either of you had any connection with the railway, you would never have eaten in this house.'

'Why do you speak so strongly, uncle?' Janse inquired.

'Because this railway is the work of the devil, planned to ruin us by his servant, the heretic Burgers. Is not that enough?'

'There is no word in the scriptures against railways,' Meninsky suggested mischievously.

Trichard spat: 'That may be; but the thing is evil, none the less.'

'After all, what harm can it do you?' Janse asked.

'What harm? You speak like a child. The game know it is coming. Once a man might feed his family with a gun. Now he must ride for miles before he can fire a shot. The railway engines will drive the herds even farther away, and then how shall a man live? Besides which, take my word for it, that means we shall have to pay taxes.'

'You'll be able to pay them. You'll send your produce by rail to Pretoria in hours instead of in days.'

'What? Pack cattle and sheep into trucks? They would die of fright before they got there, nephew. And the thing's against nature, too. Why has God given them legs and hooves if He didn't intend them to walk? Then think of the transport-riders. Their trade will be ruined, and how shall they live?'

'The railway will give them work.'

'And who will pay them for it? The farmers, I tell you.'

'The farmers will be more prosperous. If the line goes near it, the value of your farm will increase.'

'What good will that be if I do not wish to sell it? If my land becomes valuable, foreigners will soon be after it. I know what they are. The railway will bring them along like a swarm of locusts, fossicking for gold and diamonds all over my land.'

'Have you gold or diamonds here then, uncle?' Meninsky inquired with carefully-affected innocence.

Trichard's dark eyes narrowed with suspicion. 'I neither know nor care, nephew; but I hope there are none. They say that men who know what to look for can find diamonds everywhere.'

Meninsky laughed: 'If it comes to that, uncle,' he said, 'there may well be diamonds in the moon.'

The farmer puckered his bristling eyebrows and grinned sardonically. 'No, no, there are no diamonds there, nephew. How do I know? Why, I'll tell you – because, if there were any diamonds in the moon the damned English would certainly have annexed it! Is that true, or isn't it? No, nephew, wherever the English go there is trouble to follow. You know that as well as I do. Even now, at the gold-fields, I hear they have put up their flag and defied the Republic. That also will have to be dealt with,' he added gloomily.

'Yet the Lydenburg gold may pay for the railway, uncle, and save you from having to pay the taxes of which you're afraid. There is nothing wrong about gold in itself, particularly in a poor country. That is why my friend and I are going to look for it.'

The farmer stared at him reproachfully. 'This man told me before you were trekking to Lydenburg, but said no word of gold. And I thought you were honest men! Now take my advice, nephew: turn back while there's time. There are hundreds of starving folk at the gold-fields already. They find less and less and the gold will soon be finished. Then what will you do among so many thieves and murderers and men of Belial? Turn you back, my friends, while there's time, for I'll tell you another thing: wherever these foreigners go, drink and guns go with them. The English have never known how to handle Kaffirs: they do not see that with natives what once has been given can never be taken back. Now the guns that the Kaffirs have bought in the diamond-diggings go north every day. There is a chief who rules the Bapedi – Sekukuni's his name – who would make of the Lulu Mountains a new Basutoland. He swells himself up, this fellow, because he has guns and powder and knows that Cetewayo and the assegais of the Zulus are behind him. And one day soon – mark this well! – Sekukuni will come down from the hills and eat up the foreign riff-raff that fouls the gold-fields – you know as well as I do that all foreigners are cowards and cannot shoot – as easily as old *erdvark* gobbles up an ants'-nest. That is why I tell you: "Go back!" And I tell you this too: when the people of a country do evil in the sight of the Lord and make traffic with the heathen, as these men at the gold-fields have done, then be sure that God will turn the Amalekite against them and deliver them into his hands even as the children of Israel were delivered. For so it is written.'

He relapsed into sullen silence, and spoke no more that night. Next day, when he bade them farewell, he watched them depart with a brooding solemnity, impervious to all the assaults of Meninsky's impish humour, of which the memory remained for many days in Janse's mind. To him, who had lived all his life on the peaceful Witwatersrand, the menace that lay in the neighbourhood of unconquered tribes, stamped deep as it was on the memories of his elders, had never seemed real. He had thought of native wars as belonging to a vaguely romantic past. Yet to those who, as this man Trichard, lived on the High Veld frontiers, that peril was so actual and pressing as to be rarely out of their minds. Behind them they saw the Zulus, divided yet still unsubdued; north of these another war-like nation, the Swazis; and now, northward again, the new-risen, newly-armed power of Sekukuni's Bapedi – a half-circle of swarming black hosts outnumbering them by a hundred to one.

In the Southern Transvaal, again, he had not been aware of the quality of this hostile preponderance. The only Kaffirs he knew had been the timid, degenerate remnants of unwarlike peoples that had drifted back to the land they had once inhabited when the *Voortrekkers* drove their Zulu oppressors northward beyond the Limpopo: a poor-spirited folk, parasitic on the white man, who had so utterly lost their tribal identity that it seemed fantastic to think of them as potential enemies.

It was not till he heard frontier farmers, such as Gert Trichard, speak, that he realized the depth of the passion, bred in fear, which made them so bitterly resent the sale of arms in Kimberley. The English, secure and numerous behind the Vaal River, had greedily, cynically sold the natives these arms; but it was the back-veld Boers scattered on the frontiers who would have to face the bullets; and as Janse reflected on this, his mind, which was half-Dutch and half-English, became, as it were, a symbol of that divided land, impatient, even as Adrian was, of the Boers' obstinate ignorance, yet indignant against those careless injustices which he could not deny that they had suffered. He was becoming aware, indeed, of what to him was a new Africa: the darker and greater Africa which his forbears had purchased so dearly in blood and in fire; the vast, tragic background against which the triangular drama of his two races and their common enemy, the dispossessed native, was posed.

Three days later they came to Lydenburg. It had a mournful name, Janse thought – the Town of Sorrow – and seemed a sad little place, for all its ambitious display of no less than five stores and canteens, its bank, its jail and its courthouse, from whose flagstaff the four-coloured Republican flag drooped in discoloured tatters. And indeed this town, which had once been called New Origstad, was a monument to the first Origstad, forty miles father north, which had been rotted with fever and abandoned not many years since. Faded grasses grew in its streets; the sparse houses themselves lay buried in thickets of weeping-willow, whose vivid tresses – the only visible green – gave the place the air of a cemetery set in the midst of a stony wilderness.

So Janse thought; but Meninsky's mind had no room for such gloomy reflections. The little man was on the top of himself. This dead dorp was what he had called their 'jumping-off place', the gate of the gold-fields. No sooner had they outspanned in the vast, empty market-square than he must be off to the landdrost's office to get their diggers' licences and collect information from a Jewish bar-keeper with whom he had made friends on his previous visit.

'You'd better leave this to me, mate,' he told Janse seriously. 'I know just what I'm after and how to set about it, and in a job of this kind one head's better than two – though God only knows what sort of a head mine will be by the time I've finished,' he added lugubriously; 'you don't know the way these beggars shift square-faced gin! However, drunk or sober, it's got to be done. Keep an eye on what's in the wagon, or it's liable to vanish, and expect me when you see me.'

Janse lounged all day under a bucksail slung from the tilt of the wagon, at grips with the geological primer Meninsky had brought from Kimberley. It was nearly dark when the Peruvian returned, his diminutive figure advancing with unusual dignity over the grass-grown outspan. In his right hand he brandished a bottle which he used as a tight-rope-walker uses a balancing-staff. The solemnity of his face in the firelight was not encouraging. When Janse welcomed him he shook his head and flopped down on the ground without speaking.

'I see you've bad news,' Janse said.

Meninsky raised his head slowly and winked. He spoke with deliberation: 'First of all, understand, I'm drunk. No … drunk's not the word, old cock, I'm bloody well pickled. Two blooming quids' worth of square-face gone down the drain, as you might say; two quids' worth and nothing but me to show for it! Don't light your pipe, mate! If you put a match near me this instant you'll see me go up in smoke, so be careful. But I've

95

got what I want and my head's clear enough. First of all, here's the licences: a pound apiece, and cheap at the price. Now get pen and paper and put down every word I say, although it seems rubbish. Are you ready there, now?' He proceeded to dictate a detailed report of his day's investigations.

'Hendriksdal. Farm belonging to Jan and Hendrik Muller. Thirty-three miles due east. Keep the Mauch Berg always on the south – no, damn it, the north. Remember the Eisenberg. Get hold of a chap called Maclachlan. Alluvial gold in most of the spruits running into the Sabia River, or Sabi Lala, at foot of the Berg. Geelhoutboom ... yes, that's it. Don't forget the Devil's Knuckles. Nuggets big as beans and one as big as a sovereign. Erasmus's farm even better. Follow reefs of quartz down from the Berg where the rock can be seen. Dig three feet below the surface. Red clay on the top, then gravel-quartz in fragments, then limestone, then cindery stuff that looks like slag; below that, again, soft black soil which pans out like tar, with veins of pipe-clay in it. Best finds hid under large boulders. Epsom Salts and Water's Quinine Wine. Where did I put that bottle? Ah, here it is. Well, now, have you got all that down?'

Janse nodded.

'Thank God. Then I'll go to sleep. We'll be off in the morning. Good night, mate.'

He rolled over slowly and lay like a Kaffir, his thin legs tucked up, his face pillowed on folded arms.

(4)

The thirty-three miles' trek to the Maclachlan's camp was a nightmare. It took them a week. Even with an empty wagon the pull-up out of the flats of the Spekboom valley would have been stiff enough. Under the monstrous load they carried such gradients were well-nigh insuperable. Piet's oxen were stalwart, stout-hearted beasts, but this toil was too much to ask of them. Three times in the first day's trek they gave up; the shirkers leaned inward against the chain, edging away from the weight of the yoke. Only the big red front ox, Slingveld, which Piet had let go with regret, wedged his hinder hooves in such foothold as he could find, lowered his massive head and bent his great body like a well-strung bow until the very sight of the bulging,

96

knotted back-muscles became intolerable, for it seemed as if they must crack. And at last even Slingveld gave in; though the pride of his mighty strength would not let him slump down like the rest. He stood upright still, though the muscles of his back still quivered and his legs shook, looking round at his fellows with a mild reproachfulness in his yellow eyes.

They would have managed the tired team better, Janse thought, if they had known the beasts longer or been more skilled in the handling of oxen. The teamster's job, over such heart-breaking tracks as these, demanded such cunning and knowledge as neither he nor Meninsky possessed. It was a white man's job, too. Old Cobus the Hottentot's ideas of encouraging a spent team were limited to lashing and goading them. When he doubled the tail of one wretched bullock and bit it, Janse lost his temper and kicked him, and then was sorry for it. There was only one thing to be done, as it seemed: to let them lie as they would till they got their wind, then leave the front-oxen and after-oxen to themselves, and do what they could to encourage or harass the shirkers.

When they stopped for the third time the ingenious Meninsky was seized by an inspiration. Why not harness the thirteen donkeys in front and let them pull too? Old Cobus grinned in their faces at such a fantastic proposal; but Meninsky rummaged away in the bowels of the wagon until he had found his gear, and six spans of donkeys were harnessed in front of the oxen. At this offence to his dignity even Slingveld rebelled. Not an inch would he budge with an ass's buttocks in front of him; and indeed, when this unnatural insult had been removed, the whole team apparently decided to show what they could do, and started off again without any violent persuasion.

For some time after leaving Lydenburg they had been able to steer with confidence by the spoor which preceding wagons had sunk in the brick-red earth; but when, as they climbed, the ground grew stonier, this obvious aid to direction was lost. The track – if track it were – twisted so bewilderingly, clinging close to the mountain's precipitous contours, that it was no longer possible for them to feel sure of their orientation. Their only fixed landmark in this welter of contorted stone was a single magnificent peak which Meninsky's still somewhat fuddled memory identified as the Mauch Berg, the highest point in that part of the Quathlamba range. He had been told to keep that on his left: that was the one thing he clearly remembered. But now, so far as the trend of their general direction could be guessed at (and that was not easy), it seemed as though they were leaving the Mauch Berg behind them.

'Give those poor beasts another breather and get out your compass, for God's sake,' Janse said. 'I'm ready to swear that no wagon has ever passed this way before. You say this valley we're bound for lies thirty-odd miles due east of Lydenburg?'

'If that's what I told you last night, then it's right.'

'Then Lydenburg ought to be lying due west of us. Let's go back to the last rise we passed and check the direction.'

Meninsky trudged back with him unwillingly. The rocky road had torn his *veldskoene* to shreds; blood oozed from his swollen feet. But wherever Lydenburg may have lain it was now invisible, sunk deep in the trough of the Spekboom River, beyond fold after fold of stone.

'Well, let's look at the compass, anyway,' Janse said.

He examined the disc impatiently in the failing light. It told them, as clearly as they could calculate from the position of a bluff under which they had almost certainly passed a few hours since, that they were travelling north-north-east, the best part of a quarter off their track.

Janse stared at Meninsky accusingly.

'Are you sure that you had to keep the Mauch Berg on your left? When you told me that last night you corrected yourself?'

'If I said to the left, then it's right,' Meninsky protested.

'Pull your gin-sodden wits together, you drunken swine, and think!'

Meninsky shook his head hopelessly.

'Why the devil did you souse yourself like that?' Janse shouted, and the echoes laughed back at him.

Meninsky smiled blandly, but rather piteously.

'Now, look here, mate,' he said, 'be reasonable. Just reflect. If I hadn't got pickled and taken drink for drink – and, mind you, I loathe the damned stuff worse than poison, honest to God – we should never have known that the ruddy Mauch Berg existed, right *or* left. We should never have known we had to go east to Maclachlan's – if that's what the beggar's name is as you tell me. We should still have been hanging round Lydenburg and lost a whole day when every moment's worth money.'

'You've landed us in a damned mess.'

'Well, if I said left, it *is* left, and it's no use quarrelling over it. Let's get back to the wagon and turn in. My feet are frozen. Come on. Give us an arm.'

They stumbled back in the dark to the point where the wagon lay stranded. Old Cobus had kindled a fire and skidded the wheels with rocks. The oxen lay down by their yokes, still breathing heavily. Their blood-warm breath froze on the air in white clouds with each exhalation. Meninsky sat down by the fire and took off his *veldskoene*, which stuck to his swollen feet with clotted blood and serum. He looked so small and pitiful that Janse felt sorry for him and regretted his bitterness. Sitting silent, hunched in their blankets, they ate the first meal that day: bolting lukewarm mealie-pap and chewing shredded biltong. Meninsky would have opened a bottle of *brandewyn* if he had dared; but the look in Janse's haggard eyes was forbidding. When they had finished their meal they crawled into the wagon and wedged themselves, glad of each other's warmth, into the small space left between the load and the tail-board; yet neither of them could sleep for very tiredness, and for the cold that gnawed into the marrow of their bones. Meninsky rolled himself up in a ball with limbs retracted, like a little black spider. Janse lay with his short leg outstretched. It grew numb with cold; it felt like an excrescence of icy lead attached to his living body.

About midnight the thunder which had been muttering distantly all day, broke full overhead – not with a single isolated clap, but in a series of crashes that overlapped and merged into one appalling volume of sound that not merely shook the air with its blast, but seemed to rock the foundations of the precipices from which it re-echoed. At this height, on the very roof of the continent, their wagon, poised perilously as it was on a narrow shelf of friable stone between an abyss below and columnar bastions of dolomite above, appeared pitifully insecure and vulnerable. The sheer force of vibration seemed sufficient of itself to dislodge it, or to overwhelm it with fragments of rock torn away from the beetling crags and sent crashing downwards. Yet, oddly enough, though this tumult of sound never ceased overhead, the lightning discharged from the pitchy sky in broad bands of liquid fire, which split asunder in jagged streaks as it neared the earth, seemed to leave the flank

99

of the cliff, to which, like a lizard on a wall, the wagon was clinging, untouched. All its fury and spite were concentrated on a single isolated peak a mile or more farther south, into whose conical shape the forked flashes from all quarters of the sky buried themselves in such rapid succession that it seemed as if the rocks that composed it, perpetually enveloped in flickers of livid light, must surely be riven and fused and molten. The very intensity of this concentrated malignance was terrible to behold. Meninsky and Janse watched in mute and awed fascination.

Of a sudden the Peruvian's body stiffened; he struggled to his feet and pointed excitedly.

'Janse . . . Janse,' he cried. 'I've got it! D'you know what that is? It comes back to me now, God help me! That's one of the things I was told. That's the mountain they call the Eisenberg, mate: a solid mass, they said, of magnetic iron. That's why all the lightning strikes it. What's more, old cock, don't you see that's what's played the deuce with our compass and put us out of our reckoning? It's pulled round the needle eastward, how much you can't reckon; but I'm ready to bet you a thousand pounds to a tickey we're on the right line after all. And the ruddy old Mauch Berg *is* on the north as I told you to start with!'

'Well, maybe you're right,' Janse admitted gloomily.

'There's no "maybe" about it. I know that I'm right, as I always was. Now I reckon we'd better try to get some sleep.'

He curled himself up again in his spider-like ball. Janse envied him his astonishing faculty of shutting his ears to the thunder's incessant roar, his eyes to the lightning-flashes. He himself was incapable of achieving this masterly abstraction. He lay awake shivering till the thunder's violence was spent and no more trace was left of the storm than the flickering moon-like radiance of lightning still silently washing the sky behind curtains of cloud. After an hour or more he fell into an uneasy sleep, only to be awakened again by the drumming and lashing of rain on the wagon's tilt and the savage clamour of new-born torrents unloosed on the hills, plunging downward and sweeping the tumbled boulders along with them. Soon the tilt was sodden, and water began first to drip, then to pour from the sun-rotted canvas. The track on which the wagon and oxen lay marooned was a foaming water-course. Janse could hear the fierce water chuckling past as it rose axle-high, and knew it

100

might rise still higher. After all, one might just as well be drowned, he reflected, as struck by lightning. He lay stiff in his sodden moleskins. But Meninsky still slept like a child.

It was no wonder their compass had played them false, apart from the powerful pull of the Iron Mountain. When light came next morning they saw that a great part of the rocky flank over which they had been travelling was composed of magnetic iron. Crystalline particles clung to the iron tyres as the wagons floundered onwards over a track that had been scoured clean and hard by the rain. More than once in the day they came upon patches of spongy haematite which still carried the spoor of wagons that had gone before them; and this was a blessing indeed, for that day the air that blew over the Berg from the Low Veld was so sodden with moisture that no sooner had it reached the summit than it condensed into milky vapour, through which they moved rather by faith than by sight. Yet now, though the road was still scattered with monstrous boulders that the torrents had hurled across it, the going was easier, and the oxen, for all their wretched night, were rested and seemed in better heart. As for Meninsky, now that the Lydenburg square-face had cleared from his blood, there was no terror on earth that could daunt his mercurial spirits.

So they came, at the end of the third day's trek, to the edge of the Berg's escarpment. Meninsky, who had guessed that they must be near it, had forced the pace all day and refused to outspan at the usual hour; for he realized that the descent which lay before them was the most perilous part of their journey, and was anxious to reach the pass before sundown, in order that they might begin it with new strength and a full measure of daylight. When he had given the order to halt and outspanned the tired oxen, he took Janse by the arm.

'Come along, mate,' he said, 'I can tell by the sky that we're not very far from the pass. There may not be much to see in this light, but I'ld like you to have a squint at it. The first time I took a look over, all unexpected like, is a thing I shall never forget, not as long as I live. I'm not much of an artist, nor anything of that kind, Janse, but damn my eyes if the sight didn't knock me out flat!'

They trudged over a shelf of stony ground on which grass grew thin, for the force of uprising winds had scythed it perpetually. Before them rose a low rampart of craggy rocks that dipped in the middle to reveal what should have been another horizon. But no horizon was there. Meninsky steered straight for this gap. By the time they neared it, the last light had gone from the sky.

'Just a couple of minutes too late, I reckon,' Meninsky said regretfully. 'Still, seeing as we're here, we may as well have a look. Mind your step, mate: I don't want to lose you.'

They moved forward cautiously into the triangular dip. Janse strained his eyes, gazing forward into the darkness.

'That's the Low Veld,' Meninsky whispered in an awed, rapt voice.

There was nothing to be seen. Though Janse's eyes were directed downwards over the lip, no solid earth was visible. He might just as well have been gazing upward, he thought, into unfathomable depths of sky. And, indeed, when his sight at length became adjusted to the vastness of this empty air, it seemed as if this were no illusion of fancy – as if, indeed, the earth were flat and they had come to the edge of it and stared over into space; for, out of the blackness beneath them lonely stars appeared to be born, not sparkling with the white fire of the true sky's diamond-like coruscations, but burning sullen and red, like planets, as Janse thought, slowly fading into extinction.

'Do you see?' Meninsky said. 'Them's the lights of the Bathonga villages – there's always war between them and the Swazis now – or maybe the fires that some hunter or transport-rider has lit to keep off the lions. Four thousand feet beneath us. Only think of it! Four thousand feet down. . . . Well, come on: there's no more to be seen, though that's where we'll be tomorrow with any luck. You pray God for the old wagon's timbers before you sleep this night, mate.'

On the third day, at dawn, they went down. . . .

In itself the downward passage of the Berg was actually more hazardous than any adventure they had faced before, being nothing more than a series of falls, in which the wagon, its wheels skidded with reims and chains, lurched and jolted from ledge to ledge of an irregular stony stairway. It was a laborious progress, hindered, every few yards, by the necessity of levering boulders and fallen crags from the track, off-loading stores from the wagon to lessen its weight, jacking-up wheels from crevasses into which they had sunk, regulating the pull of the oxen when they started to haul, lest the wagon, floundering and swaying and bumping from rock to rock, should be over-balanced – perhaps even overturned – for sometimes, where the narrow shelf sloped steeply sideways to the brink of a precipice, the wagon, even off-loaded, tilted so dangerously that it seemed as if the least jerk would send it crashing to splinters, carrying the oxen along with it. Then, while Cobus coaxed the clumsy team forward, step by step, Meninsky and Janse anchored the swaying monster with stay-ropes of knotted reims. They dug their heels into the crunching gravelly debris, and hauled till their sinews cracked, while the great mass, against which their own weight and strength seemed so puny, moved onward at last into safety. Then, streaming with sweat, but triumphant, they loaded the dumps they had jettisoned, and the wagon moved on again, having gained, perhaps, a few yards of smoother progress.

And yet, during all the delays enforced by these anxious manoeuvres – in which Meninsky, poor teamster as he was, displayed such masterly patience and ingenuity and unsuspected strength – Janse was conscious of the overwhelming magnificence of the scene against which their antlike labours were set. From the moment when they had topped the ramparts of the Berg, above which, even now, the moist air of the plains, condensed as it met their sudden coldness, towered upwards in spoutings and billows of dazzling mist, he had been aware of a landscape transcending in richness, as well as in savage majesty, any other on which he had set eyes.

Above rose the cloud-topped pillars of stratified dolomite, sheer bastions of a cyclopean fortress – an unbroken wall of perpendicular stone, so forbidding that it was hard to believe that any human traffic – let alone their frail selves, with their overloaded wagon – could ever have succeeded in piercing it. As they wound their way with such painful slowness through the welter of fallen rocks that ice and water had split or torn from the escarpment's face to form a terraced glacis, there was nothing immediately about them but a stark desolation of sun-bleached stone; but below, in the kloofs (where, but for the grace of God, the wagon might well have lain splintered to matchwood), Janse's sun-dazzled eyes beheld a miracle of green loveliness.

Between the tops of the forest trees, where blue monkeys swung chattering on airy trapezes, and birds of bright plumage restlessly fluttered, there shone many hundreds of feet beneath them, green dells where gigantic tree-ferns uplifted their feathery fronds above streams that plunged downward in drumming cataracts or slid, placidly gliding, from pool to glassy pool, or rippled, with glancing lights, over beds of pebbles between banks of maidenhair fern, unbelievably green. From those cool green depths the streams mocked his blistered lips and parched throat; they taunted his ears with their distant watery music. And then, as he lifted his dusty eyes from that moist chasm, whose very walls were lined with draperies of lacy stag's-horn moss dripping with rain or spray, he could see, even farther beneath him (no less than three thousand feet, as Meninsky said), the land in whose thirsty sand the bright water would lose itself: that trackless expanse of bush and savannah which men called the Low Country, stretching eastward, ten days' journey and more, to the faint lilac line of the Lebombo Hills. And beyond that, again, lay the sea. He had never set eyes on the sea.

Yet it was not only by the sense of liberation and of power with which the command of these vast, mysterious expanses exalted his spirit that Janse was stirred that day. What moved him even more than the prospect's grandeur and amplitude was its loveliness. In all his life up till now he had only known the rolling plains of the High Veld; and here, as it seemed to him, he had found a new Africa – not merely richer in the variety of its beauties but, for all its unfamiliarity, strangely near to his heart and satisfying to his aspirations. Though he had never seen it before, his eyes were oddly attuned to it. He had a feeling that here he could never be lonely even in solitude, or doubtful or restless or bitter or apprehensive. This was his spiritual home: the land for which, unconsciously, he had craved.

This mood of dream-like exaltation possessed him through all the laborious vicissitudes of the long descent. It reached its rapt culmination that evening in a visionary moment which he would never forget. An hour or so before sunset, when they cleared the last rocks of the terraced glacis and saw the tremendous shadow of the Berg lengthening slowly behind them, they came to a tumbled region of grassy, rounded hills divided by watery valleys through which ran the track of red earth, now once more defined, yet so softly-surfaced that the measured shuffle of the oxen could no longer be heard – nor any other sound, indeed, but the squeak of an axle or the groans of the wagon's long-suffering timbers.

It was a moment of sweet relief in which men and beasts alike rejoiced in the knowledge that the worst of that heart-breaking trek must surely be over. Even Meninsky, that tense bundle of active nerves, relaxed and was silent, forgetting his swollen feet. Many runnels of limpid water crossed the track, and at these the oxen would pause, span by span, to splash themselves and let their cracked hooves luxuriously sink into the tawny sand. As the leaders stood there, swishing their tails with pleasure, small yellow butterflies, which had lighted on the wet sand to sip its moisture, rose in clouds to settle again upon the tall reeds and grasses and the thorn-trees, newly-fledged with emerald leaf, which dipped their roots in the subterranean water. Brilliant sun-birds flashed to and fro in streaks of living malachite; mouse-birds threaded the traceries of new green with their tapering tails; in their oval nests that weighed down the boughs of the taller acacias until they swung near the water's surface, colonies of sociable weaver-birds chuckled their tender love-songs.

All the life that was gathered about these tiny streams and spruits had an air of gay innocence. It suggested not merely the spirit of Spring, Janse thought, but the spirit of hope eternal. Wherever he looked his eyes were caressed and delighted by signs of new growth. For some time he had noticed here and there on the lower hill-slopes irregular patches of native cultivation where the red soil was pierced by shoots of green mealies and kaffir corn; and now, as the valley opened itself into a wider basin, a sight met his eyes which touched him even more deeply. On the hill-side above were clustered the beehive huts of a humble village, their grass roofs golden-brown in the latter light, from the midst of which a thin spiral of milk-white wood-smoke rose straight into the air. On the slopes that fell to the stream a small herd of wide-horned cattle moved slowly, cropping the new grass as they strayed, while above, on the stony flank of a kopje, a mixed flock of sheep and goats, tended by a small naked child, dappled the hill-side with brown and white. Janse could hear the lambs bleating as they pestered their mothers for milk; he saw the kids leaping sideways and spring-ing from rock to rock and then foolishly tossing their heads as though they were giddy.

After the savagery of the Berg there was something subtly moving to him in this sunset pastoral; the spirit of Eden pervaded the amber air; he felt as though by some miracle he had been transported backward into a world which had never lost its primal innocence, a world untouched by time. And then, as they reached the level of the village, there came to him a revelation of beauty more poignant, perhaps, because it was human. Here the stream, above a little ford, had been deepened to form a watering-place, a still pool where dragon-flies sunned themselves on the floating leaves of blue water-lilies; and towards this, advancing obliquely to meet them as they drew near, came a winding file of young women with gourds for the carrying of water poised on their heads. They moved slowly, silently, superbly erect, unconscious of anything but their task, with the grace and stateliness of a classical frieze come to life. The sun, dipping red to the line of the Berg, enriched the nut-brown nakedness of shoulder and torso and thigh till their oiled skins glowed with a sheen of satin, so that their slender bodies, from head to foot, appeared to be transfused with warm light. It was a revelation of beauty which Janse was to remember all through his life, yet brief as it was entrancing. For even as he gazed the sun sank behind the crest of the Berg and the transfiguring light departed. The girls saw the wagon-tilt floundering out of the dip, and the stately frieze was broken. They turned and fled, running backwards with ungainly movements; they clustered together in fright or affected fright, laughing shrilly, babbling like a flock of starlings, and screaming who knew what provocative obscenities. And now the veld was plain veld, not a meadow in Eden, and the village no longer an enchanted place but a circle of squalid huts roofed with faded grass.

'Them there donahs have got their black eyes on you, Janse,' Meninsky chuckled. 'You'd better look out. I could never fancy black women myself; but then, as they say, tastes differ. I reckon we'd better outspan as soon as we're clear of the stink of the village. I'm just about finished, I don't mind telling you, and so are the oxen. They've earned every penny you paid for them, and more, this day. Suppose we try the next rise? I'll go on and have a squint and see what the ground's like.'

He went onward rapidly, limping and hobbling. There was no end to his stores of energy. As he reached the brow, Janse saw him turn round and wave his arms, beckoning excitedly. He himself plodded on with difficulty at the tired oxen's pace.

When he drew within earshot he heard Meninsky shouting:

'Come on, you ruddy old slow-coach. Here's a sight for sore eyes.'

Below them he saw the green hill-side furrowed with cut water-races and a camp of half a dozen or more bucksail tents huddled together like white birds at rest. A single fire twinkled beyond them, and its rising smoke trailed away into the pit of Sabi valley and the darkening plains beyond.

'That must be Maclachlan's,' Meninsky said. 'We've hit it first shot. *Now* what's wrong with your uncle's compass, I'd like to know – or his drunken memory, either?'

(5)

The camp, which from a distance had looked so inviting, presented, at closer quarters, a desolate sight. The first of the scattered tents which Janse approached were deserted, having been left to rot where they stood. The bare red earth in the midst was littered with gnawed mealie-cobs like the centre of a native village. The only tent apparently inhabited was pitched on cleaner ground at some distance from the rest. Here a thin trail of smoke still rose from the newly-lit fire they had seen from above, and Meninsky, nosing his way round the back of the bivouac to see if he could discover a living soul, almost stumbled into a group of four men who lay sprawled on the ground, so engrossed in a game of cards that the Peruvian's sudden appearance startled them. One of them, a tall red-bearded wraith of a man, reacted more quickly than the rest. He jumped to his feet and snatched a gun that stood propped against the canvas.

'Here, what are you doing sneaking round here and who the hell are you?' he shouted.

'Steady on with that gun, old cock,' Meninsky said. 'I don't like the way it's pointing. It might be loaded.'

'It's loaded all right. What d'you want?'

'I've a message for Mr. Maclachlan.'

'Maclachlan, is it? Well, Maclachlan's not here.' He spoke in an oddish mixture of Cockney and Irish. 'What's more, if he was here,' he went on, 'I'd know what to do with him! Mr. bloody Maclachlan's gone down to the coast with Valentine on his way to Durban to persuade some poor innocent beggar that

107

knows no better to put up the cash for machinery to work his reef. You'd better go there if you want him. You've come to the wrong shop.'

'Unless he's got any gin with him, Mike,' another voice drawled. It was a sensitive, cultivated voice, strangely out of keeping with the unkempt exterior of the man who had spoken, a fellow much slighter and younger than his companions.

Meninsky lied brazenly. 'Gin, did you say? Not a drop, mate.'

The young man shook his head reproachfully. 'Then what the hell is the good of your coming here and disturbing our game of poker? If you'll take my advice you'll clear out before Mike gets annoyed. He's a short-tempered bloke, and not any too safe with a gun. Are you, Mike?'

The red spectre cursed him and put down his weapon.

'That's more friendly,' Meninsky said. 'Don't let me interrupt you, gents.'

He sat down on the grass beside them. The younger man laughed.

'What do you want with Maclachlan?' he said.

'I've a message for him from Mr. Cohen of Lydenburg.'

The young man surveyed Meninsky's torn *velskoene*. 'The devil you have. Come on foot?'

'We've a wagon outspanned over there.'

'What? A whole damn wagon and not one bottle of gin! I'm ashamed of you, Isaac.'

Meninsky sat up with a start. The young man laughed softly. 'Oh yes, I know you,' he said. 'Seen you often in Kimberley.' He turned to the Irishman. 'This little bloke's all right, Mike. He's only a *smous*. Not worth powder and shot, you know – even if you hit him first time. What are you doing up here, Meninsky? Going down to the Bay?'

'That's about it,' Meninsky agreed. 'Just taking a holiday. Thought of having a look at the gold-fields on the way.'

'The gold-fields? Oh yes, I seem to have heard of them. Seen any gold-fields about, Mike?'

'I have surely,' the red-bearded man agreed. 'I've seen all I want to last me a lifetime, bad cess to them!'

'Things not going too well?' Meninsky inquired.

'That is what me'tutor used to call a meiosis. If you want to know what that means you can borrow Mike Haffernan's dictionary. Or, if you prefer it, just go and dig in the creek for a

108

month or two. There are plenty of abandoned claims. You can have mine for a fiver – no, damn it, five bob, if you like. The gold's petered out, Isaac – and even if it hadn't there's no water left to wash dirt with. It gave out last month, just a fortnight before the gin. If you want to know the truth, this place is a bloody fraud, anyway. Your Mr. Maclachlan picked the eyes out of it before he declared his find. He sold me my claim. By the way, now I come to think of it, you can have it for fivepence. If you've sixpence on you I'll borrow the change from Mike. That reminds me, by God! What about a hand of poker? Mike's marked all the cards; but a smart little Yid like you should be able to skin him blindfold.'

The red man looked up angrily: 'Is it mocking me you are, Charters? One of these days I shall stop your mouth the way you'll not be able to open it!'

Things were blowing up rather too dangerously, Meninsky thought. He rose to his feet and backed away from the party. 'I reckon I'd better be getting back. My mate'll be wondering.'

'What? Off already, Isaac?' the young man protested, with excessive politeness.

'Let'm go. The sooner the better will I be pleased,' the red man grunted. 'There'll never be light to finish this hand as it is. I'm raising you and be damned to you, Charters.'

The young man took no notice of him.

'Look here, Meninsky, if you're going to the Bay you'd better take Bosmann with you. Four lunatics are enough in one camp: we don't want five.'

'Who's Bosmann?'

'You'll find him up in the canteen if he's still alive. If he's dead, by the way, you and your mate might bury him, if you don't mind. Mike'll lend you his prayer-book to read the funeral service – unless you've any religious objections to Christian burial. So long, then. I may step round and have a talk with you later. I've a damned good mind to go with you down to the Bay.' He looked at his cards, then tossed four chips into the pot. 'All right, Mike: I'll see you,' he said.

Meninsky made his way with difficulty back to the wagon where Janse awaited him. 'Where have you been?' he asked anxiously.

The Peruvian flopped down with a sigh. He scratched his bristly black head. 'Now you're asking!' he said. 'Wherever it was it was more like a bad dream than anything else: a mixture of Bedlam and Parkhurst with hell round the corner. There's four men over there, mate, and every damn one of them's mad or bad or both.' He described his strange interview. 'That young chap Charters, you know, he's born a toff – the kind I'd feel bound to tip my cap to if I was back home in England. He knew me before I knew him. Well, that's not to be wondered at. The last time I set eyes on him at the diggings he was driving a slap-up spider tandem, as smart as be damned, with his baby face and a long cigar in his mouth. Now his eyes are gone in. There's nothing left of him but a beard and a voice. He looks like a ghost, and a nasty sort of ghost. There's something wrong here, Janse. I'm damned if I know what it is, but I don't like the look or the smell of it. Maybe Bosmann can put us wise.'

'Who the devil is Bosmann?'

'He's in the other part of this madhouse: the padded cell, by all accounts. Keeps the canteen. Charters passed me the wink to get hold of him. There may be something in it. We'd better see. But I reckon we'll take a lantern and a couple of guns with us – just in case.'

They walked round the scattered tents, flashing the lantern-beam into each. At the top of the rise stood one larger than the rest which had a notice-board, crudely inscribed, announced as The Squareface Canteen. Inside it, surprisingly, the light fell on the motionless figure of a fat man (or a man who had once been fat) who sat chewing the stem of an empty pipe on an upturned whisky-case. He had a large, solemn face and a bald scalp, pale as a bladder of lard. When the light swept across him he jumped up with a start and a cry. His hand trembled violently as he took his pipe from his lips.

'Ach! I thought you was Haffernan,' he said. 'What you want here? Who are you? I have noding to sell you ... noding. No, not one drop. They haf cleared me out, dry as a bone: my stock, my money. There is noding left now but de bottoms of one sack of mealie-meal full of vorms. After dat I starve from hunger. De Kaffir is gone and he steal my gun too. What you see is all dat I have. And now, I t'ink, de fever begins. I soon must be sick.'

Meninsky laughed and slapped him on the shoulder. 'Cheer up, old cock! Me and my mate here don't want nothing off you. All you need, by the look of it, is a square meal and a drop of something hot. Come along with us to the outspan: we'll soon put you right.'

The poor devil needed a good deal to put him right. His legs were so feeble that they would hardly support the weight of his sagging paunch. However much of his shivering might have been due to the approach of a bout of malaria, the main cause of it was sheer terror of Mike Haffernan's party. As they crossed the deserted camp, his hunted eyes searched the darkness apprehensively for the first sign of movement on their part. Added to this, he was evidently so weak with starvation that his stomach would not accept the food they gave him. It was only when Meninsky had forced him to swallow a stiff dose of hot grog that a faint flush reddened his ashen cheeks and took the fear out of his pitiful eyes.

'Now tell us all about it, cocky,' the Peruvian said.

It was a pitiful tale. He had stumbled on this place – it was called Mulder's Spruit – as a prospector, rather more than nine months ago. At that time the story of Maclachlan's discoveries had leaked out and a new 'rush' had begun. Diggers were like that, he said: no sooner did a story of rich finds of gold get abroad than they swooped down on it in hordes, appearing like vultures out of an empty sky. Within a few weeks of his coming a camp of tents and huts had sprung up at Mulder's and nearly a hundred miners had pegged their claims.

'But Maclachlan had got there first,' he told them. 'He and his friends had prospected the creek with cunning and knew all that was there. That also I saw – for I am not wholly one fool,' he went on, with the pallid ghost of a smile. 'They could not find much gold, I see, but they must have drink, so I sell my claim that I pegged and buy the canteen from a man that is sick and ready to die called Prout, a Welsher. Ten ounces of gold I pay for stock and all, that is thirty-six pounds, and business is not so bad. What the diggers have they spend. But then the diggers they hear told of new finds farther north in the Blyde Valley creeks. There is summer and too much water; they work to the waist, and then there comes the fever. So like vultures again they go. Only twelve tents are there left. I am here, with many debts and nobody to buy, and I cannot move after them, for I, too, now have the fever. You see how it is?'

He had stayed there, it seemed, fever-stricken and helpless, through the summer and autumn and winter. One by one the remaining diggers had vanished, till at last he found himself alone in the deserted camp, living on, as best he could, in the hope that fortune would change, consuming what was left of his own stocks of meal and canned food, crawling out with a gun when recessions of fever would let him, to kill a small buck for the pot – 'though I am no shooter,' he said.

And then, six weeks ago, when the first rains came round again, Mike Haffernan and his party had arrived and taken up their abode in two of the abandoned tents.

'At first they are polite and, as you say, sympathetic. They come to me friendly and pay for the food and drink. But I know from the first that this Haffernan is a bad man. One day I see him stripped of his shirt, and his back it is marked with deep cuts of the lash: he has been a criminal. The others are dumbheads, they do what he say. Only the Englishman, Charters, he is an onlooker; he lets the others do and smiles and says noding. And him I fear most of all. The red Irishman he has the strength: when he drink a bottle of square-face he is an animal. But this other one has a cold head full of brains. That is why I fear him . . .'

Bosmann shook his moon-like face desolately.

'And now comes the end. They have no more money. Also they have no gold. In winter it rains not, the spruits are dry, and they cannot wash dirt. There begins a reign of terror. First they give me what you call "good-fors" that are good-for-noding. Then they say that this is not needed, and what can I do? They take what they wish. If I did not give they would kill. And four nights ago this Haffernan and the two others come full of my drink and say they must make a finish. You see it is three men to one, and I am helpless. They strip the store bare and laugh at me; they tear down the shelfs for firewood and break up the empty bottles. In the night I send my boy with a brief to the Landdrost in Lydenburg. He goes, and when he is gone, my gun is gone too. He will never come back; he is gone with the gun to Sekukuni's country from where he came. That is the end, my friends.' His green face wore a ghastly smile – 'and now, with permission, I go to be sick.'

He rose hurriedly and staggered away from them into the darkness. In the distance they heard him retching.

'That poor fat tick's had a pretty thin time,' Meninsky murmured. 'What are we going to do, Janse?'

'Take him out of it, I suppose. Will he face it? That's the question.'

'If I were in his shoes I would; make no mistake! We've no stores to spare, though.'

'We can't think about that.'

'No, you're right,' Meninsky agreed. 'We can't think of that. And, mind you, if once we can pull him round, he may be useful. He's been a prospector. He's worked this country before and he knows the ropes. "Cast thy bread on the waters": it was a Jew who invented that, and the best of charity is, it often pays a good dividend.'

Out of the darkness the shaken form of Bosmann returned.

'I am relieved,' he said, 'and feel better. My head, too, is clear. While I vomit I have been thinking. Now it is you, my friends, who are in danger. Haffernan knows you are here with this wagon. There is no law. They are desperate, these swine, and have no fear. In the night, when you sleep, they may do to you what they already have done to me and make off with the wagon. You should watch all night and be ready. Better still, you should inspan and go while there's time.'

Meninsky laughed: 'If there's any of them monkey tricks going, boss, they're liable to get as much as they give and more than they bargain for. We can both of us shoot pretty straight, so that's all right. Let 'em try it! As for inspanning tonight: can't be done: neither us nor the oxen are up to it. See my feet? Well, my head's just like them, only worse. All the same, I'm with you: I don't fancy the place nor the company, and I reckon we'd better be pushing on before dawn. If the spruits has gone dry and the best of the gold been found, like you say, and there's all that fever about, this is no place for Isaac. Time's money, they say. But the question is, where to go, boss?'

'You must go Nord-East, my friends. The Nord is no good. There you run into Sekukuni. That fellow is growing big, my Kaffir boy tell me, and soon will give trouble. And there is more gold Nord-East too. I have heard this from a friend named Brunner who come here and die and never pay me. That is where I had wanted to go before I was ruined. But now it is too late.'

'Too late be damned, boss!' Meninsky said cheerily. 'Why don't you come along with us and show us the way? You need looking after.'

'Do you want to take with you a man who will die?'

'If you're going to die you may just as well be buried, and we'll see to that.'

Bosmann shook his head. 'You don't know this Haffernan. I dare not go. They're like wild dogs. They will follow me.'

113

'You've got Haffernan on your nerves, boss. He might follow you if you were worth following maybe, but now they've skinned you, you ain't. You just tuck yourself up in the wagon and go to sleep, and we'll wake you for breakfast.'

Bosmann's pale face worked with emotion: 'You mean what you say? You will take me? God bless you, my friends. I begin to believe in Him once again, for you are the good Samaritan. *Nicht wahr?*'

Meninsky laughed. 'You've got the wrong end of the stick. I'm no good Samaritan, boss, though I am a passable Jew with an eye to the main chance; and my pal here's an Afrikander.'

'Whatever you are,' Bosmann said, with tears in his eyes, 'the good God will reward you.'

(6)

It was not long before their charity began, as Meninsky had hoped, to 'pay a dividend'. When they had removed those prime causes – starvation, fever and loneliness – which had lowered his resistance and magnified in his mind that morbid dread of Haffernan and his crew that had become, in the end, a persecution-obsession and had reduced him to dithering terror, the unfortunate Bosmann emerged as a pleasant and helpful companion. No doubt Haffernan had robbed and misused him and taken a cruel schoolboy's delight in his victim's distress; but neither he nor his friends had been quite as sinister as poor Bosmann's sick mind imagined. The worst of his sufferings, Janse decided, had probably arisen from his complete inability to understand the alien humour with which Charters and Haffernan, in their different ways, had freakishly embellished their persecutions. His mind was radically serious and literal. Whether it were with him or against him, he simply could not see a joke.

Even when he had come to himself, Meninsky's mercurial Cockney wits bewildered him. When the Peruvian talked nonsense – as he did for hours at a stretch – Bosmann would sit solemnly, mildly staring, his short-sighted eyes owlishly magnified behind his round steel-rimmed spectacles. So far as knowledge – and even intellect – went, he was superior to both of them. How he had come to be stranded in Africa he never

114

confessed, though he implied that his exile had been due to some sentimental complication – which seemed plausible enough, for the cast of his mind was romantic; but he had in his youth, it appeared, been a student (if not a graduate) of Heidelberg University, and was variously equipped with all sorts of useful knowledge, including a smattering of metallurgy. Having abandoned any attempt to keep pace with Meninsky's levity or to understand his picturesque idiom, he attached himself, with solemn devotion, to Janse, who found profit (as well as amusement) in a type of mind and a kind of knowledge he had never encountered before. This small, plump, middle-aged man, with his wistful myopic eyes and his large pale face, was not merely the first friend of his own sex he had ever made, but also a perfect foil to the Peruvian's oriental exuberance.

As for his promise to redeem his debt by guiding them to the ore-deposits of which he held the rather indefinite secret, Bosmann performed it religiously. He was not merely a competent guide, well-versed in bushcraft, but a prospector with eyes quick to notice geological conditions indicating a promise of gold. He did nothing haphazard. Whenever these appeared he took careful bearings with his sextant – the only part of his personal belongings that had survived the disaster of Mulder's Spruit – and jotted them down for future reference. More than once Meninsky, inflamed by his prophecies, and eager to get to work, was for stopping and taking the chance of a payable find; but in this (as in most other things) Bosmann's purpose was adamant. This part of the foothills of the Berg was too populous for his liking. Every few miles they came upon signs of prospecting work: rock bared and shallow shafts sunk and, here and there, rudimentary water-races and furrows and flumes which had been hurriedly made and abandoned. Wherever the gleam of a tent or any other sign of human presence was seen, Bosmann diverted their course and hid their progress in some patch of indigenous forest or ferny sunken kloof.

'These diggers they are like sheeps,' he said. 'As soon as we stop in one place where we can be seen they will say "Ha! These fellows they have found easy gold!" and sheep-like come flocking. And then there will not be water enough. I have seen. I know it. No ... where we find gold there must be no white men to see.'

'All right, boss. Have your own way,' Meninsky consented.

'But we're going a devil of a distance. When we reach the equator you might just tip me the wink. I should like to have a squint at it.'

'The equator?' Bosmann answered, with mild reproof. 'But that you cannot squint, my friend. It is imaginary.'

'Only fancy that, now! Then why the hell do they make such a fuss about it?'

'That is because ... Ach! I see you are joking again. You can never be serious!'

'I'll be serious enough when the right time comes, boss,' Meninsky said.

But the right time did not come for more than a week of hard trekking during which they never covered more than nine miles in a day. The north-eastward course, which they checked with Meninsky's compass hour by hour, led them against the grain of the land, across a complicated system of watery ravines leading downward from the face of the Berg to feed the Olifants River.

All this country revealed the strange dream-like beauty which had possessed Janse's heart on the day when they dropped to the foot-hills, in its mossy kloofs drenched with spray and shadowed by feathery tree-ferns, in its tumbling torrents. Here and there a humble village, spread on more open slopes, gave glimpses again of that pastoral life which had seemed to him so Eden-like and innocent; but the flocks and herds were scanty, and the natives even more shy. They belonged, Bosmann said, as he knew from the shape of their huts, to the people called the Bathonga, a poor tribe struggling for existence and crushed between the upper and nether millstones of the Basutos and Swazis and ravaged by both.

In such matters Janse found Bosmann extremely knowledgeable. His mind had an ethnological trend. When they lay listening at night to the distant grunting of lions' and jackals' quavering cries he would often descant on the racial destinies of South Africa.

'Here we are,' he would say, 'we three men. You are English and Dutch and French, as you say, and I am pure German, and Meninsky, he is a Jew. The Teuton, the Latin, the Jew: that is the five best bloods and brains in the world to make a new country. This great land is all ours to make, my friend, and yet we must quarrel instead of making one new nation of overmen. And while we lose time, disputing who shall be first, we do not

116

see the one thing that is most important. Our white empire is for a hundert years, or perhaps, two hundert, no more. That is not too short for such Empires. And then, after us, comes the dis-owned, the Kaffir whose land we have besat on, to take it back. That is the *Schicksal*, the Fate you say, of South Africa, though the white man will not admit it, and you and I shall not see that day, thank God!'

A sinister reminder of what that day might be was brought to their minds towards the end of their first week's trek from Mulder's Spruit. During the last forty-eight hours Janse had been aware of a comparative infrequency of Thonga villages. Around such as they passed he had noticed a curious absence of life: no cattle grazed on the slopes; no women came with gourds and pots to the water-places. More than once, where a village had stood, lay circles of blackened ashes. And then, of a sudden, one evening, they came on the cause of this desertion. In a narrow ravine they found their way barred by a company of twenty or thirty natives. These people were very different from the timid, fugitive Bathonga, men of splendid stature, erect and finely-muscled, with thin hips and wide shoulder-girdles. They stood in the neck of the kloof against the skyline like statues carved out of ebony, each one motionless, with a gun in one hand and a stabbing assegai in the other. When he saw them the Hottentot Cobus, who was leading the oxen, dropped his rein and scuttled to the rear.

'Where are you running to?' Janse called.

'*Bapedi, baas,*' he cried. 'Sekukuni's Basuto. I go for the guns.'

'Leave the guns where they are and get back to your leaders, you yellow devil,' Meninsky shouted. But Cobus was gone. Already the oxen had halted.

'Don't let them stop. Keep them going, Janse,' Meninsky said.

Janse hurried forward, to take the *voorlooper's* place and restart them.

'That is right,' Bosmann said. 'Above all, we must not show fear. Now I go to speak with them. I have learn Sesuto.'

He ran forward, quickly overtaking the oxen, and advanced up the slope in front of them. He was a comical little sight, Janse thought, in his short, tight jacket and a broad-brimmed hat, much too big for him, sunk over his large, pale face. As he approached the natives the magnificent figure of an *induna*

117

stepped out and towered over him. He stood six foot three at least; encircling his head he wore the *isigoko*, a ring of fibre covered with twisted sinews attached to the roots of unshaven hair and blackened with beeswax; and a bunch of black widow-bird plumes increased his stature. Bosmann gravely saluted this dignified figure with upraised hand, and the *induna* returned his salute with equal gravity.

'Where are you going and what do you want here, Umlungu?' he said.

'We go north, but more towards the rising sun. We do you no harm. We are travellers.'

'You lie, Umlungu. We know you are searching for gold. This is Sekukuni's country, and the gold you look for is his.'

'Yet I have seen Bathonga kraals.'

The *induna* threw back his lordly head in contempt.

'The Bathonga are only Sekukuni's dogs. The young men you see have washed their spears in their blood and burnt their kraals. This is Sekukuni's country, I say. You cannot pass here.'

'We shall not go farther towards the sun,' Bosmann mildly assured him. 'Even now we turn east.'

The *induna* grunted. There was no more parley between them; but he stood aside to let the wagon pass. When they had cleared the neck and looked backwards, that group of ebony statues still stood superbly poised against the sunset on the crown of the hill.

'I do not think now we need fear more trouble,' Bosmann said. 'It is not Sekukuni's country here, although he claims it. Did you see the young men's spears?' He shuddered. 'Every one of them was glazed with dry blood like a varnish. They have finished. Now they go home.'

Even so, they took turns to keep a look-out that night, and each man, including Cobus, who had turned up from the bush before dark, slept with a loaded gun at his side, fearing not so much violence to themselves as the theft of their oxen, on which the young warriors of the Bapedi had set envious eyes – and, as ill luck would have it, in spite of the fire they lighted, a lion took one that night, and the one they could least afford to lose; the big red front-ox, Slingveld. It was because, as Bosmann explained, the raiding Bapedi had driven away the game and the lions were hungry. But that was not much consolation to Janse, who had lost his best leader and a sixteenth part of the price of Witfontein.

At intervals during that restless night Bosmann had been busy with compass and sextant, making stellar observations whenever the sky was clear. He jotted down the results by candlelight and compared them with the figures contained in a notebook which, for the first time, he produced from a pocket in the leather belt he wore next his skin. Janse leant over his shoulder to see what he wrote, but could make nothing of it. He read: '*A Tauri: Aldebaran. Observed altitude:* 90.37.0; *lat.* 23.58.59. *A. Orionis: Betelgeuse, Observed altitude:* 117.21.30; *lat.* 23.58.2. *Index error* 2′ *minus. Mean latitude,* 23.58.2.' When he asked Bosmann what these figures meant, he would not explain.

'They mean only that we are growing very near. That is all,' he said mysteriously.

Next morning, as they advanced, under his intructions, on a line bearing farther east, his manner betrayed an increasing excitement.

'At noon I take a new observation,' he said; 'but that shall only confirm what I know already. We have travelled well: praise be God, we are nearly there.'

He was most concerned, it appeared, with the relations of two prominent features in the tumbled landscape: the western end of what at first seemed a camel-backed ridge, but later resolved itself into a series of three sharp peaks, and a densely-wooded kloof running up into the Berg in the direction of a slight depression or notch in its unbroken rampart. As they drew nearer the kloof, which at its lower end expanded into a level open valley through which a stream ran, Janse saw that the sides of its northernmost wall were streaked with bands of quartz, shining white against the green. They moved slowly onwards until the fore-oxen had reached the brink of the stream and put down their heads to drink. There Bosmann, his mild eyes shining, his voice oddly shaken with emotion, gave the word to outspan.

'This is the place,' he said. 'In the morning we begin.'

'In the morning? What's wrong with this afternoon, boss?' Meninsky protested.

'Tomorrow, as the Boers say, is also a day. This afternoon we prospect. But first I thank the Lord.'

119

The odd little man sank down on his knees with head lowered, his hands over his eyes. Meninsky and Janse watched him praying with a sense of mingled discomfort and reverence.

Later on in the day they explored the kloof. Through its bottom a limpid stream of moderate swiftness flowed between banks cushioned with fern into which their feet sank deeply. They might well have been the first men who had ever penetrated that solitude, Janse was thinking, when, of a sudden, they came upon a series of oblong excavations. They were six or seven feet deep and looked like graves that had been dug and abandoned, for already the rampant herbage had choked them and overspread the heaps of soil that lay beside them. Bosmann gazed at them sentimentally.

'This is where my poor friend make his prospect,' he said, 'before the fever came and drove him away. See, there is the dam he built in the river, but the floods have broken it. We will now name this place. We will call it Brunner's Rest in his memory. Now we go to examine the reef.'

They left the moist bottom and clambered up the precipitous slope that faced northwards, hauling themselves upward from ledge to ledge of passable foothold by the wiry brushwood that clung to its arid face. Here the tree-ferns which grew lower down gave place to spiked aloes and gaunt candelabras of elephant-hided euphorbia, which lifted their desiccated fingers to the sun as in vain supplication. It was a sinister climb which taxed Janse's crippled leg. Every other bush was draped with the gauzy sloughs of snakes; and once, as his hand groped upwards, he saw the flash of a cobra's brown mail as it whipped through the bushes and vanished beside his feet. Meninsky, agile as a monkey, outdistanced them all, and had reached the scar of quartz while Janse and Bosmann were still toiling painfully upwards. When they landed, panting, beside him on the narrow ledge, Janse saw that the crystalline quartz dyke was not white but stained rusty pink. Through its substance, diagonally, ran a darker vein. Bosmann chipped a fragment of this with his hammer. The fracture, snow-white and glistening, showed a serpentine network of granular yellow threads standing out in high relief like a delicate filigree.

'This is what is called wire-gold,' Bosmann said in a trembling voice. 'Here is great wealth, my friends.' Meninsky and Janse examined the fragment eagerly, incredulously, in turn. It was the first unmined gold they had seen. 'But such ore must be blasted and crushed,' he went on, 'and we have yet no machinery. This must wait, though we know where it is. First of all we dig for alluvial.'

Though it was hard for Meninsky to resist starting work at once, they accepted the man's prudent advice and rested that evening. They were all of them tired out, physically and emotionally, and suffering the effects of reaction. They sat round the fire with a bottle of Janse's mother's peach-brandy. Meninsky, who could not keep still, brought out his concertina and played music-hall songs, while Bosmann, made sentimental by liquor, was persuaded to sing the yearning songs of his homeland until his eyes filled and his cheeks streamed with tears. They all slept soundly that night. In the morning Cobus reported that three more of the oxen, which had been ailing during the last few days, were dying of red-water. Though they knew they could not recross the Berg with a loaded wagon and only six spans, this disaster did not depress them. They were above all such circumstances. For they had found payable gold.

(7)

They set to work digging and washing in Brunner's creek next morning. Meninsky had already mastered the job in theory, but Bosmann, who had practised it, was tacitly given the part of leader. It was odd, Janse thought, how a chance circumstance beyond their control – nothing less than the deflection of a compass-needle by a mountain mass of magnetic iron – should have altered not merely their first destination but their whole plan of campaign. But for that, they might still, at this moment, have been fossicking among the hordes of hungry alluvial diggers whom, like flotsam, the tides of rumour swept helplessly to and fro along the cliffs of the Berg. Now, instead of being dependent on the problematical kindness of fortune, they had been led straight to a prospect that was not only apparently rich, but also unknown to any probable rivals – and that by a man much more 'knowledgeable' than themselves, who, but for their chance arrival at a precise moment, might easily have been dead and buried along with his secret.

The first principles of digging for alluvial, as expounded by

Bosmann, were simple and logical. They were based on the known existence of a gold-bearing dyke high up in the wall of the kloof, and on the supposition that, during the gully's gradual formation – first by slow atmospheric action, combined with alternations of drought and moisture, heat and cold, and then, later ón, a channel once having been made, by the more violent erosions and attritions of running water – the whole mass of rock (including the reef itself) which had once filled the gap must have been disintegrated and washed away along the bed of the stream. Here, at points where the valley twisted because of the projection of some more resistant rock, it was reasonable to suppose that the new-born stream had formed pools or eddies in which the water-borne debris – and particularly the parts of it which were heavier because they held gold – would be concentrated, and allowed, by the slowing-down of the current, to sink to the bottom and form a conglomerate mass of gold-bearing soil.

Such a favoured spot, in Bosmann's judgment, was the flat reach of the stream beside which Brunner had sunk his pits. As the dead prospector's digging had proved, there was a depth of no more than seven feet of soil, with detritus and debris embedded, between the present level of the ground and the face of the bed-rock beneath it.

In this, with picks, spades and crowbars, they set to work excavating, and found the task, to begin with, surprisingly easy, for the upper layers of red earth were soft with moisture. It was only when these had been stripped and they had reached the next, where the clay was stiffened with densely-packed gravel and smooth water-worn boulders that could only be prised from their beds inch by inch with pick and crowbar, that the pace of their digging, begun so light-heartedly, showed signs of flagging. At the hour when they started, the morning air had been cool; the great fronds of the tree-ferns had shadowed them from the rising sun; but now, as the sun climbed higher, its rays beat down on them as fiercely as if the moist air of the kloof had the concentrating power of a burning-glass. By ten o'clock they were forced to strip off their shirts and work naked to the waist. Meninsky, whose skin was protected by pigmentation, withstood the glare easily; but the fair-skinned Janse and Bosmann were soon scorched and blistered in spite of the sweat that streamed from them.

Bosmann, indeed, was a pitiful sight. At the best, his physique could never have been impressive, his pale body widening, pear-shaped, from the narrow shoulders to the lax paunch. Now, his muscles softened by sedentary living and all the tissues of his body sapped and wasted by fever, he was obviously incapable of any sustained physical effort. His hands, too, unused to labour, were soon bleeding and ragged with broken blisters. Only Meninsky, wiry and tough as a Basuto pony, horny-handed, without an ounce of superfluous fat on his small, swart body, appeared to be unaffected by either the heat or the toil. As he worked, he sang and chattered and joked continually. There was nothing that could daunt his spirits or break his strength.

By late afternoon, between them, they had dug a pit three feet deep and excavated no less than six cubic yards of earth mingled with water-smoothed boulders and shale and gravel. It seemed little enough to show for such a prodigious expenditure of labour; but Bosmann, who was by this time reduced to a pitiful state of exhaustion, appeared to be satisfied – particularly when he discovered fragments of quartz among it.

'Today we have done enough,' he panted at last. 'Tomorrow morning, when it is cool, we wash and pan this dirt.'

Janse gladly agreed. The muscles of his back were so strained by digging that he could hardly straighten it; his trousers were sodden with sweat; his lame leg had gone stiff and painful, it refused to obey him.

'Yes, tomorrow. I'm just about done,' he said. 'Come on, Meninsky.'

Meninsky crawled out of the pit and faced them angrily.

'Tomorrow? What the hell do you think you're talking about, a pair of white-livered *skelms*? The sun won't be down for another hour, and before it sets I'm going to see that my day's work's not been wasted. Where's the blasted pan? Give it here!'

He snatched up the wide iron prospecting-pan from the ground and scooped into it from the broken earth at the bottom of the pit as many handfuls as it would hold. He ran to the bank and immersed the pan in the stream, with the outer edge slightly depressed. As the pan filled, he shook and rotated it, making the muddy water sweep round the 'dirt' and allowing it to escape over the tilted edge. By this time both Janse and Bosmann were kneeling beside him and watching anxiously.

'Is that right, boss?' Meninsky inquired.

'Yes, that's right,' Bosmann said in an eager whisper, 'but I have more practice. Give it to me.'

'All right. Mind you don't fall in, mate.'

Bosmann had forgotten his tiredness. His pale eyes were intense and excited behind their sweat-smeared lenses. He handled the heavy pan with a loving dexterity, picking out from the sodden surface the larger lumps and pebbles, some of which, because they were of quartz, he laid carefully aside. Again and again he dipped the pan in the stream and sluiced it with a delicate circular motion and tilted it. He kept on filling the pan until the water that flowed away from it was no longer muddy and in the bottom lay a deposit of clean, heavy sand. And now he displayed his virtuosity. Half-filling the pan with clear water, he rose to his feet. With a quick, dexterous twirl of the hands he set the pan's contents spinning in a whirlpool that swept the lighter substances to the edge. In its centre there remained a small nest of rounded particles, some inky black, some shining bright yellow with a pure soft lustre. The inner edge of dark sand was fringed, too, with a thin line of gold.

Bosmann gazed at the tailings lovingly:

'There is your colour, my friends, he said. 'This dirt is rich ... rich.'

All three hung over the pan, with greedy, fascinated eyes.

'Are all them black bits gold too, boss?' Meninsky asked.

'Perhaps they are gold. If you flatten them with a hammer or cut it with a knife, the gold is like lead. But I think the black is mundic.'

'Where's a knife? Better try.'

'I try no more tonight,' Bosmann answered him firmly. 'I have done what I promised you, and that is enough. I have brought you to payable gold. Tomorrow, if I can move my poor legs, we must seriously begin. And that is another thing.'

After that moment of exaltation it was indeed an anticlimax to settle down to the arduous and unspectacular labour of building their sluice-box for the washing of gold. For this, since the prospect on which they had decided to concentrate lay in a flat part of the valley, where the stream itself flowed slowly and sunken between deep banks, it was necessary to bank up a 'head' of water at a higher level and lead it down-hill by furrows dipping at a gradient steep enough to give the flow force. It was easy enough to release the stream from one of the natural pools in the higher part of its course, but more difficult to excavate the furrow and give it a regular 'fall' over ground that was generally uneven and occasionally stony. It proved to be harder still to make the race hold water when it was made. Though the 'head' they obtained from the stream seemed sufficient to supply a strong current, by the time it reached their dump it had dwindled to a trickle. They lined the furrow with puddled clay throughout all its length, but still it leaked, and in the end they were forced to tap the stream lower down, and construct a flume lined with the yellow-wood planks Meninsky had brought in the wagon.

Next, under Bosmann's direction, they made their sluice-box, an oblong receptacle, square in section, about a foot wide and twenty feet in length. Half-way down the box they inset a ripple, a transverse ledge two inches in height, and at its lower end another, paving the length between the two ledges with heavy flat stones. Then the work of washing began. It took all three of them – and old Cobus as well – to do the job properly. At the head, Meninsky, the strongest, shovelled in the 'dirt' that the Hottentot dumped at his feet. In the middle length Janse was kept busy freeing the upper division of the box from the heavier stones. At the lower end, Bosmann, whom the labour of making the flume had knocked out and made unfit for any task more strenuous, kept the tail-race free from accumulations of silt, which, left to themselves, would have backed up the flow and flooded the upper compartments. When the water ran clear, Meninsky diminished the current and began to work down by hand what was left in the upper division, picking out any stones that remained – apart from fragments of quartz – and scraping out all the sludge on a scoop of tin, which he emptied carefully into the pans where Bosmann, who had the knack, would deal with it later.

During the first day's work they did little more than wash the first of Brunner's dumps. The dirt must have weighed rather more than a ton. It yielded seventeen pennyweights of fine gold, apart from the problematical amount contained in a number of fragments of quartz, which would have to be crushed before the value of their contents could be assayed.

It seemed an exiguous result from eight hours' labour – that residue of fine yellow grains in the middle of the pan, whose total value was no more than three pounds sterling; yet, as Bosmann explained, alluvial gold was naturally patchy, and a

125

find of a few grains in one day might be followed by that of a nugget as big as Maclachlan's famous pair, the 'Emma' and 'Adeliza', which the Burgers government had bought for a hundred and thirty pounds. And indeed, the next day's washing produced ten ounces, including a bean-shaped nugget of nineteen pennyweights.

Meninsky was over the sky with delight when the weight was known.

'Ten ounces at three pound fifteen an ounce: that makes thirty-seven pound ten. Divide that by three, and you get twelve pound ten apiece. Seven times twelve pound ten makes eighty-seven pounds ten for the week. That's three hundred and fifty a month and four thousand two hundred a year, which is the interest on one hundred thousand pounds of capital! We're not quite millionaires yet, mates, but we're well on the way to it. I'm not greedy, I reckon I could rub along pretty tidy on a cool thousand a year – what do you say, Janse?'

'I say that you're asking for trouble, talking like that,' Janse said.

They got it, anyway: for the next two days' washing, which exhausted Brunner's dumps and the greater part of their own, produced not a single nugget, and no more than a faint show of 'colour' – gold so fine that it was difficult to weigh.

'It looks like we're booked for the workhouse,' Meninsky said. 'We're down to five bob a day. Why, a chap can earn more than that as a labourer at the diamond-diggings.'

During the next week they had to do without Bosmann's help, for he went down, that night, with another attack of fever. He lay sweating and shivering alternately under the wagon's tilt, almost too feeble to concentrate on giving advice. It was unfortunate that Meninsky's elaborate preparations had not included a supply of quinine. They had nothing with which to treat Bosmann but the mildly medicated bottle of Water's Quinine Wine he had picked up in Lydenburg. Janse saw Bosmann swallow the dregs of it with some apprehension; for though on the healthy High Veld, he had had no acquaintance with fever, he knew that Vee Boers, such as his Uncle Barend, who habitually drove down their cattle to graze in the Low Country, had learnt to avoid these altitudes like the plague as soon as winter was past.

And now spring was advancing. They knew this not only from the increasing power of the sun, which made physical

126

labour impossible for a white man in the middle of the day, and at all other times a torment, but also from the steamy moisture which made the close air of the kloof seem lifeless and hardly breathable. Yet work they must; for now they were no longer concerned with the relatively easy task of washing the dirt which Brunner had excavated. They had to keep the sluice-box filled with what they dug for themselves; and in this poor Bosmann, frail at the best of times and now weakened by fever, was almost useless.

Though their muscles had become better accustomed to digging and their hands calloused by the friction of pick and spade, though Meninsky, always cheerful and indefatigable, did the work of two, this was no labour for white men. In the more frequented foothills of the Berg, they might have hired native labourers; but this patch of country had been abandoned by the Bathonga as being too near Sekukuni's guns and spears for safety.

Moreover, the rains, which had broken first on the night when they came to the edge of the Berg, had begun to increase in volume and frequency. Though their days were usually serene, black tatters of watery vapour drooped from the mountain barrier; the eastern horizon was ringed with stationary masses of anvil-shaped cloud. At sunset the weight of oppression became intolerable, and relief only came when the sky could no longer sustain its contents of moisture and electricity, and cracked overhead, to release a deluge of rain.

Those black nights were a pandemonium of noise and falling water; but when the sun rose cloudless at dawn into the rain-cooled sky, Janse thought he had never seen the foothills more beautiful. Now every leguminous tree was airily fledged with emerald leaf and bowed beneath the weight of its trusses or panicles of bloom, blood-red and scarlet, snow-white and golden and amethyst. The whole face of earth was green, and from it there sprang, miraculously, flowers in myriads – tulips, lilies, violets and primulas. Birds were noisily courting and building; a ceaseless hum of insect-wings thrilled the air. The face of the Berg, too, rose green to its pinnacles, which seemed strangely near, and down every cleft in its barrier white torrents thundered.

With the rains, as well as beauty, there came disaster. In a single night water swept away not only the heaps of soil they had excavated, but the plank-lined flumes they had built with

127

such care, and the wooden sluice-box. The stream from the kloof swept knee-deep beneath the wagon where they were sleeping, and carried their timber along with it a mile past the camp. All the falling slope was strewn with pebbles and boulders and fragments of quartz spread glittering in the sun.

'Well, I reckon that there cloudburst, or whatever it was, has washed more dirt in an hour than what we have in a month; but it damn near washed us and the ruddy wagon away as well. And they say the rivers of Africa ain't got no water!'

It was not merely the destruction of their flume and sluice-box that frustrated them. When the scattered sodden planks had once been assembled they could easily have 'knocked these up' – as Meninsky called it – again. Their main enemy was the stream itself, which, after that first outburst of spite, showed no signs of returning to the condition in which they had found it, but remained a fierce torrent, plunging from ledge to ledge of the kloof in loud cascades. Over the flats where they had started to strip, the water spread in a pool more than three feet deep; beneath it lay drowned not only the most promising strata of alluvial soil, but also the tools they had carelessly thrown aside out of sheer fatigue on the day when the flood-water came, and – most galling of all – more than twenty ounces of gold, the gains of a hard week's work, which Bosmann, jackdaw-fashion, had secreted in a tin under a ledge of rock. For the moment it was useless to try to salvage this cache, so deeply was the whole smothered in silt.

Nor, until the water subsided, could there be any question of further digging in the spruit. Janse and Bosmann, in fact, were not entirely sorry, for one was still weak with recurrent bouts of fever and both had worked themselves out. But Meninsky was furious. He regarded himself as the object of some private spite on the part of Nature.

'How long do you reckon this water will take to go down?'

Bosmann shook his head with a mild and irritating fatalism.

'Who knows? Perhaps it will flow all summer, till the rains finish,' he said. 'That is, what you say, the devil of gold-mining. It is always the same. At Mulder's Spruit there was no water, and here too much . . . too much.'

'You don't tell me we've got to wait here doing nothing for three ruddy months? That'd send me balmy. Let's have a shot somewhere else.'

128

'That would not be so clever, my friend. Suppose we go and some others come and find what we leave? You know the Gold Law? Perhaps not. I will tell it you. If a claim is abandoned for more than one week, any person who finds may "jump" it. And we are outside the law as it is, I remind you also. He who finds payable gold has the duty to report to the Government. That we have not done. In these parts, God be thanked, the Government comes not. But the danger is there. No, no, we must stay where we are.'

'What about the reef? Can't we start working there?' Meninsky persisted.

'The land is too steep. All the rock you break would slide down the slope and fall in the water. We could not carry it here. If we did, we could not crush it without machinery.'

'Well, we shall want the machinery sooner or later,' Meninsky said. 'If you'll show me what you want I'll set about making it.'

He threw himself into that job with a new release of energy. What they needed, Bosmann said, were the parts for a 'dolly', a rudimentary stamp consisting of a sturdy post, seven feet high, the trunk of a tapering tree, and a flexible cross-bar, six or eight yards long, attached to the top of it. The thick end of the cross-bar must be firmly bedded in earth and kept down by the weight of heaped rocks: to the tapered end must be fixed the hard bole of a tree, three or four feet in length and heavily shod with iron. This, the ramming end of the stamp, must be placed in such a position that, when the flexible cross-bar was pulled down by hand, its iron-tipped weight would descend on the fragments of quartz, fed into a sluice-box through which water flowed, and crush it – after which the resilience of the anchored cross-bar would lift the ram once more to its first position.

The job of selecting and fashioning the wood for the 'dolly' was after Meninsky's heart. He had felled six trees before he found one that Bosmann accepted as suitable. While he worked in the bush, Janse took out his gun. Now that green, sweet grass was springing, the game which had been driven away by the Bapedi and the flight of the unfortunate Bathonga had gradually returned to the foothills, and he was able to shoot a number of rheebok and partridges for the pot. The fresh food put them all in better heart, and the oxen, too, grew plump and glossy-coated from feeding on the new grass.

But still the rain never ceased, and still the bottom of

Brunner's Spruit remained flooded, the ground unworkable. Bosmann was not a cheerful companion. His bouts of fever continued to lay him out with a calculable periodicity.

'In two hours' time,' he would say, 'I shall begin to shiver. I tell you now, Meninsky, and you will see by the watch I am right.'

And, of course, he was; but the manner in which he gloated over the accuracy of his prophecies irritated the Peruvian.

'I'm just about sick of you and your fever, boss,' he said crossly. 'It's a ruddy nuisance to all of us, not a thing to take pride in. And the way you talk of it anyone'd think you was the only beggar in the world that had ever had it.'

'But that is not so, my friend. I am not the first nor shall be the last,' Bosmann said with sinister satisfaction. 'This fever, it come from the air, what you call miasma. Miasma is heavier than common air. It hang in the valleys about two thousand feet when the rains have come, from middle September to May. Now we are in December, and I think this place where we are is about eighteen hundert and seventy feet. If you had brought a barometer I could tell you for certain.'

'Well, I ain't brought no barometer, and what's more, you don't need one here. It's safe to say, by what I can see, that it'll rain every day. As to fever, I've never believed in meeting trouble half-way. If it comes, it comes.'

It came, in fact, three days later. Janse was the first to go down with a splitting headache, followed by a rigor that made his teeth chatter. Bosmann, who always had an irritating explanation for everything after the event, said he had picked up his dose (as was possibly true) by sitting out late by a watering-place on the chance of killing a kudu, and returned drenched after dark. Whatever the cause may have been, the effect was devastating. For the whole of one night he lay in a muttering delirium, and when he came to his senses next morning, felt shattered and hopeless. Meninsky had sat with him all night and restrained him with difficulty from staggering out to plunge his burning body in the stream. Janse had already learnt to admire the stalwart spirit this little man showed in every emergency, without realizing the devotion and tenderness of which he was capable. He could not have been better nursed and tended if his mother had been at his side.

'By God, you're a good friend,' he said.

'Don't you believe it, mate,' the Peruvian said with a wink. 'I know how to feather my own nest. First of all, if you'd drownded yourself, I should have had to bury you, and I didn't fancy it. What's more, if I got fever myself, I wanted to make sure you'd look after me the same way. Whatever I done, you may bet your boots on one thing, and that is that my eye was always on the main chance.'

And no sooner was Janse back on his feet than the roles were reversed. Meninsky himself went down with an even more violent attack, in the midst of which, to make matters worse, Janse and Bosmann were laid out together. They were three sick men, lying helplessly side by side for two days under the dripping bucksail, while the deluge sluiced down without ceasing. Janse lay listening to the lashing of the rain and Meninsky's delirious chatter. The Peruvian's tongue never stopped making calculations on compound arithmetic that ran into millions. The ceaseless activity of that fevered brain with its spate of mounting figures became a sheer nightmare. He could only shut it out by stuffing his fingers in his ears and concentrating on his own thoughts, which sought refuge, of themselves, in the breezy heights of the Witwatersrand, in his abandoned Witfontein, and – with even more bitter longing – in the cool beauty of her for whose sake, he supposed, he was suffering this senseless exile, Lavinia Haskard.

It was not ruddy well good enough, Meninsky declared. It was time they got out of it. Here they had hung on like fools, through the four worst months of the rainy season, going rotten with fever, without the remotest chance of getting on with their work before the middle of May.

Bosmann passively resisted every suggestion of retreat. Supposing, he kept on saying, that as soon as they turned their backs, some other party arrived and jumped their claims?

'They can't possibly work them any more than we can,' Meninsky said. 'What's more, by the time we come back, the odds are that the miserable beggars will be dead or dotty with fever.'

'If you and Janse go, then I stay behind,' the German said obstinately, 'And wait till you come.'

Meninsky put his foot down.

'It ain't my job to stop you committing suicide, boss,' he said, 'but we can't afford to lose you. You're coming uphill along with us. Do you understand? And if you start turning mulish,

131

by God, we'll tie you up and carry you; so the sooner you drop this damn nonsense the better for all of us.'

They off-loaded the bulk of the less perishable stores from the wagon. It was a work that their wasted muscles could hardly achieve, but they knew it was impossible for the diminished team (three more oxen had died) to haul any considerable weight. They made a zigzag course over the flank of the foothills and established themselves at last on a shelf fifteen hundred feet above the pestilent valley. Though the cold air of the heights brought out the fever that remained in their blood, its thin sweetness gradually gave them new life. Below them – so near, in fact, that the white bucksail which covered their dump of stores was plain visible – they could see Brunner's Spruit and the deadly mist that lay in the bottom at dawn. And still the rain fell, and still the cataracts thundered.

CHAPTER TWO

(1)

ONE evening towards the end of summer, Adrian Grafton stalked into the house at Wonderfontein in a state of cold fury. He was red with dust from head to foot, having covered the whole distance from Pretoria without a halt.

'Like Paul, I've been fighting with beasts at Ephesus,' he told them. 'I've finished with this dirty business now, for good and all. I've fought till I'm sick of it, but it's no use going on fighting if the other side never plays fair. Such a crowd of sanctimonious lick-spittles and double-dealers! The President was a fool to have trusted them. By the time he gets back, things will have gone beyond his control. No, he shouldn't ever have taken the risk of going; although, if he hadn't gone to Europe to raise money, the Republic would certainly have been bankrupt in another six months.'

John Grafton smiled. 'That is nothing new, my son. The Republic has never been anything else but bankrupt since I can remember. In early times being bankrupt didn't matter. It was a family business. We were all of us in the same boat, and the money we owed, we owed to one another. It's the foreign loans that have wrecked us. Foreigners don't understand our ways. When they lend money they expect to draw interest in cash and have some security for their capital. That's not unnatural.'

'Security? Haven't we thousands of square miles of the best land in Africa?'

'Land's worth next to nothing in itself. It's the work men put into it that makes it valuable. And the bulk of our folk won't work, Adrian. Why should they? They've never been used to it, and they've not done so badly without it. A man lives only once, after all. They've never starved as people did in England when I was a boy.'

Adrian shook his head impatiently: 'You're as bad as the rest of them, Father. You refuse to see anything beyond the beacons of your own farm. Times have changed – and that's something that only Burgers has realized. A state that is weak

133

and poor is at the mercy of its neighbours. Every one of the English annexations proves that. If we don't make any attempt to develop our resources and put our house in order, somebody better qualified will step in and do it in spite of us. If we're ignorant we go to the wall. And we can't develop, I say, without foreign capital. We must borrow money.'

'We have borrowed money – and look at the result.'

'It's too soon to look for results. That's my point. We must have time. Burgers has laid the foundations. Now, as soon as his back is turned, his enemies have started to undermine them – not so much because they're ignorant, as out of sheer spite. Every single thing the President has put in hand – with the Volksraad's approval, mind you! – is being deliberately neglected or destroyed. The railway survey's been suspended. The material we've bought for the line lies rusting at Delagoa. Why? Because a few transport-riders who have votes have started to grumble! Then the new law we passed to extend secular education: it's simply been shelved. Why, again? Because the old gang of Dopper predikants don't want our folk to be educated, or their game will be up. Then the question of Government lands in native occupation. The natives have got to live somewhere, haven't they? Unless we are just, we lay ourselves open to the accusations the English are always making against us. Yet, everywhere, land that has been set apart for the Kaffirs has been parcelled out and peddled by members of the Raad to their personal friends. Even small things that don't really matter, such as the new coat of arms and the new flag that Burgers designed, are being changed with no other object than spiting him. We've fought them on every point; but it's no use our going on fighting without a leader. The dumb vote of the Dopper majority has beaten us every time.'

'Who's the villain in the piece?'

'Ah, that's not so easy to answer. The Vice-President, Joubert, who hates Burgers like poison, takes the lead; but the more subtle malice comes, I think, from Paul Kruger, who has twice as many brains as Joubert, and three times as much influence. He rarely opens his mouth in the Raad; when he does, he appears to favour moderation; but outside, on the burghers' stoeps and under the wagon-tents, he plays a dark game of his own and the back-veld vote follows him blindly. The devil of it is, there are many things I admire in Oom Paul. I can't help respecting his intellect. On the surface we're excellent friends. But he's no friend to Burgers – nor even to Joubert, for that matter. When the President comes back, Kruger's brains may find their match. It's possible that Burgers may force him to come out into the open, though that will be as difficult as pulling an *erdvark* backwards out of its hole. We shall see. In the meantime, I wash my hands of the whole ugly business.'

John Grafton smiled at his son: 'You take it too hardly, Adrian. I've lived in this country more than thirty years, and the one thing I've learnt about politics is that no two leaders have ever been known to agree except when they put their heads together to destroy another. For myself, I think you're much better out of it for good.'

'No, that I shall never be. I love my land too much, Father, and I believe in its future. When Burgers returns. . . .'

'In the meantime, it's good to have you home for a while, Adrian,' Lisbet said. 'We have almost forgotten what you look like, my son, and your father needs help.'

They needed Adrian's help less, in fact, that year. The rains, which had brought nothing to Janse but frustration and fever, had come as a blessing to Wonderfontein. This was the third good season running since the lean years in which drought and lung-sickness had threatened to nullify the accumulated gains of thirty. The depleted flocks and herds had increased without further mishap; green crops of food and fodder had flourished abundantly; and since the welfare and prosperity of her husband and her sons were all that really mattered to her, the tenor of Lisbet Grafton's life, during this period, had been serene. Though her thoughts grew tender and anxious at times for her long-lost Andries and for poor Janse – from whom, since he trekked away with Meninsky, they had had no word – it was a great solace to her to have Piet and Adrian within reach.

As for Piet – he was not, save under occasional compulsions of conscience, of very much use to Wonderfontein. That long-headed young man, with characteristic prudence and energy, was throwing himself into the reorganization of Jans's derelict farm. He had sold his surplus wagons and transport oxen at a time when, thanks to the continued growth of Kimberley, prices were still high. With the proceeds, added to his considerable savings, he had plenty of money (which Janse had lacked) to spend. With his eye on intensive development and quick profits, he was ready to pay wages for native labour not greatly inferior to those that were offered in Kimberley.

135

His father and Adrian shook their heads over what they regarded as reckless extravagance. But Piet, as usual, knew what
he was doing. In his transport-riding to Kimberley he had not
only studied the markets but also made valuable business connections. He had realized that in a community where ready
money flowed as freely as water (and almost more plentifully)
and where opportunities for spending it were limited, it was not
the time-honoured staples, corn and wool, but luxuries of a
more perishable nature, such as fruit and fresh vegetables, that
were most eagerly absorbed and bought at any price. Traffic in
this kind of produce had a further advantage. If it was bulky,
it was also light and made transport speedy. Wagons loaded
with such stuff could make three return journeys to Kimberley
in less time than one packed with Boer-meal spent in making
two.

For the growth of green produce and fruit the poor depth of
the soil at Witfontein, of which he had made a buyer's point at
the time of his purchase, was less of a disadvantage than in the
growing of forage or corn; for fruit-trees are shallow-rooted,
and stony ground gives good drainage, in which they will thrive,
while vegetables and salads are in the nature of catch-crops.
The one thing they needed most (and that Witfontein lacked)
was plentiful supplies of water; but Piet realized this from the
first and, as soon as his orchards of stone-fruit and citrus (the
last a more daring speculation) were planted, he set himself to
the systematic collection and conservation of every available
spot of moisture that Witfontein could produce: digging a network of contour-furrows, with nicely-calculated gradients, to
spread the water of the 'fountains' over the slopes; sinking two
wells that might possibly serve him in times of emergency,
building a series of puddled dams to imprison the rain-water
which, in the season of thunderstorms, ran to waste down the
southern face of the Rand. For water, he knew, was the life-
blood of that arid soil, and he would rather put money into the
storage of water than into anything else.

When he had laid these foundations, and almost spent himself out, he turned his swift, practical mind on to Janse's dilapi-
dated house. That weather-worn structure of sun-dried brick,
which had served Janse well enough and had been loved by him
as the centre of his workaday world and the refuge of his secret
dreams, was an offence to Piet's orderly eyes. There seemed no
reason why, when work was slack and his Kaffirs were at a

loose end, he should not rebuild it – or better still, plan another, in which his wider ideas would not be restricted by the modest scale that had contented Janse. From the first his eyes had been attracted with envy to the house the Haskards had built for themselves high upon on the ridge above Brakfontein. Though it still remained empty – Major Haskard's lungs had been behaving well at the Cape, and no business took him farther north than Kimberley – Piet often rode round that way to inspect it with critical and admiring eyes. He had made himself an adept at picking other folks' brains, and this house, in its planned convenience, its use of sun and shade, above all in its shapeliness compared with the boxes of masonry in which people of his race and station were generally content to live, satisfied his sense of what was due to himself – not merely to himself as he was, but to himself as he intended to be. So he made careful drawings and measurements, decided to turn Janse's handiwork into a shed for cattle and horses, carted three wagon-loads of galvanized iron from Kimberley, baked bricks of the clay excavated from his new furrows and dams, and began to build on a site more convenient for water, a hundred feet high up the slope.

Once more Adrian and his father were shocked by an ambitious project so much in excess of his needs. Piet countered their criticism:

'If I ever want to sell Witfontein, my new house will easily have doubled the value of the property.'

'But no farmer would ever want such a house,' Adrian said.

'No Boer, perhaps. Most of your friends, Adrian, don't even know what a real house looks like. If it weren't for their wives they'd be living in wagons to this day. That's the trouble with you. In politics you're proud to consider yourself an enlightened liberal. At heart you're a voortrekker, as conservative as your great-grandfather, and hate everything new. Do you imagine that anyone coming from Kimberley or the Cape would consent to live in a hovel like Janse's?'

'Why should anyone in his senses want to live on the Witwatersrand, unless he happened to be born here?'

'Major Haskard settled at Brakfontein, didn't he?'

'I still say the whole affair is a ridiculous waste of time and money. If you want to get rid of your savings I can't stop you. This fad of yours of planting fruit seems just as foolish to me.

You will never grow good fruit such as they have at the Cape, or even Pretoria, in this soil and at this altitude.'

Piet laughed. 'That is true. But I don't want to grow good fruit. I want to grow fruit that will sell. The market I mean to serve doesn't know what good fruit is; but I'm ready to bet it will buy every basket I send it. If they won't buy it fresh why, damn it, I'll dry what's left over. Never fear: I know what I'm after.'

'Well, that's more than I do, anyway,' Adrian muttered contemptuously.

'I never supposed you did,' Piet said quickly, twisting his meaning.

'Children . . . children!' Lisbet entreated.

They were always like that, these two, at cross-purposes or on the edge of quarrel; and Adrian, though slow to anger, could be formidable when he was roused. Their differences, which often hurt and sometimes scared her, were due, she supposed, to the preponderance in Piet of his father's racial strain, which made him not merely look but actually think like an Englishman, whereas Adrian (like Sarie) was pure Dutch all through, from his pale golden beard to his *velskoene*. It was her duty as well as her pride to smooth over these divergences; her understanding, no less than her love, being the flux that could reconcile and unite. Now, seeing the flush of anger slowly rising on Adrian's temples, she intervened with a smile.

'Perhaps,' she said, 'Piet is building a bigger house to put a wife in; and I hope he is. That is what you should have done long ago, Adrian. Here am I, an old woman, without a single grandchild to nurse, and none of my sons but Andries married as yet. Why, when your father and I were your age, Adrian, we already had nine children: only Maria had not been born. You spend too much time on your quarrelsome politics, which are really not very important. I think you are wrong.'

Adrian laughed. 'I'm beginning to agree with you, mamma,' he said. 'As for my not marrying – you're partly to blame. I've been spoilt. If you'll find me a wife like yourself, I'll marry her tomorrow.'

'But in that case,' Piet said, 'I should probably be after her myself – and get her, too. You can't marry a wife unless you've a home to give her.'

'You'll be lonely in that great house all the same, Piet,' Lisbet said.

138

'Not if I go to live with him, he won't,' Maria put in eagerly. 'Will you have me for your housekeeper, Piet? I should have to bring Janse's donkey with me, of course.'

'What? Two of you? That's a grave question,' Piet teased her solemnly. 'I might possibly make such a sacrifice for your poor mother's sake. I can't see any other reason.'

Maria laughed: 'Try again, then.'

There, too, Lisbet thought, the strange distribution of different bloods in her family told. Just as Adrian and Sarie and Andries resembled one another (with poor Janse, a sort of odd hybrid of English and Dutch and Huguenot, in between), so Piet and Maria, the youngest, had much in common – including a capacity for teasing one another and for seeing each other's jokes. When she heard Maria's low, eager voice and saw her standing there, bright-cheeked, slim and tall and straight as a bamboo-shoot, with laughter in her grey eyes, she was moved by an access of tenderness for this child, the baby of her long family.

A baby no longer. During the last three years Maria had shot up prodigiously. Now, at seventeen, she was taller than Lisbet herself, and nearly as tall as Piet, but she had never 'filled out' as most girls with Dutch blood in them did. Her figure was not only slight, but flexible; her movements had grace, like those of a sapling swayed by the wind; there was about her the air of a woodland in spring, more native to the oak-woods of the Cape or the green glades of her father's dim homeland than to the treeless expanse of the High Veld on which she had been born. There would never be any doubt as to Maria's marrying, Lisbet thought – the idea of marriage still persisting in her mind from the talk that had gone before; if they had lived more in the world, young men would have been buzzing round her like flies already. No, in Maria's case the difficulty would be to find any young man suitable to handle a creature whose mind and body were so delicately, so sensitively made, without brushing away the bloom or breaking the ardent spirit. She could not see her Maria, so gay, so vivid, so tender, condemned, for want of a better opportunity, to the static drudgery of sharing a back-veld farmer's life. It would be a crime to permit such a sacrifice. Well, the child was still young, just turned seventeen. Perhaps time would avert it. Perhaps she might even marry an Englishman, Lisbet thought, though she could hardly believe that all Englishmen were as gentle and straight and tender with women as her husband, John Grafton, whom she still adored. Indeed, the second-rate Englishmen – and there were plenty of them about in these days – were much less desirable as husbands than the average back-veld Boer, who, for all his uncouthness, was usually solidly reliable and faithful to his wife. Lisbet sighed to herself as she smiled on Maria's eager face. It was almost a greater responsibility to have daughters who would certainly marry young than sons who would not. . . .

(2)

There was a high potential of vague amorousness in the air that surrounded Wonderfontein in early autumn that year. A powerful and scandalous part of its influence emanated from the huts of the coloured heople who, when Kaffir labour ran short, had settled on the eastern boundary of John Grafton's land. They were half-caste folk bearing the good Dutch name of Erasmus, which proudly commemorated their bastard origin, and had come trekking west indolently with a broken-down donkey-wagon from Griqualand East, which the head of the family, whose name was Adam, had found too 'hot' for him.

Adam himself was a shambling man with a tawny beard, which he made the most of to counteract the effect of his high Hottentot cheek-bones and his little dark eyes. He was also, by habit and inclination, a liar and a thief, though John Grafton, hard driven for labour, had been glad to employ him in spite of these disadvantages, for he was handy with cattle and (when he was sober) an excellent teamster. Erasmus's wife, Lydia, on the other hand, was a much lighter-coloured Cape woman, with perhaps – for that race is old – the blood of several white cross-matings in her veins, together with a strong dash of the Malay, which gave her a narrow nose, even faintly acquiline, and an oval face, with cheek-bones not over-prominent. Most of the Hottentot that was left in Lydia expressed itself in her adiposity and in a slovenliness that made this group of huts, on the edge of the lands, where the Erasmus family-party swarmed promiscuously and apparently throve in the dust like a hatch of fleas, an offence to every sensibility.

There was an enormous brood of them, of many gradations

140

in colour and age – from dark bronze to a dusky ivory, from crawling brats to slim boys and girls in their teens; and two of these elder girls, in spite of their filth and degradation, were beautiful, delicate-featured things with soft, golden-brown hair and shy eyes which had the light that dances in tawny-sanded brooks. The Erasmus girls were quick to mature; by the time they had reached fifteen they were women; and no sooner were they women than Barend Prinsloo's lusty blue-eyed sons became aware of them.

Neither Adam Erasmus nor his wife had any objection of their daughter's promiscuity. Indeed, they encouraged it and were even rather proud of it; for both (and particularly Adam) despised and loathed the Kaffir, and were glad of any connection that could bring them nearer the white men in the next generation. When the elder daughters grew ugly, there would be more to follow. The rearing of such a desirable family was a lucrative trade.

Lisbet Grafton knew of these happenings. She was not unduly squeamish, having spent part of her girlhood at the Cape, where such relations between the meaner kind of white men and brown women were not uncommon – as indeed the existence of the coloured race proved. But she had much family pride; and the fact that the new off-white babies who swelled the population of Erasmus's compound were her brother Barend's grandchildren and shared her own Prinsloo blood, revolted her. She often wished she could persuade her husband to sweep the squatters away; but she knew that this wouldn't be fair, for their coming had solved all his labour difficulties, and Erasmus's boys, who were growing up, were already useful on the land.

If she hated for itself the sight of the Erasmus girls brazenly flaunting their white-skinned babies all over the farm, she disliked even more what this exhibition suggested. Though nothing could ever have convinced her that Adrian or Piet was likely to descend to the depths in which Barend's half-savage boys had sunk their racial pride, she could not deny that these golden-brown creatures were physically attractive. She knew Adrian to be grave by nature and Piet a hard-headed young man, but in matters of this kind all men were unaccountable, even to their mothers, and she dreaded lest either of them should fall in a moment of weakness or opportunity. That was why, though she

141

hated the idea of losing them, she was doubly anxious to see both her sons safely married. The two girls were fortunately in no danger. They could wait.

Yet it was Sarie, that dark, silent creature, who married first. At the Christmas Nachtmaal, when the whole family had trekked into the dorp for an extended course of Mr. Blair's Jeremiads, Sarie's sombre charms had attracted the attention of one of their old friends and neighbours, the Oosthuizens of Langlaagte. Soon after their return to Wonderfontein, young Hans Oosthuizen had ridden over on a Sunday afternoon in the acute discomfort of black broadcloth, a rainbow neckerchief and white *velskoene*, thus announcing his intentions in the traditional way.

The occasion was almost as thrilling to Maria as to Sarie herself, who received the young man with such deliberate indifference that Maria began to wonder whether she had not been mistaken – whether she herself might not be perhaps the object of this ceremonial call. Though she considered young Hans Oosthuizen as nothing more than an amiable lout and would have laughed at the idea of accepting him as a suitor, the mere possibility of having a grown man in love with her made her more than usually impish and vivacious.

For some dreary hours Hans Oosthuizen's shyness prevented him from showing his hand. He hardly looked at Sarie and never once spoke to her. He spent the whole afternoon in ingratiating himself with the males of the family, soliciting Adrian's opinions on Burgers' politics and asking John Grafton's advice on matters of farming; refusing blankly to rise to any of Maria's attempts to inveigle him into lighter conversation. For all the interest he showed in the two girls, one might have supposed that this was no more than an ordinary social visit – though Maria knew that he wouldn't have put on his Nachtmaal clothes unless he were bent on something more serious.

It was clearly no use attempting to bring Hans Oosthuizen to the point of declaring his intentions by mere encouragement. The sun set and the evening meal was brought in. It looked to Maria as if even now his courage would fail him. It was only when evening prayers had been said and sung, when the whole family had shown their intention of retiring for the night, that the young man rose with a brick-red face and moved towards the bench where she and Sarie were sitting.

'He's going to speak to one of us,' Maria thought. 'Oh dear, I do hope to goodness it won't be me. If it is, what on earth shall I do? I can't run away; but I can't stay with him; because, though I'm sure he's nice, I think he's simply awful.'

She moved aside instinctively, and was greatly relieved when Hans Oosthuizen leant across her and hoarsely whispered in Sarie's ear. Maria heard the time-honoured formula: '*Sarie ... Sal ons opsit?*'

Sarie nodded. 'So it isn't me after all,' Maria thought thankfully. She was thankful in one way and yet rather hurt in another. Though she didn't really like Hans Oosthuizen and shrank from the thought of his touching her with his huge calloused hands, it would certainly have been exciting to 'sit up' with any young man and to be told, however clumsily, that he loved her. If the love he offered was hopeless, so much the better.

But Sarie, that dark, warm, silent creature, apparently knew exactly what was expected of her. She rose quietly and went to a cupboard and fetched out the butt ends of two wax candles, which she fixed in a pair of brass candlesticks. She lit the two candles and set them in the middle of the table. Hans Oosthuizen too knew his duty. When the last good nights had been said and the two girls, with Maria leading, had moved towards their bedroom, he thrust his great leg across the door and barred Sarie's way. Sarie laughed – Maria had never before heard her laugh like that – and returned to the *voorhuis,* closing the door behind her.

Maria undressed with a fluttering heart. There was something oddly disturbing in the thought of what might be happening behind that closed door. Of course, this love-making was no business of hers; yet she couldn't help feeling that since every girl sooner or later had to face it, she owed it to herself to take this, her only likely opportunity, of finding out what it was all about. When she had put out her light, she wrapped herself in a jackal-skin kaross, crept to the bedroom door, and put her right eye to a hold that had been chiselled out to hold the peg that locked the latch in its hasp. She had no qualms in looking or listening, for she felt certain that, in the circumstances, any prudent young woman would have done the same.

The scene revealed by the light of the guttering candles which Sarie had selected to cover the duration of her *opsit* was one of the most decorous propriety. Hans Oosthuizen, once having

143

made sure of her, had planted himself on the rest-bench by the hearth and relighted his pipe, while Sarie had taken cover behind the long dinner-table. Hans stolidly smoked and occasionally spat without uttering a word. In a ceremony of this kind, the young man's intentions having once been established, it was clearly the young woman's duty to make conversation. Sarie did this, as usual, with difficulty.

'We have had good rains this season at Wonderfontein.' she began. 'Have you had the same at Langlaagte?'

'Yes ... The rains have been good at Langlaagte. Very good rains.'

'Father's mealies are looking well.'

'We have good mealies too.'

'The predikant preached very well at Nachtmaal, I thought; though the sermon was rather long. Two hours is enough.'

'No sermon can be too long,' Hans said sententiously. 'If it is good.'

'That is right; that is true; but Mr. Blair is growing old; I think he forgets when to stop. He looks very ill. ... I shouldn't think he will live very long,' Sarie added cheerfully. 'Perhaps we shall have a young man in his place. I expect he'll be married.'

Hans Oosthuizen spat deliberately, but did not answer. The trend of the conversation was getting dangerous.

'After all it is better that a predikant should have a wife,' Sarie went on meditatively. 'Otherwise, folk will always gossip, and that makes trouble. It is the same now with my two brothers, particularly Adrian; a man who is so looked up to surely ought to be settled. Piet, of course, is still young – he is even younger than me; but I think he will find a wife before Adrian.'

'All the same, I like Adrian better than Piet.'

Sarie would not be side-tracked: 'Yet Piet is more clever. You should see the fine house he has built on poor Janse's place! There will be room in that not only for a wife, but a large family as well.'

'I saw Piet's house as I rode here today. He must have money to waste. It is three times the size of ours at Langlaagte,' he added gloomily.

'Even so, the size of a house isn't everything,' Sarie said. 'You have better land at Langlaagte than Piet has at Witfontein. Oh yes, and a fine house too. Those beautiful gum-trees ...'

'You like Langlaate, Sarie?'

'Of course I like it.'

'Well enough to live there?'

'Hans. . . . Why ask such a question?'

'Ah. . . .' The young man knocked out his pipe and rose from the rest-bench. He crossed the room on tiptoe, approaching the table; and Maria, seeing his vast shadow obscure the flames of the candles, which were now guttering low, was seized with a sense of shame or guilt or fear of discovery more compelling than her former curiosity. She hurriedly took her eye from the hole in the door and scuttled back to her bed, where she lay with a fluttering heart and ears still strained to listen. But now no sound came from the room beyond save whispers and sometimes low laughter.

A full half-hour passed before Sarie lifted the latch and came to bed. The opened door showed no light in the *voorhuis*; both the candles were out. Maria, lying mouselike, pretending to be asleep, heard Sarie's slow movements and the swish of her clothes as she undressed in the dark. She had never before, Maria thought, taken such a long time to undress. When Sarie had slipped into bed, she lay on her back looking up, as Maria guessed, with open eyes, into the dark thatch where insects were stirring. She made no attempt to turn over and go to sleep. It was silly, Maria thought, for them to lie side by side wide awake without speaking; so she said, at last:

'Sarie . . .'

'Yes.'

'Are you going to marry him?'

Sarie laughed the same unfamiliar, soft laugh:

'Of course I shall marry him. The Oosthuizens are a good family. They are not strangers. They came up with Mamma and our grandparents at the time of the great trek. And Hans is the eldest son: he will have Langlaagte.'

That seemed a horribly unromantic reason for wanting to marry him, Maria thought. But then, Sarie had always been very matter-of-fact.

'I suppose you'll have heaps and heaps of children,' Maria said.

'I hope so,' Sarie said fervently.

And married they were, two months later, with no end of junketing. First of all there had been a long service in the whitewashed church at the dorp and an even longer sermon from Mr. Blair, in which he had made it clear that matrimony was no primrose path, but a way thick-set with temptations and pains and torments, with the gulf of death gaping black at the end of it. He was much less concerned, it appeared, for Hans and Sarie than for the enormous family which he took it for granted that they would produce – the procreation of which, indeed, was the only purpose for which they were being married. This led to a dissentation that lasted half an hour (and was obviously directed at Adrian) on the iniquity of Burgers' new measure for Secular Education, and a bitter review of the heretical President's personal record which lasted even longer. After that the whole congregation drove off to the Oosthuizen's farm at Langlaagte, where there must have been twenty neighbours' wagons outspanned beneath the blue gums, and then there was feasting, enlivened by much peach-brandy, and even a German fiddler who played music for dancing which, had he known of it, would have given Mr. Blair his theme for a sermon that would have lasted for more than three hours.

On the whole, Maria enjoyed her sister's wedding. She liked being a bridesmaid, and felt very lovely and elegant, compared with the Oosthuizen girls, in the sweeping dress of green-striped figured silk which Lisbet had 'made up' out of the eighteenth-century fabrics still carefully folded and stored in her bottomless wagon-chest. She enjoyed dancing the boisterous country-dances too – particularly with Piet, who was so lively and jolly and light-footed and saw the same jokes as herself. The whole evening, in fact, would have been a complete success from her point of view, if, towards the end of it, a middle-aged farmer named Grobler had not caught her in a dark corner and tried to kiss her. She wouldn't have minded being kissed just once, to see what it felt like, if her assailant had happened to be one of the younger men; but Paul Grobler, who weighed seventeen stone and had sixteen children, was not sufficiently romantic to justify the ordeal even as an experiment. When once she had escaped from him she never again left Piet's side.

By the middle of April Piet's grand new house was finished. It still needed, as he declared, a woman's hand to make it habitable. He pleaded for Maria to come and stay with him and help to put things straight; and Lisbet, who could never deny him anything, allowed her to join him, although, now that Sarie was married, she found it awkward to dispense with Maria's help.

For Maria this long visit to Witfontein was a great adventure. She had never before slept under any roof but that of Wonderfontein or in any bed save the one she had shared with Sarie. It was exciting to find herself in complete command of a brandnew house in which every domestic detail had to be planned from the start, and delightful to feel that her beloved Piet depended on her. They had great times together, laughing all day over the comical vicissitudes into which her inexperience led her; but she took her job very seriously, and Piet's grave approbation – in which there was always a twinkle of fun – made her proud of herself. Life was always rich and amusing in Piet's company. If ever she married – for Sarie's wedding had awakened her mind to that strange possibility – she felt she could only marry a man like Piet, who would share her private jokes and laugh at the same things as she did. But, of course, there was nobody like Piet, and never would be. So probably she would never marry. In this brilliant early winter weather, when the air was so bright and crisp and stimulating, that didn't seem to matter in the least.

And now came a new excitement. Major Haskard, feeling himself under the weather at Table Bay (as well might any man with indifferent lungs when the winter mists droop from the mountain) and deciding that nothing but the High Veld could save him from running downhill, hurriedly whipped his wife and Lavinia north again to Brakfontein, leaving Edward to sail to England and complete his education at Cambridge.

The farm had lain empty now for more than two years and suffered from the neglect of the natives he had left in charge of it. Moths had fretted the fabrics of the upholstery; during the rains, damp had penetrated the outer wall that faced south; Lavinia's piano had gone out of tune; over all the contents of the house was spread a fine powder which boring-insects had dislodged from their minute galleries in the underseasoned beams that supported the thatch. Mrs. Haskard, a discouraged woman at the best of times and now worn out by her husband's morbid activity, found herself quite unable to deal with this desolation, threw up the sponge and took to her bed. Lavinia, whose talents were even less domestic than her mother's, sent an anguished appeal for help and advice to Janse at Witfontein, in answer to which Piet came, and with him Maria.

The Haskards had never met Piet before, and remembered Maria only as a coltish child of fourteen. At first they seemed disappointed not to find Janse, whom they had all of them liked as a slightly uncouth but sympathetic oddity with a pitiful eagerness to share their alien culture and profit by its example. There was nothing pitiful about Piet. From the first he earned Major Haskard's gratitude and won his confidence by the smiling assurance with which he took their difficulties in hand. Nothing seemed any trouble to him. Beneath his firm touch all their physical embarrassments magically vanished. Though the ravages of moths were beyond repair, he soon patched up the leaky walls and promised, when next they went south, to strip the roof and rebuild it. He was always jolly and brisk and practical. He spoke English easily, with only the faintest of accents; what was more, he could see Major Haskard's dry jokes without having them explained to him, as no Dutchman had ever done. Major Haskard prided himself on his little jokes, which even his wife did not always see at once. Piet could talk intelligently about Kimberley too, for he knew it well, and give him what seemed to be shrewd advice on farming matters in which Haskard was an amateur. When Piet took him to Witfontein and showed him the house he had built, his new system of irrigation and maiden orchards, Major Haskard was even more deeply impressed. This young man was no airy theorist, but had a good head screwed on tight. The best type of colonial: would to God there were more of them! As he remarked to Lavinia, it was hard to believe that Piet and that poor chap Janse were actually brothers. And Lavinia coldly said 'Yes.'

He took to Maria too, for he had reached the time of life when middle-aged men like the company of attractive young women – particularly when their wives are invalids, as poor Mrs. Haskard – thanks mainly to the exactions of an invalid husband – was. He himself had begun to 'pick up' and rid himself of his neurotic fears for the condition of his lung, which had never really been serious, as soon as he set foot again on the High Veld. He felt like a young man again, he said: and certainly, so far as Maria was concerned, he behaved like one.

148

He had always had an attractive 'way' with women, which was due, he believed, to the dash of Irish in his blood, and found it no strain on his waning powers to exercise his charms on this ardent, delightful creature whose freshness and innocence seemed so much in keeping with the wild, sweet High Veld air.

There was no serious intent in Haskard's display of his mature fascination: he had no need to be anything more than his bluff and hearty self, with an occasional exhibition of wistful tenderness (an old man with a groggy lung) and a certain teasing courtesy which implied that Maria was not only delicious but also a young lady to whom respect was due. But Maria, who had never known any attentions like these before, took them very seriously. She was touched by the bravery of Jim Haskard, this doomed man who faced his uncertain life so gallantly; she was awed by his various knowledge (he seemed to know something about everything), by the fluency with which he expressed himself, by his exquisite manners; she was flattered by the fact that he, a man of the world, did not find it beneath him to talk with her as a familiar and treat her as an equal; she even admired the dashing cut of his clothes.

It was a shame, she thought, that his family should take such an exceptional person for granted; for Lavinia's attitude towards him, she could see for herself, was dutiful but uninterested, while Mrs. Haskard, as he hinted, was too delicate (and no wonder!) to give him the attention he deserved. She was sorry for Haskard, also, because, in revealing moments of self-pity, he confessed, rather wistfully, that his life had been a failure; that the future held nothing for him, an ageing, ailing man, whose only remaining pleasure was to be found in the sentimental – yet faintly melancholy – contemplation of ardent, hopeful young things like herself.

'I'm an old, old man, my dear,' he would say; and Maria, of course, as was expected of her, vigorously denied it.

'You don't seem at all old to me, and you oughtn't to talk like that,' she reproved him gravely.

'Ah, if only you knew, my child,' he said. But the reassurance, on which he had counted, stimulated him to prove that he wasn't as old as he pretended to feel by an astonishing display of alertness of body and mind.

He was at his best when they went riding together, cantering side by side through the crystalline, sun-drenched winter air. Major Haskard was a good horseman: he rode short-stirruped and erect, like a cavalry-man, and the clean cut of his riding-breeches and highly-polished leggings seemed to Maria, by contrast with the slouching seat of Adrian or her father or even of Piet, an expression of his physical and cultural superiority. When they knee-haltered their horses and sat down to rest, gazing idly over the golden plains that stretched to the humps of the Magaliesberg, he would question her, lazily, teasingly, about the innumerable small things that made up her life. At first she was too shy to talk; but by degrees he coaxed her into a frankness which, because of her innocence and freshness, he found delightful. He liked, for itself, her low voice, the hint of a Worcestershire burr in her speech, which came from her father, and an occasional turn of phrase which betrayed the Dutch influence.

Maria had never talked so much in her life to anyone – not even to Piet; she had certainly never found it possible to talk with such freedom. She told him, amusingly, the story of Hans Oosthuizen's courtship of Sarie, confessing how she had spied on them during their *opsit*. She told him of the dance at the wedding and of the man who had tried to kiss her.

'Well, some day before long,' he said, 'some other young man will ride up in his Sunday clothes and put his leg in front of the bedroom door. I'm surprised it's not happened long before this. I suppose you know how attractive you are, Maria?'

She blushed. 'What nonsense you talk! If you only knew what these young farmers were like. I shall never marry anyone at all unless I'm in love.'

'And you've never been in love? Not the very least bit?'

'Of course not. I never even think of such things.'

Yet she was, in a sense, already in love with Haskard; that is to say, she felt for him an overwhelming admiration and tenderness, a kind of protective emotion, devoid of any sexual feeling, which made her resent the lack of appreciation his family showed him and want to supply the deficiency. She was his slave; there was nothing, she thought, that she would not gladly do to make this lonely man happy. He was so humble and sweet and natural with her, and yet, as she knew, so wise.

'I'm glad you and I are such good friends, Maria,' he said. 'You're far better for me than all the tonics the doctors have given me. You've made a new man of me: I feel twenty years younger. That is,' he added wryly, 'I feel just as I was three years before you were born.'

'There you go again! It's really wicked to talk like that,' Maria said gravely.

Mrs. Haskard, who had now recovered sufficiently to take the air, watched this unequal friendship with weary amusement and some concern.

'You should really be careful, Jim,' she said, 'or you'll turn that poor little thing's head.'

Major Haskard laughed. 'Don't be ridiculous, Laura.' But her warning pleased him. In a sense the reproof implied a compliment. Of course, it was only a joke; yet it proved to his anxious valetudinarian mind that he was neither so ill nor so decrepit as he had persuaded himself. He had begun to take a new interest in his derelict farm, and was full of new, confident plans which Piet's transformation of Witfontein had suggested. If he chose to unlock a little of his capital – and, with diamond-dividends mounting, he had plenty to spare – there seemed no reason why he should not make Brakfontein pay. When he was not riding or flirting with Maria, he spent most of his time with Piet, whom he found precisely the kind of man he had always wanted to develop the place and keep it going during his absence.

Piet realized the impression he had made and used it cunningly. He had always known that the Brakfontein land, though sorely neglected, was better in quality and more richly-watered than Witfontein. As he had ridden over it, he had often reflected on what he would do with it if it had happened to be his own. When Haskard consulted him, a detailed plan lay ready, filed and docketed, in his practical mind.

'It's no good talking in general terms,' he said. 'If you really intend to develop this farm as it should be developed and are not afraid to spend money on it, I'll go into the matter thoroughly and let you know exactly what I should do in your place.'

'All right. Go ahead,' Haskard said.

Within a week Piet returned to Brakfontein with his plan worked out on paper in every technical detail. As a man who prided himself on his business acumen, Haskard was surprised at its shrewdness, its thoroughness, its grasp of the situation. In

151

his costing figures Piet had relied on his own experience. Labour, planting, materials, machinery: all were accounted for. Haskard, hurriedly glancing at the grand total, was surprised to find how modest it was. He could do everything that Piet suggested almost without feeling it. The prospect tempted him.

'There are only two things left out,' he said regretfully, 'and those, I'm afraid, are the most important. Supervision and Management.'

'If you work to my plans, they won't be difficult.'

'I can't work to your plans, my dear fellow, for more than four or five months at a time. That's the trouble. In winter the High Veld suits me; but when the rains break in summer it's no place for me. Apart from which, don't forget I have other interests at the Cape and in Kimberley which I can't possibly neglect. Then there's the question of labour.'

'That's not so difficult as it was. I can get any number of apprentices from the Landdrost, who's a friend of mine.'

'Apprentices?'

'Natives brought in from the western border where there's been so much fighting.'

'Doesn't that sound a bit like the slavery we hear so much talk about?'

'The children are much better off on a Boer's farm than they'd be if they were left to starve in their kraals. What you want most of all is a capable manager. In any case, as you've seen, the house suffers by your absence.'

'Ah, now you're talking! But where can I find a responsible man? Do you happen to know of one?'

'Not one that I'd trust with a morgen of land if I couldn't keep my eye on him. You see, the things that we've planned are outside the Boer's ordinary experience. I like the Dutch personally: I'm half a Dutchman myself; but nobody can say they're adaptable or progressive. Why not leave your son here?'

'Edward has three years at Cambridge in front of him. He's a nice boy, but by no means brilliant. He'll probably scrape into the army by way of the yeomanry. In any case, I can't see him burying himself in the middle of Africa. He's a sociable creature.'

Piet had known what the answer would be when he put his question. He had also known what he intended to say next.

There came a long pause.

'There's one idea,' he said, with deliberation, 'but I don't know if it will appeal to you. . . .' He hesitated.

'Why don't you go on?'

'If you like it, it might save you money too. Here it is, for what it's worth. Our lands "march together" – that was your phrase, I think? – and my own orchards won't be coming into full production for two or three years. In other words, though of course I must keep an eye on them, I shall have a certain amount of time on my hands. If you'd like to leave the whole business to me, as your manager, I think I could see it through to your satisfaction. Of course, if you don't approve . . .'

'But, my dear fellow, that solves the whole difficulty. An excellent idea! Of course, you would have to be properly paid. I have no idea . . .'

'We can discuss that later. After all, it's a friendly arrangement, between neighbours and friends, as you might say.'

'Yes, yes: but I know we shan't quarrel over that. The main point that occurs to me is that we shouldn't be wasting time. We have only three months of dry weather in front of us. If we waste them we lose a whole season. In fact, we ought really to begin on the groundwork at once.'

'The sooner the better. I'd much rather start while you're here.'

'So from today, let us say, you're my manager? What about fifteen pounds a month to start with? It doesn't sound much, I admit.'

'It will do for me very well – provided that later on, if all goes well, I can have a commission.'

'Of course you shall. That's the most satisfactory way.'

They were both of them pleased with their bargain: Haskard principally because, little as it had cost him, his High Veld farm had lain on his conscience as an investment that gave no return, and again because, though he had no executive ability, he fancied himself as a director of other men's work and as a good judge of character in the choice of subordinates, and Piet Grafton, it seemed to him, was the perfect man for the job. Piet was pleased, first of all, because Haskard's fifteen pounds a month, a pittance by the standards of Kimberley, was enormous by those of the High Veld. His capital was almost exhausted, and this regular salary would free his hands for new developments. He had been itching for months to get his hands on Brakfontein, not only because it was worth developing but because the ample springs on its western boundary would enable him to bring many more acres of the higher Witfontein land under the plough. The problem of irrigating both farms was really one, and when he made his plans for Brakfontein he had always contrived them with his own land in view. As he pointed out to Haskard, and as Haskard agreed, it would be to the advantage of the two farms if their system of furrows were connected and water conserved and distributed for the benefit of both.

Haskard entered upon the project with enthusiasm. To tell the truth, apart from the fact that it suited his lungs, he had little use for Brakfontein. Its air gave him new vigour, indeed; but, so far, there had been no direction in which that access of energy could be expended. He was a man of ideas: on the High Veld he found himself out of touch with the world in which they were generated. He was a sociable creature: the loneliness of Brakfontein bored him. His imagination, once kindled, flamed up so quickly that the scope of Piet's plans appeared to him too restricted. If it were merely a matter of money, he said, Piet need not consider it: more capital could easily be found. He had always enjoyed a gamble and disliked the idea of spoiling the ship for a ha-porth of tar.

'Better wait for a while and see how it pans out,' Piet said.

He knew it would be an error in tactics to appear over-eager, and was anxious to err – if he erred at all – on the side of moderation; for he had read Haskard's temperament rightly as one subject to moods and swift changes, and wanted to gain, first of all, a reputation for caution and sobriety.

In this he succeeded. Nor was it only in farming matters that Haskard came to rely on him. In every trivial domestic emergency that worried his wife (and Mrs. Haskard was not born for pioneering) Piet showed his resourcefulness, his good humour, his common sense. He had deft hands and a mechanical mind. Even the out-of-tune piano yielded to his manipulations. Lavinia herself, explaining what was amiss, was surprised to discover the accuracy of his sense of pitch. In Janse such an accomplishment would not have appeared so surprising; but then Janse would never have tuned her piano!

It was natural that, among themselves, the Haskards should

154

often compare the two brothers. They had all of them in a way been fond of Janse, a sympathetic lost soul born out of his proper environment, pathetically aspiring and sensitive, and handicapped, as they could never forget, by his lameness. And yet, of the two, Piet undoubtedly fitted himself more easily into the Brakfontein household – not because his mind was better equipped than Janse's, but because it was more adaptable. There were no dubious half-tones about Piet: he was black and white; one always knew (or thought one knew) where one was with him. His manners, considering his origins and education, were exceptionally good. As Major Haskard said, without any intent of patronizing him, he was a 'natural gentleman'. In his dealings with all sorts of men during his transport-riding, Piet had acquired a good deal of social tact; and his attitude towards women, of whom he knew less, was marked by a disarming modesty which quickly appealed to them. Within a short time both Mrs. Haskard and Lavinia had succumbed, as completely as Haskard himself, to Piet's unassuming charm.

Lavinia enjoyed Maria's companionship too. Of course Maria was very much younger than she – in experience if not in years – and, in many ways, astonishingly ignorant; but, for Lavinia, the society of anyone of her own sex in that remote wilderness was something to be thankful for. She took pleasure in Maria's quick wits and agreed with her father in falling a victim to the child's freshness and innocence.

'If Maria had been sent to a really good school at the Cape,' she said, 'she would have been terribly attractive. If it weren't for those awful clothes you would say she was a pretty girl too. Don't you think so, father?'

'Pretty? Pretty? Well, hardly that,' Major Haskard said cautiously, with an eye on his wife. 'I'll agree she's a nice little thing. Something rather appealing about her.'

Now that the 'groundwork' of the farm-planning was under way, he rarely went out riding with Maria, with the result that she spent more and more of her time in the house with his daughter. At first Maria had found Lavinia Haskard intimidating – for Lavinia, who in this way resembled her mother, did not easily make friends – and had been awed as much by her elegant remoteness and silence as she was subdued by an apparent coldness beside which her own warm enthusiasms and impulsive affection appeared slightly improper. Even so, she admired the perfection of Lavinia's frigid, classical beauty so

155

ardently that, by degrees, she was able to penetrate her icy defences. Though she couldn't quite force her way into Lavinia's heart (if she had one) she managed, at least, to thaw her into a sort of friendly companionship which, if still reserved, was no longer distressingly awkward. Lavinia was so silent, so self-contained, that, try as she would, Maria could never be positive about what she was thinking: yet, in spite of these inhibitions, she loved her as passionately as she had admired her from the first. That was how she was made. She could never do anything by halves.

Piet, too, spent a good deal of time in the house at Brakfontein when the day's work was over. Major Haskard was riding his new hobby so furiously that he was never happy unless he was talking about their plans, and grudged every moment Piet spent away from him. Piet had become more intimate with the family than ever Janse had been, and took his place among them with a familiarity that Janse had never achieved. While the men talked – it was Major Haskard who did most of the talking – the women listened humbly. Sometimes, when they had finished talking, Lavinia played or sang. But all the time, whatever they might be doing, Maria noticed that Piet was conscious of Lavinia's presence – and she, compelled by the sheer force of this concentration, of his. No doubt, her romantic mind leapt to the conclusion, they were in love with each other.

It was not Maria's idea of a love-affair. There was nothing tempestuous or exalted about it. So far as she knew, Piet rarely spoke to Lavinia, or she to him. Piet's manner towards her was always the same: easy, courteous, and matter-of-fact. In the rare instances when she had surprised them alone together both had shown a disappointing lack of embarrassment and had admitted her at once to their conversation. Perhaps, after all, her romantic imagination fathering the thought, she had been mistaken. She hoped she had not; for the idea of having Lavinia for a sister-in-law to be adored in perpetuity, entranced and excited her.

As a matter of fact, even if he wasn't passionately in love with her (and in his case, though he was a normal young man, passion would always be subordinate to more material interests), Piet had thought a good deal about Lavinia during the last few months. He had admired her as much – though in a different way – as had Maria. His hard, clear mind approved of her elegance and her physical distinction. It was not repelled by her coldness, which he guessed to be deliberately protective rather than natural to her. He respected her capability, her culture – even her habitual silence, since most of the young women with whom he had been acquainted were inclined to talk too much and not to the point. Whatever her defects as a potential lover might be, he had no doubt as to her temperamental and physical qualifications as a wife.

There were other factors involved. Major Haskard was presumably a rich man and the owner of the Brakfontein land which he had always coveted. He had not forgotten the hint which Haskard had dropped (and for which he had angled) as to the improbability of his son and heir, Edward, ever being interested in that part of his inheritance. He was by no means certain how long Haskard's interest in the Grakfontein developments would last – or how long, being the invalid he was, he would last himself. He desired Brakfontein passionately. He was inclined to desire Lavinia. In any case, since sons were an asset and a comfortable home was another of his ambitions, it was high time, as his mother said, to be getting married.

As for marrying Lavinia Haskard, he was under no illusion as to his social and financial qualifications. He had no property but his own farm and no money save what Major Haskard had contracted to pay him. He was not, in the accepted English sense of the word, a 'gentleman'; and though he knew Haskard liked and trusted him, a back-veld farmer, comparatively uneducated, was hardly the kind of son-in-law he would expect. On the other hand, this was not England but South Africa – a country in which social distinctions were more or less merged in the greater difference between black skins and white; a country in which one man was as good as another and himself, as he firmly believed, a shade better than most.

Still, the problem was ticklish. He set about solving it with characteristic restraint and self-confidence. He declined to thrust himself on Lavinia's attention. She could see what he was for herself and form her own opinion. He pursued identical tactics with Mrs. Haskard, whose somewhat dim personality would not, he presumed, weigh heavily on either side. It was on Lavinia's father that, unobtrusively, he concentrated his fire. His was the key-position in his hazardous adventure. And in that part of his tactical plan he succeeded beyond his hopes. By the end of the winter he had Major Haskard safely pocketed, convinced that his 'best type of colonial' was no boaster, but an honest, capable, and extremely intelligent young man.

But by now time was pressing. Already, with the first sprinkle of spring rains, Major Haskard was growing restless; he had scared himself into a cough and begun to pine for the drier air of the Cape. Mrs. Haskard, recognizing the familiar signs, had begun to pack. The moment had come, in fact, when Piet saw that it was time to take bolder measures.

It would be unwise, he decided, in spite of conventions, to approach Haskard first. His only – at any rate his best – chance lay in presenting Lavinia's father with an accomplished fact. Piet awaited his opportunity and found it, only three days before the date fixed for the Haskard's departure, at an hour when her mother was fast in the toils of packing and her father was taking a last sentimental ride over the veld with Maria.

He found Lavinia putting music together. He stood by the piano and watched her.

'No more music for me,' he said sadly.

'We shall come here again next year.'

'Are you sorry you're going, Lavinia?'

'Yes ... I suppose I'm sorry in a way. One always is. The High Veld winters are lovely. One feels throttled, after this air, when one gets to the Cape.'

'Then why don't you stay here?'

She laughed. 'What on earth do you mean?'

'You know perfectly well what I mean. If you don't, you ought to.'

As she bent over her music, hiding her face, he took both her arms and drew her towards him and kissed her lips.

'I've been wanting to do this,' he said, 'for three months – ever since I first saw you. Now do you know what I mean?'

This catastrophe – for as such Mrs. Haskard, who came of a county family, chose to regard it – postponed their departure from Brakfontein for nearly a week. Major Haskard, when once he had got over the first shock, was more tractable: he did not so much resent Lavinia's marrying Piet as her marrying at all. If he had only had a spare daughter (or could have arranged for the loan of Maria) he would have minded less; but he had come to a time of life when, as he said – and his wife noticed – he liked to have 'young things about' and he was not unreasonably proud of Lavinia's looks, for which he regarded himself as mainly responsible.

In the crisis, Lavinia herself displayed a surprising degree of resolution. She had been in love with Piet, she discovered (though before he kissed her awake she had hardly noticed it), just as long as Piet had loved her. Before that kiss she had not been sure what kind of man she wanted or whether she wanted any man at all. Now her mind was made up: she wanted Piet, and none other.

'This comes,' Mrs. Haskard, who hated the High Veld, declared, 'of taking impressionable girls into outlandish places. It's not fair, as I've always said. We should have sent her to England as soon as she turned eighteen, like dear Edward. *He* won't marry a colonial, thank goodness!'

'Don't thank goodness too soon, my dear,' Major Haskard said. 'He may yet fall in love with a girl in a Cambridge tobacconist's, as I did, you know.'

'I didn't know, Jim; but anyway, you didn't marry her.'

'No. Too much competition,' Major Haskard said wistfully. 'Really, Laura, you know, I've nothing against this boy Grafton. His father's a decent fellow, most highly respected. His mother comes of a good old Cape family, the Celliers. I've seen a good bit of Piet; he's not intellectual, but I think he'll do well in a country that has a future like this. They'll be comfortably off, too, by Transvaal standards, with the salary I give him, together with Lavinia's allowance, and later on, his commissions. When we come up here in the winter you won't have any more housekeeping worries, and we shan't lose touch with Lavinia, as we probably should have done if she'd married an Englishman. On the whole, there's quite a lot to be said in favour of it. Of course, when I'm gone, Lavinia will have the farm, and that, with all the money I'm putting into it, should be worth quite a lot.'

'Well, two things I insist on,' Mrs. Haskard said firmly. 'If they're going to be married they must be married properly, under English law and in an English church at the Cape. And she must come to the Cape to have her babies, too.'

'There's plenty of time to think about them,' Haskard said.

Two months later Piet rode to the railhead and went down to Capetown, and Lavinia and he were properly married in the Cathedral. There were four bridesmaids in pale blue organdie, and each of them wore a brooch of small Kimberley diamonds in the shape of an Irish harp, 'the gift of the bridegroom', which Major Haskard paid for.

159

Maria was sad to be left behind at Wonderfontein. She would have liked wearing pale blue organdie much better than the frock of sprigged silk her mother had made her for Sarie's wedding. And she would have loved a harp-shaped brooch. She had no jewellery at all save the diamond which that lanky boy C. J. Rhodes had given her nearly four years ago. And that stone was still uncut.

CHAPTER THREE

(1)

PRESIDENT THOMAS FRANCIS BURGERS returned from Europe in the new 'Colonial Mail' liner, *Dublin Castle*, two thousand nine hundred tons, and stepped ashore at Capetown into a hornets' nest. Stories of what had been happening in the Transvaal met him as soon as he landed, in letters of sympathy from friends and in the gossip, usually malicious, on which 'political circles' in Capetown throve. He was an ailing man and not a happy one. His mission to Europe, for which he had paid out of his own depleted purse, was a failure. He had nothing to show for it but a commercial treaty with the Portuguese and a new loan, at usurious rates of interest, from Amsterdam. All his attempts at concluding protective alliances with Belgium, with Holland, with Germany, had failed; and now even more serious domestic troubles threatened him. There was not the least chance, his friends wrote, of his being re-elected to the Presidency next year.

Burgers wasted no time in Capetown, but pushed straight through to Bloemfontein. After a hurried consultation with Jan Brand, the Free State President, he crossed the Vaal drift and headed north for Pretoria, prepared to face and anxious to join battle with his enemies. On the last night of his journey he arrived, to Adrian's astonishment, at Wonderfontein.

Maria was excited to see in the flesh this man whose name, revered or vituperated, had held such a predominant place in her elders' talk during the last few years. She had expected him to be a little more than life-size, for he was the first of the great ones of the earth on whom she had ever set eyes, and was disappointed to find him no demi-god, but an ordinary travel-stained traveller in a black tail-coat. He looked mortally tired. His luminous eyes were inflamed with dust, his tawny beard was dishevelled. It was only when he spoke that she realized the fire that still burned in him for all his tired eyes, and the personal charm which had made her brother his slave.

Burgers sat with his fine head bowed in his hands and listened while Adrian recited his tale of the hostility and discontent that had accumulated during his absence; how, presuming on the acting President's laxity, or even encouraged by him, the backveld burghers had shirked the paying of taxes; how the railway material lay rotting and rusting on the quay at Delagoa; how, through lack of confidence, the land which had been pledged as security for Government loans had ceased to have any negotiable value; how the traders and shopkeepers settled within the Republic itself were growing restive and beginning to talk of a British annexation as the only cure for the country's ills.

Burgers listened to him in silence, with no more interruption than an occasional challenging flash of the eyes or an impatient gesture of his sensitive hands.

'But you see, nephew,' he said at last, 'all these troubles are economic. We want money ... money. Without it we cannot govern. You say nothing of the Lydenburg gold-fields, which are our only hope?'

'Joubert hates the gold-fields, I think,' Adrian said, 'and Paul Kruger's thoughts are as his, though he rarely speaks them. They grudge the gold-fields success because the diggers are foreigners. And the diggers themselves, from what I hear, are ready to take the law into their own hands if the Government won't administer it. They have fallen on bad times, your honour. There is no great reef on which they can settle to work. Gold is everywhere, so they say, but it's patchy and small in quantity. They move to and fro like game when the veld is poor. Sometimes the gold is guarded by fly-belts, and their transport-cattle are stung and perish before they know they are in them. There is red-water, too; and many men die of fever – when they don't die of drink. I know we want gold, State President; but I've no great liking myself, I confess, for the diggers.'

Burgers nodded: 'They are evil, I know – but for us a necessary evil. It is all, as I said before, a matter of money. We are too lazy, too unadventurous, too corrupt. There is no denying it. Therefore our credit is bad. As things are, we cannot go on without help from outside. We can only get that help in one way, I'm afraid. By Federation.'

'By Federation, your honour?' Adrian cried. 'Do I hear you – of all men! – say that?'

The President smiled sadly and shook his head. 'Ah, I know what you feel, my dear fellow; but sooner or later one has to

162

submit to hard facts. In my early days, as you know, I frankly believed in Federation. Then came the rape of the diamond-fields. The Cape robbed us; the Free State went back on us and sold its birthright. My thoughts swung round violently. I said: "Let's be shut of the lot of them and build our own railway and put our finances in order and live our own lives." It was because of those thoughts, I know, that the burghers elected me. But, vast as it seems, this South Africa of ours is a little world, and a black world, too, in which we, the small sprinkling of white men, shall be forced in the end to depend on one another. We can't stand by ourselves: that's the bitter lesson I've learnt. I know now that unless we accept Federation we shall be lost. I have talked with Jan Brand, and he agrees with me.'

'That thought shocks me, State President,' Adrian said. 'Is there no other way?'

'Yes. An even bitterer way. A British Annexation.'

'God forbid!' The voice, surprisingly, was John Grafton's.

Burgers shook his head: 'God forbid it, indeed! I echo your words, my friend. And yet, I think, you are English?'

'That is true, your honour. I love England in duty, as a son loves his mother; but I do not like its laws. This is now my country. I have lived here safely and happily for thirty-five years. If the British came north and annexed the Transvaal . . .'

He floundered for words. His air was so passionate that Lisbet laid her hand on his arm.

'Peace, peace, John,' she whispered. 'You know you have nothing to fear any longer.'

Maria gaped with astonishment at the inexplicable scene. She had never known her father so agitated before. 'Nothing to fear,' her mother had said: 'nothing to fear any longer.' Yet one would almost have said he was afraid . . . 'Afraid of what?' she wondered. He rose from his seat and made for the door as though fear pursued him and he were trying to escape. Lisbet followed him anxiously and drew him back again.

'Well, there goes one good republican, anyway,' the President said. 'And you, nephew, are another. Will you gird on your sword and buckler and come to Philippi with me tomorrow, Silas?'

Adrian smiled. 'Your honour need have no doubt of that, though dynamite would be better. I can see the journey has tired you, sir. You need sleep.'

'Yes, yes. I am tired: I cannot deny it,' Burgers said.

He went to his room, his head bowed, his hands clasped behind him, like a man who carried the weight of all Africa on his shoulders.

They rode to meet trouble, and found it. The news of Burgers' landing had reached Pretoria in front of him. In Pretoria there was plotting and whispering, not so much in the Raad itself as on the stoeps where members met to smoke and drink coffee in the morning, and at the outspan, where a man might slip round and visit his friends in secret at night without being compromised. The hostile Raad knew that Burgers would put up a fight. There would be tirades of accusation and counter-accusation; more exhibitions of the heretic's dialectical skill (for his brains, like the devil's, were sharper than theirs in an argument); more flights of the famous oratory. But it also knew that these things did not count. The only things that counted now that the spell was broken were the votes that had been planned, the combinations that had been arranged in the tobacco smoke of the stoeps or under the wagons' bucksail tents in the darkness of night. The President might rant or rave or coax or cajole or refute what his enemies said by the ultimate argument – scriptural quotation; but the back-veld, united now, had measured him for his coffin. He might brazen it out for the remaining year of his presidential term, or resign, as the people's voice had forced Pretorius to resign, but his days were numbered: the land would soon be free of him and his works and his *verdomde* Hollanders.

So the Raad sat, solidly, sullenly, voting Burgers down. It was enough that a measure should have come from him (and more than enough if it happened to be near his heart) to ensure its crushing rejection. All the cherished plans his eager brain had formed on his voyage from Europe went the way of the reforms he had made before he sailed.

He was sick and losing his nerve. At last, in desperation, he consulted Adrian and three or four others who were all that remained of his party. Should he fight it out to the end or resign?

It was for him to decide, they said; they could not advise him: but the advice that was implicit in their refusal to say the hard word had the unexpected effect of stimulating his resistance.

'My conscience is clear,' he said. 'I've done nothing, and shall do nothing, that I do not believe to be right and for the good of the country. If you trust me and will go on supporting me, I'll hold on till the end. We are religious men, all of us, I think; and religion teaches us that right must prevail. I go on, in the hope that an angel may trouble these stagnant waters.'

It was a dark angel that troubled them. Towards the end of the session news came from the north that Sekukuni was up. The Bapedi were driving diggers and herdsmen away from the lands they claimed. They had swept down from the north, stealing cattle as they went, to within a few miles of Lydenburg itself, and had sacked and set fire to a mission-station. To the Landdrost of Lydenburg, who sent messengers to warn him, Sekukuni had replied that he no longer acknowledged the Republic's authority. All the north, the gold-fields included, was calling for help.

And that help must be given, the Volksraad, unanimous at last, agreed. This was not the usual kind of native rising – one of those inter-tribal squabbles or epidemics of cattle-lifting in which the white man was only indirectly involved: small fires that could be trampled out in a week by the hoofs of a hurriedly-raised commando. It was a more serious revolt. For years the mountainous north had been in a smoulder. Now it was well alight. Though Sekukuni and his Bapedi might not in themselves be so formidable, his country, of late, had become a black Alsatia, a refuge for outlaws and fugitives of more warlike tribes. There was another incalculable factor in this revolt: the results of the persistent sale and smuggling of guns from Kimberley, against which, again and again, the Boers had protested. For the first time in the history of the Transvaal the native had been given the chance of fighting the white man with his own weapons and wiping off old scores. And there was still one more thing to be feared. Those who knew the native best had begun to suspect that Sekukuni was not playing a lone hand; that his revolt had been fomented – and, if he succeeded, would certainly be supported – by a more powerful enemy, Cetewayo, the friend of the English, who had set himself to revive the Zulu nation. How many guns were there hidden in Zululand? Nobody knew.

Sekukuni's revolt, in short, was something more than it seemed. It was a secret and formidable challenge to the white man's predominance – not merely in the Northern Transvaal, but on all the Republic's borders. The whole of black Africa,

165

from the Zambezi to the Cape, was watching the outcome and waiting. If it were not dealt with firmly, the whole veld might soon be ablaze.

Burgers dealt with it firmly. He was not, in the least, a man of warlike disposition. Yet, harassed as he was, he could not help being thankful that the thunder of approaching war had drowned for a while the mutterings of his unruly Volksraad. This was not the moment, he pleaded, for civil dissension. He held out his hand to his enemies and begged them to help him give Sekukuni a lesson.

They accepted it grudgingly. Even now they rebelled against Burgers' 'big ideas'. The punitive expedition he planned was to be on a larger and more expensive scale than anything ever attempted previously in the Transvaal. What could be more fantastic, for instance, than sending a party with camels to drag up the new Krupp guns, which had lain rusting in Delagoa, over the coastal swamps and the wooded Lebombo range? He insisted on commandeering no less than two thousand mounted burghers, and on assembling in Pretoria a train of four hundred wagons – a wagon to every five men – which, on trek, three abreast, would form a convoy over five miles in length. This was not, the old hands protested, the Boer manner of warfare, which made mobility the first of military virtues. If they had their will they would have ridden out in the good old way, with a sack of meal, and biltong stuffed in their saddle-bags. They knew more about fighting natives than any predikant living. And who was going to pay for war on that scale?

Burgers answered the question with a magnificent gesture: 'I will pledge my private fortune to the last penny,' he said.

Then the question of leadership arose. Burgers talked it over with Adrian who, ever since his return from Europe, had been his chief confidant.

'There is only one man to command,' Adrian said, 'and that is Paul Kruger.'

'Would Kruger be loyal to me?'

'Perhaps not. But if he commands he will have to win; and if he wins you get the credit – or some of it. There is no other burgher with a quarter of his experience in warfare. That man is a warrior. Only think: as a boy of fourteen he fought against Moselikatze; he fought the English at Boomplats; he fought in Schoeman's rebellion; he fought against Makapan in the Zoutpansbergt.'

166

'The Executive Council must make the appointment; but I will ask Kruger first,' Burgers said.

Kruger listened to his persuasions and flatteries sullenly and shook his heavy-featured head.

'I cannot lead this commando, if you come, State President,' he said. 'With your merry evenings in laager and your Sunday dances, the enemy will even shoot me behind the neck, for God's blessing will not rest on our expedition.'

'Come, come, Mr. Kruger,' Burgers said. 'If you are general, surely you can forbid anything?'

'Do you think the burghers would listen to anything a general said when you, the State President, set them an example?'

'I think they listen a good deal to you already, Mr. Kruger.'

'To me? No, no. But they still can listen to God's word, Mr. President. Our fathers, under Andries Pretorius, destroyed Dingaan and Moselikatze because they and their leader were God-fearing men and kept the Sabbath. So it is written: *Five of you shall chase an hundred, and an hundred of you shall put ten thousand to flight.* And again, in Joshua: *One man of you shall chase a thousand.* But you, State President, you know no Sabbath, although you have been a minister. You ride through the land and in and out of town on Sunday. You know not the church and God's service, to the scandal of many pious folk. That is why the harvest is bad and the people murmur. If your honour will read the twenty-sixth chapter of Leviticus you will understand. *Ye shall keep my sabbath*, it says; and if you do not: *Ye shall sow your seed in vain, for your enemies shall eat it.* I will have no lot or part in this matter, Mr. State President. These are my thoughts. I have spoken.'

'Those are not all Paul Kruger's thoughts,' Adrian said. 'If he will not command, I am sure there is something behind it.'

'There is always something behind with him. I think he's too clever for me.'

Burgers put the matter to his Executive Council of four, announcing Kruger's refusal and proposing Joubert. Joubert also refused the command – reluctantly, Burgers thought. Like Adrian, Joubert could not fathom Kruger's motives, but found them suspect, and so deeply respected his canniness that he dared not commit himself. Perhaps Kruger, his rival for the next Presidency, hoped that he would spoil his candidature by associating himself with the heretic?

'Is it not right,' Kruger said at last, 'that the State President himself should command, even as President Pretorius took the command against Dingaan, and Joshua and the Judges of Israel led their people in battle?'

'I am no man of war,' Burgers said.

(Yet the prospect tempted him. What could establish him better with the people than a great victory?)

'We will appoint a burgher who knows all about fighting to act under you,' Kruger said, 'and call him the *Veggeneraal*. Nicholas Smit is the man. And Joubert, as before, shall be Acting-President in your absence.'

So Burgers, that volatile man, half-doubtful yet half-intoxicated by dreams of military glory, accepted the command. The burghers rode in from the back-veld, two thousand of them, to join the commando. The camels dragged up the German guns from Delagoa. Four hundred commandeered wagons overflowed the Church Square, while their oxen stripped the town lands of their last blade of verdure. On the Sunday before the great caravan's departure, Burgers went to church in state – and the predikant preached on the twenty-sixth chapter of the Book of Leviticus.

On the same day Adrian said good-bye to the family at Wonderfontein. He had no need to serve, being exempt as a member of the Volksraad; he went, not because he wanted to fight, but because of his personal devotion to Burgers and his anxiety to show the President's enemies that his friends were still loyal. Maria was deeply moved by his departure. He was a romantic figure, she thought, riding off to the wars on his *blouskimmel* stallion, erect in the saddle, with a smile on his lips and the wind in his golden beard.

Lisbet, though she smiled and waved to him as he rode away, had no such romantic enthusiasms or illusions. She knew what war meant and had suffered from it. The only bright spots in the picture for her were that Piet was still safely away at the Cape on his honeymoon, and that Adrian might possibly bring back news from the north of Andries and her poor Janse.

During the last year things had not been going any too well
with poor Janse. The months they had spent in their summer
rest-camp, high up on the Berg, had been marred by an irksome
sense of frustration and inactivity. If he had been alone, Janse
could have contented himself with the secret meditations that
were so great a part of his life, and with the overwhelming
beauty of his surroundings; the superb headlong swoop of the
Berg's vast forest-shagged face; the green kloofs, misted with
rising spray and loud with echoing water; the endless plains of
the Low Country rolling away to eastward – that dreamy expanse over which gigantic storms stalked by day, and by night
lightning flickered unceasingly.

But Meninsky was not so easily satisfied. His mind chafed
against this enforced inaction. He was restless and bored and
impatient with nothing but a vague future to set the teeth of his
mind in. Bosmann was calm enough by comparison; but his
placidity, as Janse knew, was that of a sick man. Though
his fever had burnt itself out for lack of new infections, it had
consumed his reserves of strength in the process. There was
obviously something organically wrong with him, for there were
times when Janse found him fighting for breath; and when he
moved, with dragging feet, Janse saw that his legs were swollen.
The air was too thin for him, Bosmann said, at this altitude, he
would be able to breathe again all right when they returned to a
more reasonable level; but, though he agreed with him, Janse
began to doubt whether, once having got him down, they would
ever get him up again.

The results of their first season of digging had not been encouraging, or fulfilled Meninsky's exalted calculations. Though
their first pannings – the proceeds of Brunner's prospecting pits
– had shown high values, the contents of gold in the ground
they had stripped for themselves had been small. Once or twice,
in the clay that was caked on the under side of boulders, they
had found nests of small nuggets, weighing at the most a few
pennyweights, but none of any size. They had never yet washed
a load of dirt in the creek without finding 'colour'; every cubic
foot of ground was undoubtedly auriferous; yet it took a great
deal of fine gold-dust to make up an ounce, and an ounce represented little more than a sovereign apiece. Indeed, by the time

they had been flooded out of the kloof and forced to take to the mountain, their gains, for nearly three months of enthusiastic labour, amounted to thirty-three ounces nine pennyweights, and the results of the later pannings seemed to suggest that, in that part of the kloof, the gold was petering out.

Meninsky surveyed these meagre gains with puzzled resentment.

'Looks to me, boss,' he said, 'as if this chap Brunner of yours has sold us a pup. I don't mind working myself to the bone, but I like to see something for it. Thirty-three ounces nine pennyweights! That's roughly a hundred and twenty pounds in three months. Divide that by three. A bit over thirteen pound a month each. Call it three pounds ten a week, and have done with it. Why, I could earn more than that as a clerk in an office in Kimberley!'

'That is true,' Bosmann said, 'and yet there may come a day when you find a twenty-ounce nugget in your first washing. At Geelhoutboom they found one of twenty-five pounds. You think of this work as an industry, Meninsky. It is not. It is a gamble. You think of yourself as a gambler, but you have not the necessary patience. We know now that in this same creek alluvial gold may be anywhere. At this moment, beneath your feet where you stand, Meninsky, there may be another nugget of twenty-five pounds.'

'My God, if I knew there was, I'd soon have the beggar out!'

'But you do not know. That is the point: We treat with alluvial that has been evidently washed into pockets: very rich in one place and very poor in another. This is not a reef where the gold lies all in one leader.'

'Then why the hell are we wasting our time over it? For Moses' sake let's fit up the dolly and get on with the reef. I don't want to spend the rest of my ruddy life pottering about here while all the bright boys from Petticoat Lane are piling up fortunes in Kimberley. Look here, boss: I made up my mind when I come to this country that I'd be a millionaire by the time I was fifty.'

Bosmann shook his head: 'That I do not think you shall be,' he said solemnly.

Meninsky took up the challenge: 'You just wait and see, mate.'

They rigged up the dolly and set to work on the reef. It was a strenuous labour, in which Bosmann, dragging his swollen legs, could take no part. From the pit of the kloof he watched them clinging like flies to the face of the cliff, hacking away with pick and crowbar and dislodging fragments of glittering quartz that went crashing down one by one and awoke gigantic echoes. This was far harder toil than mere digging. They worked stripped to the waist. The sun, beating back from the facets of crystalline rock, scorched their backs to blisters. It was almost as hard to collect the quartz they had mined from the snake-infested brushwood into which it had fallen. Many pieces were awkward to handle and too heavy for one man to carry. The fractures, sharp as broken glass, tore their palms into shreds, so they made slings of reins to lift them. Yet, slowly, the dump of rock by the side of the sluice-box grew. The broken quartz was lovely to look at. The red-veined hyaline matrix sparkled in the sun, and here and there a fine network of wire-gold shone with a softer light and flattered their eyes with its promise.

When they had piled a heap of three tons or more, Bosmann told them they had enough to start work on. 'But before we can feed it into the box,' he said, 'it must be broken again; these pieces are much too large for the dolly to break.' They sat down beside the dump and attacked it with hammers, binding flaps of leather on their foreheads to protect their eyes from flying splinters. Bosmann sat down with them and handled a hammer himself. This was the first manual work of which he had found himself capable since they had come down from the Berg; but before he had been long at it he began to tire; Janse could see how his breathing laboured, how the flabby muscles of his forearms jerked and trembled, and persuaded him to give in.

'It is true I am not so strong as I was,' he said pathetically.

'Never mind, boss. Nobody can say as you haven't shown willing,' Meninsky said. 'Me and Janse can manage this little lot all right. Though, God knows, I never reckoned as I should finish up breaking stones like a ruddy roadman at fivepence an hour. That only goes to show, don't it?'

What it went to show remained to Janse a mystery. He was thankful, at any rate, to be off his feet again, for the cramped position in which they had worked on the face of the cliff had strained and twisted the sinews of his lame leg. It took them more than a fortnight of hammering to reduce the heap of mined reef to fragments of a suitable size, and nearly another six weeks to crush it with the dolly.

The crushing, though the thought of having the help of some sort of machine was an encouragement, was a wearying task. It was a labour in which Meninsky's surprising strength and ingenuity counted for little. The strain lay in the monotony of the rhythm with which the weighted iron-shod ram did its work, rising and falling, pounding the fragments of quartz to powder with blow after blow. If their ears had been accustomed to any mechanical noise, this endless series of dull percussions would have been more tolerable. But they were used to what was nearly absolute silence, and the persistent thudding of the dolly got on their nerves and made them touchy.

It did not take much to get on their nerves by now. That was partly, Janse supposed, the effect of the fever, which had returned as soon as they reached the lower levels. As Bosmann said wisely, after the event, they had left the Berg a month too soon as a sop to Meninsky's impatience. The Peruvian and he had a violent quarrel over this, which was only ended by Janse rating both of them. Bosmann remained unreconciled and querulous for a week; but Meninsky, as usual, 'came round'. He was always ready to laugh at himself; though even he found it hard to laugh at anything in the middle of a bout of malaria.

And the dolly, when once they had mastered its mechanical secret (which was to allow the cross-member to do most of the job by its own resilience), worked surprisingly well for so rude a contrivance, reducing two hundred pounds of broken quartzite to powder in one day's hours of light. From the sluice-box the sludge was washed into a race lined with blankets treated with quicksilver, and the resulting slate-coloured amalgam, in which gold and mercury were combined, was afterwards heated, until the mercury volatilized to separate them.

On the vertical face of the reef which they had attacked, and where wire-gold was visible, the values proved to be excellent. Their best samples (the first) yielded an average of sixty-five ounces of gold to the ton: a result which made Bosmann shake his head – it looked, he said, more like a 'blow' than a lode or leader. Meninsky refused to have any of this cautious talk. Performing prodigies of mental arithmetic, he announced that they were now earning a hundred and thirty-eight pounds a week, or seven thousand one hundred and seventy-six pounds a year. It would take them no more than four years at this rate, he declared, to clear the ten thousand apiece on which he had set his heart. The first ten thousand pounds, he had always been told, was the most difficult step in the building up of a million. After that it was child's play: the money just grew of itself.

It was characteristic of Meninsky's calculations that he had forgotten to make any allowance for the rainy seasons in which work was impossible, and typical of the ebullience of his nature that he had failed to envisage the chance of the reef's (or the blow's) petering out; nor did he take into account the time that would almost certainly be lost through fever, the possible intrusion of other prospectors, which might lead to a 'rush', or the even more dangerous menace of Sekukuni. And so infectious was the little Jew's enthusiasm that both the others, in different ways, fell victims to it and allowed it to colour their dreams – which, for Bosmann, were centred in a visionary vine-wreathed porch, high upon the banks of the castled Rhine by Durkheim, where an elderly man of substance could sit sipping cooled *Liebfraumilch*, and for Janse, rather less definitely, in a white African farm with a shaded stoep, a farm immune from floods or drought or fever or locusts, where life was made sweet by Lavinia Haskard's music and serene by her presence.

But, of course, within a few months, the rains came again, and again they were driven up on the slopes of the Berg till summer was ended; and during their second spell of intensive digging, the reef's values began to fall off. The leader (if leader it were) appeared to dip vertically downward and could now only be reached by driving tunnels or adits into the face of the cliff. Even if they could manage to do this – and they were ill-equipped for such large-scale operations – Bosmann thought it a wildish gamble and not worth risking. He still clung to the opinion he had based on the deposit's unusual richness that what they had found was a 'blow' – a mass of fused gold that had sunk into a pocket of rock during some distant volcanic convulsion. It would be sounder, he said, to abandon their search for the lost lode and to concentrate once more on the alluvial in the kloof bottom.

During all this time Bosmann's weakness steadily increased. There was no longer any question of his helping with anything but advice; the slightest exertion or even movement embarrassed his breathing. Recurrent bouts of fever had weakened the others too. Short spells of work, stripping soil from the bedrock, soon exhausted them. This was no longer a jolly pastime, but a grim duty.

Meninsky bitterly resented this failure of strength, and even more his inability to sleep, which was one of the results of prolonged malarial poisoning which he shared with poor Bosmann. During the day he rarely spoke; but in the cool of night, when Janse would gladly have slept, he made up for his silence by talking perpetually – not so much of the future, now, as of his rapscallion past and its memories.

'D'you know, Janse,' he said one night when a prowling leopard had kept them on tenterhooks, 'I've just remembered a rum thing that I heard when I was a lad in Poland. There was an old Jew used to come round to my dad's, perhaps once in a couple of years, with all sorts of yarns about what he'd seen on his travels. A pedlar he was, and he carried his pack all over the Turkish Empire and parts of Russia. He must have been devilish old – and, my God, he was dirty! My mother always spring-cleaned the house as soon as he'd gone.

'But this story I've just remembered. . . . It seems like yesterday. He'd been lugging his pack, this old chap, through Asia Minor – Anatolia, I think it was – when, one day, he come on a village. Not a man, not a child to be seen in it; only a few old women, who looked as though they were starving. He asked what was up: he supposed some gang of bandits must have been up to their tricks like he'd seen in Armenia. They wouldn't tell him at first, but, being a Jew, he stuck to it, and at last one old harridan said the whole village had gone digging.

' "Digging where and what?" he says.

' "They've gone to the caves," she told him, "to dig for the treasure of Iskander. I don't rightly belong to this village," she says: "I'm a foreigner here, and I wish as I'd never set foot in it. All the people in this village are mad. They've been digging for generations, from father to son. Treasure-diggers, that's what they are. If you've any sense you'll have nothing to do with them."

'Well, this made the old boy sit up. He asked her where the caves were; and, after a lot of talk, she finally told him. He'd seen a hell of a lot of things in his life; but this, he said, was the rummiest he'd ever set eyes on. There was a great cave sunk in the hillside. You could just see the mouth of a passage leading into it. Outside, on the veld (or whatever they call it there), there was great mountains of earth, like the spoil-heaps on the banks of a coal-mine; and in and out of this tunnel or passage there come pouring a stream of kids, boys and girls, stark-naked, with baskets of earth on their heads, which they tipped

174

on the mounds. Like a ruddy blooming ants' nest it was, he said
– and not a sound, mind, but the patter of their feet as they ran
to and fro. Why, not one of them even looked at him.

'"Well, this is a rum go," he thought. So after a bit, he
decides to follow the tunnel and see what's happening inside.
The best part of sixty yards he went, feeling his way, with them
kids brushing past him in the dark, until at last the tunnel
opened out, as it were, into a ruddy great cave. He couldn't see
the top of it; but it was full of great fluttering bats, he said, and
it stank like the devil. And there they were, in the light of a lot of
smoky flares, men and women, stripped to the waist, a hundred
or more of them, just digging, digging, digging away for their
lives. They didn't even trouble to look at him – much less speak.
Not one of them turned their eyes. Their skins were all deathly
pale – sort of greenish, like potato-shoots in a cellar, he said.
There was no sound but the clink of picks and spades and
shovels and the patter of kids' feet as they ran to and fro with
their baskets.

'It was about the maddest, most awful thing, he said, he'd
ever seen. When he'd watched them a bit he went over to one
old man and spoke to him in Turkish. The old chap stopped
work for a moment and stared at him. His eyes were dead
black, he said, just like holes in his head. He asked him what
they were doing.

'"We're digging," he said.

'"But what the devil are you digging for?"

'"The treasure of Alexander, of course," he says, reproach-
ful-like.

'"How d'you know it's here?"

'"Because our fathers have told us."

'"Have you ever found any treasure?" the pedlar asks. You
bet, if there was any treasure, he was a Jew and meant to be in
on it!

'"Not yet," says the old man, "not yet."

'"How long have you been digging?"

'"I cannot remember. I began when I was a boy. And my
father began when he was a boy. That is what we are: we are
diggers, diggers for treasure.'

'"And will all these children dig, too?"

'"Of course they will," he says, "as soon as they're strong
enough. First they carry, then dig. It is our life."

'The old chap turned away angrily, as though he thought the

175

pedlar was a damn fool asking such questions. He spat on his hands and went on digging like the rest.

'By this time, what with the stink and them ruddy bats that never stopped fluttering, my dad's pal thought he'd better get out and be sick before he went mad. He just turned and ran like a hare, he told us, till he reached the fresh air and the light.'

'And then . . .?' Janse asked.

'That's all, mate. Rum story, ain't it?'

Meninsky was silent. A little later Janse heard him chuckling in the dark.

'What is it?' he said.

'Nothing much, mate. It's only struck me: when you come to think of it, there ain't a lot to choose between them and us. Digging, digging away for the Treasure of Alexander. Is it a mug's game or isn't it?'

Next morning, his fever gone, he had apparently forgotten his story and its grim implications. They went on stripping and washing dirt for a couple of weeks with indifferent results. Then another sinister incident came to disturb their waning confidence.

Janse had been out with his gun one evening. It had become more than ever necessary to shoot for the pot, as their provisions of meal were running low, though, as Meninsky said, they could always fall back on the donkeys the lions had left. Of late the growing scarcity of game had been noticeable; the big herds of palla and wildebeeste had deserted the foothills, and Janse counted himself lucky if he could bring down a single duiker or steenbok or pick up an odd brace of guinea-fowl. That day had been fruitless: he had not fired a single shot. Then, just as he started homeward, he thought he saw something moving in the long grass and brought up his gun to his shoulder. As he aimed, a cry stopped him firing. An emaciated, grey-haired native came crawling out of the grass. He held a split stick in his hand. In the cleft was a letter which he presented to Janse. It was a shaky scrawl written in English, and addressed to an unfamiliar name in Lydenburg. Janse unfolded the letter and read it.

Dear Friend (it ran),
Your Kaffir, Jim, met Mr. Swanston and myself on the point of death with six Kaffirs. I have been prostrated and reduced to a skeleton. Swanston also has been in a fearful

176

state; in fact our sufferings during the last two months have been such as I cannot tell you on this scrap of paper. Poor Frielinghaus died at some Kaffir houses. Williams, who was with Jones, drowned himself in the delirium of fever. Pray don't blame Jim; he has, I fully believe, saved my life by his attentions to me when raving with fever in the creek. I am better and Jim leaves me today. We will try to make our way back to Lydenburg, as a mission Kaffir who spoke to mine says that Sekukuni is getting ready for war. Today some of his young men threatened to drive my Kaffirs out of the creek and broke the races, saying this was his land and he doesn't want any diggers or prospectors about, or, if found, will wash his spears in them. That is all for now.

Towards the end, the handwriting had begun to straggle. The signature was illegible.

Janse hurried back to the camp and showed the letter to his companions. 'This means some beggars are working to north of us,' Meninsky said.

'It means more and worse than that,' Bosmann said. 'It means we must trek. If Sekukuni's young men are out, it is not gold but lives that are in danger.' For the sick man that he was he showed a quick grasp of the situation. 'This old Kaffir, Jim, must hurry on over the mountain to Lydenburg to warn his master, who will tell the Landdrost. Any white man he sees on the way, he must tell them that Sekukuni brings mischief. And we, we must trek this night. You, Janse, tell Cobus now to gather the oxen and inspan. You, Meninsky, see to the gold. That is all that matters. Everything but the very lightest things and the guns and powder we must leave, for we have only five spans of oxen, and these will not take a loaded wagon over the Berg.'

'You want me to leave behind all the stuff I brought from Kimberley? You speak for yourself, boss. I'll take what I damn well like.'

'I speak for all three, Meninsky; and you will take what I say. And I say one thing more: even if the wagon is lightened, as it shall be, we cannot go over the Berg by the way we came. Five span of oxen not used to work will not do it; they are stuck half-way. Even my weight will be too much – for I cannot walk. So we go the long way, due south, till we hit the Transport Company's road. There is a hill called Pretorius Kop, where

177

they build a rest-house, and on that road we may find wagons coming up from the Bay who will lend us a fore-span to pull us over the Devil's Knuckles. And now I can speak no more. It is for you to do.'

Indeed, this recital had nearly exhausted poor Bosmann. As he sat watching them keenly, propped up in the wagon and gasping for breath, and Cobus brought back the diminished team and inspanned, Meninsky and Janse loaded the gold and the few light personal belongings from which they hoped they need not be separated. During this process Janse found the Peruvian's eccentric attachments a nuisance. He could not bear to part with anything for which he had paid what he called 'good money'. If he had had his way the whole interior of the wagon would have been stuffed with junk. But Bosmann stood firm and Janse backed his decisions, and Meninsky, forced to jettison most of his worthless treasures, looked on with tears in his eyes. It was odd, Janse thought, that in so desperate an emergency, the little man should have so utterly lost his sense of proportion.

'Can't you see,' he said, 'that with a few ounces of gold, you can replace all this stuff you're so anxious to take with you?'

'Yes, yes, I can see that all right, mate,' Meninsky said dolefully, 'but you didn't have to scrape up the money to pay for them things and haggle over them like I did. If you had, you wouldn't like parting with them any more than me. It's kiss-me-good-bye. Next time we come here, I don't mind betting every ruddy one of them'll be gone.'

'Next time ...' Janse thought. He wondered if any one of them would ever set eyes on Brunner's Rest again. Or, indeed, if they would ever reach the High Veld alive.

It was hard enough to reach Pretorius Kop, as they did on the fifth day of their flight. The bullocks, though glossy-skinned and plump, were out of condition, and missed the leadership of the big, red front-ox Slingveld. This country was slightly higher than the Brunner's Rest creek, and, in comparison with that sombre gully, airy and cheerful; until they were clear of its mighty shadow Janse did not realize how heavily the perpetual imminence of the Berg had weighed on his spirits. It was a fairly open country, too, lightly sprinkled with patches of deciduous thorn-trees, with slades of grass between where buck were grazing, and occasional outcrops of broken or whale-

178

backed granite, the haunt of baboons and klipspringers. Pretorius Kop itself was one of these rocky landmarks, easy to recognize and to steer by; and, as luck (for once) would have it, at the moment when they arrived, a convoy of three loaded wagons westward-bound from the Bay had just outspanned for the night.

Their owners were the first strange white men Janse and Meninsky had seen for nearly two years. All three were Englishmen of the hard-bitten type which transport-riding breeds; big, bearded fellows, heavy in movement and speech.

When Janse warned them of Sekukuni's rising they gave one another good-natured winks and laughed at him.

'You're just about two months late with that news, mate,' one of them said. 'The Boers are marching on Sekukuni already. One of these wagons here is loaded with rifle-ammunition and shells for the German guns, that we're bringing up from the Bay to Lydenburg.'

'Will you give us a haul over the Devil's Knuckles?' Janse said 'I've lost half of my team with red-water.'

'Ay, I reckon we'll manage to find you a fore-span for that, mate – provided you can keep up with us. We've no time to waste.'

The ascent of the Berg with a light wagon and fifteen span of well-conditioned oxen was a very different matter from their first desperate climb. These three men had ridden the road from the Bay so often that they knew all its dangers and difficulties by heart: where to swing wide or hug the face of the cliffs; where to get all the oxen leaning on the yoke for a 'heave together'; where to water them or give a 'blow'; when to use the whip or to spare it.

Janse left the whole job to their expert direction, while he and Meninsky walked beside the wagon, providentially relieved of all responsibility and congratulating each other on this fine turn of luck. During the last year they had been too much alone, driven in on themselves, too receptive, unconsciously, of each other's ills and forebodings. The company of these good-humoured fellows, who seemed not to have a care in the world and took life so easily, infused them with hope and courage. As the wagon wound slowly upwards into more rarefied air, their spirits were curiously lightened. They were so elated by this sudden change in their outlook that they forgot all about Bosmann sitting alone, propped up in the lumbering wagon.

Alone, and fighting for his life. . . . Even by the time they had climbed the fifteen hundred feet to Pretorius Kop, Bosmann's flagging heart had felt the change of altitude. Now, with every foot of the next two thousand, the distress became greater, the strain more intolerable. He heard Janse and the Peruvian talking and laughing in the road behind him. Could he have spared the breath or the strength he would have shouted and begged them to stop, if only for a moment, to give the fluttering heart a chance to relax and adjust itself to the ever-increasing embarrassment. But he knew he had neither the breath nor the strength to make himself heard above the rumble and clatter of the wagon, the shouts of the teamsters, while the relentless spans carried him up and up into the throttling thin air.

And soon he had not even the will to shout for mercy. He was no longer a sentient man, but a dimly-conscious mechanism of muscle-fibres, all striving to the same end – not merely the muscles of the ribs and the diaphragm, but those of the nose and face and the thin strands that lay hidden beneath the skin of his throat – all pumping in the air that had less and less life in it. He could no longer hold himself up. A swing of the wagon dislodged him from the heap of karosses against which he was propped. He rolled over, helplessly, face-downwards, twitching like a fish out of water. His heart raced like an engine without a governor in one last, supreme effort. It faltered. It stopped.

Janse found him there, fallen on his face, and called to the others. The three transport-riders peered into the wagon, solemn and puzzled, while Meninsky and Janse bent over the huddled body, hopelessly waiting for any return of life. Then one of the teamsters took out his pipe and rubbed tobacco into it.

'Poor beggar,' he said. 'That's bad luck, that is – to kick the bucket just when we got to the top. But there it is, mates. There's nothing left but to bury the poor little sod. We'd gladly give you a hand; but this contract's urgent, and we ought to be trekking on by rights. See you later in Lydenburg.'

They dug Bosmann's grave on the top of the Berg, where the great dolomite bastions fell sheer to tumbled green hills and the dreaming plain.

'We'll let him lie facing the Low Country,' Meninsky said. 'Although it killed him, I reckon he loved the Low Country.'

A few hours short of Lydenburg a party of mounted men appeared on the skyline. When they had watched the wagon for a moment they came cantering towards it. Their leader, a youngish veld-kornet. rode up and saluted Janse.

'Who are you, and where have you come from, and where are you going?'

Janse told him.

'What? Grafton? Are you then a brother of Groot Andries and Adrian? I know them both: I am Devenaar; but I did not know they had a brother who is lame. This is your wagon?'

'Mine and my friend's,' Janse said.

'Your friend? He looks like a Peruvian,' the veld-kornet said scornfully. 'But you are a burgher, of course, and though you are lame you can drive a wagon. The general wants wagons, so now you are commandeered. Report yourself to headquarters as soon as you get to Lydenburg.'

The troops swerved and rode rapidly away.

'Well, it looks like you're off to the wars, mate,' Meninsky said, 'though that long-haired beggar don't seem to have taken much of a fancy to me, thank the Lord.'

'I shall see my brothers, at any rate,' Janse said. 'And Adrian, who's a friend of the President, may make things easy for me. Do you want to come with me?'

'Come with you? No ruddy fear! Wars are not in my line, mate. Not the fighting part, anyway. Though, mind you, in wartime there's usually money to be made buying cheap and selling dear to the Government. I might even sell those damn donkeys, you know. But, first of all, we must take this gold to the bank and divide it.'

'What about Bosmann's share?'

'The less said about Bosmann the better. We'll report his death to the Landdrost to be on the safe side: if he had any heirs, you may bet your boots they'll damn well show up like a lot of vultures. If they don't show up – well, so much the better for us, mate.'

'I don't like that,' Janse said. 'We ought to declare Bosmann's property.'

Meninsky sighed. 'All right, all right, have your way. But if you're going to do that, I can tell you it's the last you'll see of it.

Unclaimed estate. The Government mops up the lot: and why the hell should they? That's the only thing I've got against honesty, Janse: it costs more than anything else I know of. They say that it pays. If ever you hear of it paying, just let me know!'

They handed into the bank two hundred and eight ounces and seven pennyweights of gold, and, deducting Bosmann's share, drew out five hundred pounds, which they split between them, balancing the value of Janse's wagon and team against that of the mining gear and materials the Peruvian had provided.

'Two hundred and fifty,' Meninsky said reflectively. 'It's one or two short of the ten thousand on which I'd counted. But it's something. It's more than I've ever had before. Not so bad, when you come to think that Barney Barnato started life in Kimberley on a parcel of bad cigars.'

'You'll go back to Kimberley, then?'

'That's about the ticket. Unless something extra happens to catch my eye on the road. Anyway, the post office at Kimberley will always find me, and if I do strike it rich, I'll soon put you in the way of it, never fear that. I'll write you care of the bank here in Lydenburg. You've been a first-rate pal, mate, and good Jews, like me, never forget.'

By evening Meninsky had found a berth in a convoy returning light to Pretoria. He and Janse said good-bye on the Lydenburg outspan, already crowded with the advance-guard of Burgers' four hundred wagons. Meninsky had bought a ready-made suit of a particularly unpleasant purple: 'Half-mourning for Bosmann's money,' he said with a wink – a gold Albert chain, with no watch attached to it, and a billycock hat, which he wore on the back of his head. Janse laughed at him.

'You look like a clown in a circus, Meninsky.'

'There you are wrong, mate,' Meninsky said gravely. 'I look just what I am.'

Janse watched the ridiculous figure strutting away. He was sorry to part with Meninsky. Of the few men he had known in his life he had found none more trustworthy, more kind-hearted, more generous, more vivid, and – yes – more innocent than the little Peruvian. He felt he had lost what his life had lacked most: a friend.

With a genuine feeling of regret he drove his wagon to Headquarters, as he had been bidden, and received a written acknowledgement, one of those 'good-fors' which had lately become the chief currency of the Transvaal Government. He inquired for Adrian, but was told that he was not in camp. He was attached, it appeared, to the President's personal staff, and would not be likely to leave Pretoria until the whole force was collected and the advance began.

'But your other brother, Groot Andries, is here,' a burgher told him. 'You will find him among the Zoutpansberg commando, on the other side of the square.'

Janse threaded his way between the wheels and the disselbooms of outspanned wagons. The sun had set and an apricot sky swiftly darkened. The air grew dim with fumes of milk-blue woodsmoke rising up straight from the fires the Kaffirs had kindled to cook the doughnuts of meal fried in fat, which the burghers called stormjaers. In several bivouacs a sheep had been killed or a buck brought in by a hunting-party, and here hunks of meat were grilling on ramrods and a smell of charred flesh filled the air. Alongside of the Zoutpansberg commando's encampment a larger fire had been lighted. By the light of the flames a wide circle of men played yokeskeys for hands of tobacco, hurling pointed pegs from the oxen's yokes at others pinned in the sand.

Janse scanned the circle of fire-lit faces in search of Andries, but could not find one that resembled what he remembered. Suddenly, the veld-kornet who had stopped his wagon earlier in the day caught his eye and recognized him.

'Ah, the little brother, the lame one!' he cried. 'What did I tell you, Groot Andries?'

A bear-like figure detached itself from the group and came lumbering towards Janse. This uncouth fellow could not be Andries, he thought; yet, when he came nearer and held out his hand, he perceived, through the thickets of beard and whisker, a faint resemblance to the brother he had almost forgotten. Andries had always been taller than the rest; but this rustic figure was monstrous in every dimension.

'Devenaar told me he'd met you and commandeered your wagon,' he said. 'But what are you doing here – and what have you done to yourself? You're shrunk to a skeleton.'

'Nobody can say that of you!'

Groot Andries gave a great bellow of laughter and the Zoutpansberg men laughed too.

'That is not my fault, brother. I come from a country of elephants. That must be the reason. What news of Wonderfontein?'

'For that we must wait for Adrian. I've been digging gold for two years.'

'And your farm?'

'Piet bought it.'

Groot Andries shook his huge head. 'That is bad, that is bad. A man should not sell his land. In our country we don't like gold-diggers. It's those *skelms* who've made all this mischief with Sekukuni and brought us to this.'

'Have you left your wife behind in the Zoutpansberg?'

'No, no. Things are far too unsettled up there for women. Nothing but trouble with Kaffirs. You know we had to burn Schoemansdal? They're in laager, the women and children, now, at Marabastad. I do not like war, but something had to be done. I hope, this time, the Kaffirs will get their lesson for good and all.'

'This is a mighty commando. I cannot count all the wagons.'

Andries shook his head. 'It is not a matter of numbers or human strength. They say that the President will lead us, and that is not good. A light man who knows not the word of God. A Sabbath-breaker! They say Adrian is with Burgers.'

'Adrian has always believed in him.'

'And we, of the Zoutpansberg, have always been against him. There is only one man for this war, we say, and that is Paul Kruger. If Kruger refuses to lead, there must be something wrong, and no good can come of it.'

He went back, with a heavy face, to his game of yokeskeys.

Next day Burgers, with his four adjutants, including Adrian, rode into the camp and joined Nicholas Smit at Headquarters. He came full of excited hope and enthusiasm. Up till the last moment he had been working night and day in his office at Pretoria, trying to clear up the administrative arrears that had accumulated in his absence. Now the back of that thankless task had been broken. There was one more to be done. He looked forward to a crushing victory over Sekukuni and the pacification of the turbulent North. When once that was out of the way – and it would not take long – he could get on with his job.

The burghers received him coldly. For all the notice they took of his flamboyant arrival, he might have been a private citizen. He was appalled, even more, by the sullen listlessness he found in the camp, particularly among the men who had ridden in from the settled areas. They had obeyed the summons to go on commando, but it was clear they resented it. With each day of forced inactivity discontent was growing. It would be wise, Smit told him, to give them something to think about.

'Then we will trek tomorrow morning,' Burgers said.

Janse went round to Headquarters in search of Adrian. A solemn young man with a long face and jutting lower lip received him and told him that Adrian was busy attending Burgers. He could not say when the conference was likely to be over. More than twenty men were already waiting to see the President, with requests or complaints of one kind and another. He surveyed Janse's haggard face and torn clothes with a kind of cold curiosity.

'It's not much good hanging about here,' he said; 'but if you'll give me your name, I'll let Grafton know that you came here.'

'I'm his brother Janse.'

'In that case you'd better wait, after all. By the way, my name's Struben – Fred Struben. I'm another of the President's adjutants.' The young man hurriedly and rather shamefacedly glanced at Janse's lame leg. 'What are you doing here? You've surely not been called out on commando?' he said.

'My wagon was commandeered yesterday,' Janse told him. 'I'd come over the Devil's Knuckles on the way from the Low Country.'

'Ha ... I thought as much,' Struben said. 'There's quartz-dust on your clothes. You've been digging. Is that it?'

'Yes. Northward, along the foot of the Berg.'

'Any luck?'

'Better luck than some of them. The climate is bad. Too much fever.'

'But you've been working a reef. The quartz-dust shows that. What sort of values?'

'Pretty good to begin with. It was petering out when we left.'

'Ah, that's always the trouble,' young Struben said. 'The gold's scattered in patches down there. I've been there myself prospecting: that's how I know. But some day we're going to

185

find the great reef where all the gold comes from. And then . . .'
His cold, serious eyes grew bright – 'then we'll all make our
fortunes. You must tell me more about this later on. It's the one
thing I'm interested in. Now wait here a moment: I'll try to get
hold of your brother.'

A few moments later Adrian came out with a worried face.
At the sight of Janse he gasped.

'Almighty! What have you been doing to yourself, Janse?' he
cried. 'You're nothing but a scarecrow. I must find you some
clothes.'

Janse laughed. 'I've not seen myself for two years, so I don't
know what I look like. Are you so ashamed of me, Adrian?'

'I'm distressed. You're shrunk to a shadow. You've been
ill?'

'Just hard work and fever. There's nothing to worry about.
When can we meet and talk quietly? I'm longing for news.'

'The talk and the news will have to wait. I shan't have a
moment tonight. We're all in a muddle, and shall be until we
get started. Come round to Headquarters tomorrow when
we've outspanned, and I'll have some decent clothes ready for
you if I can find any. You must have a horse too.'

He went back to the President's tent. Janse watched him go
anxiously. This was not the serene Adrian he knew. It was clear
that the tensity of Burgers' nerves had been playing the deuce
with his. Janse made his way back to his wagon, which, in his
absence, had been fitted with four new spans of indifferent
oxen. For all the apparent confusion there must, somewhere,
have been a controlling intelligence at work. The whole camp
was now buzzing with activity. Men were shouting and running
to and fro in the firelight. The order to trek at dawn had spread
rapidly, and they had something more than their doubts and
grievances to think about now. From the bivouac of the Zoutpansberg commando came a sound of deep voices growling in
unison. He could recognize some of the words. They were singing the metrical version of the Sixty-eighth Psalm:

'*Let God arise and let his enemies be scattered: let them also
that hate him flee before him. As smoke is driven away, so drive
them away; as wax melteth before the fire, so let the wicked
perish at the presence of God. . . . Oh, sing unto the Lord,*' he
heard, '*sing praises unto his name; extol him that rideth upon
the heavens by his name JAH, and rejoice before him.*'

186

It rolled forth before dawn, that vast cavalcade, into the hostile North: the greatest force that had been mustered and set in motion since the days of the Great Trek, forty years before. Three abreast the wide trail of swaying wagons crept forward. The red dust, rising from sixteen hundred wheels and twenty-five thousand hooves, rose into the sky and hung there like cloud – so densely curdled that, when the sun rose, its dull disc threw a baleful light on the gleaming wagon-tilts, as though it were bleared by fog. The State President and his staff led the column, riding clear of its noise and dust. Behind them came the Krupp guns and their German artillerymen; around the slow-moving convoy, far out on the veld, hovered the mounted burghers, advance-guard and flankers and rear-guard, spreading a curtain of skirmishers to protect the wagon-convoy; while beyond these, again, another armed force shadowed them – the horde of Swazis, Sekukuni's sworn enemies, who had leapt to arms as soon as they heard that his day of reckoning was come. The whole convoy moved with a painful deliberation, slowing down, pausing, halting, at every donga or spruit that scored the dry bush, while the men in advance hacked down trees from its path or packed the dips with faggots to ease its crossing. And when the last wagon had passed there stretched behind it a track, forty yards wide, resembling the path of a hurricane; a scar on the face of the veld like that left by a timber-slide.

Janse's wagon, as befitted its state of decrepitude, had been allotted a place at the extreme rear of the convoy, where the air was dense with the dust of those that went before. There was no question of getting into touch with Adrian during the day's trek, for a distance of no less than four miles, an hour's walk at the best, separated the head of the column from the tail, and he had no horse. In all his mining adventures he had never known any physical discomfort to compare with this torment of dust; his eyes, his nose and his throat were clogged with it, his skin, beneath his clothes, was caked with it. Though they stopped for a 'blow' in the middle of the day, the cloud still hung over them; it seemed almost to thicken, indeed, as the particles slowly descended.

At four o'clock in the afternoon, when he felt he had come to the end of his tether and was nodding asleep, with sheer tiredness, on the wagon-seat, an order came back from the laager-commandant for his file to swerve to the left. Janse followed the wagon in front of him and soon saw that the other outer file, on the columns right, had been ordered to stop, while the one in the middle went on and, at a fixed point, split east and west at right-angles, to form with the others a triangular laager, enclosing at least a square mile of veld.

It took them more than an hour to perform this evolution; and when the last gap had been closed, there was a scene of great animation: men running excitedly this way and that with sticks in their hands to knock down the small buck and hares that had crouched in the grass and been caught in the space between the divergent lines. Janse had no energy left for this hunt. He had a feeling that a new bout of fever was on him, for his head split with aching and his gritty eyeballs burned like hot cinders. He left Cobus, who seemed none the worse for the dust and the glare, to outspan the oxen and drive them afield for grazing in the last hours of light. He flung himself down on the floor of the suffocating wagon and, somehow, slept.

When he awoke it was dark, and his premonitions of fever had vanished. The dust had gone, too. There was even a sense of exhilaration in the chill air. The trek-oxen had been brought in from grazing and lay chewing the cud contentedly under the lee of the wagons to which they belonged. The whole laager smelt like a gigantic byre with their sweet heavy breath. Each field-cornetcy had its own bivouac, and the triangular wall of wagon-tilts was flushed with the light of numerous fires. The whole laager was wrapped in a pleasant sense of well-earned relaxation and security; for, out on the veld, in a wide perimeter, strong outposts (or *Brandwagte*) kept watch and guard – more for the sake of establishing a discipline than as a necessary precaution against surprise, since the column was still in what might be counted as 'friendly' country.

Janse rid himself from the day's dust as well as he could in the firelight and limped, picking his way between the bivouac-fires and the tired oxen, to the Headquarters tent. Young Fred Struben, still on duty and acting the part of a watch-dog, challenged him, but smiled when he recognized him and let him pass to a corner hard by the President's wagon where Adrian sat smoking, propped up by his saddle, his golden beard gleaming in the light of a lazy fire. Groot Andries sprawled opposite, dwarfing Andrian with his enormous bulk. When they saw Janse coming, both his brothers looked up and smiled. Janse was astonished, now that he saw them together, by the closeness of the family resemblance.

'Come along, sit you down and smoke,' Adrian said. 'It's been a long trek today, and Andries says the dust has been bad.'

'Not so bad for those that ride in front,' Andries said in a deep voice that rumbled like distant thunder.

'Quiet ... quiet, Boanerges, or you'll wake the State President! He's asleep just behind us, and I think it must be the first time he's slept for a week. That man is all nerves. Neither Struben nor I can keep him quiet.'

'Paul Kruger will keep him quiet before he's finished with him,' Andries said, with a rumbling laugh. 'But there ... we mustn't start quarrelling, brother, the first moment we meet after so many years.'

'No, no; let's forget about politics,' Janse said. 'What we want is news of Wonderfontein.'

Adrian smiled and shook his head. 'Things don't change much at Wonderfontein. We have had three good years since you left, Janse. No more drought or locusts or lung-sickness. Yes, now we are going ahead. And the folk at Wonderfontein don't change much either. The old *baas* is older and greyer – but then, he's nearly sixty ...'

'Fifty-six,' Janse said.

'He looks older than that. He's a man who's lived a hard life. He must have been middle-aged at twenty, I think, when I was born. As for mother, she doesn't alter. She has no age. She has the heart and the shape of a girl. I wish I could find one like her. You're an old married man, Andries.'

'Eight years, and seven children. It's a warm country, the Zoutspansberg; we breed fast up there!'

'The Witwatersrand's not so bad. Our sister Sarie's begun to compete with you.'

'What? Sarie's married, then?' Janse exclaimed.

'She married soon after you went north. Young Hans Oosthuizen.'

'Of Langlaagte? That's not much of a farm,' Andries said contemptuously. 'You should see my soil and my veld! In the Zoutpansberg ...'

'That's all very well, if the Kaffirs would let you live on it,' Adrian said.

'If your damned Government would leave us alone we'd soon finish with them! You get more like the English every day. If I had my way ...'

'The Oosthuizens are a good family and old friends,' Janse said, 'and Sarie was born to be a farmer's wife and to mother a big family. She has children already, you say?'

'One ... a boy. And another coming. They lose no time.'

'And our little Maria?'

'Our little Maria no longer. A fine young woman, Janse. You should have seen her at Sarie's wedding in the silk gown mamma made for her. A capable young woman too. For a time she kept house for Piet in his grand new home at Witfontein.'

'Ah, Witfontein ... don't speak of it,' Janse said. 'That pulls at my heart.'

'If you saw your Witfontein now you wouldn't know it. We were doubtful, father and I, at first. We thought Piet was too ambitious and would lose all the money he'd saved. But that boy has more brains than any of us. He always knew what he wanted. Your old house is the stables now, Janse. ...'

Janse shook his head: 'It was good enough for me.'

'But not for our Piet. His new house is built higher up, with a covered stoep and an iron roof and six rooms, if you please! The whole farm is transformed. He's planted hundreds of fruit-trees ...'

'Fruit-trees on the Witwatersrand?' Andries growled. 'The poor fellow must be mad! Now if you were talking of the Zoutpansberg ...'

Adrian laughed: 'So we all of us said. And yet you should see how they grow. A picture, as father says. It's mainly a matter of water. Piet has spent most of his money on that; he's made furrows, built dams. The whole farm is a network of furrows that follow the contours: he can lead water anywhere.'

'Not on the west – the Brakfontein side,' Janse said. 'There the slope is against him. Don't I know every inch of it?'

'Ah, but that's where the young devil's been so slim. As you say, the western half of Witfontein's waterless. But the Brakfontein springs break out higher up the slope; and Piet can do anything he likes with his father-in-law.'

Groot Andries slapped his vast thigh. 'Almighty! Young Piet married too?'

'And married money, my lad,' Adrian laughed. 'When I left

190

he was still on his honeymoon at the Cape. A grand wedding, by all accounts. And the girl – you don't know her, Andries: Lavinia's her name – is likely to be an heiress. Her father, James Haskard, they say, has big interests in Kimberley.'

'What? Piet's married an Englishwoman? That's bad – yes, that's bad,' Andries said.

'Yet I think she's a good girl, Andries. You know her well, Janse, don't you?'

'Yes ... I know her a little,' Janse said, with an effort. He laughed nervously. 'Not so well, perhaps, as I thought.'

'A beauty, too, in her way – though it isn't my way. The great point is that mother likes her, and father too. And she seems to be very much in love with our Piet. Her mother was not too well pleased with the arrangement at first; but the girl got her way in the end. She's a will of her own, never fear: she and Piet are well-matched – they both know what they want and get it. As for Piet, he's not only got hold of the girl, but the land as well. For the present he's running the Haskards' farm along with his own at a handsome salary. When the old man dies – Haskard's not really old, but his lungs are weak – Brakfontein will go to the girl, and Piet gets the lot. The young devil takes no chances: the English make what they call a marriage settlement, and he has it on paper in black and white. Yes, he'll be a rich man.'

'If I were he,' Andries said, 'I'd sell out as soon as this old man died and buy farms in the Zoutpansberg. The Witwatersrand isn't only poor; it's too near to Pretoria. He'll have Burgers' damned Hollanders sniffing round all the time after taxes. This railway tax, now. What will a railway do for us in the Zoutpansberg? I ask you that, and you know the truth. Not a thing. It will not help us at all – so why should we pay for it?'

'The old story,' Adrian said impatiently: 'we hear that night and day in Pretoria. The answer is clear to any man who takes the trouble to think. This railway, we say, will make the Republic wealthy and independent. You none of you see that the Republic is one: the time is long past when a man could say: "I belong to Lydenburg" or "to Potchefstroom" or "to the Zoutpansberg". We are all burghers of the same state. If the state prospers, its members are prosperous. If it grows rich, they grow rich.'

'But *I* say,' Groot Andries roared, 'there are things worth more than riches. We in the Zoutpansberg . . .'

So they ran on through the usual rambling course of a political discussion that appeared to lead nowhere. Janse sat with his head in his hands, hearing only a babble of words bereft of meaning or reason. He was trying to control himself, to pull his wits together. This disaster had fallen on him too suddenly. From the moment when his talk with his brothers had begun he had restrained himself from mentioning the Haskards' name, simply because it was uppermost in his thoughts and he felt the very eagerness of his voice might betray him. During his long meditations under the Berg he had never been able completely to dismiss from his mind the fear that some unknown rival, more brilliant, more confident, and more acceptable than himself, might discover Lavinia. It seemed natural enough that any man who came near her should fall in love with her, and when he thought of his own pretensions to a place in her thoughts he was shocked by their slenderness. Yet somehow, for all this humility, there had been moments, when his lonely imagination warmed and took fire, in which he had dared to believe that some memory of himself – if only that of an odd, inarticulate adorer – must remain with her. At times, in the exalted state betwixt sleep and waking or in the hallucinations of fever when thought ran beyond his control, he had even persuaded himself that by sheer mental concentration he could force his own image into her consciousness, and make her remember him.

Now, with one casual word, Adrian had not merely dispersed this airy edifice of extravagant hopes, but razed its foundation. Lavinia was lost to him, gone beyond hope and for ever. In one tragic instant past, present and future had abruptly ceased to have any significance. Though he continued to breathe, and felt his pulse beating fast, and heard, as it were at a distance, his brothers talking, the man in whose body these automatic impulses and sensations took place was not, surely, himself, but another. They resembled the contortions of a snake whose back has been broken; the twitching of the tail that has been severed from a lizard's trunk; the awful automatism of a horse which he had once seen continuing to graze when a charging buffalo had ripped out its guts. For he, surely, was dead if ever a man was dead.

Something of this hopeless agony must have shown itself in his face; for suddenly, out of the babble of meaningless words, he heard Adrian speaking to him.

'Janse ... Janse! What's the matter with you? Hold him, Andries: he's going to faint!'

Andries clutched his arm and steadied him. Janse had not even known that his body was swaying. He dragged himself back to life again and forced himself to smile.

'It's this fever,' he gasped. 'I'm full of it. Take no notice, I shall soon be better.'

As he spoke, his features started to work in spite of himself. His teeth began to chatter, though not with fever.

'Come into the tent,' Adrian said. 'You'd better lie down.'

'No, no. I'll get back to my wagon,' Janse said. 'I'm used to it now, I shall be better tomorrow morning.'

He pulled himself on to his feet, refusing Adrian's help. Before either of them could stop him he was limping away, uncertainly, into the dark. Adrian watched him go with anxiety, but Andries was in no way perturbed.

'Yes, that's fever he's got,' he said solemnly. 'You could hear his teeth chatter. But it's nothing to worry about, as he says. I know all about it. We have plenty of that in the Zoutpansberg.'

Adrian laughed out loud for all his anxiety and slapped his brother's great back.

'Is there anything you haven't got in the Zoutpansberg, old Andries?' he said.

(5)

When you see a writhing, broken-backed snake or a severed lizard-tail twitching in the sand, your first instinct, Janse thought, is to remove the obscenity from your eyes, to stamp on it and crush it under your heel and destroy it utterly. It made no difference, he thought, to the snake or the lizard: those twitching fragments had no feeling; they were dead; yet this mockery of life was unnatural and hateful and best out of sight. He resented the thought that curious eyes might observe his own pitiful contortions, the spectacle of a dead man limping among the living. It would be far better, he thought, to have done with it for good and all, and the sooner the better; to seek, on the first opportunity, a complete destruction in the most obvious way – by means of a Kaffir bullet or an assegai-thrust through the ribs. The prospect of such a death, and one so easily attainable, made a grim appeal to the romantic side of his nature. It pleased him, ridiculously perhaps, to think of himself as a hero of an exploit that would be long remembered – as a lame man riddled with fever, whom the strong had despised, leading them all and hurling himself, with fantastic bravery, on the Kaffirs' spears. He looked forward, with an eagerness that he found amusing, to the coming encounter with Sekukuni's hordes and the chance of sacrificing his life in a flare of glory which would cost him nothing – the cream of the grim joke being that only he would see it!

In the meantime the fever with which he had pretended to be stricken was on him in earnest. For the best part of a week he lay sweating and shivering, a prey to fantastic nightmares, on the bottom of the wagon, while old Cobus drove the team. Several times a day Adrian cantered back through the column's dust to the rear, to see what he could do for him. Once or twice the vast form of Groot Andries loomed over the tail of the wagon. Young Fred Strubens, too, visited him, endlessly talking about gold. Wherever he went, he confessed, he carried with him a geological hammer. When he saw an outcrop of rock he would ride away from the convoy and chip off likely samples and crush them to powder and pan them when they bivouacked at night. This long-faced young man, with the big ears and jutting underlip, had no other interest, it seemed, than the quest for gold; and gold was the last thing Janse wanted to talk about; in a life that was now unimportant this metal, on which he had set his mind for two years, seemed even less important than anything else.

But young Struben, despite his obsession, was a kindly soul. He gave Janse stiff doses of quinine – a supply of which, along with his hammer and pan, he always carried with him as a matter of routine. They made Janse deaf, but they cleared his blood of fever. This was the worst 'go' he had ever had. When he emerged from it, in spite of the numbness and emptiness of his heart, he felt oddly, morbidly, elated and – paradoxically – hopeful (though what he hoped for he could not say) in a world divorced from familiar realities.

One day the column checked suddenly in the middle of the morning. Janse lifted himself on his elbow: he thought he heard shots. This was by no means unusual. Every fourth or fifth day of the trek the convoy had been outspanned to give the cattle rest, and drives had been organized to round up a herd of impala for fresh meat. But the firing that morning was of a greater persistence and intensity than usual, and the usual triangular laager was formed at the point where the convoy halted.

In the evening Adrian rode round to the wagon and told him that the Potchefstroom commando had had a brush with the enemy. They had surprised an *impi* of Matebi's Zulu refugees in the flats and driven them back on the chiefs' hill-top kraal with heavy casualties.

'Tomorrow, before dawn, we shall attack Matebi's Kop,' Adrian said, 'and try to cut him off from Sekukuni. The Swazis are making a war-dance tonight. If you listen hard you can hear them singing and stamping. It's a nasty position to attack, all rocks and schanzes; the Kaffirs will have plenty of cover from behind which to shoot, and the ground is too rough for horses. Burgers calls it "Matebi's Gibraltar". However, the devils can't hold out long: the Pretoria commando is sitting tight on their only water-supply. It may be a stiff job; but you're out of it, anyway.'

'I could sit a horse now,' Janse said.

'I've told you that horses will be useless.'

At three o'clock in the morning firing began. Janse could hear the sharp crack of rifles and the deep detonations of long-barrelled elephant-guns. A little later the northern sky flared red – the Kop had been stormed and Matebi's grass huts were burning – but by daylight the fighting had ceased. There was a smell of smoke in the air, and millions of smuts and wisps of charred grass that had been sucked up into the sky as sparks by the draught of the conflagration continued to fall on the laager like flakes of black snow.

The fight had been short and fierce, Adrian said, and Matebi's smuggled guns were less to be feared than many had expected, for the Kaffirs generally fired high. He himself had escaped with a skin-deep graze on the shoulder, but Groot Andries had had his hat knocked off by one bullet and another had ploughed its way through the flesh of his flank.

'I told him he'd better crawl on his belly in future,' Adrian said. 'He's such a big mark that not even a Kaffir could miss him. But he says they're used to that sort of thing in the Zoutpansberg – all he wanted to put the wound right was a dab from a tar-bucket. I love old Andries. He must be rather like our mother's cousin, Jan Bothma who saved all their lives at

195

Blauwkrans. The worst part of the whole affair was the end, when the Swazis ran loose. How those savages hate the Zulus! The whole of that burning kraal was drenched with blood. They went mad, and nothing could stop them. Women and children too. No, no ... I can't bear to speak of it. But war is war, as they say; and a Kaffir war is bloodier than any other.'

'Did the President take part in the attack?' Janse asked.

'Yes, indeed – though Struben and I did our best to keep him out of it. It's hard to imagine anyone who looks less like a soldier, and he wouldn't carry a rifle. And yet he's completely fearless. As I've always said, there's something big as well as lovable about Burgers – something glowing and passionate. He believes in himself, his mission and his destiny, so strongly that he not merely feels but looks invulnerable. Of course, his enthusiasm carries him away. That, I think, is his weakness. To-night he's talking as if the whole war were over. "The little Gibraltar has fallen," he says. I confess I find it frightening. His Gibraltar, if only he knew it, is the Raad in Pretoria, where Oom Paul is watching and waiting to see what happens.'

'The old buffalo bull in the grass,' Janse said.

Adrian nodded. 'And yet, do you know,' he said, 'the more I see of Paul Kruger the more he impresses me. I've watched him a good deal lately; and, much as I love the State President and much as I'm fascinated by him, there's a quality in Oom Paul which, in spite of his old bull's cunning, I have to respect. I believe, in a way – and I hate to admit it – that he's a bigger man than Burgers. It's not only his strength of body and intellect. He has wisdom and moderation. A massiveness, too. That bulk is as hard to move as a granite kopje. And that, I believe, is the root of the difference. Paul Kruger's just as much part of this land as if he had actually been hewn out of it, while Burgers, for all his imagination and gifts, is a foreigner. If we could only make these two men see eye to eye and work together! We can't, alas, and that is our tragedy.'

The speedy fall of Matebi's 'little Gibraltar' had put the whole commando in better humour. This was the first Transvaal war in which the Kaffirs had been equipped with firearms to any considerable extent, and the engagement had proved that the unfamiliar weapon was hardly more formidable in their hands than the assegai. It had also shown that the presence of

196

the heretical President did not necessarily condemn them, as had been prophesied, to defeat.

Many of them felt, indeed, that a smaller levy would have sufficed to deal with Sekukuni, and some, more impatient, were for breaking away and riding home to their farms.

It was the amiable Nicholas Smit's authority rather than Burgers' that held them together. With Sekukuni, he told them, half-measures were useless. The eyes of all black Africa were on them. If this rebellion within their borders were not completely stamped out there would be more trouble later – not only with the unsubdued Bapedi, but with Cetewayo, who, backed by the English – that political card always paid for playing! – was probably behind it. What was wanted now was a quick and crushing victory which would give Cetewayo something to think about: Sekukuni in chains, his tribe scattered, his kraal sacked and demolished! And then no more irksome commando duties for a lifetime. He could almost promise them that.

For a while the column pressed on more eagerly and more swiftly towards Sekukuni's Great Place. Even so, Burgers fretted at the slowness of the advance. He saw every moment of this protracted campaign in terms of money, and thought of his empty treasury. He wondered, too, what was happening in Pretoria and what new surprises his enemies were preparing for him behind his back. He began to see how shrewd Paul Kruger had been in playing on his vanity and forcing him, against his judgment, to accept this command.

And now, as they trekked north into the mountains, with desultory skirmishing all the way, the pace of the column slackened seriously. In broken country such a huge convoy became unmanageable. It was no longer possible for the wagons to travel three abreast, while, in single file, they sprawled over so many miles that it was difficult to defend them. Then horse sickness appeared in its most fatal form: the variety known as *deng sik*. Few of the burghers who came from the south had salted horses; there was distress and discontent in the camp when they saw beasts they had bred and broken standing miserably apart, with dull eyes and staring coats, their lungs clogged with frothy mucus. Adrian lost his favourite sleek dapple-grey, and Janse the commandeered hack which Adrian had found for him. This assuredly, men declared, was a visitation from God which would not have afflicted them under a more acceptable leader who kept His Sabbath.

Janse was sorry to lose his horse, poor thing though it was: not only because the wretched beast's sufferings pained him, but also because when he was mounted, strangers did not notice his lameness and (as he imagined) stare at him. He was proud of his horsemanship, too, being of a lighter build and a better rider than Adrian; and the possession of a horse had enabled him to escape from the convoy's dust and to ride out on patrol courting the heroic death he had decreed for himself.

By the time they had reached the foothills of the Lulu range, in which Sekukuni would be forced to stand and fight, the horse-sickness had taken such toll of the great commando that half the burghers were forced to march on foot.

'Your Government will have to pay for this,' Groot Andries told Adrian sullenly.

'Why do you call it "my" Government? It's no more mine than yours,' Adrian answered irritably. The strained atmosphere of Headquarters was more than ever on his nerves.

'This means taxes,' Andries growled.

'All government means taxes. And all wars are expensive. But this one was necessary.'

'Four hundred wagons and two thousand men! How many men had Pretorius against Dingaan? If you'd only thought to give us a free hand with Sekukuni, we, in the Zoutspansberg . . .'

'You in the Zoutpansberg couldn't even hold your own against Makapan, who chased you out of Schoemansdal. You're just talking nonsense.'

'I'm only saying what all my neighbours are saying.'

'Then they're talking nonsense too. Was there ever such a people? The trouble with our folk has always been that they'd sooner quarrel with each other than fight their enemies.'

'Well, the Zoutpansberg men are all sick to death of this war of yours,' Andries said.

'So am I. And that's why I say "For God's sake let us finish it!" We can't go back now. The campaign is nearly over.'

It reached its climax, indeed, within a few days. In that tangle of hills and kloofs it had not been easy even to find Sekukuni's Great Place. Several scouting detachments, led astray by false guides, had been ambushed in the attempt and had only escaped with losses. But now the cumbrous force confronted the main

198

mass of the enemy. From the brow of the hill on which they were laagered they could see Sekukuni's kraal, a huge circle of beehive huts densely clustered at the base of a bold mountain ridge honeycombed with caves and craggy with schanzes. From the smoke that went up from it, they could see that the kraal was occupied; but the site of the decisive battle, they guessed, would not be in the kraal itself, but on the steep slopes beyond it where the scattered rocks gave cover to its defenders.

That same evening Burgers held a council of war to which the leaders of all the regional commandos were summoned. It was decided that next day, before daylight, a small body of mounted men, under Veld-Kornet Roos of Pretoria, should cast a wide circuit to northward, enveloping the enemy's rear and occupying the ridge behind him. At dawn, as soon as the mounted force had shown itself on the crest and engaged the enemy, the main body should cross the dongas that separated them from the kraal and deliver a frontal attack. The second part of this strategical plan was disliked, for the intervening slopes were too rough and the dongas too deep for horses to be used to advantage, and it was contrary to every tradition of Boer warfare to fight on foot; but Smit supported the President loyally, and at length, with reluctance, the scheme of attack was accepted.

'I only hope to God they won't change their minds,' Adrian said when the council was over. 'The mere fact that they think the plan is the President's makes them jib at it. If only we had one strong man here to whom they'd all listen.'

'A man like Paul Kruger?' Janse chaffed him.

'Yes, a man like Paul Kruger. Why not?'

Adrian had prevailed on the President to let him join the Pretoria commando.

'And if you'll find me a horse I'll go with you,' Janse said.

'This is no job for you,' Adrian told him.

Janse knew he was thinking of his lame leg, and flushed with anger.

'On horseback I'm just as good a man as you, Adrian, and a better shot.'

'You stay by your wagon. That is your place. You were not commandeered to fight. And why in God's name should anyone want to fight who doesn't have to?'

'Then why don't you stay with the President yourself?'

'You're arguing like a born fool. That's a different matter.

I'm going with Roos because I know it's important that one man at least from the Headquarters staff should be with him. The burghers are in an odd mood, and I don't much like it.'

Janse saw it was no use pressing him. In the middle of the night he limped round to the sleeping Zoutpansberg bivouac and unhaltered Groot Andries's mare, a big-boned chestnut. When the mounted commando assembled he joined it, knowing well that in the dark there was small chance of his being recognized.

He laughed to himself as they rode out into the moonless night. Here, at last, was the great adventure for which he had been waiting so long; the strong draught of danger, the cup of fearless sacrifice, which alone could purge his soul of its hidden misery. The thought of the peril that lay ahead of him was oddly stimulating. It filled him with a strange, reckless gaiety. He was exalted and fey.

When they were well clear of the camp he rode forward to Adrian's side.

'Good morning, brother,' he whispered.

Adrian turned on him furiously.

'You're an even bigger fool than I thought you,' he said. 'You've no right to be here. I order you to go back.'

'And be shot at sight by our outposts? No, no, I can't say I fancy that kind of death. It's too late. Now I'm here, you'd much better make the best of it.'

'Where did you get that big horse?'

'It's Andries's horse. I borrowed it.'

'Andries will thank you for that. It's salted. It's worth a hundred pounds.'

'If it's killed, I'll pay him.'

'What if you're killed, too?'

'In that case I shan't miss the money.'

Adrian only grunted.

'Who's that you're talking to, nephew?' the Veld-kornet said. 'He's not one of our men.'

'It's my brother Janse,' Adrian said. 'He's no right to be here. He's a fool. A damned fool.'

The Veld-kornet laughed. 'That's the kind of fool I like.'

They rode on through the dark. Low clouds, caught in the mountain-tops, quenched the glimmer of starlight. There was no sound save the occasional metallic clink of a rifle and the soft thudding on the earth of six hundred unshod hooves. Yet this silence, to Janse, had a strange, awful beauty of its own, in tune with his exalted mood. It was through such a silence, he thought, that men should ride to their death; if indeed death awaited them. For the first time since the blow that shattered his hopes had fallen on him he was aware of a sensation of tenderness – not merely for Adrian, whom he had always loved for his goodness and his simplicity, but for these shadowy men among whom he rode, and of whom he knew nothing.

Oddly enough, in this silent journey, he felt less lonely than usual. He was not to them the shy alien who had learnt to shrink back into himself at the faintest suspicion of scorn or pity, sensitive, unaccountable misfit limping through life with his incomprehensible dreams and his shortened leg, but a man like themselves, accepted without question as one of their brotherhood in the community of danger wherein, as in death all men are equal. Janse was strengthened – and softened too – by the moving sense of human comradeship-in-arms, this mutual dependence of body and spirit, which is the one thing of beauty, perhaps, that emerges from the brutality of war.

He felt this now, in the dark, as he rode silently at Adrian's side; he felt it even more strongly later on when they had reached their allotted position and the glow of dawn reddened the faces of the group of horsemen mustered behind the ridge. They were not, of themselves, an impressive collection. Most of those who had been chosen were solid men of middle age and experience, hard-featured, weathered, and heavily-bearded, and some of them, in their ruggedness, looked almost savage. Yet Janse's heart warmed when he saw them, for he knew it was from them, invisible in the night, that he had drawn the novel, inspiriting sense of companionship that had stirred him so deeply. These men were of his race who spoke his own tongue and now, together with him, were about to face death.

The detachment dismounted. They deployed, advanced to the crest, and stood for a moment silhouetted against the sky. Two shots crackled out from the schanzes below. Sekukuni's outposts had seen them. A bullet, aimed high, sang over Janse's head like an angry wasp. Another passed through his hat. Adrian pulled him down beside him.

'Hold your fire and keep low,' he said. Only shoot when you're sure of killing. When you see the whites of their eyes, as our forefathers said.'

The whole line held its fire, lying flat and taking cover. Far below, on the rock-scattered slope, Janse saw a confusion of black shapes running to and fro, pouring out of the gates of the kraal like peppercorns spilt from a broken cone of paper. Then he saw this confusion resolve itself into an orderly formation of a black central mass and two horns curved like the claws of a scorpion. The Kaffirs were hundreds of yards out of range, but puffs of black smoke and the following sound of shots showed that some of them were already wasting ammunition, though the guns of the nearer outposts now were silent. The central mass, though packed closely, was never still. It was like dark volcanic mud in a state of ebullition: it seethed, and bubbled, and now and then black figures leapt out of the midst like stones shot up from a crater. And then, all of a sudden, the half-fluid mass appeared to gather itself like a breaking wave and surged forward. Long after he saw the movement take place Janse heard the howl that accompanied it.

'That is good,' Adrian said. 'We have drawn them this way. They don't even think what's behind them. God has made the Kaffir's mind in that way. In a heated moment they can only think of one thing at once. They still follow the tactics of Chaka: while the centre charges, the horns will fold in on both sides. It's a pity they're coming up-hill. Though it checks the force of their charge, the fall of the land will correct their high aim. Until we have broken their front we must still keep low.'

The Kaffirs advanced up the slope at a trot. Sixty yards, and then forty. The temptation to fire was hard to resist. The wave swept up to the outposts and carried them along on its face like fragments of driftwood. As it came within range of the crest a ragged fire broke from it, and a hail of lead spattered the rocks behind which the commando was lying. One fragment, a red-hot ricochet, singed Janse's hat. He heard Adrian say: 'Now!' He had already chosen his target; a tall man who looked like the *induna* who had challenged their passage on the way to Brunner's Rest. He stood there, magnificently posed, with a heavy *roer* pressed to his shoulder. As he fired, Janse fired too. The *induna* leapt high; seemed to twist in the air and pitched forward on to his face.

'I have killed a man,' Janse thought, with a sudden sensation of awe. 'Yet if I hadn't, he might have killed me. This is what I wanted.'

There was no time for thinking. He was reloading his rifle

with the rest. As he aimed and fired again he heard a sharp cry. The burgher on his left had been hit, and rolled over groaning. The Kaffirs, too, were clumsily reloading their guns; but before they could aim, a third, shattering volley struck them. Gaps appeared in their closely-massed ranks. Their attention seemed to waver. Men were shouting, gesticulating wildly, pointing to the rear – and there, at the foot of the slope, Janse saw leaping tongues of red flame and black columns of smoke pouring into the sky. Sekukuni's Great Place was ablaze.

'Good work,' Adrian cried. 'That's Roos and the men from Pretoria. Keep it up . . . keep it up!'

The burghers were keeping it up. As the black mass stood hesitating between the call of the fired kraal behind and the invisible enemy in front, withering spatters of leaden hail continued to sweep them. Some moved forward, some backward; they wavered; they turned; they broke into a rabble and ran down the rock-scattered slope, leaving their dead and their wounded behind.

'Come along,' the Veld-kornet shouted. 'Horses, quickly – and follow them.'

Janse ran back and scrambled into the saddle. The burghers were laughing and shouting to one another. He saw Adrian leading the charge far ahead, but could not catch up with him, for Groot Andries' big bay was too heavy and clumsy-footed to move fast over broken ground. As he coaxed the nervous beast forward he felt a quick stab of pain in his leg and heard a hoarse cry. A wounded Kaffir, fallen among the rocks, had hurled an assegai at him as he passed. The blade ripped through his trouser leg and pricked the belly of the horse, which leapt in the air and all but unseated him. Janse slewed round, ready to fire from the saddle. He saw the Kaffir's face bloodless beneath his skin's pigment and streaming with sweat. He put his gun to his shoulder and aimed point-blank. But he could not fire. He wrenched the assegai out of his leg and rode on as fast as he could after Adrian, cursing himself for a fool. . . .

Down in the main laager things were not going so well. Veld-kornet Roos and his Pretoria commando of sixty had done what was asked of them. As soon as the mounted men were seen on the horizon they had crept over the dongas and set fire to the kraal. Now the turn of the main body had come. They had moved out reluctantly. The men on the crest were mounted:

why should they go on foot? It was unnatural to fight Kaffirs on foot. It was not the way of their fathers.

Veggeneraal Smit rallied them. If they did not advance, he said, Roos's small storming party would be isolated and enveloped. Even now, as they could see, the main body of Kaffirs, driven back from the crest, was retreating on the burning kraal.

A large number refused to go forward into the dongas. President Burgers moved to and fro among them, entreating them to follow him, but they held their ground sullenly. Who was he, a mere predikant – and a heretic at that – to teach farmers how they should fight? He abandoned the hopeless task in despair, and hurried forward with Struben to join the *Veggeneraal*.

Smit, too, was in trouble. He had induced a small force of no more than two hundred to follow him into the first of the transverse dongas. Here a desultory fire from the rocks on the farther side had met them. The Kaffirs were firing downhill, to better effect; half a dozen men had been lightly wounded and several more seriously. From the outskirts of the burning kraal they could hear sustained firing. By this time the broken *impi* had re-formed, and Roos and his sixty men were heavily engaged.

'We must go to their help,' Smit said. 'We have nothing but scattered outposts in front of us and we are two hundred. We can drive them back easily. Come along, then. Follow me!'

Only a handful followed him. Smit turned on the rest of them angrily:

'Are you frightened of a few Kaffirs, you men who fought at Blood River?'

'At Blood River we had our horses and the Zulus had no guns. Why should we be killed just to please the heretic? There are a thousand men in the laager. If they come and fight, we will fight, but we will not fight alone. Go back and tell them that, General.'

Smit raged and Burgers entreated; but nothing would move them. They lay scattered all over the donga, each man taking cover as best he could.

'We stay here till the others join us,' they said. 'We have made up our minds.'

'You had better go back to the laager, General,' Burgers said, 'and see what you can do.'

'If I go, your honour, they'll follow me. You had better go

yourself.' The poor man was almost distraught. 'This is a shameful thing . . . shameful.'

Burgers left the donga, followed by sulky looks. They watched his unmilitary figure, with his tawny beard, his pale, agonized face and his black frock-coat, picking his way through the scattered rocks. A shot rang out and he ducked. The men shouted with laughter.

'The State President is less of a coward than you,' General Smit said bitterly.

Burgers looked for his horse. It was gone. There was no time to search for it. He returned to the laager on foot. The huge triangle was already broken. Many drivers were already busy inspanning their oxen. In the middle of the camp groups of Boers surrounded half a dozen orators who stood upon wagon chests and harangued them. He thrust his way into the midst of these centres of revolt. As he mounted on one of the limbers of the Krupp guns, the small groups of dissidents dissolved and crowded round him, hostile and curious. He raised his hand for silence, but the crowd buzzed like an angry swarm. He shouted above the tumult, and at last they consented to listen. The man was an orator and had never spoken with a more passionate eloquence.

'Have you come all this way, from every corner of the Republic, to betray your comrades? Have you come for a second-rate tribe like the Bapedi to call you cowards – you, whose fathers scattered the hosts of Dingaan and Moselikatze? Cannot you see that the eyes of all Africa are on you today – not merely the eyes of the white folk who trust you – our Afrikander brethren in the Cape and the Free State, your wives and your children – but the eyes of the black men, too? What will Cetewayo say when he hears of this shameful thing? What will the English say of us?'

'Who cares what the damned English say?' a rough voice shouted.

'I care what the English say, burgher. Because I am an Afrikander and proud of my race and yours which has never known such a shame as this. And I care that God Almighty, who looks down on us now, should see that His people have lost the valour of righteousness.'

The crowd broke into murmurs. 'Who is this man to speak of God – this renegade predikant condemned by the Church he disgraced, this godless Sabbath-breaker?' The mass surged

205

towards Burgers threateningly. 'Away with the heretic – away with him! We will have none of him!'

A small group of miners from Lydenburg levelled their rifles and kept them at bay. Burgers raised his voice in a last, despairing effort.

'The Republic has chosen me as its leader,' he cried. 'I stand here by the people's authority. In the people's name I command you.'

The crowd burst out laughing: 'The people? Who are the people? We are the people. We have heard enough. You are not our leader. This war is not ours. It is time to trek homeward. *Huis toe! Huis toe!*'

The cry swelled to a deep-throated chorus as the angry crowd scattered.

'Stop .. stop!' Burgers cried. He leapt down from the limber and forced himself through them. 'If I am not the people's leader, then shoot me before you disgrace me!'

His words were drowned in the cry *'Huis toe! Huis toe!'* It spread through the camp, gathering volume. They were pulling the wagons out of line and turning the oxen's heads southward. The space where the crowd had been thickest was empty now. Dishevelled and hatless, Burgers stood in the midst of it. Von Schlickmann, the German gunner, rode up to him at a gallop and saluted.

'Your honour,' he said, 'Veld-kornet Roos needs help, and the men in the donga still refuse to move. The *Veggeneraal* must have reinforcements.'

'You had better find them, Schlickmann. I can do no more. The burghers are breaking camp. You see for yourself.'

'But this is a general mutiny! There is only one thing to do: what Bismarck would certainly have done. Let me turn the guns on them, President.'

Burger shook his head: 'I am no Bismarck, Schlickmann. I'm more like Napoleon the Third at Sedan. *Trahi . . . trahi!* These men say I have blood on my hands already. I want no more.'

Roos and his small detachment of Pretorians were now in a desperate fix: behind them the burning village; in front a numerous enemy, growing bolder, no sign of the main body moving up in support. Even the mounted men riding down from the crest had checked their descent. They, too, were bewildered, waiting for the general advance.

'We cannot stand here and be butchered,' Roos said, 'or be

driven back into the flames. Come along, then, and let them have it! God fights on our side. Remember Blood River!'

The ragged detachment moved forward by degrees, pouring volley after volley into the black mass in front of them. The horsemen above, encouraged by their advance, swept round right-handed and charged the Kaffirs' flank. It was a ticklish moment, yet it ended as all such encounters had ended before. Caught between two fires, Sekukuni's host wavered and broke and ran for the hills.

There was no question of any pursuit that day. Once freed from the threat of destruction, which, had Sekukuni known it, would have been so easy, the battered detachment's only desire was to return to the camp and find out the cause of the breakdown. When they reached it, they saw the laager already broken and the dust of departing wagons rising in the distance. Of all that great convoy which had set out from Pretoria only the German guns and the Lydenburg and Middelburg commandos – some five hundred frontiersmen, who knew what the Kaffir menace meant – remained, preserving some semblance of discipline.

Burgers, haggard, disconsolate and humiliated, held another council of war that evening. It was decided that what was left of the force, under Commandant Ferreira, should relieve the laager in which women and children were congregated at Kruger's Post, and establish a number of permanent forts to the north of Lydenburg: it was a plan of passive resistance – but what more could be done? As for President Burgers, he had finished with soldiering. His place, as he said, was now in Pretoria, where he would have to face a more bitter enemy than Sekukuni.

'I shall go back with the President to face the Volksraad,' Adrian said. 'But what about you, Janse? Have you had enough of war?'

Janse laughed: 'I think one honourable assegai wound is enough for me.'

'The bullet that went through your hat must have been pretty near, brother. You are evidently not meant to be killed.'

Janse himself was beginning to wonder. He was a very different person, he had to confess, from the embittered man who had ridden out in the dark that morning (could it be only that morning?) determined to find a quick solution for his misery in an heroic death. It was the imminence of death which

207

had shown him that life, after all, was worth living. The fey calmness of the predestinate victim, the willing sacrifice, had given place to a saner serenity. That bitter exaltation was gone. He had come, as it seemed, to himself – not to the brooding, suffering, fever-racked self which he knew, but to a new self, more courageous and clearer-eyed, still solitary, perhaps, but prepared to accept the buffets of fate as they came.

'Let us make a plan,' Adrian was saying. 'You had better come back with me to Pretoria, and settle down to rest at Wonderfontein for a while. You will lose the remains of your fever there, and I know how much mamma has missed you.'

Janse winced in spite of himself. The old wound was still tender. This sudden pain warned him that he was not, perhaps, quite so strong as he had imagined. The prospect of revisiting Witfontein and seeing Piet and Lavinia together was the acid test of his newly-won courage. It would be tempting the Providence that had healed him to face it.

'Not yet ... No, not yet,' he said. Adrian stared at him, mystified. 'You see,' Janse continued hurriedly, 'I have business in Lydenburg. My money's there in the bank, and I expect a letter from Meninsky.'

'Still dreaming of gold? I should have thought the fever had cured you of that.'

'I think I shall buy some spans of good oxen and go transport-riding between Lydenburg and the coast.'

'In search of more fever?'

'Ah, well one gets used to that. This time I shall have quinine and know better how to deal with it. But it's an odd thing, you know, Adrian: when once you've lived in the Low Country, your mind always goes back to it. There's something mysterious and subtle about it, the spirit of it – I can't say what it is – that pulls at you all the time; and when once it has taken hold of a man I doubt if he can ever be happy far away from it.'

'Well, well. . . . There's no accounting for tastes,' Adrian said. 'Old Andries has odd ones too, with his "We in the Zoutpansberg. . . ." As for me, I belong to the High Veld.'

At the bank in Lydenburg Janse found a long letter from Meninsky awaiting him.

Dear old pal [it ran],

Well, here I am back in the ruddy red dust and not doing so bad, thank you kindly. Kimberley's grown no end. Hardly knew my way about it. The same old gang of bright boys from Whitechapel still making hay while the sun shines and guzzling fizz. Diamonds don't look like giving out. The diggings go deeper and deeper. But there's a lot of leakage and buying stones on the sly – as yours truly knows, having done a bit on his own – and until they shut up the Kaffirs inside barbed wire I don't see what's to stop it. Apart from that, all going champion. I bought the soda-water plant that young Rhodes had and am doing a nice side-line in the retail rag business: the first thing the mine-native sets his heart on being a pair of trousers, though God knows why. If you can spare me two hundred, Janse, I'll double it for you in two months. Think it over, mate, and send to me care of James Ferguson, Kimberley. When I've touched a thousand I reckon I shall get a licence, set up as a diamond broker, and grow moustaches like Barny. I've got a book on diamonds by a cove named Streeter, but I reckon you learn more about them by seeing and handling them. And, mind you, I'm still dead sure there's money in gold. Everyone knows what a diamond is, it's just plain carbon, and when the scientific blokes get on to it they'll soon be turning diamonds out by the gross. But you can't manufacture gold, and, as you and me know, it's not too damn easy to find it.

Talking of which, a rum thing happened to me, mate, on the way down here not far from Lydenburg. Where we outspanned one night there was a dirty old Kaffir sitting alone on the Veld. One of them witch-doctors he was, with a doll-oss, or whatever they call it: bones out of a snake and a sheep's foot, a couple of shells and two or three bits of horn. The drivers told the old boy to clear – and no wonder, he stank like a badger! – but, as you know, I always like to have a wag with a nigger: you never know what you may pick up. I asked him, joking-like, if the doll-oss knew who I was. He said, 'Yes, I'd come from Sekukuni's country and I'd been digging gold.' Not so bad for a start. Then I said, did the doll-oss know of any gold hereabouts, and the old chap got quite excited. He said, 'No, no, inkoos, it is not here, it is not here. It is pambele – pambele (which means, I reckon, a hell of a way from here). It is high up over the white rand where they go down on the road to Natal. There are the yellow cows,' he says, 'and the yellow milk.' Damn funny, ain't it? It sounded as if he meant the Witwatersrand, where, as you and me

209

know, there isn't as much as a ruddy pennyweight of gold, or anything else worth looking at. Still, you know, I can't get it out of my mind. You see the old lad was dead right about my having come down from Sekukuni's country. And how the hell did he know that? Well, that's all tonight. I often wish we was back at Brunner's Rest, and I often think of you and poor old Bosmann ... especially when I've got fever ... for which I touch wood!

Janse went to the bank and sent Meninsky two hundred pounds. With the remaining fifty he bought new spans of oxen and set off for Delagoa. He had never been farther east than Pretorius Kop, and was longing for the smell of the Low Country. He wanted, too, to cross the Lebombo, that faint line of blue hills over which, from the summer camp on the Berg, his eyes had so often brooded. And he wanted to see the sea.

CHAPTER FOUR

(1)

LISBET was waiting anxiously for Adrian's return; but it was more than six weeks before he came home. During the following months he was rarely seen at Wonderfontein. Even when the Raad was not sitting he felt it his duty to stay in Pretoria and stand by the President.

The first session showed the hostility which Burgers and his party – or the shrinking remnant of it – must be prepared to face. Long before his return from Lydenburg the deserters from the front had brought back their own explanations and excuses for the fiasco. The President, and nobody else, was to blame, as might have been guessed. To begin with, the campaign had been planned on a far too ambitious scale, in keeping with Burgers' notoriously extravagant nature. No man with the faintest glimmer of military sense would have dreamt of dragging a convoy of four hundred wagons and two thousand men into that tangle of mountains. In any case it had been unnecessary to tear so many burghers away from their farms and families – as was proved by the fact that a mere fraction of the force, the loyal Middelburg and Lydenburg commandos, had sufficed to burn Sekukuni's Great Place and drive him northwards. Under a more experienced leader, Paul Kruger for instance, two hundred men, in six weeks, would have settled the Bepedis' hash!

Again, the very cumbrousness of that slow-moving wagon-convoy had defeated its purpose. It had been against the Boer tradition of speed and mobility in native warfare; its slow movement had been the direct cause of the grievous losses from horse-sickness. In this policy, as in most others, it was clear that the President had been advised by the devil. He might say he had quelled Sekukuni, but what of the cost, in time, in money, in horseflesh? The Republic would now have a pretty bill to face on the score of compensation alone. And where could that money be found?

Burgers had his answer. New taxes. An emergency war-tax, ranging from five to ten pounds, on every farm.

The Raad listened to the proposal in silence. For once, Burgers lost his nerve, which the unfamiliar strain and anxieties of the campaign had already weakened.

'If you refuse to pass this decree,' he stormed at them, 'the Republic will go bankrupt – it will become a laughing-stock and a by-word among civilized nations. It is time that the members of this Volksraad realized their responsibilities and stood up to them like men instead of sulking like children. During my term of office I have never yet touched a penny of the President's salary. I have advanced to the Treasury the whole of my private fortune. Twenty-two thousand pounds I have given out of my own pocket. Twenty-two thousand pounds, honourable gentlemen! And yet now you object to each landowner having to pay a maximum of ten!'

'Twenty-two thousand pounds is a great fortune,' an old member agreed. 'The State President is lucky to have so much money to lend. But I will not vote for this war-tax. I am an old man, your honour; but so large a call as this has never been made in my memory.'

'The State has never before needed to make so large a call.'

'But for what has been wasted on this big commando, which has done so little, it would not need to now.'

'It is the State's duty, honourable member, to protect its citizens from the inroads of savages.'

'Isn't it rather,' another member suggested slyly, 'the State President's personal desire to protect his friends the foreigners at the Lydenburg gold-fields?'

'The Lydenburg men at least were not cowards. They did not run home like the rest of you,' Burgers said hotly.

Yet, before the session ended, the Raad had passed the new war-tax. A little too submissively, Adrian thought, though Burgers himself was triumphant. Was it, Adrian asked himself, because they knew well that it would never be collected, and that the fact of its imposition was only another nail driven home in the State President's coffin in time for the Presidential election next year? He hardly knew what to make of it. Though his affectionate loyalty to Burgers never wavered, though he was still awed by the President's intellect and fascinated by his fiery imagination, he was beginning to wonder whether, in certain political conditions, expediency was not of more importance than rightness.

He confessed as much to the family at Wonderfontein when, at the end of the session, he had hurried away from Pretoria to attend the funeral of his parents' old friend, Mr. Blair, who had died in his sleep at the age of seventy-seven. He talked the whole matter over with his father and Piet, whose judgment, as that of a man of the world, he was beginning to respect.

'Ten pounds is not easy for many of us to come by in these days,' John Grafton said: 'but I should not mind paying it if I thought we had value for our money. That is what I doubt, Adrian. Was this war really necessary – or did the State President think it would pull the people together and make him more popular?'

'If he did, the poor man was sadly mistaken. But no, that's not Burgers' way. We could not allow Sekukuni to overrun the whole Lydenburg district, father. It would make Cetewayo think he could do the same; and then there would be no end to our troubles. If you lived on the frontier you would realize that.'

'The truth of the matter is, Adrian,' Piet declared, 'that the Republic's got itself into a mess and Burgers can't pull it out of it. If I ran my farm on such unbusiness-like lines I should be bankrupt within a couple of years – and deserve to be bankrupt. Your friend's an intelligent man and is doing what he can. But what can any man do almost single-handed – for that's what it comes to – against the sheer weight of ignorance and indolence and prejudice that you find in nine out of every ten back-veld farmers? The bulk of this country's still trying to live in the seventeenth century, and this is the nineteenth. Burgers is right; he's right all the time and every time. The poor fellow happens to have been born two hundred years too soon, and, with all his virtues, he just isn't strong enough for the job he's tackled. He's the right man in the wrong place. He must know that himself. And because he's impatient (as God knows he's every right to be!) he's getting on people's nerves. The position is perfectly simple and obvious.'

'But the solution is neither simple nor obvious,' Adrian said. 'The President is right. We're all agreed on that. Is he right for us? That is quite a different matter. Am I serving my folk and my country when I support a man – good man though he be – whom most of the people, however unreasonably, dislike and distrust? Suppose Burgers goes on fighting for what he believes in? We know – I begin to be sure of this now – that he can never

213

win with Kruger and the predikants against him. If he comes near to winning, what will be the result? By the time we have reached that point, if we ever reach it, our country will have been rent in twain, like the veil of the temple, from top to bottom. And if once we are utterly divided, it seems to me, we shall be at the mercy of those who covet our land. The English will step in and annex it, as they annexed the diamond-fields.'

'And a damned good thing if they did!' Piet said. 'Then, at least we should have some semblance of order and firm government, and not be shivering in our shoes because of Sekukuni and Cetewayo. The day the English flag goes up in Pretoria . . .'

'Which God forbid!' Adrian muttered . . .

'. . . your land, I say, will be worth five times what it is today. I'm not talking wildly. Look at the difference it's made to Kimberley already. Of course, you don't know – nor do you, father. You've neither of you ever been there, nor yet to Capetown for that matter. You like living in the seventeenth century. And I don't. That's the principal difference between us.'

'That is foolish talk, Piet, and you know it,' John Grafton said. 'Your father-in-law's converted you. Since you married Lavinia you have become more English than the English themselves. That's what happens to converts. You've never lived under the English law. I have, and know more about it. In the Transvaal, at least, we are free.'

'Yes, free to hang ourselves. And the sooner we get it over, the better.'

Adrian shook his head.

'Burgers would certainly never submit to annexation. If it comes to that we shall all of us have to fight. And who knows? – perhaps such a war may be the only thing that can heal our dissensions and draw the people together.'

'Fight? Fight against England?' Piet scoffed at such an idea. 'Why, you talk like a child, Adrian! We, a handful of farmers who can't even beat Sekukuni, against a great Empire like that?'

'The Americans fought the English and won their liberty.'

'I'm glad you have taken to reading history, Adrian; but there are other examples. Napoleon, for instance.'

'Other nations in Europe, the Dutch or the Germans, might help us.'

'In that case I, too, should be fighting,' Piet said, 'but not on your side.'

Adrian returned to Pretoria deeply troubled in mind. From the moment he reached it he felt that the atmosphere of the capital had changed. In the past, the inhabitants of Pretoria, who were mainly officials and traders, had not taken the deliberations of the Volksraad very seriously. In its twisty intrigues, its display of farce or comedy, it had generally been regarded as a mild substitute for a permanent theatre with a limited repertory. By now it was not only among the President's political opponents that discontent with his regime was growing. The contractors and merchants who had equipped the commando against Sekukuni were anxious about their money. The railway-tax and war-tax were not coming in. The Republican paper currency was worth as little as its 'goodfors', pound 'blue-back' notes were fetching a shilling apiece. The officials – even the President's Hollanders – were short of their salaries. Cetewayo – encouraged, as people said, by the English in Natal and the negrophile bishop, Colenso – was arrogantly massing his warriors on the eastern border. The railway, from which so much had been hoped, showed no signs of advancing inland from Delagoa. The borrowed money which had been poured into it had all been wasted. On the surface, indeed, the country appeared to be calm, but this calm was not healthy: it sprang partly from pessimism and political apathy and partly from a vague presentiment that, with things as they were, something was 'bound to happen' before long.

The old talk about 'Federation' began to crop up again. Not only the foreign traders, but staunch burghers too, had been heard to murmur the forbidden word 'Annexation'. After all, people said, the rule of the British, distasteful as it might be, would be better than no rule at all. Burgers' Government, supine and divided as it was, was incapable of ruling. Would Kruger or Joubert be any better? they asked. The answer was doubtful. The state was too rotten and rickety now, its resources were too feeble, for any power from within to give it stability and save it. As it was, disintegrating and bankrupt, it seemed hardly worth saving.

Depressed by this gloomy fatalism, Adrian had expected to draw courage and comfort or at least stimulation from Burgers; but the President was no longer the man he had known. The strain of continual struggle and frustration had begun to tell on him. Though at times he showed flashes of the old fire, the old gay confidence, it was clear that his mind was shadowed by dreary foreboding. He knew he was a beaten man, and an ill man, too. He no longer spoke of the future. When he talked with Adrian it was always the empty Treasury (two hundred and fifteen thousand pounds owing and nothing with which to meet it!) or of the rumours of native unrest in Zululand.

'We can't face our creditors,' he said, 'and we can't – or won't – fight our enemies. The Volksraad listens and watches, but the members won't raise a finger to help the Republic or support its authority. Was there ever in history such a people as this? I would rather be a policeman under a strong Government than the President of such a state! We are unable – or at least unwilling – to help ourselves. Very well. In that case, if we are to survive, somebody else must save us. Isn't that clear?'

'Do you mean the English?' Adrian asked.

'My dear fellow,' the President answered irritably. 'When a man's on his death-bed he doesn't worry his head about the colour of his medicine. Unless he's a fool he swallows it.'

So, in Pretoria, the Volksraad went on sitting and squabbling over trifles, and in every pulpit throughout the land the predikants quoted Leviticus and denounced their enemy, the heretical President; and then, one day, on the eve of Christmas, a horse-wagon, escorted by twenty-five riders in the uniform of the Natal police, drove up to the outskirts of Pretoria, and was hauled through the streets in triumph to the Church Square. Adrian, standing on the stoep of the Raadsaal, heard the sound of distant cheering; he saw the wagon go by in a cloud of dust, and a tall, smiling man on the driving-seat, who acknowledged the cheers.

That evening the streets of Pretoria buzzed with excited talk. The newcomer was Shepstone, Theophilus Shepstone: a name to conjure with! He had come – and none too soon! – to 'put everything right', as the Special Commissioner of the Crown Colony of Natal, to talk about Federation – just to talk about it in a friendly way, nothing more, be it understood. Now this, people said, was the man for whom they'd been looking: no *verdomde Engelsman*, but a born Afrikander, the son of a

216

missionary, who understood the Dutch point of view as well as the English and could speak the *taal* fluently: what was more, the one man in all Africa whom Cetewayo respected and feared and called 'my father Sompseu'.

Late at night, Shepstone made a formal call on the President. An anxious crowd waited outside in the street and escorted him back to the outspan. Many questions were shouted at him. He answered them all with a smiling good humour and salty phrases that made the crowd laugh. He had come to Pretoria to help, he said, not to interfere; he had been commissioned to tender advice, for what it was worth, and not to make threats. Next day, to make his position clear, and with Burgers' approval, he issued a statement in Dutch and English:

> '*Recent events in this country* [it ran] *have shown to all thinking men the absolute necessity for closer union and more oneness of purpose among the Christian Governments of the Southern portion of this continent; the best interests of the natives no less than the peace and prosperity of the white races imperatively demand it, and I rely upon you and your Government to co-operate with me in endeavouring to achieve the great and glorious end of inscribing on a general South African banner the appropiriate motto* Eendracht maakt macht *or Union makes Strength.*'

Federation! The blessed word had been openly spoken at last!

That was all for the moment, and, for Pretoria, where officials and foreigners predominated, enough. Hopes – and credit – began to rise. There was nothing spectacular or arrogant about Mijnheer Slypsteen (or Whetstone), as the Boers called him. From the moment of his ceremonious arrival the escort of armed police had tactfully retired into the background. He was no more than a friendly visitor – endowed, indeed, with the prestige of his exalted position, yet essentially a quiet, unassuming man, only anxious to 'help' (as he said) and to 'talk things over'.

He was ready to 'talk things over' with ordinary citizens no less than with members of the Government or of the Volksraad. Burgers driving into market with produce, minor officials, storekeepers, all were welcome to take a seat in his tent on the outspan and smoke their pipes and sip his excellent sherry. He was particularly fond of children and 'talked things over' with

217

them too, sending them home with expensive presents – a concertina, a locket, perhaps a bracelet. He was 'a dear old man', just like 'one of ourselves'. In the three months during which he remained in the Church Square outspan, several newly-born children were actually christened 'Theophilus' or 'Theophilia'. *Most excellent Theophilus*: a good, Biblical name! He was a rich old man (though not really so old) as well as kindly. It appeared that he had actually helped a couple of indigent backveld farmers to pay their war-tax!

Apart from these social and charitable diversions 'Mr.' Shepstone contrived to get in a good many hours of hard talking with President Burgers and other members of the Raad. Burgers was inclined to be wary at first. Whatever was going to happen (and who could say what?), it would suit the book of his enemies to saddle him with the full responsibility. He wisely refused to consult with Shepstone on matters of state except in the presence of Kruger and Joubert. At the appointed hour Kruger duly arrived, but Joubert excused himself, and after a few moments, in which he did not speak a word, Kruger remembered a previous engagement and left the conference.

'You see what these fellows are after,' the President complained to Adrian. 'It's the old story all over again. They're waiting to see how the wind blows. If it blows against me, they'll wash their hands of me: if it's with me, they'll come in at the last and take all the credit. Paul Kruger's too slim to run the risk of having anything he has said recorded in black and white. But that doesn't mean that he isn't consulting with Shepstone. I still have some friends – or he, at least, has some enemies – who keep me posted on the old devil's movements. He went round in the dark last night to Shepstone's tent and stayed talking with him for two hours. Joubert's talked with him too.'

'What does Shepstone want?' Adrian asked.

'You know what he wants. You've seen his proclamation. He agrees with me that the time has come for some scheme of Federation.'

'He agrees with your honour?'

'You know it has got to come, nephew.'

'And what next?'

Burgers smiled and shook his head.

'If your honour will not answer me,' Adrian said, 'I must tell you. We are poor, and our brothers in the Free State are poor. Natal and the Cape are rich and have the power of England

218

behind them. In any such partnership it is riches and power that count. It will not be long before Natal and the Colony swallow us. We shall lose the independence for which our fathers fought. I have gone with you many years now, State-President, but I fear I can go no farther.'

'Et tu, Brute?' Burgers said sadly. .... 'Well, well, you have told me this to my face, which is more than the others do.' He held out his hand. 'I am grateful for what you have done for me. If we must part, we part friends.'

Adrian left him, deeply moved, carrying with him a memory of that fine, agonized face which would always remain. There had been tears, he thought, in the President's eyes. There were certainly tears in his own.

The negotiations and consultations, secret and open, dragged on. Shepstone was fighting what his friend Cetewayo would have called 'the fight of sit down', listening to Burgers, listening to Joubert and Kruger, listening to anyone who would talk to him – and saying remarkably little. Two months went by. Still the Special Commissioner sat in his tent. Folk visited him in hundreds and talked to him. He was sympathetic to everyone – to the foreign traders anxious for annexation to save them from bankruptcy; to the back-veld farmers whom the predikants had assured that their country was being betrayed; to the frontiersmen, who had seen Cetewayo massing his *impis* and feared an attack; to the Lydenburg miners, who complained that violence and anarchy were wrecking the gold-fields. Yet, though they all told their tales, not one of these visitors was able to gather, from Shepstone's impassive face, the least hint of what he thought or was authorized to suggest or intended to do.

Out of this perplexity and uncertainty and delay, crops of whispered rumours hatched out like flies under the summer sun. Shepstone was keeping the Volksraad quiet, the annexationists said, while British troops were massing on the Vaal River and waiting the signal to march in. Shepstone's guile was dividing the Volksraad (as though it could be more completely divided than it was already!) and trying to drive the two parties into a civil war that would give the British an excuse for intervention. Shepstone had bribed the President to hand over the country to him, gagged and bound. Shepstone was in league (and communication) with Cetewayo: if his sinister plans miscarried he would let loose the Zulus. Shepstone was the devil incarnate –

and an angel in disguise. Whatever the end of the situation might be – Federation, Annexation, a Civil or Native War – anything would be better than this intolerable suspense.

The Volksraad continued to sit and to wrangle over domestic trifles. The fate of the country did not appear to worry them. They discussed tax-exemptions, distribution of native lands, new ways of raising money, a new constitution. The men who crept round to talk with Shepstone at night denounced his continued presence in Pretoria as a breach of the Republic's sovereignty – as indeed it was. Tempers were growing ragged – and Burgers' temper, excusably, grew more ragged than most. They rose to a climax of fury when a member of the Executive, Jorissen – a mere Hollander – challenged the rights of three members who had not paid their war-tax to vote, and charged them with high treason. When Burgers supported Jorissen, the storm broke.

'You talk of high treason, Mr. State-President – you who have sold your birthright – *our* birthright – for a mess of pottage!'

Adrian watched the lamentable scene from his seat on the President's right. He saw Burgers rise to his feet; his body was trembling, his eyes sparkled, his face was flushed, the whole man was on fire; all the passion of suppressed resentment, prolonged frustration, flowed at last from his lips in a torrent of bitter words.

'It is you,' he cried, 'you members of the Raad and the farmers who have lost the country, who have sold your independence for a *soopje*. You have ill-treated the natives, you have shot them down, you have sold them into slavery. And now you have to pay the penalty. To the uttermost farthing.

'The State Attorney, Mr. Jorissen, has said that members who have not paid their taxes are not competent to vote in this assembly. You say, in reply, that this or that man must be released from taxes because the Kaffirs have driven him off his lands and occupied them.'

('That is right . . . that is just!')

'It is right, you say. By this, then, you proclaim to the world that the strongest man is master here, that the right of the strongest prevails?'

('That is not true.')

'Mr Marais says it is not true. Then it is not true what the honourable member, Mr. Breytenbach, has told us about the

220

state of the Lydenburg district; then it is not true either what another member has said about the farms of the Zoutpansberg? Neither is it true, then, what I saw with my own eyes at Lydenburg, where the burghers have been driven off their farms by the Kaffirs, and where Johannes was actually ploughing the land of a burgher? These are facts. They show that the strongest man is master here. That is the state of anarchy into which we have fallen. I challenge any honourable member to deny it.'

They did not deny it.

'Now I tell you,' Burgers went on, 'that we should not delude ourselves by entertaining the hope that matters will mend by and by. It would only be self-deceit. I tell you openly matters are as bad as they ever can be: they cannot be worse. These are bitter truths, and members may turn their backs on me; but then I shall have the consolation of having done my duty. The question that is troubling many men's minds at this moment because of the visit of the Special Commissioner, is that of our relations with our English neighbours . . .'

('What have the English to do with this?')

'I will tell you: just as much as we have to do with our Kaffir neighbours. As little as we can allow barbarities among the Kaffirs on our borders, so little can the English allow that in a state on their borders anarchy and rebellion can prevail. Have you heard, do you know what has recently happened to Turkey? Because no civilized government was carried on there, the Great Powers intervened and said: Thus far and no farther! And if this is done to an Empire, will a little Republic like ours be excused when it misbehaves?'

('Why talk of the English? It is the English, and only the English, who have ruined us. Like strong bulls of Bashan they encompass us, as a ravening and a roaring lion. Will not other Powers succour us if we complain to them, seeking justice?')

'Yes, justice is still to be found, thank God, for the most insignificant; but, honourable members, it is precisely justice that will convict us. If we want justice we must be in a position to ask it with unsullied hands. I ask you: Whence has arisen this urgency to make appeal for interference from elsewhere? Has that appeal been made only by enemies of the state? Oh, no gentlemen; it has arisen from real grievances. Our people have degenerated, I say, from their former position, they have become demoralized; they are not what they ought to be. And the result?' He paused; then spoke slowly: 'Today a bill for eleven hundred pounds was laid before me for signature. I would sooner have cut off my right hand than sign that paper, for I have not the slightest ground to expect that when the bill comes due there will be a penny to pay it with. That is what we have come to!

'And shall I tell you, gentlemen,' he went on, 'the principal thing that has brought you to your present position, the one thing to which you will not give attention?'

('We have no need to be told. We know. It is you who have borrowed money at interest and spent it like water.')

Burgers waved the accusation aside: 'No, no, gentlemen. It is not this or that thing which has impeded your way. You, yourselves, have stopped the way; and if you ask me what prevents this people from remaining independent, I answer you that the Republic itself is the obstruction, owing to the inherent weakness and incapacity of its people. And whence this weakness? Is it because we are deformed, because we are worse than other people? Is it because we are too few or too insignificant to occupy this country? Those arguments do not weigh with me. They are not true; I do not consider them of any importance. Our people, I say, are as good as any other people; but I tell you again, they are completely demoralized; they have lost faith in God, reliance upon themselves, and trust in each other.'

('The State-President is not the man to speak of faith in God. As for trust – we have trusted you too much and too long.')

'Listen gentlemen. . . . The Great Powers, with all their greatness, all their thousands of soldiers, would fall as quickly as this state has fallen – and even more quickly – if their citizens were to do what the burghers of this state have done. If the citizens of England had behaved towards the Crown as the burghers of this state have behaved towards me, their President, and my Government, England would never have stood as long as she has – not even as long as this state has stood. Remember: we owe obligations to other countries. Those countries know that the fire which has nearly consumed this state will, if felt by them, very soon consume them also. In several of the cities of Holland there are people who have subscribed for a single debenture because they thought that men of their own blood were living in Africa. What is the reward of their faith in us? The interest, up to July last, has not been paid. In January of this year two thousand and fifty pounds is due for interest, and there is not a penny to meet it.'

('Yes, because we are being strangled – because we are cut off. The time for talking is past. Let us break our way through! *Vat nou jou roer!* Take up your gun for it! That is our way. *Dit is die gewoonte van die Boer!*')

Burgers flung wide his arms in despair.

'To take up arms and fight as you say is nonsense. To draw the sword would be to draw the sword against God, for it is God's judgment that the state is in the condition it is today, and it is your duty to inquire whether you should immerse in blood the thousands of innocent inhabitants of this country – and, if so, what for? For an idea. For something you have in your heads but not in your hearts. For an independence, as you call it, which is not prized. Let us make the best of the situation, gentlemen, and get the best terms we can. Let us come to an arrangement with the British Government in a bold and manly manner. Let us agree to join hands with those of our brethren in the South! And then . . . and then from the Cape to the Zambezi there will be one great people.'

He paused once again. His eyes searched the faces of those who had listened in sullen silence. They rested for a moment, affectionately, pleadingly, on Adrian Grafton. Adrian bowed his head; he refused to meet those eyes. In spite of himself he had been deeply moved, but he dare not let himself weaken. 'The man is growing hysterical now,' he thought. 'He's broken. He's lost his judgment.'

'Yes, there is something grand in that,' Burgers said in a rapt, low voice; 'something grander even than your idea of your own Republic; something that ministers even more to your national feeling. And will this be so miserable, after all?' His voice rose again, strong and challenging: 'Yes, this will be miserable for those who refuse to be under the law, for the rebel and revolutionary? But it will be welfare and prosperity for all men of goodwill, for men who believe, as I do, as most of you do, in law and order.' He spoke in a more formal tone. 'It is now my intention, gentlemen, to submit to this Raad a new measure, to be called the "Permissive Act", embodying proposals for a scheme of Federation embracing all the independent states of South Africa.'

The Volksraad broke up in confusion. By that evening the details of Burgers' speech were being discussed on the stoeps and in every street in Pretoria. The traders were full of excited hopes: they were saved; Federation was coming. They crowded round Shepstone's tent and cheered him as the author of their salvation: Shepstone smiled and waved his hand to them, but said nothing. They started a huge petition in favour of Burgers' 'Permissive Act', sent it out to the back veld in search of signatures, and succeeded so well that within a few weeks they were able to boast that they had accumulated three thousand from among the Republic's eight thousand electors.

Though he could hardly believe it, it seemed to Adrian as though the tide had turned with a vengeance. He was half in a mind to ride home to Wonderfontein and leave the distracted Raad to die, without watching its death-pangs; but the hope that, at the last moment, some new leadership which he could accept might emerge from its confusion and apathy, kept him still in Pretoria.

The next session was even more chaotic than the last. Burgers brought in his Permissive Act. It was firmly rejected. The Raad members would not even grant it the favour of a long debate. And Burgers, by all appearances, was pleased with the result! The whole situation seemed farcical and inexplicable. Encouraged, paradoxically, by his defeat, the President went on to propose a new constitution which granted to his office new rights: a seven years' term; the power to make all appointments, to draw up all laws, to veto the Raad's decisions, to summon or dismiss it at will. Then the Volksraad woke up. For the first time in Burgers' presidency Kruger showed his strong hand. If the new constitution was passed, he said, the state would become a dictatorship, not a Republic. Burgers was censured – and yet the new measure was passed to a Committee; and the Committee reported in its favour! Outside the Raadsaal an angry crowd of three hundred armed Boers made a demonstration against the rejected Permissive Act. Confusion worse confounded!

'It's not only the President who's losing his senses,' Adrian thought. 'The whole Volksraad's going stark mad.'

He determined to go and interview Shepstone for himself. The Commissioner received him, smiling as usual, and addressed him in Dutch. Adrian answered in English. 'That is my natural language,' he said.

Shepstone bowed and encouraged him to speak. He spoke for an hour while the Commissioner listened impassively.

'We want to know where we are,' Adrian pleaded at last. 'We are fed on nothing but rumours and don't know what anyone in authority believes or what to believe ourselves. We're deafened by a continual roar of conflicting talk. The shadow of Annexation looms over us and darkens every mind. Tell me frankly, then, can nothing be done to avert it?'

Shepstone spoke, without raising his eyes:

'You are half English in blood,' he said, 'and more than half English in temperament I will be frank with you, Mr. Grafton. It is too late . . . too late.'

'The people will never accept it, sir.'

'They will have no alternative. Even your leaders – the President, Kruger, Piet Joubert – don't know their own minds. They blow hot and cold. I can tell you, in confidence, what is going to happen. Tomorrow I shall go to the Volksraad and proclaim that the Transvaal – the South African Republic – has been annexed to the British Crown. You and others will protest. Paul Kruger and Joubert will protest. The President himself will protest, to keep noisy people quiet, although, between you and me, he fully agrees to the terms of the Annexation, which are just and generous. After that you will have no more cause to complain of uncertainty. From the beginning, twelve years ago, this end has been inevitable.'

'And if we take up arms, Commissioner?'

'If you don't submit, my friend, I'm afraid you will have to take up arms in any case – but not against England. I have dispatches today from Utrecht and Wakkerstrom. Cetewayo is up, and the Zulus will overrun you.'

'You encourage the Zulus to attack us?'

'You do me an injustice, Mr. Grafton,' Shepstone answered reprovingly. 'I think I may even say that your question calls for an apology. You should not forget I am an Afrikander, like yourself, to whom the idea of encouraging native aggression against any white man is abhorrent. Please get this quite clear: I have not encouraged Cetewayo. But I can restrain him from attacking British territory. That is what I am proposing to do as soon as the country is annexed – the day after tomorrow.'

'I see. You have got the better of the President and the Executive Council by threats.'

'Wouldn't it be fairer to say that the President and the Executive have acknowledged the force of reason? If a man feels incapable of defending himself it is wise to make powerful friends. If he is bankrupt . . .'

'I thank you, sir,' Adrian said. 'I have heard enough.'

'And after the event, you know,' Shepstone went on calmly, 'one can always protest . . . one can protest till one's blue in the face, and so save one's bacon.'

Four days later, on April the twelfth, eighteen hundred and seventy-seven, the Proclamation of Annexation was read, amid cheering crowds, at Pretoria, while the *Vierkleur* was hauled down and the Queen's flag hoisted. No violence was used; not a drop of blood was shed. President Burgers left for the Cape, broken-hearted and bankrupt. Paul Kruger took office under the new administration – with an increase of salary. Adrian Grafton rode out of Pretoria and swore he had finished with politics. He took with him, folded in his saddle-bag, the *Vierkleur* flag – green, white, red and blue – of Burgers' design, which had flown over the Headquarters' tent during the campaign against Sekukuni.

(3)

Adrian reached Wonderfontein late that evening in a mood of dejection. The house, in contrast, appeared to be more brilliantly lighted than usual; wide beams of light, issuing from the windows on either side of the stoep, illuminated the glossy leaves of his mother's orange-trees, their golden orbs of fruit and their luminous waxen blossom which, at this season of the year, distilled a nocturnal perfume that, whenever he smelt it, had power to touch him profoundly. It was the perfume of youth; and tonight he felt very old – too old, indeed, too depressed and too irritable to risk an encounter with strangers.

To make sure of avoiding this he approached the house quietly and, having mounted the stoep, peered in at the window. Only his parents and Piet were there; the unusually brilliant light proceeded from a paraffin-lamp, for Wonderfontein a great novelty, which his brother had insisted on buying during his last visit to Kimberley to ease the strain of mere candlelight on Lisbet's ageing eyes. Piet, as usual, appeared to be on top of

226

himself, a picture of prosperity and easy self-confidence. Adrian noticed that he had adopted his father-in-law's mode of dress: a full-skirted riding-coat, cord breeches and highly-polished leggings. He heard him explaining the mechanism and expatiating on the virtues of the new lamp, and making his gift the text for a dissertation on the superiority of everything English over everything Dutch. When Adrian stalked into the house, Piet gave him a casual nod, then went on talking. Adrian stood and watched him, waiting for him to finish, and hating him in his heart for every word he said

'So now you'll be able to sew after dark, mamma, without blinding yourself, and dad will be able to read.'

'Are you really certain it's safe, Piet?' Lisbet said timidly. 'I'm sure I shall never dare to light such a thing myself for fear of its exploding.'

Piet laughed: 'Of course it won't explode. How old-fashioned you are! It's the latest and best I could buy, just imported from England.'

'And the oil. ... When this is finished, how shall I get more?'

'We have plenty of oil at Witfontein. You need only send for it. But if the flame rises you must be careful to turn it lower, or the chimney-glass will be smoked and may crack – and then it will not be so easy to get a new one. And look here ...'

Adrian felt he could bear this chatter no longer.

'Take that damn thing away, Piet,' he said, 'and let us go back to our candles. I don't want to see any English muck in this house.'

As Piet stared at him in astonishment, he picked up the lamp and tilted it dangerously; the flame licked the chimney-glass, which split with a crack.

'Adrian. ... Adrian. ... What are you doing?' Lisbet gasped.

'Here, give it to me,' Piet cried, 'or you'll set the house on fire!'

He took the lamp and turned down the wick hurriedly. Adrian laughed. The small outburst of violence had eased his tension. He took the faded *vierkleur* from under his coat and flung the bundle on the table.

'Will you take care of this for me, mother?' he said.

'Why, what is it, my son? A flag?'

'Our flag, mother. It was hauled down at Pretoria this

morning and the Queen's flag run up in its place. Keep it safely for me. We shall need it again some day.'

Piet stared at him incredulously. 'Is that true, Adrian?'

'Too true. Your British friends have annexed the Transvaal. No doubt that's good news to you.'

'Good news? My dear fellow, it's the best news I've ever heard! So Shepstone has brought it off! Don't you realize what this means? It means that in twenty-four hours every morgen of land in this country will have doubled in value. It means . . . my God, Adrian, if only you'd let me know this was going to happen I'd have bought up every scrap of Republican paper money on which I could lay my hands been here and Potchefstroom! We could have made a small fortune.'

'A fortune out of your neighbours' misfortunes. Yes . . . that would have been slim – and like you – my little brother. You've learnt to be a good Englishman!'

'Misfortune be damned! If only you'd try to be honest with yourself you'd have to admit that this is an act of Providence: the only thing that can save your country, as you call it, from utter bankruptcy. This means a new start for all of us. It's the signal for full speed ahead. As for slimness. . . . Sneer as you will, the fact remains that anyone who knew what you must have known and didn't move a finger to forestall the rise in the value of everything ought to be called . . . well, let's put it mildly and say not exactly wideawake. I don't mind betting some of your fellow-members – and some of your most sanctimonious patriots at that! – have feathered their nests pretty well. When I think of what you might have made, and what you have lost . . .'

Adrian shook his head. 'I've lost what I valued most – far more than I could ever have gained if I'd been as slim as you, Piet. I've lost my independence. I've lost my freedom. I've lost . . .'

Piet broke in impatiently: 'Independence be damned! What is the use of that without government? The baboons on the kopje are independent, if it comes to that. You fellows have used the word so much that it's lost its meaning. No bankrupt state can boast of its independence: it's tied, hand and foot, to its creditors. And no state so weak as ours can call itself independent either. We depend on our neighbours for our very existence. If they didn't protect us, Cetewayo would gobble us up. As for your "freedom" – that's only another of your big words: it

228

means next to nothing as soon as you come to examine it. Are the folk who live now under the British flag at Kimberley, at the Cape, in Natal – any less free than ourselves? I'll tell you the truth, Adrian: the only freedom of which we can boast in this country – if boast we must – is freedom to snap our fingers at any kind of authority. That's what I call licence, not freedom; and the less we have of it the better for all of us! Equal rights, security, justice that's the true freedom. And that's what the British flag gives us. Isn't that so, dad?'

John Grafton did not answer him. Throughout Piet's hot harangue he had sat like a man apart, hearing nothing: face drawn, hands clenched, eyes staring before him. Adrian shocked by the sudden change in him, hurried to his side.

'What's wrong, father? What is it? You're ill?'

John Grafton pulled himself together with difficulty.

'No, my son, I'm not ill. This news you've brought is graver for me than for either of you. It means – I shall have to leave Wonderfontein.'

'Leave Wonderfontein?' Piet protested. 'You don't understand, dad. This is the beginning of better times for all of us.'

'Better times, perhaps, for you, Piet; but it's a sore blow to me: the thing I've been dreading most for thirty-eight years.'

Lisbet knelt beside him and put her arm round his shoulders.

'You had better tell the boys everything, Jan,' she said. 'They are old enough now to know, and perhaps they may help us. Their heads are clearer than ours.'

John Grafton kissed her. 'It's time they were told, my dear. If my fears are justified they will soon have to know in any case. I am too overwhelmed to think; and perhaps, as you say, they are wiser than we and can see things more clearly.'

'But what is this mystery, father?' Piet exclaimed.

'Sit down, my son, and I'll tell you. It's all an old story. Only your mother and Mr. Blair and myself have ever known the whole truth of it. And now Mr. Blair is dead. . . .'

He began his long tale from its bitter beginnings in the old, unhappy times of the Reform agitation in England. He told of the Grafton Lovett Enclosure Bill; of how he, John Oakley, an ardent youth, had tramped up to London, a pitiful village Hampden, and lodged his protest before the Committee of Parliament; of how, on his disillusioned return to Grafton Lovett, he had been caught up, innocently, in a poaching affray, imprisoned and tried for his life and then finally sentenced to a term of fourteen years' transportation to Macquarie Bay, in Tasmania. He spoke without bitterness – the memory was too old to be bitter – of the horrors of the convict-ship *Minerva*'s voyage to the Cape; of how, when her boats had put into the shore for fresh water, he had escaped with a fellow-convict and staggered on through the night-terrors of the Assegai Bush to their grandfather Adrian Prinsloo's farm, Welgelegen, where he had found shelter and kindness and safety. He told them how he and their mother, who guessed his secret, had fallen in love, and how the Great Trek, on which the Prinsloo family were then embarking, had providentially carried him over the Vaal, out of reach of the British law – a free man at last, bearing a name that it did not know. He spoke calmly, dispassionately, as though he were telling the story of an acquaintance long since dead rather than his own:

'I can hardly believe such things happened to me,' he said. 'But look, even now, on my ankles, I carry the scars of the chains. There are scars of old fear on my spirit as well. I had almost forgotten they were there; but this change of wind has awakened the pain that I have not felt for nearly forty years. If this country is taken by the British, I cannot stay here any longer in safety. It's a hard thing for a man of my age; but there's nothing else for it: I must go.'

'But all this is such ancient history, father,' Adrian said. 'These things happened before I was born.'

'The British law is different from ours, my son. It has a long arm, as they say, and a longer memory. It never forgets. It's records are there, and my name appears in them.'

'But you have changed your name, father,' Piet said. 'John Oakley no longer exists. Not a soul in the world, but mother and you and we two, is aware that he ever existed, while eight thousand people have known John Grafton for forty years and respect him as a good citizen and a law-abiding man. I think these fears are quite groundless.'

John Grafton shook his head.

'You may be right, Piet. Your mother tells me the same; but it is impossible for any man to measure another's fears – and this fear, in the back of my mind, has never died down. It has made me an awkward, silent man, as you know. It has haunted my dreams. It was this fear that drove us out of Natal before you were born, Adrian. It is what has kept me from going with

230

Piet to Kimberley. Whenever I've seen the British flag or a British uniform – whenever I've spoken with Englishmen – it has come back to me. If the British take over this country, their police will come with them. They are thorough, these people; nothing ever escapes them. They will want to know who this Englishman, John Grafton, is, and where he has come from and how he happens to be here. They are capable of finding out everything; and then you, my sons, will be shamed.'

'But we know you are innocent, father,' Piet protested.

'You know I am an undischarged convict. That is a matter apart from all questions of innocence or guilt. This is my home, my sons: it will break my heart to leave it. I am not a young man to begin life over again. But how can I stay, with such a threat hanging over me? I am thinking of you and your mother as well as myself.'

'For me you need not think, father,' Adrian said indignantly. 'I do not acknowledge the British law in this country, and never will.'

Piet was silent. As Adrian spoke, there came to him a vision of Mrs. Haskard, his mother-in-law, that thin and tight-lipped paragon of the conventions. He was ashamed of its unworthiness and put it out of his mind.

'But supposing you felt yourself forced to leave Wonderfontein, father,' he said, 'you could not go to the Cape or Natal or West Griqualand. Where could you go?'

John Grafton passed his hand over his brow: 'I don't know, I don't know, Piet. At present I find it hard to make my mind work. There is your brother Andries' farm in the Zoutpansberg which is near the frontier . . .'

'And beyond that the Matabele! No, no, father, that won't do,' Adrian said emphatically. 'The Zoutpansberg is for young men who are used to danger; a frontier life is no life for mother and you.'

'You need take no account of me, Adrian,' Lisbet said. 'I am not afraid of danger or hardship: I've seen too much of them. Where your father is happy I can be happy too. It is only while this terror broods over him that neither of us can have peace. You say he has little or nothing to fear, and I agree with you; but if he feels that he is not safe any longer at Wonderfontein, why, then he must go, and I, of course, shall go with him. It's far better to put an end to this uncertainty.'

'But we're going round this matter in circles, mother,' Piet said. 'Let us get to grips with it and try to see where we stand. At present we only know that Shepstone's annexed the Transvaal and that from now onward it's going to be part of the British Empire. As a fugitive – if you like to put it that way – father feels his liberty's in danger. After forty years of freedom, I myself don't believe that it is – nor do you, nor does Adrian; but we're arguing in the dark; we've none of us any grounds for that opinion until we know exactly what this annexation implies and how far it goes. For instance, for all we know there may be an amnesty. That's what Adrian ought to be able to tell us.'

'Here is Shepstone's proclamation,' Adrian said. 'I haven't even read the stuff: I had no stomach for it. You can see for yourself what it says.'

Piet took the crumpled paper from Adrian and read it methodically, following each line with his blunt-ended capable forefinger and muttering to himself as he read:

'And I further proclaim and make known that the Transvaal will remain a separate Government, with its own laws and legislature . . .

'Its own legislature: mark that well, father! You see what it means? It suggests that the subject state will remain under its own laws; in other words, that the British law, of which you're afraid, will not run in it . . . *and that it is the wish of Her Most Gracious Majesty that it shall enjoy the fullest legislative privileges compatible with the circumstances of the country and the intelligence of its people. . . .* Ha, that's one for the back-veld, anyway, Adrian! Next . . . ah, yes: *That arrangements will be made by which the Dutch language will be practically as much the official language as English. . . .* "Practically" is good. . . . *All laws, proclamations and Government notices will be published in the Dutch language; in the Legislative Assembly –* you see, we've not done with the Volksraad! – *members may, as they do now, use either language, and in courts of laws the same may be done at the option of suitors to a cause. The law now in force in the state. . . .* Listen, here's the important paragraph for which I've been waiting. . . . *The law now in force in the state will be retained until altered by competent legislative authority.* And the Legislature, as it said before, remains the private affair of a separate Government. We are to make our own laws or keep the laws that we have. The "law now in force in the state" has nothing against you, father; the English law cannot touch you unless the new Volksraad, elected by the voters who put in

232

the old one, decide to bring the English law over the border – and I can't see the majority of the electorate doing that. You've nothing to fear. You've nothing to run away from. You can spend the rest of your life at Wonderfontein without giving this wretched business another thought. Isn't that perfectly clear?'

'It would seem to be clear,' Adrian said.

'It seems to be clear enough,' John Grafton admitted.

Piet laughed. 'Then that's settled. Let's hear no more about running away from Wonderfontein; let's all forget the story you've told us this evening. My name's Grafton, anyway. It's a good name; it's served me well and I've no mind to change it. John Oakley, if ever there was such a man, was lost or drowned forty years ago, and John Grafton, my father, is well known as a Voortrekker and inscribed on the burgher-roll of the South African Republic, while you, Adrian, it seems, are still an honourable member of our Volksraad!'

'I will have nothing to do with the government of this country under a foreign flag. I've finished. I wash my hands of it.'

'A foreign flag! You make me angry, Adrian, with your obstinacy. You're a prominent member of the state whom your own people trust. Will you leave your electors in the lurch? I admit that, in spite of his excellent intentions, your leader, Burgers, has failed. . . .'

'He's done worse than that: he's betrayed the Republic and sold it into the hands of the enemy. And the rest of them are no better than he: Paul Kruger, Jorissen, all the members of the Executive with the exception of Piet Joubert, have knuckled under to Shepstone and kept their appointments.'

'Of course, and why not? They've acted as reasonable men – to tell the truth, rather more reasonably than I expected. Can you imagine a more generous document than this Proclamation? The people keep what they prize: their language; their own form of government; their old laws and the right to make new ones. They gain what this country has always lacked most: new funds to develop it; protection against the natives whom they were powerless – as your war against Sekukuni has shown – to resist; the chance of becoming solvent and strong and self-respecting; the backing of the greatest empire the world has ever seen. What more could you ask?'

'We have lost the *vierkleur* under which you and I were born, Piet.'

233

'The flag invented by Burgers – whom you call a traitor – to be more accurate. For myself I'd much rather live under a flag that commands respect than one which is only laughed at, like this fancy bit of bunting.'

'This is a matter on which we have never agreed and shall never agree, Piet,' Adrian answered quietly. 'Only one thing I tell you. Though you scoff at this flag of ours and call it a bit of bunting, there have always been men who were ready to die for such things, and I am one of them. That is why I have told our mother to keep it in safety – for, as surely as there's a God in heaven, the time will come when we shall see it flying over Pretoria again. There are the seeds of war, I say, in this annexation.'

Lisbet took his arm and kissed him: 'My son, my son. ... What do all these things matter so long as we're safe and happy and not divided? For my part, I think that anything is better than a war – but then, I am a mother of four sons who would have to fight in it. Let us do as Piet says, and forget what has happened this evening. All I ask of God now is that your father and I should be permitted at least to end our lives in peace.'

Book Three

CHAPTER ONE

(1)

THE annexation made little difference to Wonderfontein or any other place in the back-veld, though casual reports from Pretoria suggested that the capital was indulging in an unexpected orgy of patriotism and adulation for the new flag. Shepstone himself was becoming a more important and popular figure than any State President had ever been, the hero of a renaissance of confidence – and therefore of business. The value of land and property of all sorts was rising; the depreciated republican paper-currency, now backed by British gold, recovered its face value. The town, which had been dying of inanation, took on a fresh lease of life. Arrears of salaries and government debts were paid in full. New officials, imported from the neighbouring colonies, replaced Burgers' hated Hollanders – the only section of the urban community (apart from a small minority of obstinate 'patriots', some of whom had thriven on the pickings of the old regime) that remained irreconcilable.

Then the troops of the British garrison marched in, horse, foot and artillery, bringing with them a new market in which money was lavishly spent, and a gay social life which the Pretorians – and their wives and daughters – found more to their taste than the monotony of their former existence in a sleepy dorp. Young soldiers, whose duties were mainly ornamental or ceremonial, must be entertained. There was an endless round of dances and picnics and shooting-parties and evening concerts performed by the regimental bands. The old shopkeepers began to demolish their stores and enlarge them; arrivals from Natal and the Cape set up new 'emporiums' in which the latest novelties and fashions from Europe were displayed. Though the state was bankrupt, it appeared that the people had money to burn.

Even the Boers trekking in from the back-veld found their produce snapped up eagerly at high prices, and were finally convinced of a change for the better when the war-tax against which they had grumbled was suddenly remitted. They saw men of substance and family – Holtzhausen of Middelburg, Joubert of Potchefstroom, Nel of Rustenburg and Lourens Geldenhuis of Pretoria, accepting office in the new Executive which Shepstone appointed. Though they signed mass-petitions against annexation and subscribed, under force of public opinion, to the thousand-pound fund which was being raised to send Paul Kruger to England with a deputation pledged to protest against it and, if possible, to get it reversed, they were compelled to confess that under the British rule they were none the worse off – and perhaps even better – than before. If Shepstone fulfilled his promise – of a new Volksraad elected by a free vote in place of the old one which had voluntarily prorogued itself, and of complete self-government in domestic affairs – there would be little to complain of. So far, indeed, no arrangements for the election were being made; but their country was one in which men were easy-going and had never been disposed to hurry unnecessarily. '*Alles sal erg kom,*' they said. 'All will come right: tomorrow is also a day.'

Meanwhile, from the back-veld pulpits, the predikants thundered; and, in the end, the Boers' good friend Mr. 'Slypsteen' went back to Natal, and a new Pharaoh who knew them not was sent to rule over them – a lanky, olive-skinned soldier, Colonel Lanyon by name, who, some said, had nigger blood in his veins and, in any case, was a martinet, all spit and polish, determined to take no nonsense from anyone and to run the undisciplined Transvaal rabble like a well-drilled regiment. They were living now under a military dictatorship. Lanyon's officials adopted their chief's autocratic tone. There was no sign as yet of representative government, nor even of the promised elections being held. They would never be held, the bitterest said, so long as the soldiers were in charge: Owen Lanyon hectoring it in Pretoria, another soldier, Sir Bartle Frere, at the Cape, and yet another, Sir Garnet Wolseley, already filling the country with redcoats marching on Sekukuni, who, encouraged by Burgers' failure (and perhaps by Cetewayo), had popped up again.

When volunteers were called for to join in this new northern campaign, the mass of farmers returned a sullen refusal. If this Government did not represent them, they argued reasonably, why should they trouble to fight for it? Let it do its own dirty work! Pretoria might still be more English than the English, but the back-veld was Dutch to the marrow, growing more irreconcilable every day and seething with discontent.

Adrian Grafton took a prominent part in spreading the ferment of disaffection. At the moment when he had finally lost faith in President Burgers, a chief whom he had not merely admired but personally loved, he had sworn that he would have no more truck with politics for the rest of his life. The fact that Paul Kruger, who carried more weight in the country than any other leader and whom he felt most like following, had jumped at the chance of taking office in Shepstone's administration, had disillusioned him even more than Burgers' failure to stand firm. These damned politicians, he told himself, were all equally unreliable: idealists, such as Burgers, lacked strength and staying-power, men of action, such as Paul Kruger, had strength enough but used it to their own ends.

The one man, to his mind, who had emerged with credit from the sorry capitulation was Kruger's rival, Piet Joubert, who had refused to serve under Shepstone; but Joubert, in Adrian's view, did not possess the large qualities, intellectual or personal, he looked for in one who should lead his folk through the wilderness; though he shared Piet Joubert's ideals, he doubted his capacity; if a national movement were to arise and succeed against such enormous odds it must be headed, he felt, by a bigger man than this; to support such a leader (already weakened by Kruger's hostility) would be to court immediate failure and, by failing, to prejudice a future success when the right man arrived.

For the moment he threw himself into the work of the farm, deliberately isolating himself from every sort of political association and trying, in this way, to forget his own bitterness and the indignity into which he felt he and his fellow-citizens had been tricked. Even so, he was restless. For a time he played with the idea of breaking away and joining his brother Andries up in the Zoutpansberg, where land went begging and the influence of the new Government could hardly be felt; but the disappointment his mother showed when he spoke of this scheme made him quickly abandon it. She was the only person on earth at this time towards whom his bitter heart was capable of feeling tenderness.

'You want to leave your old father and mother so soon? Why must you be always so restless and so unhappy, my son?' she pleaded. 'What is done is done. You know that you cannot alter it. Why can't you forget these grievances and settle down like our Piet?'

'You know I am not like your Piet in anything, mother, and never have been.'

'I don't want you to be like him in many things,' Lisbet said. 'It is right that you should be yourself. But I want you to be happy as he is, and one source of true happiness you have rejected. You ought to be married, Adrian. It is wrong that a man of your age, a fine man like yourself, should not have a place and a family of his own. Even if you marry now, by the time your sons have grown up to be men you will be nearly as old as your father. It is only because I know how much you are missing that I sometimes feel angry with you.'

He smiled at her seriousness. 'Are you angry now? Will you find me a wife, then, mother?'

'Indeed I will not. That is one thing a man must find for himself.'

'If you'll find me a woman exactly like yourself I promise I'll marry her.'

'Ach, what nonsense you talk! There are plenty of nice young women about if you'll only look around for them at the next Nagmaal. I'm old, and I want to be able to see your children, my grandchildren, before I lose my sight.'

'You want to see grandchildren born under the British flag – a pack of little *rooinekke*?'

She laughed, for she knew he was half teasing her.

'See now, what I will do, Adrian,' she said. 'When your wife goes to bed I will take her the *vierkleur* you gave me to keep and spread it over her. Then you can boast that your sons have been born beneath the Republican flag, and that will content you, perhaps, though I'll wager that she, poor child, will be past caring what shape or colour of flag they are born under.'

'If that is a bargain,' Adrian said, with mock seriousness, 'I'll see what can be done.'

Yet, for all his mockery, he had taken her words to heart. This was the first time, since the day when he went into politics, that he had had leisure to think about marrying, and when once the idea of its possibility had entered his austere mind it was not long before he had found a mate and married her. His bride was not, as Lisbet had hoped, one of their neighbours' daughters, but the sister of the new predikant, Mr. Blair's successor, a young Cape Dutchman named Strijdom, educated at Stellenbosch, who shared, like most of his colleagues, Adrian's extreme nationalistic views.

It was this community of interests which, pronounced unequivocally from the pulpit, first drew Adrian and the predikant together. He was astonished and encouraged to find that the apathy he had lamented among his fellow-citizens was not shared by his brother Afrikanders at the Cape. There the seed of a nationalist movement had been sown by a young journalist named Jan Hofmeyr, the editor of a Dutch newspaper, *De Volksvriend,* who had founded a political body known as the Farmers' Protection Society, and entered parliament as the leader of an Afrikander Party. By his side – or a little in advance of him – stood the predikant du Toit, who himself had founded another group, the Society of True South Africans, and a second Afrikaans newspaper called *Die Patriot*, the organ of a new body soon to be known as the Afrikander Bond, which was planned to embrace not only the Dutch at the Cape, but the citizens of the Transvaal and the Orange Free State, and professed as its object the making of a united South Africa under its own flag. Both du Toit and Jan Hofmeyr were personal friends of Strijdom. It was his admiration for their enthusiasm and reliance on their support that had induced him to accept the ill-paid cure left vacant by Mr. Blair's death. He had determined to go to the Transvaal as a missionary in the interests of national unity, and the blow of the British Annexation, falling on him soon after he had taken up his post, had strengthened rather than discouraged his resolution.

He was a slight man, tense and pallid, with a thin ascetic face and dark eyes that smouldered in sunken orbits beneath a wide intellectual forehead and black eyebrows, unusually heavy, that met at the root of the nose. He was full of quick gestures and nervous movements; but for all his apparent physical frailty his nerves were of steel. He refused, on principle to speak English or even High Dutch. In the pulpit he made of the elementary Akrikaans speech an instrument of flexibility and even of beauty, enhanced by the fire in his eyes, an unerring theatrical instinct, and a voice to which the passion of his thought gave moving overtones. Adrian had no sooner heard him preach than he fell a victim to the charm of this man who, physically and mentally, was so different from himself. He had always had a weakness of zealots and oratory (as witness his blind passion

239

for Burgers); but Carel Strijdom possessed, in addition to Burgers visionary enthusiasm, a practical and uncompromising quality and a faith which spoke straight to his heart. The time for compromises, if there ever had been one, was over for Adrian – so completely that he had even become impatient of the Kruger deputation's visit to Europe.

'But there you are wrong, my friend,' Carel Strijdom assured him. 'Paul Kruger is longer-headed than any of you. This is a complicated game, and he is playing it shrewdly. He will gain three things by this visit. First of all he will see for himself how the land lies in England; he can learn what support he may expect in the English Parliament. The Liberal leader, Gladstone, has already spoken strongly against annexation; so has Chamberlain; so has Hartington. Before long it is possible that these friends of ours may be in power. Again, Kruger is playing for time. He knows that the Transvaal burghers are too stunned to think. Every day of Lanyon's autocratic ways and Wolseley's barrack-room braggartry increases the feeling against the English: every month during which Shepstone's promises of popular representation remain unfulfilled makes the people feel sorer and binds them together.'

'Kruger consented to serve under Shepstone. For me that's enough.'

'You judge even that too hastily. It proves my third point: the virtue of moderation. It shows he was ready to give annexation a trial, even though he abhorred it. And this mission to Europe, again, shows the world (and remember: England is not the only great power that is interested in the future of Africa) that we are reasonable men, willing to discuss our grievances and seek our rights calmly, not savages eager to win them by bloodshed.'

'We cannot make war on England. Burgers was right when he said to take up the sword would be useless.'

'Yes, Burgers was right when he spoke those words,' Strijdom agreed. 'At that time he knew that the Transvaal would be forced to fight its own battles. The Republic was hopelessly divided. The Free State has no quarrel with the English. President Brand himself studied law in England and gave them the Diamond Fields. But this annexation has given the Free Staters something to think about: they must see that their turn may come next. And the movement which Hofmeyr and du Toit have started in the Cape is gathering force every day. By the time Paul Kruger comes back the situation will be very different from what it was when he left. Over the whole of South Africa – apart from Natal, which is utterly barren – he will find the seeds of an Afrikander nation shooting green; and that crop will flourish and be white to harvest before long. The success of that harvest depends on a very few people who are prepared to devote their lives to it. In this country, alas, the fields are widely scattered, but the word of the Lord has told us what we should do. *Pray ye therefore the Lord of the harvest*, He said, *that he would send forth labourers into his harvest*. There are times when one feels very helpless. Still, it is good for folk like Suzanna and myself to know that we have such a stalwart labourer as you working with us, Grafton.'

His sister was always present during these ardent colloquies. She was younger by two years than he, and ten years younger than Adrian: a slight, dark girl, resembling her brother in his physical fragility, distinction of body and intensity of spirit – with the difference that while Carel Strijdom was capable of volcanic outbursts of eloquence, in which words poured forth like molten lava, she was by nature (or habit) silent; her dark eyes, though no less alive, were more gentle than his, and her fervour, though no less passionate, glowed within her rather than flamed.

At first Adrian had found this transfusion of spiritual heat which, insulated, as it were, by her silence and contradicted by the cool pallor of her skin and the frailty of her person, made Suzanna seem slightly inhuman, somewhat intimidating. He knew little of women, and she was unlike any woman he had ever known. Yet the influence of her proximity could not be evaded; whenever he talked with her brother, and she sat with them in silence, he was even more conscious of her presence than of his. In the beginning he had been far too shy to look at her; but when, later, familiarity conquered his shyness, he was surprised to perceive that she was beautiful and so strangely moved by this revelation that, when once he had seen it, he could not keep his eyes off her.

Nor was her nature quite so remote and unearthly as he had imagined. When they had exhausted their lofty political discussions and descended to the plane of common social intercourse, he found that she could be natural and human and

241

friendly. The society of Suzanna and her brother was different from any to which he had been accustomed. There was a whimsical vein in both of them that found vent in a gaiety which Adrian's grave mind found puzzling and yet delightful. He was not given to joking himself; and the Strijdom's variety of humour (which played a part in their lives as important to them as their political fervour) was at times too quick and subtle for his comprehension. He had been rather shocked, indeed, by Carel's display of impish levity, having previously accepted the standards of clerical behaviour set by Mr. Blair, to whom nothing in life had been a fit subject for joking. It was not only their humour, which even leavened their politics, that made him feel awkward. They were both of them far better educated, knew more of the world, and were in every way more alive than he. Carel Strijdom had a brilliant scholastic record at Stellenbosch; Suzanna, too, had studied history seriously at Leyden. Compared with either of them, intellectually, Adrian was a child – yet such a charming child in his naïvety that both took pains to avoid making him conscious of his inferiority, and welcomed him for what he was.

Adrian accepted the Strijdoms' friendship humbly and gratefully. Within a few months he had become an intimate of this delightful household. Whenever he could be spared from Wonderfontein he rode over to the dorp; but now he was drawn there less by his admiration for Carel than by the fascination of Suzanna, with whom – and for the first time in his life – he had completely fallen in love. Rather hopelessly, too; for he could not persuade himself that such folk as the Strijdoms (and particularly Suzanna) would have tolerated the company of a fellow so clumsy and simple as himself except for the fact that he shared their political sympathies.

By this time he admired Suzanna as fervently as he loved her. There was no end, it seemed, to this frail and ardent creature's variety. She was, among other things, an excellent cook and housewife. In its shining cleanliness and material comforts the predikant's house was superior to any he had ever frequented, even in Pretoria. But what impressed him even more was the adaptability with which, while sharing her brother's professional and political life and his intellectual interests, she contrived to make himself, an uncouth denizen of an alien civilization, equally at home. There was no detail in his workaday life that, when his first shyness had been conquered, he could not discuss with confidence in her understanding and sympathy. He wondered if even Carel realized how richly he was blessed. What a wife that woman would make!

As for Suzanna: she had never taken Adrian's qualities at his own humble estimate. Though she admitted that, by the more cultured standards of the Cape's old civilization, he was clumsy and uninstructed, she came of a race (and of a country) in which social or intellectual snobbishness is rarely found. On his first appearance she had accepted him as a comrade in politics, a man who had thought and felt deeply on such subjects and had been driven by his conscience to range himself on her side. When she came to consider him as a person she had been struck, not unnaturally, by his complete sincerity and by the simplicity which made him, in the isolation to which the wife or sister of a newly appointed predikant in a back-veld dorp was condemned, a charming companion. Her mind was more subtle than his, and the company of a man so much less complicated than her brother or herself, who were too much alike, was something of a relief. If she sometimes found herself treating Adrian as a child, there was nothing amiss with that: it gave scope to a protective, quasi-maternal instinct which Carel was far too adult and self-reliant to satisfy. When she considered him as a man, the oppositeness of their natures and physical types, together with the proximity of Adrian's strength, his handsomeness, his virility, was sufficient to attract her. There was little coquettishness in her nature; she did not encourage him to make love to her, yet she did not repel him. When she realized the increasingly emotional nature of their relationship she was flattered – and pleasantly fluttered too.

It took Adrian, doubtful of himself, a long time to nerve himself to a proposal. Suzanna felt sorry for his embarrassment, but would not help him. When, at last, he asked her to marry him, she accepted him without hesitation – not only because she loved him, but also because she felt she could help him and that, together, they could better serve the cause which was so near her heart. Her brother welcomed the match. In his generous nature there was no room for jealousy. He had always liked Adrian, as Suzanna loved him, because they were so different, and respected him, too, as a sober and honest man. Maria was thrilled by the event – as by everything else that savoured of the romantic – and Lisbet, soon satisfied by Suzanna's neatness and modesty and by seeing that she was obviously devoted to Adrian, was thankful to see her son 'settled'.

The only thing that troubled her was that the couple had rejected the idea of building a house for themselves on the Wonderfontein land and had decided to buy a farm farther north, in the foot-hills of the Magaliesberg, nearer Pretoria. This was a more densely-settled district in which Adrian believed that his influence as a political missionary could be more effectively used than in the thinly-populated Witwatersrand district, where his brother-in-law, Carel Strijdom, would carry on the good work. It was with mingled regret and happiness that she saw Adrian collect his stock from the lands, and watched the dust of his wagons move slowly north-west. Now that he and Andries and poor Janse had flown from the nest at Wonderfontein, she had only Piet left; and Piet, too, had made a life for himself in which, though he always made her welcome, she never felt quite at home. It was no use complaining, she told herself. Such was the fate of all mothers. Yet this last flitting made her feel, for the first time, that she and her husband were growing old.

(2)

Perhaps, Lisbet thought, it was better, on the whole, that Adrian and Piet should not be near neighbours. Slow to anger as Adrian was, it would have been hard for him to tolerate Piet's exultation at finding himself at last under the British flag. Major Haskard had been no less pleased than Piet by the annexation. The only thing that had ever restrained him from putting more money into Brakfontein was the possibility of racial disturbances endangering the property and of vindictive anti-foreign legislation making it hard for aliens to own land in the Transvaal. He was so pleased, indeed, by what he called 'the great news' that as soon as he heard it he forgot all about his lungs and hurried northward before the autumn rains had exhausted themselves.

'Now at last I feel I can breathe freely, my dear fellow,' he told Piet as soon as he arrived. 'It's positively a physical comfort to realize that one's living in a country with a civilized government, to think of the good old flag waving over Pretoria, and a chap like Lanyon, who'll stand no nonsense – and an Irishman too, begad! – stepping up into Shepstone's place. I knew him well in Kimberley.'

'On the whole, I would rather Shepstone had stayed,' Piet said.

'No, no. . . . He's a colonial, my dear boy. Too fond of the Dutch and too easy-going for my liking. A civilian, too. What these fellows need most is a taste of discipline.'

'They may need it, but they won't like it.'

'So much the worse for them! I'll back Owen Lanyon to make 'em toe the line Trust a soldier for that! It's pleasant, too, having a garrison in Pretoria. Not merely because it gives one a sense of confidence, but because it's nice to have people within reach who figuratively as well as literally speak one's own language. Taking them all round, the officers of the British Army are the salt of the earth. When Edward comes out – I told you, didn't I, that he's given up Cambridge and slipped into the yeomanry, and hopes, before long, to get himself seconded to one of the regiments out here? – we shall be able to have great times. I expect he'll keep the house full of his brother-officers. The poor lads get bored in stations like these with nothing to do but a bit of shooting. We'll get 'em along and give them a good time. That will brighten things up a bit for us too. Something to look forward to, eh? We shall have to keep our eyes on little Maria, though, with young soldiers about. She's a stunner, by Jove! Upon my word, I should hardly have known her. Well now, what about saddling up and having a look round the orchards?'

Haskard always began to bubble with energy and enthusiasm as soon as he set foot on the High Veld. They rode over the sunlit lands together and he was delighted with all he saw. The leaves of the peach-bushes had turned red, but were not yet fallen; the citrus-groves dotted the slopes with a velvety corduroy of darker green.

'Now that we know where we are – politically, I mean, Haskard said, 'there's no reason why we shouldn't launch out a bit more. Luck's been running remarkably well for me in Kimberley. If you want money you've only to ask for it. What's the next move?'

Piet answered him warily. Though he had made a good beginning and would soon, with any luck, be showing a reasonable profit, he was by no means sure that their enterprise could make rapid headway against transport difficulties. Since the day when he had first made a conquest of Haskard the scale of his ambitions had changed. He had completed the job with which he had been entrusted with characteristic thoroughness; but now that he had tasted money his appetite for it had grown. Fruit-farming, under conditions that were by no means ideal, was all very well, he felt, as the pastime of a rich man who didn't care so long as it paid its way. Thanks to his salary rather than to his sales he had actually covered his original expenditure and had begun to put money by. His orchards were there and flourishing, a reserve on which, at the worst, he could always fall back and make a living; but even at the best, the income from them would never satisfy his desires or give his intelligence the scope it demanded. Fools were making money hand over fist in Kimberley. It seemed wrong to him – who knew he was no fool – not to take advantage of Haskard's Kimberley connections and influence while the going was good.

'The next move?' he said. 'Well, to tell you the truth, sir' – he was always punctilious in this form of address, which he knew Haskard liked – 'I don't think we ought to expand or put more land under cultivation until we are sure of our markets. You know what the difficulties of transport are, how they eat into our profits. I don't want to produce more stuff than we can conveniently handle. If our production once overruns us there'll be a tremendous waste. We've broken the back of the job. Everything is in order and a routine established. From this point until we reach full production there's not a great deal to be done. As a matter of fact, during the last six months I don't honestly feel I've been earning my salary.'

'Nonsense, nonsense, my boy! Your scruples do you credit; but, after all, that's a trifle which doesn't hurt me. If you don't feel you're earning it, you'd better regard it as Lavinia's contribution to your joint income, though, in my opinion, you've earned every penny of it and more.'

Piet smiled. 'Well, it's very generous of you, sir, to put it that way; but it still leaves me not quite happy. I'm young – and perhaps a little ambitious too, and I feel I'm not really using my energies to the best advantage. After all, I must look to the future; I'm the father of a family – I suppose Lavinia's told you there's another one coming?'

'Yes, yes. We were both delighted to hear it. The more the

better! There'll be plenty for all of them when I'm gone.'

Mr. Haskard's face fell. The allusion had reminded him of his lungs, which he had momentarily forgotten: he became conscious of a slight pain in his side: the result, perhaps, of the sudden change of altitude. He should have been more cautious.

'Don't even speak of such things, sir,' Piet was saying. 'I've never seen you look better than you do today. But that,' he persisted, 'isn't quite the same, is it?'

'Perhaps not. Yes, I see your point. What d'you want to do then?'

'You were speaking just now of your holdings in Kimberley. You say things are going well, sir. I wonder if they mightn't go better if you had somebody whose interests are identical with yours looking after them on the spot? Things change quickly in these days At a distance it's easy to miss opportunities. I was wondering . . .'

'H'm. . . . So that's what you mean. There may be something in it. But you can't leave the farms to look after themselves.'

'I think I could get a reliable manager for half what you're paying me.'

'But Lavinia . . .? No, my dear boy, her mother would never consent to your leaving her alone at Witfontein.'

'I should have no need to leave her alone for long at a time. I could go to and fro without any difficulty: the journey need not take more than forty-eight hours. As it is, Maria spends half her time over here. I could arrange for her to stay with Lavinia while I was away, and run up quarters for the manager near to the house; besides which, in the winter, we both hope that you will be here, sir.'

'I shall have to think about this,' Major Haskard said.

The more he thought of it, the more the idea appealed to him. He was an indolent man by nature, and his hypochondriacal state made him often suspicious of those who served him. He had no such doubts about Piet. In two years the young man had proved himself to be hard-headed and reliable. The more he had to do with him, the better he liked him. On general principles it was wise to keep business 'in the family'. The only obstacle to what now seemed an admirable arrangement was Mrs. Haskard's almost certain objections.

Piet knew this as well as he did, and doubted his powers of dealing with them unaided. The best channel of approaching the difficulty was through Lavinia herself. Since the birth of her son she had been more interested in the child than in him, and the coming of the next, which was due towards the end of the winter, would keep her too busy to worry about his short absences. He knew he could count on her taking her part in preparing Mrs. Haskard for the announcement. In the meantime, realizing the importance in any argument for the new scheme of the accomplished fact, he engaged a Cape coloured man, an expert in fruit-growing, whose brains he had picked during his honeymoon visit to Capetown, to come up to Witfontein as assistant-manager at a little more than half his own salary. From the first he had had no doubt as to what his father-in-law's decision would be. He guided him so gently and tactfully and with such a loose rein that, by the time the new manager arrived, Major Haskard was convinced that he himself had originated the idea – with the result that, in the middle of the winter, Piet was ready to start for Kimberley with letters of introduction and a Power of Attorney in his pocket.

'You'll need to keep your eyes pretty wide open, my dear boy,' Haskard said. 'On the whole, you'll be safer if you steer clear of foreigners and stick to Englishmen. I've given you letters to two sound fellows, George Hull and Charles Rudd. And you might have a word with Rhodes – he's a canny young man.'

'What? A tall chap with a beard who talks your head off? I think I know him.'

'No, no, that's his eldest brother Herbert. He's up in the north somewhere. The fellow I mean is called Cecil. A rum, silent cove, you'll find him, but clever as be damned. Kept his terms at Oxford and comes of a family of soldiers. His brother's an old Etonian and an officer in the First Dragoons, the Royals, you know.'

Piet did not know, but nodded

'I'll look him up,' he said. 'I think I remember him too. A sullen, untidy young devil with a squeaky voice.'

It was a great moment for him when he rode into Kimberley, no longer the dusty transport-rider of his earlier days, but well-mounted and well-dressed, a man of substance with his father-in-law's credit behind him. He made straight for Cotty's, where Haskard had told him he would be likely to find his friend Rudd; but neither Rudd nor George Hull was there: he would be most likely to find them, he was told, at the de Beers mine, on the outskirts of the town. As he rode down the main street in which, even since his last visit, many of the old landmarks had given place to buildings more imposing and permanent, his eye was caught by a face that seemed familiar, though the figure to which it belonged was not. He hesitated and pulled up. The figure advanced with a smile and held out his hand.

'Why, Meninsky?' Piet cried.

'That's right, mate. Put it there!'

'I should never have known you,' Piet said.

'To tell you the honest, I hardly know myself, mate.'

The Peruvian had certainly changed. He had put on flesh and lost some of his insect-like activity of movement. He was dressed in a light alpaca suit with a fancy waistcoat, patent-leather boots, a flamboyant necktie fixed by a diamond pin, and a straw hat, with an equally vivid band, which he wore rakishly tilted on the back of his head. He stood smiling, a ragged cigar in the corner of his mouth.

'What are you doing now, then?' Piet inquired.

'Well, now you're asking: a bit of everything. All's grist that comes to my mill, mate, so long as there's oof in it. Claims, soda-water, ice-cream, real estate, diamonds – good ones as well as rubbish, and no questions asked where they come from – kaffir-truck and Brummagem gas-pipe guns: I'm not particular. If I had been particular I shouldn't be where I am now.'

'And where are you now?' Piet laughed.

'On the top of the ruddy world, boy. No, straight, I'm not joking. I learnt my lesson along with poor old Janse. Want to know what it was? Just this, mate: The way to get on is to handle things, not to produce them. As long as you're handling them, buying and selling, they don't even need to exist. Never hold the baby: that's my motto in life, and it's served me champion. Speaking of which, you look as if you'd not done so badly either. Want to sell that horse, by any chance? I can find you a buyer. Ten per cent commission, and I'll promise you a good price.'

Piet explained his position.

'Cor! You've not half fallen on velvet! What a thing it is to be a good-looking chap, and what a chance you've got! Nothing of that sort ever comes my way. What's the news of old Janse? I've wrote to him several times at the bank in Lydenburg, but I don't get no answers.'

'He's still transport-riding between there and the Bay, so far as I know.'

'I've got money waiting for him: just on a thousand pounds.

'A thousand pounds? For Janse?' Piet was surprised and vaguely disturbed. It wasn't exactly jealousy; but he was thinking what he could do with that thousand pounds. It was ridiculous that Janse should be better off than himself.

'Ay, he gave me two hundred to play with,' Meninsky said casually, 'and I can't stop the damned stuff growing nohow. Look here, mate, if at any time you need a word from the horse's mouth, like, or want any information about people or property . . .'

'Thanks, Meninsky. I won't forget. What about a drink?'

The Peruvian pursed his lips and shook his head.

'Not for me, mate. I've only two vices. This is one' – he waved the ragged cigar in the air – 'and the other's not what you think it is. No, this is my vice.' He took out a handful of shining sovereigns and spun one in the air with a ping. 'Heads or tails, mate?'

Piet called 'tails'.

'Bad shot. It's the lady. Toss you double or quits?'

Piet called again and won.

Meninsky dropped the coin back in his pocket.

'Well, there you are: that's my life. I was born a gambler, mate; and so far the gamble's come off. Don't forget what I told you about inside information and so on. Anything that I can do for a brother of Janse's . . .'

'You can help me now. I'm looking for a fellow called Rhodes.'

'Go out to de Beers and you'll be certain to find him; but don't be surprised if you come back with a flea in your ear. He's a queer-tempered beggar, that.'

Piet rode on his way. The de Beers mine now resembled a grid-iron, or rather a kind of gigantic waffle-iron. It consisted of a circular bowl, more than a hundred feet deep, divided into separate claims or compartments by a rectilinear network of narrow elevated roads, running straight between the sheer precipices on either side, along which the conglomerate dug every day was carted to its owners' washing-ground on the fringe of the town. At close intervals along the outer edge of the circular pit were set box-like erections that housed the handwindlasses of the aerial tramways by which buckets of 'blue-ground' were hauled up from below. The system of wires, converging beneath and deviating above, gave the impression of a huge spider's-web spun of steel, along whose radial strands the buckets, ascending and descending with a murmurous rumble like that of far thunder, resembled minute black insects perpetually crawling to and fro. From the bottom of the chasm, where the blue-ground was broken by blasting, and from its rim, where the contents of the bucket were tipped, rose a cloud of dust that was like the smoke of a smouldering fire.

Piet left his horse tied to a fence on the outskirts of the mine and picked his way over one of the bars of the grid to the place where, a digger assured him, young Rhodes would be found. He discovered him sitting, his back propped up against a packing-case, on the edge of the chasm, a loose-knit, slovenly figure, his hands in his pockets, gazing down, in sullen abstraction, into the depths of the 'paddock' below. When Piet called his name, he turned round and surveyed him coldly with blue eyes that seemed even bluer for the red-scorched skin that covered his cheeks and his aquiline nose. Apart from the ragged blond moustache which he had grown and a grimness of feature which aged him, he was merely a more robust version of the lanky invalid who had visited Wonderfontein six years before. His falsetto voice, too, was the same.

'What d'you want,' he squeaked, 'and who are you?'

Piet explained his visit:

'I think we've met before. I gave you and your brother Herbert a pull through a drift, and you stopped the night with us at Wonderfontein.'

'Wonderfontein. . . . That's on the Witwatersrand. Yes, I remember. I remember a nice little girl who brought me a cup of coffee.'

'My sister Maria. She's grown up now.'

'Well, what can I do for you?'

'My father-in-law, James Haskard, wants me to talk with you.'

'I know Jim Haskard quite well. A perfect sportsman. Hunting, shooting and fishing and polo and pig-sticking. Charming fellow. In other words, he's a loafer. What does he want us to talk about?'

'Things in general. Kimberley. The future.'

'Well, we can't talk here. Come and see me this evening. I'm pigging it at the moment with eleven other fellows. Ask where "The Twelve Apostles" live. Anyone'll tell you. So long!'

In the evening Piet visited 'The Apostles'' diggings. They were a tin hut calculated to hold four or five occupants at the most. In the middle of the smoke-misted room, round a table littered with the remains of the evening meal, bottles, glasses and empty tins, the twelve men, and surely a good many more, were clustered – playing cards, telling stories, laughing, drinking and talking. The close air smelt stale, of alcohol and Boer tobacco. Half-way down the table, his chair tilted back on its hinder legs, his hands in the pockets of his shrunken white-flannel trousers, Cecil Rhodes sat staring moodily at the festoons of flypapers, black with buzzing victims, that hung from the ceiling. When Piet entered, he greeted him nonchalantly, with an unfriendly stare and a casual nod, then turned to talk with his neighbour. It seemed an extremely odd way in which to receive an invited visitor. Since nobody else in the room appeared to take any notice of him, Piet decided, after a moment's awkward hesitation, that he might just as well go.

As he moved to the door, Rhodes came lumbering after him.

'Here, Grafton, where are you off to? Come and sit down. Have a drink.'

He grasped Piet's upper arm familiarly and drew him away from the door, and Piet resented this warmth as much as the former frigidity: he had an instinctive distaste for being handled. Rhodes brought the drinks and pulled two chairs into the far corner of the room.

'We can hardly hear ourselves talk in this racket,' he said. 'Here's looking to you! Come along with your questions, then. What can I tell you?'

It was he, in fact, who asked most of the questions. He wanted to know, first of all, how things were going in the Transvaal. Was the annexation accepted as generally as was said? Were the predikants calming down a bit? How did Lanyon compare with Shepstone, and how had Wolseley 'gone down'?

Piet answered him as best he could. He had heard enough from Adrian to know that the annexation was much less in favour than it had been. That was partly, he said, because of the delay in instituting the representative government which Shepstone had promised; partly the fault of the soldiers, and partly, again, the result of Lanyon's personality.

'He's a fellow without any tact,' he said. 'He hates and despises the Dutch and makes no attempt to conceal it.'

Rhodes shook his head. 'We can't afford to hate them,' he said. 'I like the Dutch. I like their homely courtesy and their tenacity of purpose. Apart from that, they're the majority in this country and we have to work with them. But the Government's making a damnable muddle of this with their chopping and changing: Shepstone, Frere, Lanyon, Wolseley: one damn governor after another. The people in the Transvaal don't know from one minute to the next whom they have to deal with. And what makes it worse is the fact that officials at home can't get it into their narrow heads that it's impossible attempting to govern a complex people from a distance of six thousand miles and treating them like tiresome children. The only hope for this country is to break down these local barriers of interest and trade, to build a great continental railway that will link up Cape Colony with the Transvaal by way of the Free State, and to set up a system of government that embraces all three with a uniform fiscal and native policy. Federation. That is the word.'

'I heard you use it six years ago at Wonderfontein,' Piet said.

'Well, I don't often change my mind,' Rhodes chuckled, 'unless it pays me. And you? You believe in it?'

'Poor President Burgers once said the right thing: "From the Cape to the Zambezi there should be one great people." '

'That's Jan Hofmeyr's policy too. But under what flag?'

Piet smiled at the intensity of this catechism:

'I've nothing personally against the Union Jack.'

'And, good God, I should hope you haven't! It's the only one that can protect us and allow us to expand. The Cape and the Transvaal talk as if they were great independent nations. They're nothing of the sort: they're only the population of a third-rate English town spread over a continent. The Cape to the Zambezi, you say. . . . I'll ask you something else, Grafton. Why stop at the Zambezi?'

His voice rose to a high falsetto that Piet found embarrassing.

'Isn't that biting off rather more than we can chew?'

'If we don't bite, someone else will. Since the Franco-Prussian War there has been a new Germany. Do you ever look at the map of Africa? I'm fond of maps – always have been.' He

253

rose clumsily. 'Don't move; stay where you are.' He lumbered off into his bedroom and brought back two canvas rolls: one a map of Africa, the other a Mercator's Projection of the world. He unrolled the first and spread it on his knees between them. Piet noticed that he was breathing rapidly, as if he were excited. He laid his plump palm on the peninsula of the Cape and drew it slowly upward till it reached the Nile.

'I want to paint all that red,' he said, 'from Capetown to Cairo.'

He paused and threw back his short-necked head in a gesture of challenge; his blue eyes were blazing.

'Have you ever read Ruskin? No, of course you haven't. Why should you? He gave a lecture at Oxford not very long ago, and his words made such a deep impression on me that I learnt them by heart. They're odd sentiments for an elderly Slade Professor of Art. He was talking about the future of England, and he said that we English had "a destiny now possible to us, the highest ever set before a nation to be accepted or refused." "Will you youths of England," he said, "make your country again 'a royal throne of kings, a sceptred isle,' for all the world a source of light, a centre of peace? This is what England must do, or perish. She must found colonies as fast and as far as she is able, formed of the most energetic and worthiest of men; seizing any piece of fruitful ground she can set her foot on, and there teaching her colonists that their chief virtue is to be fidelity to their country and that their first aim is to be to advance the power of England by land and sea." '

Piet smiled to himself at the high, rolling phrases. He had no idea who Ruskin might be, but the old fellow was evidently pretty well pleased with himself. This was more or less Major Haskard transported to a poetical plane. The arrogance of the English, in this mood, had always seemed to him comical.

'You know, Rhodes, I'm not really English,' he said. 'I'm a mongrel: my mother's pure Dutch.'

'That makes no difference.' Rhodes swept his modest reservations aside. 'Your father's English. You've been brought up to think like an Englishman. That's the only thing that matters. Our citizenship isn't a question of race: it's a common mode of thought and behaviour, a common ideal. Darwin gives us the key to it; it's a question of Natural Selection and the Survival of the Fittest. We happen to be the best people in the world, with the highest ideals of decency and justice and liberty and peace,

254

and the more of the world we inhabit, the better it is for humanity. Ourselves, our colonists, and the Americans: we all stand for the same things . . .'

He paused, setting his lips pugnaciously and gazing into the space of the smoke-clouded room. He bent over the map, repeating that slow, possessive gesture, as though he were gathering into his moving hand the hundreds of thousands of square miles the area of printed paper represented.

'All red . . . all red,' he murmured. 'And that was my reason,' he went on, 'for saying: "Why stop at the Zambezi?" Why stop at Africa? That's what Ruskin meant, I believe, when he spoke of our destiny – "the highest ever set before a nation to be accepted or refused". I maintain that knowing our own fitness to rule, we've no right to refuse it. We, the English-speaking people, have the power to gather the whole civilized world into one great Empire: every inch of it that is fit for white habitation. What about the whole continent of South America, the seaboards of China and Japan, the Holy Land, Mesopotamia, the Malay Archipelago? It's our duty to build up this irresistible power. When once that is done, war, man's greatest misfortune, will become impossible. However . . . you and I had better begin with Africa. Have another drink?'

Piet accepted it, though his brain was already buzzing with this heady eloquence. Cecil Rhodes, having exhausted his vaulting theme for the moment, descended to matters more personal:

'What are you and Haskard doing on the Witwatersrand?'

'Growing citrus and stone-fruit.'

'That's a new idea, isn't it? Will it pay?'

'I shan't make a fortune.'

'All the same you're a lucky devil. I envy you, Grafton. That's because I come of a farming stock, I suppose. I respect the man that produces. I'm only a tradesman. We take out, but we don't put anything back again: at least most of us don't; and I never forget that there's a bottom to every mine. Still, I've got to make money. I don't care for it for its own sake; but it's a power, and I like power. Without money you can't do anything, and I've a great deal to do. What's brought you to Kimberley?'

'I'm having a look round Haskard's interests. He needs a man on the spot. He told me to ask you for advice.'

'Tell me what his interests are, and I'll give it you for what it's worth.'

They talked about diamonds and the future of Kimberley. From the first moment Piet judged that this young man, for all his high-flown political ideals of Imperial expansion, was a practical genius in matters of business and knew his subject thoroughly. He explained the defects of the diamond-mining industry in its present state: the wastage of energy and mining material inherent in multiple ownership; the losses by theft, inevitable so long as native labourers were not strictly controlled; the traffic in liquor by which they were demoralized; the price-fluctuations which made estimates of profit impossible so long as production and sales were not restricted. He dealt with this limited industrial problem in the same large way as he had handled the future of the British Empire. In both cases he needed dictatorial powers. First, amalgamation, and then a managed output.

'I shall get both, sooner or later,' he said. 'That's why I have to make money. It may be the root of all evil, but it's also the root of all power, and power's what I want. You should keep these things, which have got to come, in mind when you consider Haskard's investments. Bring me a list of them tomorrow, and I'll tell you frankly what I think of them. We've talked enough for this evening. What about a night-cap?'

Next morning when he awoke Piet wished he had kept count of his drinks; he felt bruised, like a man who had been swept along for hours in the tail of a tornado. The only thing about which he felt certain was that he had encountered an overwhelming personality, less like a human being than a force of nature. He couldn't say that he liked Cecil Rhodes. There was something unsympathetic to him in the combination of that large, slovenly body, with its restless, jerky movements, and that shrill falsetto voice. And yet like or dislike seemed rather beside the point: the scale of this odd young man imposed respect. He felt that a new influence – though not necessarily a pleasant one – had come into his life and that he could not easily escape from it.

Meninsky, meeting him next morning, examined him quizically:

'You look like you've had a thick night, mate. Them beggars can't half shift it. How did you get on with young Rhodes?'

'All right. We'd a pretty wet evening and talked a good bit.'

'Talk? I tell you that chap can talk the hind-leg off a donkey when once he gets going. He'll talk for three hours, and then shut up like an oyster for a couple of weeks. And next time you meet him he'll stare right through you, the same as if he'd never set eyes on you before. You just wait and see.'

For once Meninsky was mistaken. During the month he spent in Kimberley Piet saw a great deal of 'young Rhodes', who had obviously taken a fancy to him – finding in him, perhaps, the embodiment of one of his favourite theories: an attractive, intelligent and lively combination of the two racial strains on whose union, he believed, the future of South Africa rested. Though he pounded away at his Imperial theme, he gave shrewd advice, not only on Haskard's business, but also on Piet's own modest investments. When Piet rode home to Witfontein his thoughts were still dominated by this strange encounter. Unconsciously, he would find himself thinking: 'Rhodes would say this' or 'Rhodes would do that', – an odd condition in one who had previously prided himself on his independence of judgment and did not like to think of himself as a disciple of anyone. Rhodes' singular appeal, indeed, was not to his intellect nor yet to any recognizable emotion: it was, rather, one of those manifestations of personal magnetism, unconnected with either, which are the empirical cause of some of the most fervent human loyalties. From the day he left Kimberley, Cecil Rhodes (whom he did not particularly like or even admire) was Piet's master, and he Rhodes' man. The mysterious influence displayed itself even in trivial things. When he met Maria, for instance, after his return to Witfontein, his first words to her were:

'I've been seeing an old friend of yours. Can you guess who it was?'

'I've no friends that I know of in Kimberley. Who was it?'

'Cecil Rhodes.'

'What! that funny, untidy boy who came with his brother? I never knew that was his first name, and I don't like it much either.'

'He asked after you. You were apparently the only person he remembered at Wonderfontein. You ought to feel complimented, Maria. I think it's quite possible he may become a great man – or is one already.'

'Oh, Piet! With a voice like that? I remember he was reading Greek, and he gave me a diamond.'

'A diamond? Let's have a look at it. I'm an expert on diamonds now.'

She brought the stone and showed it him.

'Well, yes. .... It's a diamond all right – though I don't think it's a very good one.'

'I can quite believe that. After all it was only a joke. I shall keep it, all the same. He told me . . .' She stopped abruptly; but Piet did not notice the hesitation.

'You'd better,' he said. 'Some day you'll be proud of it.'

(3)

In the winter of the following year Edward Haskard returned to South Africa in a new and glorified version. He had gone down from Cambridge, taken a Yeomanry commission, and through the influence of one of his father's old friends, who commanded it, scraped into a county regiment of no great distinction which made no objection to his being transferred, under the new Regimental Exchanges Act, into the Ninety-fourth Regiment, the Connaught Rangers, which was not only Irish, as befitted his ancestry, but also happened to be serving in South Africa, an unpopular station and the country of his birth.

Here, again, because of his family connections and origins, he quickly dropped into an ornamental job on the staff as aide-de-camp to the Commander-in-Chief of Her Majesty's forces in Natal, Sir Frederick Thesiger. In this post he had practically nothing to do, and did nothing so unobtrusively that he was scarcely missed at headquarters when he went on the long periods of leave which the general granted him. Naturally, he stayed with his parents at Brakfontein, but spent the greater part of his time with his own generation: with Lavinia, to whom he had always been deeply attached: with Piet, whom he had not known before and was surprised, remembering Janse's more difficult temperament, to find 'a cheery cove', and with Maria, who, now that Lavinia's second child, Cecilia, had increased her domestic reponsibilities, had become almost a permanent member of the household at Witfontein.

Maria liked Edward Haskard. She was disposed, having known so few, to like any presentable young man, and Edward, in his externals, was far and away the most distinguished specimen of his sex she had ever beheld. He had always been a healthy good-looking boy; but Trinity and the Army had smartened his appearance considerably. Whether he wore his scarlet

258

tunic, with its bright buttons and emerald facings, or the civilian clothes which were cut for him by his military tailor, Hawkes of Savile Row, he was always 'turned out' with the perfection of a newly-hatched butterfly. Not a hair of his glossy head was ever out of place, being fixed in position by a pomade of highly-scented bear's-grease, the greenhouse odour of which, combined with that of violet powder and shaving-soap, surrounded him with a perfumed aura and pervaded the house wherever he went. His main physical glory and care, at the moment of his arrival, was a heavy military moustache which had not, as yet, reached perfection, but which, carefully parted in the middle and sedulously stroked and combed to encourage its growth, gave an odd contradiction, in its manly ferocity, to the rather boyish mouth it adorned.

Maria, at first, was overwhelmed by young Haskard's external magnificence. He appeared to her unaccustomed eyes as an incarnation of one of the heroes, usually Guardsmen, whose strength and silence had thrilled her in reading the novels of Ouida, which she had found in the Haskards' library; but Edward, as she discovered as soon as his novelty had faded, was far too Irish to be silent and, in spite of the moustache's ferocity, anything but strong. By comparison with Piet, that close-knit bundle of hardened muscle enlivened by quick, practical wits, Edward Haskard appeared lamentably flabby in body and in mind. The contrast showed him up so completely that Maria felt more than ever kindly to him; but it destroyed the least chance (if there had been one) of her finding him romantic or falling in love with him.

When he fell mildly in love with her (Edward did everything by halves) she was naturally flattered and, with some qualms of conscience, mildly encouraged him. Even if she had no intention of marrying him, it was pleasant (and not in the least risky) to receive the attentions of such a polite and well-bred young man, so experienced in the technique of the kind of flirtation which would have appealed to du Maurier's charming young ladies in intervals between games of croquet in the garden of a country rectory.

Edward Haskard was a very perfect carpet-knight. He knew all the tricks of the parlour: was an adept at holding wool to be wound, turning over pages of music, supplying a cushion or footstool when one was needed, handing round cups of tea – even at singing sentimental ballads (usually Irish) with an extremely melodious and manly baritone voice, and listening to Lavinia's songs with ecstasy in his fine violet eyes. Piet granted him other accomplishments; he was an excellent shot with rifle or scatter-gun, and a fine horseman – although he would persist in describing point-to-points and runs with the Quorn in Leicestershire; he was physically strong, for all his appearance of softness; yet when Piet came into the house from the veld, with his dusty clothes, his clean-shaven, sun-scarred face toughened like leather, his brisk gait and his keen, merry eyes, it seemed to Maria as though a fresh breeze had entered with him and blown the fumes of scented bear's-grease away.

Major Haskard was actually a little jealous of his son's attentions to Maria, pathetically lamenting and exaggerating the burden of his advancing years, in the hope that she would reassure him that he was not so old as he felt. Maria did this willingly. On the whole she still enjoyed his company and his flatteries more than Edward's, for he was an old hand at the game and did not play it with his son's forlorn, sentimental seriousness. She had come to the conclusion that, if ever she were to marry, her choice would most probably fall – not on an elderly man like Jim Haskard, but certainly not on one of her own age so callow as poor Edward. Though she enjoyed flirtations, she was still entirely heart-free; and, soon after this, the cause of Major Haskard's jealousy, which resembled that of an old raven which falls on its offspring and dashes them into the sea, was removed by Edward's being recalled to Natal to grace, if not to assist, General Thesiger's mobilization against Cetewayo in the Zulu War.

She had never felt quite so tender towards Edward as on the day when he rode away in his scarlet uniform, the buttons of which she had polished with her own hands in the spirit of a 'Lady' burnishing a crusader's casque. She felt almost compelled to give him a glove, a gage to wear in his helmet and fling, if the opportunity should arise, in Cetewayo's face; knowing nothing of war, she still saw it as a romantic adventure; but her anxiety not to commit herself deterred her, though there were tears in her eyes when Edward turned in his saddle and threw her a kiss. He was so young, so innocent.

There was a great deal of feeling among the English in the Transvaal about this war. Maria heard Major Haskard and Piet discussing it hotly. Haskard himself was, of course, too old and too much of an invalid to serve in it, and Piet, as a family-man with responsibilities, considered it unnecessary to volunteer; but both of them felt indignant at the general refusal of the Dutch to take their share.

'After all,' Piet declared, 'it's much more their job than ours. We've set out to crush Cetewayo in their interests. The British do all the fighting and spending, and they take all the benefit.'

'It's the old, old story, my dear boy,' Haskard said. 'The fault of the Dutch has always been "giving too little and asking too much". It was precisely the same last year, when we polished off the appallingly bad job the Boers made over Sekukuni. I made a note of what Wolseley said at the time. Just listen to this: "I couldn't help feeling that the battle we were engaged in was essentially a Boer battle, but there were no Boers there. There were two thousand British soldiers and volunteers of European and Afrikander origin raised in the country, and I asked myself, in whose cause is this battle being fought? Why are we left to fight it out by ourselves, when these ignorant men, led by a few designing fellows, are talking nonsense and spouting sedition on the High Veld?" That's what Garnet Wolseley said. A fine fellow, Wolseley. Only forty-six, and a general! An Irishman, like myself, by the way,' he added modestly.

'But the trouble is now,' Piet maintained, 'that it isn't a matter of a few designing fellows. The whole damned country's gone sullen. D'you know that Paul Kruger, whom I've always regarded as a moderate man, was asked by Frere to raise a commando when he passed through Natal, and refused? Quite ready to give his advice on native warfare and all that. But to risk his skin? Not a bit of it! When they pressed him, he came out with a real try-on: said he'd take five hundred burghers and mop up Zululand if the Government would give the Transvaal its independence, and that the annexation had made friendly co-operation impossible. Joubert takes the same line. There are a few decent men left, like Piet Uys, thank heaven, but the rest are all shirkers.'

'Well, well, we can do without them, thank God!' Haskard said. 'Trust Fred Thesiger for that. Edward says it's going to be a walk-over, and he's on the spot. We shall soon have news.'

They had not long to wait for it. On the tenth of January the ultimatum to Cetewayo expired and the redcoats advanced in three columns into Zululand; ten days later the Twenty-fourth Regiment of eight hundred men was almost annihilated at Isandhlwana, and blood-drunken Zulus were tossing the spitted drummer-boys from spear to spear; on the next day the remains of the shattered Twenty-fourth, seventy men, under two lieutenants, in a laager of flour-bags and biscuit-tins, held up five thousand of Cetewayo's best warriors at Rorke's Drift – not more than five miles from the spot where the Voortrekkers had camped on the day of Dingaan's destruction. It was not till July, at Ulundi, that the Zulu power was broken, at the moment when reinforcements of ten thousand troops had arrived in Natal, and the Haskards received news from Edward that he was coming home for a month's leave, bringing with him two brother officers, one of whom had been wounded in the final advance.

'We must give these lads a good time,' Major Haskard said. 'By Jove, they deserve it! You can take them out shooting, of course; but it's a pity we haven't a bevy of pretty girls to entertain them. That's what young men home from the wars fancy most – or did in my day.'

CHAPTER TWO

(1)

MARIA was certainly ready to make any reasonable sacrifice on the altar of duty. She looked forward to the visit, in fact, with pleasure, for excitements of any kind were rare at Wonderfontein. The Haskards could only accommodate one visitor in addition to Edward at their farm; so it was decided that Piet and his wife should 'put up' the other, and that Maria should stay at Witfontein too, to relieve Lavinia of the burden of his entertainment. Major Haskard, meanwhile, was making all sorts of plans, based on his memories of country-house life in the West of Ireland, for a series of picnics and shooting trips, a card-party, and, as a crowning festivity, a dance at Brakfontein, to which a number of the neighbouring young people, selected by Piet, would be invited.

On the evening of the visitors' arrival Maria found herself increasingly and unreasonably nervous. She was not at all sure how Edward would expect her to receive him – nor, for that matter, what her own reaction would be; and, indeed, when he did appear, her heart softened towards him dangerously; for the campaign, with its exposure and short-commons, had hardened and aged him – he was no longer so overwhelmingly smart and well-groomed; his tunic was stained and torn and the bright buttons tarnished; his superb moustache, now fully-grown, looked almost too large for his pinched face, and the lips beneath it were firmer. She had never before felt so kindly towards him, and the fact that he was a hero home from the wars made her feel he was entitled to special treatment, even though she wasn't in love with him. If he wanted to kiss her, she felt she would have to let him.

Edward's companions appeared even more war-worn than himself. Both belonged to his regiment. The elder was a senior lieutenant named Martyn, a thick-set, unattractive man, with a brusque staccato utterance, who had escaped the perils of the campaign through an unromantic visitation of boils and veld-sores. Though he was the heir of a small squire in Galway, he had none of the western Irishman's irresponsible charm – that social quality which Major Haskard exploited so skilfully; perhaps it was not easy to be mercurial, Maria thought, with a stiff neck trussed up in bandages and a carbuncle at the nape of it. This forced immobility prevented him from turning his head, with the result that his eyes appeared to be set in a disconcerting stare. Though she felt sorry for poor Mr. Martyn in his affliction, she hoped it would not be her lot to make conversation for him at Witfontein.

Edward's second friend was an Englishman: a subaltern attached to the Ninety-fourth, named Richard Abberley, who had been wounded by an assegai-thrust in the left shoulder during the fight at Kambula. It was not, he protested, a very serious wound; but infection had delayed healing, and the doctors still insisted on his wearing a sling.

Nature could not have provided a more complete contrast to Martyn than Richard Abberley. He was a slim, tallish boy, fair-haired and delicate-featured, with grey eyes, which smiled before his lips, and an unusually quiet voice. He was inclined, Maria discovered, to smile at most of the things that amused her; there was always a flicker of humour lurking in the corner of those eyes which, gentle as they were, had a boldness and candour that reminded her of Piet's. His face, she decided at first, was almost too young and sensitive for a soldier's; it was still pale and transparent from loss of blood: and yet, beneath that delicacy there was a sense of firmness which – even though he looked like a boy – made her feel that, in spirit, he was more adult than Edward, for all his manly moustache.

Richard Abberley's mind was certainly quicker than Edward's, and his manners, though less studied, were easier. She was meeting, in fact, a good specimen of a type with which she had never before been acquainted: that of the well-bred, intelligent young Englishman of the land-owning class, the product of many generations of country living and easy circumstances, so sure of himself and of his position as to be perfectly natural with people of a different social environment – including the daughter of a back-veld farmer in the Transvaal. The fact that Maria, if not exactly beautiful, was a girl of his own age, fresh, high-spirited, ingenuous, and endowed with a quick sense of humour, made the adjustment easy for both of them.

It was at once a relief and an excitement to her when Mrs.

Haskard decided that Martyn, as the greater invalid of the two, was in more need of her attention, and handed over Abberley to Piet and Lavinia at Witfontein. Maria took him home with her. On the way, she was astonished at his inquisitiveness. He had never been on the High Veld before, and his lively mind was eager to master the lie of the land. He asked her innumerable questions in his quick, quiet voice: where was Kimberley, where was Pretoria; what was the name of that line of humped mountains to the north-west; what were the names of a bush or a bird or a herd of buck in the distance? Nor would he content himself with indefinite answers; she soon found she could not evade his curiosity by hedging.

'How terribly exact you are, Mr. Abberley,' she complained.

'Well, it's no good half-knowing things, is it, Miss Grafton? he said.

Nobody had ever called Maria 'Miss Grafton' before: the form of address enhanced her dignity, no doubt, yet she found it comical.

'I wish you wouldn't call me that, Mr. Abberley,' she said. 'We don't use surnames much here. My father's always "*Oom Jan*", though mother calls him the "*out baas*", and she's *Tante Lisbet*. My name is Maria.'

'A lovely name,' he said. 'My mother's is Mary. Mine's Richard, though most of my friends call me "Dick".'

'I much prefer "Richard".'

'As a matter of fact, so do I. I think it's quite a good name, but it takes some living up to. A Richard feels bound to behave quite differently from a Dick. What did you say your mother called your father?'

'The *ou baas*. It just means "the old master" – the head of the family.'

'I must learn Dutch,' he said seriously.

'You'll find that quite easy.'

'You only say that because you've always spoke it. I'm rotten at languages. Most Englishmen are. Will you teach me a little, Miss Gra . . . Sorry, I mean Maria?'

'If you'll teach me English. When you say that you're "rotten" . . .'

'Ah, that's just the slang of the moment.'

She laughed. 'But that's just as bad. "Slang" means "snake" to me.'

'To me it means ... well, I'm hanged if I know what it does mean. It's just loose, colloquial English. I shall have to be careful.'

They laughed together. She liked his eyes when he laughed.

'Why do you want me to teach you Dutch? My High Dutch is shocking.'

'While I'm serving here it's my job as a soldier to learn the language of the country.'

'Isn't that taking your job very seriously?'

'Of course it is. It's a family failing. My father's a colonel on the reserve, and my grandfather before him fought at Waterloo. Besides which, it's the way I'm built. I want to know everything ... everything.'

'You're not very like Edward Haskard. He was born in South Africa; but I doubt if he'd understand a word if I started talking Dutch to him.'

Richard Abberley smiled. 'I don't suppose he would. He's a charming, kindly soul, Edward. I like him enormously. It was extraordinarily nice of him to invite me up here for a week or two before I go on to Pretoria.'

'Are you sure your wound will be quite all right so soon?'

'Oh, yes. I'm getting sympathy on false pretences. It's nearly healed: I don't really need this sling. But I ought to change the dressing tonight. The only trouble is, it's not easy to get at.'

'I'll change it for you.'

'Why should you? I'll get your brother – he is your brother, isn't he? – to give me a hand.'

'I want to do it for you,' Maria said.

'The "ministering angel"? All right, Maria, you shall.'

It gave her acute pleasure when he called her 'Maria'. The familiar word, on these unfamiliar lips, had a caressing sound – 'But I shall never be able to call him "Richard" as easily as that,' she thought.

He seemed to be equally unselfconscious, and consequently 'at home', with Lavinia and her small son, James. Maria felt a little jealous, indeed, since she had already established a right of property, when he and Lavinia talked about England and discovered common acquaintances who had entertained him at Capetown on his way through.

'I ought really,' he said, 'to have disembarked there – or possibly at Port Elizabeth, and to have hurried up to join our regiment at Pretoria; but, with this Zulu trouble, they wanted all available officers and men in Natal, so they pushed me, and the draft I was bringing out, on to Durban. I'm glad they did, as a matter of fact.'

'You mean you enjoyed the war?'

'Good heavens, no! If anyone ever tells you they like fighting, Mrs. Grafton, just don't believe it. Of course, it's all good experience, and I got a "mention". But I was merely trying to make a pretty speech. I meant, quite honestly, it was nice to be here.'

'I hope you'll be comfortable,' Lavinia said.

'I shall be in heaven. Don't forget we've been roughing it on half-rations or less for nearly four months. This'll be the first time I've slept in a bed since I landed in Africa. And I like being spoilt. Maria is going to dress my shoulder this evening and start teaching me Dutch tomorrow.'

'You won't get much time for that, if I know my dear father,' Lavinia said. 'Your programme's mapped out for you as thoroughly as a visiting royalty's. Tomorrow, I think Piet said, he's arranged a shooting-party.'

'Well, you know, we've had rather a lot of shooting and being shot at lately,' he said mischievously, 'and, as a matter of fact, I can't shoot with my arm in a sling. I'm afraid I shall have to stay at home and learn Dutch.'

'But you said . . .' Maria began.

She was going to say he had told her the sling was unnecessary, but the reproachful glance and the smile he gave her compelled her to stop. The rest of the sentence was a secret between them. It was run to share secrets.

'Well, Maria will be able to teach you Dutch far better than I could,' Lavinia said, as though she were proud of the fact.

'He never asked you, my dear,' Maria thought.

That evening, before he turned-in looking rather pathetically wan with tiredness, she bathed and dressed his wound. It was an ugly, glancing gash from an assegai. The wound was dry and the dressing had stuck to it, and she knew she was giving him pain; but when she hurt him he only screwed up his eyes and smiled.

'I'm so sorry,' she said.

'You needn't be sorry. Your hands are as light as – what shall I say? – as falling plum-petals. I have to show off a bit because I want sympathy.'

'That's not true,' she said. 'I know it hurt, because I saw you blink.'

'Well, perhaps it did hurt a trifle. You're very literal, aren't you, Maria? The truth, the whole truth, and nothing but the truth.'

'I suppose I am. But a horrid wound like that isn't exactly a thing to joke about.'

'Then this time I'll tell you the truth; I've enjoyed myself thoroughly.'

In spite of the shock that the jagged wound had given her – the first sight of it had sent a ridiculous shiver of pain, or something near to it, up the back of her thighs – Maria had enjoyed herself too. The submissiveness of this young man had made her feel not merely tender, but important and, in an odd way, possessive. By this act, the intimacy of which endowed it with a vague ritual significance, she had established indefinite, but inalienable, rights over him, which she was prepared to defend. It had made him her own private property, and nobody else's. When she had left him that night those moments returned to her in the memory of the white muscular shoulder through which the assegai had torn. Abberley looked so slight in his uniform that she would never have guessed how well-muscled, how strong that shoulder was; yet the skin that had been so brutally used was smooth, white and delicate – of a satiny texture, finer even than her own – a skin, she thought, of which a girl might have been proud.

Next morning he was up earlier than herself. It was a still day, with all the brilliance of the High Veld winter, the sun rising blood-red and a bloom of rime on the ground. She met him coming back from a walk with the sun in his happy eyes. He had discarded his sling, and waved to her from a distance.

'I walked nearly to the Haskards',' he said. 'Not a sign of life there as yet. They don't know what they're missing.'

'I hope you've not tired yourself, Richard.'

He laughed: 'Tired? I'm sure I don't look it. I slept like a log. How could I be tired in this sparkling air? I'm hungry, if that's what you mean. I believe I smell bacon.'

'You shouldn't have taken off your sling,' she said anxiously.

'You've cured me completely. But don't let anyone know. I must put it on again before Edward comes.'

Again that strangely-sweet conspiracy. . . . They walked back to the stoep together talking and joking as naturally as if they had known one another all their lives. After breakfast Edward and Piet rode over together to collect Richard Abberley for the shooting-party.

'I'm awfully sorry, you know,' he said, 'but my arm won't come up. I suppose I shall have to keep it still for a day or two.'

Maria thought that Edward eyed him suspiciously.

'You can ride over quietly to Brakfontein and lunch with my mother.'

'I'd just as soon stay here, if I shan't be a nuisance.'

He glanced at Maria slyly. Piet looked at her too and laughed. She was angry with him for calling attention to her like that, and went back to the nursery to Lavinia's babies.

'I'm not going to run after him, anyway,' she thought. 'If he wants me, he'll have to fetch me.'

When the others had ridden away he sat smoking on the stoep: she knew he was there because she could smell the tobacco. Then she heard him get up and walk restlessly to and fro. She was forcing herself to talk to Lavinia, but her divided attention made her lose her thread. She heard his steps as he entered the house, walking from room to room. He appeared in the doorway and smiled.

'What about my lesson?' he said quietly.

She sighed. Do you want me, Lavinia?'

'No, go and give him his lesson for goodness' sake and keep him quiet.'

'Thank you, Mrs. Grafton,' he said gravely.

'Shall we sit on the stoep?' Maria asked him.

'Isn't the day too lovely for that? Couldn't we walk to the top of the ridge and see what's on the other side? I can never see a skyline like that without wanting to look over.'

'It's farther than you think, the air is so clear. We'd much better take the ponies.'

'All right – but I think you South Africans are awfully lazy,' he said. 'You ride everywhere. In a couple of generations you'll have no legs left.'

They saddled the ponies. Richard made a stirrup of his hand to help her to mount.

'I wish you wouldn't do that,' she said. 'I'm not used to it.'

'Well, see what it feels like, anyway,' he insisted.

She placed her foot in his hand and was conscious of her rough *velskoene*. He lifted her into the saddle easily, then vaulted into his own.

269

'You used your left arm, too,' she reproached him. 'You may be very strong, but you're not very sensible.'

'I'd forgotten about it, to tell you the truth, Maria. And that isn't a matter of strength, it's just knack. I'm used to it.' (She felt faintly jealous.) 'You see, my sisters hunt,' he went on, 'with the Worcestershire.'

'How many sisters have you?'

'Two. Lucy and Annabel, bless them!'

'That's why he's so natural with girls,' she thought.

'What do they hunt?'

'Why, foxes, of course,' he laughed. 'That's what hunting means in England.'

'There's no reason to laugh at me. I didn't know. I'm not English.'

'I know. Edward told me your mother was Dutch, but I can't believe it. I should have taken your brother Piet for an Englishman any day. And you ... why, you're just about the most English thing I've ever seen – so English that you make me feel homesick.'

'If it's true what you say about me, you oughtn't to feel home-sick at all.'

'You're too sharp for me. Well, as a matter of fact, I don't ... not when I'm with you. That's the delightful part of it.'

'So that is the second untruth you've told since I've known you.'

'You told me yesterday I was too exact. I mean. . . . What do I mean? I mean that here, in the middle of Africa, where everything's different, it's astonishing to find oneself talking to somebody like you who reminds one all the time of one's home. You see, you might have stepped right out of a Worcestershire orchard. You don't seem quite to belong here.'

'Oh, yes, I do. I'm as African as I can be. I love Africa every bit as much as you love your England.'

'That's what makes it exciting. You've got the best of both worlds. Your very name, Grafton . . .'

'Well, that's my father's, of course.'

'I know. But the point is that it's the name of our village: Grafton Lovett in Worcestershire.'

'Our village sounds very grand. Do you mean you own it?'

'I suppose my father owns most of it; but I never shall. My elder brother will have it. He's in the Worcestershires. I'm what is known as a penniless younger son. We aren't a bit important, you know. The only thing about us is that we've lived in the same place for over four hundred years. And that's not important either. There must be lots of peasant families who've lived in Worcestershire quite as long as we have.'

'What is this "Worcestershire" you're always talking about?'

'In my brother's case, it means the regiment. But Worcestershire – the county – I don't know what you'd call it here – is . . . well, for me it's the most perfect place in the world; it's the centre of my life and my dreams; it's what I care most about; it's . . .'

'Here's the top. Suppose we sit down under this thorn-tree while you get your breath, Richard?'

'Very well. But I've hardly begun. When I start on the subject of Worcestershire . . .'

They knee-haltered their ponies and sat down at the foot of the leafless acacia. Its bare boughs gave no shade, but Maria, flushed with the climb, took off her cotton *kappie,* and the shadow of the twigs fell criss-cross on her cheeks. Below them the golden plains dappled with game rolled away to the feet of Magaliesberg; but though this was what he had come out to see, Richard Abberley turned his back on it. He flung himself at Maria's feet and sat there, with folded arms, gazing at her so intently (and, as she thought, critically) that she felt herself blushing and had to speak:

'I wish you'd go on, and tell me more about your family and your country,' she said.

'Well, my father's a soldier – or was – and my mother's a darling, and my sisters, as I've told you already, are nice, lively young persons. The place where we live is right in the middle of England; you couldn't get nearer its heart if you tried, and the people are just as English as they can be. Like you. It's not a large county: you could drop it down into that plain, at our feet here, and lose it; but then, like you again, it's full of the most astonishing variety: the north's quite different from the south and the east from the west. There are hills all round it, and all the hills are different: I mean they have different shapes, and a different feeling. Then there are three jolly rivers – Severn, Avon and Teme – all different and all running more or less south. The Severn's the trunk of a tree, upside down on the

271

map, and the others are its branches . . . Like this . . .'

He scratched the shape of the river system with a stick on the tawny earth.

'And we – we live right in the middle, just here, with the big hills I spoke of to look at on every side. It isn't a plain; it's a tumbled sort of country of hills and twisting valleys, every one with a tiny brook in the bottom of it. There are farm-houses and villages scattered everywhere: you'd never guess they were there until you come on them, they're so hidden in woods and orchards. Some of the farms are lovely buildings, hundreds of years old, and lots of them moated . . .'

She did not know what 'moated' meant, but she let him run on: he looked so entranced and happy in his narration.

'Round us, at Grafton Lovett, there's a regular cluster of little villages with delicious names: Chaddesbourne – that's where our cousins, the Ombersleys, live; Monk's Norton – two maiden aunts of mine, Lettice and Annabel, live there in a Carolean house. No expectations, unfortunately: they're wedded to the Church – all these little places have churches, I ought to have told you. You can hear the bells ringing on Sundays. You go from one village to another by winding lanes with high banks and hedges full of honeysuckle or wild roses, or, sometimes, by field paths. You don't even know what a field is. You see, the country isn't open like this; there's a network of hedges everywhere with a few acres of meadow or tilth enclosed inside them. And the whole country smells sweet because of the flowers in the hedges and those that grow in these fields, cow-slips, primroses, meadowsweet.'

'It sounds as if it were always spring in Worcestershire,' Maria said.

He laughed: 'I believe you're right; but that's the way one remembers the things of one's childhood. I was back in spring at that moment, when you interrupted me. My father and I were riding through the lanes to a great Elizabethan house called White Ladies, belonging to the Pomfrets, a Norman family that settled there long after us, as a matter of fact.'

'I don't like the sound of those lanes,' Maria said. 'With all those hedges how can you ever breathe in them?'

'Oh, we've all the fresh air we want. We're quite healthy and live to great ages. All the people like us live the same quiet sort of country life. We keep very much to ourselves: I expect we're terribly snobbish – my aunts are, anyway. But that isn't because

272

we object to new people. It's rather because we know they can't possibly understand our way of life: we have such a lot to do, and our interests would bore them; we belong to the soil, and they don't.'

'You mean you're all farmers, like us?'

'Well, we own a lot of farms, of course, and we have to look after the tenants, naturally. Farmers are not quite the same in England as they are here. They don't all of them own their land.'

'Fancy farming land you didn't own! I should hate doing that!'

'Well, they seem to like it all right; the landlords spend most of their time in what you might call pottering about, but they're always busy – at least my father is. And it's a perfect life. I don't know ... the whole countryside is so quiet and friendly and green. You can have no idea of its greenness, Maria.'

'You've never seen the High Veld in spring. I don't believe that anything could ever be greener than that.'

'But our country's green all the year round, you see.'

'Then it must rain all the year round.'

He laughed: 'Well, it does, more or less. But it's friendly rain; not a deluge like the thunderstorms, day after day, down in Zululand, that jolly near washed the lot of us into the Tugela. You wouldn't mind it a bit. In fact, I'm sure you'd love it. It makes the air soft and kind to the skin. All the girls have complexions like yours – that's one of the reasons why I say you're so English. That reminds me: what about learning a little Dutch?'

'It's too late to begin now,' Maria said. 'We ought to go home; Lavinia will be wondering.'

'What a bore! I could stay here for ever – with you,' he said.

'No, you'll miss your friendly rain,' she said. 'There won't be another drop here before September.'

'I said "with you",' he reminded her.

So the days slipped by, in the brilliance of the High Veld winter, with its flawless blue overhead, the golden veld beneath, and between, the crystalline depths of pellucid air. Richard Abberley throve on that air and on the fresh food of Witfontein. His body looked firmer; his face lost its pinched look, its transparent pallor; his grey eyes brightened in contrast with his bronzed skin. The wound, too, healed rapidly and soon required no more dressing, though he still occasionally, for protective purposes, carried his arm in a sling and continued to evade Edward Haskard's invitations. He looked so well, indeed, that Edward grew more and more obviously suspicious of his motives, and Maria was troubled.

'I think you ought to go out shooting with them, at least once or twice,' she said.

'I shall get all the shooting I want when I rejoin at Pretoria,' he told her.

'But it looks so unnatural, deserting the other men.'

'I shall see all the men I want to see in Pretoria, too. But I shan't see you, Maria ... at least, not very often. I suppose I shall be able to ride over here easily enough when I get leave?'

'It's only about thirty miles. Adrian used to ride to and fro when he was in the Volksraad.'

'Do you think I've exhausted Piet's hospitality?'

'You don't know South Africa. We always like to see strangers.'

'So I'm still a stranger, am I?'

'Oh, dear, can't I ever say anything without your catching me up? You know quite well Piet will like you to come.'

'Would Edward?'

'What on earth has Edward to do with it?'

'That's just what I wanted to know.'

'Of course, we all like Edward.'

'You don't like him – you, personally, I mean – you don't like him particularly? I just want to know that. You see, I've a feeling he does ... like you, Maria.'

She shook her head: 'If you mean ...'

'Yes, that's what I did mean. So there's nothing that I – as a man of honour and all that – need worry about?' She smiled, but was silent. 'All right, then, we'll say no more of it. Poor old Edward! Do you realize that I've been here more than a week, and I've never yet seen your father and mother or the place where you live?'

'You wouldn't think anything of Wonderfontein. It isn't a grand house like this. It's just an ordinary farm. It wouldn't interest you.'

'It would interest me enormously. I believe you're trying to keep me away from it. That's not playing fair. You encourage me to talk for hours about my home, and then . . .'

'No, no, it isn't that, Richard.'

'Then we'll ride over this afternoon – or walk, if you like. Is that a bargain?'

She was glad, in a way, he had forced her to take him there. It wasn't that she was ashamed of it or of her parents; she had only wondered how he – who evidently regarded Piet's and the Haskards' grand scale of existence as rough and ready – would fit into the primitive severity of Wonderfontein. She was also a little afraid of her father's reaction: John Grafton always went speechless and drew back into his shell when Englishmen were about.

That day, at least, they saw Wonderfontein at its best. Enveloped in the superb light of the winter afternoon, it had a modest, homely grace of its own that seemed the more dignified for its lack of pretentiousness. It looked as if it had been lived in and loved – as if it were a home. In the hues of its tawny sun-baked brick and amid the rich growth of her mother's long-established garden, it seemed nearer to the soil and more natural than either of the new houses. Lisbet welcomed them in the garden. She was wearing a full-skirted cotton dress and a sun-bonnet. She eyed Richard keenly and kindly when Maria, fluttered by the occasion, introduced him.

'It is you, then, who have stolen my daughter from me all these days, Mr. Abberley?' she said, with the lilt in her English speech she had learnt as a girl at the Cape.

'Do you blame me for wanting to steal her, Mrs. Grafton?'

'No, that I won't say. Maria is a good child, and she doesn't see many young people. She's my baby, you know.' Maria laughed and slipped her arm round her and kissed her. 'She has coaxing ways, too, as you see. She gets everything she wants out of us.'

'That also is easy to understand.'

'I think you are probably rather like her in that, Mr. Abberley. Come in, now, and I'll make you a cup of tea, which is what every Englishman wants, or used to when I was a girl.'

'How clever of you to remember such things, Mrs. Grafton. But you're right. We're creatures of habit. I should like nothing better.'

Lisbet led the way to the stoep. They entered the *voorhuis*. It was cool and dim inside, sweet-smelling and specklessly clean;

275

the old stinkwood furniture shone with long use and with its nut-brown patina of wood-smoke.

'You are a soldier, I see, Mr. Abberley,' Lisbet said. 'When I was young and gay at the Cape we used to see a great deal of the officers of the garrison. That's where I learnt my English, such as it is. And, of course, my husband is English.'

'I've been asking Maria where her father came from, but she couldn't tell me.'

'He came from the Eastern Province. My father's farm, Welgelegen, was not far from Grahamstown.'

'Ah, yes. But I mean before that.'

Lisbet gently evaded him. 'You know there were a great many settlers from England about that time. Now your tea is ready. Our menfolk always drink coffee, so you mustn't blame me if it isn't exactly to your taste.'

A shadow darkened the doorway: John Grafton stood there. He caught the colour of Abberley's uniform tunic, and drew back quickly. He might even have escaped without being seen, had not Lisbet's quick eyes seen the movement. She knew what it meant, and hurried to reassure him.

'Come in, father,' she said. 'It's only Maria, who has brought with her Piet's guest, Edward Haskard's friend, Mr. Abberley.'

John Grafton came forward and shook hands without looking at him. 'You are welcome,' he said.

A good type, Richard Abberley decided. Though this was hardly the kind of man he would have expected to find as Maria's father, he was impressed by the quiet dignity of John Grafton's bearing and by the refinement of his features which contrasted so strikingly with his farmer's clothes – the thick moleskins, the open shirt-neck and the ragged, wide-brimmed straw-hat, all of which hardly seemed to fit in with Maria's exquisiteness. Her mother . . . yes, there the connection seemed more reasonable. From the moment when Lisbet had greeted him in the garden he had been impressed by the physical distinction of this white-haired woman, whose face was so young and innocent and whose clear hazel eyes showed the candour he knew in Maria's: by a distinction of manners, too – for she had done the honours of their home, which by the standards to which he was accustomed, was hardly more than a labourer's cottage, with the tact and poise of a great lady. But this dour, bearded man, who now, as though seeking concealment

276

instinctively, had retired into the shadow of the embrasure that contained the hearth and sat sipping his tea without speaking, was another matter. His remoteness negatived the serene warmth of the reception Maria's mother had given him. Abberley felt that he wasn't welcome, and in his innocence couldn't imagine why. Yet John Grafton's favour was so important to him that he had to make an effort to ingratiate himself.

'Your son Piet, and Maria,' he said, 'have been my good angels, sir. I came up from Natal a week ago, and they've made a new man of me.'

John Grafton nodded his head. 'Ay, Piet's a good lad. I reckon he'll make you comfortable. I heard tell of you. You've been in the wars, they say?'

'We've been trying to settle Cetewayo's hash, sir; and by now I think we've pretty well succeeded. We found the Zulus good fighters.'

John Grafton smiled: the smile made his face suddenly charming.

'I know all about them, and so does my wife. They nearly had us at Blaauwkrans, forty years ago.'

'That was under Retief, sir?'

'Pretorius . . . Andries Pretorius. They called the place where the big fight was Blood River. We reckoned we'd broken them then; but the Zulus are a masterful tribe.'

He was getting on rather well now, Richard Abberley thought. As he listened to John Grafton his mind had been troubled – not so much by the words he used as by the curve and the intonation of his speech – its broad vowels and a faint burr in it, both of which were familiar.

'You've been a long time in this country, I understand, sir?'

'More than forty-two years. A long time.'

'Then, of course, you weren't born here?'

John Grafton put down his cup and rose from his seat. He looked from side to side, as though he were anxiously measuring the possibility of escape without any breach of politeness. Then, apparently, despairing or changing his mind, he sat down again.

'No,' he said, 'I was born in England.'

'I asked you, sir, because of your name. It struck me the first time I heard it. You see, it's the same as that of the village in which I was born, the place we belong to – Grafton Lovett, in Worcestershire.'

John Grafton's body stiffened: he gripped the arms of his chair:

'What did you say your name was? I didn't catch it at first.'

'My name's Abberley, sir. Richard Abberley.'

'Abberley.... Yes.'

'You know it?'

John Grafton hesitated. 'Yes.... At least I've heard it. Many years ago, many years ago. When I lived ... in a place called Dulston.'

'That's a long way from us; but still, it's in Worcestershire, sir. Isn't it strange that I should have come so many thousands of miles to find myself, by sheer chance, in the house of a fellow-countryman? No wonder I told Maria she might have stepped straight out of a Worcestershire orchard. That explains it, doesn't it?'

John Grafton did not answer him. He rose slowly and moved to the door.

'You're going, John?' Lisbet said.

'Yes, my dear. I must see the cattle kraaled before it is dark.' He turned to Abberley and held out his hand. 'Good-bye, Mr. Abberley,' he said. 'I must go about my business.'

'I hope I may see you again, sir, and that we may have a long talk about Worcestershire. When my leave is over I hope to be stationed at Pretoria.'

'Pretoria's a long way from here, Mr. Abberley – and Worcestershire's even farther. My memory for those old times is not very good – no, not very good. I wish you good day, sir.'

'Your mother is wonderful, Maria: so sweet and young and dignified. Her eyes are like yours. But your father I can't understand.'

'He's not easy to understand. Most people find that, Richard. I've never known him anything but silent like that. It's his nature. Adrian's nearly as quiet as he is. He's had a hard life, you know, and he's not a young man any longer; and I don't think he likes the English very much.'

'That's ridiculous. If he's English, he must be proud of it. And your mother's so different. So warm. From the moment I saw her I felt completely at home with her. But I could make no headway with him – not an inch.'

'In spite of all your well-known charms? That must have been a disappointment!'

'It seemed as though he disliked me at sight.'

'I don't think he disliked you. Why did you want to "make headway" with him?'

'You know that perfectly well. Because he's your father.'

'I shouldn't worry, if I were you.'

Yet she, herself, was troubled.

'When I suggested that I might be riding over from Pretoria . . .'

'Well, it *is* a long way, as he said.'

'If it were twice as long it would make no difference to me.'

'We had better hurry,' Maria said, 'or we shan't get in before dark.'

'There'll soon be a moon.'

'We can't wait for the moon, Richard.'

She touched up her pony and shot on in advance of him. When he had caught up with her he returned to the subject:

'When I heard him speak I could have sworn he came from our part of the country; and you see, I was right.'

'I thought you were rather *rude*, asking all those questions?'

'But I wanted to know, Maria.'

'Was it really so important as all that?'

'Of course, it was immensely important to me. Haven't I told you all along how I felt you and I had more in common than I could explain? Now I know where that feeling came from. Your English ancestors and mine must have been born under the same stars and lived side by side for hundreds of years. That's why we've never been strangers.'

'The same stars, Richard? What do you mean? Aren't the stars the same everywhere?'

'My sweet child, of course not! Your stars are brighter than ours – or seem brighter; but there are not nearly so many of them. Do you see that great dragon sprawling northwards over the ridge? That's Orion, the hunter.'

'I didn't know stars had names. How clever you are.'

'You see which I mean?'

'Yes . . . I think so.'

'Come nearer and let me show you.' She obeyed; he slipped his arm round her shoulder and pointed: 'There . . .'

'Yes. I'm certain now.'

'Well, at home, at this moment, he'd be hanging over the south. I'm not positively certain, but that's where I think he

279

would be. And instead of the empty black space that's over us here, the English sky will be crowded with all sorts of brilliant constellations which we can't see: the Great Bear and Andromeda and Cassiopeia's chair, and Aldebaran blazing away in the middle; while all those little groups over there in the south – the Southern Cross (you surely know that?) and the False Cross, and that great big star Canopus, which is the brightest you've got – aren't even visible in England. I'd never set eyes on one of them before we drew near the Equator.'

'Well, the moon's the same, anyway, I suppose.'

'Not a bit of it! Your moon's all the wrong way round. I mean: our moon, when it's waxing, looks like a "D", while yours faces the right like a "C". It'll be up in a moment. I'll show you just what I mean.'

Maria shivered. 'It's much too cold to stay star-gazing here. Let's go on.'

She knew she had disappointed him, yet she couldn't help herself. During the last few days, since he had regained his strength, their relationship had changed: she had felt that he was much less in her power than he had been when he was an invalid; the initiative had passed, as it were, from her hands into his. Though she knew she loved him – she had loved him, she told herself, from the very first – his growing predominance frightened her. After all, this young man was a stranger, an alien, in race, in culture, in station, in everything, a visitant from another hemisphere no less mysterious than the stars of which he had spoken and which she had never seen. Like a comet rather than a star he had soared into her empty sky and filled it with unfamiliar splendour and light. In a few days more – she had already begun to count them – he would be gone, the light would have faded, and perhaps it would never return. Though she knew little of such things, tradition had taught her that men were lighter in their loves than women. If she gave him her whole heart, as she feared she had given it already, and let him ride away with it, she knew that, being what she was, she could never recover it. Though she trusted him utterly and reproached herself for her unworthy reservations, she distrusted herself for trusting him. It was hard for her to believe that she, who was nothing more than the casual companion of a convalescent holiday, could fill his whole life as he already filled hers. She did not doubt that she filled it at this moment; nor could she believe that, once having loved, she would not love

280

him for ever; yet the whole romantic circumstance of their meeting – his tense mood, of a man who has only just escaped death; their complete isolation and constant propinquity, the miraculous beauty of the setting of sundrenched or star-lit veld in which their love's lot had been cast, the conjunction of his masterful youth and her own ardent innocence – made her wonder if the exalted mood which had swept them both off their feet were not almost too intense, too high-pitched to be durable – on his part at least.

Therefore, on this homeward ride, though she yearned to surrender to her heart's inclinations, Maria withdrew herself from him and rode by his side in silence, not trusting her tongue. She knew he was conscious of this deliberate withdrawal, that it puzzled and irritated him. He, too, was so moody and silent, so like a sulky child, that she could not help feeling more than usually tender and sorry for him – and a little for herself.

'What ridiculous creatures we are,' she thought, 'behaving like this!'

They rode up to the lights of Witfontein without speaking another word. As they dismounted and handed over their ponies to Klaas the Hottentot, the bright disc of the moon sailed slowly above the black ridge they had crossed on their ride back from Wonderfontein and dimmed the stars.

'There, you see: it's just as I told you,' Abberley said. 'It *is* the wrong way round. That should teach you to believe me.'

Maria could not help laughing at his aggrieved tone.

(2)

The full moon, which was due in three days, had been an important factor in Major Haskard's plans for his guests' entertainment. It was to be celebrated by a dance – the first that had ever been given at Brakfontein – to which all the young folk from the neighbouring farms (except Barend Prinsloo's savage sons) were to be invited. Major Haskard had left the list of invitations – as he left most other things – to Piet, relying on his son-in-law's taste to see that the guests were presentable and that their dancing would not be too rowdy for Mrs. Haskard's sense of propriety.

From the moment when the plan had been announced Maria had been wondering what she should wear. She had outgrown the frock which her mother had improvised for Sarie's wedding, and possesed no other that seemed suitable for such a grand occasion. She had meant to consult with Lisbet on the afternoon when she had taken Richard to Wonderfontein; but his oddly disturbing encounter with her father had driven the project from her mind – and now she had only two days in which to get ready.

'I'm going over to see mother again tomorrow morning,' she told him as they said good night.

'All right. What time shall we start, then?'

'I shall be gone before you're awake.'

'Are you ready to bet on it?'

'I want to go alone, really – if you don't mind.'

'I shall mind a great deal. Our time's growing dreadfully short. Why shouldn't I come with you?'

'I want to see mother alone. How jealous you are!'

'Of course I'm jealous. I don't want to miss a minute of you. Even if you want to talk to your mother alone, we should have the ride over and back again. What's the matter with you tonight, Maria? You've changed suddenly; I don't understand. What is all this mystery, anyway?'

'There's no mystery at all. I want mother to find me a frock for the Haskards' dance. You'd only be in the way.'

'That's a polite way of putting it! What's wrong with the one you're wearing?'

'Oh, Richard, don't be so foolish!'

'I'm not. It's the kind I'm used to. It suits you perfectly. Of course, if you want to break all the young men's hearts by dolling yourself up . . .'

'You know I don't want to break anyone's heart. I want to look nice. Why shouldn't I do you credit?'

'You look quite nice enough for me as you are. What time shall we start, then?'

'I've told you I'm going alone. I think it's time you devoted yourself a little more to Lavinia. After all, she's your hostess.'

'I shall be waiting for you in the morning,' he said.

But she was gone, and half-way to Wonderfontein, before he opened his eyes.

'How you grow, child!' Lisbet said. 'It seems only the other day that we made you the new dress for Sarie's wedding. You're too long-legged for the ones I wore when I was a girl; but your grandmother was a good deal taller than your aunt Anna and me, and must have been slender enough, poor soul, before she had her family. Let us look in the Welgelegen wagon-chest, the one that wasn't burnt, and perhaps we may find something that will only need a few stitches, though you've given me little time for such a task.'

Maria followed her eagerly. The wagon-chest, which had come from Welgelegen and, before that, from the farm at the Cape, in the French Hoek valley, where her grandmother Jacoba Celliers had been born, and had finally survived the destruction of Blauwkrans, had always held a mysterious attraction for her. There was no end to the enchanting variety of its carefully-folded contents – the faded elegancies of an earlier, more settled life, the bunches of bright-hued ribbons, the frilled cambric *kappjes*, the filmy wisps of Mechlin lace, the Kashmir shawl (which one of Jacoba's naval flames had brought her from India more than seventy years ago), the coquettish toy-like silk parasols with their folding ivory sticks. Besides rolls of material there were several dresses of figured Lyons satin, immaculate and unfaded for all their age, and one lace-fichued gown of rustling taffeta, with strips and flounces, on which, as soon as she saw it, Maria's eyes fastened greedily.

'Can we try that one, mother?' she said.

'You can try it, my little heart, but I know it won't fit you. That was your grandmother's wedding-dress. How they must have laced her in! I put it on once myself, but the waist wouldn't meet by inches, and I'm sure you're no slighter now than I was then. Besides, I'm afraid the silk is faded in parts and has cut where it had been folded. That's the way with taffeta.'

'Do let me try it, mother.'

Maria stripped to her shift, and Lisbet, watching her, thought how slim and straight and graceful she was, this child of hers who, almost without her being aware of it, had become a woman. 'She's still only a child,' Lisbet thought; and yet, seeing Maria's eager face and flushed cheeks, remembered how excited she herself had been when she had stayed at the Cape as a girl even younger than Maria, and had been taken by her friends, the Truters and Cloetes, to dances at which English officers of the garrison had appeared in the splendour of their dress uniforms. There was one of her partners, an Ensign named Fellows, who had quickly been taken with her, pursuing

283

her everywhere and insisting on taking her out sailing in Table Bay. Indeed, if her mother hadn't considered her education complete and brought her home again unexpectedly to Welgelegen, hundreds of miles away, she might easily have married him instead of John Grafton. 'If that had happened to me,' she reflected, 'how different my life would have been! But then, I,' she thought modestly, 'was not nearly so attractive as Maria is with her tall, graceful shape, her jet-black brows, her honey-coloured hair and her slim white shoulders. No wonder that English boy has fallen in love with her! I hope they won't break one another's hearts, that's all – though hearts are more easily mended, thank heaven, than one dreams at that age! I must ask her about him.'

'Yes, it suits you, my darling,' she said; 'but I'm sure it won't meet at the back. I daren't put any strain on it. See, the taffeta's split, as I told you, though of course we might use the lace at the neck.'

'Oh dear, it's beginning to tear already,' Maria said. 'You'll have to take it off me: I could never get out of it myself. But do be careful.'

Lisbet laughed and carefully extricated her from the dress. Maria threw back her tousled head and laughed too.

'What a tiny waist she must have had! I always thought she was fat – what Mrs. Haskard calls "stout". And what a pity! It would have been perfect, wouldn't it? The right length and everything.'

'Perhaps rather too grand, too elaborate. After all, it's a wedding-dress, and you're not getting married, are you? There's one more here, I know, and I think it will suit you better. Yes, this is it.'

'Isn't that rather too sober-coloured?'

'We'll try it and see.'

It was a full-skirted frock of heavy lustrous foulard, in which dove-coloured stripes alternated with others more pale to which the silk gave here the opalescent sheen of an oyster-shell and there the dull gleam of platinum.

'I can get into this much more easily,' Maria said, 'and the waist's not too small. Oh, mother, I think it's lovely. I wish I could see myself.'

'You'll be able to see yourself in Lavinia's mirror when you get back to Witfontein. The length is perfect. I shouldn't have thought your grandmother was so tall.'

'It will hide my shoes, thank goodness!'

'How particular you are!'

'Well, isn't it natural to want to look nice – with so many strangers?'

'Tell me about your stranger, Maria.'

'Who, the young man who came with me yesterday?'

'Yes. Mr. Abberley.'

'You like him, don't you? Oh, mother, say that you like him.'

'Yes, I think he's a nice boy. I've always liked young English-men. After all, I married one.'

'But father didn't like him.'

'You mustn't misjudge your father. He suffered a great in-justice in England – that was why he came here – and he's never been able to forget it. The sight of a redcoat fills him with alarm.'

'He couldn't be alarmed by Richard.'

'So that is his name? There's no doubt about your liking him.'

'I like him better than anyone I've ever known, mother.'

'My little one! You haven't known many men, have you?'

'Enough to know how different Richard is. You didn't see him at his best. Father's attitude puzzled him. He didn't know what to make of it.'

'No ... I quite understand. How long is he staying at Wit-fontein?'

'Only two more days. After that Mr. Martyn and he will go to Pretoria and Edward back to Natal. But Richard will come over here, I know, as often as he can.'

'If he didn't come, would it hurt you very much, child?'

Maria laughed. 'But he will come, mother. He's said that he will.'

Lisbet smiled and kissed her.

'What a thing it is to be young!' she said. 'Come, let us try to make the dress fit you. A few stitches will do it. You'll be coming home again as soon as these visitors are gone, I sup-pose?'

'Yes, as soon as they're gone and Lavinia doesn't need me.'

'We shall be glad, your father and I, to have you home again. You're the last of my babies. The house seems silent without you.'

Richard Abberley had been furious when he woke and found that Maria had slipped him. His first instinct had been to saddle a pony and ride after her to Wonderfontein. He rejected this idea. John Grafton's reception of him had not been encouraging; it might be even less friendly if he arrived without being invited. His next thought was to give her a taste of her own medicine by joining his friends at the Haskards'. The dose would have been salutary for her, but hardly polite to his hostess, Lavinia; added to which, Maria might return within a few hours – that was the reason, perhaps, why she had started so early. He would not willingly miss a moment of her company; and the thought of her distress at finding that he had gone (for he had a goodish opinion of himself) filled him with an anticipatory remorse that affected him deeply: in this absence she appeared to him gentler and sweeter and more tender than ever before; he would rather suffer anything, he told himself, than hurt or offend her. He contented himself as best he could by mooning about the house; attempting to read, with little success; being polite, with even less, to Lavinia, and playing with the children. It was the middle of the afternoon before Maria returned, to Lavinia's relief.

'For heaven's sake take that young man of yours away, Maria,' she said. 'He's been like a lost soul or an animal in a cage, following me about all over the house. Thank goodness Piet never worries me like that. Young men at a loose end are awful. Did you find your dress?'

'Yes, it's perfect.'

'Put it on this evening and let us see.'

'No, I don't think I want to. I'd rather wait till tomorrow.'

'Well then, go and console your friend.'

She found him sitting on the stoep in an attitude of despondency. As she approached, he did not look up.

'I've come home,' she said humbly.

He did not answer. His face and neck were red. She laughed to herself. 'What a baby he is,' she thought.

'I've come home, Mr. Abberley,' she repeated.

'So I see,' he said bitterly. 'A nice trick you've played me. You might have stayed a bit longer while you were about it.'

'Richard, don't be so foolish!' she said.

'Well, you've found the right word for me, anyway.' He turned and faced away; she saw that his lips were trembling. 'I suppose I'm a fool to have thought you cared a damn for me –

and an even bigger fool to have fallen in love with you!'

'Richard . . . Richard . . .'

'Maria, my sweetheart, can't you understand that life simply means nothing to me, nothing whatever, without you? That I grudge every single moment when I can't see you? That our time is so short? Here we are, with only tomorrow left – and half of that going to be wasted by Haskard's ridiculous dance – and you've stolen a day from me, a whole day! If that wasn't cruel!'

'I could never be cruel to you, Richard,' she said. 'I love you too terribly for that.'

'Maria. . . . You mean that? My God, I can hardly believe it.' He laughed. 'I don't know what I'm saying. Tell me again.'

'That I love you? Surely you must have known it. Oh, from the first moment.'

'From the first moment. My dearest. . . . It was the same with me.'

'Isn't that how it should be?'

'Of course. But that makes it all the more wonderful, the more strange. I still find it hard to believe my own luck . . . what a word for it! But words are no good for a thing like this. Don't let's stay here, my darling. Let's go where we went that first day – on the top of the ridge by that thorn-tree. Let's be alone and try to find out where we are.'

'It's too late, Richard. In half an hour it will be dark.'

'Dark? What are you saying? The whole world is ablaze with light!'

So their last day came. It was full of bustle and distraction; during the whole of it they found it impossible to snatch a minute for themselves. Major Haskard was on the top of his form: preparations of this kind were just 'in his line'. He took charge of the whole affair, like a chief of staff: clearing the large living-room of its carpets and furniture, dusting the yellow-wood floor with french chalk, carting Lavinia's piano over from Witfontein, superintending the cutting of sandwiches and the concoction of jugfuls of 'cup' which he made from Cape wines and liqueurs.

'I'm sure you're putting in far too much brandy, Jim,' Mrs. Haskard complained.

'Nonsense, nonsense, my love. We must keep the wheels well-oiled if we want them to run smoothly. You don't know how heavy these Dutch folk are. This is the first dance we've ever had, and I want to make it a success for the boys' sake, if not for our own.'

It was all very jolly and exciting, but extremely fatiguing. Maria was kept running to and fro perpetually until her legs ached. Richard shadowed her all the time. She had never appeared to him more ravishing than she did now, with a clean white apron tied round her print dress, her cheeks bright with exertion and excitement. Once or twice he managed to catch her on the wing and steal a quick kiss when nobody else was looking. Strangely sweet to him were these hurried contacts. Her lips were so cool and soft, her young body so warm and full of life in his arms; and though she pretended to protest, being certain that someone would see them, he knew that her ardour was as frank as his own; that she was his and he was hers and that nothing could part them.

Lavinia and she had to leave Brakfontein earlier than Piet to give themselves time to dress, and Richard rode back with them. Maria was chattering eagerly with her sister-in-law all the way. He marvelled at the contrast of her irrepressible brightness, her glowing vivacity, the intense concentration of life that was in her, with Lavinia's obvious fatigue. She sounded almost too light-hearted, too frivolous, he thought, considering the gloom of approaching separation that now hung over them. Her gaiety appeared to him high-pitched and fey; it was almost a challenge to fate; and the fact that she devoted herself to Lavinia and seemed unconscious of his presence, made him vaguely jealous.

'You hardly spoke a word to me,' he complained.

'You funny darling! Wasn't I thinking of you all the time? What do words mean, anyway? What does anything matter now?'

She kissed him swiftly and left him.

He waited for them on the stoep, watching the sun go down: the last sun that would shine on their too-brief love until he found a chance of getting leave from the regiment. He would have to start from Witfontein before dawn next morning to join his comrades on their ride to Pretoria. As the two girls dressed in Lavinia's bedroom, he could hear Maria's low voice and sometimes the sound of her laughter. It was that low voice and that laugh, he believed, that had first attracted him, though one could not divide or classify her charms: she was wholly exquisite.

They took an unconscionable time over their dressing. The stars came out. It had been a moment of peculiar sweetness, he remembered, when, pausing alone on the veld which had seemed as vast and lonely as the sky, they had gazed at the stars together. A light glowed in the living-room. Maria had slipped away first, and he hurried to meet her. She was wearing the dove-grey foulard which her grandmother had worn, with its full skirt and its tiny waist. She moved slowly towards him with a composure, a dignity that filled him with unfamiliar awe. She was carrying a candle whose placid point of light illuminated the sheen of the striped silk with a radiance of moonbeams, enlivening, against the dark background, the milkiness of bare arms and throat. She seemed at that moment not merely unsubstantial, with the loveliness of a phantom, but ghostly too in the dimension of time – as though she were the shadowy reincarnation of a beauty that had vanished long since. She threw back her head and smiled at him, slowly, tenderly, the grey iris of her eyes dilated to blackness. She swept him a formal curtsey.

'Will I do, sir?'

He shook his head impotently, without speaking, and caught her in his arms as she rose from her curtsey; her body glowed with warm life through the smooth silk beneath his hands; their lips met and lingered.

'I love you, Richard,' she said. 'Oh, my love, be careful. Look what I've done! How careless!' The wax from the tilted candle had spattered the floor. 'And I'm sure Lavinia will guess how it happened.'

'Well, why on earth shouldn't she?'

'She's coming, darling. Be careful.'

They separated quickly as Lavinia entered.

'What are you children whispering about?' she asked suspiciously. 'You must put something over your shoulders, Maria, or you'll be frozen in that thin frock. I'm afraid we shall be late as it is.'

In the space of bare earth around the farm-buildings at Brakfontein, knee-haltered horses stood shivering under their blankets, and a number of unharnessed cape-carts were scattered,

More than twenty guests, including Edward's friends from Pretoria, had already arrived; the house was crowded; the windows blazed with light.

'I wish we could stay outside. This is the last I shall see of you,' Abberley grumbled.

'We shall see each other all evening.'

'That's not seeing each other.'

'Well, we shall have the ride home when it's over.'

'With Lavinia watching us? Thank you!'

'Well, what does it matter now, anyway, as I said before?'

It was an uproarious evening. Major Haskard's 'cup' had been only too thoroughly laced. He himself was indefatigable in throwing the young people together, though his efforts were hardly needed, for the Dutch neighbours were adepts at dancing and let themselves go. Lavinia and Mrs. Haskard took turns in providing the music. There were waltzes, polkas and quadrilles through whose formal figures the boys and girls from the farms moved even more deftly than the young soldiers from Pretoria. In between these they clamoured for their own country-dances – *Vat jow goed en trek, Ferreira* and the rest – and sang as they danced.

Maria had plenty of partners. Edward Haskard, with one jealous eye on Abberley, absorbed her as much as politeness allowed him, and saw to it, as their host, that the visitors from Pretoria had a good deal more of her company than did Abberley, whom, whenever Maria and he were together, he watched with anxious eyes: Abberley had had a good run (and rather too good) for his money, he thought, and he wasn't going to neglect this chance of getting a bit of his own back.

As for Richard, the whole of that evening was a foretaste of purgatory. When he saw her dancing with others he could not suffer the thought that grosser hands than his should feel the glow of Maria's sweet warmth through the dove-coloured silk. When he danced with her himself he detested the scrutiny of interested eyes which his self-consciousness told him was fixed on them. He wished to heaven that he could have found any plausible excuse to stay behind at Witfontein – though in that case, no doubt, he would have been consumed by a blinder and fiercer jealousy.

'I can't bear to think of anyone touching you,' he said, 'let alone see them.'

'They don't touch me, my darling. Can't you understand that

290

so far as I'm concerned, there might be nobody here but you and me?'

'That's all very well. It's them, not you, I'm thinking of. That prancing old satyr!'

The mythical beast in question, as he was forced to explain, was Major Haskard, who was renewing the sentiments of his youth with fine abandonment and a complete disregard for the consequences to his faulty lungs on the morrow.

'Poor Major Haskard,' she said. 'Why should you call him such names? He's known me ever since I was a child.'

'That makes it no better,' Richard said gloomily. 'The way he mauls you and goggles at you with his lecherous old eyes.'

'That's another word I don't know,' Maria said. 'You use such odd ones.'

'Well, it means . . .' he began.

But there their dance ended, and he lost her again.

It was true, as she said, that there was nobody else in the room, for her, but themselves; and yet she was enjoying herself. During the last twenty-four hours she had reached a pinnacle of ecstasy from which nothing – not even his difficult mood – could displace her. She loved and was loved. The music, the rhythmical movement, were no more than an accompaniment to this supreme state of exaltation. In dancing, no matter with whom, she found a physical release for the surplus of life and feeling which, if she had been alone, would have forced her to sing. If she smiled on her partners, it was only for happiness; if her eyes glowed with tenderness, it was not for what they saw, but for what was within her. It was her love, above all, that made her lovely that night (as she knew she was lovely) and that which made men desire her – Major Haskard, breathing his compliments in a hushed voice heavy with whisky; Edward, languishing and inarticulate behind his ridiculous moustache; the young officers, who swore there was no girl to come within miles of her in Pretoria – was the emanation, natural as the perfume of a newly-opened flower or a ripening fruit, of her own unrealized desire for Richard Abberley. Though she answered their questions and laughed at their compliments with her smiling lips, neither her heart nor her mind was with them. She was only aware of her lover. She did not even have to look to see if he were there, and, indeed, forbade herself to look for fear of being moved beyond all endurance by the sight of his needlessly tragic face. She did not share his possessive jealousy.

The more he danced with others, the better she was pleased; for she knew that, whomever he danced with, he must be, like herself, possessed.

So the full moon came up and climbed to the zenith and drenched the outer veld with its silver and slowly declined. After midnight the dancing became a little too boisterous for Mrs. Haskard's decorous sense of propriety; she was more angry than ever that Jim had put so much *dop* in his 'cup,' and retired to her room. But not even this gesture of disapproval could quell the dancers' enthusiasm or stop them dancing. When Lavinia's thin hands became limp and nerveless with playing they were not disconcerted; the young men and girls from the farms insisted on making their own music, singing breathlessly (and occasionally out of tune) as they danced. They would show these short-winded, half-hearted *rooineks* what a Boer dance was!

By the time they had finished and streamed out of the lighted house to saddle their horses or harness them to the cape-carts and shouted their last good nights, the moon lay low in the west and the veld had lost its bright silver.

'I shall fall asleep in the saddle before we get home,' Lavinia complained.

'I'll wake you as soon as we get there, darling,' Maria said.

'But I really mean it, Maria.'

They did not care how long she slept. Richard edged his horse nearer to Maria, so that he could hold her warm hand; yet she found found him strangely silent. Her fingers closed upon his:

'You're not still feeling cross, Richard?'

'Of course not. I know I was foolish, but that couldn't be helped: it's the way I'm made.'

'Then what is it?'

'I've had rather a blow. One of those fellows from Pretoria brought me bad news – the worst possible news. Two companies of the regiment have orders to go to Lydenburg with Colonel Anstruther. The odds are I shall be sent.'

'To Lydenburg? That's where my brother Janse is.'

'What do I care for your brother Janse? Don't you see it may mean that I may not be able to see you for months?'

'Never mind, my dear. You'll be able to find some reason for going back to Pretoria, and you'll be sure to get leave. If we decide to be patient . . .'

'Patient indeed! Maria, listen: as soon as I get back to Pretoria, will you marry me?'

'Of course I'll marry you. How can you ask?'

'There may be difficulties. I shall have, first of all, to get the colonel's permission. They don't like married subalterns much in ours; so, maybe, I shall have to send in my papers – resign my commission. And that means, perhaps, I may have to go back to England and earn my living in some other way. Do you understand? If I had to do that, you wouldn't mind coming with me?'

'I couldn't live without you, my love,' she said.

When Maria had safely shepherded Lavinia to bed, she came back on tiptoe to the sitting-room. The night was cold, but they sat side by side on the sofa and kept each other warm. They spoke very little. There seemed to be no need for speech. They sat there, remote and enraptured, till the sky in the east grew grey, and a dim light, creeping through the windows, illuminated their pale faces, their cavernous eyes.

'I must saddle-up,' Richard said. 'The others will be waiting for me. They already think I was mad not to have turned in at Brakfontein. I don't want you to come out to see me off in the cold, my sweet, and I won't say good-bye. There must never be any good-byes between you and me, Maria.'

They kissed again and he went. She did not follow, but stood at the door and watched him saddle his horse and mount and ride rapidly away. She closed the door and went to her room and undressed in the dusk; but her body was mortally cold and she knew that she had no hope of sleeping.

When the sun was up, she put on her cotton dress, the one that Richard had admired. She called the boy to kindle a fire to warm her frozen limbs and drank a cup of sweet, hot coffee which made her feel as though she were coming to life; yet the life which came back to her seemed strangely aimless and empty and detached. She stood on the stoep and let the heat of the morning sun diffuse itself through her. At last, moved by a sudden impulse, she went to Lavinia's writing-desk, found pen and ink and paper, and began to write in her rather childish hand.

Dear Mr. Rhodes [she wrote],
    *My brother Piet says you remember me, though I can
hardly believe it. I wonder if you remember also that you*

once gave me a diamond and made me promise that when I was going to be married you would have it cut for me and set. Well, now I am going to be married, though not just yet. His name is Richard Abberley and he is an Englishman, an officer in the 94th Regiment. I do not think any girl has ever loved anyone so much as I love him, but it's no use writing about that, as I can't express it and you would probably laugh at my attempt. But I am sending you your diamond that you gave me because I think you meant what you said that day. At any rate, I hope you did, and that the ring won't be awfully expensive. I would much rather that it was simple, and I'm sure that Richard would too, though he doesn't know that I'm writing.

With kind remembrances,
Yours sincerely,
Maria Grafton.

PS. – The piece of thread, between the knots, will be the right size.

CHAPTER THREE

(1)

PIET had not been unduly alarming when he warned Cecil Rhodes in Kimberley that matters were going badly for the English in the Transvaal. More than two years had now passed since Shepstone's Annexation, and still the elections he had promised had not been held, nor did his successor, Lanyon, show any signs of holding them. Paul Kruger's deputation returning from Europe had brought nothing back with them but disappointment. Messages sent from the Cape had preceded their arrival in London, discounted their representative character, and queered their pitch. A mass meeting, assembled at Kleinfontein, received their report, decided to raise a new and more numerous petition of protest, and authorized the delegates to visit Europe again.

But even at this point the folk were still divided: some favouring a stiffened resistance and being prepared, as a last resort, to take up arms, others urging the moderation which Kruger himself advised – partly, perhaps, because his visit to England had opened his eyes to the extent of British power; partly, again, because he saw that active resistance would be hopeless until the people were of one mind, and partly, no doubt, because he knew that his rivals' dissensions weakened their personal prestige and brought nearer the moment when he would be able to realize his ambitions and assert his own predominance. His subtle mind saw that the effect of the grievances which sprang from Lanyon's autocratic regime would be cumulative. Like the buffalo-bull in the grass, he was prepared to wait until his enemies, English and Dutch alike, placed themselves in a position of tactical inferiority. Instinctive wisdom told him that Time fought on his side.

During this period of brewing tempest Adrian Grafton took a large part in organizing and strengthening the opposition in the back-veld. His mission had many suspicions to contend with. His intimate association with Burgers, now universally reviled, made him an object of distrust in circles swayed by the

Dopper predikants, who could forgive the ex-president's heresies less easily than his political failure.

Against this disadvantage Adrian could set his handsome presence and personal popularity as a good fellow and an honest, if temporarily misguided, man, who had now renounced his pernicious allegiance. But there was more in it than this. Marriage had modified his nature, not, as one might have expected, by softening, but by stiffening it. Before, though he had been manly and resolute and, above all, conscientious, it had been easy-going, and had lacked that hard core which the spirit of a few others (such as Paul Kruger) possessed. The complementary qualities of Suzanna reinforced this weakness and made good this deficiency. Though she did not advertise her power over his thoughts and took care to conceal her intellectual superiority (a quality which, particularly in a woman, was liable to awaken suspicion), being, to all appearances, a submissive and dutiful wife, it was she – and, through her, her brother – who had changed him. She was the foreign body implanted in his spirit (occasionally, perhaps, a mild irritant) around which, layer by layer, the pearl had been formed. She was, again, the inward focus of light and heat from whose glow, when his energy flagged, its fires were rekindled.

In this way, Adrian, who had previously been considered merely a 'moderate', or progressive in his support of Burgers' idealism, had become a prominent figure among the militant irreconcilables, and had assumed, under his brother-in-law's direction and his wife's inspiration, a kind of roving commission among the disaffected elements in the Transvaal. As he rode far and wide it took him into odd company, for revolution makes strange bedfellows. It reconciled him with relations, near and remote, from whom in the past he had been divided: such as his uncle Barend Prinsloo and his half-savage brood; his aunt Anna, who had married a near relative of Paul Kruger, in the Magaliesberg, and her sons, and with a more distant cousin in the Potchefstroom district, Piet Bezuidenhout, a fine specimen of the 'old Boer' and son of that rebel (or martyr, as many called him) whose death (or murder) at Slachter's Nek and the executions that followed it remained, at a distance of more than sixty years, the most bitterly remembered of ancient wrongs. Together with these, the strongest influence in the district his activities covered was the Veld-kornet of Potchefstroom, Piet Cronjé.

Adrian himself had little in common (and Suzanna less) with

these new associates, who differed from both of them in their culture and mode of life – since Adrian had been reared in the mild and gracious atmosphere of Wonderfontein, and his wife in the intellectual air of Stellenbosch. But the one thing they shared was a deep-rooted hatred of everything that the English stood for; and also strong had this passion grown in Adrian – increased rather than tempered by the fact that he had to admit he had English blood in his veins – that he not merely accepted their manner of life as natural and proper, but even gloried in its downright uncouthness and savagery as a contrast to the smoothness and slipperiness of English ways, as an outward expression of the true Boer spirit which for two centuries in Africa had resented authority and had always been ready to court destruction by resisting it – the Huguenot spirit which had survived St. Bartholomew's Eve, the spirit of the Dutch, which not even Alva could subdue. He was mild-natured, and therefore the more susceptible to counsels of violence. He was a convert, and therefore more zealous than his converters: a renegade from that part of himself which was English, and therefore more convinced of his rightness than any loyalist. Up till his marriage the discordant strains had been fairly equally balanced, with a resultant irresoluteness. Now that the influence of his wife, who was stronger than he, had tipped the scale, he became even more uncompromisingly Dutch than Suzanna herself.

When Kruger came back from Europe empty-handed, Adrian had stood in with Vorster at Kleinfontein, demanding that the People's Committee – their substitute for the promised but non-existent Volksraad – should demand independence and, if necessary, set out to obtain it by force. At the time when the Zulu War broke out and the English appealed for help, he had not merely refused it, but had even toyed with the idea of profiting by their embarrassment and persuading his countrymen to support Cetewayo. Such an action, he knew, would violate one of the first Afrikander principles: the solidarity of all white men against the black; but in his present mood no such scruples weighed with him. When the Zulu War was over and Cetewayo crushed, he felt that a great opportunity had been missed and that the chance of a successful rising had vanished; for now the British Government's hands were free, and a greater concentration of troops than ever before had assembled on the border of Natal.

Adrian appealed to Paul Kruger. It was odd to think how he

297

had been driven to accept this man, whom he had previously suspected and disliked as the author of Burgers' downfall, as the one leader on whose strength and wisdom he could rely. Kruger listened to his fiery reproaches impassively. The experience of his two visits to Europe had aged his old enemy. His coarse hair and the beard that fringed his massive face were streaked with grey. He sat on the stoep of his farm at Rustenburg and smoked and spat as he listened to Adrian.

'You were one of the sheep that followed Burgers, nephew,' he grunted, 'and now it seems you have become a lion. You say that Time has helped the British to shake off their difficulties; but I tell you that Time fights for us too. You think that I move too slowly. Well, such is my nature. I have fought in too many wars to have any liking for bloodshed; and perhaps I know better than you what is behind this affair. You say we have come back from Europe with empty hands; but our heads are not empty. We have listened and watched, and I tell you now that we have more friends – yes, even in England – than you are aware of. This Government has thrown aside our petition; but the English are fickle folk who never know their own minds for long at a time: there will be an election in England before long; the tide is turning, and I think that our good friend Gladstone and the Liberals will come into power. Then I shall talk with a man whom I know, and all will come right.'

'In the meantime we cannot say what we feel. We have no Volksraad.'

'That is not altogether a bad thing. The more men are stifled the greater their discontent grows; the more we are discontented, the stronger and the more united we shall be when strength is needed. There is another handful of dust which shows how the wind is blowing. The High Commissioner, Frere, is coming up from Natal to talk with us and to hear our grievances. And Frere is no Lanyon. I spoke with him at Durban and I think he is a just man. Let us have a great gathering to meet him. The best thing we can do, nephew, is to let him see our strength: people talk too much – an armed protest, a *gewapende protes*, carries farther than all your shouting. And that is where you can help: see to it that, when Frere comes next week, there are plenty of burghers with rifles waiting to receive him at Kleinfontein.'

Adrian scoured the veld, carrying summonses for the great meeting. The results of his canvass discouraged him. His views of the universal discontent had been coloured by the talk of the small circle of friends whom he frequented because they thought as he did. In the remoter districts he found himself faced with a depressing apathy and inertia. When persuasions failed, he resorted to threats, to which many surrendered unwillingly. Yet the result was not bad: by the appointed day a commando of over three thousand armed men had assembled in laager at Kleinfontein.

They waited a week – two weeks, three weeks – and still Frere did not come.

'He never intended to come,' the hotheads complained, 'or if he did, our friend Lanyon has stopped him. This is the usual insult: he treats us like fools or children.'

Some joked, though the jokes were bitter, quoting scripture:

'This man is like Baal,' they said. 'You'd better call him louder. *Either he is talking, or he is pursuing, or he is on a journey, or peradventure he sleepeth and must be awakened!*'

'Perhaps he has *bought five oxen and goes to prove them,* or maybe, *he has married a wife and therefore he cannot come!*'

But many had gone beyond joking. They felt that they had been needlessly dragged away from their farms, their wives and their families, and might just as well ride home again. Adrian and his friends did their best to persuade them to remain, but by the end of three weeks the great gathering had begun to melt away.

And then, finally, with genuine excuses for his tardiness, Sir Bartle Frere arrived – and Lanyon with him. Adrian watched him ride into the camp unarmed, with a small staff behind him, a soldierly figure, grey-haired and grey-moustached, with a kindly, intelligent face, in which only the eyes were stern. Though he hated all that he stood for, Adrian could not help being impressed by the natural dignity of this elderly man who had served his country so faithfully. As he rode slowly up to Erasmus Farm, between the two sullen files of unarmed burghers, Frere raised his hand in a courteous salute that was not returned; as he advanced to the tent in which Joubert and the other leaders awaited him, the sullen files closed in behind. Adrian felt sorry for Frere, and even a little ashamed. He did not feel sorry for Lanyon, that swarthy autocrat with his rigid uniformed figure and his black drooping moustaches.

'I am sorry, gentlemen, to have been delayed and to have

299

kept you waiting; but that, you know, was not entirely my fault. We have been kept busy in Zululand. But now I am ready to listen to your grievances.'

Piet Joubert was the spokesman: a handsome, heavily-bearded man. His eyes were set closer together than Kruger's; his face lacked Kruger's craggy massiveness, and his voice the power of that which issued from Kruger's pugnacious lips. He spoke fluently, and with a politeness that Adrian found exaggerated. It was not until the end, when he spoke of the Annexation, that the passion for which Adrian had been looking made his voice tremble.

'Suddenly,' he said, 'without any preparation, without any cause on our part, when we were in temporary difficulties with Sekukuni and when we had succeeded in bringing him to peace, it pleased Sir Theophilus Shepstone to avail himself of those temporary difficulties – to take our state by stealth and murder our liberty, to steal what we value most: our independence.'

'One moment, Mr. Joubert: what do you mean by your independence?'

'Your Excellency knows well what I mean. All was written down clearly and signed by both parties in the Sand River Convention. Must I repeat the words? "The right to manage our own affairs without let or hindrance and to govern ourselves, according to our own laws, without any interference on the part of the British Government." '

'That is an old story, Mr. Joubert. The convention was signed before the Transvaal Republic . . .'

'The South African Republic,' Kruger put in.

Frere smiled: 'As you will, Mr. Kruger. Before, as I say, the South African Republic existed. Now, I want you, gentlemen, to listen to me,' he went on calmly, 'so that you may understand exactly why I am here. I am Her Majesty's High Commissioner, sent out here to see that all her colonies in South Africa are defended from infringement and from being assaulted by any enemy. I have come unattended because I do not wish to have any other weapons than those of reason and right with me. I think you have made some grave mistakes and got into a very dangerous position by bad advice, and I should be glad if any knowledge or experience that I have or any power given me by the Queen, can help you out of that position and enable you to get what I consider is meant by independence.'

'We think the meaning is clear, your Excellency,' Joubert said.

'Well . . . I am afraid that I and some of you may not exactly agree as to what is right, and what is freedom, and what is independence. We come of the same stock, one of the most honoured stocks of all white men. We hold the same religion and hope to be guided by the same Word of God; but, of course, different men see things with different eyes.

'Now the first thing I was assured of before I came here, was that the whole people were unanimous in their approval of the Annexation.'

'You have seen our latest Petition?'

'Yes, I have seen it. But never, until I came into the Transvaal, had I any reason to doubt that you were unanimous.'

'We are unanimous now, Your Excellency, though not in the way you think. This great gathering proves it.'

'Evidently the Press, and some of your delegates, have been misinformed. Let me tell you this: I have never passed a day without meeting Dutch burghers who inform me that they have nothing to do with this movement. I have asked no questions. Their information has been volunteered. Only the other day, a man rushed into my bedroom and asked me anxiously whether there was any truth in the rumour that the Annexation would be reversed. Again and again, men from outspanned wagons have ridden up to ask the same question. There was not one of them who wanted the Republican Government again. They wanted a good, firm Government, and nothing more. For myself, I think you have got it.'

The tent murmured with angry disapproval; but Frere went on:

'Now, as to what you call "this great gathering": I should like to know how many burghers are here of their own will. I think, to be frank, there has been intimidation. Last week, on my way here, a woman came crying to me: "There is my husband out in the camp," she said; "I hope they will soon send him home." I asked her why he had gone to the camp. "Because they threatened to shoot him and cut him in pieces and make biltong of him," she said. "How can I stay here on the veld without him?" she asked. "I'm not safe in my bed." Another man came to me in a grave state of alarm. "Give me notice if you are going to give up the country," he pleaded, "and I will leave it." I know

301

also that some of your burghers have pulled up travellers and compelled them to join you. That is not liberty; that is not independence. You have a free power, as you know, to meet to discuss politics. But if one man is compelled to go against his will, it is no good talking to me about freedom.'

'We have two thousand here, your Excellency, who have come of their own free will.'

'Yes, you have two thousand here, and you call them the people of the Transvaal! Mr. Joubert, gentlemen, you know you are not agreed. It was not Sir Theophilus Shepstone who put an end to the Republic; it was men amongst yourselves. You made President Burgers supreme, and he brought in people who were not farmers or Afrikanders to assist him. Do you want that again?'

'Major Lanyon has brought in English troops. What is the difference?'

Frere waved the question aside. 'Have you freedom of speech here? You know you have not, though in the Cape and in England you would have it. What you call freedom is not enough. Together with it there must be protection of life and property. Is there that, I ask you, gentlemen, when men are compelled to attend a political meeting and threatened, if they refuse, to be made into biltong? I agree, it is essential that all men should have the franchise and that those who pay taxes should have a voice in making laws. This has been too long delayed, I admit, and I give you my word it shall come. That is what I offer you: the same kind of independence as men have in the Cape.'

He paused ... 'One word more: there are rumours about, I am told, that we are on the point of commandeering wagons and young men and taking your land away. Of course, there is not a word of truth in them. As I told Mr. Joubert before: the Transvaal had a great opportunity at the beginning of this Zulu War. We asked him and Mr. Kruger for your help against a common enemy. You may be quite sure we won't do that again. For the rest – all those things which make up what I call independence, I can give you. I can promise that they shall be the objects of any Constitution that is made for the Transvaal; that you shall be able to go where you please, and do what you please – all within the Law; that you shall be protected in your lives and property while you obey the law; and that you shall have the power to make your own laws with reference to everything within the Province. What more can I say?'

Joubert rose and spoke slowly: 'I should mislead your Excellency if I said that the folk of the Transvaal would be content with anything short of their independence.' (Frere shook his head at the obstinate repetition of the word.) 'Independence in the Cape or in England is held by people who have voluntarily chosen their sovereign or voluntarily stand under that sovereignty – unlike us who have never consented to such a sovereignty. A slave, however kindly treated, desires liberty, and will exchange for such slavery, freedom, even though it entails much misery.'

Adrian saw in Frere's face a rising irritation; his forehead flushed red beneath his grey hair.

'Mr. Joubert,' he said angrily, 'I think we have had enough of this tall talk. You must know that it is sheer nonsense, this talk of being a slave!'

Joubert paused and went on.

'We bought this land, your Excellency, with our property and our blood. When we got the country we could never believe that Her Majesty's Government would repudiate our right. We feel that the circumstances of the Annexation have brought a stain on Her Majesty's name. Would she wipe it out with our blood? Well, we are willing to be ground and crushed rather than suffer oppression and injustice. We will rather perish by the sword of the Zulu and the Makatee than suffer injustice in our own country. I think, sir, that any Englishman would say the same.'

Frere raised his eyes. His anger had cooled. He spoke quietly:

'And you, Mr. Kruger?'

'After hearing what your Excellency has said, I am more discontented than I was before. I think the Queen has been misled in regard to the Annexation. According to my view, the honour of Her Majesty would be this: that if Her Majesty finds she has been deceived, she will not allow her crown to be stained, but will make truth prevail and will give back what has been unjustly taken.'

Frere shook his head:

'Mr. Kruger, you do not help me. You have none of you, from first to last, from the time when you returned from England until now, said anything practical as to what the Queen's Government can do. You have kept on repeating: "We will have our independence" – and when I ask you what that is, you say "our independence as at the Annexation." We are all of us here free men, also practical men; and instead of talking about slavery, like Mr. Joubert, we ought to speak about how we are to be self-governed. I will make one thing clear: I will say that nothing that has been done up to this day shall incur any penalties. And I will forward a Memorial for you if you wish it. The one unpardonable offence – and I fear some of you have come very near it – is inviting natives to take part in a war against white men. I have no more to say.'

He rose and left them. During two days of heated debate they wrangled over the wording of the Memorial Frere had undertaken to forward. Once again, but for Kruger's moderating influence, the tone would have been provocative and defiant. In the form which they adopted at last, it was resolute, but reasonable. Throughout the discussions Adrian supported Kruger with his voice and his vote. The compromise was not easy: it implied a change of front which discredited him with his more violent friends: but, watching Oom Paul and Joubert side by side, he had made up his mind, once for all, which leader to follow.

It was harder still, as he had foreseen, to justify his attitude to his wife. When he rode home from Erasmus Farm and told her what had happened her scorn was withering.

'So that is all you have done,' she said, 'to draw up a Memorial! Can't you see that the time for Memorials is past? Even if the High Commissioner forwards it, do you think for one moment it will ever get to the Queen or the British Parliament? It will be shelved, exactly as the two petitions were shelved. And what's in your Memorial, anyway? Is there a word about our language, about our flag? You've been tricked once again. You should never have let Frere go until he had summoned the Volksraad.'

'He promised that it should be summoned, Suzanna.'

'So did Shepstone. And what has come of it?'

'Kruger trusts him, and I have made up my mind to trust Paul Kruger.'

'While I think that he is betraying us. Who knows what treacherous tricks he may have been up to in London or what he has got out of them, you know he likes money.'

'His plans may be wrong; but I will never believe him a traitor.'

304

There came a coldness between them which Adrian, who was still fiercely in love with her, found hard to bear. Suzanna was now far gone with their first child; she looked ill and haggard and irritable; and Adrian, unused to the psychology of this state (or to any female psychology), felt that she had changed and turned against him. Politically, nothing was working out as Kruger had hoped and prophesied. Frere was censured by the Home Government, and compelled to resign. His place as High Commissioner was filled by Wolseley, a second and stronger Lanyon. No steps were taken to summon the Volksraad, as Frere had promised. Gladstone had come into power and stood by the Annexation. A new stringency showed itself in the collection of taxes – not merely of the recent railway-taxes the British had decreed, but of the arrears due to the old Republican Government, which Shepstone had wisely remitted. Throughout the Transvaal, Adrian's old friends, the extremists, were getting the upper hand. Powder-jumping became the fashion. It was no unusual thing for a party of six or seven armed men to ride up to a store, without an official permit to buy ammunition, and strip it of shot and powder at the muzzle of the rifle. Since their leaders would not help them, the people were arming themselves. Adrian was compelled to admit that Suzanna had been right and now had the laugh of him.

(2)

One evening, late in the following year, his old friend and cousin Bezuidenhout arrived at the farm in a state of fierce indignation and claimed his help.

'Now see what they have done to me,' he cried, 'these damned bloodsuckers who gather the taxes! They have sued me for twenty-seven pounds five, instead of the fourteen pounds that I owe them.'

'You need not pay more than you owe by law, cousin,' Adrian said.

'I have offered the Landdrost the fourteen pounds that I owe, on the condition that it should go to the Republic when the country is given back to us. He refused to accept my offer. The case was adjourned. And now, when it comes up again, see what he has done! He has added a bill of costs, as they call it, for thirteen pounds five, which brings the sum up to what they first

305

demanded. That is the justice Frere promised us!'

'I think you would be right to resist.'

'To resist? Indeed I resist it,' old Bezuidenhout roared: 'I have seen van Eck, the Attorney, and he had advised me to refuse to pay a penny more than I owe.'

'Well, that is good. Van Eck will fight in the court for you,' Adrian soothed him.

'That is good, you say! But before he can fight for me, the sheriff has taken my wagon and dragged it into Potchefstroom to be sold. You should have been there, cousin. That was a fine sight, I tell you! A crowd of a hundred men with their guns in front of the Landdrost's office. They would have beaten the life out of him if he hadn't hidden. Then on to the Square, where they'd put out my wagon to be sold. The sheriff gets up on the wagon, as pale as a bucket of lard, and starts asking for bids – poor devil, I didn't envy him! – but no sooner does he open his mouth than Piet Cronjé jumps up and catches him by the scruff of the neck and heaves him out into the crowd. They say he was kicked: it's lucky for him he got off with his life. Then the men made a guard round my wagon. They sent for oxen and inspanned them and drove them back to the farm. A great day . . . a great day! There were a hundred of us, I tell you.'

'There will be trouble for this,' Adrian said.

'Trouble? That's what we want – Piet Cronjé and Koetze and Basson and all the rest of us. What's more, it's started already. Lanyon sent Commandant Raaf down from Pretoria with a warrant to arrest Cronjé and myself. He brought three men with him; but we, as I say, were a hundred, so he had to go back. If he'd tried any tricks we'd have shot him. I tell you, cousin, the blood of the people is up. It's reached a point when they will have no more of this nonsense. Now Raaf's sent a message to say he's coming tomorrow to Fendersdorp to take us away. Let him try it: that's what I say! Paul Kruger is coming this evening from Rustenburg, and you must come too. The word has gone round. We shall have some fun, I can promise you. We can count, I reckon, on more than three thousand guns. That will make him open his mouth. Now I go to spread the news farther. The day of deliverance is at hand, cousin. You will be there?'

'If Paul Kruger is coming, then I will be there,' Adrian said.

He silently took down his rifle and filled his bandoleer. Suzanna watched him with burning eyes.

'So it has come at last,' she said, 'the red-letter day, the day of deliverance.'

'The red-letter day,' he repeated darkly. 'Yes, that is right; for I think it will be written in blood. This is war, Suzanna.'

'Then are you afraid of war?' she asked bitterly.

'I am thinking of you and the child. ... I love you, Suzanna.'

'Do you want our child to be born a slave, then?' she said. 'As for me – if I thought it would help, I would take up the other gun and ride at your side – yes, big as I am I would go with you. Ach, why was I born a woman?' she cried. Her voice broke on the words. Then she stretched out her arms and caught him and fiercely clung to him. 'My love, my dear love, my own darling,' she said, 'do you know how I love you?'

They stood clasped in each other's arms with joined lips. He was shaken by that moment of parting, whose terrible strangeness and sweetness were almost more than he could bear; for, along with the sombre sense of foreboding that darkened them, there rose within him a proud exaltation before which those other clouds which of late had dulled their first rapture, had veiled her from him, were swept away. They were more truly one at this moment, he felt, than ever before. She took his head in her thin, dark hands and gazed at him long and tenderly.

'When you come back, my love,' she said, 'perhaps our child will be born.'

At this a new terror chilled him.

'Is it so soon then? In that case I cannot leave you, my love. No, I cannot go.'

She laughed: 'What cowards men are! Have you forgotten, then, that you yourself were born in a wagon when your mother was alone? Such a little woman, too! You know I have twice her strength, and I am not afraid. I am a Boer wife, Adrian; we face these things as they come. *Dit is onse gewoonte.*'

'No ... I cannot go,' he protested.

'Then I will ride with you. Saddle a horse for me.'

And in the end she prevailed on him to go.

It was dark when he drew near to Fendersdorp, but the sky was red with the fires of a mighty concourse. Bezuidenhout had

307

not exaggerated. Adrian judged that there must be more than four thousand men in the camp. Their mood had changed from the sombre sullenness which had marked the conference with Frere at Erasmus Farm. It was high-spirited, light-hearted and confident. There was in the air a manifest feeling of relief that the time of half-measures and hesitations was over; that it had come at last to the arbitrament of the sword. He rode between the scattered camp-fires and up to the house in search of Paul Kruger; but Kruger had not yet arrived. Was it possible, he thought, that Suzanna's intuitions were right; that this man whom he trusted was holding back after all? Piet Cronjé affirmed that Kruger was certainly coming. Adrian had to leave it at that. He knee-haltered his horse and settled down to sleep: the whole night was haunted by panic fears for Suzanna.

At dawn the commando assembled and prayers were said. The men shouldered their rifles. Some gathered in front of the farm; others rode out on the veld to scout for the officials' arrival. About ten o'clock a cape-cart, with two travellers, was sighted in the distance. Two brave men, Adrian thought, to invade such a nest of hornets. A quarter of a mile from the farm, four armed horsemen converged on them and compelled them to halt. Adrian saw them, apparently protesting, as they were hustled on to the backs of two led horses, and then again, within a few yards of the house, commanded to dismount. He knew one of them. Raaf, the Dutchman, who, a week before, had demanded Cronjé's surrender. He marched up, pale but determined, his warrant in his hand, unalarmed, it seemed, by the hostile thousands who watched him.

Bezuidenhout, Cronjé and Basson stepped out to meet him. Cronjé gave him good day.

'I know what you want, Commandant,' he said; 'but this morning, as you see, I have company, and I have no time to waste.'

'I have no intention of wasting your time,' Raaf told him. 'I have here a message from Her Majesty's Government. If you will give me your word that you will hand yourselves over to justice at Potchefstroom on a given day, I will promise not to imprison you.'

Piet Cronjé laughed: 'To justice, you say, Commandant? If we did justice to you we should tie you up here and now! If you have anything to say, you had better say it to Paul Kruger, who has come here to advise me.'

As he spoke, Adrian saw that thick-set figure moving forward. Kruger shook hands with Raaf and listened, nodding his head.

'I only arrived here from Rustenburg last night, Commandant,' he said. 'I was sent for, but before I came I was not aware that matters were so dark and threatening. I have come here to try to prevent the shedding of blood. All these men you see are armed and determined to fight. If it is in my power, I shall do all I can to keep them from coming to blows. For years I have striven to do this; but this is the last, the final effort I shall make: if they won't listen to me, I must wash my hands of it; but I can truly say that I have done my utmost. These three burghers say that your prosecution is unjust and that they will not undertake to surrender themselves to your authority. So . . . what have you to say?'

Raaf paused and reflected. He stuffed the warrants in his pocket.

'Mijnheer Cronjé,' he said, 'I am going to make you an offer. I do it on my own responsibility, and I may be blamed for it. Our Government Secretary, Mr. Hudson, is now in Potchefstroom. Will you and your friends consent to meet him there?'

Kruger turned to Cronjé and nodded: 'The terms are fair, Piet. You should meet him and see what is to be done.'

Next day the whole commando moved on to Potchefstroom. They hung on the ridge above the town like a threatening cloud. A bodyguard of two hundred or more rode into the square, from which Bezuidenhout's wagon had been rescued, and where the Secretary, Hudson, awaited them: a pleasant civilian official, Adrian thought, rather overwhelmed by his present responsibilities, yet anxious to assert a control which he knew he could not enforce.

Paul Kruger took Adrian by the arm and drew him aside:

'Let Piet Cronjé speak for them,' he said; 'it is our duty to watch, but we have no standing here.'

'All I ask of you three,' Hudson said, 'is that you should submit yourselves, when I call on you, to the Government's authority. Will you give me your word for that?'

'Your Government is not ours,' Cronjé shouted, so loudly that all could hear him. 'We do not admit its authority. We have never been the Queen's subjects, and never will be; nor will we pay taxes that we, the folk, have not passed by our votes. If we pay taxes, we acknowledge you, and that we will never do. That is where we stand.'

A roar went up from the crowd; it swayed and bulged forward towards them.

'This is treason, Mr. Cronjé. Consider your words. They may be used against you.'

'Then if that is treason, we're in good company. There are more than two hundred traitors of my sort in the square at this moment, and three thousand more outside. If you want to arrest us, take us!'

Again the crowd roared. It was an ugly sound, Adrian thought, this deep voice of the multitude. Kruger edged his ponderous way towards Hudson and took him by the sleeve.

'The people are getting excited,' he said. 'If you touch these men I cannot answer for what will happen. For your own sake it's better you should go.'

'I must perform my duty, Mr. Kruger.'

'You know as well as I do, you have not the strength to do your duty. I am trying to help you. See now, next week we are holding a meeting of the people at Paardekraal. The Government knows my position. I am not a light man. I give you my word that, until that meeting is over, these three men will keep quiet. If you're wise, you will take it, before it's too late. I tell you I do not like this.'

Hudson gazed at the turbulent masses in front of him while he hesitated.

'Very well, Mr. Kruger,' he said, 'I will take your word. I do this under protest, be it understood.'

He turned and walked back slowly into the Landdrost's office.

Outside the town Adrian mounted and rode hurriedly home. It was a seventy-mile ride from Potchefstroom to the Magalies River. A summer storm travelled with him, illuminating the veld with livid flickers of lightning and drenching him to the skin before he reached his farm. He tied up his horse and stalked, dripping as he was and numb with fatigue, into Suzanna's bedroom. She lay there, mortally pale, so still that for a moment he feared she was dead. He flung himself down beside the bed and clasped her limp hand. She opened her eyes; they were meek, subdued wondering: all the fire had died out of them, but her blanched lips smiled.

'Ah, Adrian,' she whispered, 'I thought you would come to-night. I'm glad you have come.'

'It is over?'

'Yes. . . . A long time ago. I don't know. My head won't remember. He is here beside me, our son. Lift the blanket and look at him, but don't wake him: I think he's asleep.'

Adrian gazed at the red, puckered face with awe and curiosity. The baby, dazzled by the light, began to cry fretfully. He felt singularly awkward and helpless.

'But you, my love . . . ?' he said.

'Oh, don't worry about me. I am tired, that's all. The Hottentot woman helped me. I want to know all that happened.' –

She listened, with closed eyes. There was a strange beauty in the dispassionate calm of that bloodless face. Only her voice, though toneless and feeble, had passion in it.

'So Paul Kruger has failed us again,' she said. 'I feared that would happen.'

'I don't think he has failed us. He is cautious, and that is good. He wants to make sure of our strength before he acts. We have a whole week before us in which to let everyone know what happened today and bring in the waverers. When we meet again at Paardekraal, the people will speak with one voice. Their temper is very different from what it was.'

She was silent. 'Perhaps you are right,' she said at last; 'but now, more than ever, there is work to be done, and you must do it. Take off your wet clothes, then, and rest by me for a while. Tomorrow you must leave us again, your son and me. Seven days seems a short time – and yet it may be too long. Now that they've come to this heat, they must not be allowed to cool. That is your business now, Adrian.'

He lay down beside her and slept with her hand in his.

Suzanna need not have been concerned about the temperature of the great meeting at Paardekraal. Up to now, though feelings of resentment and discontent had been general enough, they had lacked co-ordination. The Bezuidenhout case, in itself a trivial injustice, had the seemingly miraculous effect of one of those minute saline particles which, dropped into a saturated solution, causes it to crystallize. It had brought three thousand men under arms within a few days. During the next week, thanks to the general infection and the efforts of Adrian and his friends, this number was doubled. The fact that the Government proclaimed the meeting illegal, in contradiction of Frere's latest promises not to infringe the right of free assembly, gave the movement an even greater impetus. On December the eighth more than seven thousand armed men assembled at Paardekraal.

There was a feeling amongst them that it was 'now or never'. The British troops in Natal were disorganized by the losses of the Zulu War: they were tired of campaigning, and still suffering from shortness of food; the increasing number of desertions from the ranks was becoming ominous. The small garrison in the Transvaal had been split up into detachments and scattered all over the country. The only cavalry regiment, the King's Dragoon Guards, had been withdrawn and dispatched to India. And apart from this inspiriting evidence that the powers of the Government had been weakened, the Transvaalers had reason to believe that their cousins in the Cape, under the sway of the growing Afrikander Bond, would support them. When, after a furious week of unceasing propaganda, Adrian rode his fagged horse into the camp at Paardekraal and saw the thousands of stern, determined faces around him, he felt that, at last, he was in the presence of a united people.

The course of the next two days' deliberations confirmed this. Even Paul Kruger, still clinging to moderation and conducting a conciliatory correspondence with Secretary Hudson, in which he implored him to refrain from more provocation, was swept away by the vehement tide of opinion. The folk had not come there to listen to speeches, but to elect their own Volksraad, to choose their leaders, and to proclaim their rights. A triumvirate was appointed: Piet Joubert, ex-President Pretorius, and Kruger himself. A week later, at Heidelberg, the British allegiance should be formally disowned and the Republic proclaimed, whatever might be the consequences.

On his way eastward to Heidelberg Adrian diverged from his course and called in at Wonderfontein. Lisbet was shocked to see his haggard face and dishevelled figure, and her heart fell, for rumours had reached them by way of their natives of the disturbances in Potchefstroom and the great Paardekraal gathering.

'You bring us bad news, my son?' she asked anxiously.

'The best news in the world, mother: you have another grandson.'

'And Suzanna's all right?'

'Since the day he was born I haven't seen her. I've covered nearly five hundred miles in a week.'

'That means trouble, I know.'

'It means freedom at last, God be thanked. The people have risen against the annexation. This time they'll stand firm.'

Lisbet shook her head.

'This is war, then, Adrian?'

'Perhaps. . . . But I do not think so. We are too strong. We have seven thousand men under arms, and every moment more are joining us.'

'Does Piet know about this?'

Adrian's face darkened.

'How can I tell, mother? I neither know nor care. I must go on my way, but there is one more thing that I want of you. You remember, three years ago, I gave you something to keep for me?'

'The flag? Burgers' *vierkleur*?'

'Yes, that's what I want. It has risen from the grave. Tomorrow it will be hoisted in Heidelberg.'

She went to the wagon-chest in the bedroom and brought it back with her. She unfolded the sun-bleached bunting and spread it out on the table, with its broad green vertical band and its horizontal bars of red, white and blue.

'It is faded and torn,' she said.

Adrian laughed: 'And yet it has come alive again! If we have to fight, this is something worth fighting for, mother.'

She sighed. 'I know men love fighting, Adrian; but it is we, the women who have borne them, who have to suffer. It tears my heart that young men should die for these strips of canvas. If I had my way I would burn all your flags, no matter how they were coloured.'

He smiled and kissed her.

'There are some things in men's lives,' he said, 'that not even the women who bore them can understand.'

When he had ridden away, she called Klaas to bring her a horse and hurried over to Witfontein to warn Piet and the Haskards.

At that hour, far away in the north-east, Janse, with his wagon, was approaching Lydenburg.

For three years – ever since the end of the Sekukuni campaign – he had been 'riding transport' from Delagoa Bay to the gold-fields, first of all under contract with the Gold-fields Transport Company, and later 'on his own'. There had been no lack of work: though Burgers' grand railway project, so hopefully begun, had well-nigh given up the ghost in the swamps of the lower Komati River, there was still a considerable traffic in goods between the Bay and the High Veld; though the Lydenburg gold-fields had not fulfilled their promise, there were still adventurous spirits eager to try their luck who, together with those who had tried it and lost and been broken, passed to and fro in driblets over the transport-road.

But, although he worked hard, Janse had not prospered materially. In the first year, when he was still ignorant of the deadliness that lay hidden beneath the fascinations of his beloved Low Country, he had suffered crushing losses from tsetse fly, that cross-winged devil of the bush which made certain belts of territory fatal to oxen and horses. It was only by dire experience and from the empirical counsels of those who had suffered before him that he learnt over what parts of the track this winged menace bred; how, by cunning divergence, the widest fly-belts could be avoided or his beasts protected by trekking only at night, when the tsetse slept. And even when he had mastered this peril to his cattle, he had not been able to protect himself from the malaria which made the first forty miles inward from the coast uninhabitable to white men. Recurrent fever had taken a heavy toll of his strength; his eyes had lost their brightness, his face its colour; he limped to and fro, between Lydenburg and the sea, a spare, sallow-skinned, solitary, hard-bitten man.

And yet, for all these afflictions, Janse was happy. He could think of no human lot which would have suited him better. His nature was not averse to solitude; the few human contacts he made – with the hopeful newcomers, the broken derelicts, the friendly natives, the half-savage Portuguese hunters of the Lebombo – were all, oddly enough, in keeping with their surroundings. He had never recanted the passion he had conceived for the Low Country. This was the Africa of his heart. He was still enthralled by its mysterious wildness and cruelty no less than by its strange beauty. Whenever he climbed the face of the Berg, to the poort on the verge of the High Veld where Bosmann lay buried, he would look back on the Low Veld with yearning. That vast solitude was the home of his bruised spirit, its refuge, its kingdom. Its life was the life he had chosen, with which he was in tune.

That evening, when he had crossed the Devil's Knuckles and skidded his wagon-wheels for the long descent into Lydenburg, he was stopped by a mounted patrol of the Ninety-Fourth. As the three men, a sergeant and two privates, converged on him, he was reminded of the evening, three years before, when Veld-kornet Devenaar had swooped down on himself and Meninsky and commandeered their wagon. The sergeant rode up and roared at him in halting Dutch.

'Where are you going and where have you come from?'

Janse answered him in English.

'Well, thank God you can talk a Christian language,' the sergeant said. 'I've bust up my poor lungs with shouting this ruddy lingo. You're the very chap we've been looking for. We're short of wagons, and this here will come in handy, though I must say it don't look up to much.'

'What – are you going to commandeer it?'

'Commandeer it? What do you take me for? Do I look like a Dutchman? No, my lad, the Colonel will give you a tiptop price for it: a damn sight more than it's worth, and cash on the nail. This is a Government job, mind. They're chucking money about. You'll have nothing to worry about.'

'What is the meaning of this?' Janse asked. 'Another war?'

'War? What are you talking about? Never on your life! We've got orders to move to Pretoria three weeks ago, matey, and just about time. I've had enough of this ruddy hole to last me a lifetime. We should have been gone by now if we hadn't been short of transport.'

On the edge of the outspan another detachment stopped him.

'What d'you want for that wagon, mate?'

'I've no intention of selling it.'

'Don't be a damned fool. I'll give you a straight tip, my lad: we're that short you can ask what you ruddy well want and get it. They'll pay you as much as a hundred and fifty pounds, and ten pound apiece for your bullocks. That's not to be sniffed at! What's more, if you like to sign on as a driver for the trip to Pretoria, they'll pay you two pound a day, and everything found.'

Janse turned the proposal over in his mind. His recent losses had left him short of cash; the wagon was rickety and his oxen were in poor fettle. In Pretoria, the central market of all the High Veld, there would be plenty of newer wagons and better oxen for sale. With more than three hundred pounds in his pocket, he could fit himself out again and have more than a hundred to spare. It would be foolish to miss such an opportunity. He decided to sell.

They set out two days later: a thin, mile-long column straggling over the veld. Ahead marched the regimental band, the colonel and his company commanders riding in front of it, then came the main body of nearly two hundred rank and file under their subalterns; behind these, thirty ox-wagons, water-carts and ambulances.

Janse found himself placed in the immediate rear of the men of 'A' Company. The men marched at ease, with their green-faced red tunics unbuttoned, for the December sun beat down fiercely, and owing to their garrison life they were out of condition. By midday the heat and the glare became almost intolerable, and the lieutenant in charge, a tall, slim boy, fair-haired and grey-eyed, allowed the men to dump their heavy equipment on Janse's wagon, which was loaded with boxes of ammunition. Some even unshouldered their rifles and proceeded to stack them on the top of the cartridge-boxes.

'No, no, that won't do, Sergeant-Major,' the young man said.

'Very good, sir.' The man saluted. 'Here, pick up them ruddy rifles! Call yourself soldiers?'

The men took them back reluctantly. They were a good-tempered lot. The relief from so many months of forced inactivity in Lydenburg and the prospect of returning to Pretoria had put them in a gay mood, in spite of the broiling heat. They talked and joked as they marched. In their speech Janse recognized echoes of Major Haskard's faint brogue, which made him remember some things he would rather have forgotten: even now, at a distance of nearly four years, the memory of Lavinia hurt him. When the column halted for a rest in the middle of the day, the young officer brought his rations to the shady side

316

of the wagon where Janse was sheltering, and sat down beside him.

'Do you mind if I come here?' he said.

'Not at all, sir. This is the only shade you'll get anywhere today,' Janse said.

'Why, you're English! I thought you were a Dutchman.'

'I'm half-English, at any rate: my mother is Dutch,' Janse said.

'I didn't mean that I thought you any the worse for it,' the young man explained.

Janse laughed at his tact. 'I should think you are very English, sir. Much more English than the men. Sometimes I can't understand what they say.'

'Yes, I'm English all right. The Regiment, of course, is Irish. They're the Connaught Rangers, you know, and a jolly good lot. You were born in South Africa, I take it?'

'Yes. A long way from here, on the Witwatersrand. I don't suppose you've ever heard of it. It's . . .'

'Yes, I know where it is. I was there a few months ago. A good place to be born in. Yes, I've happy memories of the Witwatersrand,' he added, a little wistfully.

A bugle-call rang out. 'Step to it! Fall in there, you lazy beggars!' the sergeant-major shouted. The men picked themselves up reluctantly and fell into column of fours. Janse saw no more of the young English officer that day.

In the evening bivouac a rumour reached the tail of the column. Two Englishmen named Barrett, who lived in Middelburg, had warned the Commanding Officer, Colonel Anstruther, that there might be some trouble ahead; but headquarters, so the men said, had discounted their story. The night had been cooled by a deluge from one of those crashing thunderstorms which were usual on the High Veld at that time of the year; in the early morning the air was sweet, the dust of the wagon-track had been laid, and marching was easy; but by the middle of the morning a blistering sun beat down through the humid atmosphere, and once more the sweating soldiers piled their equipment on Janse's wagon. Some even discarded their rifles again, and this time, neither Janse's friend nor the sergeant-major noticed them. Janse, perched on the driving-seat in shade and comparative cool, saw how the long column in front of him laboured. The steady thud of marching feet in the dust was a painful sound. Sweat streamed from the soldiers' red

317

necks and stained their scarlet tunics. He called to the subaltern and offered him a lift.

The young man laughed: 'Oh no, that would never do. I must march with my men. Thanks, all the same,' he said.

At midday, mercifully, the sun clouded over. Bulging masses of tawny cumulus ringed the sky, foretelling another tempest which seemed likely to break before sundown. They packed in the sulphurous sky; the air beneath them was dense and tepid and, somehow, ominous. The marching men no longer chattered or joked or sang.

Of a sudden a halt was called. Three horsemen, with rifles slung on their backs, had appeared on the ridge to westward and cantered up to the head of the column. The men stood and muttered, wondering what had happened. The break in the rhythm of marching made them feel their fatigue. Then a message came back from the front and the column re-started. There was nothing to worry about, it was said. The Boers who had ridden up and merely reported that they were on their way to a big meeting of some sort. These damned Dutchmen were always holding meetings of one kind or another.

Janse looked at his watch. It was only half-past two. Three more hours of purgatory, he thought, for these poor devils. He was sorry that the young Englishman had not accepted his offer of a lift. He saw him plodding ahead, on the left of the column, and thought how well he carried his tall slim body. The sight of a boy like that, so easy-mannered and frank, yet so conscientious and soldierly in a matter of duty, made him glad of the English blood in his veins. They were an aristocratic race, these English, for all their renowned stupidity. There was something gay and gallant, too, about this soldiering; to step out, however tired one was, to a military march such as that which the band was now playing, though, at that distance, it was little more than the rhythm of the drums that he heard.

Suddenly, the drum-beats stopped. Again a halt was called. At this point there was a dip in the land where a small spruit crossed the road. On the left stood two farms with clumps of trees beside them; on the right a wooded kloof, out of which the spruit's water ran. Janse remembered that the Peruvian had told him the name of the place on their journey east from Pretoria. It was called Bronkhorst Spruit, after the owner of one of the farms; the other belonged, as he knew, to a kinsman of his mother's, Solomon Prinsloo.

He jumped down from the wagon-seat to stretch his cramped legs. Over the falling ground he could see the long column stretched out before him in a wide arc. On the rise beyond, a cluster of mounted men stood silhouetted against the sulphurous sky, and down the slope slowly rode a single horseman, carrying a white flag. As he saw this an order came back for the column to close up. The company immediately in front of him moved forward. Janse noticed that some of the rifles they had piled in the wagon had been left behind. He heard the clicking of locks being opened and cartridges slipped in.

The man with the white flag rode on towards the halted column. A corporal, Conductor Egerton, was sent out to meet him.

'Is the general there?' he was asked.

'The Commanding Officer's here – Colonel Anstruther.'

'I have a letter for him.'

'Come with me to the troops, and then you can speak to him.'

'I'm not allowed to do that. It's against my orders.'

'If you'll ride on a bit, I'll ask him to come and meet you.'

He went back and reported. From this point of vantage Janse could see the small group of officers discussing what should be done. Then the colonel tossed back his head and strolled forward, followed by two of them. The band, which had stopped playing when the column halted, struck up 'God Save the Queen'. The tune, which Janse knew as that of a hymn, came back over the distance slowly and plaintively.

'Well, what do you want, my man?' the colonel said.

'Frans Joubert sends you this letter, general.'

'What's in it?' Anstruther asked.

'That's more than I can say, general. Open it and read it.'

Colonel Anstruther read the letter and crumpled it angrily in his hand. He laughed: 'Your commander forbids me to go to Pretoria.'

'Yes, that is the message. If you cross the spruit it will be a declaration of war. What do you say to it, general?'

'I'm going to Pretoria. That's all.'

'My general gives you five minutes to consider over the matter and what your plan will be.'

'I tell you: I'm going to Pretoria, man,' Anstruther answered angrily. 'I'm ordered to Pretoria, and there I shall go.'

'Do you mean War or Peace, then?'

'I've told you: I've got orders for Pretoria, and to Pretoria I'll go.'

He turned on his heel and began to walk back. The two others followed him.

'War or Peace?' the burgher repeated.

Anstruther swung round again:

'Take back my answer,' he said.

The Boer pulled round his horse. He rode for a hundred yards at a walk, then broke into a canter.

Janse heard the order: Extend in skirmishing order. The men who had forgotten their rifles ran back to the wagon to get them, but before they could reach it quick firing had broken out, not only from the crest ahead, but also from either side of the column and in its rear. The Boer marksmen, concealed behind rocks and bushes, were picking off the officers first. Then they turned a withering fire on the whole column and swept it from end to end. Janse threw himself down on his face and crawled under his wagon; but no sooner had he reached this vain shelter than the oxen, three of which had been hit, stampeded, and one of the wheels passed over his leg as the wagon lurched forward. The whole road was a confused shambles of wounded men and plunging oxen.

Janse saw a woman run forward from the wagon behind him. She was Mrs. Fox, the sergeant-major's wife, who had seen her husband fall and left her children to bind up his wound with shreds of her apron.

'That is what I should be doing,' he thought.

He scrambled to his feet, convinced that the wagon-wheel had broken his good leg; but before he had pulled his wits together, the firing stopped as suddenly as it had begun. The 'cease fire' had sounded, and the men who had clustered round the spot where Colonel Anstruther had fallen were waving white handkerchiefs in token of surrender.

'I had better leave a few men to tell the story,' the colonel had said.

That fierce fusillade had lasted exactly ten minutes. Out of two hundred and fifty-eight men, fifty-seven had been killed outright and a hundred and one were wounded, with an average of five wounds for each man.

When the firing ceased, Frans Joubert rode down, accompanied by Paul de Beer, the English-speaking Boer who had

320

carried the white flag, to the group which surrounded Anstruther.

'This is our general,' de Beer said, 'and this, Oom Frans, is
their colonel.'

'Tell the colonel not to be angry, nephew,' Joubert said. 'This
is his fault, not ours.'

Anstruther smiled as de Beer translated.

'Tell your general,' he said, 'that all he did against me was
honest; and bring all your wounded burghers nearer, so that the
doctor may attend to their wounds. They behaved well, and
they are good shots. God be with you!'

Janse found that his leg was not broken after all. He went
limping over the blood-stained ground in search of his young
English officer. He found him trying to sit up, clasping a leg
whose thigh-bone had been smashed by a rifle-bullet. Blood
spurted red from the thigh: he was coughing and spitting blood,
too, from a wound in the lung. Janse put his arm round his
neck and propped him with his knee.

'I'm afraid I'm finished,' the young man whispered. 'It was
bad luck: we hadn't a chance.' He spoke slowly, with difficulty
dragging the words from his blood-stained lips. 'The Witwatersrand ... you remember. There's a letter ... my tunic
pocket ... here, on the right. I can't reach it. ... Will you see
that it ... gets to her?'

'Yes, I'll promise you that,' Janse said.

The young man drew a deep shuddering breath; his head
rolled over; the weight that Janse supported grew heavier; he
lowered the slim young body gently to the ground, where it lay
motionless, appearing to breathe no more. He thrust the letter in
his pocket and staggered away.

The Witwatersrand ... That was the uppermost word in his
bewildered brain. If war had come, and this massacre was the
beginning of it, every Englishman and woman in the Transvaal
was now in danger. His father had burgher-rights, and in any
case, Adrian might protect him. But Lavinia, and the Haskards?
His first duty seemed clear: to make for Witfontein as fast as he
could, and to warn them.

Amid the blood-stained confusion he found a loose horse and
scrambled into the saddle. As he mounted, a hurly figure rushed
forward and seized the bridle.

'Where are you going?' he shouted.

Janse recognized in an instant the shaggy, bearded face of Gert Trichard, the *ve-bor* who had entertained him and Meninsky on their way to Lydenburg – the man who distrusted railways – and the old man recognized him.

'So it's you, nephew,' he said. 'What did I tell you and that Peruvian? You went to the gold-fields, and now you have got into trouble.'

'It's not my fault I'm here, uncle,' Janse lied. 'The English commandeered my wagon in Lydenburg and made me go with them. Now I'm free, and I want to go home.'

'The general has ordered that nobody shall leave this place without his authority.'

'But I am a burgher. I am no Englishman. I want to go home to join my brother Adrian, whom you know. Things have come to a fine pass if a burgher of the Republic can't go where he wills.'

'That is true,' Gert Trichard admitted grudgingly; 'but some burghers are traitors, and I find you here with the English.'

'Against my will. I am no traitor, uncle. My brother will answer for me.'

'Will you give me your word to ride straight home, and not to Pretoria?'

'I give you my word.'

'Then perhaps I may let you go. But you will ride straight home, and if any question you on the way you will tell them nothing of what has happened here?'

'I give you my word for that too.'

'Then go. But if you are shot, it will not be my fault.'

The warning was not unnecessary. As he galloped away, Janse heard cries behind him and a shot whistled over his head. He leant forward low in the saddle. The horse was a good one and fresh. He made straight for the farm on the rise, and was soon out of gunshot and over the brow on his way to Witfontein.

He reached the crest of the Witwatersrand in the small hours. The sky was still packed with thundercloud and the night pitch-dark, but the country was so familiar here that he could have ridden blindfold. It was only when he had crossed the ridge and began to drop down on Witfontein that he found himself baffled by Piet's new plantations and water-furrows. The sight of the large, new, whitewashed house which had been built on the slope above his old dwelling made him feel a stranger. No doubt Piet had bettered the property and quadrupled its value; but this well-ordered domain was no longer the old wild Witfontein he had loved. The place had changed so much that he could no longer feel sentimental about it or wish to recover it. That was all to the good, he told himself. In the new scheme of life which he had deliberately adopted there was no room for regrets, nor for any tie that restricted his spirit's freedom.

Yet, as he drew near to the house where she slept, he could not rejoice in the same emotional independence with regard to Lavinia. Her image was the only one that he could not exorcize from his memory. Though he had lost her for ever – and indeed had never possessed her – he could not face the prospect of seeing her without a trepidation and a foreboding of acute pain which made him flinch from the task which duty had laid on him. How would she look, he thought, and what would she say when she saw him? He halted for a moment to brace himself for this distressing encounter, then dismounted and limped up to the stoep.

There was no light in the house, as seemed natural enough at that hour of the night; but, apart from this, he had a feeling in his bones that it was empty. No window was open, and every shutter was closed. He hammered on the doors at front and back. Only hollow echoes answered him. He went down to the stables which once had been his home. They, too, were empty. He shouted to wake the natives that might be about and peered into the huts where they slept. The whole farm was deserted.

He walked back to his horse and rode on slowly to Wonderfontein, relieved in two ways: by his knowledge of Lavinia's safety, and by the satisfaction of knowing that he had mastered his emotions sufficiently to try to save her. Only one other duty remained: the delivery of the letter which the dead officer had entrusted to him. He took it out of his pocket to read the direction – and this was easy now, for the clouds had cleared from the sky and stars shone briliantly. One corner of it had been pierced by the bullet that entered the young man's lungs, but the address was clearly written in a bold hand. He saw:

Miss Maria Grafton,
Wonderfontein,
(on the Witwatersrand)
S. Transvaal.

and, as he read those words, Janse's eyes filled with tears that were the culminating expression of the feelings of that tragic day. 'Poor little Maria ... poor boy!' he thought. 'What a cruel world we live in! Why in God's name do we live in it?'

He looked up to the blank and glittering vault.

(4)

Witfontein had been empty, in fact, for more than forty-eight hours before Janse reached it. Some days before that, the rumours of the Bezuidenhout riot at Potchefstroom and the mass meeting at Paardekraal had reached Piet and set him thinking. At first he had not been inclined to take the vague news very seriously. During the last two years he had become so deeply engrossed in the management of Major Haskard's affairs and in laying the foundation of his own fortune that the centre of his life had shifted from the Witwatersrand to Kimberley. He knew that there was a good deal of political unrest in the Transvaal, and that 'poor old Adrian' had been dragged into it up to the neck by that little firebrand Suzanna, whom he admired for her intelligence, but disliked, as he disliked all extremists. Political unrest, after all, was endemic in the Transvaal; for lack of any more profitable excitement – such as speculation in diamonds – it had always been the Boer's favourite form of amusement; there people were never happy unless they were talking and meeting and looking for trouble.

But when Lisbet arrived with the alarming news that Adrian had called in to retrieve his flag and had assured her that within a few days it would be hoisted at Heidelberg, the Annexation renounced and the Republic proclaimed, Piet was ready with plans to meet the emergency.

His position was complicated by the presence of James Haskard at Witfontein. Though he refused to believe that this foolish insurrection could survive for long the pressure the British Government would bring to bear on it, he realized that, for a time at least, Haskard's liberty was in danger. It would be no joke for a man of his father-in-law's age, an invalid, used to luxury, to be rounded up and thrown into a prison-camp; it would be unfair to his own children and to Lavinia, who was expecting another, to expose her to any unnecessary risk or excitement; moreover, he himself had no intention of being caught up in a war. Wars were not in his line.

'The sooner we clear out of the country, the better,' he said.

'Do you think it's a serious as all that?' Haskard asked.

'You never can tell. I'm taking no chances with you and Lavinia, and I don't want to be dragged in either.'

'How could you be?'

'Well, if the Republic's restored – even though it's only for a few weeks – I shall be considered a burgher – and called out on commando. I'm in the first levy – from eighteen to thirty-four. I'm not going to fight against England, and I don't want to be shot as a deserter.'

'We'd better make straight for Kimberley, then?'

'No; I think that's too risky. It means passing by Pot-chefstroom. which is the centre of all this mischief, and it's possible – though I don't think it's likely, mind – that they may have some trouble in the Cape: the power of the Afrikander Bond is not to be sniffed at. My idea is to make a bee-line for the Free State frontier, crossing the Vaal at Viljoen's Drift, and then trek on to Natal. I'd prefer to feel that the British army's in front of me at a time like this.'

'That's an excellent idea. We should be able to link up with old Edward, too. If there is any fighting he'll give us ring-side seats. When ought we to start?'

'Immediately. There's no time to be lost.'

They had shut up the house and were off before dawn next morning. Maria went with them. Piet had begged her to come. In Lavinia's present condition the long trek would be sufficient disturbance without burdening her with the care of two children: little James was nearly seven – a delightful child, but, as Haskard confessed, a 'limb of the devil' – and Cecilia, now cutting her first teeth, a 'handful'. Lavinia, too, had been nervous and querulous of late. Her delicacy of physique and her natural refinement were not adaptable to the primitive conditions of life on a back-veld farm, and the strain of three pregnancies in quick succession had told on her. She knew she had lost her looks, and regretted them. She was her mother's daughter, in short, and though she still loved Piet, there were times when his abounding health and energy got on her nerves and made her feel an indefinite grievance against him.

She was only too thankful to hand over the care of the two children to Maria; and Maria, who adored them both and had energy to spare, was delighted to undertake it. To her this sudden, forced exodus was welcome as an adventure and, above all, as a distraction that would keep her mind from brooding too anxiously on Richard Abberley. She had only heard from him once since the day he left Pretoria, and that precious letter, long since learnt by heart, was scant food for her hungry love. It was true that, by going to Natal, she was increasing the distance between them by some hundreds of miles; and yet, if war were inevitable, she felt she would be happier there, among his people, than alone at Wonderfontein. There was even, she told herself, the exciting possibility that the Ninety-fourth might be withdrawn from Lydenburg and transferred to Natal, where the bulk of the British forces were concentrated. If he heard she was there – and she felt sure that Edward would contrive to send him a message – he would be happy, at least, to know that she was in safety.

So they forded the River Vaal at Viljoen's Drift, crossed the treeless veld of the Orange Free State towards Harrismith, and descended the face of the Drakensberg through Van Reenen's pass by the road which her voortrekker forbears had followed under Retief – and which Piet, in his transport-riding days, had used on his trading-trips to Pietermaritzburg. But when they had crossed the Berg they turned north again, making straight for Newcastle, where Edward was stationed as a member of General Colley's Headquarters Staff.

'We shall be just in time for the fun, my boy,' Major Haskard said, rubbing his hands. 'Once a soldier, always a soldier! The old war-horse, what? *He paweth in the valley and rejoiceth in his strength. He saith among the trumpets, Ha, ha! – and he smells the battle afar off.* You see, I can quote scripture, when I like, as well as any damned Dutchman! Where does that come from, Piet? I'll bet you a pound you don't know.'

They were in plenty of time for the 'fun', Edward Haskard assured them. He was a very business-like Edward, Maria thought, and his moustache had grown more ferocious than ever. As for the war – if they chose to dignify it by such a name – his new chief, General Colley, was sending the Boers an ultimatum next day. They were encamped, he said, on the heights above Laing's Nek, but against modern artillery and gatlings and the rocket-tubes of the Naval Brigade they couldn't possibly hold it.

'We shall go through the poor devils like butter,' Edward said. 'Well, that's their fault, not ours. Why d'you look so solemn, Maria?'

'Oh, I don't know, Edward. It's you who sound so bloodthirsty.'

She was thinking of Adrian.

'Well, my child, war is war, you know,' Major Haskard boomed sententiously. 'You have all the luck, Edward. Two campaigns on Active Service at twenty-two. Two medals already. I wish I was your age, my lad!'

Next morning they watched a mixed column move forward from Newcastle. A military band played them out. Maria had never heard a band playing before, or seen bodies of men in bright uniforms swinging along on parade. She was delighted by the brilliancy of the dazzling tunics of the Fifty-eighth, by the blue and white of the Naval Brigade, and even more by the green-black uniforms of the Sixtieth. ('But if it's riflemen you prefer, you should see the Royal Irish, my child!' Major Haskard said.) The sun shone on the band's brass instruments, on the officer's swords, on the sleek steel barrels of the seven-pounder and four-pounder guns. In comparison with this professional pageantry, the uniforms of the Natal Mounted Police, who followed, seemed terribly tame. It was a gallant, inspiriting spectacle, this setting forth on the paths of glory to the sound of martial music that made one long to fall into step. All the same, she felt glad that Edward was staying behind, and thankful, even more, that her Richard was still safe in Lydenburg.

That night Major Haskard listened attentively for the sound of gun-fire. The heavens thundered, but there was no thunder on earth. In point of fact, by nightfall the column had made no more than six miles. They marched five next day, and came within sight of the precipitous track that led to the Nek; but still no shot was fired. Next morning Major Haskard swore he heard firing; but it was not until they saw Edward that night that they heard what had happened.

At dawn the guns of the Royal Artillery and the rocket-tubes of the Naval Brigade had begun to plaster Laing's Nek. After twenty minutes' shelling, observers reported that the body of Boers defending the Nek had retreated, though reserves were still occupying the heights out of range. An attack was launched on either side of the road, the mounted squadron on the right, the Fifty-eighth on the left; but before either were half-way up the steep slope they had been caught by an enfilading fire and decimated.

'A bad business,' Edward said, 'but it won't happen again. They've no guns, but they have these damned Westley-Richards rifles, effective at six hundred yards, and they're first-rate shots.'

It happened again, a few days later, at the Ingogo Heights: a drawn battle in which Edward himself received his baptism of fire and a bullet that grazed a rib.

'I can't think what's up with you fellows,' Major Haskard complained.

'The trouble is, they're more mobile than we are,' Edward explained. 'You never know where the beggars are till they've potted you, and when you get there they've gone. In the Nek, the ground favours that odd sort of warfare and makes their position pretty nearly impregnable. But the general's a cunning old bird. He's got a new plan. I'll tell you about it later.'

He made Piet the recipient of this momentous confidence.

'Look here, you know this country pretty well, don't you?' he said.

'I've ridden over the Nek once or twice,' Piet told him guardedly.

'Do you know an isolated hill called Majuba or Amajuba, overlooking the Nek and the country behind it from the west?'

'I know what you mean.'

'I thought as much, and I told General Colley so. You're the very fellow we want. The old man has authorized me to give you the general idea. It's to move up by night to the Majuba with five or six hundred men and occupy the top. When we're up there all right, the guns will bombard the Net, and the main body will advance under cover of an enfilading fire from the Majuba. In other words, the Boers will be outflanked and will have to retire. The whole thing's ridiculously obvious and easy as winking. The point is – we want a bloke who knows the country, the conditions and that, to act as a guide up the Kaffir path that leads to the top. I mentioned your name to the general and he simply jumped at it. It's not everybody you can trust on a job like this, but your being my brother-in-law . . .'

'I've never been over this path,' Piet said defensively.

'But you'll know what to do. Veldcraft, and all that sort of thing. Anyway, I thought it would give you the chance of going up with us – the general is in it himself. You'll see the whole concern from beginning to end, and I know you'd not like to miss it. You're invited, anyway. If you can't undertake to guide us, you can chum up with the war correspondents.'

Piet thanked him, with no great enthusiasm. It was just like old Edward's dunder-headedness to let him in for this; and he couldn't very well refuse General Colley's invitation without appearing to funk it. He felt he had a right to feel sore – for he had come to Natal to get out of the war and not to plunge into it.

'I suppose you realize,' he said, 'that, properly speaking, I'm still a Transvaal burgher, and liable to be shot as a traitor if I'm found in your company?'

Edward laughed: 'Well, as far as that goes, my dear fellow, we're all liable to be shot.'

The plan took a couple of weeks to mature, for they had to wait for the dark of the moon. Though the force assembled, with three days' rations, soon after sundown, no member of it, outside the staff, had any idea where he was going. They were five hundred and forty-four rifles in all, of the Naval Brigade, the Ninety-second, the Gordon Highlanders, and a company of the Fifty-eighth Northamptonshire Regiment. They set out at ten o'clock. It was so dark that it would have been easy, Piet thought, for him to get lost on the way or sprain an ankle; but Edward had introduced him to one of the war correspondents, a talkative, generous young man named Edmondson, who had already loaded him with tins of sardines and stuck to him tight.

They went up in single file, over the Kaffir path that skirted the edge of a cliff with a sheer drop of a hundred feet. Piet could smell the aromatic scent of trampled brushwood. The tread of a thousand feet moving forward cautiously was barely audible to his ears, though the dogs in O'Neill's farm, down in the valley, heard it and began to bark. At the end of every hundred yards the straggling column halted, moving on again at a prearranged signal which imitated the whistle of a frog. Within a quarter of a mile of the top, the path petered out and the climb became precipitous; they clutched the bushes and pulled themselves up on their hands and knees.

It was still pitch-dark when the force reached the crown of the Majuba and spread itself out over the shallow depression on the top. The men lay down exhausted, scattered all over it. An irritable officer, with a strong Scots accent, hurried to and fro among them, blaspheming beneath his breath:

'Get out to your posts, men,' he said, 'and then you'll have plenty of time to rest. Come along: get a move on!'

The war correspondent and Piet made their way through this confusion to the lip of the land. They could see, beneath them, the Nek, and behind it the main Boer laager, in which lights were still burning, and dim clusters of tents on either side of the road. At this point, facing the enemy's left, the land sloped gently from the brim, over gullies clogged with scrub and fern, and natural terraces. On all other sides the Majuba appeared to be unassailable.

'Good Lord – what a chance!' the war correspondent whispered. 'With rockets and gatlings we could wipe out the whole damned camp. I didn't see any guns, by the way: I suppose they'll bring 'em up later?'

'Don't ask me,' Piet said. 'I know nothing whatever about it.'

The eastern sky paled, and soon the heights of the Elandsberg appeared to be swimming in lakes of liquid fire. A small group of Highlanders, who had recovered from their fatigue, advanced to the ridge and gazed down on the sleeping laager.

'Come up here, you beggars!' they shouted.

Though their shouting could not be heard, their figures, etched black against the lightening sky, were seen by the Boer outposts. The laager buzzed and seethed like an ant's nest that has been given a kick. The plain was dotted with galloping horsemen and others on foot, streaming out of the camps to right and left. Piet watched this swarming activity of minute, fore-shortened figures with fascinated eyes. He saw oxen inspanned and tents struck and a confusion of dots that were men running hither and thither.

'It's a regular panic,' he said. 'Where the devil are those gatlings and rocket-tubes?'

Now that he saw the Boer force breaking he was moved by an uncontrollable impulse of hatred and cruelty. Those scattering dots were not men to his mind, but mere symbols of the rebellious spirit which he loathed. He would gladly have

330

handled a gatling himself and sprayed the helpless thousands with bursting shrapnel.

But the gatlings had not come up; nor yet had the guns from the British camp at Mount Prospect opened fire on the Nek. He borrowed the journalist's glass and scanned the most distant ridge in search of guns or redcoats, but could not see any sign of movement. Either the plan for an attack had miscarried or else the advance was hidden by a fold in the land.

General Colley, too, was concerned. As soon as the sun was up, his heliograph began to flicker, but no answering flashes reached him. The men were beginning to feel that all was not well. A few were collecting stones and putting up cover of a sort. The same irritable officer, a tall man with a leathery face, stalked into the midst of them.

'What the hell's the good of that?' he said in a rasping voice. 'You'll only get hit by splinters.'

A tough-looking sergeant of the Gordons smiled and saluted:

'Oh, it's all right, sir. It's good enough for what we shall want up here.'

'They ought really to be digging trenches,' the journalist said.

'What's that?' the officer snapped. He gazed down at the young man and Piet with a ferocious fixed stare. 'The general says that the men are too tired to entrench. It's his funeral, not ours.'

He took out the glass eye which accounted for the fixity of his stare and washed it carefully in water tipped into his palm from his water-bottle. Then he stuck it back again.

'That's better,' he said.

Piet and his friend decided to breakfast, opening a couple of tins of sardines with a borrowed bayonet. The men, too, were munching their rations. Edward Haskard came over to Piet with a sardine-smeared crust in his hand.

'Got plenty to eat, you fellows?' he asked.

Piet nodded with his mouth full.

'I say . . . has something gone wrong?' he asked.

'Every damned thing's gone wrong,' Edward said. 'Wood ought to have advanced to the Nek by now, and the artillery hasn't opened.'

A shot rang out on their left.

331

'Stop that damned firing, there!' Edward shouted.

The culprit was an officer who had snatched a rifle from one of his men. He grinned sheepishly. 'Sorry, Haskard. I saw a chap climbing up the gully below here, and had to have a pot at him.'

'Well, you know what the orders are, Lucy,' Edward said.

He went back to headquarters.

But now, in spite of the orders, sniping continued – there must be plenty of targets, Piet thought – and half an hour later a more sustained fire broke out from the heathery slopes below. Bullets whined overhead and occasionally a ricochet stripped through the grass. The men lounged in the sun and laughed.

'Will the beggars try to rush us?' one asked.

'You dinna ken the Boers as well as me, man,' the stocky sergeant said. 'If they do . . .' He tapped his bayonet-scabbard significantly. 'Better get a sleep while you can, boys, and settle your breakfast.'

The general was wandering restlessly round the lines with Edward Haskard in attendance. From time to time he approached the crest overlooking Mount Prospect and searched it with his deer-stalker's telescope. A sergeant came running up from the rear on the left:

'Mr. Lucy's compliments, and he wants reinforcements, sir.'

'What? Anything wrong?'

'Nothing wrong, sir. The fire's warming up a bit on our side, sir.'

Colley turned to Edward:

'Heliograph for the Sixtieth to come up in support. And reinforce Mr. Lucy.'

'Very good, sir.'

But now bursts of fire from the slope were coming in volleys. Another group of Highlanders came up from the rear carrying two wounded men to the well where the doctors were stationed. The officer with the glass eye was collecting reserves:

'Will you step up quick, there?' he shouted. 'Rally on the right! I say, rally on the *right*!'

The men had their backs to him and were rushing to the left. Highlanders, sailors and Fifty-eighth were all mingled in one confused mass.

'This is no place for me,' Piet thought.

He crawled towards the head of the path by which he had come up. Nobody took any notice of him. The hurriedly-mustered reserves stood packed four deep behind a breastwork of stones: the front rank could see nothing below but the muzzles of the Boer rifles – two hundred of them spitting ferocious volleys at thirty yards' range, drawing the fire in front while their comrades crept up on the flank.

Piet heard a yell of 'Fix bayonets!' He saw the blades flash in the sun and heard the rasp of steel. The one-eyed officer was shouting above the din of musketry: 'Now, men of the Ninety-second, don't forget your bayonets!' Others were calling on the Fifty-eighth and the Naval Brigade: 'Show them the cold steel, men: that'll check them!'

But still there was no order to charge. Piet heard snatches of talk:

'Why doesn't he let 'em have a go at it with the bayonet while their blood's up?' ... 'That'll come in a minute. You'll see the Ninety-second charging in a second. ... They may, but I don't like that run on the right: I don't like this hesitation.'

A wounded Highlander staggered back from the dressing-station and tripped over Piet's leg: 'Here, who the hell are you?' he snarled. 'You look like a Boer. Get out of the way. I want to have another shot at the devils.'

Shouts came from the front: 'Now, my lads, wait till they show up. Fire low! Fire low! Now give it them! Be steady; cease firing there! What are you aiming at? Extend to the left! Will you deploy there? Deploy! What the devil d'you think you're doing? Come back, or I'll shoot!'

Piet saw the smoking revolver in the officer's hand. He was caught up in a rush of men of different regiments surging towards the gap for which he had been aiming. As he pulled himself over the brim and rolled down the slope, he saw bearded figures swarming over three sides of the top of the Majuba. He clambered back to the track and was carried on again by the flood of fugitives. His companion the journalist appeared miraculously just in front of him.

'Hello! Is that you?' he panted. 'Lord, what a go!'

They were plunging downward together under a dropping fire from the crest, till, suddenly, Piet's companion threw up his arms and toppled sideways. Piet, caught by his legs, tripped over him and fell with him. He spun over and rolled down the face of the screes, until his head struck a rock which stopped him and knocked him senseless.

When he came to himself he found his face sticky with blood, and there was a singing in his ears. That was the only sound he heard. It seemed that the firing on the Majuba had ceased. He propped himself up on his elbow and moved his legs to see if a bone were broken. A little higher up the slope he saw a party of Boers searching the brushwood for wounded men or fugitives whom they could make prisoners. His numb mind began to work. If he were recognized by any neighbour, he knew he would be finished: a firing-squad was the least that he could expect. One of the searchers appeared at a distance not unlike his uncle Barend. 'What a chance for the settling of old scores,' he thought, 'if he finds me!'

The journalist was lying beside him, unconscious or dead. Piet didn't waste time in finding out which. His brain was now brilliantly clear. He crawled over to the body and ransacked its clothing in search of the only thing that might save him: the pass officially issued to every war correspondent. He found it in the breast-pocket and opened it eagerly. *Hugh Edmondson. Aged thirty-two. Born at Durban, Natal.* He must not forget his new name! He folded the pass and stuffed it into his pocket.

Only just in time ... Within a moment of his having rolled over on his face the searchers converged on him. They were a party of five, two boys and two older men led by a shaggy, short, brown-eyed veld-kornet, who looked rather like a Newfoundland dog. The two boys rolled Edmondson's body over and emptied his pockets of the remaining tins of sardines. The small, shaggy man poked Piet in the ribs with the muzzle of his rifle. Piet pulled himself up laboriously on to his knees.

'This one's not hurt much,' the veld-kornet said in Dutch, 'and he isn't a redcoat, although he looks like an Englishman. Who are you?' he bawled.

Piet shook his head. 'I don't understand Dutch,' he said.

'The man is a fool: he doesn't understand what I'm saying. Better bring him along.'

Piet offered him Edmondson's permit. The veld-kornet frowned at it with puzzled brown eyes. Piet pointed to Edmondson's name, and then tapped his own chest.

'War correspondent,' he said.

'War correspondent? What's that? Do you know what that means, Jan Greyling?'

The second of the older men shook his head.

'I should search him, uncle.' The two boys pinioned Piet and ran through his pockets, triumphantly finding another squashed tin of sardines that had broken his fall.

'He is not armed: he has no revolver,' Jan Greyling said.

'That is nothing,' the veld-kornet replied, with a sagacious wink. 'He may have thrown it away, as the redcoats threw their rifles. Keep him here, till I've fetched the Commandant.'

After a while he returned accompanied by a larger man whose face was shadowed by his hat. As he advanced, Piet felt sure that he recognized those ponderous movements; then he saw a great golden beard and heard a voice that he knew:

'War correspondent, uncle? That is one of those skelms who writes all the lies about us in newspapers.'

'Then he'd better be shot, Commandant,' the veld-kornet said simply.

'Wait a bit. We'll see. Hugh Edmondson ... I don't know that name.'

Piet found himself gazing straight into Adrian's blue eyes. He met them without flinching. He saw the blood mounting through Adrian's neck and cheeks to his temples and a look of bitter scorn on his bearded mouth. He looked Piet up and down, from his blood-stained head to his feet. Then he folded the pass and thrust it into a pocket in his flapped moleskin trousers.

'This fellow isn't even worth shooting, Veld-kornet,' he said. 'He's a poor sort of white man. The English are welcome to him. Let him go.'

One of the younger men aimed his rifle as Piet turned his back. Adrian knocked it up and caught him a buffet on the head that sent him spinning.

'It's time you learnt to obey an order,' he said.

They signed an armistice at O'Neill's, the farm of the barking dogs. They sent parties up the Majuba to bury the dead – including the unfortunate Colley, shot through the back of the head – and to succour the wounded. Paul Kruger rode over from Rustenburg and a treaty of peace was debated while the British Army, now reinforced from Natal, fumed and fretted with impatience to wipe out the shame of folly and defeat. But the Gladstone Government had made up its mind to climb down, and the soldiers had no say in the settlement which gave back the Transvaal Republic (or the South African Republic, as Kruger still insisted – and why quarrel over two words?) its old independence, under a mild form of suzerainty in the conduct of foreign affairs and the indefinite promise of an adjustment of borders. A commission to settle the details would sit in Pretoria.

Major Haskard and Piet were among the loudest and most bitter opponents of the Peace. Piet declared that nothing would induce him to return to Witfontein and submit himself to the humiliation of living under the Republican flag. He was still shaken – naturally enough, as Haskard agreed – by his experience on the Majuba. (He made no mention among them of his encounter with Adrian.) When he had recovered, and deposited Lavinia and her babies at the Cape with his mother-in-law, he intended to go back to Kimberley and take care of Haskard's interests.

They hung on in their camp at Newcastle until Edward Haskard, astonishingly unwounded, was released. Edward looked horribly thin and depressed. He had been treated quite well, but he couldn't get over his anger or his anxiety to 'have another crack at them'. He sat in the outspan telling them the stories of what had happened to the scattered garrisons besieged in the Transvaal, at Potchefstroom, Pretoria and Lydenburg. (When he mentioned Lydenburg, Maria pricked up her ears.) But the worst thing of all, he said, was the disaster to his own regiment at Bronkhorst Spruit.

'Bronkhorst Spruit?' Major Haskard asked. 'That's new to me.'

'Of course. My brain's gone to pot. I forgot. You've not heard of it. It was our Lydenburg detachment, simply cut to pieces on the road to Pretoria. They picked off the officers first: poor Colonel Anstruther; Sweeny, Nairn, and the Adjutant, Harrison, and those two nice fellows who came up with me to Witfontein: Pat Martyn and Richard Abberley.'

'Richard Abberley?' Maria gasped.

'Yes, your friend, Maria.'

'He's . . . killed?'

Maria rose unsteadily. She put out her hands before her, groping, as though she were blind. She walked out of the circle of firelight on to the veld and was lost to sight.

'Well, I've gone and done it!' Edward said anxiously. 'I'd no idea it had gone so far as that. You'd better go after her, Lavinia.'

'No, I'd rather leave her alone,' Lavinia said. 'She won't want me, poor child.'

336

'Then I'll go . . .'

'For goodness' sake stay where you are, Edward,' Lavinia snapped. 'She's much better as she is. You don't understand.'

'It looks like a nasty shock. But she's young; she'll get over it,' Major Haskard said.

Lavinia went round by sea to the Cape with the children and Piet; but Maria would not accompany them for all their persuasions. She wanted to be alone, she said. She wanted to go back to her mother at Wonderfontein. They found her a place on a wagon bound from Maritzburg to Pretoria. She travelled home in a dream. John Grafton met her at Heidelberg and drove her to Wonderfontein. She was so silent and pale that he could not understand her – 'like a little ghost,' he told Lisbet, 'a little ghost.' Next day, her mother gave her two packets that had been waiting for her: one from Kimberley, containing a diamond ring wrapped up in a pencilled scrawl of congratulations; the other a letter with a bullet-hole in the corner.

Book Four

CHAPTER ONE

(1)

PIET came up from the Cape to Kimberley and threw himself into the job for which he felt himself best qualified: the quick making of money. His strategic position was excellent. Thanks to the steady advance of the railway he was able to keep in touch with Haskard in Capetown as well as with the manager of the farm at Witfontein. He was on British territory, and therefore safe, but within easy reach of the Transvaal, and therefore able to ascertain how the findings of the Royal Commission, now wrangling in Pretoria over the rights of the restored Republic, would affect himself.

An amnesty had already been granted, to all who had taken up arms against the British Crown; but nothing, so far, had been decided about the positions of burghers who had joined or followed the other side. So far as he knew there was nobody of any importance in the Transvaal, apart from Adrian, who had recognized him on the Majuba and could denounce him as a traitor; but the gleam he had seen in Adrian's blue eyes was a warning light, and the pass, which Adrian had pocketed, a trump card which, at any moment, might be played against him. So, until feelings simmered down (as Adrian's, from what he knew of him, seemed unlikely to do), he felt that the climate of the Transvaal would be none too healthy for him. Kimberley was the place.

Not that many people in Kimberley worried their heads overmuch about politics: they were too busy digging for diamonds and buying and selling them and forming syndicates and peddling claims. He found, of course, a general feeling of disgust for Colley's failure and of humiliation at Gladstone's climbdown; crowds were always ready to cheer the Union Jack (now formally hauled down in Pretoria) and to indulge in any other demonstration of loyalty that cost nothing: but the world, for most of them, was no larger than that small pitted and scarified patch of ground on which they strove and haggled, sand-girt and separated from any other considerable centre of habitation by hundreds on hundreds of miles of desolate aridity. Their horizons were very little wider, Piet thought, than those of the natives who sweated, four hundred feet down, in the bottom of the pits, with the great bastions of rock and the twanging wires above them.

At the moment the little the folk in Kimberley saw was none too pleasing. The deepening of the diggings into the blue ground had brought with it disastrous falls of rock and subsidences. A man who had gone to bed pluming himself on the richness of his claims might hear, in the night, a rumble of distant thunder, and wake to find himself ruined, the floor which contained his wealth buried beneath thousands of tons of fallen reef. Though the Mining Board undertook the clearing of debris, its charges were heavy enough to swallow up all his capital before he could make more profits. There was loss of life, too – not that native lives counted for much, but black labour was not so plentiful as it had been, nor yet so manageable. With every yard they went down into the earth the cost of production and the charge for pumping had risen, and the fierce competition of producers, each fighting for his existence, had brought down prices with a run.

What was more, no claim-owner could be assured that half the stones found would reach his pocket. The natives had learnt to spot a good diamond at sight, and knew its value in terms of women and drink and fire-arms. They secreted stones in their ears and their cheeks and under their tongues; they even swallowed them; and around their kraals there hovered perpetually the noctural hordes of Illegitimate Diamond Buyers, elusive anonymous gentry on whom nobody could keep an eye. A bad business. . . . The new blue-ground broken was richer than any that had been crushed before; and yet the industry was declining. Along the limited horizons of Kimberley clouds brooded heavily.

They would never lift, Cecil Rhodes said, until the industry was organized and the small competitive producers brought into line. Amalgamation! Restriction! He kept hammering in the words with his quick, nervous movements of the hands just as, a few years earlier, he had hammered in the word Federation. It was ridiculous to say that the industry need decline. There was more potential life in it now than ever before. Hadn't people said it was finished at the time when the yellow-ground ended and the blue-ground, actually incomparably richer, began? He had backed his own faith with every penny he possessed or could command, and fortune had smiled on his courage – the new shafts he had sunk at his own expense had not yet touched the bottom of rich reef. He believed in diamonds: the smallest form of readily negotiable wealth on earth. It was ridiculous, too, he said, to suggest that the market was nearing saturation:

'Was there ever a woman,' he squeaked, 'who would confess she had too many diamonds? Give me the power,' he said, 'to hold this industry in my hand, to amalgamate, to restrict, to control I.D.B., and I'll soon show you what it's worth! But one can't do these things unless one has laws to support one. That's why one has to go into Parliament.'

'Without any ulterior motive connected with that red map of yours, I suppose?' Piet chaffed him.

'Ah, that will come later ... later. My map has just had an ugly stain on it; but that's nobody's fault but our own – or rather our Government's. If those stupid fellows at home would keep their hands off the men on the spot and stop imagining themselves competent to rule a grown-up community with a mind of its own at a distance of six thousand miles, one might get somewhere. But they don't and they won't. They've not learnt a damned thing during the last hundred years, since they lost the American colonies – just as, forty years ago, they did their best to lose Canada. They look upon us, a young nation, a vigorous nation, as a pawn in their game of party politics. Do you think Gladstone cares a brass farthing about the Transvaal except as a stick to beat the Tories about the head with, or as a sop to offer the Nonconformist Conscience? Well, well, some day one will be able to do without the Imperial factor!'

'And bang goes the British Empire!'

'Not a bit. The Empire's bigger than any of them dream. It's a thing one can't destroy: as I told you before, when I quoted Ruskin's lecture, it represents a mode of thought, an ideal – the only one I believe in. It's the right ideal, and so it's got to go on. Do you know, my dear fellow, it wouldn't keep me awake if I thought that some day the Empire was going to be ruled from Ottawa or Sydney – or even New York, for that matter? Still, my job is Africa. Federation is the first step. One must go on working for that in Parliament.'

'Majuba has put a spoke in that wheel,' Piet said.

'It's taught some who didn't know it that the Boers, *qua* fighters, are brave men, and that's something gained. We've got to make friends with the Dutch: I say it again! They're the majority: we can't do without them. We've got to make them join with us in taking the North for South Africa – for we've got to go north, and pretty soon, too. I've always tried to understand them, to make friends with them. I'm doing my best to make friends with Jan Hofmeyr now, and I believe I shall get round him.'

'What? You, an imperialist, join with the founder of the Bond?'

'Why not? He's South African, like yourself – like me, if it comes to that. He wants the same things as I do, though he expresses himself rather differently. All sensible men want the same things, Grafton. Why, even Paul Kruger has started stealing one's powder! Only the other day he was talking about "Africa for the Afrikanders – from the Zambezi to Simon's Bay". "The Zambezi," mark you, not "the Limpopo". It's right, of course, but somehow, from him, I don't like it.'

'You could never work with Paul Kruger.'

'Just give me the chance! If one were Prime Minister of the Cape, I'm ready to bet one could get round him. One can deal with most men if one sets one's mind to it. Or one can square them. Don't forget, the Transvaal is poor.'

If one were Prime Minister of the Cape . . .

The words remained in Piet's mind. On the face of things it appeared fantastic that a man of his own age, still under thirty, who had only just entered Parliament, should talk like that. Yet on Rhodes' lips they did not seem unreasonable. During the last few years he had changed and developed enormously. He was no longer the gawky, forbidding youth whose moods alternated between long, sullen silences and bursts of shrill eloquence. His lanky body had filled out. In his shaggy Oxford tweeds it appeared almost massive. His face, too, was fatter, the hooked nose seemed less predatory, the mouth more firmly composed. He had the air of a middle-aged man of experience. His presence radiated a new sense of cool power rather than the old hot aspiration. He had set himself a fixed course, and was following it with confidence and determination. Every move was mapped out, every contingency provided for. He told Piet he had made his will.

342

Piet smiled. 'My dear Rhodes, you look as if you'd live to be ninety.'

Rhodes tapped his own chest significantly.

'Only a few years ago a doctor gave me six months to live, with my lungs; and my heart's groggy too. You never know. I've made a good bit of money and I'm going to make more, and I don't want to see it chucked away when I'm gone. Talking of doctors, you don't know Jameson. Now that's a fellow! And you don't know Neville Pickering. A charming lad. He and I are living together: I've left the "Apostles", you know. You must come round and meet him and the Doctor.'

Piet liked young Pickering, a fresh, jolly boy almost extravagantly English, but found it hard to share Rhodes' enthusiasm for his other new friend. He was a little, dark man, with a small, intelligent face, half-humorous, half-cynical, wispy hair, and wide-set black eyes, one bigger than the other. He was jerky and shy, but concealed his shyness with an affected detachment and a harshness of speech which was salted by a strong Scots accent and a quick laugh, which did not always ring true. He sat languidly hunched in his chair, sometimes smiling to himself, sometimes mischievously tossing into the conversation a provocative scrap of commentary or a cynical joke that Rhodes pounced on and tore to pieces. In his smallness, his darkness, his quick alternations of bored languor and mercurial vivacity, he was a complete foil and contrast to Rhodes. Perhaps, Piet reflected, it was this that had made them friends; and however little Piet 'took to' him, he certainly made Rhodes talk.

Rhodes talked endlessly during those lamp-lit sessions in the little tin shack at Kimberley. In his political faith and in his dominant obsession concerning the sacred mission of the British Empire, he had not changed. But his spoken 'thoughts', as he called them, were more and more concentrated on the north – 'our Hinterland'. He was uneasy about the north. Though he had refused to let Piet draw him on the subject of Colley's failure and Gladstone's 'scuttle', he regretted the mishandling that had made war inevitable.

'If one had treated the Boers decently,' he said, 'none of this need have happened. It's complicated my friendly relations with Hofmeyr and the Bond, and put back Federation for God only knows how long. It's made our own people sore and bitter against the Dutch; and it's made the Boers cock-a-whoop,

343

because they think the British can't fight and that the Government hasn't the spunk to back us. From now on, they'll imagine they can do what they like. I told you, Grafton, that Kruger was talking about the Zambezi. That's a new note. It means, if they can, they'll try to cut us off from the north. And that means we're ditched. I tell you the Cape has got to take Bechuanaland.'

'When you're Prime Minister, Rhodes,' Jameson put in elfishly.

Rhodes waved him aside:

'You may laugh, but that's what it must come to. That strip between the frontier of the Transvaal and the Kalahari is our Suez Canal, and I'm going to have it! They're settling the boundaries now in Pretoria; but that means nothing: boundaries be damned! You know what the Boers are. A fellow goes off with his wagon into new country; he likes the look of the land and sends for his brother, then his aunts and uncles and cousins come rolling along, and before you can say Jack Robinson there's a new Republic. That's what's happening now. I tell you it's got to be stopped, and I'm going to stop it. There may be trouble ahead. If there is, we three shall be in it.'

Piet was not so sure about that. Still, he listened to all this talk of high politics, and listened more eagerly for any hints relating to diamonds that fell from Rhodes' lips. He had always respected Rhodes' judgment and vision in matters of business; now he spoke with even greater authority, for he had lately floated the de Beers Mining Company with a registered capital of two hundred thousand pounds. If Rhodes were determined to force the mines to amalgamate, Piet thought, he would certainly do it, and make sure that this own company's claims were the nucleus of the amalgamation and reaped its first profits. This period of faltering confidence was a buyer's opportunity. Piet sold out a large part of his own holdings and Haskard's at a slight loss, and invested the proceeds either in de Beers or in contiguous properties which, when the time for amalgamation came, would be in a position to hold out for a fancy price. For the moment he did not make money in any quantity. He was trusting to Cecil Rhodes to make it for him later.

In this busy life he often encountered Meninsky and talked with him. It was his business, he had decided, to use other people's brains without giving anything away: and Meninsky had proved by his progress that his were worth using. During the last few years the Peruvian had prospered exceedingly; but prosperity, though it had fattened and coarsened his body and slowed his vivacity of movement, had not altered the quality of his mind. He was still, like Piet himself, the born middle-man: a charming and comparatively honest parasite on all the activities connected with diamond-mining. Though he was too much of a gambler to miss an occasional chance of handling diamonds, the bulk of his business was concentrated on buying and selling other things on commission. Increasing wealth had not modified his manner of life. He still lived in a galvanized-iron shack on the outskirts of Kimberley, more fit for a native than a white man. He still fared frugally and drank water, when most of his fellow-Hebrews – 'the bright boys from Whitechapel,' as he called them – had a taste for champagne. Yet, for all his eccentric humility and unobtrusiveness, or, perhaps, because of them, the odd little man had become something of a figure in Kimberley. If he was a universal provider, he was also a universal friend.

When Piet pumped him on what he thought of his latest investments, Meninsky was much more chary than of old in offering advice.

'Don't talk to me about diamond shares, mate,' he said. 'I've no use for the damned things; I've finished with 'em. In the old days, when they went up I felt like jumping over the moon, and when they went down it was like a load on the stomach. Let 'em go up and down, I say now: it's no odds to me. What I want is a quiet life and a good night's sleep. High or low, so long as they go on digging, I get my profits out of the stuff they use, without any risks.'

Piet let fall a hint on the possibilities of Amalgamation. Meninsky narrowed his boot-button eyes.

'You've been talking to Rhodes,' he said.

'Well, why shouldn't I talk to Rhodes?'

'I never said you shouldn't. I've nothing against him. I've nothing against anyone: that's where I score. But do you see that chap over there?' He jerked his head backwards.

'What – that little chap in the check suit and billy-cock hat? I don't know him. Who is he?'

'Well,' Meninsky said, 'if you'd asked me that a few years ago, I should have told you he was Harry Barnato's brother, Barnett Isaacs – distant connection of mine by old Abraham's marriage with Sarah . . .'

345

'I can quite believe that part.'

'But if you ask me today I say: "Oh, that's Barney Barnato: Harry Barnato's his brother." '

'I'm none the wiser, Meninsky.'

'You will be before you've finished, mate. Under that bloody billycock there's the sharpest packet of brains – *and* of cheek – that's ever turned up in Kimberley. Come up first with forty boxes of bad cigars – well, even I couldn't smoke 'em, so they must have been pretty rank – and went in with Lou Cohen. Started off as a general dealer, the same as me, and three years later was making two thousand a week. Now he's just back from London – that's where he got that sporty suit and the wax to point his moustaches, I reckon – after floating a concern of his own with a hundred and fifteen thousand pound capital. Yes, I call that quick work, mate.'

'Quick enough. But what's he to do with Rhodes?' Piet asked.

'You wait and see. By what I reckon, him and Rhodes is on the same lay – Amalgamation, or whatever you like to call it. He's out to do for the Kimberley Mine what young Rhodes is doing for de Beers, working parallel, as you might say. That's a good word, ain't it?'

Piet laughed. 'Well, what then?'

Meninsky screwed up his little brown eyes: 'Know what parallel lines are? They say as they never meet; but that's where they're wrong. Them two are going to meet some day, and when they do it'll be a hell of a collision. One of 'em's got to come out on top, and one underneath; and seeing as both of them's pretty tough, I doubt if either will be much the worse for it. It's the small men underneath both of them that's going to cop it then. If once they get going together they'll squeeze the blood out of the lot of them. I'm too small for a game with them chaps. That's one reason I don't buy diamond shares any more, mate.'

'Got any others?' Piet chaffed him.

'I could give you a dozen others, if time wasn't money and I could afford to waste it. But I'll give you one.'

'Come on, then.'

'Don't you breathe it in Kimberley, mind, or you'll get me lynched – or lose me my trade, which'd be worse.' He lowered his voice to a whisper. 'I don't believe in diamonds and never

346

did. What's wrong with diamonds? I'll tell you: there's nothing *in* them. Pure carbon – the same as coal at a quid a ton. No, mate – give me gold.'

'I thought you'd got over that in the Low Veld with Janse.'

'So I did, mate, to tell you the truth. But it can't be done. I dream of gold. Would you credit it? Yes, the same dream, again and again. There's an old Kaffir witch-doctor, dirty as hell, doing his tricks, throwing the *dolosse*. . . . You know. I go up to him, just like I was awake, and ask him where the gold is; and he says, every time just the same: *"Pambele . . . Pambele . . .* It's a long way from here, *baas:* it's high up on the White Rand where they go down to Natal. *Meninge, meninge.* . . . Plenty of gold,"* he says. Funny, ain't it? The same dream coming again and again like that.'

'It's a good example of dreams going by opposites, anyway, if he means the Witwatersrand. I'll sell you all the gold on that god-forsaken ridge for twopence-halfpenny, Meninsky.'

'Well, I might go as far as twopence,' Meninsky said. 'Has Janse been home lately?'

'Yes, he called in at Wonderfontein at the beginning of the war, my mother tells me.'

'He's all right?'

'Yes, as far as I know.'

'Well, you might tell your mother to let him know, if he calls in again, that I've four thousand pounds for him.'

'Four thousand? I thought you said one.'

'I did, but it's grown since then. That's what happens to money if you mix a little brains with it.'

'You old devil!' Piet said.

'I should like to know what's been happening to poor old Janse, all the same,' Meninsky said meditatively.

(2)

A number of important things had been happening to Janse, and continued to happen to him during the next three years.

When he left Wonderfontein at the end of his hurried visit in the middle of the night after the fight at Bronkhorst Spruit, he had ridden straight on to Heidelberg, where Lisbet had told him that he would find Adrian – not that he wanted to be caught up

347

in this war, the first bloodshed of which he had witnessed, but because he had given his word to Gert Trichard, the *vee-boer* who had let him escape, that he would ride straight home and report himself to his local veld-kornet for service.

He had arrived at Heidelberg in time to see Adrian's faded *Vierkleur* hoisted, and to hear the Republic proclaimed under a triumvirate consisting of Paul Kruger, Piet Joubert and ex-President Martinus Pretorius; he had found Adrian, now a Commandant and a personage of importance on General Joubert's staff, and confided his doubts to him. This was the first time he had met his brother since his marriage with Suzanna Strijdom. He found him older and sterner and strangely changed, not realizing how greatly he had aged and changed himself. Adrian received him brusquely.

'I don't want any more of this nonsense of yours about fighting,' he said. 'You were lucky to escape with your life last time, against Sekukuni. But we're not fighting Sekukuni now. This war is a struggle to the death and we've got to insist on discipline. This time, orders are orders.'

Janse smiled at his tense severity; but Adrian was not smiling.

'Though you can't take an active part,' he went on, 'we may want every man we can muster in an emergency. You've a horse: that is good. You'd better attach yourself to the Potchefstroom commando and make yourself generally useful.'

Janse moved down with the main force from Heidelberg to Laing's Nek and was shelled by the rockets of the Naval Brigade, the 'cowhorns', as his comrades called them. He heard the sound of far firing that drifted over from the fight on the Ingogo Heights, and saw, from a distance, the miracle of the Majuba. When the armistice had been signed, Adrian took him back with him to Pretoria. Janse saw the first meetings of the new Volksraad, with the triumphant, impassive Paul Kruger intalled as Vice-President and Adrian at his side. He saw Gladstone burnt in effigy in the grass-grown Church Square at Pretoria and the Union Jack ceremoniously buried in the presence of a crowd of more than two thousand loyalists, who surged down the streets singing 'God Save the Queen' between files of war-weary burghers with rifles in their hands. He saw, as a culmination of the British surrender, the *indaba* of native chiefs, to whom the High Commissioner, Sir Hercules Robinson, presented the Boer triumvirate as their new leaders.

348

'With that sense of justice which befits a great man and a powerful nation,' Sir Hercules began . . .

Janse watched the chiefs' faces. He had never seen any more pitiful spectacle than that of these bewildered children who felt they were handed over, without any reason, to the mercy of their natural enemies.

'I am treated as a stick of tobacco, *inkosi*,' Umgombarie, the chief of the Zoutpansberg, cried. 'I have fought with the Boers and have many wounds, and Baas Kruger, there, knows it is true. I belong to the English Government. I am not a man who eats with both sides of the jaw at once: I only use one side: I am English. I have said.'

Silamba spoke: 'I belong to the English, *inkosi*, and I will never return under the Boers. You see me, a man of my rank and position: is it right that a man such as I should be seized and laid on the ground and flogged, as has been done to me and other chiefs?'

'We hear, and yet do not hear,' Sinkanhla said: 'we do not understand. We are troubling you, *inkosi*, by talking in this way. We hear you say that the Queen took this country because the people of the country wished it, and then, again, that the majority of the owners of the country do not wish her to rule, and therefore the country is now given back. But we are the real owners of this country; we were here when the Boers came and, without asking leave, settled down and treated us badly. We have now had four years of rest and peace and just rule. We have been called here today and told that this country, our country, has been given back to the Boers. This is the thing that surprises us. Did the country, then, belong to the Boers? Did it not belong to our fathers? We have heard the Boers' country is at the Cape. If the Queen wished to give them their land, why does she not give them the Cape?'

An old chief, Umyethile, spoke even more bitterly:

'We have no heart for talking, *inkosi*. Our hearts are black and heavy with grief at this thing. Our intestines are twisting and writhing within us like a snake that is struck on the head. We do not know what has become of us: we feel dead. It may be that the Lord will change the nature of the Boers, and that we shall not be treated as dogs and beasts of burden. But we have no hope of such a change; and we leave you with heavy hearts and great fear of the future.'

Sir Hercules listened to each of them, with impotent patience

349

and sympathy, as their words were interpreted. There was no more to be said on his part. He saluted them gravely and turned away. The *indaba* was over.

When the last commando had been disbanded, Janse bought a new wagon and a fine team of fly-proof mules and went down to the Low Country again. It was now mid-winter, and even in the dip of Pretoria, the chill of the High Veld was seeping into his bones and waking the spores of fever that slept in his over-thinned blood.

Since the outbreak of war a change had come over the transport-riding business at Delagoa. For some time the gold-fields scattered along the Berg had been languishing. Spitzkop, Mac-Mac, and Pilgrim's Rest appeared to have yielded most of the gold that could be won by diggers who lacked expensive machinery and capital, and Lydenberg itself, when the siege was raised and the garrison withdrawn, had ceased to be a great market and clearing-house and had relapsed into the funereal peace of its weeping-willow groves. But now, farther south, in the ferny spruits of the Crocodile River and in the kloofs of the green hills from which it was fed, fresh and ever-richer deposits of alluvial had been discovered, and a new 'rush' had begun.

Diggers flocked to this 'poor man's paradise', as it was called, in far greater numbers than had ever poured into Lydenburg. They came not merely from the face of the Berg, where luck had forsaken them, but from Natal, the country from which the new gold-field's original discoverers had hailed. In Durban and Pietermaritzburg the gold-fever raged furiously. The Press fed it with weekly reports of fantastic gains. The sheets of the *Natal Mercury* were peppered with daily advertisements of tents and mining material and boring-machines and horse-gears for stamp-driving and force-pumps and steam-pumps. Enterprising contractors even established a regular service of wagons between Maritzburg and de Kaap – four pounds ten a head, and a hundredweight of luggage free – but the bulk of the needy adventurers chose the shorter sea route from Durban to Delagoa, where they landed, half-drunk and still sick from the swell of the Madagascar channel, and waited, on the malarial flats, for a chance of cheap transport on a northward-bound wagon, or shouldered their bulging packs and set out on foot over the fever-stricken track (which, even in winter, was deadly) that led to the Devil's Kantoor at de Kaap, the point of habitation nearest to Moodie's farms, where the gold had been struck.

Janse helped in the haulage of men and stores and machinery from the Bay to the camp at de Kaap and began to make money more rapidly than ever before. The road up the Crocodile valley was not only shorter by forty miles, but also far kinder to his cattle, than his old track to Lydenburg. It took him through new parts of the Low Country, too; and this, of itself, made the change of route attractive: if he could have afforded it there was no life he would have preferred to that of a wanderer over the face of these lowlands of Africa, which had captured his heart and whose mystery still had power to excite his imagination.

Even the natives, in this part of the world, appealed to him more than the timid Bathonga. They were a taller, more warlike people, the Swazis, a tribe he had encountered for the first time as auxiliaries in the Sekukuni campaign. Janse liked them for their proud bearing, their traditional life, their comparative purity of race, their rich sense of humour. His harmlessness, that of a lame man who carried no arms with hostile intent and respected their women and property, made him welcome in the kraals whose lands bordered the track. He had set to work learning their language and studying their customs and folklore. When he had outspanned his mules for the midday break or had camped before sunset, he would often wander away to villages where he was known and sit with them round their fires, observing, talking and listening, while the old men related the bloody saga of Chaka, the Battle-axe, the black Attila (whom some had seen), and the interminable Bantu fables, of which the guileful rabbit and the wise baboon were heroes.

He loved the patriarchal peace of these firelit circles where men gossiped and laughed and told tales over their mealie-pap and women tittered in the shadows, while cicalas zizzed in the trees and the chorus of frogs in the spruits thrilled the dusk with the rise and fall of their trilling castanets. No doubt he idealized these people; no doubt their customs were cruel – indeed, much of their humour found a mischievous delight in pain and suffering; no doubt, in fact, they were capable of any savagery. Yet he had never entirely forgotten that one magical moment when, years ago, descending the Berg with Meninsky, his heart had been moved by the sight of that sunset pastoral – of flocks slowly grazing over the spring-green hills and the moving ebony

351

frieze of young women, with gourds on their heads, coming down to the watering-place where the blue lotus floated and clouds of yellow butterflies rose from their sipping, and dragon-flies, nailed in sapphire, swooped and trembled.

That memory of an imaginary Eden still coloured his thoughts. It was in the unconscious desire of recapturing it that he frequented the kraals of the Amaswazi. He had lost, more-over, that physical repugnance for the native which he had inherited, through Lisbet, from his ancestors at the Cape, so that he could see nobility in the faces of black men and beauty in the shapes of black women. They seemed to him, as Rhodes had declared to Piet, 'not very different from ourselves'.

One evening in early autumn he happened to diverge from the road in open savannah country near the Lomati River, and walked up to a Swazi village he had never visited before. It was the season of the ripening of the marula, that yellow plum-shaped fruit which the natives call *umgana* or 'friend'. On the outskirts of this village there stood three marula trees, with tall, smooth trunks and spreading crowns, in which green fruit-pigeons and bulbuls and mouse-birds chuckled and twittered as they gorged themselves, while the women and children of the village stooped below, gathering the fallen fruit into baskets and gourds for the brewing of marula-beer.

Among this laughing, chattering group, which scattered and vanished as he approached, Janse noticed one child, a girl of ten or eleven, so much paler-skinned than the rest that he took her for a half-caste and wondered by what chance she had come to be born in a spot so remote and so little visited by white men as this.

When he reached the kraal it soon became clear that the beer-drinking season, which lasts for several months, was in full swing. All the men of the village were in a state of mild in-ebriation, and the vinous smell of the marula must was in the air. By this time he had mastered the Swazi dialect, and was sure of a welcome for this alone, though, in fact, his repute as 'the lame man who told stories' was already widely spread and had even gained him the compliment of a nick-name, so that he was known already by many natives who had never seen him.

As he limped up, he was quickly recognized. The headman welcomed him and asked him to sit and drink beer with him.

'*Sala kable, inkos*' – Stay in peace,' he said, with a formal dignity.

Janse accepted the invitation willingly: on such festal occasions, when tongues were loosened and shyness abandoned, there were usually new words to be heard and strange stories to be told.

They sat round the great jars of marula-beer which the women had made, while the old men revived their memories and the young men drank prodigiously. Later on there was singing and dancing, and some of the warriors became quarrelsome; yet through all this festive confusion Janse could not dismiss from the back of his mind that fugitive vision of the little white girl who had fled from him with the other marula-gatherers. In the end he questioned the headman:

'Baba,' he said, 'when I came here this evening I had a strange dream: I thought I saw a white child among the other piccanins.'

The headman laughed: 'That was no dream, inkos',' he said. 'There is a white child.'

'I thought she might be a half-breed.'

'Our women are not of that kind. I will tell you how it is. A long time ago – I cannot say how long – a white man and a woman came and camped by us. Where they came from I cannot say; but I think it was from the sea.'

'Were they Boers?'

'I do not think so. The man was tall, taller than yourself, and he had a glass that he wore in his eye and a hammer with which he was always chipping the rocks: I think he was mad, and always weak with fever. The woman was smaller and darker. Perhaps she was Portuguese; she was like Albassini's people. I cannot say. But these two, they lived in a grass hut for a long time, not far from the river, and the man went about with his gun, shooting buck or guinea-fowl, and with the hammer, always breaking the rocks. They did us no harm, and we left them alone: their speech we could not understand. This child was born when they came here; the woman carried her, and sometimes the man carried her too, which made the people laugh, for that is not a man's duty. He carried her wherever he went, on his shoulder: that shows he was mad. He used to bring the child up to the village every day to get milk.

'Then, one evening, he came no more, nor yet did the woman. We thought they had gone. But next day one of the young men went out to set a trap and passed by the hut and, thinking they might have left something behind, looked inside. He saw the man lying there with his head blown to pieces and black with flies, and the child sitting by him. The gun, which he hoped to find, was gone, and so was the woman.'

'What did you do, *baba*?' Janse asked.

'There was nothing to do. He was dead. The young man took the child and brought her back to the village. She bit him and scratched his face like a young baboon till she tired herself out. She was starving, and yet the women could not make her eat. She lay and cried for her father. But in the end she grew tame, and I put her to run with the other children. That was many years ago. She is well-grown now, and should soon be ready for marriage.'

'Does she speak a strange tongue?' Janse asked.

'When she came, she did; but now she speaks like ourselves.'

'Perhaps she might speak to me words I could understand.'

A married woman, her body smeared with red clay and her hair pulled out into ochred rats'-tails, led the child in. She looked sullen and full of sleep, and regarded Janse with suspicious eyes: but the eyes were not those of a half-breed – they were hyacinth-blue, like Lavinia Haskard's, the sclerotic clear-white, unpigmented; her slim body, naked from shoulder to girdle, gleamed ivory-white in the gloom of the headman's hut, and her tousled hair was of the same hue as Maria's, the colour of dark honey.

Janse addressed her in Dutch. She glowered at him, not answering a word. He tried English: 'What is your name?'

A flicker of puzzled half-comprehension passed over her face; she opened her lips, but closed them again and continued to stare with the intent apprehensiveness of a young wild animal.

'What did your father call you, then? Tell me.'

She hesitated; then answered quickly in the Swazi dialect: 'I do not know . . .' And then, shyly, 'He called me Lena.'

'She is well-made,' the headman gloated. 'She will make a strong woman; but the young men will not take her to wife for fear of being put to shame by having white children.'

'That I understand,' Janse said. The child listened as he spoke; her blue eyes had lost their sleepiness; they were bright and intelligent. 'What if I take her with me, *baba*?'

The old man's face grew crafty with greed.

'She will make a fine woman, fit for hard work,' he said. 'She is worth many cattle in *lobolo*. If one of our women is worth ten, then a white girl should fetch many more. And this is no common girl; she is the daughter of a chief.'

'Come, you said the young men would not have her!'

'But that is because they don't want her. If you want her, *inkos*', it is a different thing. She becomes more valuable. I am a headman, too. I have brought her up and fed her and she is my daughter. That makes the *lobolo* higher.'

'She is worth nothing to you unless I want her. And I don't want her for a wife. I am too old for marrying, *baba*, and she is too young to marry according to our customs.'

The headman laughed. 'I am old, that is true; but you are not old, *inkos*', and the older men are, the better they like young women from what I know. I do not know what *lobolo* the white men give. It is better that you should tell me.'

'The white men give no *lobolo*,' Janse said. 'But of that there is no question. I would take this child because I think it is wrong, for you as well as for her, that a white girl should grow up among you. You say your young men will not marry her; but that doesn't mean that they won't soon be after her. The Amaswazi, I know, are a proud people. Do you want Sebusa, your chief, to find your village full of bastards, like the village of Albassini, the Portuguese, who is called Juwawa?'

'Tell me what you will pay for her, *inkos*'.'

'I will give you a yoke of good oxen.'

The old man shook his head.

'What are trek-oxen to me who have no wagon? I cannot use them.'

'I will give you ten goats.'

'Ten goats? Who has ever heard of such a *lobolo*!'

'Then I will give you a gun.'

The headman's eyes brightened, then narrowed quickly.

'What is a gun without powder and shot?'

'You shall have both. A ten-pound bag, a roll of lead and bullet-mould. I'll throw in a roll of tobacco as well.'

'You can take her for that, *inkosi*,' the headman said. 'It is true that if I keep her here she will only bring trouble. But she has grown strong on my food for many years and I must be paid for her.'

Janse turned to the child:

'Will you come with me, Lena?' he said in English.

She yawned, and nodded, solemnly.

(3)

When he had handed over the gun with its ammunition and taken his purchase back with him to the wagon, he began to wonder what sort of impulse had betrayed him into this fantastic bargain. It had sprung partly, no doubt, from the poignant likeness of those dusky blue eyes to Lavinia's. This resemblance had been the reagent which, aided by the marula-beer, had precipitated a romantic mood in which pity, sentiment, quixotic gallantry, and a sense of duty to his own colour and race had added their persuasions. As he gazed at her now, this slim-shouldered thing in her ochre-stained wrap of palm-fibre cloth, wondering what on earth he could do with her, he was forced to laugh at himself. He could think of no man on earth less qualified than he to look after a child of eleven – and a girl at that. He could not pretend to know anything about children; and here he was, a bachelor of thirty-five, rashly committed to the care and tutelage of this incomprehensible little animal of the opposite sex, combining the functions of a children's nurse and a menagerie-keeper.

When he made his bargain he had not fully realized the responsibilities it entailed. That he was prepared to accept them was proved by the fact that, that very night, he inspanned, feeling anxious lest the headman should repent of his bargain and want to go back on it. While he trekked on through the dark, the child continued her broken sleep in the wagon behind. Once or twice Janse dropped back to peer inside, and saw her lying there on the top of the mealie-sacks, curled up like a puppy. Each time he saw her, he was compelled to laugh at himself; yet there was also a certain tenderness in his laughter. This was the first time in his solitary life that any human being (if this creature were human) had been dependent on him. Her youth, her bodily fragility, and the mysterious tragic events which had shaped her small life, touched him deeply and kindled a warmth in his heart that was unfamiliar to it. He had suddenly found an absorbing interest, and a better reason for living than any he had recognized since his defeat at Witfontein. His nature was capable of great tenderness, as yet hardly

356

exercised; and his new acquisition (for as such he still thought of her) provided an outlet for much that had been suppressed.

When the child woke next morning, other problems presented themselves. It would be quite impossible, for instance, to keep her near him in her present clothes. Her wrapping of palm-cloth was drenched in the rancid oil with which Swazi women anoint themselves; it stank of this, of woodsmoke, and of the sweat of black bodies which had kept her company in the unmarried girls' hut. When they came to a spruit where pools of water were lying, he sent her down to it to wash, with a piece of soap, a refinement of civilization with which she was unacquainted, and a comb for her tangled hair.

While she stripped and bathed he possessed himself of the noisome garment and hurriedly burnt it. When she came back he provided her with the only clothing he could improvise, a clean cotton shirt of his own, much too big for her and badly torn. Her face fell at first – not that she was conscious of her nakedness, but because she had been deprived of her natural covering – but when she had slipped the shirt on, she was obviously entranced with its grandeur and novelty, and carried it with a peacock pride.

It was strange, Janse thought, that she accepted her change of ownership so easily – or as a matter of course. She did not even inquire who he was or where he was taking her. She sat perched on the driving-seat beside him and chattered, without any shyness, as they wound their way through the bush. When she talked in the Swazi dialect of the Bantu tongue, Janse made a point of answering her in English; and though sometimes she misunderstood him and repeated her questions, it became clear that, when she was forced to explore it, her small brain was stored with a wealth of English words not entirely forgotten, but preserved in a state of suspension – like the spores of fever which lie dormant in a man's blood until unusual physical strain or cold arouses them. Left to herself, she would always talk Kaffir, pretending not to understand English, because this was easier; but Janse could play that game too, and, by affecting an equal ignorance, he forced her to dredge up the submerged English words from the depths of her memory. When she spoke them, he thought that he occasionally recognized a turn of the tongue that reminded him of Jim Haskard's faint brogue. He wondered if her father – or her mother – had been Irish.

357

Her modes of thought were still those of the native mind. They were combined with a naïvety of expression which made Janse feel that he was learning more about the psychology of the Bantu from her childish lips than he had ever acquired in the Swazi villages. Her mind was limpid-clear, he found, and completely candid: a far older mind, in experience, than that of a European child of a similar age, yet, in other ways, younger. Her eyes and ears were far keener than his, for all his experience of bush-craft: they had been sharpened, like those of a small buck, by a sort of protective instinct, to catch even the faintest sound or the stealthiest movement that might signify danger. Nothing escaped those blue eyes. As Janse and she walked together she would shoot out her finger and point to some infinitesimal spoor in the dust, marking where a duiker had leapt, or a snake swarmed, over the track.

Her wits were as sharp as her senses. He supposed that her white heredity had given her a more agile brain and a greater power of associating cause and effect than is usual among natives; and she showed, moreover, a sense of verbal humour – in which the native, richly endowed with the humour of situation and ideas, is generally lacking. She was deft with her hands, having always been made to use them. When they outspanned she would run away to gather sticks for a fire, and she showed herself an adept at mixing and cooking mealie-pap, which, up till now (apart from an occasional gorge of game), had been her staple diet. She ate with the gusto of a hungry wild animal; but it was clear that she had never handled a spoon or fork. When he tried to make her employ them as he did, she persevered for a while, but soon sighed hopelessly and reverted to the use of her fingers. Janse found an amused fascination in watching her and exploring the mysteries of her incalculable mind.

When night came and he saw her nodding asleep by the fire, he wrapped her up in a blanket and put her to sleep in a nest he had excavated for her among the sacks in the wagon, where she curled herself up as before. As he laid her down he kissed her good night, to her evident surprise. He had never known anything sweeter than the softness of that childish cheek on his lips, or an emotion of greater tenderness.

He himself lay down as usual under the wagon and fell asleep instantly. In the middle of the night he awoke to the consciousness of an unusual warmth, and, turning drowsily to throw off his second blanket, discovered Lena at his side. She had crept out of the wagon so quietly as not to disturb him, and lain down close to him like a cat that seeks the warmth of a friendly bed. She slept there already, contentedly; but Janse could not resist the impulse to gather the small body to him and fold it in his arms. In the nescience of sleep she snuggled even closer, and lay with her head beneath his shoulder.

And Janse, too, went to sleep again, with a smile on his lips.

The strange couple trekked on for five days. In three more, Janse realized, this idyllic solitude would be over. By the time they reached the diggings at de Kaap, he knew he would have to make some kind of plans for the future. Though the mining community, in which he was well known, was not particularly fastidious in matters of morality, he saw that this odd association, to which he had impulsively committed himself, would lay him open to ridicule no less than to ribald commentary. Apart from these, which he was too sensitive to face with composure, there remained his responsibilities towards Lena herself. He was aware of his own disqualifications to fulfil them, and supposed that it was his duty to hand her over to some woman – and a white woman at that – who would be prepared to mother her.

And here a difficulty arose. Though the scattered population of the new gold-field now amounted to several thousands, there were only two white women, so far as he knew, at de Kaap: one a barmaid, who served in the smaller of the two galvanized-iron canteens, a good-natured lady who was in the habit of putting herself up for auction at the end of the day's drinking, and was therefore hardly an ideal guardian of youth: the other the wife of the newly-arrived Mining Commissioner, a young Natalian, who had several children of her own.

On his arrival at the Devil's Kantoor, Janse pitched his camp on the outskirts of the settlement, in the hope that Lena's existence would not be noticed. Next he put the problem to his friend and principal client, Yankee Moore, whose store – a bucksail tent furnished with a counter of empty Rynbende gin-cases and seats scooped out of the piled sacks of mealie-meal – was (after the Red Lion canteen, with its invitation to 'liquor up', and the Parsee store, where a melancholy Indian named Dhorabji Dunghboy served acid palm-beer to natives) the busiest commercial establishment at de Kaap.

He found Yankee Moore buying gold-dust, which a miner named Charlie had brought in a paraffin-tin, at three pounds ten an ounce: a discount of half a crown on the current price in Maritzburg. When the miner had emptied his tin to the last grain he turned out his waistcoat-pockets as well on the gin-case counter. Yankee Moore handed over a thick wad of Transvaal blue-backs.

'What are you going to do with this, Charlie?' he said. 'You'd far better let me keep it. There was two murders last week, don't forget.'

The miner laughed: 'No fear of that boss,' he said. 'Ten pound of this lot goes straight to the ruddy magistrate.'

'What the devil for? Do you owe him all that for a fine, then?'

'Not a penny, I don't; but I reckon I shall by Monday. Drunk and disorderly: that beggar Murphy seen me come in and has got his eye on me. When I go on the spree I pay the fine in advance.'

He slouched away towards the Government Offices, where the Transvaal flag drooped in the midday heat, then stood hesitatingly and turned into the Red Lion canteen.

'Poor old beggar,' Yankee Moore said sympathetically; 'that there chap, Charlie the Reefer, they call him, he's got the best eye for alluvial of anyone I ever saw, and a hard worker too. But keep it? No, sir: not he! He'll have blued the lot by Monday.' He locked up the safe in which he kept his gold dust. 'Well, Janse, what can I do for you? Had a good trip?'

Janse told his story and Yankee Moore listened smiling.

'Well, I'll be jiggered,' he said, 'this is a new line for you, boy.'

'I want the kid brought up decently, Yankee.'

'You've brought her to the right place, boy. Two murders a week, and the hill stiff with strawyard bulls! Delagoa's a convent compared with de Kaap.'

'What about the new Mining Commissioner's missus?'

'Well, she might do it. Got kids of her own, but I doubt if she'd fancy another – not of that kind.'

'There's nothing wrong with my kid,' Janse answered angrily.

'Better go and talk to her, then, if you've the nerve to do it. I don't happen to be a family-man, so my advice ain't worth nothing.'

Janse went to see Mrs. Wilson. He found her a pleasant, large-hearted woman who listened sympathetically.

'Yes, I'll willingly take the poor little thing in for a bit, Mr. Grafton,' she said; 'but I think, in justice to her, you should get her away from here to some friends or relations before she's much older. My husband and I have no choice, but this is no place for children. I do hope she's clean, though,' she added wistfully.

So Lena, in Janse's worn shirt, was taken along to the Mining Commissioner's house and scrubbed, quite unnecessarily, and had her hair cut and combed, and emerged in a clean print frock, which made her look like a model English school-child. Janse was astonished by this transformation; yet slightly regretful for the loss of the little grotesque who had grown so dear to him. Lena herself resented it: for the uniform which she shared with the Mining Commissioner's children symbolized the loss of the freedom she had tasted in Janse's company. She was ready to accept any code of manners, however artificial and unreasonable it seemed, from him, because it was he who imposed it on her. To be asked to imitate the behaviour of children younger than herself who sniggered at her solecisms was an entirely different matter. When she lost her temper, she stormed at them in Swazi with a spate of indecencies which, fortunately, neither they nor their mother understood.

But what Lena resented even more than Mrs. Wilson's discipline and her children's prim superiority, was her separation from Janse. She had adopted him from the first, as her own property, as she was his, and attached herself to him with a blind and passionate devotion. She asked nothing more of life than to be near him. Though she had been forced – against all reason, as it seemed to her – to submit to the banishment and imprisonment he had inflicted on her, she did not pretend to enjoy it. If he failed to appear when she expected him, she withdrew herself into an intimidating sullenness. She declined to speak English or to admit that she understood it, she even refused to eat. At such times her eyes glowed darkly in a face that was pinched with misery.

'The child really looks as if she were going to fly at one

like a wild animal!' Mrs. Wilson sighed. 'I'm positively frightened of leaving her alone with the children, for fear something should happen. She ought to be smacked by rights; but it's no use smacking her. The child never makes a sound; she just looks dumbly at you out of those great big eyes, as if she hated you. Heaven knows how she'll behave when you go down to the coast again. I really don't know what to do with her, Mr. Grafton.'

Nor yet did Janse. To tell the truth, he dreaded this imminent parting as much as Lena. The child had filled every cranny of his heart, and her exclusive devotion not only flattered him, but also touched him profoundly. On the night before his departure he gave her a lecture and saw for himself the sullen misery, the look almost of animal hatred, which Mrs. Wilson had described. Lena was obstinately silent; refused even to say good-bye. When he went back to the wagon he felt almost as miserable as she looked.

He went to sleep early, having planned to start before dawn. In the middle of the night, as once before, he awakened to find her fully dressed and sleeping beside him. The misery had left her face. Though she pretended to be asleep, he guessed she was awake. But he did not speak to her, and soon the slowness of her breathing told him she slept.

As he lay there he made up his mind that he must alter his plans, whatever it might cost him. Half an hour before dawn he wakened her.

'I'm going to take you back to Mrs. Wilson's,' he said. 'Don't you see what a fright the poor woman would have got if she'd found you were missing?' Lena only yawned like a lazy cat, and smiled. 'Now, supposing I stay here after all and don't go away, will you promise to be a good girl, and not do things like this?'

He felt, as he spoke, the hopelessness of scolding her; yet when he asked her a second time, she pursed her lips and nodded. She flung her arms round his neck, and he carried her back to the Mining Commissioner's house, where he watched her climb back through the window by which she had escaped and drop, soft-footed, inside.

He determined to sell his wagon and team and start gold-mining again. It would be a very different matter from mining as he had known it at Brunner's Rest. At de Kaap the industry was already organized on a large scale, and an outlay of capital would be necessary, not merely to pay for the Government licences and 'tribute' to the owners of the reef, but for buying machinery and employing Kaffir labour. As it happened, all his savings of the last three years were intact, and the sale of his wagon and team provided a comfortable reserve. Mrs. Wilson was unfeignedly relieved by his decision to stay, and her husband encouraged him.

'There's no doubt that there's plenty of money to be made by a man who sticks to it,' he said, 'but you'll have to hold your own – you'll have pretty tough neighbours, I warn you – and with the wretchedly inadequate police force I have, it's not easy to keep order. As a matter of fact, I think things are blowing up for a first-class row.'

'Rows aren't much in my line,' Janse said.

'Still, you may find it hard to keep out of this one. You know they're all up against Moodie?'

'I know nothing about Moodie except that my brother used to speak of him as the chap who was surveying the railway for President Burgers.'

'Yes, he was actually Surveyor-General of the Republic. That was how he first came into these parts. When he'd finished his job, and, as usual, not been paid for it, he mopped up all the odd corners and slices left over from his survey that he fancied, to make up for his salary. Thirteen farms. Eighty thousand acres. Call it a hundred and twenty square miles. Land down here can't have been worth much more than four bob an acre then; but even at that, Moodie didn't do so badly.'

'Sixteen thousand pounds? I should think not!'

'And he's done even better since. Practically all the gold that's been found – reef and alluvial – is on Moodie's farms. He's a canny fellow. He waited for the prospectors to prove the values, and kept the "field" from being formally proclaimed: he's an old hand, and knows how to pull all the political strings in Pretoria. And now he's floated a company in Natal with a capital of more than a quarter of a million – out of which he collars half the shares and twenty thousand pounds down to pay for his trouble.'

'In other words, without raising a finger, he's made the best part of a hundred and forty thousand?'

'That's it. And that's what the miners resent. If you want to dig here you have to take out a licence from the Moodie Company's agent, a fellow named Nourse. Ten bob a month for every alluvial claim of fifty square yards and a quid a month for every claim on the reef, to be increased to five pounds when payable ore is struck.'

'The Company are on velvet. They get others to do all the work and they take no risks.'

'Of course, it's your gamble,' the Mining Commissioner said. 'But the values are good, and men who work hard do well. What sticks in their throats is that the Company's claimed the right to cancel all licences at the end of eighteen months without any compensation – particularly considering the way in which Moodie got hold of the land. The diggers have formed a committee of five to look into his title, and if possible, to dispute it. In the meantime, they flatly refuse to pay their monthly dues.'

'Suppose I start digging without any licence?' Janse asked.

'I can't advise that. The land is Moodie's until the courts decide otherwise.'

'But if I buy a claim and take out a licence from Nourse and pay for it . . .'

'Then Culverwell and Co., the committee of five, will post you as a "traitor", and you may have a rough passage.'

'In which case, it'll be your job as a landdrost to protect me?'

'And much good may it do you! There are two thousand men at de Kaap, and I've only one constable to help me keep the peace.'

'If this were a British colony . . .' Janse began indignantly.

'But it isn't. This is a Republic, in which all men are free. The Boers, from Vice-President Kruger downwards, hate gold-mining and everything to do with it. I've talked to Oom Paul myself and tried to persuade him that if these diggings were properly run they'd produce enough to pay the Republic's debts. I've told him that the Transvaal might be the richest state in South Africa; but he simply won't take it in. He says the gold brings in foreigners, and he doesn't like foreigners, and there it is!'

'Well, I've got to make a living,' Janse said obstinately, 'and I'm not going to be intimidated by Culverwell, whoever he is, or by anyone else.'

'I wish you luck,' the Mining Commissioner said. 'And I reckon you'll need it!'

Janse took out a licence from Nourse, the Company's agent, and wandered on to the 'hill' in search of a promising claim. Over the whole six miles of Moodie's reef ran an unbroken line of claims that were being worked or had been abandoned. Many neighbours had pooled their properties and formed syndicates covering as much as three or four hundred feet of reef. Dollies, worked by natives and better made than the one Meninsky had constructed under Bosmann's direction, were thudding everywhere. As he passed, many miners recognized Janse by his limp and shouted good day to him. One of these, a man named French Bob, the chief member of a syndicate called 'The Pioneer Company', ran out after him as he passed.

'Have you seen any cases of machinery waiting for me at the Bay?' he asked breathlessly.

'No sign of them when I left,' Janse said. 'What are you expecting, Bob?'

'Six stamps from Deakin and Cradock damn them! They ought to be there by now.'

'That's a big load. I saw nothing of them. How are things going, Bob?'

'Pretty fair. The reef's yielding fifteen ounces a ton. Nothing wrong with that. As you see, we've got four dollies going, but our damned Kaffirs won't work. When I get in those stamps we shall crush up to sixteen tons a day. That means eight hundred quid. They won't take long to pay for themselves. For the Lord's sake keep your eyes open when you go down again.'

'I'm not going down again. I've finished with transport-riding. I'm on the look-out for a claim.'

French Bob spat. 'If you work it yourself you'll finish up by living on mealies and smoking cow-dung. There's nothing but rubbish left on the hill. If you go down in the valley after alluvial, you won't last the rainy season. Those chaps die of fever like flies.'

Janse laughed. 'I know all there is to be known about fever.

365

What I'm looking for is someone who's tired of the job and wants to clear out.'

'If a fellow's tired of the job, you may bet he's picked the eyes out of his claim, or else it's no ruddy good. What are you going to do about Moodie's licences?'

'I've applied to Nourse already.'

French Bob shook his head.

'Cast your eye over this,' he said. He pointed to a crudely-written placard, which Janse had not noticed, affixed to a post a few yards away from them:

NOTICE!!!

200 men wanted! Special constables are wanted by the Committee to turn *Traitors* to our mutual benefit off the hill. They will meet at 2 p.m. at the Committee House. By Chairman of Committee. *Now is the time to show your future intentions.*

PS. – Protection to claims will be given, being on Constable Duty.

'You know what that means,' French Bob said. 'If you're willing to stand up to two hundred men by yourself – well, go and do it! There's four loafers to every miner in this camp, and I tell you, these chaps are in a queer temper. They've torn the Transvaal flag down twice at the Devil's Kantoor, and the other day they damned near marched down with Dick MacNab to annex Delagoa Bay. Don't say I've not warned you. Most likely you won't have the chance. And I'm not going to bury you either.'

Janse found a half-worked claim which had just been abandoned on the slope above the Kaap Valley, and promptly 'jumped' it. He found that the owner had left his dolly where it stood, together with a dump of uncrushed rock in which veins of yellow grains sparkled softly here and there in a matrix of quartz stained pink with iron. He hired four natives to help him, and set them to putting the claim in order before beginning to crush. He spent Sunday at the Kantoor, and found Lena oddly subdued. The pressure of civilization was beginning to tell on her. Mrs. Wilson regarded the change as her personal triumph; but Janse, although he marvelled at it, wasn't quite sure that he didn't prefer his little wild animal in her natural state. Mrs. Wilson had taught her to call him 'father' – and that, too, was rather a shock.

On the following day he started crushing. He had no cause to complain, as French Bob had done, of his Kaffirs, for he knew not only their language but also their methods of thought, and kept them laughing at their work. It was good to be sitting up there on the crown of the ridge with the folds of green hills around him, the blue hills beyond, and the near veld sheeted scarlet with starry gerberas. He was a wiser and happier man now, he thought, than in his young days at Witfontein.

In the middle of the afternoon a stranger approached his claim. Janse guessed, at sight, that he was an Englishman. He was a tall, fair, slim young man, with the easy stride of an athlete; he wore his ragged clothes with an air; his voice was pleasant and cultivated. For all this, Janse did not like his face; it was old for his body and somehow, indefinitely, evil; its high colour, which, at a distance, had seemed to signify health, was the blotchy ruddiness of a drinker. He sat down by Janse and said:

'Good afternoon. I don't think we've met before.'

'No, I don't think we have. My name's Grafton,' Janse said.

'A ducal name,' the young man laughed. 'Mine is Charters.'

A quick memory stabbed Janse's mind.

'Weren't you digging at Geelhoutboom, a good many years ago?'

Charters gave a start; his suffused face flushed. 'How the devil do you know that?'

'A man named Bosmann mentioned your name to me.'

'That lard-faced scug?'

'You needn't worry. He's dead.'

'Well, that's no great loss,' Charters said. He changed the subject with an uncomfortable laugh. 'So you've taken Harris's claim?'

'I found it abandoned and jumped it last week.'

'Do you know what happened to Harris?'

'I haven't the least idea.'

'I wouldn't ask, if I were you. By the way, I'm afraid I shall have to ask you to show me your licence, if you don't mind.'

'Are you an official, then?'

'Yes, I'm a sort of inspector.'

'Which licence do you mean?'

367

'Oh, you've got two, have you? The Moodie Company's licence is the one I want.'

Janse handed it to him. Charters read it through and put it in his pocket.

'Look here, you can't take that away,' Janse said.

'Don't worry. I'm just checking up.'

Charters grinned and waved his hand and walked away.

Next morning a native arrived with a letter in a cleft stick. Janse snatched it from him in alarm. Only the Mining Commissioner knew where he was, and he dreaded some disaster connected with Lena. He read:

> '*Dear Sir,*
>
> '*The feelings of the diggers against you for having made an application to Mr. Moodie for terms is so great that I am requested to give you forty-eight hours to move off the hill. I will not hold myself responsible for any rough usage of your-self or chattels if you are not off within that time.*
>
> > *(Signed) H. Culverwell.*'

'There's no answer,' he told the native, and went on with his work.

In the evening he walked to the Kantoor and handed the letter to the Mining Commissioner.

'Well . . .?' Wilson said.

'It's your duty to give me protection, isn't it?'

'I've told you, I can't.'

'Well, that's straight enough. Do you know anything of a man named Harris?'

'We buried Harris last week. He'd been kicked to death.'

'And you've done nothing about it?' Janse flared up.

'I can't arrest two hundred men, Grafton. If you think that I'm sitting still, you're mistaken. I've sent a runner to Pretoria with an urgent appeal for help. Whether Kruger will answer me is another question. He ought to. I sent the Treasury five thousand pounds last month.'

'Then I shall have to throw in my hand,' Janse said.

'That's the only advice I can give. But you needn't lose heart. All the gold isn't on Moodie's land. I had a report some time ago – I oughtn't to tell you this, by the way – that three brothers named Barber, who used to work on Moodie's, have struck it rich about twenty miles south from here. I'll give you a letter to them, if you like. They're all decent fellows.'

'Twenty miles. .... That's a long way. I don't like leaving the child.'

'You needn't worry about her. She appears to be settling down with my kids quite happily. My wife says her behaviour is almost too good to be true. As a matter of fact, I've been planning to ride over and declare the new diggings a township. I thought of calling it Barberton. The boys will be pleased by that. If you like, I'll take you there, and lead the second horse back with me – unless you'd prefer to buy one.'

Next day, before the expiration of his notice to quit, Janse bought a horse and rode over with Wilson to assist at the christening of Barberton in a bottle of gin. It was true that the Barber brothers had found a reef of proved richness. Within a few months other equally startling discoveries were made: the 'Umvoti' Reef, the 'Thomas', the 'Kimberley Imperial', the 'Honeybird', and the group of four, surrounding the 'Golden Quarry', which were soon to be amalgamated under the name of the 'Sheba'.

When the 'Hottentot' Reef assayed at ten thousand ounces to the ton, even the diamond-blinded eyes of Kimberley began to take notice. The Kimberley speculators came straggling down in buckboards and cape-carts to the steamy Barberton Valley to pick up gold scrip (and sometimes malaria too) with greed in their eyes. They set up a scramble for Barberton shares, good or bad. Janse sold the ten 'Shebas' he had bought at a pound apiece for over two thousand.

The magnitude of the sum dazzled him. He could not make up his mind whether to buy new stamping-machinery for the moderately rich claim he had pegged out on the day he arrived, not far from the Barbers' boundaries, to risk gambling it in undeveloped concerns, or to hand it over to the bank (there were two of them now) as a nest-egg for Lena. The child was becoming more and more the dominating interest in his life; and he was proud to think that – quite apart from his own earnings, which might yet be considerable – the two thousand from the Sheba shares would cover her more polite education in Capetown and support her supposing 'anything happened to him'.

The problem was solved on the very day when he took his cash to the bank. As he stood in a crowd of alluvial miners who had brought in their packets of dust and nuggets to be weighed and paid for, he was startled by a thump on the back, and turned to see a familiar figure grinning at him.

'Why, Meninsky!' he cried.

Meninsky shook his head. Tears dropped from his eyes as he grinned, but he could not speak; he appeared so overcome with emotion that Janse feared he was going to kiss him.

'Oh, come along, Janse,' he said. 'Let's get away out of this. Do you know it's the best part of ten years since us two have met? And I'm damned if you've changed a hair.'

'I can't say the same of you,' Janse said. 'My God, you don't half look grand!'

'Don't take no notice of that, mate: it's only the flesh-pots of Egypt. My old heart hasn't changed; it's only my pockets that's swollen.'

'How d'you happen to be down here?'

'There's no happening about it. I come down here in style, in a slap-up two-horse cape-cart that cost me a hundred and fifty, to see what all them beggars in Kimberley's losing their heads over. And I knew I was going to see you, mate. As I come through Carolina, I says to myself, "Isaac," I says, "I'll bet you ten thousand quid to a tanner you're going to join up with old Janse." Straight, I did!'

'Pretty free with your money, aren't you?' Janse laughed.

The Peruvian puffed out his chest beneath his check waist-coat.

'I could have made it twenty and paid on the nail if I'd lost, mate,' he said.

'Well, the first ten thousand are the worst, you always told me.'

'And I never said anything truer,' Meninsky said. 'But come on: I'm a busy man, and I reckon we've both got a hell of a lot to say. Tell me your story first. There's nothing in mine worth speaking of, bar the money. You can take me wherever you like, but I'm not going to walk, so I warn you. I've given up walking.'

'It'd be better for your figure if you hadn't,' Janse told him.

They drove down to Janse's camp in the slap-up cape-cart, from the bottom of which Meninsky produced a bottle of champagne.

'I always keep a spot of fizz,' he said, 'in case it might come in handy.' (Janse remembered he had kept his donkeys for the very same reason.) 'And if ever there was a night that warranted cracking a bottle of the boy, it's this.' He knocked off the neck and poured the wine into a couple of tin tea-cups. Then he lit a cigar: 'Now, fire away, mate,' he said.

Janse told him his story. Meninsky listened, his brown eyes gleaming in the firelight. When Janse came to the episode of Lena, they opened so wide that the whites could be seen.

'Well, you are a ruddy cough-drop, Janse!' he said. 'That beats Banaghan! You, who never so much as looked at a woman, white, black or brown, going picking up pieces in Kaffir kraals!'

'She isn't a woman,' Janse explained. 'She's a kid.'

'But she damn soon will be a woman, mate, never fear. And then there'll be the devil to pay.'

'I've got money enough to pay him and settle her, anyway.'

'How much?' Meninsky asked keenly.

'Two thousand, and some over – and this claim's worth a bit.'

'Two thousand. . . . That's not so dusty – when you put it along with the other five thousand I've got for you.'

'Five thousand? What are you talking about?'

'You sent me two hundred from Lydenburg, didn't you? Well, it's grown a bit. That's all.'

'You're a marvel, Meninsky; I don't know how to thank you; but I believe I could make it go on growing down here.'

'Well, that's what I want to talk about. You know all the ropes, I reckon. Tomorrow we'll have a look round together if my legs ain't too stiff.'

'You'll have to walk,' Janse warned him.

'Oh, I can walk fast enough when I'm after oof.'

They toiled over the diggings next morning until Meninsky's cotton suit grew dark with moisture; sweat ran into his eyes from under the crown of his ludicrous grey billycock hat. In the evening, over the camp-fire, he delivered his verdict.

'Well, I've lost two stone, and I've made up my mind. It's no go, mate, and that's what I reckoned from the first it was going to be. If you're in on the ground-floor and sell out in time, then it's all serene. But them bright boys from Kimberley's been climbing in at the attic windows. They'll be screaming out for fire-escapes before long, and it won't be only their fingers they've burnt. What's your Shebas now? A hundred and fifty pounds for a one-pound share! Well, what are chaps like you and me going to get out of that?'

371

'The "Gold Quarry" they've got is the richest reef in the world.'

'There's no reef in the world that can pay three thousand per cent., and that's what it would take to pay twenty, which I reckon reasonable for a gold-mine, at the present price. Mines don't last for ever, you know. There's a bottom to every one of them.

'And I'll tell you something else,' he went on: 'I don't like this here quartz. You say Barbers' reef is yielding thirty ounces to the ton. What's the "Umvoti", next to it, yielding?'

'Seven ounces, perhaps. These fellows don't boast about figures.'

'All right. And you're near the "Umvoti". What's your yield?'

'Two or three.'

'Well, there you are! D'you see what I'm after? The values vary a sight too much for my liking. This reef's like the one you and me and old Bosmann found. It's a blow – or a series of blows. If I was buying a ham – which Moses forbid! – I should like to know it was sweet near the bone. If I was in on the ground-floor – though the basement's more in my line – well and good. But I'm not going to put the tail of my shirt, let alone the whole of it, on this. Barney told me the same.'

'Who's Barney?'

'You ask your brother's friend, Cecil Rhodes.'

Janse laughed: 'I've never heard of either of them.'

'You will, before you're much older. You're backward in history, mate. No, I say Barney's right. I can't see the bottom of these mines any more than he could, and I've come in too late. But I've not finished with gold, mate, nor yet have you. We haven't begun. When I come out from Kimberley last week, I had a look at Witfontein, just for old time's sake. Very nice it looked, too.'

Janse smiled and shook his head. 'I think no more about Witfontein.'

'That's right. Cut your losses, mate. That's my motto as well – and my other one is: don't make any. But I'm going to tell you a thing that'll make you sit up. *There's something happening on the Witwatersrand.*'

'Nothing has ever happened on the Witwatersrand.'

'You listen to me, mate. D'you know a farm named Sterk-fontein?'

'There are two of that name. One belongs to my uncle Barend.'

'No, I'm talking about the other one, farther west, not far from Paardekraal.'

'Ah, yes: that's Jacoby's.'

'Well, passing by there, I noticed some recent prospecting holes in that pebbly outcrop. You know the stuff better than I do: it looks just like them almond toffees you see in the country stores.'

'Yes, they call them "banket". That outcrop of rock runs through my farm and my father's too.'

'The devil it does! So I thought to myself: "Hello, what's all this about?" And I took up a handful or two of the stuff they'd dug and put it in my pocket. But that wasn't all. When I'd followed the line of them pebbles a bit farther east to Wilgespruit . . .'

'That's Geldenhuis's . . .'

'. . . I saw more prospecting holes dug, a dozen or more of them, and all in this pebbly stuff. I couldn't take samples of all of them, because I saw a Kaffir in the distance who looked like he was watching me. I drove over to him and asked who the farm belonged to. He said Baas Geldenhuis, just the same as you. Then I asked him, innocent-like, if the baas was looking for water. He said, No – there was plenty of water at Wilgespruit.

' "Then what are these holes for?" I says. The poor beggar didn't know; but he told me right out they'd been made by another baas named Struben from over Pretoria way.'

'Fred Struben?'

'He didn't say "Fred". D'you know the name, mate?'

'Very well. Fred Struben was on Burgers' staff with my brother Adrian. A nice fellow, mad about gold. He kept worrying me all the time, when I was half off my head with fever, about what you and I had done in the Low Country.'

'That all fits in. Here's a fellow, mad about gold, as you say, prospecting the same outcrop at places miles apart along the Witwatersrand. What d'you say to that?'

'Fred Struben's a knowledgeable chap: but you wouldn't expect alluvial as high up as that, and anything that looked less like a reef . . .'

'Now just wait a minute. The stuff in between them pebbles looks just like red sand or soil: but if you come to examine it closer, as I done, you'll see that it's nothing more nor less than broken-down quartz. But whatever it is or isn't, we're going to crush it and pan it, or my name's not Meninsky!'

Next morning they panned the seven samples which Meninsky had carefully wrapped up separately in newspapers. Everyone showed fine particles of gold. Meninsky was over the sky with delight in this proof of his shrewdness.

'But the values aren't up to ours here,' Janse said.

'Values be jiggered! Can't you see the difference between your blows and your veins and this? It's a reef that's gone soft with exposure – a reef, forty miles long, stretching over the whole ruddy length of the Witwatersrand. It's what I've been looking for, mate: what that lousy old witch-doctor told me nearly ten years ago: "*Pambele, pambele,* high up over the White Rand where they go on the road to Natal." Them's the words he used. And I've found it, the same as I knew I would.'

'You mean Fred Struben's found it.'

'What the hell does it matter who's found it! We know that it's there. You and me are in on this, Janse, and there's no time to lose. What d'you pay for a farm up there?'

'Piet gave me a span of oxen for mine.'

'Well, the price can't have altered much.'

Janse smiled as Meninsky embarked on a series of the lightning calculations he remembered so well.

We ought to be able to pick up an average farm for a hundred pounds – let's call it a hundred and fifty. Now what have we got between us? Seven thousand of yours – apart from what you can get for this claim. Call it eight thousand in all . . .'

'If I got two hundred for the claim I should think myself lucky.'

'Well, our luck's in today, mate, and no mistake, so let's say five hundred. Seven thousand five hundred. Add twenty thousand from me. I reckon I ought to be able to push that up by another two thousand five hundred, which'll give me three shares to your one. That's thirty thousand grand total – which means that between us we're in a position to buy up two hundred farms – a property sixteen times as big as George Moodie's. Why, that's over fifteen hundred square miles. We can damned near buy the whole ruddy Witwatersrand.'

'You forget that Struben's in first.'

'By a short head, that's all – and we haven't reached

Tattenham Corner yet, let alone come into the straight. I'll bet you that if I once get my nose in front I can leave Struben standing. I'm a business-man: don't forget that!'

'What's more, your reef – Struben reef – has only been proved in seven places.'

'God Almighty! I've told you I've seen it all along the Witwatersrand. It must be continuous. Look here, Janse, it stands to reason . . .'

'It's no use buying farms till you know the reef crosses them,' Janse persisted, 'and, after that, until you know its values.'

'Well, what in Moses's name are we sitting here arguing about? Of course the values have got to be proved, and you and me must look sharp about proving them, see? We ought to be getting off at once.'

'I'm not going without the child.'

Meninsky went up in smoke:

'Oh, damn you and your child! What can you do with a kid on the Witwatersrand? She's best left where she is.'

'I could leave here with my mother and my sister at Wonderfontein. I'd always intended to do that sooner or later.'

'Then go and get her,' Meninsky snapped viciously. 'I'll give you twelve hours – but not a minute more.'

(5)

Things had certainly been happening on the Witwatersrand.

They might have happened fifteen years sooner, when the German, Carl Mauch, going north to explore Matabeleland, had casually declared the reef's outcrop to be a gold-bearing conglomerate. But Mauch had gone on to discover King Solomon's Mines (as befitted a romantic) and returned, with malaria in his blood, to the unromantic job of a railway official, and died, less romantically still, by falling out of his bedroom window and breaking his neck; so the Main Reef Outcrop remained inviolate until Geldenhuis, the owner of Wilgespruit, re-discovered it and thought it might be worth showing to Fred Struben, the long-headed young man with the jutting lower lip who was 'mad about gold'.

This was happening when Janse found Lena on the Swaziland border. By the time he had settled in Barberton, Struben had scraped up enough money to form a syndicate to exploit the gold he had discovered at Wilgespruit, and continued his laborious task of tracing the outcrop over the whole extent of the ridge, while his brother Harry trekked down to Natal to buy a five-stamp mill. A month or two later, two penniless men who were tramping to Barberton, a rough fellow named Walker and a little Cornishman named Honeyball, stumbled on Struben's camp at Wilgespruit and asked him for work. Fred Struben gave them the job of building a house for him; for Honeyball was a carpenter. When they had finished building the house Struben paid them their wages, and they went on their way eastwards until they saw in the distance the group of tall gum-trees that marked the farm of Langlaagte, where the widow Oosthuizen also was building a new house to hold Sarie's growing family.

It would be a long, footsore slog to Barberton, Walker and Honeyball thought, and it was surely a gift of Providence to see a new house going up so near the one they had just finished, so they decided to ask for work again before tramping on. The widow discussed the matter with Hans, Sarie Grafton's husband; and Hans, who was not much of a builder himself, thought it would be a good idea, providing they could afford it, to make use of these experts while they had a chance. The wage the Oosthuizens offered was not attractive; but still, it was nearly three hundred miles to Barberton, and, having walked ten from Wilgespruit, both Walker and Honeyball felt like a rest.

One afternoon, when Walker was taking a stroll at Langlaagte, he came on a piece of the outcrop which seemed to him like the rock over which Struben was making so great a fuss and being so mysterious at Wilgespruit; so he took a pick and hacked out a load of it and carried it back in a sack to his hut at Langlaagte. If there were payable gold on the Witwatersrand, he told himself, it would obviously be ridiculous to walk three hundred miles to Barberton. Without speaking to Honeyball, he threw the sack in a corner, and slipped out, when his friend was asleep, to have a chat with the widow Oosthuizen, who was a lonely woman and always liked a good gossip, She welcomed him into the voorkamer and gave him a cup of coffee.

'I hear that chap Struben's found gold at Wilgespruit, *tanta*,' he said.

'Gold at Wilgespruit? Look, our family has been in these parts for fifty years. Many people have come along here looking for gold. If there were any gold they'd have found it. Wilgespruit, indeed! You might just as well talk of finding gold at Langlaagte, nephew,' she said, and laughed out loud.

'Well, supposing I did find gold on your farm.' Walker said, 'would you give me a claim or two?'

'You must ask Hans about that,' the widow Oosthuizen said cautiously, with a look at her son.

'We shall do very well without gold,' Hans Oosthuizen growled. 'You mind your own business and get on with our house.'

'Well, you can buy many things with gold,' Walker said. 'If I found gold, it would pay for the house in no time. Do you mind if I have a look round?'

'Not if you do it in your spare time,' Hans Oosthuizen said.

'Well, let's have a paper to say you'll give me three claims if I find any: I'll write one out now for your mother to sign.'

'Don't you sign any paper, mamma!'

'There's no harm in signing a paper, Oosthuizen, providing you know what's in it. I can't write it in Dutch, but I'll write it clearly in English, so that your wife can understand.'

He produced a grubby sheet of paper and a pencil and wrote laboriously, then handed the manuscript over for Sarie to read.

'What has he written there?' Hans asked anxiously.

Sarie read and translated:

'It says that should he find gold on the farm he should have three claims. That's all.'

'There! What did I tell you?' Walker said.

Hans got up in a sullen rage: 'I'll have nothing to do with it.'

'You don't have to, mate. It's your mother's property, not yours.'

'If it would pay for building the house, Hans . . .' the widow said wistfully.

'I'll have nothing to do with it,' Hans repeated, and went out of the house.

'Are you sure that's all he's written, Sarie?' Vrouw Oosthuizen asked.

'Yes, that's all, mamma.'

'Well, then, I shall sign the paper. This is my business, not

377

Hans's. His father was just the same when it came to signing anything. If there is any gold, let this fellow find it. As he says, it may pay for building the house.'

She signed the paper and handed it back to Walker.

'There now! Go and find this gold,' she said; 'but get the house finished first.'

Walker went back to the hut where the Cornishman was already asleep. The sack full of samples was too heavy to carry over a long distance, so he filled his pockets with likely-looking pieces of rock and set off, there and then, to Potchefstroom, where he had storekeeper friends who might be interested in them.

When Honeyball woke next morning, he was surprised to find his friend gone. Walker had not taken him into his confidence, yet he couldn't help feeling that this sudden disappearance was connected in some way or other with the mysterious sack in the corner. He opened it, and discovered the remainder of the samples: rough fragments of tawny conglomerate with a yellow gleam in them, not unlike the stuff that Struben had collected at Wilgespruit. He suspected, at once, that Walker had played him a dirty trick and determined to get even with him.

That same evening he walked back to Wilgespruit, where Struben was busy, excitedly crushing his first loads of rock with his five stamp steam battery, and showed him the contents of the sack.

'I'd like you to have a look at this stuff, boss,' he said.

Struben glanced at it casually. The yellow incrustations were too bright for his liking; they had not the soft glow of gold.

'Looks to me a bit like pyrites,' he said. 'Where did you get these samples?'

'George found them at Oosthuizen's, where we'm working to now.'

'If you'll leave them with me I'll pan them.'

Honeyball suddenly took fright. Walker was a much bigger man than he, and an ugly customer to quarrel with.

'I don't think I belong to let them out of my hands,' he said.

'All right. Take them away then. Just as you like. I've no time to waste.'

'Will you give me five quid for the lot, boss?' Honeyball asked reluctantly.

'I won't give you a penny until I've panned them. I've told you, they look like pyrites to me.'

Honeyball walked back to Langlaagte and went on with the building of Hans Oosthuizen's house. He noticed that some of the rock he was using for the walls was encrusted, as were Walker's samples, with gleaming metallic particles, and that put his mind at rest. 'If I'm using this rock for building, it stands to reason,' he thought, 'that the stuff can't be gold.'

Meanwhile George Walker was hawking the contents of his bulging pockets round all the canteens and stores in Potchefstroom. He got, in return, a good many free drinks, but more sceptical chaff. The Potchefstroom folk were not interested in gold. All the good it had ever brought them was the chance of exploiting the purses of the migrant hordes of prospectors and capitalists from Kimberley who had lately been pouring through their dorp – in coaches and spiders and wagons and even in hansom-cabs – on their mad rush to Barberton. The Potchefstroom tradesmen believed in the Barberton gold, although it was no business of theirs, because they had seen it. But gold on the Witwatersrand? Old George was either pulling their legs or making a fool of himself.

George Walker's pocketful of samples became a standing joke, and jokes, being scarce, had a longish life in the liquor-bars at Potchefstroom. The Walker joke came, at last, to the quick ears of a shrewd, scrubby man named Joe Robinson, a bankrupt Afrikander shop-keeper from the Cape, who had managed, by sheer persistence, to bring himself to the notice of Rhodes' friend Alfred Beit, and had been commissioned by him, on account of his prowess in Afrikaans, which was his natural language, to sift the rumours of new gold on the Witwatersrand, which had been set afloat by the news of Struben's activities.

Joe Robinson had picked up the Walker joke on the day he had dismounted from the Barberton coach at Potchefstroom and strolled into one of the bars in the hope of gathering useful information. He had laughed over it with the landlord and the other drinkers; but his canny mind had already fastened on it as something worth looking into. That same day he hired a cart and a team of mules and set out for Langlaagte, a shabby and apparently an aimless traveller. He was not, he soon found, alone – or even the first – in the field. He passed four or five farms where men in the distance appeared suspiciously to be

379

digging, and in the middle of the afternoon his progress was stopped by a more advanced excavation where a farmer named Bantjes had dug a deep trench at the end of an antbear hole. Joe Robinson pulled up his mule-cart and walked over to watch him.

'Good day, uncle,' he said. 'Are you making a dam?'

Bantjes straightened his back and leaned on his pick. He looked Robinson up and down without answering, and found him harmless enough. His Afrikaans was faultless: indeed he even spoke English with a Dutch accent.

'Whatever you're doing, I can see it's hot work,' Joe Robinson said. 'Let me give you a hand.'

He took off his coat and turned up his sleeves and set to work with the pick. When Bantjes turned his back to take a swig of water, Joe Robinson slipped a fragment of ore in his flapped trouser pocket.

'What's that shiny stuff in the rock?' he inquired.

'Who knows?' Bantjes answered cautiously. 'Do you think it is gold?'

Joe Robinson laughed:

'The English have a saying: "All is not gold that glitters." Who ever heard of gold on the Witwatersrand?'

He put on his coat again, and wished the farmer good evening. Out of sight, at the very next spruit, he took out his sample and panned it. He guessed the value a rough ten pennyweights. Nothing to shout about compared with the values at Barberton; but if the reef were continuous it was a very different story. He had carefully noted the colour and form of the rock in which Bantjes had been digging. With intermissions, the outcrop appeared to follow a definite line, and that line, as he traced it, brought his arrow straight to Langlaagte, where he claimed the customary hospitality and outspanned his mules for the night.

It was pleasant for such isolated folk as the Oosthuizens to talk with a stranger who came from the outer world of Kimberley – even with such an unprepossessing stranger as Joe Robinson. Walker and Honeyball (who had now finished work on the young people's house) had been company of a sort; but their jokes and their stories were English, and only Sarie had understood them, while this visitor was a 'right Afrikander' who knew their ways. The widow Oosthuizen liked nothing better than talking, and Joe Robinson was a patient listener. By the end of two hours he had learnt from her everything that was to be known about the Oosthuizen family's history from the time of their leaving Grahamstown with the Prinsloo party on the Great Trek, to Hans' wedding and the building of his new house – including the story of George Walker's disappearance.

'But do you think he really found gold, *tante*?' Joe Robinson said incredulously. 'If he did, I think I might be able to help you. I know a bit about gold-mining.'

'Well, that is good. Tomorrow Hans shall go round the farm with you, and you shall see for yourself,' she said.

Joe Robinson stayed for a week at Langlaagte, talking English to Sarie and Dutch to Hans and the widow. During that time he traced the reef through the whole width of the farm, and panned samples more promising than the one he had pocketed at Bantjes'. The heap of unused building-stone by the new house gave the best values of all. That was encouraging: it meant that the deeper one dug the richer was the ore. By the end of that week he had made up his mind.

'I should like to take a lease on your farm,' he said, 'with the option of buying it within a year for six thousand pounds.'

'Almighty! Six thousand pounds!'

There must be some catch in it, the widow decided, in anxious consultation with Hans and Sarie. The sum was so vast that their minds could not grasp it. Its magnitude troubled them. If Langlaagte could draw such a staggering offer as that, might it not be worth more – ten thousand or even twenty? When they went beyond three, figures ceased to have any reasonable significance.

'It would be a pity,' the widow complained, 'to leave the new house before you've even lived in it, Hans. I think you should talk it over with Sarie's brother Adrian. He is a man of weight and position. He will decide for us.'

'That's all right as far as it goes,' Joe Robinson said: 'but I can't pay you the money until I'm sure that your title is good and that I have a right to mine on the farm if I buy it. Hans had better come with me to Pretoria and see the State President.'

'Ah, yes, that is better still,' the widow agreed. 'It is better for us as well as for you, nephew. Paul Kruger is not a man who would see his own people wronged. Go and see him then, Hans, and tell him who was your father.'

Joe Robinson and Hans rode off to Pretoria together. They

found the State President smoking, as usual, on his stoep. He listened to Hans Oosthuizen's story impassively, puffing smoke from his hard, pugnacious lips and staring past him with narrowed eyes.

'Well, what is this fellow giving you, nephew?' he said at last.

'Six thousand pounds, your honour.'

'Six thousand pounds, for a poor farm like that? Either I'm mad or he is. You say he's an Afrikander. That sounds more like an Englishman.'

'He's shown me the money, President.'

Kruger puffed at his pipe: 'Has he paid you?'

'Not yet, your honour. He says if the documents are all right ...'

'I'll see that the documents are all right. Hurry up and get your money while you've the chance. A madman like that may easily change his mind. And don't meddle with gold, don't be tempted to meddle with gold, nephew. Buy good land and good cattle: that is what I call wealth. Stay on your farms and read the Scriptures, like your father before you. Learn to shoot, and pay your taxes – don't forget to pay your taxes!'

The widow Oosthuizen sold Langlaagte, which her husband had taken in exchange for a rickety wagon, for six thousand pounds, and later trekked north to Adrian's district under the Magaliesberg. Langlaagte became part of the Robinson Mine. Beit paid Robinson fifty thousand pounds for a half-share in it. Within a few years it had realized twenty-five million.

And so the great game went on – rather too fast for Meninsky. He and Janse and Lena had reached Wonderfontein a week after the sale of the Oosthuizens' farm to Joe Robinson, and by this time the news of this startling transaction had already been widely spread. When John Grafton announced it casually on the evening of their arrival, Meninsky threw up his arms.

'Six thousand pounds, Oom Jan? Six thousand pounds for Langlaagte?'

The little man was nearly in tears. Janse watched him pitifully as he saw the towering edifice of his calculations – 'Two hundred farms – fifteen hundred square miles – the whole ruddy Witwatersrand' – collapsing and crumbling before his eyes.

'We're too late ... too late. That skelm Joe Robinson – I

know him! – has got in front of us. Why the hell did I waste all that time in going to Barberton? I might have known it.'

Janse did his best to comfort him. For himself he was too familiar with the Peruvian's high-vaulting visions of wealth to take much count of them, and even a little thankful to feel that the five thousand pounds which had dropped into his lap would not be immediately scattered in Meninsky's wild specu- lations.

'We can try to find your reef and trace it over the Wonder- fontein land tomorrow,' he said.

'Wonderfontein? Why worry about that? It's your old dad's property, and if the gold's there he'll get the *mijnpacht* all right. It's no use talking about Wonderfontein. Why, in God's name, did you sell Witfontein?'

'Because I was broke and had to. It's no use talking about Witfontein either,' Janse replied.

'I know, I know,' Meninsky said bitterly; 'but you can't help thinking of what Piet's got for nothing.'

'Piet gets most things for nothing. He's one of the lucky ones.'

'Well, damn it, so am I,' Meninsky proclaimed. 'We're cut off on the east. What's the next farm to westward? My head's in a ruddy muddle: I can't think straight tonight.'

'That's my Uncle Barend's. Sterkfontein.'

'Your uncle's? There's luck to begin with: We'll go there tomorrow.'

'Not so much luck as you think. If you want to get anything out of Uncle Barend you'd best leave me behind: he doesn't like anybody from Wonderfontein. It would be fatal even to let him know that you'd been here.'

Next morning Meninsky made a wide circuit and approached Barend Prinsloo's farm cunningly – driving his cape-cart across it not from the Wonderfontein side but from the east. There were many outcrops of rock to be seen on it, but no obvious continuations of the 'banket' conglomerate in the line where he had hoped to find them; and his reception at Sterkfontein was not encouraging. But his luck was 'in' that morning, none the less; if he had arrived a day later he would not have found anyone there; for it was late autumn, and the Prinsloo family were on the point of setting out for the Low Country with their cattle for the winter grazing. Three wagons stood, with their teams lying down before them, in front of the principal house;

the stone-walled kraals were packed with livestock that had been herded ready for the trek.

As Meninsky's cape-cart drew near Barend Prinsloo and three of his sons moved out to meet him. Barend was a grizzled man now, with a fringe of ragged white hair spreading out beneath the brim of his hat, and a shaggy beard: but his eyes were still bright as a hawk's, with flecks of hot gold in them. The three sons were tall young men – not one less than six feet in height. They carried English rifles, booty from Majuba, slung over their backs, and looked as if they could use them. As they barred Meninsky's way, between the house and the cattle-kraal, their attitude was watchful and threatening.

'*Pas op* . . . Stop there!' Barend Prinsloo shouted. 'Where do you come from?'

'I come from Barberton.'

Barend looked at the horses, and passed his hand, from sheer habit, over the near beast's knees and pasterns and fetlocks.

'You haven't come far today,' he said suspiciously. 'The horses are not warmed up yet.'

'How could I come far today, uncle? The sun's not up more than two hours.'

'What are you travelling this way for?'

'Just wandering about looking for a farm,' Meninsky said innocently.

'Englishman, you lie!' Barend Prinsloo answered, and his tall sons laughed. 'You lie. You are looking for gold.'

'Why do you call me an Englishman, uncle?' Meninsky said in an aggrieved voice. 'I am no Englishman. I'm a Peruvian, as you should see; and now I come to look at this place I think I have been here before with my donkey-wagon – many years ago, yes, and sold cloth to your wife. She would recognize me . . .'

'She is dead,' Barend Prinsloo said shortly.

'That is a misfortune that comes to all of us, uncle.' Meninsky shook his head.

Barend Prinsloo passed over the condolences with a grunt.

'Where is your donkey-wagon now, then? You are no longer a *smous*. I know you are looking for gold.'

Meninsky laughed. 'If I were looking for gold I should be going towards Barberton, not coming away from it. No, no, uncle, I tell you I've too much sense for that. Those miners in

Barberton are no better than savages. They work on the Sabbath and spend all they get on drink. I am looking for a farm. If you showed me gold, I would rather be without it.'

'There is no gold here,' Barend said: 'but that does not prevent those damned red-necks fossicking all over my farm. We have had six in a week. We spend all our time riding after them and driving them off. I have told my sons to shoot the next one they see. You yourself,' he added grimly, 'are lucky to have escaped being wounded: my boys can shoot; they are not like Englishmen. Now we go to the winter grazing, and we shall see no more of them.'

Meninsky condoled with him.

'The English are mad about gold. They see it everywhere, even when there is none.' He dismounted and leant on the wall of the kraal, apparently surveying Barend's lean cattle; but his sharp eyes had already examined the stones of which it was built, and discovered, amongst them, a fragment of pebbled conglomerate. 'Yes, your cattle look sorry,' he said; 'they will be better for a feed of good grass. If I had this farm I should only run sheep. I wonder you stay here ... particularly with all these damned Englishmen wandering about. You should see the grass in the Zoutpansberg! There a man does not have to trek down in the winter to keep his cattle alive. In the Zoutpansberg, too, there is freedom; no man need pay taxes; and good Government land goes for nothing because of the Kaffirs.'

'Kaffirs? Who is afraid of Kaffirs?' Barend scoffed. 'It was only the missionaries and the English who spoilt them. Now that we have the country again we shall soon put an end to their nonsense!'

'Well, one can see you are a strong man, uncle,' Meninsky sighed, 'and have strong sons to help you; but I am growing old and weak, and my chest gives me trouble!' He coughed and patted it. 'You see? That is why, when I settle down, as I mean to do, I should not mind the Witwatersrand.' He gazed over the great sweep of downland; his fingers caressed the fragment of banket in the wall. 'I like this place of yours, uncle,' he said. 'Why don't you sell it to me?'

'I have lived here forty years,' Barend Prinsloo said. 'I have buried two wives and four children.'

'Ah yes, and you have excellent neighbours, no doubt?'

Meninsky said slyly. 'It is a good thing to have old friends near one.'

'Good neighbours? My nearest neighbour's another of these damned Englishmen, who married my fool of a sister. They know better than to come near me.'

'That is bad again. Listen, uncle, I am not a rich man; but I have my savings. I will give you enough for this farm to buy good land in the Zoutpansberg. I'll give you two hundred pounds.'

Barend shook his head. 'What's the use of money to me? If you offered me cattle . . .'

'But well-conditioned cattle are cheap in the north. With the same money you could buy more and better as you trekked.'

Barend thought for a moment: 'What about these two horses?' he said. 'I like the look of them.'

'But I couldn't possibly part with those,' Meninsky declared. 'They are both of them young and salted. The pair cost me more than the whole of your farm is worth.'

'They are guaranteed salted?'

'I would not wish to talk about them. There are no better horses in Kimberley – no, not even in the whole of the Transvaal.'

'You say "Kimberley"? You told me first you came from Barberton! I was right when I said you lied.'

The man was as apprehensive as an unbroken colt. Meninsky calmed his suspicions:

'I spoke the truth. Does one come here from Kimberley from the east? But the horses were bought in Kimberley.'

'How can I be sure they are salted, as you say?'

Meninsky smiled wearily and shrugged his shoulders:

'What does it matter to you, anyway, uncle, since they are not for sale?'

Barend's eldest son, who had been examining the horses' teeth, came back and reported:

'He has spoken the truth, father. They are both of them young, they are three-year-olds and their legs are sound. If it's also true that they're salted . . .'

Barend Prinsloo nodded, and turned to Meninsky.

'Now listen what I will do. I will sell you the farm for two hundred pounds and this pair of horses.'

'If you take my horses, what is the good of the cart to me? I am not a fool, uncle.'

'We will give you two others to put in the cart.'

'Horses broken to harness?'

'You're a fine sort of farmer if you can't break a horse to harness for yourself!'

'If you take my horses I cannot give you more than a hundred and thirty pounds for the farm. They are worth fifty pounds apiece, and more – as much as the farm. This is poor veld, and you know it.'

'Well, so let it be,' Barend Prinsloo said. 'A hundred and thirty pounds and the pair of horses. You must make up your mind at once, though, because we are trekking.'

'You drive a hard bargain, uncle,' Meninsky said. 'Am I the Jew, or are you?'

Barend laughed and told his sons to unharness the horses.

So Meninsky bought Sterkfontein and drove home, none too easily, with two spavined nags in his slap-up cape-cart, while Barend's three wagons trekked northward with his three huge sons, his herds of lean cattle and sheep, and four of the half-caste Erasmus's golden brown girls with their brood of off-white brats.

This was the only farm Meninsky was able to buy on that part of the Rand where the outcrop was visible. Though Janse and he scoured the country and lived in the saddle for weeks, they were met, whenever they tried to buy land, by fantastic demands, or the news that options had already been granted. Joe Robinson had gained a big start on them, and, backed by Beit's credit, had used it, knowing full well that the tide of hungry speculators who had flocked to Barberton would swing back to the High Veld as soon as they heard he was on the move. Joe Robinson went west to Randfontein; but the Strubens, and others who were on the spot – Henry Nourse, Jan Meyer, Dirk Geldenhuis – were busy buying options nearer to Wonderfontein. Then big money from Kimberley flooded the market; Meninsky's and Janse's pooled thirty thousand appeared a small sum. When he heard that a single farm had changed hands for sixty thousand, the Peruvian threw up the sponge.

'No use kicking,' he said; 'we're lucky to have what we've got, mate. It's a tidy bit, when you come to think of it; and we shall be able to use the money that's left on development and buying machinery – which is a damn sight better than being dependent on amateur capitalists who think they can boss you up just because they've backed you. All we've got to do now is to go on steady and sit tight till we've proved our values. After that we can begin to talk!'

(6)

As for Janse, he was by no means averse from a quiet life. At first, when he returned to Wonderfontein, he had felt – not exactly a stranger, but rather a melancholy ghost revisiting the scenes of his former life, and finding them unreal. His emotions were near the surface and hard to control. Wherever he went, familiar, small things had power to touch him and even to bring ridiculous tears to his eyes. The sight of the shiny rustbank on which he had sat as a child, of the great clasped family Bible, which gave the same old click as his father opened it, of his mother's work-basket, stocked, as it seemed, with the very skeins of wool and bobbins of thread with which, squatting on the earth floor, he had been fascinated thirty-five years ago, aroused in him an almost intolerable wistfulness.

It was odd that these humble landmarks of memory should have remained exactly as they were while he had changed so much, being no longer a boy, but a lean, weathered man of thirty-five with a sun-wrinkled face and threads of grey in his hair. Such was the lot of humanity. While he was aware of the changes in himself, he felt them less than those he observed in his parents: in John Grafton, no longer the tall black-bearded figure whose severe taciturnity had intimidated him, but a frail, white-haired man, with a stoop that had robbed him of several inches in height, whose voice had lost its resonance and its accent of command; and in his mother, who, though her hazel eyes were as bright and her quick smile as sweet, was, in fact, a little old woman, with the neat, busy hands he had always adored now bony and heavily-veined, and the skin shrunken on her temples beneath her thin silvery hair.

No doubt his own physical exhaustion after more than fifteen years of poor food and hardships spent under the sun of the Low Veld made him susceptible to this wistful mood. The icy nights of the Witwatersrand winter chilled his thin blood and brought on a series of bouts of malaria. There were mornings when, yellow-skinned and cringing, he hated the sight of that naked expanse of sere down-land over which the wind blew without hindrance from the Antarctic, making the dry mealie-stalks rattle and quiver as though they too were agued; his blanched and contracted skin yearned for the kinder air of the bush lying golden and still under the noonday sun, that warm, silent land whose spirit had healed his when it was wounded and weary.

And yet, while he shivered in the Witwatersrand, he was not entirely bereft of the Low Veld. It was present to him in the company of Lena, who surely was a living part of it and who throve in her transplantation as though this bleak ridge were her natural soil. She was still a fierce, wild little thing, tempestuous, generous, and sometimes unaccountable because her elemental mind jibbed at the apparent lack of reason in the accepted rules of civilized behaviour. For all that, in some ways she was more adaptable (being younger) than he. If she thought their ways odd and constrained, she accepted her new friends at Wonderfontein – partly, perhaps, because they were Janse's, and, to her, nothing so intimately connected with Janse could possibly be wrong – as frankly as they accepted her.

Lisbet, particularly, was enraptured to have found a new granddaughter to satisfy her boundless maternity. Lena was a little shy of her at first, repelled by the novel experience of being mothered; but, from the instant she saw her, the child took to Maria with an attachment only less passionate than that she cherished for Janse. If Janse was in the house or about it she had eyes for nobody but him: in his absence she shadowed Maria with an equal fidelity. In her loves, in her hates, in her laughter, in her rages, Lena could do nothing by halves.

This attachment was good for both of them, Janse thought, if only because of their unlikeness. Though he admired this new Maria – so different in her mature composure from the ardent child he remembered at the time when he first left Witfontein, there was something in her restraint, her quietness, her serenity, that hurt him – not only because it seemed such a negation of the Maria he had known, but also because it appeared to him forced and unnatural in one so young – in one so beautiful, too, he would have said – for Maria's slim body, her delicate features and her soft eyes, were surely beautiful. But her beauty was oddly lifeless, detached and remote. Though she was quick in movement and in speech, though she seemed full of energy and even, at times, of a high-pitched gaiety, Janse felt that these things were superficial – the expression of her will rather than of spontaneous feeling. When she withdrew herself, as she seemed sometimes to do, from domestic and social activities, her face, as he watched it, lost all its expression; her mouth became sad, and her eyes, beneath their straight brows, appeared not so much hurt, perhaps, as puzzled.

When he saw Maria in one of these disarmed moments, as it were shrunken and bewildered, Janse was moved by a deep compassion which he longed, but was afraid, to express. His mother had told him as much as she knew of the story of that brief love affair, the tragedy in which he, unconsciously, had been the last messenger. He felt it more deeply, too, because he had witnessed the end, of which Maria mercifully knew no details.

'But I have never dared to mention it, Janse,' Lisbet said. 'At first I thought that, if we left her alone, the child would get over it. But she doesn't get over it, really. You see that ring she wears on her wedding-finger? It was an uncut diamond a young man from Kimberley gave her – long ago, before you left. Yes, indeed, I think you were here on the night when he and his brother came. He gave her the stone and made her promise that when she grew up and was engaged to be married he should have it cut and set for her. It was a little joke between them. But now it is no joke, Janse.'

'Don't you think it might be a good thing, mother, if I said something about that letter? She must know I was there and that the boy gave it me. Don't you think feelings that are bottled up like that for too long without any release are almost dangerous?'

Lisbet shook her head. 'I don't think I would, Janse, unless she speaks for herself. She's more sensitive, that child, than you can imagine. In the first months it was harrowing to all of us. Not a word – and such cruel suffering that you could feel it. She is a strange child. I don't think it's easy for a man to understand. No, no ... let her speak for herself. You would risk too much. She may come to it some day.'

Janse accepted her advice – the more gratefully, indeed, because he had dreaded the results of the course he proposed, and it would have taken a good deal of courage to break through a silence that was almost forbidding in its dignity. Yet this strange, repressed mood of Maria's, and the horror behind it which was ever present to his mind, compelled him, at last, to express the tenderness and the pity he felt for her. One day when he found her standing alone on the stoep, her features, unguarded, betraying the look of emptiness which he knew so well, he limped over and took her in his arms and kissed her. She gasped at the suddenness of his embrace, and stared at him for a moment with startled eyes. Then she closed them and shook her head, and, with a quick, urgent hand-clasp, hurriedly left him.

Janse himself, left alone, was almost as deeply affected as she. When she was gone he could still feel the strength of her grip, the impression of her ring on his hand. Yet, after this sudden release of emotion on both sides, their relations subtly changed, as though this mute sharing of a secret had drawn them closer together. Though her heart was still loyal to her childhood's companion, Piet, she had discovered in Janse's awkward gesture a kinship of feeling more delicate and more understanding than that of a mere blood-relationship. She looked upon Janse as her comrade as well as her brother; and he, who had never, outside his dreams, known any such human intimacy, rejoiced in this intimacy and found it sweet.

Lena, indeed, showed some jealousy at the signs of this comradeship which her quick instincts noticed immediately; she was so passionate in her attachments that she wanted to possess them both – but particularly Janse – and resented any infringement of her claims. This possessive passion of the small human animal at once amused and flattered them, and when the child was not there they joked with each other about it.

'You must really be more careful, Janse,' Maria said, 'or some day that child will stick a knife in me.'

'Ah, she loves you as much as me.'

'Don't think that for a moment. You're her absolute property. Those great blue eyes of hers follow you like a dog's.'

Janse laughed. 'She's an odd little creature, isn't she? I think she feels more strongly than what we call civilized children.'

'I hope she'll grow out of that. It's a dreadul handicap in this cruel life. The more strongly one feels the more deeply one has to suffer. I only wish I could teach her that in time. I've grown very fond of that little thing, Janse. She's so full of life, so – how shall I put it? – so clear. There's nothing hidden in her.'

'She means a great deal to me,' Janse said. 'Do you know, when I took her away with me, I thought I'd made a fool of myself? But now I believe it was the best thing I ever did. I never realized how lonely I'd been till I found she'd crept close to me under the wagon that night.'

'Yes, I think you must be a lonely person, Janse. And yet I think women should love you; you're so gentle. Have you never been in love?'

'Once ... perhaps. But that's an old story. I've forgotten it now.'

'I think you'd make a good husband ... and a good father.'

'I'm a sort of foster-father already. As it is, I look like having to be a mother as well. Why don't you help me out and share the job with me, Maria?'

'I'll do what I can – if she'll let me,' Maria said.

They were agreed that the time must soon come when it would be a mistake to keep Lena running wild on the farm. She was, presumably, nearly thirteen, and though her manners had now been adjusted to the standards of Wonderfontein she was still, in the accepted sense of the word, entirely uneducated. Maria did not feel herself competent to instruct her: at the time of her love-affair with Richard Abberley she had bitterly regretted her own shortcomings, and had envied Lavinia for her conventional education.

'It wouldn't be fair to keep Lena here, Janse dear,' she said, 'however much we should miss her. It's unnatural for her to spend all her time with grown-up people. She ought to be mixing with children of her own age. You can see how she tends to do that from her always wandering away to the kraal to play with the Kaffir children, and to the Erasmus's huts – which is far worse. We ought to get her away from that sort of influence; and I think the best thing would be to send her to the Cape and let her go to school with Lavinia's children. Jimmy is very little younger than she is.'

'She'll hate going as much as we shall hate letting her go. She'll be so dreadfully backward compared with other children of her age, and she'll certainly give them some shocks.'

'I'm afraid she will. But that can't be helped. What's more, I'm sure she won't take long catching up: she's as sharp as a knife. So long as you can afford it ...'

'You needn't worry about that. I've nothing else in the world to spend my money on, and I've plenty to spare. The only thing that worries me is the chance that Lena may turn against it and run away. She's quite capable of finding her way home like a cat if she once takes it into her head.'

'If you like I'll take her down to the Cape myself, Janse, and stay for a bit until she's settled in. We could catch the Kimberley coach at Potchefstroom, and I could discuss the whole business with Piet on the way. Piet's advice is worth having in any practical problem – and so is Lavinia's, for that matter. You hardly had time to know the Haskards' did you?'

'I knew them slightly.'

'I'm very fond of Lavinia. She's shy, and she's cold in a way. You might find her difficult. But she's a perfect wife for Piet and an excellent mother.'

'I'm surprised that Piet never comes over to Witfontein,' Janse said. 'There must be a lot of gold on that farm, and on Brakfontein too: the reef runs through both of them.'

Maria laughed:

'You may be perfectly certain of one thing – and that is that Piet knows what he's doing. He always did.'

It is questionable if, at that moment, Piet did quite know what he was doing. The years since Majuba had been a difficult time in Kimberley. Diamond prices had slumped to ten shillings a carat owing to the lack of any restriction in sales; the multiplication and the daring of Illicit Diamond Buyers; catastrophic new falls of reef which the Mining Board, already facing bankruptcy, was unable to deal with; and, finally, an epidemic of small-pox which put the whole field in quarantine. The mining companies were calling up their share capital, the banks refusing advances on diamond shares. The amalgamation in which Cecil Rhodes had set his heart seemed no nearer. Indeed, he was now embarking on the toughest commercial struggle of his life, a fight to the death with Meninsky's friend Barney Barnato, the controller of de Beers' great rival, the Kimberley Mine.

Not that Rhodes had time to think about diamonds, or even about the gold-field at Barberton over which so many of his puzzled friends in Kimberley (not including Barnato) had lost their heads. Though he continued to consolidate his position as a diamond-owner and took advantage of the slump, knowing well that sooner or later Amalgamation would come and put everything right again, a larger problem engrossed him: the Road to the North.

Ever since his entry into the Cape Colony Parliament he had felt himself stultified by its parochial attitude and shortness of vision, limited, as he fretfully complained, by the mists of Table Mountain. It talked and wrangled over the native borders within its own territory – Basutoland and the Transkei, purely local affairs – neglecting its only possible outlet for expansion: Bechuanaland ... the neck of the bottle ... the key position ... the Suez Canal of the trade of the country. He came down to Kimberley fuming, caught up Piet and the other faithful, and swept them along in its tempestuous wake.

There was no resisting him. Night after night, in the galvanized hut he still shared with young Pickering, Rhodes walked heavily to and fro, haranguing them in his falsetto voice, threshing his way through speech to thought. He was more physically impressive now than ever before: a tall, full-chested, plethoric, short-necked man with pouched eyes and a double chin which made it difficult to believe he was only thirty. The little doctor sat hunched in his chair, smoking his chain of cigarettes, a glint of cynical amusement in his black eyes, putting in, now and again, an acid word of commentary or pawky humour that would have taken the wind out of the sails of a less determined talker. Sometimes, indeed, Rhodes would laugh with him, sitting on his own hand, his big body shaking with soundless mirth. He could enjoy Jameson's humour even when it was against him. But not for long.

While the mist-blinded Parliament in Capetown fought over the parish pump, things had been happening in Bechuanaland. The Transvaal Boers were spilling over the western boundary fixed by the Pretoria Convention, which was still, thanks to bunglers at Westminster, unratified. ('They're too slow, too slow! If we want anything done we must do it ourselves and cut out the Imperial Factor.') There were already two new Republics founded under the Dutch flag: Stellaland and Land Goshen, straddling over the Road to the North, the Suez Canal, the Bottle-Neck.

And not only that. The Germans had appeared on the coast to westward and were flirting with Pretoria. Between them they were going to hold the Balance of the Map. They could put a stop to any expansion northwards. Kruger – that was the man to be feared, and no less admired! – wanted the North for himself because he was afraid of the Transvaal being encircled; but it was the Cape that was going to be encircled, cut off, if he had his way; the Transvaalers were 'bouncing' the road to the interior. And the Cape Parliament would do nothing; couldn't see beyond their own noses. Jan Hofmeyr was the only man with an atom of vision. *He* wanted the only proper solution, a Federation of South Africa. ('Don't you see, doctor, it's precisely the same thing as the Amalgamation of the Diamond-Mines: Kruger *qua* the Transvaal like this damned fellow Barney *qua* the Kimberley Mine?') But if Hofmeyr had his way it would be a Dutch Federation, on Kruger's terms; and that meant – they knew what it meant: stagnation, parochialism, narrowness; they had only to look at what the Transvaal had made of itself in more than forty years! The Transvaalers were already imposing a prohibitive tariff on goods from the Cape. If they held the Bottle-Neck and put on their tariff too, they would have a stranglehold on the whole trade of the interior.

'When I went into Parliament,' he told them, 'I said to myself: "One must take Bechuanaland" – and what's more, one must take it damned quickly, or else it will be too late.'

'One' rode up, by invitation of the High Commissioner, dragging Piet along with 'one', and took Bechuanaland.

Rhodes amused them all by his account of his interview with Sir Hercules.

'Mr. Rhodes, I'm afraid Bechuanaland is gone. These freebooters will take the country, and Kruger, of course, is behind it," the old fellow said. Well, of course, one couldn't just leave it at that, so I asked him if I could go up and see what was happening. He was extraordinarily nice about it, but slim as the devil. "Oh, you can go up, Mr. Rhodes," he said, "but I can give you no force to back you. You must use your own judgment."

'Which is exactly what I mean to use, old boy, I thought to myself. So I asked him again: "Look here, sir, will you allow me to do what I like?" He was quite frank about it. "Yes, do what you like," he said, "but if you make a mess of it, don't forget I shan't back you up." "Well, that's good enough for me." I told him. And now we shall see.'

They went first to Stellaland, where Rhodes had made a flying visit before and settled matters with the head of the new Republic, Van Niekerk. All Van Niekerk had wanted then was

395

protection from the local tribes and from the horse-stealers, half-savage Scotsmen, most of them, who terrorized the whole district with organized native bands: black men armed against white – the unforgivable sin! Well, the Cape could give them better protection and more secure land-titles, Rhodes had persuaded him. What he wanted, he said, was an Anglo-Dutch occupation of this debatable land. And Van Niekerk, agreeing, had hauled down the *Vierkleur*.

But now, by a shocking error of official judgment, the Rev. John Mackenzie was there, rubbing everyone up the wrong way with his missionary heritage of bitter anti-Dutch feeling, determined, with the Aborigines' Protection Society behind him, to 'protect' the natives who were stealing the Stellaland cattle and fighting amongst themselves. ('That damned interfering missionary!' Rhodes grumbled. 'This is a pretty kettle of fish!') And now Van Niekerk was not so amenable. He had with him a mountainous man, a western Transvaaler, Groot Adrian de la Rey, who roared at Rhodes: 'It is no use talking. Blood must flow!'

'No, give me my breakfast, uncle,' Rhodes said. 'Then we can talk about blood.'

They stayed with Groot Adrian a week. By the time they rode on to Land Goshen, the Stellaland question was more or less settled; with land-titles properly registered, and self-government under the British flag pending annexation. A triumph of reason. But Land Goshen was in an uproar. Blood was actually flowing there. On the day they arrived Piet Joubert launched an attack on the local chief, Montsioa. When Rhodes asked him to call it off until they had talked, Joubert flatly refused.

'I don't quite understand what this fellow's up to, Grafton,' Rhodes said. 'He's here representing Kruger, but he hates Kruger like poison. He knows he can never beat Oom Paul for the presidency, so I fancy he's playing a lone hand in the hope of becoming President of these new Republics. Kruger would like to gather in Goshen and Stellaland because he wants the north; but he won't want Joubert to mop them up for himself, so I don't think he'll back him. In the meantime I'll give Piet Joubert one more chance, though I doubt if he'll take it.'

They went up to Joubert's wagons.

'Mr. Joubert,' Rhodes said, 'I'm afraid I have to warn you. If this fighting goes on, you're at war with the British Government.'

'That is no new thing, Mr. Rhodes,' Joubert answered sullenly. 'The last time was the Majuba.'

'Very well. In that case we inspan.'

No sooner were they gone than Kruger annexed Land Goshen to the Transvaal by proclamation.

They hurried south.

'This is all that bloody fellow Mackenzie's fault,' Rhodes grumbled. 'He's antagonized every Dutchman in Bechuanaland: the very people with whom we've got to work. It's time these missionaries were taught a lesson and made to keep out of politics. The only thing now is to appeal to the British Government and try to make them see sense.'

'What? The Imperial Factor again?' Piet said.

'I'd use any factor you like to keep Bechuanaland. I've got to keep it. What's more, I'm going to keep it. There are a thousand Boers in Land Goshen, and Kruger has a commando out on the Transvaal side of the border. He may have put them there to keep an eye on Joubert, or he may be waiting for a chance to jump the claim. I don't think Kruger'll fight if he can possibly help it; he's too short of money. He'd like to climb down, at the moment; but it's difficult for an autocrat to climb down when his chief rival is looking on, and the best thing we can do is to help him save his face by confronting him with a force that makes fighting imprudent.'

'This is all very complicated,' Piet said.

'Complications are just what makes life worth living: but I've never met anyone it wasn't as easy to deal with as to fight. These fellows – Kruger, Joubert, Van Niekerk, Mackenzie – are all intriguing. It's far better to tell the town-crier exactly what you are going to do. If you have an idea, and it is a good idea, and if you only stick to it, it will come out all right.'

He stuck to this one so effectively that he induced Sir Hercules to send up General Warren with a force of four thousand men, including two hundred dragoons.

'I don't like professional soldiers,' Rhodes said, 'but I know this man Warren. Met him once in a railway carriage. He'll do at a pinch.'

Warren hurried up to Kimberley – the railway was through at last – and arranged a meeting with Kruger and Rhodes at Fourteen Streams, where the Vaal divides, in Rhodes' own constituency. He arrived with four thousand redcoats – and the man who had made all the muddle: the Rev. John Mackenzie.

From the moment they met, Warren's frigid manner made it clear that he was not taking instructions or even advice from a mere civilian like Rhodes – and also that he was already in Mackenzie's pocket. When he insisted on taking the anti-Dutch missionary with him to his meeting with Kruger, Rhodes felt bound to protest.

'Mackenzie's presence will queer our pitch, General,' he said. 'This man has been writing articles about Bechuanaland full of the grossest imputations against the Dutch and against me personally.'

'I know you don't like missionaries, Mr. Rhodes,' Warren answered coldly; 'but Mackenzie knows more about this country than you do.'

'The Boers know he's fanatically opposed to them: that's one thing. But they also know he's against me: and that's another. If we appear together, Kruger will see at once that we've a divided front, and he'll bank on it.'

Warren shrugged his shoulders.

'Neither you nor Mackenzie is conducting these negotiations, Mr. Rhodes. I am solely responsible. Your capacity, as you don't quite seem to realize, is merely advisory.'

'There is one thing more, General. We have agreed that both parties shall come to this conference unaccompanied by anything more than a personal escort. I've read your orders, issued last night, and find that we're going up just as if we were marching into a hostile country, with scouts in advance and skirmishers thrown out on each side. That's ridiculous, to my mind. What's more, it suggests a feeling of distrust on our part which will be deeply wounding to Mr. Kruger and his companions. You don't know the Dutch as I do. They're a sensitive people, and they don't like scabbard-rattling. No more do I.'

'Really, Mr. Rhodes,' Warren said with a flush of anger. 'Are you in charge of this expedition, or am I?'

Rhodes left him, fuming.

'I felt like socking the damned fool one on the jaw,' he told Piet; 'but one has to see this through.'

They found Kruger and a small group of burghers, all unarmed, awaiting them in a bivouac at Fourteen Streams. Piet had never seen Kruger before; he was curious to discover what quality had enabled this supposedly ignorant man to impose his authority on the whole of the Transvaal. He found him an ncouth, unwieldy figure, shabbily dressed in tobacco-stained broadcloth, with little, red, pouched eyes, like those of a rhinoceros, and encrusted eyelashes on either side of a massive determined nose. He saw the firm, obstinate, clean-shaven mouth (in which, even on this formal occasion, his pipe was clenched) with the straggling fringe of grey beard. Warren took the lead; yet Piet could not help feeling that he, in his scarlet and gold, was the smaller man. Mackenzie, pale and venomous, stood at Warren's elbow, prompting him. Rhodes, ruddy with suppressed indignation, glowered in the background. Only once did he intervene.

'May I put one thing to the President?' he said. 'I blame only one man for the events that followed my visit to Goshen, and that man is Joubert. If he had come with me, we could have prevented any violence. And now, when the matter comes up before us, where is Mr. Joubert? Why is he not here to answer for himself?'

Kruger shook his head. 'What is done cannot be helped,' he said.

'But I asked Joubert to come with me,' Rhodes persisted, 'and to use his influence – or even force – to recall your burghers, the freebooters as one calls them, from overrunning the land.'

Kruger meditated.

'I did not see my way clear to send armed men to oppose them,' he said at last. 'I thought it better to take over the land by proclamation.'

'But this land, Mr. President,' Warren said, 'is outside the boundaries to which you agreed in the Pretoria Convention!'

'That is true,' Kruger answered with unexpected meekness. 'Yes, that is true, that is true.'

'What did I tell you, Grafton?' Rhodes whispered. 'He'll climb down. He's not ready to fight. And he's right – the old devil's right. But he won't forget this in a hurry. There's a rod in pickle for us, if Warren only knew it. Now, if he'd have the sense to leave well alone . . .'

That was not Warren's way. He hadn't brought four thousand men to the north for nothing. When the agreement was signed and Rhodes and Piet Grafton returned to Kimberley, he marched his force up north like a conqueror. He was full of bitterness against Rhodes, a mere box-wallah, an interfering, untitled civilian, who had failed to show respect to his new knighthood and his general's uniform. But he got his own back. He repudiated the Stellaland land-titles which Rhodes had guaranteed, and went so far, following John Mackenzie's teaching, as to proclaim that no men but those of English descent should be eligible for grants of land in the new protectorate: another blow at Rhodes' ruling principle of Anglo-Dutch co-operation.

'I shall have to get this damned fellow put in his place,' Rhodes said. 'Still, we've got the road to the north, Grafton: we've got Bechuanaland. Now the fun is going to begin!' He chuckled to himself. 'The next step's the Zambezi. I'm going to send Charlie Rudd to Matabeleland to have a shot at Lobengula.'

'That young man,' Kruger told Adrian, back in Pretoria, 'is going to cause me trouble. He never sleeps, they say, and he doesn't smoke.'

Trouble met them in Kimberley. In addition to the urgent necessity of getting the Governor at the Cape to put 'that damned fellow' in his place, they found the diamond industry going from bad to worse. Neville Pickering, too, was ill. He had been thrown from his horse a year earlier and had been ailing – that was why Rhodes had asked Piet to accompany him to the north – and now the mischief had settled on his lungs and was giving Jameson anxiety, though he tried to make a wry joke of it as of everything else.

Piet was amazed by the gentleness Rhodes showed in nursing his friend, and by the valuable time he willingly devoted to cheering him up. What concerned Piet more than the diamond slump, which Rhodes merely laughed at, declaring that all would come right, was the increasing number of reports of gold-finds on the Witwatersrand. He was safe enough, as he knew, in his ownership of Witfontein and in his expectations of owning Haskard's farm; but it irked him to think that he was possibly missing other golden opportunities: he had a right, he felt, to a finger in that pie.

They were worrying Rhodes about the Witwatersrand, too: that smooth, quiet-voiced Alfred Beit with his stories of the bargains Joe Robinson had struck at Langlaagte and Randjiesfontein, Hans Sauer, his pet mineralogist, continually urging him to take a hand; but, save when he dashed off to

Parliament to cook General Warren's goose, nothing could move him from Pickering's bedside.

'Is Barney in this?' he asked.

They admitted that Barnato had held back from the Rand, as he had held back at Barberton.

'Gardner Williams says the same. He calls the Rand a ten-pennyweight proposition.'

'No doubt he's right,' Beit agreed; 'but you mustn't forget the extent of this reef: it's a case where quantity makes up for quality.'

'That's all very well, Beit; but I can't calculate the *power* in these gold-claims. Understand what I mean? When I'm here in Kimberley and have nothing much to do, I go and sit on the edge of de Beers and look at the blue-ground below, and I can calculate the number of loads of blue and the value of the diamonds in the blue and the power those diamonds give me. But I can't do this with your gold-reefs. I can't trust my judgment. I've never been a gambler, like the doctor, and you can't turn me into one at my time of life.'

He refused to move, and Piet knew he would have to stay with him. If you were Rhodes' friend, it seemed, you were Rhodes' slave. Even if he could have escaped, he was still a little chary of visiting the Transvaal alone: he remembered the dead man's pass Adrian had taken from him on the Majuba and the look in Adrian's eyes. If the new field were a failure he might find himself caught in disastrous speculations: if it were a success, then the value of Witfontein would continue to rise. On the whole, though he longed to speculate, he was afraid of it, and he had little money to spare, for, during the last three years, the face-value of his diamond shares (and Haskard's) had decreased by a half. If Rhodes gave the lead, it would be quite another matter. In that case he would be prepared to plunge in up to his neck. He would have liked to have a talk with Meninsky; but Meninsky had vanished from Kimberley.

Suddenly, yielding to Beit's continued entreaties, Rhodes emerged from his sick-room abstraction.

'Sauer's brought back a bag of samples from the Wit-watersrand, Grafton,' he said, 'and these fellows insist on my going and having a look at their reef. Rudd and I are going in Gibson's Pretoria coach tomorrow morning. As you know that country, I think you'd better come with us – unless you'd like to go on with Sauer, who's walking a couple of stages ahead to avoid the suspicions which will be aroused from his being seen with a notorious character like me!'

At three o'clock next morning Gibson's ten-horse leather-slung coach went swaying over the dusty veld towards Potchefstroom, with Rhodes and Rudd wedged into the forward corner-seats, heavily muffled and hardly recognizable in its dim interior. At Potchefstroom the coach diverged from its ordinary route (such was the power of de Beers) to cross the Witwatersrand. It deposited the party finally at Colonel Ferreira's outspan, already dignified by the name of Ferreira's Camp, where men were busy stripping the outcrop, and a hut of mud and reeds announced itself as Walker's Hotel.

It was an odd experience for Piet to find himself back in the Transvaal and almost within sight of Witfontein. Though he was still a little nervous as to his political position, he felt fairly secure in such important company. Joe Robinson met the party and showed them his purchase at Langlaagte. They went on to Klein Paardekraal, which Rhodes, with his usual swiftness of decision, bought out of hand, and to Hans Duplessis' farm, Turffontein, where they crushed and panned samples from the Main Reef and its leaders, and secure a ten days' option on it for five hundred pounds, and another for two hundred and fifty on Doornfontein.

Rhodes was in excellent spirits. The purchase of land on a large scale always had the effect of stimulating him.

'If one comes of a farming stock, as I do,' he said, 'there's always a fascination in buying land.'

They went fossicking, east and west, for three days, while Esselen, the Landdrost, drew up the various contracts for Rhodes' signature. It was a 'whirlwind campaign' – 'Midlothian was nothing to this,' Rhodes declared – in the midst of which he found time to dash over to Pretoria for a conference with Vice-President Rissik and Commandant-General Joubert on the validity of sales or transfers effected before the new gold-field was proclaimed. He even met Kruger – still sore from his surrender to Warren and doubtful of Rhodes' good faith, but aware, for the first time in his life, that this accursed gold might save the Republic from another default or sheer bankruptcy – and induced him to remove the interdict on the land Rudd and he and Joe Robinson had already bought. That was a heartening triumph.

'I think one will be able to deal with the old fellow in future,' Rhodes said. 'He's a fine type: the right, old-fashioned Dutchman, whom one has to admire. If he weren't so damned suspicious and one could deal with him *qua* the farmer, not *qua* the State President, we could work together.'

'All those documents are ready for your signature, Mr. Rhodes,' they reminded him.

'Give me something to eat first,' he said.

While he sat feeding, voraciously, there came in a sheaf of messages from Kimberley which he scanned as he ate. One of these was from Jameson. It told him that Neville Pickering had taken a turn for the worse and was not expected to live. Rhodes left his meal unfinished.

'I'm off, Sauer,' he said. 'I've got to catch the mail-coach!'

'But you must sign these options and transfers before you go, Rhodes.'

'Damn you and your options! I've told you: I'm off.'

He went like a hurricane, Sauer fluttering the papers in his wake, and rode, on the top of the roped mailbags, to Kimberley and Neville Pickering's bedside. When once he had reached it nothing could move him. Sauer sent anguished telegrams imploring him to deal with the lapsing options; but not one was answered. A month later, when Pickering died, he was to realize that he had thrown away millions. But he did not care. At the graveside, hysterically laughing and crying alternately, he flung his arms round his rival Barnato's neck.

'Ah, Barney,' he sobbed, 'he will never sell you another parcel of diamonds.'

Reluctantly – for in everything connected with gold he was still apprehensive, divided between his anxiety to profit by it and to exclude the hordes of damned foreigners who alone could work it – Paul Kruger proclaimed two farms, Driefontein and Elandsfontein, as a recognized gold-field, and, ten days later, four more – Randtjeslaagte, Langlaagte, Doornfontein and Turffontein – and appointed a Commission to inquire into the advisability of founding a township. Commandant Johannes Joubert, Johannes Mayer and Johan Rissik rode over from Pretoria with the Government surveyors to lay out a site.

They took Ferreira's Camp as a centre for the new settlement, and defined a rough square, with swamps to east and west, the Turffontein marsh on the south, and on the north the broken, rocky line of the watershed. As a compliment to themselves, since each bore a variant of the same Christian name, the Commission decided to call the new township Johannesburg.

CHAPTER TWO

(1)

THUS the City of Gold was born. . . .

Like that other city of pure gold, in the Revelation of Patmos, it lay four-square, and the length was as large as the breadth. It stood firmly rooted to the core of the Witwatersrand by three slender bands of iron-grey conglomerate with pale pebbles in its matrix: the Main Reef, the South Reef, and the Main Reef leader, diagonally piercing the crust of the continent, slanting downwards to depths that, even today, not all man's mechanical prowess and ingenuity have fathomed – nor, perhaps, shall ever fathom, seeing that their foundations may well be lost in a fiery flux of rocks still molten and seething with the heat of the planet's primal avulsion.

It lay there, that small plot of measured ground, on the open veld, five thousand six hundred feet above sea-level, encompassed by marshy land on three sides and bounded on the fourth by a barren ride: a desert of dust and red earth, on which the shape of the city to come was but vaguely foreshadowed by lines of wooden pegs defining its unmade streets and the central space of the outspan where the converging trails of coaches and carts and wagons off-loaded their burdens – rusty machinery, boilers and galvanized sheets; crockery, furniture, forage and produce – incontinently dumping them there in the dust and the sun.

As yet there were no buildings more permanent than the mud and reed hut called Walker's Hotel; but already the traffic in 'stands' had begun. Corner lots on the pegged enclosures had become gambling counters to be sold and re-sold half a dozen times in a month. Everywhere there were tents. Reaching forth from the congested nucleus of Ferreira's camp, their far-scattered tilts, bleached by the sun, resembled, when seen from a distance, a litter of paper-scraps strewn haphazard, or a flock of white egrets come to rest on the shoals of a sandy estuary.

In these tents, without water or sanitation, dwelt men – three thousand of them, drawn not only from the backwash of

405

Barberton but from Kimberley, from the Cape, from Natal, from the uttermost corners of the earth to which the rumour of easy-won wealth had penetrated. Here were skilled miners from Colorado and Ballarat; Hebrew capitalists from Kimberley; mining engineers from America; builders and blacksmiths, hucksters, panders, saloon-keepers; casual labourers, down-and-outs – every imaginable sort of human riff-raff washed on to that barren ridge like jetsam cast up by the tides.

To these thousands was added an even greater concourse of natives: Malay drivers from Capetown, whose carts plied from one end of the reef to the other at exorbitant fares; Griquas, Hottentots, Cape-coloured folk, and, outnumbering all these, the hordes of raw Kaffirs who, tramping to and from Kimberley, were snatched up like metallic particles by the magnet of Johannesburg and swept, naked, underground – to have their lungs eaten away by sharp crystals of powdered quartz – or flung on the tented streets to rot their bewildered brains with Cape Smoke and *dagga*, or raw potato-spirit laced with tobacco-juice. Sometimes, in the crowded kraals where these were herded, tribal affrays broke out in which black men were killed; and that was a pity – for, even with this vast influx, labour was scarce, and the stamps must be fed and the pockets of their owners filled.

There were high wages (or pickings) for every man, black or white, who had strength to move. Never before in the history of this impoverished pastoral land had money flowed so lavishly, or been of so little value, as that which the mines of the Rand poured forth in their sluggish rivulets of grey-green slime. Money to waste: there was neither time nor care to extract all the gold that the slime contained. When the mercury had been sublimated from the amalgam, the tailings were tipped on the veld in pale pyramids which the summer sun cracked and the summer rains eroded in fissures and channels down which flowed milky torrents carrying with them millions of grains of ungained gold to be lost in the spruits that drained southward into the Vaal. But nobody recked such losses. Quick gain and quick spending was the word in Johannesburg: the gold is there for the taking; let us snatch what we can.

More gold than had ever been dreamt of! For now many miles of the pebbly outcrop had been stripped and the buried reef run to earth in its miraculous continuity. Shafts had been driven and sunk to prove its depth and the yield's consistency;

but no shaft sunk as yet had touched bottom or shown any great variation in values. This was Bonanza, as the Americans said, unfathomable, inexhaustible.

It was difficult to provide sufficient machinery to soothe men's impatience or satisfy their greed. The Cape railway had petered out like a desert stream in the sand-belt surrounding Kimberley; the railway from Natal was still crawling upwards among the Drakensberg foot-hills. Only slow convoys of bullock-wagons, toiling over the veld, hauled the massive loads of engines and stamps from the rail-heads. The mines' demands for machinery exhausted the carrying-capacity of all available transport. And the mines came first. What did it matter if the growing city was starved of everything else it wanted – except, perhaps, liquor – if the prices of foodstuffs and every other commodity soared fantastically? There would be money enough to pay through the nose for everything, if only the miners were given the power to dig and crush their gold. Wages, prices, the hungry mouths of men counted for nothing, provided the stamps were fed.

There were hundreds of these rising and falling now: the batteries filled the air with an incessant clatter and thudding. Primitive wooden headgear and hauling-winches driven by wood-fired steam were hurriedly being erected on every side – not only in the centre of the town from which Colonel Ferreira's canvas camp had been shifted to uncover the gold beneath it, but on every skyline save the rocky ridge to northward. They ringed the remaining horizons until the township was girt by a broken circle of fires that glimmered by night and plumes of white steam that blew away on the wind by day. The gleaming dumps rose beside them: they, too, shone white in the sun; and the surrounding veld was scarred with pits and trenches such as are hurriedly dug about a beleaguered city.

And still Johannesburg grew. . . .

Soon the city of canvas tents and reed huts, the primary stratum in its architectural geology, had well-nigh disappeared, though, here and there, lay remains of it – 'intrusives' (as were the gold-bearing reefs themselves) or 'accidentals' deposited on its growing boundaries in a state of attrition or imperfect disintegration. Where once the tents had been pitched, there arose a secondary formation, composed, more durably, of corrugated-iron structures on frames of wood which, because of their relative permanence, were built facing the rudimentary roads which the surveyors had measured and pegged: so that now the slow teamster, driving his ox-wagon over the veld and viewing the scene from afar, could deduce from the broken lines of dwellings and offices and licensed-traders' stores (every third of which was a drinking-bar) the rectangular plan of the city that was to be.

On the 'stands' between these, or replacing their ruins, there soon rose a third and more solid stratum of buildings with one or two storeys, constructed of bricks sun-dried in the yards on the verge of the market-square or on the farm named Doornfontein, which strengthened the parallel lines of the thoroughfares running south from Bree Street to Commissioner Street and east from West Street to End Street. In the midst of these, again, appeared more ambitious edifices of stone or hard-baked kiln-brick, with double tiers of ornate cast-iron verandas facing the streets: so that now the red dust that the south wind sucked up from the wagon-scarred veld, and the ashen dust it sheared from the dumps of tailings, whirled in clouds through long culverts floored with unmetalled roadway and lined with houses on either side.

The old mining-camp, where scattered men lived to themselves and from hand to mouth, disappeared. There was the Central Hotel, in Commissioner Street, where, at a price, a man could eat well and sleep on an iron bedstead or, at worst, on a billiard-table or on the billiard-room floor when the last game of the night was finished. There were other, humbler hotels – and some less reputable – and numbers of 'ordinaries' where meals could be had, and beer at four shillings a bottle; there were bars, of all shades of propriety, by the dozen, where whisky and gin were even cheaper than beer; there were brothels, to whose contents the Erasmus family contributed, and boxing-booths, where upstanding young fellows like Abe Bailey and Wolff Bendoff and Couper, the champion, could show their skill. There were two fiercely competitive (and sometimes scurrilous) newspapers – the *Diggers' News* and the *Transvaal Mining Argus*, at sixpence a copy. There was little, indeed, that the 'average sensual man' could complain that he lacked.

There were even churches and evangelists: the Anglican, Darragh, sent up from Kimberley to found the church of St. Mary; the Salvationist, Lieutenant Kendrick, in dusty uniform, stalking into the bars and bidding miners to prepare to meet their God or to flee from the wrath to come; the gentle Presbyterian, James Gray, with his mission-bred wife, holding his first service in the unfinished billiard-room of Height's Hotel.

But the principal god Johannesburg worshipped was gold; and the Persons of its trinity those three shelving dikes of banket – the Main Reef, the South Reef, and the Main Reef Leader. Its citizens did their god reverence in the smoke-clouded, clamorous bars; in Paddy Green's saloon, where the mails were delivered, round the tent of 'Cockney Liz', the first white woman and cynosure of the Rand; above all, in the rudimentary stock-exchange, facing the Corner House, where the traffic between Commissioner Street and Market Street was barred by iron chains, and the list of stocks was 'called' at ten o'clock every morning in a pandemonium of buyers and sellers shouting names of mines that are now forgotten: Heriot, Jubilee, Anglo-Tharsis, Moss-Rose, Walsingham, Chimes.

Everybody talked incessantly and dreamed about gold-scrip and bought it and sold it. Within two years there were more than three hundred gold-mining concerns, some sound, some worthless, some merely existing on paper or in their owners' imaginations, offering shares for sale. Men bought, not with any intention of holding their purchases, but for the thrill of a game of chance that was less scientific than poker. High stakes, quick returns were the rule: tomorrow was 'settlement day', and few brokers took the risk of selling gold-scrip 'to arrive', when, within a week, the buyers might well be gone. There was no reason behind the prodigious gamut through which shares would go rocketing one day and crashing the next in a market that had the sensitiveness of a seismograph. The first rumour of substantial values would set them soaring: the faintest whisper of doubts bring them down with a run. Representatives of the great Kimberley houses, handling millions, took part in the scramble with men who worked with picks and drills in the mines. The greater part of the gamblers, no doubt, were ignorant folk who staked all their wages and paid heavily for their ignorance; but the strange thing was that, during those first two years, despite set-backs that made a price-graph resemble the temperature-chart of a typhoid-fever patient, the general tendency of gold-scrip values was upward; for the more the gold was thrown on the market the more money flowed back into Johannesburg for speculation, and nobody in the city dreamed of putting his money into anything but gold.

There was no saying how long the vicious circle would continue to revolve; now that the fame of the Rand was noised abroad, foreign buying, by speculators in London and Paris and New York, who barely knew where the Rand was or what shares they bought, continued to keep it spinning at an even more furious pace. They called the Exchange, not unreasonably, the 'Kaffir Circus'.

What was the cause of this insensate optimism, a few sober minds (and among them Janse's) wondered? Was it the sheer isolation of this new city on the veld, where men thought and talked of nothing but gold, and, literally, breathed it, that restricted the view of eyes already dazzled, and persuaded its inhabitants that nothing else mattered? Was it the sheer potency of the force so suddenly and so surprisingly released that shook their senses; the mere vision of such prodigious growth and wealth that blinded them; the heady fumes of other men's success that inebriated them? Was this euphoria, rather, a physical effect of the sudden transference of men who had been for the most part dwellers in lowland plains to this dizzying altitude where the unaccustomed sun cheered them perpetually and the low pressure of rarefied air, relaxing their arteries, sent the blood running free and flushed their brains? Was there even, perhaps, some novel constituent in the earth of this High Veld, or some power in the radiations diffused from its broken surface, which played on their bodies and tautened their nerves so that they lived in a state of reckless and restless exaltation? Was this spiritual turbulence nothing more than the result of mass-suggestion and mass-hallucination, an epidemic infection caught from the first-comers already fevered by the quick making of millions, or was it an endemic, normally associated with the finding of gold?

These questions were not easily answered; but whatever its causes might be, the disease was universal and raged without intermission. When the stock-exchange was closed, excited brokers gathered 'between the chains', still buying and selling Gold-scrip, good or bad, became a sort of second currency Men carried it about with them in their pockets and paid for drink or women with bearer-certificates – which was a gamble on both sides; but what did that matter in Johannesburg, where all life was a gamble?

Wise men, such as Meninsky, who would not handle the stuff

ade firmer fortunes out of real estate and bricks and mortar: a house that had cost two thousand pounds to build could command a rent of fifty or sixty a month. Transport-drivers reaped such a harvest as had never been known in the best days of Kimberley. Two hundred wagons a day toiled into the market-square, and these were not enough. All the farms in the neighbourhood – even those on which no gold was likely to be found – became valuable possessions. Every scrap of green food that could be grown, every animal that could be reared, was eagerly bought as soon as it reached the market. These were halcyon days for everyone. How long would they last?

(2)

The minds of Meninsky and Janse were not concerned with such remote speculations. With the coming of middle age, Meninsky had acquired an unwonted prudence. Though he still talked extravagantly and could be carried away by his familiar excursions into 'lightning arithmetic', in which, as always, high figures intoxicated him, he was more canny than Janse in the management of their affairs. The farm Sterkfontein, which he had bought from Barend Prinsloo, was 'proclaimed' a few months later than the first four, which had included Langlaagte, but not before Meninsky had satisfied himself as to the line of the reef.

It was fortunate for them that Barend's primitive dwelling-house and farm-buildings, which the Gold Law of the Republic excluded from the land open to be 'pegged' by any citizen who had paid his poll-tax, covered the richest part of it; and Meninsky took care that the *Mijnpacht,* the tenth share reserved for the owner, and the sixty *Vergunnings,* or Preference Claims, which the law allowed him to assign to his friends, should be grouped compactly around this rich area which he had assayed. For the rest, he was not concerned as to how many claims should be pegged by the competing diggers who, on the day appointed, swooped down on the farm like a flight of locusts: he knew that the pick of the farm was his already, and that out of the licence-fee of a pound, payable monthly for every claim of four hundred feet by a hundred and fifty, ten shillings would come back to him and Janse as joint owners, producing an income sufficient for their own claims' development.

411

In this matter, too, he revealed his native shrewdness.

'I'm not going to be in a hurry about it, Janse,' he said. 'The land's ours for keeps now, and nobody else can touch it. If the reef's what I think it is, what I *know* it is, the boom's not begun. The big money isn't moving yet. Beit's in it, I know, and your brother Piet's friend, Rhodes, has formed a company. But Kimberley hasn't quite made up its mind – and, mark my word, as soon as it does it'll lose it. Barney hasn't got going. He's holding off for a bit, waiting for the excitement to cool down, just the same as me; and two can play at that game! When he does decide to come in he'll come in with a rush, and all the Bright Boys will come rushing after him and push up prices. That's the kind of boom I'm looking for! Meanwhile, all we've got to do is to go on steady, stripping the reef that we've traced and noting the values. When the boom's at its height we put Sterkfontein in the shop-window and let them scramble for it. They'll get that excited they won't care a damn what they pay.'

'Sell Sterkfontein?' Janse said. 'Why, we've only just bought it!'

'For a hundred and thirty pound and a couple of middling nags. I shall get eighty thousand for it – or even a hundred.'

'But we've ordered machinery!'

'Oh, an odd thousand here and there for eyewash is nothing to worry about. We've got to have something to show them. If they come along and see nothing's been done, they'll ask why it hasn't; but if they see two poor beggars like you and me unable to work a proved, slap-up propertly like this for want of capital, then every damn one of them will think what a job he could make of it. I know what I'm doing, mate.'

'But we can make money by working it,' Janse protested.

'Now, look here, mate,' Meninsky reproved him, 'the whole trouble with you is, you won't learn. You've forgotten the lesson we got along of old Bosmann, the motto I've made all your money on. The beggar who does the work ain't the one that makes the money. The secret of life is buying cheap and selling dear. We've bought cheap, and when the time comes we're going to sell at the top of the market. Got that clear? I might as well chuck the lot if you haven't! And meanwhiles we'd better be getting along with Wonderfontein. Don't forget you've a share in that, too – or will have, some day.'

Though, during this time, Janse lived with Meninsky in

Barend Prinsloo's house, they both of them spent most of their evenings at Wonderfontein. It was a quiet place now that Maria and Lena had gone to the Cape, and a little melancholy, in spite of Lisbet's bright equanimity.

'Let's run over and cheer them old folks up, mate,' the Peruvian would say – and, indeed, they needed cheering, though they did not always respond to his comical efforts. John Grafton was growing old, even older than his years, and found it difficult to adjust himself to the feverish activity that surrounded him. Without Adrian – who was now involved more deeply than ever in politics, sharing the two Rustenburg seats in the Volksraad with his new leader Paul Kruger – and Piet, engrossed in Rhodes' fight for the amalgamation of the Kimberley mines – he was saddled, single-handed, with the task of managing the farm, and even with that of working it; for the wages extravagantly offered by the mining companies to natives, and the natural gregariousness which lured them into the compounds, had robbed him of his best labour.

Even the wretched Erasmuses, poor workers as they were, found jobs in Johannesburg at rates of pay that were beyond his means, returning to Wonderfontein on Saturdays with insolent hordes of coloured riff-raff who made night hideous with their orgies. If he had been a young man, he would have turned the squatters off his farm; but he had no energy to waste in quarrels or disturbances, and, in spite of all he had spent on it, he saw that Wonderfontein was 'going back', and lamented it, impotently.

'Never you mind, *ou baas*,' Meninsky said. 'Why the hell should it matter to you if the farm goes to blazes? The value lies in what's underground, not what's on the top of it. You just wait till Janse and me have prospected it thoroughly and traced out the reef and settled the part you want to keep for the *mijnpacht*. Then, when it's proclaimed, you'll pick up more than enough to buy yourself twenty farms, and far better than this, if you're so minded. You have nothing to worry about for the rest of your natural now, nor your missus neither. Just think what that ought to signify to a man who's been scraping a living with the sweat of his brow – if you take my meaning!'

John Grafton smiled.

'I take your meaning, Meninsky, but you don't take mine. Money isn't important' (Meninsky gasped at the sacrilege) 'to a man of my age; but Wonderfontein is my home. I've lived here

413

contentedly for more than forty years, since the day when I set up the beacons and Adrian was born, and I'd liever die here, too, than anywhere else. No, no, it is foolish trying to tear up an old tree by the roots even if the soil into which you transplant it is better.'

'Who's talking about old trees?' Meninsky rallied him. 'How old was your missus's dad when he trekked from the Cape with Retief?'

'That was a different matter, Meninsky. The Prinsloos were discontented and seeking their freedom and ready to suffer for it. But here I am free and contented. They were wanderers, too, by nature. All Boers are wanderers: their homes are their wagons. We English are bound to the soil and put down deep roots. My home is here. Even if the farm is proclaimed and I grow to be rich, I shall stay at Wonderfontein.'

'Well, there's no harm in growing rich, anyway,' Meninsky said, 'particularly if you happen to be a family man; and whether you stay here or no, Janse and me are going to see that you get your dues.'

They prospected Wonderfontein systematically and traced the reef and stripped it. Janse himself did most of the work, for which, by now, he was well qualified, and discovered that the values were not inferior to those they had assayed on Sterk fontein. He even found time to give his father a hand on the farm. Though he couldn't help feeling, with Meninsky, that this was a waste of labour, he performed it willingly; for the High Veld air and its freedom from fever had restored the health and strength he had lost in his wanderings. It was also a labour of love; since now that he spent more time in his father's company he found him no longer the aloof, restrained, and rather for bidding figure he had known in his boyhood, but a shy, gentle man, much softened by age, and more simple than he had ima gined, whose sweet nature no less than his frailness appealed to his sympathy. He began, as never before, to realize the cause of his mother's devotion and tenderness.

Yet life in those days seemed oddly silent and lonely at Won derfontein. Janse missed Maria; he missed Lena even more. Not that the distance between him and them seemed so form idable as it would have been before. Letters came, by rail and coach, from the Cape to Paddy Green's post-office in Johannes burg in less than a week, and Maria wrote regularly. Her news was encouraging, though the surroundings from which i came were hard for him to visualize. She herself was enraptured with the soft air and the loveliness of the Peninsula: the eastward face of the mountain, dark with firs or shimmering with silver-trees; the hot richness of vineyards, green in the cup of Constantia and Tokai; the sands of False Bay which were white as the surf that came charging in on them, line after line, out of the Indian Ocean; the beauty of the gabled homesteads set in shady oak-woods, with their stylized eighteenth-century graces and their musical names – Vergelegen, Meerlust, Paarl Vallei, Morgenster: a world almost incredibly remote from the bare and wind-swept Witwatersrand.

'I think England must be green like this,' she wrote, innocently; and Janse, reading the words, shook his head, for he knew where her thoughts were taking her.

Yet there seemed to be sufficient distractions in Capetown to keep her mind from broodings in that direction. Major Haskard, naturally, knew all the best Capetown Society, and was proud, as well as pleased, to take her about with him. There were plenty of parties and picnics and admiring young men in the naval base at Simonstown, and rides over the sandy flats and under the crags of the Mountain, and shopping-expeditions with Lavinia to Capetown, where all the luxuries of the world were displayed behind plate-glass windows. She mentioned one or two of the young men by name – they were all of them sailors – but betrayed no preference. One encounter had evidently impressed her. Outside the House of Assembly, with Piet, who had run down for a short visit from Kimberley, she had met his friend Mr. Rhodes, who, people said, would some day be Prime Minister. She had shown him her ring (this was the first time she had ever mentioned it to Janse: that seemed a good sign) and he had laughed at her and told her the stone had a flaw in it and wasn't a good one. The interview had been short, and apparently awkward.

'I should never have known him but for his voice,' she wrote. 'He's not lanky, as I remembered him, but a big, fat man – not exactly fat, but coarse and, compared with the men you meet here, really dreadfully untidy. Piet says he's a woman-hater; and I can quite believe it, though men seem to like him. Piet, of course, is quite gone on him. (That's the latest "slang", which doesn't mean "snake" by the way!)'

As for Lena, she told him, the child had settled down splendidly and seemed to be perfectly contented. (Janse felt a

415

slight pang at this fickleness.) She was going to school every day with Piet's elder children, Jimmy and Cecilia. The school-mistress said she was sharp as a needle, and that the fact that she knew practically nothing but what Maria had taught her was not really a disadvantage, because it made her anxious to catch up with the other children.

'She's shot up like a growing mealie-stalk,' Maria wrote, 'and is going to be disturbingly pretty in a year or two when she's got over the awkward stage, with those great violet eyes of hers – so like Lavinia's, and yet so much more lively. She really is an odd little creature, Janse. Of course, she's attached to me (I think), though that's probably for your sake; and she's quite *polite* – her manners just now are almost too good – to Lavinia. But I really think she's rather like Mr. Rhodes: she doesn't like women; and even with men she's discriminating. I mean, she clearly adores Major Haskard – though *he* "has a way wid' him": don't I just know it! But I don't think she likes Piet very much – which, of course, is a shame and ridiculous – and she shows it, which makes it far worse. Her chief passion is for Jimmy – or James, as we've now got to call him – and I can't really blame her. He's such a nice, generous boy, Janse, with a lot of Piet's charm and frankness and occasionally a look that reminds me of you, which may be why she's so "gone on" him. (I must really get out of using that phrase; but it's catching: a sub-lieutenant told me he was "gone on" *me* yesterday!) I'm afraid there'll be the "divil and all to pay" – as the Major says – when James is packed off to England next month. I didn't tell you, I think, that Mr. Rhodes has taken a fancy to him and has insisted on Piet sending him what he calls "home" to a school where his brother Frank was, called Eton, I think. Piet protests that he can't afford it, but Major Haskard has come to the rescue, so now it's all settled. As Piet says, if Mr. Rhodes insists on a thing, it's got to be done. He gave Jimmy two sov-ereigns the other day, and Jimmy gave one to Lena. I asked her what she was going to do with it, and she said: "Buy a present for Jimmy." So you see how it is! The child is so serious and intense in her passions that I really think I shall have to stay at the Cape until after Jimmy has sailed and smooth over the parting, although it's high time I came home – for my own sake and darling mother's and everyone else's. I shall probably wait till Piet comes down again and travel up with him. He and Major Haskard are awfully excited at the moment (as they

416

always are) about money and shares and things. Mr. Rhodes is winning his great fight over Amalgamation – whatever that is, I'm simply tired of the word – and they're going to make their fortunes. The latest idea is gold on their farms. They're getting a Mr. Bite (what a name!) to look into it. I hardly dare come back home when I think how my lovely Witwatersrand (yes, I *do* love it best of all) will be changed . . .'

Well, thank heaven Maria was so happy, or sounded so happy, Janse thought. Her news of Lena amused him. He quoted the words that described her 'passions' to Meninsky.

'You may laugh, mate,' Meninsky said; 'but don't forget what I told you. If you had to adopt a kid, you'd ought to have chosen a boy. Before many years are gone – mark my words – you'll be in for a pack of trouble with that little monkey.'

Janse told him what Maria had said about Alfred Beit's interest in Witfontein.

'That's good news for all of us,' Meninsky said seriously. 'There's big money there. And don't forget that Haskard's farm and Witfontein are next to Wonderfontein and that Wonderfontein's next to our little bit. Four farms on the reef in a line! That's property, mate, and no mistake. I've a damn good mind to drop a line to Barney.'

'If Beit's after it why should you do that?'

Meninsky exploded: 'My god! They say fools must be reared. To get them bidding against one another and run up the price, you poor simpleton!'

'I only heard about Beit in a private letter.'

Meninsky shook his head pityingly.

'And what the devil has that got to do with it?' he said.

(3)

Although Lisbet missed Maria, she did not complain of her daughter's long absence at the Cape; she welcomed, indeed, any change of surroundings or unusual activity that might divert the child's mind from her secret tragedy. She missed Piet, of course, too, but could set against the loss of him the unexpected return of Janse – a happier, serener Janse than she had ever known – and her growing pride in Piet's success. It pleased her to know that her youngest son, whom she still regarded as a child, had established his reputation as one of the 'coming men' in South African industry and finance. What hurt her more, because she could not understand it, was her almost complete separation from Adrian who, up to the time of his marriage, had been his father's right hand, his natural successor, and a tower of strength and reason in every emergency.

Since the night when he had called in on his way to Heidelberg to retrieve President Burgers' flag, she had hardly set eyes on Adrian and knew little of his activities save what she gleaned at the quarterly Nachtmaal from Suzanna's brother, the Predikant, Carel Strijdom, that hot young man whom she could never accept as a suitable substitute for Mr. Blair. It was from him – not from Adrian – that she had learnt of the birth of Suzanna's babies, no less than five of them in quick succession. It seemed strange to her that a man with such a strong sense of family tradition as Adrian should not have brought his children to see and be seen by their grandparents. This was not like Adrian, she told herself, unless he had changed. She supposed that the powerful influence of Suzanna had changed him – as, indeed, it had.

The only occasion on which he had stayed at Wonderfontein was on the day, at the height of the Johannesburg boom, when the farm, proclaimed a few weeks before together with Witfontein and Brakfontein, had been thrown open to 'claim-pegging'. Adrian's visit had been a godsend: it was a great comfort to feel that she and her husband were protected by the presence of a strong man set in authority, from the violent hordes which streamed out from the Mining Commissioner's office in Johannesburg and swarmed, cursing and fighting, over the whole of the farm.

The events of that day had resembled a nightmare for other reasons. An hour after Adrian's arrival, Piet, too, had turned up, brimming with confidence and good humour. As he appeared in the dooryway, smiling, she had seen him catch sight of Adrian. She had watched that smile fade from his lips and the gay words of greeting die on his tongue. She knew that he and Adrian had never been friends, but the mingled alarm and repugnance she saw on Piet's face were beyond her comprehension, and Adrian, though more composed, seemed no better pleased by the meeting.

As usual, she had tried to smooth away this mysterious, bristling hostility.

'This is a great day for me, father,' she said, 'when we have three of our sons together. If only Andries were here too!'

Janse greeted Piet, but Adrian only stared at him. Never before had the contrast between her two sons appeared to Lisbet so full of boding: Adrian, shaggy, massively-built and severe, his roughly-clothed, bearded figure overtopping Piet's by a head as they faced one another; Piet spick and span from his close-cropped hair and clean-shaven face to his well-cut cord breeches and polished leggings. Piet was the first to recover from their mutual embarrassment.

'Hellow, Adrian, old fellow,' he said, 'it's a long time since we've met.'

Lisbet thought how frank and friendly he looked as he held out his hand. Adrian did not take it.

'Not since the Majuba,' he answered slowly in Dutch.

'But that is a long time ago,' Piet laughed uneasily.

'Not so long but that I remember it,' Adrian said, in Dutch again.

'But neither of you ever told me you'd met,' Lisbet put in desperately. 'And after all, as Piet says, that's a long time ago, Adrian. Are we not at peace now, my sons, and all our quarrels forgotten? Under this roof, where both of you were born, there should be no divisions between you. It is not kind to me.'

Adrian put his arm round her and kissed her.

'There are some things a man can neither forget nor forgive, mother. I will go away – that is better – and come back later.'

He put on his wide-brimmed slouch-hat and walked out, passing Piet on his way but not looking at him.

'Adrian ... Adrian!' Lisbet cried after him, reproachfully. But he did not turn back. 'Piet, what does this mean?' she asked.

Piet laughed. 'You know what it means, mother. You say we're at peace; but that will never be true as long as men like Adrian and Paul Kruger are living. They've got what they said they wanted: their independence. They've got far more than that now. Their state was bankrupt, and now it's rich. And who's made it rich? Who discovered this gold and brought money and brains to develop it? The English, the Jews, and the loyal Afrikanders from Natal and the Cape! Can you tell me the name of a single Boer in Paul Kruger's set who has contributed a thought or a penny to their prosperity? Are they grateful to us for saving their damned Republic? Not a bit: they resent all intiative and try to frustrate it because they have none themselves. They bleed the gold-mining industry gladly enough without any compunctions. Do you know what the revenue of the Republic was sixty years ago? Sixty-three thousand pounds. Do you know what it will be this year? Over three-quarters of a million! That's pretty good blood-letting! And while they bleed the mining industry, they starve it – by selling monopolies and pocketing the bribes they get for them; by piling on duties against everything the mines need to keep them alive; by refusing to let any railway that brings goods from a British port even enter the country. Kruger's cutting his own great nose off to spite his face – let him do it: I don't mind that – but he's also doing his best to kill the Witwatersrand, which is the only part of his wretched Republic that has any life in it. Out of sheer bitter obstinacy. And Adrian, like a damned fool, follows him. Until Kruger and everything that he stands for is broken, I say, there'll be no peace or freedom or decency in this country. And he will be broken, mother. You can take my word for it.'

Lisbet shuddered. 'By another war, Piet?'

'The last one was not a war. It was stopped, thanks to Gladstone, almost before it had begun. That scuttle is what we're paying for now.'

'I cannot bear the thought of another war,' Lisbet said.

'Well, perhaps it won't come to that. There may be a revolution without any bloodshed. It is a matter of figures. Even now the newcomers hold a majority of the wealth of the country. If Johannesburg goes on growing as it's growing now, they'll soon outnumber the old inhabitants and want a share in the government; and if Kruger denies them that, they're going to take it – by force, if necessary.'

'I hope I may not live to see that,' Lisbet said.

'There's no need for you to see it, mother. If the syndicate that's interested in my farm and Haskard's buys Wonderfontein as well, as it will probably want to, you'll have enough money to live wherever you like.'

'Your father will never leave Wonderfontein.'

'But that's quite ridiculous. You can't sell it without the *mijnpacht,* in the middle of which the house stands. That's probably worth sixty thousand pounds by itself.'

'It's worth more than that to me, Piet,' John Grafton said, 'if I can be left in peace.'

'But you won't be left in peace, father, if you stay here.'

Tomorrow they'll have the right to peg claims within a few hundred yards of the house. Half a dozen, a dozen mines may spring up on these claims. You can't go on farming in the middle of them, with dumps and batteries all round you – quite apart from the fantastic folly and waste of leaving the best part of your reef undeveloped.'

'Is this *mijnpacht* mine, Piet, or isn't it?' John Grafton said.

'Of course it's yours. But we all have an interest in it – Maria, myself and the other three boys – and I think it's only right we should be considered,' Piet went on hotly.

'Dead men's shoes, my boy? I'm not ready to die just yet. But when the time comes, I mean to die and be buried at Wonderfontein.'

'It's no use your saying any more about this,' Lisbet said quietly. 'Your father has made up his mind, Piet, and we must abide by it. It would break my heart, too, to leave Wonderfontein, where we'd lived so long and so happily and all my babies have been born.'

'The point is that it won't be Wonderfontein any more, mother,' Piet answered angrily.

He confided his grievances to Rhodes when he got back to Kimberley. Rhodes was amused but not moved by them.

'One can understand how the old man feels,' he said; 'one respects him for it. One has to respect a man who has love for the land: it's a very English motive and deep in the blood of all of us. I feel it myself. The Dutch haven't got it in quite the same way. They like land, of course, but they like it *qua* grazing; they haven't a feeling for it, a sense of attachment for any particular place. They're willing to sell their farms on the Rand not so much because of the money they get – they don't know what to do with it – as because they like solitude and room to breathe in. They're a race of claustrophobics. I can sympathize with that too. I want room to move and breathe in! (Prophetic words!) In fact, if one hadn't been forced to become a tradesman, for reasons outside oneself, I'd have preferred to be a farmer myself – like my grandfather who kept cows on the outskirts of London. You never knew that before, Grafton, did you?' He laughed his shrill laugh. 'However, there's not time for everything. Time's always been my enemy, and always will be.'

So much to do. . . . Even as his big body had reached an early maturity – nobody looking at this man who was still under forty would have given him less than fifty – so his mind, by nature ponderous for all its wide range, had lately attained the utmost height of its power and clarity. The schemes he had hammered out in solitude or as he talked with his chosen friends, were reaching their final shape; his life-work was planned.

First, the diamond-fields, which had given him what he called calculable 'power': he had won his fight with Barnato's quick wits and 'dealt with him'; the Amalgamation of all the big interests was on the way – as for the small ones, now the devil could take the hindmost! Next the gold-fields: it was true that he had made a late start (as had also Barnato) and had thrown away his best opportunities when he bolted from Ferreira's camp to Pickering's death-bed, leaving a welter of lapsed options behind him; but he had founded the Goldfields Company, from which wealth, however incalculable, was already providing him with more of the power he needed. And then, Parliament: that was a business less to his liking, for he knew he was no orator; the people at the Cape were instinctively jealous of Kimberley, and would be even more jealous of the Rand; even the English-speaking folk, on whom he felt he should have been able to count, were suspicious of capitalists, hidebound in their racial prejudices; he had aroused double suspicions by his alliance with Jan Hofmeyr and the Bond.

Not that that mattered to him: he had always been convinced that the greater South Africa on which his mind was set could never be created without the help of the Dutch majority, that all civilized men, irrespective of race, should have the right and the glory of sharing in it. He could subscribe to every tenet (but one) of the Bond's doctrine of 'Africa for the Afrikander'. That one exception, the question of the flag, could be 'dealt with', like everything else, later on, when the accomplished fact of a greater South Africa was presented to them. Self-interest, the strongest of all human motives, would then come into play and convince the Bond that a small people could not control a continent and hold it without the backing of one of the great maritime powers – of which the most enlightened, the strongest and the most generous was surely the British Empire. That was the only way, his bitter experience with Warren had taught him, in which the Imperial Factor should be allowed a place in his schemes. And what weak man could reject the protection of the strongest? As Prime Minister of the Cape Colony – it was all very well for the doctor to snigger – and with the Bond behind him, the end of his plans was in sight.

There was only one obstacle in the way of their realization: Paul Kruger – the one man whom, in all his swift triumphs, he had been unable to 'deal with', as he had dealt with the wily Barnato, the secretive Hofmeyr and Groot Adrian Delarey roaring out 'Blood must flow' up in Stellaland. One had settled that part of the business, though hardly in the way one would have wished. Bechuanaland, the Road to the North, the Neck of the Bottle, had been saved. It was under British protection. But what of the North itself? Kruger had his eye on it: that solid block of claims from the Vaal to the Zambezi. If Kruger got the North, reinforced by the gold that was flowing into his treasury from the Rand, he would command what the British wanted – trade, and what the Dutch wanted – land; the Transvaal would become the predominant state in South Africa; he could force the rest of South Africa into Amalgamation, Federation, on his own terms – as parts of an expanded Republic under the Vierkleur, a Dutch Republic. He could practically compel them to come in by shutting them off from the North with a series of tariff barriers. Already the gold from the Rand was enabling him to revive the railway from Delagoa. It was the shortest route to the gold-fields. All their trade would pass over it. It would make the Transvaal independent of the Cape, of the British Empire. If he held that as well as the North, he could snap his fingers at everybody. And now the Germans were coming in from the west coast to join up with him. Therefore, one must take the North.

Night after night, during Rhodes' flying visits to Kimberley, Piet heard the same arguments built up to the same violent climax, and watched Jameson slyly provoking his friend to greater vehemence. It was not only a matter of talk: Rhodes' words, as he knew, had a way of materializing. As he had told Piet on the day they met Kruger at Fourteen Streams, he had sent Charlie Rudd scouting to Matabeleland, and he and the missionary, Moffat, between them, had extracted a sort of treaty from Lobengula, in which the chief had agreed to refuse the entry of any foreign power into his country. One had secured, in short, an option. But, if Kruger moved, could the British Government be trusted to take up that option? *This* Government – with the record of the Majuba behind it? Would the Cape Government give a hand? Would Hofmeyr and the

Bond, who held the balance of power, do anything to restrain their dear cousins in the Transvaal from wiping the British eye? Why, they were so anxious to please Kruger that they wouldn't even push their own railway forward to the Transvaal! No, no. Something much more definite than an option was needed! But what? The strongest of all political arguments: the accomplished fact. And how best to accomplish the fact?

The answer was battered out slowly by the busy hammers of his brain in thought and in talk. When it had taken shape, he was all resolution. There was nothing original about this shape, he explained: it was based on the solid foundations of historical example.

'You fellows don't read enough history,' he reproved them. 'An intelligent chap like you, doctor . . .'

'Too many damned confinements!'

'But you know what the East India Company was? The beginnings of the Indian Empire. Clive went to India because there was trade there already. A great man, Clive! We go to the North because there is gold: the trade will come after. It's no new idea settling a country by joint-stock enterprise. There are several chartered companies in existence already: the Niger Company, the Imperial East Africa Company, and the African Lakes Company. And the Germans are working on the same lines: Lüderitz call his concern the German Colonial Company, and Bismarck's behind him. I'm tired of this mapping-out of Africa in Berlin. It's our map, not theirs. Very well, what we want is a company of our own with a royal charter, and I'm going to London to get one. I shall find more imagination there in a week than in a year at the Cape.'

'You'll want cash as well as imagination,' Jameson said.

'Well, I'll give the people at home a chance to subscribe. If they won't I'll get de Beers and the Goldfields to back me and do the rest myself. I know Beit will come in with me. De Beers alone can put up a quarter of a million. One will get the charter all right: there's no fear as to that; but while one's away awkward things may happen, particularly after the newspapers tumble to what's going on and start blathering about it. The North will be full of fellows trying to jump my claim. Concession-hunters, like Maund; possibly Kruger himself. And that won't do. One will have to take precautions. One will have to keep Lobengula on ice until one gets back.'

'You've got two men up north at the moment, smart fellows both of them. What's wrong with Rochfort Maguire? Very much in your style. All the best men come out of Oxford, I understand,' Jameson added venomously.

Rhodes flushed and laughed: he could always take Jameson's jokes.

'In my style, perhaps; but not quite in Lobengula's. It's a far cry from the high table at All Souls' to Matabeleland. I agree he's a first-class man, all the same.'

'Well, Thompson, then?'

'Yes, I admit he's a good fellow, too. I've nothing to say against him or Maguire *qua* individuals. But they both need a rest, doctor; they're stale; they've been there too long to act quickly if trouble comes up. Maguire's got a fine brain, and Thompson's a man of courage; but Thompson will never forget seeing his father with a ram-rod pushed down his throat, and I can't say I blame him. No, I want Lobengula kept sweet until I return, and I know who I want to do it. You and Grafton here are the men for the job.'

Jameson laughed: 'Good God, man, what are you talking about? I've got my practice!'

'All work and no play. It's time you took a holiday. You can get in a partner. It'd be the making of you, doctor. You need a rest.'

'Like Rochfort Maguire and Thompson! You want me to throw up the best practice in Kimberley for the chance of getting an assegai in my guts.'

'Well, you've always been a gambler: you can't deny that. And this isn't a gamble. When the job's over you can go back to your damned practice if you like: I'll admit you're not a bad doctor. But here you've the chance of a lifetime. You'll make more in six months than you could make in a year rolling pills in Kimberley. I'll see that you come in on the ground-floor with a large allotment.' His tone changed: 'But, after all, the money is nothing. This is a job that's got to be done: we've got to get hold of the North; we've got to queer Kruger's pitch and stop him expanding. You're an Englishman, doctor. . . .'

'Be damned if I am!'

'Well, a Scotsman. What's the difference? You're not a Mackenzie, anyway. It's your duty – that's how I put it – your duty to see that the whole of South Africa isn't lost to the British Empire.' He turned on Piet suddenly. 'What about you,

Grafton? It's time a good Afrikander taught this mercenary fellow a lesson.'

Piet hesitated – not doubting the answer he would give but how he should give it. He had an enormous respect for Rhodes as a man, and believed in him. He agreed with every word of Rhodes' argument – the logical developments of the thesis which had begun ten years before amid the smoke and din of the Twelve Apostles' shanty. He knew that Rhodes, kind and generous as he was as a friend, was a bad man to cross. If the challenge had been thrown at him only a few years earlier, when he was still dependent on Rhodes, he could not have evaded it. But he was now a rich man: the owner of one farm and heir to another on the Witwatersrand, and Rhodes' offer of an allotment in the new Chartered Company seemed less tempting when he remembered the ram-rod which had been thrust down Thompson's father's throat.

'I shall have to think about this, Rhodes,' he said. 'I'm not a bachelor like you and the doctor: I've a wife and four children, and another one on the way. And I can't get in a partner, as you suggested to Jameson. I've my own *mijnpacht* to develop at Witfontein and my father-in-law's alongside it. Haskard's not a young man any longer, and all his affairs are in my hands. You see . . .'

'Yes, I see,' Rhodes broke in contemptuously, '*I have married a rich father-in-law, and therefore cannot come.*'

'But I'll think it over, you know, and discuss it with Haskard.'

Rhodes looked him full in the face with those blue, imperious eyes, and smiled, without speaking. The smile and the look were enough. Jameson screwed up his elfish eyes and was also smiling through his screen of cigarette-smoke.

'Look here, Rhodes,' he said, 'I've been thinking it over, too. You needn't smile: 'I'm perfectly serious. I'd like to see Lobengula – they tell me he suffers from the gout. I doubt a judicious exhibition of colchicum might even be more efficacious in extending the British Empire than an Oxford accent. When d'you want me to start?'

Rhodes slapped him on the back: 'Tomorrow, my boy, tomorrow.'

So they parted. Jameson went north to ease Lobengula's gout with his magical colchicum, and Rhodes, without waiting for the result of Piet's 'thinking it over', returned to the Cape on his way to England in search of his royal charter.

That was now an easier task than it would have been a few years before. He arrived in London, with all the prestige of a multi-millionaire, at the height of the first boom in 'Kaffir's', at a time when the City's eyes were turned on South Africa. He held all the best cards: the self-confidence which success had given him; Germany's threat to join in the Colonial scramble, and Kruger's determination to profit by it; his own boundless resources, by which, as he tactfully hinted, Her Majesty's Government would be relieved of immediate expenditure, and the assurance that if his petition for the charter were refused, he was prepared to go forward without it. In the composition of his Board of Directors he showed equal shrewdness (he had not fought with Barney for nothing!) by giving seats on it to one prominent – and noble – member of each of the great political parties, and making sure of the Irish vote, which might hold the balance of power, by a gift of ten thousand pounds to its leader, Parnell. Even his old nuisance Mackenzie and the Aborigines' Protection Society were placated by an undertaking to regulate the liquor traffic in the new territories and not to interfere with missionary activities. When he had got what he wanted and said good-bye to the Prime Minister, asking, in confidence, how much land he should take, Lord Salisbury replied: 'Take all you can get, Mr. Rhodes, and ask me afterwards.'

It was a famous victory, won only just in time. While he was on the sea, returning to Capetown with its spoils, the mines on the Rand struck a zone of pyrites and the market broke; but though he lost heavily, Rhodes did not care: he still had his diamonds behind him. He sent his Pioneers, English and Dutch, and his newly-raised Mounted Police, a thousand strong, to skirt Lobengula's country and occupy all Mashonaland up to the Zambezi. There they ran up the flag at Mount Hampden, overlooking the site of Salisbury, the new capital of Charterland, soon to be known as Rhodesia.

Without the support of Hofmeyr and the Bond, Rhodes could have done none of these things.

'Well, you have had your way,' Jan Hofmeyr said. 'Now I hope you'll let us down lightly.'

'Let you down lightly? Nothing of the sort!' Rhodes declared, 'I mean to take you with me.'

CHAPTER THREE

(1)

MARIA came back alone from the Cape to Wonderfontein after a series of harrowing scenes with Lena over Jimmy's departure to England. At first the child appeared to be inconsolable. She felt the loss of Jimmy (as she felt everything else that involved her affections) so intensely that Maria hardly knew what to do with her. She was glad she had stayed at the Cape to tide over the break; for Lavinia was far too deeply engrossed in the cares of her own growing family to have much sympathy left for this passionate little stranger. Her nature, in any case, was so coldly unresponsive and – apart from a steadfast devotion to Piet and a tigerish instinct of protection for her own children – so incapable of expressing the generous emotions she may, quite possibly, have felt, that Lena had never given her heart to her.

Two months passed, indeed, before Maria felt she could leave her; and even then Lena's principal interest in life was centred on the long letters she wrote every week to Jimmy in England. Maria took it as the highest of compliments that Lena showed these letters to her and to nobody else. Beneath their childish phrasing she recognized a passionate single-mindedness which she could understand, though they made her feel very old and cold and lifeless.

Though she had often been homesick at the Cape and knew her mother needed her during this crucial period, she found it hard to adapt herself to the changed conditions at Wonderfontein. The *mijnpacht* in the middle of which the farm stood was now encircled by a deep zone of mining activity. On the west, the Sterkfontein reef was rapidly being developed; on the east, at Witfontein, the Beit syndicate were already sinking shafts; on the north the dense nucleus of Johannesburg thrust out tentacles of brick and galvanized iron in every direction. This was no longer the Wonderfontein she had known and loved. It had lost its great lonely vistas of veld. It had lost its

428

peace, its sweet silences. She felt not merely homeless amid the familiar surroundings and faces of home, but disorientated and imprisoned. It seemed to her that the most stable thing in her life, that plot of ground hallowed by so many memories, had been despoiled and taken away from her. The loss was bewildering and irreparable.

Wonderfontein, in fact, was now the only farm on the line of the central reef still occupied by its original inhabitants. Piet had long since abandoned Witfontein and was building himself a luxurious new home on the Doornfontein estate, which was rapidly becoming a fashionable suburb. Meninsky and Janse, having played off the Barnato group against the Beit Syndicate, had sold their *mijnpacht* for an enormous sum and left Sterkfontein. Though Janse still remained faithful to his parents, he rarely found time to visit Wonderfontein now. In partnership with Meninsky, he was investing his new capital in real estate: building-sites; corner-stands on the fringe of the growing city where roads were still unmade; a plot on the east of the Market Square where, beneath a cluster of tin shanties, Meninsky's sharp eyes had discovered a passable clay for brick-making. They had an office in Pritchard Street, behind which they lived; but Janse, with an eye on Lena's return, was already planning a modest house in Doornfontein, not far from Piet's new mansion.

There was hardly any limit to the scope of the Peruvian's diverse activities. He had so many irons in the fire that Janse, his partner, abandoned all hope of keeping count of them; for no sooner was one hot for the anvil than it was discarded (though never at a loss) and another thrust in. How Meninsky contrived to know where he stood at any given moment was a mystery; the accounts he kept were sketchy and generally chaotic. Yet somehow or other, their joint fortune steadily increased under his apparent mismanagement. He still clung to his two golden rules; to have nothing to do with gold-scrip, and to use his own powers of mystical divination in buying everything cheap and selling it at a profit, no matter how small.

'Do you mind my telling you long ago, Janse,' he said, 'as it was the first ten thousand that counted and was hardest to come by? Well, look at us now! At this rate we'll soon be talking about the first quarter of a million, and that's only a beginning It's funny to think of all them poor beggars crowding black as flies round the stock exchange over the way there, thinking about nothing but gold-shares, on the top of the sky one morning and ruined the next, when if they'd the sense to ease off and look round for a moment they could pick up just as much without moving an inch and, what's more, without any risk. They may win or lose, but it makes no difference to us. All the money that's won or lost, or the best part of it, stays here in Johannesburg. You've only to stay quiet and open your pockets, and in it drops.'

'Just so long as the gold lasts,' Janse said.

'It's going to last our time, mate; and that's all that matters to me. Why, Janse, the reef's barely scratched yet. Them that said it was nothing but a shallow river-deposit have got the right answer already. No shaft that's been sunk so far has ever bottomed it. That's the reason why Barnery Barnato's come in so strong. He knows when he's on a good thing: you may take that for gospel. And the one thing in the world I'm prepared to gamble on is old Barney's luck. Yes, I'd bet you ten thousand pounds to a farthing, and take no risk, that before twenty years are gone, there'll be a quarter of a million people living on the Rand. And where are they going to live, mate? Where the whole business started: Johannesburg. Nobody's likely to build a new city when there's an old one at hand. If you chose to buy land and sit tight while the values go up, you could be certain of touching that million we talk about in twenty years' time. But I can't sit tight and do nothing. I like to see money on the move. And it's moving faster and faster.'

It was moving rather too fast.

As the deep shafts drove down they struck water. In a little time men were working up to their waists in it. This, of course, was a common experience in all mining ventures; it had been met, and faced, and dealt with at Kimberley. When the earliest rumours of the check reached Meninsky, he hurried down to the diamond-fields, bought every available piece of pumping-machinery, chartered transport-wagons, dragged back his purchases in triumph to the Witwatersrand, and re-sold them at profits which even he found fantastic.

But this inundation was a slight blow compared with the ill that succeeded it. On the deeper levels the character of the reef suddenly changed. It became pyritic; and, with the admixture of pyrites, the extraction of metal from even the richest ores became difficult. Though amalgamated plates took up the free

430

gold as well as ever, every grain of gold contained in the pyrites escaped.

For this second ill there was no known remedy. Panic seized the Rand. The share-market crashed, and small men who had flattered themselves on the possession of paper-fortunes became penniless in a night – not only penniless but also out of work and hopeless of finding any. Within a few months, a third of the shops in Johannesburg had put up their shutters; a third of the newly-built houses had been abandoned. The Market Square was cluttered with furniture and pianos, thrown out hurriedly for a quick sale, which nobody would buy. The population which had ridden on the mounting wave of the Rand's prosperity made bonfires of their belongings (including their gold-scrip), then took to flight and scattered, stampeding back towards Kimberley – which had troubles enough of its own – and Natal, and the Cape. The firm of Grafton and Meninsky found themselves left with acres of unsaleable land.

Meninsky took the reverse philosophically.

'Well, I reckon things like that are all in the game. It was a good thing I raked in so much on the pumping-machinery. Do you know, mate, I've a damned good mind to buy it back?'

Janse laughed at him. 'Going in for the scrap-iron business?'

'Not so much of your scrap-iron! I look at it this way, Janse. There's still miles of outcrop that hasn't been worked in the hands of small companies. They can all go on developing that, and 'll have to, to satisfy their shareholders. Of course, like the rest, they may come to pyrites in the end; but before they've used all the payable reef they'll strike water – and that's where my scrap-iron comes in. A man must pick up what he can in bad times like these, mate.'

'I shall have to put off building my house,' Janse said.

'Put off building be jiggered! You've got to live somewhere, ain't you? And you're still a rich man. What with the building-trade slackening off as it is, any contractor 'ld jump at the job, and you'll get it done cheaper than when things was booming. You go ahead! And I'll tell you summat else, Janse, about this pyrites. Do you think that all these big guns like Barney and Wernher and Beit, with the whole investing public behind them and millions to play with, are going to sit down and do nothing about it when they know all the gold is there? Not likely! I don't mind betting they've got chemists at work. If it cost them a million pound to get round this bit of trouble, it'd be cheap at the price. Before long – mark my word – they'll find out how to get all their values out of pyritic ore. When they've found it, they naturally won't let on – and I, for one, won't blame them. But I shall know, all the same. When I see the big houses beginning to buy up gold shares on the quiet, then I shall know it's kiss me good-bye to the ruddy pyrites – and perhaps I shall break my rule and have a flutter in gold-scrip myself unless you stop me. And then, mate, make no mistake, you and me will come into our own. If once they scotch the pyrites, there's nothing in heaven and earth that can stop Johannesburg.'

Janse smiled at the little man's indomitable spirit: he was as young, as invincibly hopeful in mind today as he had been in their darkest hours at Brunner's Spruit. For all that, their troubles were not over. On the top of the blow the pyrites had dealt them there fell another: the Great Drought.

No such drought had ever been known in the Transvaal, and famine and thirst stalked after it – not only because the green crops withered before they had fruited, but also because the wagons which brought in the food on which Johannesburg lived stood marooned on the bone-dry veld, with the oxen and mules that hauled them lying dead of thirst in their tracks. Wells shrank and dried up; there was no water left in the spruits, little water even in the city – save the foul, unwanted water that drowned the abandoned mineshafts and galleries. The supply of provisions sank to the level of starvation; the prices of the diminished food-stocks rose to five times their normal level: five pounds for a bag of mealie-meal, five shillings for a pound of sugar – and how could the haggard men, out of work and already barely able to subsist, face these?

It was the fault of the Government, they said, the fault of that sullen, obstinate man Paul Kruger, who sat smoking complacently on his stoep in Pretoria, refusing to give the Rand the railways it needed to keep it alive: a man who thought only of his own people and hated from the bottom of his soul the outlanders, who had already made his bankrupt state rich.

But Kruger's own people were suffering only a little less than the folk in Johannesburg: their crops were desiccated, their flocks and herds dying of thirst. Even at Wonderfontein, the abundant spring which had given the place its name was beginning to fail, and the remains of John Grafton's stock grew parched and wan for lack of water. From the mines which had sprung up on the farm outside the *mijnpacht*, long trails of men carrying buckets and paraffin-tins came every day to beg for the precious liquid. There would soon be trouble, they said, among the natives in the compounds. Johannesburg itself, already cowed and depressed, had been stung by starvation into a dangerous restlessness. Food-shops had been broken into and pillaged, suspected food-hoarders attacked and beaten in the streets. There was even talk of making a hunger-march on Pretoria to compel the Government to act.

Janse had seen for himself these signs of sullenness turning to violence, and dreaded the danger that threatened Wonderfontein from gangs of hungry men who imagined that food in plenty was still to be found on the farms. He, too, was shocked by the Government's apparent supineness in dealing with the distress in Johannesburg, the city to which it owed its present wealth and prosperity.

'Why don't you try to get hold of your brother?' Meninsky said. 'He's a great pal of Kruger's by all accounts, and might get the old boy to do something.'

Janse took his advice and rode over next day at dawn to see Adrian in the Raadsaal. It was nearly twenty years since he had made a similar journey, driving his wagon into Pretoria to meet Meninsky. Now he rode straight through the centre of Johannesburg and up over Hospital Hill, where the first permanent buildings had been erected on the site of the tents in which Mother Adèle and the Sisters of the Holy Family had nursed the camp-fever patients of earlier days. (The Government, he reflected, had not been so unenlightened or ungenerous over that: they had allotted revenues of more than twenty thousand pounds to the new hospital.) As he reached the top of the ridge and looked backward Janse could see beneath him the rising City of Gold, the irregular line of ashen-grey tailing-dumps flushed by the rose of dawn; the vast hangars that housed the batteries, the headgears of latticed steel, the gigantic wheels of beam-engines slowly pumping up water and discharging it into the dams; the trolley-lines along which the slow trucks climbed like beetles to tip their tailings over the face of the dumps; the Kaffirs' 'compounds' of galvanized iron which had replaced their old hutted kraals: mine after mine, stretching east and west along the line of the Main Reef Road.

And then, as he crossed the crest, he saw before him a vista which – but for the well-marked wagon-road – had hardly

433

changed since he had seen it on that adventurous morning twenty years ago: the dun veld, still houseless and treeless, rolling northward, at his feet, to the humped masses of the Magaliesberg and the virgin waste beyond them – rolling eastward to the great escarpment that frowns over the Low Country. That watershed of bare stone, insignificant in itelf, was now the dividing line between two worlds, two epochs, two kinds of civilization; and in the depths of his heart he knew which of the two he would rather choose, though fate, it seemed, had chosen the other for him.

He found his brother at the outspan where, during the sessions of the Raad, he still lived in his wagon. Adrian looked Janse up and down with a critical eye. Janse was as conscious of his city clothes, under Adrian's scrutiny, as once, in the presence of strangers, he had been aware of his limp. When he spoke of the ticklish state of affairs in Johannesburg, his brother's face clouded.

'Talk to Kruger about Johannesburg?' he said. 'You don't know what you're saying.'

'You must make him show some positive interest in these wretched people. Otherwise they will feel they've been treated badly – just left to starve; and I, for one, can't blame them. They know they provide the bulk of the country's revenue and feel they're entitled to some consideration.'

Adrian shook his head: 'It's easy to talk about "making" Oom Paul do anything.'

'But you still have some influence with him?'

'A little, perhaps. He knows, or ought to know, I'm a loyal supporter – and that's more than can be said for many of the rest. I like the old man, in spite of his obstinacy. As a leader we've no alternative except "Slim Piet" Joubert, who has none of the solid qualities and few of the old Boer virtues I respect in Oom Paul. What's wrong at the moment, Janse, isn't our leadership: it's our form of government. That was all very well in the old days when we were nothing but a scattered community of farming-folk; but now the country's grown too big for it – too big and too rich. After Majuba, when we'd regained our independence, we imagined that we should be able to live our own lives in the way our fathers lived theirs. But we can't; and the tragedy is that so few of our people realize it. The greater part of them hate the name of Johannesburg.'

'The Republic's grown rich on Johannesburg, Adrian.'

'That is true. But are we any the better for having grown rich?'

'For better or worse, Johannesburg's part of us.'

'Yes, part of us. Like a cancer. It grows and grows, and in the end it will kill us. I remember what Joubert said a few years ago: "This gold will cause our country to be soaked in blood." He was right.'

'It will be soaked in blood all the sooner if you shut your eyes to what's happening.'

'That also is true. But what can we do with these foreigners?'

'Make friends of them. That's the advice Jan Brand gave Kruger.'

'Friends! You cannot mix oil and water. How can one make friends with people who don't understand one's language, who don't even worship one's God? Why, only the other day, they invited the President – a strict Dopper if ever there was one – to patronize one of their godless orgies – a ball at Johannesburg in honour of Queen Victoria!'

Janse laughed. 'That wasn't exactly tactful; but I expect they meant well. What did Kruger say?'

'He gave the right answer. He said that a ball was Baal's service, for which reason the Lord had commanded Moses to kill all offenders.'

'To my mind, a slap in the face was not the right answer, Adrian. There are all sorts of people in a state, and it is not for the head of a state to reprove those he doesn't happen to agree with. If he wants a united people, that's the wrong way to go about it.'

'You can't change a man's nature. Kruger's an old-fashioned Boer, and he's not a young man, either. He knows that for every foot he gives them these people will take a yard. And so he does what is natural to him: he stands firm.'

'Like Moses, who said: "Sun, stand thou still upon Gibeon, and thou, Moon, in the valley of Ajalon"?'

'He, too, is a righteous man, and knows that the Lord whom he trusts will sustain him. But his lot is not easy. There are strong forces working against him within the state, among our own people. If he had not been afraid of Joubert's treachery he would never have given way to the English at Fourteen Streams and granted them their road to the North. It is that disappointment, more than anything else, which has hardened him.

435

He loses his temper more easily now. If he's crossed in the Raad, he bellows with anger. To mention Johannesburg to him is like waving a red rag to a bull.'

'I told you some years ago he looked like a buffalo-bull.'

'And a wounded buffalo – for that's what he is – is more dangerous than any lion. I know the old man, and I think I know how he feels. He's hedged in on three sides: on the south by the Rand; on the west by the British in Bechuanaland; now he's being headed away from the North by Piet's friend Rhodes. And that isn't all. He knows that, thanks to Joubert, the people are also divided; many think he has served too long and resent his autocracy. He sees a new Presidential election in front of him, and until that is over, he dare not stand and fight; for he hesitates to put his trust in anyone – even in loyal friends like myself.'

'But isn't that all the more reason,' Janse said, 'why he should try to make friends with the growing majority – in other words, these foreigners on the Rand?'

'That would be giving Joubert another stick to beat him with. His attitude towards them is the one thing by which he can hope to hold the back-veld together. I can't blame him there: I've no liking for foreigners myself. But what I do blame him for is his turning his back on our friends at the Cape, on the Bond and Hofmeyr. That friendship's the one thing Suzanna and I and her brother have always fought for and prayed for; but Oom Paul will have none of it. "How can I trust them," he says, "when Hofmeyr is Rhodes' friend and the Afrikander Bond supports Rhodes in Parliament? If the Cape Dutch are our friends, why didn't they stop the British from taking Bechuanaland?" So he puts heavy Customs duties on all produce from the Cape! I spoke hotly of this in the Raad – it was a matter so near to my heart that I couldn't keep silence – I told them those duties will destroy all our hopes of racial unity. But the old man had his will: if he can't get it any other way he does it by shouting you down. "The Cape produce all goes to Johannesburg," he said. "Let the Cape farmers put up their prices: Johannesburg will pay all they ask; it has to live, so it cannot do otherwise. All their customs receipts go into our treasury. The Cape need not lose, and we gain; so both of us should be satisfied."

'But that isn't all,' he went on, his candour gradually getting the better of his loyal prejudices; 'Kruger's offended the Free

436

State too. He suspects and despises President Brand because he's accepted a title from the British Government and has allowed the Cape to carry their railway through to Bloemfontein. Brand refused to renew our old commercial agreement because Kruger insisted on its being bound up with an offensive and defensive alliance which might drag the Free Staters into war with the British – which is the last thing they want. So now Kruger's raised his duties against the Free State as well. This is a serious business, Janse. We're gradually becoming isolated.'

'You're isolating yourselves – or allowing Kruger to do it for you.'

'Yes, and Kruger is isolating himself from his own people, too. Every man who questions his verdicts, however reasonably, is frowned on by him and his "Yes-brothers". His distrust drives him farther than that. With the increase in the revenue, we've naturally had to extend the Civil Service; but neither Dutch-speaking Cape Afrikanders nor Free Staters nor Transvaal burghers have any chance of employment – you see, men from the Cape might be influenced by Hofmeyr, and the burghers by Brand or Joubert. No, he's turning to foreigners, Germans and Hollanders, and giving them the pick of all the new posts.'

'That was what his own party complained of in President Burgers!'

'I know ... I know. If poor Burgers had lived to see this, he would have had the last laugh. Now, the only man Oom Paul trusts – if he really trusts anyone – is a newcomer named Leyds. Heaven knows where it all will end.'

'Yet, in spite of these things, you defend him,' Janse said.

Adrian sighed. 'Well, I don't find it easy to change my loyalties. I admire Oom Paul. He's a far bigger man than the rest of them. I respect the strength of his will and his intellect. Though he may be wrong – and I wouldn't confess that I thought so to anyone but you – I'm certain of one thing: the old man's a great patriot. He's given his life to our country.'

'At this rate he may lose us our country.'

'I would rather it were lost under him than under Piet Joubert. Though I don't understand what he's after – and he won't trust me sufficiently to tell me – I think he is probably right. Oom Paul's fighting what Kaffirs call the "fight of sit down", and while he sits down, the Republic's accumulating money. A million and a half in the last twelve months! He knows that money means power.'

'That's a lesson he's learnt from Cecil Rhodes,' Janse said. 'Will you take me to see him? I've promised to speak for some of my friends in Johannesburg.'

'I'll take you – but that doesn't mean you'll get anything out of him.'

'I may as well try.'

They crossed the Church Square to the President's house. Even in green Pretoria the drought had been felt: no water ran in the furrows, the rose-hedges were yellow and wilted; though it was still early morning, the heat of the brazen sky was pitiless. Paul Kruger was sitting in his accustomed place on the stoep surrounded by a group of the men whom Adrian had called *Ja broers*. He acknowledged Adrian's arrival with a surly nod, then his little sore eyes fell on Janse.

'Who is this stranger?' he asked suspiciously.

'My brother, President.'

'Your brother? He looks like a foreigner.' He nodded to Janse. '*Kom, sit*. Where do you come from, nephew?'

'I come from Johannesburg, your honour.'

'From Johannesburg. Ah . . . And what do they say in Johannesburg?'

'They say little, because they are starving. They need your help, President.'

'Men who till their land and look after their cattle like our burghers do not need help. The Johannesburgers have plenty of gold. Why don't they buy food with it?'

'They cannot buy food, your honour. This drought has held up the transport of food from the railways, and the prices of what is left have risen to more than poor men can pay. They say that if you had let the railways reach Johannesburg things would be different.'

The old man puffed at his pipe. Then a slow smile, childish and not without charm, spread over his heavy features.

'These people, nephew, remind me of a baboon I once had which was so fond of me that he would not let anyone touch me. But one day we were sitting round the fire, and the beast's tail got caught in it. He now flew at me furiously, thinking that I was the cause of the accident. The Johannesburgers are just like that. They've burnt their fingers in speculations, and now they must blackguard Paul Kruger!'

'They could not foresee this great drought, President.'

438

An old man who was sitting at the President's elbow broke in bitterly:

'But has your honour heard what the Johannesburgers have done? It came to my ears only yesterday, and I could hardly believe it. They have shot off bombs into the clouds to bring down rain! Is not that a defiance of God, which will bring down a visitation from the Almighty? If one of my children fired towards heaven with a revolver, I should certainly thrash him. If people mock at the Almighty in this way, I say they deserve to starve. It is terrible to contemplate.'

Kruger puffed at his pipe and pursed his heavy lips.

'Did the bombs bring down rain, my friend? They did not? Then it seems the Almighty has given His answer.'

'If your honour will hear me a little longer ...' Janse began.

'Go on, nephew. Go on.'

'I think this is a serious matter for the Republic. Whether these people deserve their privations or no, they are growing desperate. When men see their women and children in want of food they turn ugly. Four years ago there were only three thousand foreigners in Johannesburg; now there are twenty-five thousand, most of them men – that is nearly as many as ourselves. They are talking now of a march on Pretoria.'

'They have no arms, nephew; and even if they had, these fellows can't shoot.'

'That is true, your honour. In that way I don't think they are dangerous, and I know you could stop them. But supposing there should be a rising against the Government: wouldn't that give the British an excuse for saying, just as they did in Burgers' days, that our house was divided against itself and needed putting in order? And wouldn't they be glad of such an excuse? Their army has not forgotten the shame of Majuba.'

'What more do they want from me, these people?' Kruger asked angrily. 'We do not interfere with their lives. We have treated Johannesburg generously. The Gold Law is a just law. The poll-tax hurts nobody. We have not grudged them money or land for public works.'

'They want railways, President. They say that a great city and a great industry cannot go on living without railways. They need a line from the south: this famine has proved it.'

'The drought is an act of God. Evil-doers cannot escape

439

chastisement, and they have had their desserts. And supposing I let them have their line from the south to Natal, what would happen to our transport-riders – why should they be ruined? The Johannesburgers know that the line from Delagoa will soon be finished. That it is shorter than the other two railways and will be cheaper. When it reaches them they will have nothing more to complain of.'

'But now they are starving, President,' Janse persisted, 'and a starving city of twenty-five thousand souls is dangerous.'

The old man grunted and puffed at his pipe.'

'See, now, what I will do,' he said at last. 'I will tell Leyds to issue a decree that a bonus of twenty pounds shall be given to each of the first two hundred and fifty wagons that bring food from over the border into Johannesburg. Yes, five thousand pounds I will spend on them. That should content them. And when I go to Blignaut's Pont to meet Loch, the High Commissioner, to settle about Swaziland, I will meet the Johannesburgers also, and talk to them about railways. I will send orders to Captain von Brandis to call a meeting on the open space we have given them which they call the Wanderers' Ground. After that they will understand. Tell your friends in Johannesburg this. Now it is time to go to the Raadsaal.'

He rose heavily and knocked out his pipe on the rail of the stoep, nodded curtly to Janse and moved away, followed by his escort of black-coated 'Ja-broers'.

'The old man was in a good humour this morning,' Adrian said.

Within a week the subsidized food-wagons were rolling into Johannesburg, and the city was saved.

(2)

Paul Kruger asked Adrian to go with him to Blignaut's Pont for the Swaziland Conference. The President had grown too stiff and bulky to ride a horse with comfort, so they drove over to Johannesburg in a two-horse cart. The meeting summoned by von Brandis had been widely advertised, so that when they reached the Wanderers' pavilion the ground was dense with a sea of pallid faces all looking towards them. Adrian had never seen so vast a concourse before. Compared with this multitude, the commando that had marched against Sekukuni seemed a negligible host. Some had flocked there out of mere curiosity to gaze on the President's legendary figure; but many more had come in a hostile mood, determined to give expression to their discontents. From time to time a wave gathered and swept over that sea of faces; the whole mass swayed forward threateningly to the pavilion rails where the police stood on guard; and, now and again, the buzzing undertone of the crowd was raised to a snarl or a growl like that of a famished beast. It was an ugly sound, Adrian thought, this composite voice of united Johannesburg; it suggested a power that he found malignant and hateful; in its deep sustained bourdon it seemed even more threatening than when it was raised; and when Paul Kruger stepped out on to the platform, which was draped and surmounted by the Republican flag, the silence that fell on the press of pale faces, still surging and swaying, had a sinister effect.

Kruger stood there for a moment without speaking, his brooding eyes fixed on the anonymous multitude, a portentous figure, massively towering above his companions; he rose like a pillar of rough-hewn granite, immovable on the verge of the swaying crowd. Adrian's heart warmed with pride as he saw him, the chosen leader of his race – a man whose sheer physical prepotence imposed itself now, without any effort on his part, on these alien hordes. He realized also, as never before, that Paul Kruger was an old man. The narrow brow above those pouched eyes was heavily furrowed. The unkempt, straggling beard that framed that pugnacious mouth was white with age; his massive trunk beneath the hunched shoulders was swollen to a paunch that threw the tight double-breasted frock-coat into wrinkles; his long arms hung loose from the body like those of an ancient baboon. Yet the mere presence of this uncouth old man compelled silence. Even the gruff, uneasy bourdon of the crowd's voices ceased.

Kruger drew in his breath; he raised his sunken head challengeably, and spoke in his rasping voice:

'Burghers, Afrikanders, and Uitlanders . . .'

'Uitlanders? We're as good South Africans as you are, and better,' an angry voice shouted. 'You treat us with contempt.'

'*Bly stil!*' the old man thundered. 'I have no contempt for the new population: only for men such as you.'

But by now the spell of silence had been broken. Once more the crowd found its voice. It rose to an angry clamour of booing and shouting. 'We want the railway. . . . Down with the bloody concessions. . . . We want our rights . . . we want votes. . . .'

Kruger held up his hand; von Brandis pleaded for a hearing; but still the uproar increased. In the middle of the ground someone started to sing 'Rule, Britannia!': the arrogant tune gathered strength and swelled to an overpowering volume. Paul Kruger turned his back on the crowd and began to leave the platform. As he did so, the bawling multitude swarmed over the rails, breaking through the line of police; they stripped the drapings of the four-coloured flag from the platform and tore them to shreds and trampled them underfoot. Adrian planted himself firmly behind Kruger, prepared to defend him, while von Brandis tactfully hurried the old man away to his house.

All that evening disorders continued. As the crowd broke through the pavilion and found that the President had gone, it burst out of the Wanderers' Ground and pursued him to von Brandis's house. Their mood was jocularly provocative rather than violent. They had shouted the old man down, and the affair had become a joke. When they had torn up von Brandis's railings and trampled his garden and tired out their voices with singing 'Rule, Britannia!' and 'God Save the Queen', and, paradoxically, giving three cheers for von Brandis himself, they allowed themselves to be shepherded away by the police and dispersed.

'Jan Brand urged me to make these Uitlanders my friends,' Kruger said, 'and now see what they are! One might as well speak to a pack of baboons on the kopje! They cry out for the vote. Let them cry as long as they will. If I gave them the vote – I have said it before – our people would lose this country. But know this: never again will I set my foot in Johannesburg.'

He drove on with Adrian next day to Blignaut's Pont, and to an even more serious defeat. All the way down to the Vaal, he sat dumped in the cape-cart moodily brooding and smoking, barely uttering a word. His temper was not improved when he learnt that Rhodes, whom he now regarded as his chief enemy, would be present at the conference.

'What does this young man want now?' he growled. 'He's suborned Hofmeyr and Brand; he's taken Bechuanaland, tricked us out of Land Goshen and Stellaland, and brought up his railway through them; he's bought over Lobengula's concession and marched his men North to the Zambezi with British

442

support. Do you know his men told Lobengula they were "sent by the Queen"? He's hemmed us in on three sides. What next does he want? I will tell you: he wants to cut us off on the fourth side as well – to cut us off from the sea, so that the Cape railways may carry all the trade to Witwatersrand. He would even destroy our own railway if he could. Leyds has heard from Europe that he is actually trying to buy Delagoa Bay from the Portuguese. The Portuguese are my friends, and won't let him have it; but who knows, if the money he offered them were big enough, what they might do? That is why the Republic must have a protectorate over Swaziland, and power to build another railway, if necessary, to Kosi Bay. We are not so poor as we were in Burgers' days. We can make Johannesburg pay for it.'

Whatever Rhodes' intention may have been, he appeared to take little part in the conference at the Pont. Adrian saw him restlessly hovering in the background, holding a watching-brief for the Cape. He found it hard to believe that this elderly man was the same person as the boy with whom he had crossed swords twenty years ago at Wonderfontein. The attitude of the new High Commissioner, Sir Henry Loch, was suave and patronizing. He behaved as the representative of the paramount power, securely conscious of his strength but disposed to deal gently with an uncouth, unlettered old peasant who could hardly be expected to understand the finer points of civilized diplomacy. But Paul Kruger was not so simple as he supposed. Adrian had never more deeply admired the old man's tenacity, his command of a nice situation, his intellectual subtlety. He was not going to be bounced or rushed, as Sir Henry soon found, by any display of superior airs and graces, or even by any threat of military interference.

He clung to his point. He wanted a port for the Republic; he wanted access to the sea through Swaziland. In return for this he was willing to make unpalatable concessions: he would enter a Customs Union; he would not oppose the Cape railways reaching his frontier and might even consider their extension to Johannesburg; he would renounce – this was what Rhodes was after – all claims to extend the Republic's territory to the North or to enter into treaties with natives beyond the northern boundary. He argued his case so tenaciously and so skilfully that, in the end, Loch gave way and a Convention was drafted.

'But I can make no promise, your Excellency,' Kruger said,

'that my Volksraad will ratify the proposals on which we have provisionally agreed. After the insult to our flag in Johannesburg the other day, their feelings will certainly be sore.'

'Yes, I heard your honour had trouble in Johannesburg,' Loch replied, 'but I also hear that the Volksraad usually accepts your views. After this frank and friendly discussion, I know I can rely on your word to sustain the spirit of our agreement.'

Paul Kruger kept his word. He kept it strictly, at the risk of losing his own power and dividing the people his personal influence had united, when, a few months later, a petulant dispatch from Loch complained that a formidable trek of armed burghers had assembled on the Limpopo and was preparing to cross the river and invade the Chartered Company's territory. It would be impossible to settle the Swaziland question, he said, unless this invasion were stopped. When the dispatch reached Kruger he sent for Adrian.

'There is trouble up in the Zoutpansberg, nephew,' he said, 'and I think Piet Joubert's behind it, though two men, Barend Vorster and Adendorff, are leading. If I don't stop them from crossing the Limpopo, I shall not get my way to the sea through Swaziland.'

'If you do stop them, President, Joubert will be able to say that you favour the British against your own people. That will make a fine cry for him in the next election.'

'That is so. But I have given the High Commissioner my word – he need not have reminded me of that – and I must have my way to the sea. You will go to the Zoutpansberg with orders from the Government that this trek must be stopped.'

Adrian rode north and crossed the Zoutpansberg; he dropped down into the plain through which the winter-shrunken Limpopo flowed sluggishly: a sandy expanse of sparse bush scattered here and there, with elephant-hided baobabs. The spoor of many wagons that had floundered through the sand led him at last to Floris Drift where, on the southern side of the stream, Adendorff's trek lay encamped. As he rode into the camp, a stentorian voice called him by name:

'What, brother, have you then come to join in the fighting?'

It was Groot Andries, more monstrously bear-like and shaggy than ever, who folded him in an enormous embrace.

'I've come to stop you fighting, Andries,' he said.

'You're too late for that, brother. We cross the river

444

tomorrow. You're just in time for the fun.' He laughed uproariously.

'I bring orders from the Government to turn you back,' Adrian said.

'It'll take more than orders from Pretoria to do that,' Groot Andries said. 'We in the Zoutpansberg have no great liking for Kruger or his Volksraad. They say the Republic is rich, but the Government still makes us pay taxes; and none of the money from the mines comes our way. And what have they done for the Zoutpansberg? Answer me that, brother! They say Kruger is a strong man. Then why did he hand over Bechuanaland and Goshen and Stellaland to the English when we were ready to fight for them? That is not what we call strength in the Zoutpansberg: that is what we call weakness and treachery. Who won the battle at the Majuba: we, or the English? We have beaten them once, and can beat them again!'

'Oom Paul is slimmer than you think, Andries,' Adrian told him. 'He has made a good bargain with the English. In return for our giving them a free hand here in the north, they have promised us a way to the sea.'

'A way to the sea?' Andries laughed contemptuously. 'What use is a way to the sea to us in the Zoutpansberg? Can our cattle drink sea-water or graze on the sands? What we want is good grazing and less Government interference. We shall get both of them here in the North, and a Republic of our own – the old kind of Republic, where a man can do as he likes without being bothered by laws and decrees and taxes for building railways that only the foreigners will use. And we'll have a new President, brother, who understands what the farmers want and 'll keep quiet and won't interfere with them.'

'Slim Piet, I suppose?'

'It's nothing to me who he is, so long as he leaves us alone. As for these orders of yours from Pretoria, you may just as well take them back where they came from, brother. What right has the Transvaal Government to stop us from going north if we want to go north? If Paul Kruger starts telling us where we shall go and where we shall not go, why, then he's no better than the English who tried to stop our fathers from trekking over the Orange River with Piet Retief! If I want to trek, I shall trek, and Paul Kruger won't stop me. And so say all the rest of us in the Zoutpansberg.'

445

'Still, I think you'd be wise to turn back.'

'Who can make me turn back?'

'The English, Andries. You're only a hundred men, and without the Republic's support, which Kruger won't give, you must know you can't possibly face them.'

'You shall see. The Zoutpansberg burghers are men: they have not gone soft and faint-hearted like you town-folk in Pretoria. The English can't shoot. I reckon that I'm a match for any ten of them. How many Englishmen were there on the Majuba, and how many were we who beat them? Answer me that!'

Adrian interviewed Barend Vorster and Adendorff and gave them Kruger's orders, which they refused to accept. They showed him with pride a concession they had obtained from a minor chief, one of Lobengula's underlings.

'This means nothing,' he told them. 'If you act upon it, Lobengula himself will reject it, for he's tied to the Chartered Company. He may even attack you – and remember, the Matabele have a thousand rifles which Rhodes gave them for his concession. If you get into trouble, as I've warned you already, the Republic will not support you.'

'When once we're over the river,' Adendorff said, 'the Republic will have no authority over us. You can tell Paul Kruger from me that he's made a mistake. If he tries to check our movements in this way, he'll find that the voters won't follow him; he'll lose the election and Piet Joubert will become President. We are not the only folk who are tired of him and his ways. Tell him that from me. We shall cross the drift tomorrow.'

Three men from the camp crossed Floris Drift on the following morning, to be disarmed and arrested by the Chartered Company's police who were posted on the other side. They returned, under escort, next day with another: a little, pale, baldish man with a dark moustache and black, humorous eyes who walked fearlessly into that crowded camp of angry giants, announcing himself as Dr. Jameson. He appeared to be rather amused by the whole situation and addressed them good-humouredly.

'You fellows, you know, have got hold of the wrong end of the stick, and if you're not careful you'll find yourselves in a devil of a mess. Here you are, all the lot of you armed to the teeth, disowned by your own Government and preparing to

446

"take on" another, and that seems to me just foolish. You can't force this drift or any other in face of Maxim fire; you'd be cut to pieces. You're only a hundred strong, but I've got all the Bechuanaland Police in the rear. But why should you want to start fighting? There's no earthly need for it. The door's open, so long as you choose to come in on reasonable terms and drop all this nonsense about an armed invasion. The Chartered Company wants settlers – the more the merrier – and it wants fellows like you who can rough it and ride and shoot. Mr. Rhodes would far rather have Afrikanders than foreigners. We're willing to allot you land, and good land, if you come into the country as *bona fide* settlers, prepared to accept the Company's authority and abide by the law of the land, which is a perfectly good law, the same as the law at the Cape. There's no catch in the offer I make you. It's all fair and square. You're welcome in this fine country, every one of you – so, upon my soul, I can't see what you're wanting to fight for. You'd much better behave like sensible fellows and come along peaceably. That's all I have to say.'

That same evening a number of wagons, including two that belonged to Groot Andries' eldest son, crossed Floris Drift. Their crossing marked the end of the Adendorff trek. It marked, also, the end of the northward expansion of the Transvaal. The little Republic was enclosed on three sides; and the fourth would never be open.

(3)

Meanwhile, encircled as it was, the Transvaal grew richer, and Johannesburg greater. Meninsky's foresight had been even keener than he knew. The chemists had been at work. Three of them, in Glasgow, the Forrest brothers and MacArthur, had been working on a process for the extraction of gold from pyritic ore, and claimed that, by the use of a dilute solution of potassium cyanide, all the gold which had refused to amalgamate in the presence of pyrites could be separated, shredded and deposited on zinc.

At the time when, thanks to the slump and the drought, the already shrinking city seemed to be approaching its nadir, MacArthur arrived in Johannesburg with an experimental plant, prepared to demonstrate his process. He set up his cyanide plant on the Salisbury Mine, and invited the leading men of the industry to watch the proceedings and subject them to the severest of tests. For two days and two nights they stood on guard over MacArthur, checking the quantities and nature of every reagent, the dimensions of all apparatus. On the evening of the third day there emerged from the oil-fired smelting-furnace a small ingot of gold, the weight of which proved that eighty per cent of the metal contained in the sample of pyritic ore had been extracted – far more than had ever been gained from non-sulphurous ores by mere amalgamation. Johannesburg heaved a deep sigh of relief. The Rand was saved!

And now, like a giant refreshed, the city arose, rejoicing, to run its course. Even Meninsky, sanguine as he was by nature, was astounded by the rapidity of its recovery and its unsuspected reserves of strength. A tidal wave of wild speculation, the magnitude of which made the first boom seem a trifling affair, carried prices above any level that had ever been dreamt of. Meninsky, whose brain was always liable to be intoxicated by high figures, broke all his resolves and implored Janse to let him throw their joint capital into the rising market.

'Barney's buying shares like a madman,' he said, 'just as I told you he would. If we don't get it now, it's going to be too late.'

But Janse stood firm.

'You told me to keep you from buying gold-shares if ever this happened,' he said. 'We both of us made up our minds to stick to land.'

'But damn it, mate,' Meninsky entreated him, 'don't you see that if we took this chance we could make enough to buy more land? Don't you see I'm after that million?'

'We can make it without any risk or excitement if we hold what we've got. Aren't you satisfied when you see that the value of every square yard of land we possess has gone up a hundred per cent in the last six months?'

'What's a measly hundred per cent?' Meninsky said bitterly. 'Five hundred's more in my line.'

'What could you do with all this money even if you made it? What you've made is of no use to you. Your cigars smell as foul as ever, and you still persist in dossing down on a mattress in a back room in Pritchard Street. You don't make a splash, like the other "bright boys" as you call them.'

'You don't understand, mate,' Meninsky answered pitifully.

'I don't want to *do* anything with money. I want to *make* it. Can't a bloke have his fancies the same as anyone else? There'll never be such a chance again as long as we live. You're not fit to live in times like these, Janse, honest you're not. You've no more imagination than a ruddy stockbroker.'

The market went on soaring, sky-high. It seemed as if nothing could stop it. Barnato was building a new Stock Exchange, but even that, people said, would not be large enough to cope with the flood of business. He was competing, too, with Meninsky, in the real-estate business; floating companies and reconstructing them every day of the week. Though small fry engaged in the gamble, this was the day of the big fish, and some sharks among them. Little mines were bought up by the dozen, absorbed and digested by the big groups and syndicates. Now that pyrites had ceased to be the menace that had been imagined, all far-seeing eyes were fixed on the new Deep Levels. It was the old story of Kimberley, where the faint hearts that had failed when the 'yellow ground' ended, sold their claims in the 'blue' to men of greater vision and courage.

Prospecting shafts were sunk to a depth of three thousand feet. Even at that level the reef kept its modest but payable yield. And with every few hundred feet the reef dipped down, the land above it doubled in value.

If only those wretched railways would come! Until they arrived, the Rand must still starve for coal and iron and machinery. There was even a calculable loss on the interest wasted while the slow wagons were hauling the ingots of gold to railhead: thousands of pounds' worth sterilized by this ludicrous lack of speed. Yet slowly and surely the lines from the Cape and Natal and Delagoa were crawling forward, like tortoises, in a neck-and-neck race. Paul Kruger and his friends watched their progress with mixed feelings. He knew they would bring money to his treasury. He knew also that they might bring redcoats to the Transvaal.

Though they continued to excite Meninsky, Janse was no more deeply moved by these developments than was his father, John Grafton, dreaming away his declining years and running his little farm above the fantastic, unquarried wealth of Wonderfontein, or than Maria, submitting to the passage of time and watching her parents grow old amid surroundings that had lost all resemblance to those of the home she had loved. As the mining activities of the central Witwatersrand increased, the farm became compressed and encysted, as it were, within the barriers of scar-tissue. It was not only that Wonderfontein's horizons were shrinking: the very veld had lost its ancient greenness. In winter, when dry winds swept over it, the surface of the land was powdered with blown dust from the growing dumps of cyanide-tailings. It entered the house through every window-cranny and lay drifted like silt or snow. One breathed it and smelt it wherever one went. It became a normal constituent of the air.

John Grafton appeared (or affected) not to notice it. He had made up his mind to stay on the farm as long as he lived, and Lisbet, deferring to him in all things as was her wont, accepted the infliction cheerfully. But the isolation to which she was condemned, this death – or slow process of dying – in life, weighed heavily on Maria. She was now – though she could hardly believe it herself – a woman of thirty-three. The years that had gone since the tragedy of her lover's death (and, strange to say, healed it) had passed over her head unnoticed and left her little changed. She was still young in heart and in body, resilient in spirit; still beautiful, with less evident brilliance but greater poise and composure. This was no sort of life, she knew, for a woman of her age and temperament.

Not that she had any lack of admirers or opportunities for escape. By this time John Grafton had become, among the newcomers, a legendary figure: the old Englishman who, in spite of all the temptations of wealth, still clung to his ancient pastoral life on that small plot of land, on the very edge of Johannesburg, which surely must be worth millions. Even the most powerful and confident of the new race of mining-magnates had abandoned their attempts to buy the islanded *mijnpacht* of Wonderfontein. Its gold must lie there untouched, they realized, until the old man died. It was some comfort to know that he was now seventy-three and every year growing feebler, so that the time for the great deal would soon come.

Meanwhile, mine-captains and engineers and managers from the neighbouring concerns were frequent visitors at Wonderfontein. They came first out of curiosity to see this strange portent and to listen to the stories John Grafton told of the Great Trek and his early days on the Witwatersrand. They stayed, and came again, because, in their hurricane life, the ancient, ordered peace of Wonderfontein was sweet to them, being nearer to what they called 'home' than anything they had found in this great, raw country of their adoption. In the end they usually fell in love with Maria, who was 'different', again, from the garish Johannesburg women and was also, providentially, a considerable heiress.

Maria did not mind them falling in love with her. They were most of them young and keen and decent fellows. Their visits and their admiration brightened her life and gave her new interests; yet when it came to falling in love herself, her heart was always subject to a strange inhibition. Though she no longer mourned for Richard Abberley, she could not forget him. She knew that the passionate rapture of those brief, sweet days in which they had loved, so fresh and clear and tender, could not be experienced again; that in the seasons of human life there could be only one spring. She was kind and gentle with her admirers because their honest admiration flattered her and demanded a certain respect. She liked more than one, but knew that she could love none of them: for no sooner were they gone than their images faded and became oddly blurred and insubstantial compared with that of her first and only love, though they were living, and Richard dead for more than ten years. Her mother noticed (and confided to Janse) that she seemed to prefer middle-aged – or even elderly – men to those of her own age. Perhaps she did this deliberately, not only as being more consonant with her sober mood but also because she dreaded making comparisons between those who were younger than Richard, whose image was eternal and incomparable.

If Maria showed any preference – and Lisbet, who was anxious to see her happily married, kept an eye on such matters – it appeared to be for Carel Strijdom, the predikant, the brother of Adrian's wife Suzanna, who had been chosen by the Synod to fill one of the earliest Dutch Reformed pulpits in Johannesburg. Carel found himself as little in sympathy with this Babylon of godless foreigners as John Grafton himself, and often sought refuge at Wonderfontein, not merely because of the family connection but because of the contrast its life provided to that of the alien city. Maria welcomed his visits, without any thought of sentimental complications. She liked him far better than his sister (the family intensity which had so greatly changed Adrian's life sat better on a man than on a woman), and was fascinated by the quick, hawk-like movements of a mind that was stronger-winged and wider in its flight than any she had known before. In addition to his intellectual gifts, she admired in him that complete directness and simplicity which is sometimes the highest quality of the single-minded, and a whimsical, an almost childish vein which refused to take anything save his religion and his political ideals with an exaggerated seriousness.

This frail, dark, middle-aged man, with his smouldering zealot's eyes, was the most gentle and charming of companions. She pitied that ardent frailty, yet when she was with him she felt herself stimulated, and long after he had gone it seemed to her as though her wits had been screwed up to a higher pitch. His sly, flashing humour, indeed, had at first been too quick for her; but when once she had tuned her mind to it and grasped its tempo, it became a particular delight; for jokes had become a rare thing at Wonderfontein in those days. She had found it all the more difficult because, on principle, he would speak no language but Afrikaans, a tongue which, although she had understood it from a child, she had always regarded as an inferior, elementary dialect. On Carel Strijdom's lips, she discovered to her surprise that it was not merely expressive but capable of poetry. Whenever she broke into English he reproved her.

'Why should you, a born Afrikander, speak a foreign tongue? Is the language of your own country not good enough for you?'

'You forget I'm half-English, Carel,' she said.

'Suzanna and I are half-Huguenot French; but Afrikaans is our language. It has sprung from the African soil, and its sound is as sweet to me as the music of our birds, which foreigners say cannot sing. What is more, you speak it beautifully, Maria. You have a low voice: "*An excellent thing in woman*".'

'You see! You have to finish your sentence in English.'

'That is because, as yet, we have no poetry of our own, and man cannot live without poetry. But some day a great Afrikander poet will be born, and then we shall not have to borrow.'

'I think you should be a poet yourself.'

'Ah, no. I have written poetry. But the poets are usually silent, tongue-tied men, and I spend all my life haranguing people from the pulpit and chattering about politics.'

Their intimacy ripened quickly. Whenever he had time to spare (though that was not often) Carel Strijdom came over to Wonderfontein and talked with her. She knew that, living alone in Johannesburg, his life was as solitary as her own, and she pitied it as she pitied his physique, which seemed always too fragile for the flame that illumined it. Her attitude was half admiring and half protective, in a way that was almost maternal; she was so far from falling in love with him that the thought of a romantic relationship never even occurred to her until, one day, he suddenly questioned her about the ring she was wearing.

'I have been wondering what the ring on your third finger means,' he said, 'or if it means anything.'

'I wear it in memory of a man I loved, Carel.'

'And whose memory you still love?'

'I suppose so.' She smiled, but her eyes were darkened and the smile pitiful. 'It was a long time ago. I was only a child. He was killed at Bronkhorst Spruit.'

'An Englishman?'

'Yes. A friend of Edward Haskard's. He was very young, too.'

'I'm sorry I spoke of it, Maria, if it still hurts you.'

She smiled. 'It doesn't hurt so much now,' she said.

He did not refer to her ring again, and she was glad of a delicacy which, indeed, she would have expected of him. It was she who brought it into their conversation again, telling him, one day when they were talking politics, that the stone had been given her by Cecil Rhodes.

'Cecil Rhodes?' he said. 'I had no idea you even knew him.'

'And you wish I didn't?'

'Far from it. The man's an idealist – and heaven knows, such people are rare in this benighted country. I only met him once, many years ago, when Jan Hofmeyr sent me to see him on behalf of the Bond – that was before they became friends, you know. I said to him: 'Mr. Rhodes, we want a united South Africa"; and he said: "So do I." I said: "There is nothing in the way of it," and he said: "No, there is nothing in the way of it – we are one." Then I gave him Hofmeyr's offer: "We are prepared to take you as our leader: There is only one thing. We must, of course, be independent of the rest of the world." He looked at me for a moment. Then he shook his head slowly. "Mr. Strijdom," he said, "you take me either for a rogue or a fool. I would be a rogue to forfeit all my history and tradition; and I would be a fool, because, if I consented to that, I should be hated by my own countrymen and distrusted by yours." So it came to nothing.'

'You're sorry it came to nothing?'

'In a way I'm sorry, for I was charmed by this man. Of course, Hofmeyr and he are now friends and working together. He believes in the things we believe in. I don't always relish his methods; sometimes they shock me and sometimes they frighten me. But he's a true South African. He has the large visions of genius, and the nature of genius is ruthless. If only he were not an Englishman!'

'That shows you are prejudiced, Carel.'

'Of course I'm prejudiced. I can't help it, although I regret it; it's deep in my blood. I know too much of our race's tragic history, from Slachter's Nek onwards; but I think my mind has grown cooler and fairer as I have grown older. I have come to see that, though we are kin, a great gulf separates us Cape Afrikanders from the folk in the Transvaal. The man who stands now in the way of unity is not Cecil Rhodes but Adrian's friend, Paul Kruger. Ah, it's all too complicated: it would be simpler for people like myself if Kruger were not a true patriot and an honest man. I believe he is both; but I know that his policy is mistaken, and that his obstinacy is killing the thing we all desire. It alienates everyone – it's even alienated Hofmeyr, the gentlest, the best, the most charitable man in the world. That makes me despair of South Africa.'

'If only this horrible racial antagonism could be killed! It has caused so much bitterness and suffering already. As you know, I have suffered myself. Is there no way out of it?'

'Only one way: that people like you and me, who love our country, should join hands in fighting against it by prayer and goodwill. It is the greatest happiness to know that you are with me in this, Maria; for in a place like Johannesburg a man who thinks about anything but money is bound to feel lonely.'

Maria was touched by his confession of loneliness; yet when, a few weeks later, Carel Strijdom asked her to marry him, she found that she could not accept him.

'Ah, you think I'm too old,' he said, so pathetically that she warmed to him.

454

'No, no, it isn't that, Carel,' she said. 'I've never even thought of your being older than myself, and you know I'm fond of you. But marriage – that's something different. I don't think I want to be married – I can't tell you why. Don't keep away from me just because I've had to say this. I should miss your friendship terribly if you did.'

He laughed, unhappily: 'I shan't keep away from you, Maria, because I couldn't do it if I tried; I love you too dearly. You'll always be the most precious thing in my life. Even if you won't marry me, I want all of yourself you can give me. Let's say no more about this and go on as if I had never spoken. Let's be just the same as we were. I shan't trouble you any more in this way; and yet, do you know, I feel convinced that some day you'll marry me.'

She was thankful that he had taken her refusal so patiently, for she felt that if he had pressed her, her liking and sympathy for him and her pity for his loneliness might have betrayed her into a weakness she would have regretted. Under their pact of oblivion, Carel Strijdom visited Wonderfontein as regularly as ever; but they were not 'just the same'; the quality of their friendship had been changed by his declaration, and there was no longer the old frankness between them; for, however loyally he dissimulated it, she felt the heat of his passion and could not meet his dark, smouldering eyes without being self-conscious.

She was more at ease and therefore happier, on the whole, in the company of Piet and Janse, which made fewer demands on her feelings and was uncomplicated by such weakening emotions as pity or charity; but, as time went by, she saw less and less of them; for both were busy men, and the homes they had built for themselves on the northern ridge were separated from Wonderfontein not only by the mile-wide zone of mine-scarred veld on either side of the dusty Main Reef Road, but by the whole intimidating breadth of Johannesburg.

Piet's new house was a palatial edifice of red brick with neo-Gothic features, befitting his station as a leader of the gold-mining industry and an important member of the new Chamber of Mines. He had trailed with him to Johannesburg clouds of glory reflected from his association with Rhodes, who, in spite of Piet's refusal to go with Jameson to Matabeleland, still favoured him – as might have been expected, for the sentimental streak in the great man's character showed itself most in his loyalty to the friends of his youth. Again, in return for the sale of the Witfontein and Brakfontein *mijnpachte*, Piet had acquired interests that entitled him to a seat on the board of Beit's holding company, and he was actually chairman of the Brakfontein mine, familiarly known as the 'Brak-Deep.'

In appearance, as well as in fact, he was now a successful man – popular too, because, for all his keen wits, he was never out of humour and made no enemies. In the new plutocratic society of Doornfontein, Lavinia and he were well liked as a handsome and hospitable couple, with a highly proper domestic life and a charming family of children; while old Major Haskard who, in spite of his lungs, had survived his wife and had come to live with them, was regarded by the newcomers (without in the least deserving it) as one of the Pioneers of the Rand. He had become more garrulous, and exploited his brogue more than ever, in an old age which allowed him, without giving offence, to take those fatherly liberties with young ladies which had always been his favourite amusement.

Janse's house, where Maria felt herself more at home than at Piet's, was a much more modest affair: a galvanized-iron bungalow with long, shaded stoeps, concealed by quick-growing plantations of wattle and blue-gum. Though it had little in common with the Witwatersrand she had known and loved in her childhood, Maria found in Janse's tree-shaded garden the only spot in Johannesburg where she could forget for a while the neighbourhood of the growing city and its mines. During the last few years she had developed an increasing affection and sympathy for Janse, both of which were more deeply rooted than her childish adoration of Piet. Success had altered Piet, and not, so far as she was concerned, for the better. Though, superficially, their gay comradeship remained unchanged, she felt she could no longer make him the confidant of anything that affected her deeply, such as Carel Strijdom's proposal; and though he adapted himself to her company and made a fair pretence of maintaining the old intimacy, their friendship was not what it had been – the world he inhabited was not hers. But Janse – although in all probability his material success was equal to Piet's – had not changed. She found him always the same: a spare, limping man, with a clean-shaven face deeply lined by past privations, grey, unruly hair, and the kindest mouth and eyes. If she could ever have met Janse's double,

456

Maria would have married him without the least hesitation.

Janse and she had a great deal in common – not merely in their natures but in their interests – and nothing bound them more closely together than their quasi-parental relationship to little Lena. She was little Lena no longer. The last time they had seen her, during a hurried (and, for Janse, embarrassing) visit to the Haskards' house at the Cape, he had found her a self-possessed young woman of sixteen in whom he could not recognize the passionate little savage he had caught running wild in Swaziland five years before, the child who had crept under the wagon and shared his blankets on the road to de Kaap. Though Lena had kissed him dutifully and made it her business to entertain him during his stay, he had felt that the three years of separation had made them strangers. He had been dazzled, and even a little intimidated, by an unexpected matureness and beauty and elegance which troubled him – for in all his visions of her he had stupidly continued to think of her as a child. In her company an unaccountable shyness and silence had come over him; for he was awkward with women in any case, and more awkward than even when, as with Lena, a brilliant youth and loveliness made him feel clumsy and shabby and old.

Lena herself was neither shy nor silent with him; civilized life had not robbed her of her impulsive frankness – which Lavinia confessed to finding an embarrassment at times – but with Janse's pride in the beauty and intelligence of this transformed creature there was mingled doubt as to his competence to sustain his part of the parental responsibilities he shared with Maria. He remembered Meninsky's warning and admitted its rightness, for he had never before in his life felt quite so helpless. There was a comical side in that helplessness which Maria found more amusing than he.

Indeed, it had been something of a relief when Lavinia – who was in process of transferring her household from the Cape to Piet's new grand house in Doornfontein, and was finding the adolescent Lena, whom she had never liked any more than Lena liked her, a considerable addition to her anxieties – proposed that the child should be sent, with her own daughter, Cecilia, who was now fourteen, to complete her polite education in England.

'If you don't mind the expense, Janse,' she said – for she could never believe that her brother-in-law was richer than he looked – 'I'm sure that will be the best thing to do. Lena's much more precocious than ordinary children of her age; she's so quick – I hardly like to say "cunning" – that she twists poor Miss Hatherleigh round her little finger. Young men – and not only *young* men – are beginning to notice the child, and, of course, she knows it. I won't say that she actually encourages attention; but, if you know what I mean' (Janse knew what she meant precisely), 'she's a child of nature – and there it is! You see, the trouble is that she's so *unusual*, and so attractive, too, that people here make too much fuss of her, and that's rather turned her head. She thinks she can get round everybody – and she isn't far wrong. What she needs is a little wholesome discipline of the kind she'd get in a first-class English girls' school like Cheltenham, with a really strict headmistress, where she wouldn't feel herself quite so important and mistress of the situation. I don't say she's not a sweet child, Janse, but there's a streak of wildness in her, which I'm sorry to say father encourages, that, if it's not checked, may lead to real unhappiness. And of course you must have noticed her shocking colonial accent. As a matter of fact, Cecilia's is almost as bad. Heaven only knows where they've picked that up. They certainly don't hear anything of the kind at home.'

Janse hadn't, in fact, noticed Lena's accent, which was much like his own and Maria's. The thought of being deprived of Lena for three more years, when he already felt he had almost lost her, did not please him. Yet, as Maria pointed out, she was now at a difficult age, and the sobering influence of new surroundings and a more formal discipline might make the future easier for both of them.

'After all,' she said, 'we want to do the best for her, and there's no question of your not being able to afford it. I only wish to goodness I'd had her opportunities when I was her age. Do you realize, Janse darling, that you and I and the rest of the family are quite uneducated? I know we're all very nice, but just think what we've lost! These Cape people are very pleased with themselves; but they aren't really educated either. I adore South Africa; but there's no denying it's dreadfully out of the world. The best education can only be found in Europe. That's why I think Mr. Rhodes was so wise when he made Piet send Jimmy to Eton. It'll give the boy a self-confidence he couldn't otherwise have had.'

458

Janse laughed: 'It will. I know your self-confident English-man! There are plenty of those on the Rand. On the whole I prefer our home-made article.'

'Ah, but Jimmy's schooling won't finish with Eton,' Maria said. 'Mr. Rhodes has his own ideas about that. When he came out here himself the first time he was only seventeen, and he only went to Oxford afterwards. So, as soon as Jimmy's finished his public-school education (they call them "public", Piet says, because they're so awfully private) he'll put him straight into the Mashonaland Mounted Police.'

'As a commissioned officer, I suppose, with a letter to the Commandant or whatever he's called informing him that he's under Rhodes' protection?'

'Not at all. That wouldn't be like Mr. Rhodes.'

'It would be very like our dear Piet.'

'No, no. He'll go in as a trooper, and rough it. That's the whole idea. I think it's a good idea, too; both parts of it – the English and then the African; but you've dragged me away from what I was beginning to say about Lena's going to Europe. It was a good thing for Jimmy; but I think it's even more important for a girl – particularly for one like Lena, who's sharp enough to take every advantage from it. You know, her brain's much keener than mine ever was or will be. She has a marvellous memory: she'll pick up languages easily. And Lavinia says she's a real talent for music. I think she ought to spend the last year at a finishing school in Paris or Florence or Dresden.'

'She'll be so "finished", if you have your way with her, that she'll end by despising us for a couple of ignorant savages.'

'No, Janse, I think you're quite wrong. Lena isn't that sort of child. The most charming part of her is her capacity for loyalty and affection. If she once loves you, she might possibly kill you, but she'd never forsake you. And I know she loves both of us – you particularly.'

'Well, you'd better tell her what's been proposed, then.'

'No, I think you ought to do that, Janse. She's really your property, and she'll do anything for you. But, for heaven's sake don't forget you can't drive her, Janse.'

'Very well, then. I'll do my best.'

It was a curious interview. Janse could quite understand why Maria had handed it over to him. It made him aware, for the first time, of the enormous strength of Lena's character as compared with his own. This child of sixteen, whose future he was arranging, made him feel oddly incapable and unimportant.

'I thought I was going to keep house for you in Johannesburg, Janse,' she said reproachfully. (From their earliest days, at de Kaap, she had always called him "Janse".) 'Has all that been changed?'

'No, no, darling, not at all. After all, you're still a little bit young for a housewife.'

'Just you try me, and see! I can make the most lovely *bobotie* and *sosaties* and all the Cape dishes – and pumpkin fritters and *konfyt*. And I think I've learnt most of what poor dear Miss Hatherleigh can teach me. Of course, if you don't need me . . .'

'There's no question of my not needing you, child; but I want you to have the best opportunities I can possibly give you – better than any I ever had, or your Aunt Maria.'

'Oh . . . so this is Aunt Maria's idea.'

'It's mine just as much as hers. I should have thought you'd have jumped at it: the chance of seeing the world, not only this little corner of it.'

'I don't believe the rest of the world can be half as nice as South Africa.'

'It might be worth while seeing for yourself; and it's such a fine opportunity for you, with Cecilia going to England at the same time.'

'But I *want* to keep house for you, Janse. You oughtn't to be living alone.'

'I've lived alone most of my life, darling. A year or two more won't hurt me.'

She caught him up quickly: 'You said three years just now. Wouldn't two be enough? I'm sure I shall hate it: I don't like Englishwomen.'

'You don't know any Englishwomen.'

'I know Aunt Lavinia.'

'That's not very grateful of you. She's been very kind to you, Lena. You ought to love her.'

'Oh, Janse dear, you don't love people because they've been kind to you. You don't love people for . . . *reasons*!' She paused for a moment: he wondered what she was thinking. 'If I go to England,' she said suddenly, 'shall I see Jimmy?'

460

'If you stay with Major Haskard's relations during the holidays, you'll be almost certain to see him.'

'Then I'll go,' she said, almost eagerly. 'That is, if you're not pretending, and really don't mind.'

CHAPTER FOUR

(1)

THE GOLD-MINING BOOM was still at its height when Janse returned to Johannesburg. The deep shafts were going down everywhere; the deep levels were being developed. In a single month a hundred and seventy-five thousand ounces of fine gold had been produced: the Rand was within sight of an income of eight million pounds a year. The population of the city itself had grown, in six years, from the sprinkling of pioneers in Ferreira's camp to a total of more than a hundred and seventy-five thousand souls. The railway from the Cape, accelerated by a Rothschild loan which Rhodes had secured, had reached Johannesburg; Kruger's answer to this, the line from Delagoa, 'Oom Paul's hobby', as Cecil Rhodes called it, was nearing Pretoria. And yet this abounding prosperity did not suffice. The Rand was not happy.

Appetite comes with eating, they say. The great mine-owners, rich as they were, grew fretful because they were not so rich as they thought they might be. Though the gold-law was fair enough, railway-rates were still too high and the expense of heavy haulage still embarrassed them. They were bled by high tariffs, which Kruger, reluctantly forced to accept the line from the South, had imposed to protect his own railway from Delagoa. They could pay them – even thus embarrassed, they were declaring enormous dividends – but they detested paying through the nose to a state that clearly regarded them with a grudging hostility. After all, there was no denying that the great city they had made was the principal pillar of that state; its heart; the source and motive power of its life.

And now, as if this sustained and heroic blood-letting were not enough, the old man in Pretoria, backed by his subservient Raad and encouraged by his foreign advisers, had discovered a new method of bleeding them, by granting monopolies to his friends. There was a monopoly in the dynamite without which no reef could be broken that cost the industry more than half a million a year and provided a handsome rake-off for certain

462

members of the Government. There was a liquor-monopoly, too, which allowed the concessionaires to poison the native labour in the mines with inferior alcohol. Even a jam-monopoly! They knew that the old man had his knife into Johannesburg. He had not forgotten – and would never forget – the trampling of the Transvaal flag on the day when he had been howled down on the Wanderers' Ground. But they dared not protest; for, if they protested, they knew that their burdens would only be increased. The Government was a malevolent autocracy; yet it had the whip-hand; if they would live, they must keep on good terms with it. So they went on making what money they could, and suffered their wrongs in silence.

The common folk of the Rand were less prudent and less complaisant, for they had less to lose. They were not concerned with the profits made by the mines, but with the high cost of living, which hit their stomachs and was due to Kruger's tariffs. They knew that the Uitlander population was not much more than double that of the Transvaal burghers, yet paid nine-tenths of the taxes. They asked how much of these taxes they paid came back to them in public services, and the answer was: next to nothing – an ignorant, corrupt, tyrannical police-force composed of men who could not speak their language; a pittance of two shillings a head for their children's education; an inadequate water-supply and a defective sanitary service! Where did all the money go then? It went, they were told, along with the vast bribes already paid by concession-hunters, to feather the nests of corrupt Volksraad members – the President included.

What was the cure for these evils? The only cure was the franchise: the natural right of the majority in a state to representation in its government and a voice in the spending of the money received from the taxes they provided. They were not, generally, anxious to get the vote for its own sake: the greater part of them was still English, and Englishmen, as a rule, are not politically-minded; but they wanted the better conditions of living to which, among such abundant wealth, they felt that they were entitled; they wanted, as human beings, to have a fair share in the prosperity which they had made. They had no intense racial feelings, and cared little under what flag they were governed provided they were governed justly and generously and allowed to live their own lives. So they demanded the vote.

With Paul Kruger still in power and in a bitter mood, they might as well have asked for the moon. Still the mine-owners held their peace; but the Johannesburg folk formed a new political body, the Transvaal National Union, which laid down the principles for which the majority of Uitlanders stood. A mass meeting, well disposed towards the Republic but not towards its Government, passed a resolution and forwarded a modest request for the vote to be granted to all male white citizens of full age who had resided for two years in the state and who occupied or owned property to the value of a hundred a year.

A deputation waited on the President in Pretoria and put the Union's case. Kruger listened sullenly and replied evasively. For himself, it had always been his policy, he said, to unite the two sections of the people; but there was a new Presidential election in sight, and if he, a candidate, gave a pledge for granting any extension of the franchise, the people would reject him, for that would deprive the burghers of their only privilege. In the meantime, they had better go back to Johannesburg, cease to hold public meetings, and be satisfied with his policy of uniting the people.

The deputation was not satisfied. It pointed out that the franchise could in no way deprive the old burghers of their one privilege, for the simple reason that all the newcomers were congregated in one or two electoral districts and, even if represented, must necessarily be in a minority. They knew they could not have power, but at least they were entitled to a voice in the Volksraad's discussions.

'I have given you a Second Chamber,' Paul Kruger said. 'That is already a great concession.'

'But the Second Chamber,' Charles Leonard, the lawyer, pointed out, 'has no say in any of the functions of government. In the very year when the Second Chamber was created, the Volksraad stiffened the conditions of franchise. A man must have lived in this country ten years before he can vote, and fourteen before he can take a seat in the Volksraad – which, practically, amounts to exclusion for life of all the businessmen established in the country. I assure your honour our only desire is for union,' he said, 'and to be law-abiding subjects of the Republic; but your honour's method of depriving newcomers of the vote will perpetuate their discontent.'

'Well, why don't they then leave the country?' Kruger said angrily.

'They can hardly be expected to do that when everything they have in the wide world is vested here.'

'You can send the Volksraad a Memorial,' Paul Kruger said. 'I cannot break the law, but I will give attention to a Memorial.'

(Did he sardonically remember the rejected Memorial he himself had taken to England at the time of the Annexation?)

A petition signed by thirteen thousand aliens was presented to the Volksraad. The Raad received it with laughter and turned it down without a debate; for by now the Presidential election which had tied Kruger's hands, as he said, was over, and Joubert beaten, and his hands were no longer tied. He used them to tighten the fetters. Any alien who desired to vote might, after two years, renounce his nationality and become a naturalized burgher, without any rights but the useless one – after two more years – of occupying a seat in the impotent Second Chamber and voting in the election of landdrosts and other local officials – except on the gold-fields! After ten years more, being thirty years of age, he might obtain full burgher rights, provided the majority of burghers in his ward signified in writing, their desire that he should obtain them – and providing the President and the Executive saw no objection to granting them! But Johannesburg had only been in existence for six years, so that, in effect, the first-comers must wait eight more for the vote, even if – as was most unlikely – they had been naturalized soon after their arrival.

At this the feeling in Johannesburg grew so strong that Janse, presuming once more on his position as Adrian's brother and remembering the success he had achieved with Paul Kruger at the time of the Great Drought, took his courage in his hands and visited the President again.

'I appeal to your honour, as a loyal burgher,' he said, 'to open the door, if it were only a little, to these people – not only for their sakes but for ours. They will welcome the least generosity open-handed: I can assure your honour of that.'

Kruger took him by the arm and led him from the stoep into the roadway. He pointed to the Vierkleur flying from the top of the new Government Buildings which the money of Johannesburg had made.

'Do you see that flag, nephew?' he said. 'If I grant the franchise to these people I may just as well pull it down.'

465

'But that, President, is the flag under which they wish to be governed. All the Uitlanders are not English: they have come to Johannesburg from every country in the world.'

'If they don't like our laws they can always go back to their countries,' Kruger said.

War broke out in the Northern Transvaal against the chief Maloboch. It was a petty war, and no great commandos were needed; but the old man took the chance of showing his power (or his spite) by commandeering British subjects in Pretoria. There were memories among them long enough to remember how the Boers had declined to help Wolseley against Sekukuni after the Annexation. A wave of fierce indignation arose.

'We Uitlanders are not good enough to vote, and yet we must not only pay their taxes but fight for them!'

Five men were arrested because they refused to fight. They appealed to the Cape. The High Commissioner, Loch, hurried up to Pretoria to protest. As he left the station, with Kruger sitting beside him, a crowd of Englishmen unharnessed the carriage-horses and dragged the High Commissioner to his hotel. It was a harmless piece of high spirits, apart from a single sinister incident. One of the crowd mounted the box of the carriage and stood there, violently waving a Union Jack. The folds of bunting flapped in the President's face, and Paul Kruger, in one of his rages, was seen to lash at them with his stick. When the carriage reached the hotel, the crowd abandoned it, and left the old President sitting alone in it.

It was a good joke, people thought, when the story was told in Johannesburg. But Kruger, at his age, could not see jokes of that kind. The second 'flag incident', like the first, was a nail in the coffin of the Uitlanders' hopes; and the fact that the President had to climb down and give way to Loch's threats was another.

His bitterness always increased. When he drove to Krugersdorp, the town that had been named after him, to address a political meeting, his heart spoke from its depths:

'People of the Lord,' he began, 'you old people of the country, you foreigners, you newcomers, yes – even you thieves and murderers . . .'

'Now we know what the old devil thinks of us,' Johannesburg said.

But the National Union did not despair of its constitutional battle. A new petition of right was drafted, and signed by thirty-five thousand citizens. It could be (and probably would be) rejected, the Union knew; but at least it would be debated, for, although Kruger had won his electoral battle with Joubert, the Progressive Party in the Raad was no longer negligible.

Janse, who knew how much was at stake, and had lately, with Piet, been taking an active part in the Union's propaganda, paid another visit to Pretoria to find out from Adrian what the Volksraad's attitude was. Adrian was perfectly frank with him.

'I've been sitting on the committee which was appointed to report on the franchise petition, with Lucas Mayer in the chair. Yours wasn't the only Memorial by any means. There were others, from every part of the back-veld, protesting against any extension of franchise.'

'With how many signatures?' Janse asked.

'Well, a thousand or more.'

'But ours had thirty-five thousand signatures.'

'Not all of them genuine, according to the men on the spot. One was William Ewart Gladstone. Mr. Gladstone is not a burgher. That is making fun of us.'

'That, no doubt, was some poor fool's idea of a joke; but I can give you my word that the bulk of the signatures were genuine: you must know that for yourself, Adrian. What did your committee decide?'

'I've no right to tell you that; but I think you can guess. The result was a foregone conclusion.'

'You're playing with fire, Adrian.'

'It's a question of politics. In the last election Oom Paul's majority wasn't any too big, and we can't afford to show any weakness, or Joubert and the Progressives will jump at the chance of getting us down. Whatever my personal feelings may be, I have to remember that I represent Rustenburg, and that the burghers of Rustenburg have petitioned against any extension of franchise. The back-veld has put us in power, so we have to consider it.'

'So you'll vote against the petition?'

'I shall vote as Paul Kruger votes.'

Janse went to the Raadsaal to listen to the debate. The surroundings were spacious, very different from those in which, eighteen years before, he had watched the death-throes of President Burgers' regime; but neither the character of the assembly nor that of the speeches he heard had changed a jot. Lucas Mayer, the chairman of the committee which had considered

467

the Johannesburg Memorial, presented its report. By a large majority it recommended rejection. He himself believed that the franchise law must be changed. Even the committee, most of whom were against him, recognized that; but he would rather the Raad submitted the proposal to the country. If the country rejected it, the Raad would have to stand or fall with the burghers; but at any rate they would be acting according to the will of the country and could not be blamed for the consequences.

Janse saw Kruger's face go grim. The last thing in the world he wanted was another election. But he held his peace. One of his supporters, a man named Tosen, rose to speak for him. Mr. Tosen was not going to take his orders from Johannesburg.

'When proposals come to extend the franchise,' he said, 'they must come from the old burghers, not from the Uitlanders; and the old burghers, I say, are against any such extension. It stands to reason that newcomers cannot have so much interest in the country as its old inhabitants. As for Mr. Mayer's proposal to appeal to the country, I warn you against it. It would be contrary to Republican principles. Yes, I repeat, it would be contrary to the principles of Republicanism; and if the newcomers are admitted to the franchise, the old burghers will soon be deprived of all their rights. They will not dare to vote or exercise any of their privileges. The persons who have signed this petition say they are peaceful and law-abiding citizens; but they have given us a sign that they are not law-abiding, because they are against the law. The Electoral Law is there, and they ought to abide by it. I shall resist to the end any attempt to alter the law as it stands at present. I speak on behalf of my constituents as well as myself.'

Still Oom Paul was silent; but the voice of Johannesburg was heard at last. Carl Jeppe spoke.

'Who are these people,' he asked, 'who demand from us a reasonable extension of the franchise? There are, to begin with, almost a thousand old burghers of the Republic, and nearly a thousand more who complain that the franchise has been narrowed by recent legislation. This petition has practically been signed by the entire population of the Rand. There are not three hundred people of any standing who have not signed it. It contains the name of the millionaire capitalist on the same page as that of the carrier or miner, that of the owner of half a district next to that of the clerk. It embraces also all nationalities: the

German merchant, the doctor from Capetown, the English director, the Afrikander teacher from the Paarl – they all have signed it. So have – and that, sir, is significant – old burghers from the Free State, whose fathers, with yours, reclaimed this country. It bears, too, the signatures of some who have been born in this country, who know no other fatherland than this Republic, but whom the law regards as strangers.

'Then, too, there are the newcomers. They have settled for good: they have built Johannesburg, one of the wonders of the age, now valued at many millions sterling; they own half the soil; they pay three-quarters of the taxes. They are not persons who belong to a subservient race. They come from countries where they freely exercised political rights which can never be long denied to free-born men. In capital, energy and education they are our equals. All these persons are gathered together, thanks to our law, into one camp. Through our own act, this multitude is compelled to stand together, and to stand, in this most fatal of all questions, against us. What shall we do with them now? Shall we convert them into friends, or shall we send them away empty, dissatisfied, embittered? Dare we refer them to the present law, which first expects them to wait fourteen years, and even then pledges itself to nothing but leaves every-thing to a Volksraad which cannot decide for another ten years – a law which denies all political rights even to their children born in this country? Should we resolve now to refuse this re-quest, what will we do when, as we well know must happen, it is repeated by a quarter of a million? What will become of us or of our children on that day, when we shall find ourselves in a min-ority of perhaps one in twenty, without a single friend among the other nineteen – among those who will then tell us they wished to be brothers, but that we, by our own act, made them strangers to the Republic? Old as the world is, has an attempt like ours ever succeeded for long? Shall we say, as a French king did, that things will last our time, and that after that we reck not of the deluge?

President Kruger rose at last. It was astonishing, Janse thought, how, by sheer physical prepotence, this old man still held the Assembly. He spoke in his harsh, slow voice.

'I wish to say a few words on this subject,' he said; 'and the first thing I have to say is that the persons who signed this monster petition are unfaithful, and not law-abiding.'

'I deny that,' Carl Jeppe said.

'Yes: I repeat that,' Paul Kruger roared. 'I repeat, unfaithful.'

'Mr. President, I say they are not.'

The Chairman called for order. The President went on:

'I will say, then, that they are disrespectful and disobedient to the law, because they are not naturalized. Now, can you contradict that? No, you cannot. Nobody can. The law says they must be naturalized, and they are not. For that reason I say I am against granting any extension, saving in cases like those I mentioned the other day. Those who go on commando are entitled to it, but no others. Those persons who show that they love the country by making such sacrifices are entitled to the franchise, and they shall get it.

'These Memorials from Johannesburg are being sent in year by year, and yearly threats are made to us as to what will happen if we do not open the flood-gates. If the dam is full, before the walls are washed over, a certain portion of the water has to be drained off. Well, this has been done in the case of the commando-men. They are the clean water which is drained off and taken into the inner dam, which consists of clean water, but I do not wish to take in the dirty water also. No, it has to remain in the outer dam until it is cleaned and purified. The Raad may just as well give away the independence of this country as give all these newcomers, these disobedient people, the franchise. These persons know that there is a law, but they wish to evade it. They wish to climb the wall instead of going along the road quietly, and these persons shall be kept back. They shall be kept back.'

He sat down heavily, amid long-continued applause. The *Jabroer*s had got their cue, and two of them, a man named Otto and another named Prinsloo, excitedly challenged the genuineness of the Memorial's signatures.

'I have looked through the petition from Potchefstroom,' Prinsloo said, 'and I find in it the names of my next-door neighbours who have never told me a word about their signing such petitions, so they cannot be genuine.'

'And I,' Otto cried, 'am ready to say that the petition from Otto's Hoop contains many forgeries. The Johannesburgers who signed their names in that wonderful fat book on the table there are as the State President says. They are not law-abiding, and I will have none of them. The Raad is always being told that if the franchise is not extended there will be trouble. I am tired of these threats. I say: "Come on and fight, then! Come on!"'

The Chairman rapped his desk violently and called: 'Order, order!'

But Otto would not be silent.

'Yes, sir,' he shouted. 'This poor South African Republic which they say they own three-fourths of – they took it from us, and we fought for it and got it back.'

'Order! Order!'

'They called us rebels then. I say they are the rebels. Those persons who signed the Memorial in that book are rebels.'

The Chairman rose:

'Mr. Otto, will you keep order? You have no right to say such things. We are not considering the question of powers, but the peaceful question of the extension of the franchise today. Kindly keep to the point.'

'Very well, I will. But I call the whole country to witness that you silenced me and would not allow me to speak out my mind.'

'All this is beside the point, sir,' Carl Jeppe said, 'and much of it out of order as well. Members are afraid to touch upon the real question at issue. They simply try to discredit the Memorial by vague statements that some of the signatures are not genuine. We are informed by certain members that a proposal for an extension of the franchise should come from the burghers, by whose verdict we are to stand or fall. That is not the law. The proposal must come from the Volksraad.'

'That is right. We do not want it put to the country,' Kruger broke in. 'This business has been repeated from year to year until I am tired of it. And why should we worry and weary the burghers once more? There is no need for it; there is no uncertainty about it. The burghers know their own minds, and their will, which is supreme, is known. The way is open for aliens to become burghers: let them follow that way and not try to jump over the wall. If they become naturalized they can vote for the Second Chamber; they can vote for officials – and that is more than they can do in the Cape Colony. There they can only vote for Raad members.'

'Which they cannot do here.'

'Why should they want more power here all at once? What is the cause of all this commotion? What are they clamouring for? I know well. They want to get leave to vote for members of the

471

First Raad, which has the independence of the country under its care. I have been told by these people that "if you take us on the same van with you, we cannot overturn the van without hurting ourselves as well as you". I say: *Ja*, that is true – but they can snatch at the reins and drive the van along a different route.'

'There is one matter,' Carl Jeppe said, 'that I must refer to before his honour finishes: and that is the State President's remarks calling the petitioners disobedient and unfaithful.'

'So they are. Disobedient and unfaithful,' the President repeated.

'But the law compels no one to naturalize himself. How then can the petitioners have disobeyed it? Of course, we prefer them to naturalize; but can we be surprised if they hesitate to do so, when they have to wait so long for any benefit? First a probationary period of ten to fourteen years. In addition to that, the law lays it down distinctly that the naturalized citizen can only be admitted to full citizenship ten years after he has become competent to vote for the Second Chamber, and that he cannot vote for the Second Chamber before he is thirty. The child born in this country of unnaturalized parents must therefore wait till he is forty years old – a middle-aged man – before he can vote, although at sixteen he may be called up for military service and die for the country of his birth. When such arguments are hurled at me by men of our own flesh and blood, born Afrikanders from all parts of South Africa, I must confess I am not surprised that they refuse to accept citizenship on such unreasonable terms. I hope the State President realizes the force of my argument.'

There was no doubt about that; but he would not answer it. The old man was growing weary.

'It is true,' he said, 'as Mr. Jeppe maintains, that these people are not compelled by law to naturalize; but if they want burgher rights they must do so. Then they will get the franchise for the Second Chamber. Let them be naturalized first. If they come nicely to the Raad after that, the Raad will have something to go to the country with and they will receive fair treatment. But if they refuse to be naturalized and reject the Transvaal laws, can they expect the franchise? I answer "No." Let Mr. Jeppe go back to Johannesburg and give his people good advice. Tell them that if they are not disobedient and do not refuse to be naturalized they will not regret it. Let them do as I advise, and I, myself, will stand by them, yes, and support them.'

The motion to reject the Memorial and to refer the Memorialists to the existing laws was carried by sixteen votes to eight. Adrian Grafton voted for it.

'The Raad has given Johannesburg an ultimatum,' Janse told him. 'There will be no more petitions. Nothing can settle this now but fighting, and there is only one end to the fight. Our country is gone. Paul Kruger has taken away our independence more surely than ever Shepstone did, and you have helped him.'

Adrian gazed at him sorrowfully.

'Well, if we must fight, we must fight. How could I vote against a man I have trusted for nearly twenty years? Oom Paul may be wrong; but he is a man who has never made war so long as he could help it. I think he will find some way out.'

'The Lord has hardened his heart, as He hardened the heart of Pharaoh,' Janse said. 'There is no way out.'

Paul Kruger had no intention of showing them a way out. His victory in the Raad over the Progressives had given him a sense of power and increased his vindictiveness. The Lord hardened his heart. He chastised the hated Johannesburg now with scorpions. The Dutch language alone must be used in the courts, in the schools, in the markets. My land is my land, and my tongue is my tongue, he said – though the land was no longer his land and the majority of its inhabitants did not speak his tongue. Taxation increased; monopolies became multiplied and even more scandalous. Bills were passed curtailing the liberty of the Press and forbidding public meetings. When the railway from Delagoa at last reached Johannesburg an even more powerful weapon, the one for which he had longed, fell into his hands. It was, none the less, weaker than he had expected; for, although the line from the coast was shorter, it had been more expensive to construct and was more costly to run, so that the Cape railways could actually carry goods more cheaply in spite of their longer haul, and the Johannesburg traffic still ran over them. The monopoly of transport for which he had hoped had failed him.

There was an easy answer to that for an incensed autocrat. The Netherlands Railway Company – which Rhodes, through

473

Rothschild, had partly capitalized – was compelled to treble its rates for the fifty-two-mile run between the Vaal and Johannesburg – prohibitive rates that would force the importers of the Rand to use his own railway.

It did not force them to do so. The temper of Johannesburg, conscious of its strength no less than of its frustrations, had now grown sterner. At such monstrous rates, the Rand declared, not a single ton should be carried into Johannesburg, nor could any political stratagem force them to use the Delagoa line. Merchants and mine-owners together hurriedly improvised a wagon-transport service of their own. As soon as the freight-trains reached the Transvaal border, their goods were off-loaded and dragged through the drifts and over the veld to Johannesburg by mules and oxen.

This was precisely the sort of enterprise to suit Meninsky, though, in this case, the making of profit was not the first consideration. He took to the veld again, scouring the plains of the Free State, buying up wagons and teams and hiring transport-riders. By the end of a couple of weeks the new service was organized, and two hundred loaded wagons a day were plunging through the great drift of the Vaal at Vereeniging. Meninsky returned to Johannesburg, at once elated and wistful.

'D'you know, Janse,' he said, 'I was actually sorry to come home? To see all them wagons taking the drifts was a sight for sore eyes. It took me back to the days when I was poor as dirt and trekking from farm to farm with the good old donkey-wagon. Them was the days, mate: we'll never see their like again. Last night when I come back to Joh'burg and seen the dumps and all this great mass of brick and stone, I says to myself: "Isaac Meninsky," I says, "what the devil's it all about, this ruddy great ants' nest? Can you look yourself in the face, in a manner of speaking, and put your hand on your heart and swear honest you're any better off now – with the best part of a million pounds you can lay your hands on – than you was in them days when every tickey counted?" And the answer was "no", Janse. I tell you, the answer was "no".'

'Which means you're what you've always been: a romantic sort of bloke,' Janse replied.

'I don't know what you mean by that,' Meninsky said. 'But I know one thing for sure, and that is that life's a ruddy rum business, and the grass on both sides of the fence is much of a muchness.'

474

Paul Kruger made his reply to the wagon-transport. He threatened to close the Vaal drifts to the passage of goods and produce from overseas, to set up a barbed-wire fence around the Republic. Johannesburg laughed at his threats; but the old man was as good as his word. He closed the drifts and set armed guards to turn back the wagons.

It was an ill-judged move – not only because it defied the terms of the London Convention and put him in the wrong, but also because it infuriated the Cape and Free State Afrikanders and threw them into the Johannesburgers' arms. The High Commissioner reported to the Imperial Government and asked for support. Joseph Chamberlain, the new Colonial Secretary, replied that, before he authorized an ultimatum, he must have the assurance that the Cape Government would share in the cost of any necessary military measures and transport Imperial troops over their railways free of charge. The Cape Government, with the support of the Afrikander Bond, assented. An ultimatum was forwarded to Pretoria. This was the signal for a wild, indiscriminate boom in the Kaffir Circus; for war would mean the overthrow of the Republican Government; the end of economic chaos; the inclusion of Rhodesia in a federated South Africa. From the Cape to the Zambezi, all red! 'Chartered' shares, of a pound, shot up to nine pounds in a week.

But, at the last moment, Kruger grudgingly reopened the drifts. He climbed down – as he had climbed down at Fourteen Streams, and at Blignaut's Pont, and in the commandeering dispute. He climbed down without any loss of pride, because he knew he was not ready to fight. But he had united South Africa at last. Against the Transvaal.

(2)

It was about this time that Jimmy and Lena returned to the Cape together from Europe. Piet went down to the coast to meet them. He relished the excitement of long journeys, and was always ready to dash off to Capetown or Kimberley on business: rapid movement and swift decisions ministered to his sense of his own importance and power. This time, though the pretext of his journey was meeting the young people, his principal mission was to interview Cecil Rhodes on behalf of the mining magnates and to enlist his support in the National

475

Union's struggle against the intolerable state of affairs in Johannesburg.

It was clear that the situation of stalemate which had followed the oligarchy's rejection of the Rand's monster petition for the franchise could not last. As Janse had told his brother after the debate, the day of petitions was over. It was a sheer waste of time making any further appeals to Pretoria. Constitutional methods, patiently pursued, had failed and would fail again. There was only one way in which to assert the rights of the bitter majority: by a revolution within the Republic itself.

Since Kruger's last rebuff, the arbitrary closing of the Vaal drifts, an important change had come over the movement for Reform in Johannesburg. Hitherto the big 'owners', the capitalists, had taken no active part in it; not one of them had taken office under the National Union. Its leaders and spokesmen had been businessmen and lawyers, such as the Chairman, Charles Leonard. They had been regarded – even by the Transvaal Government, as a moderating influence – as, indeed, was natural; for they had more to lose by violence than anyone else.

But now, by sheer force of reason, the capitalists had been compelled to come into the Reform movement, though, so far, their contribution had been limited to the provision of a secret political fighting-fund. It is no crime to be a capitalist, yet the mine-owners were wise enough to see that, in a popular movement such as this, 'big money' would always be suspect. They had entered it cautiously, without committing themselves; but the time had now come when a benevolent neutrality was not enough.

Each of the great houses contributed a member to the Reform Committee. Wernher, Beit and Co. sent Lionel Phillips, a born financier with a crystalline intellect and an artist's imagination; Rhodes' Goldfields Company sent his soldier brother, Frank – who had few qualifications apart from his august relationship, considerable charm, some military experience, and transparent honesty – and his consulting engineer, an American, John Hays Hammond. Meninsky's friend, Barney Barnato, was not represented.

It was several years since Piet had seen Rhodes. He found him, as always, delightful, for the 'old man' was always at his best with the friends of his youth, full of warmth and affection. He was eager and proud to show Piet the superb setting of his

ew house at Rondebosch, Groote Schuur, with its superb fall-
ng prospect, beyond masses of blue hydrangeas, to the sandy
flats that are the neck of the peninsula, and, behind, the slopes
dark with pines or shimmering with silver-trees that swept
upward to embrace the bastions of Table Mountain. The
gracious setting provided a contrast to Rhodes' ruggedness. Piet
had never seen him in better form or humour. He had reached
the apogee of his influence and wealth; he had been flattered by
powers and principalities; the whole continent he had converted
appeared to be within the grasp of his blunt-fingered, restless
hands – the whole continent, saving that obstinate nucleus of
the Transvaal, which he seemed disinclined (though he knew
what Piet's mission was) to discuss.

He talked, rather sentimentally, of old times in Kimberley,
the best days of his life, he said, of which Piet's presence reminded him; and he talked of the North – *my* North, as he
called it now, with some justification; of the recently-pro-
claimed British Protectorate of Uganda and the strip of land he
had acquired from the Belgians through which his telegraph
line would soon be linking South Africa with the Sudan; of the
railway which, later, would follow the telegraph line.

There was no boastfulness in his enthusiasm for what he had
done – rather, Piet thought, a morbid anxiety to assure himself
of his own achievement. For all his apparent energy and fervour, the strain of the last few years had told on him. His body,
though still massive, had a shrunken look; his loose clothes, as
shapeless as ever, hung away from it, just as the folds of skin
hung away from his aquiline features; he was rapidly growing
grey; though his cheeks were still highly-coloured, their colour
was not that of health, but the permanent flush of a network of
congested arterioles in the sagging skin. He breathed heavily on
the least exertion. His manner, too, was more restless than ever;
the manner of a man whose nerves were uncomfortably
strained.

That was why, perhaps, he did not want to discuss the Transvaal, though it was like a fleck of grit in the eye, and he could
not forget it. He had called Kruger's bluff over the closing of
the drifts; but the old devil had now gone to ground like an ant-
bear or a porcupine, and couldn't be shifted. Rhodesia,
magnificent as it looked on the map, over which he saw the red
wave steadily stealing northward, was not enough. In some
ways it had disappointed him. The new and greater Rand he

had promised his Chartered shareholders was not materializing. There was gold enough in Ophir, God knew; but the gold was widely scattered. No reef had been discovered in the new territory remotely comparable with that of the Witwaterstrand – nor even with Barberton. And the Rand could never be his to handle and mould in his masterful hands, as he wished to mould everything, so long as Paul Kruger stood in the way.

'They told me the old man was sick and swollen with dropsy,' he complained; 'but the doctor has scotched that story: he saw him some time ago and says he's as strong as an elephant and likely to outlive the lot of us! If only one had a Johannesburg! But as long as he's there we haven't a hope of it; and yet, if we had it, one could unite the whole country tomorrow. Then you would have a great commonwealth; then you would have a union of states; then, apart from the mother-country, there would be nothing in the world to compete with South Africa There is no place to touch this, Grafton; there is no place to touch it – for the beauty of its climate and the variety of its products. And yet we stupid human mortals are quarrelling over the equality of rights, instead of thinking of the great country that has been given to us.'

'That is just what I've come to talk about, Rhodes,' Piet told him.

'I know, I know. . . . But my position is very delicate. *Qua* Managing Director of the Goldfields one has as much right as any man living to be interested in the fate of Johannesburg. I have taken an interest, indirectly, through Frankie and Hammond. But *qua* Managing Director of the Chartered Company one can't compromise one's position; and *qua* Prime Minister of the Cape Colony, one's supposed to be on friendly terms with Paul Kruger's Government. Caesar's wife and the rest of it.'

'We appreciate that,' Piet said; 'but the obvious fact remains that we can't move a step without you. You hold the key to the whole situation in the railways, the Chartered Company's railway and the Cape's, which are our only lines of communication with the outside world. We must move: it's our turn now that the Raad has rejected the petition: but we feel we must know how far you're prepared to go with us.'

'How far do you yourselves mean to go? You must tell me that first.'

'Well, we've drafted – to be more accurate, Charles Leonard

has drafted – a sort of Declaration of Rights. Do you mind if I read it?'

'Not at all. Read away.'

It was actually no more than a recapitulation of the monster petition already rejected by the Raad. As Piet read it Rhodes walked to and fro on the stoep within ear-shot, occasionally nodding his head in approbation, until he came to the final paragraph which demanded free trade in all South African products. Then he slewed round suddenly.

'*That* is what I want,' he declared emphatically. 'That is all I ask of you. The rest will come in time. We must have a beginning, and that will be the beginning. If you people get your rights, the Customs Union, Railway Convention, and all the other things will all come in time. But how are you going to get your rights?'

'There is only one way to get them. By revolution.'

'A revolution within the Republic. Yes. A bloodless revolution.'

'It cannot be bloodless, unless we are strongly armed. That, of course, is a paradox; but then, we're a peaceable people: I don't suppose there are more than a thousand rifles all told in Johannesburg. But Kruger's been buying armaments. In the fort at Pretoria he has ten thousand rifles, a dozen field-guns and twelve million rounds of small-arm ammunition. Against those we're, naturally, helpless. We can't arm ourselves either. Apart from what the big mining-houses give us, we haven't a farthing.'

'What arms do you need?' Rhodes was happier at once when it came to dealing with figures.

'If we had six thousand rifles with a million rounds and three Maxims, we ought to be able to manage. With them we should be able to seize the fort at Pretoria. There are only a hundred men stationed there, and most of those are asleep after nine o'clock.'

'Well, you shall have your rifles. We're buying large quantities of arms for the B.S.A. Police and the Rhodesia Horse. They can come to one of the Goldfields' mines through the storekeeper at de Beers. But you'd better settle all details like this with the doctor and Frank. Jameson's going to Johannesburg shortly to see his brother.'

'Very good. That brings me to another point,' Piet said. 'You remember, at the time of the Drifts dispute, the Cape

Government had a force posted on the Bechuanaland boundary?'

'Remember?' Rhodes laughed. 'My dear fellow, I had 'em sent there. If the old devil had chosen to fight on the Drifts dispute, they'd have gone in, and so would the British, and all this trouble would have been over.'

'Still, I think it was the force on the frontier that made him climb down. Now, if Jameson could find some business that took the police to the boundary, and stayed there to hold what you might call a watching-brief for us ...'

'That's difficult. That's damnably difficult. I don't want the Chartered Company dragged into this, Grafton.'

'You're in it, Rhodes; and you *are* the Chartered Company.'

'In South Africa, yes; but not so much at home where most of the capital is held. We're a joint-stock company, and I have to consider my shareholders. I can't mass police or troops in Bechuanaland unless the home Government hands it over to the Company or to the Cape, and they're being damned sticky about it. What I think one might get is a narrow strip all along the frontier for the railway.'

'That's all you would need – for the present.'

'Yes. . . . That gives us a "jumping-off" place. But, supposing we get it, and supposing that Jameson is there with his watching-brief, as you call it. I don't want him to ride in, if it can possibly be avoided – though, of course, if the Rand revolution succeeds, he would be justified in riding in to restore public order.'

'That is rather the idea. We must wait to see how the cat jumps. We'd much rather Jameson didn't ride in unless we find we need him. But we must have him there, within call. Of course, nothing's settled as yet; but the rough plan would be to give him a letter of invitation which the Reform Committee would sign, saying that a conflict appears to be inevitable and that, unless he rescues us, thousands of unarmed men and women and children – to say nothing of property – will be at the mercy of well-armed Boers. The letter would be undated, and the doctor would keep it in his pocket and fill in the date if it had to be used. He might never have to use it.'

'Exactly. That is my point. The initiative must come from Johannesburg. The question is: will the Reformers play up and do their part?'

'Nearly forty thousand signed the last Memorial.'

'My dear fellow, signing a paper's a very different thing from risking one's life. There's another thing which appears to me awfully important: the revolution must be a domestic affair, spontaneously generated from inside. It mustn't have the appearance of being a British conspiracy. If once that is suspected, I warn you I shan't be able to answer for the Cape, and the Free State will be dead against it.'

'I think Leonard's Manifesto makes that quite clear. The first clause, which I read you, says: "We want the establishment of this Republic as a true Republic." It couldn't be clearer.'

'Yes, yes. That's all right.' But his face was still dubious and heavy with thought. He went on: 'The devil of it is that we're still in the middle of a boom. When one's making money hand over fist, one doesn't want to do anything to upset the cycle, and one thinks precious little about one's political rights. That's human nature.'

'I think the general discontent will be strong enough to carry us through. Johannesburg hasn't forgotten the closing of the drifts; and the speech in which Kruger toasted the Kaiser on his birthday and implied that Germany was backing him has rubbed people up the wrong way. There's a strong feeling against Germans and Hollanders – particularly against Leyds, who appears to have Kruger in his pocket.'

'Yes, Leyds is a clever fellow: a sinister influence. With his brains and the old man's obstinacy they're a pretty tough team.'

'If we're armed, and Jameson is posted on the border, we shall be tough enough, too.'

'Well, you shall have your arms through Kimberley, and I'll do what I can about Jameson, whom you'll soon be seeing for yourselves. Apropos: what's happened to that boy of yours?'

'I'm expecting him on the mail-boat.'

'Good. You'd better send him along to Mashonaland at once. I'll give you a letter to the doctor. He'll soon knock him into shape. The boy won't feel a stranger. There's quite a number of old Etonians up in the north. How old is he?'

'Rising nineteen'

'The lucky young devil! Nineteen. ... When I was nineteen I was just going north with my brother. It was then that we met, my dear fellow, and you hauled us out of that donga. Twenty-three years ago. ... 'Well, I suppose I can't complain: I've managed to do a good bit in those twenty-three years. But there's still a hell of a lot to be done. If I could only be sure of having ten more in front of me . . .'

'You look good for twenty,' Piet said.

Rhodes shook his imperial head, and smiled. 'I wish I were as fit as you are.'

It was the last impression Piet had of him: that of a weary Titan, bowed beneath the weight of his present achievement, yet asking for more; a man inwardly locked in a desperate struggle against Time. He was struggling, too, had Piet only known it, against an ill of which he knew nothing. Within that massive chest, the walls of the great aorta were giving way and the artery itself swelling into the aneurism that, in seven years' time, would compress the heart until it could beat no longer.

(3)

Piet was delighted by the first sight of his son waving his straw hat from the promenade-deck of the mail-boat as it swung into the quay. He had always been what Meninsky would have called 'a family man', affectionate with his children and proud of them – not merely for themselves but as the inheritors of the name and fortune he had established from such humble beginnings, and as choice representatives of the new aristocracy of the Rand.

Jimmy – or James, as he now must really be called – did not disappoint him. The air of England had obviously suited him. He stood six feet high and straight as an arrow, a well-grown boy, without any suggestion of weediness. Though there was a hint of his mother's blood in the distinction of his features – Major Haskard had always been called a 'distinguished-looking' man – his body had the Prinsloos' solidity, his hair was as golden as Adrian's had been in boyhood, and his figure combined the Afrikander's stalwart strength with the natural grace of a well-bred young Englishman. His speech and his manners were English, too; he spoke as Frankie Rhodes spoke (and what could Piet ask better?) and the deference with which he treated his father, whom he called 'Sir', was combined with a complete, if unassuming, self-assurance which Piet – who at times, in polite society, felt unnecessarily forced to assert himself – would have given the world to possess.

He was even more deeply impressed by the appearance of Lena, whom he had been so far from recognizing when he saw her at first that he supposed his son had picked up some fashionable Englishwoman in the course of the voyage. Lena was now what James Haskard would have described as a 'thundering beauty'. She was dressed in the height of the latest Parisian mode (Janse had always been lavish with her allowance) in a violet dress whose bodice, fitting close to the slimmest of waists and closely following the lines of a generous figure, was surmounted at the neck by a filmy collar of frilled lace which revealed the whiteness of her throat. On her honey-coloured head she wore an impudent toque trimmed with Parma violets and supporting a veil through which could be seen those deep violet eyes, so like in hue to Lavinia's, yet so much more lustrous and lively, and cheeks whose softness had the bloom of a ripening grape.

When Piet gazed at her, modestly waiting for Jimmy to introduce him, she burst out laughing and kissed him.

'Oh, Uncle Piet,' she protested, 'don't you know me? Am I so dreadfully changed as all that?'

Piet found the impulsive embrace and the touch of her smiling lips on his cheek through the net of her veil a novel and disturbing experience: he was not used to being kissed by 'thundering beauties'. But Lena was not at all shy. She was, in fact, even more natural than Jimmy, and equally sure of herself; and though the astonishing amount of her luggage and the disclosure of its elegant mysteries kept them hanging about the customs for more than an hour, Piet was proud to be seen in the company of such a brilliant and lovely creature.

Even so, he found it hard to get over the change in her, and even harder to accept the frank intimacy which she was willing to share with him. She and James were so obviously denizens of another world and of another age than his. As the slow train steamed northward over the Karroo and he listened to the young people's eager, foolish talk, Piet felt singularly out of date, and ill-educated. They alluded familiarly and enthusiastically to things and people he had never heard of – speaking not only of shipboard events and friends, whose interest was already beginning to simmer down on dry land, but of new plays and books: of du Maurier's *Trilby* at the Haymarket, which had taken the world by storm; of Miss Marie Corelli, whose latest, scandalous masterpiece, *The Sorrows of Satan,* they had both (and Lena certainly shouldn't have) read. She had also, it seemed, acquired the unfeminine accomplishment of riding a bicycle – Piet hoped to goodness she wouldn't do any such thing in Johannesburg. When she and Jimmy weren't talking nineteen to the dozen, they sang Miss May Yohe's coon-songs: 'Honey, my Honey' and 'Linger Longer, Lucy', and though Lena's low voice had a sensuous, provocative sweetness, Piet disliked this sentimental cult of the negro, whom, as a good South African, he refused to romanticize. Though they were both of them thoroughly satisfied with themselves, he resented the younger generation's detachment from what he regarded as 'life' – partly, no doubt, because it made him feel old.

Piet disliked feeling old. There was one thing on which he soon made up his mind. Lena's nature, soft and luscious as she appeared, was very much stronger than Jimmy's. The boy was an enraptured slave; this lovely little devil could do just what she liked with him. He was not at all sure it had been prudent to let them travel out from England together. However, this non-sense – if nonsense there was – would soon come to an end. He was glad to think that, within a month at the most, Jimmy would get his orders to report to Police Headquarters in Rhodesia and come under a sterner and healthier influence than that of this exigent child. He was beginning to question the wisdom of Rhodes' further plan: that, after a year or two in the police, Jimmy should return to England and finish his education at his own college, Oriel. He was already, Piet thought, quite sufficiently anglicized. Far better put him straight in the mines, where Rhodes' influence and the family fortune would help him. Much as he liked and admired the English, Piet didn't want an Englishman for a son. As for poor old Janse and this pretty baggage of his. . . . He laughed when he thought of the dance she was going to lead him.

It wasn't, in fact, quite so furious as Piet anticipated. From a child, Lena's life had been swayed by her tumultuous affections, and however greatly she herself might have changed, her devotion to Janse was unchanging. He need not have feared that, after two years of running wild with unlimited money and admiration in Europe, Lena would find her new life in the small house at Doornfontein tame and unexciting. There was now, in her affection for Janse, a new element, that of pity for this gentle, grey, lame man to whom she owed everything; and her ardent nature was capable of great tenderness. She was shocked by the discomfort, approaching sordidness, in which he lived. Much of her energy (and a little of Janse's money) found vent in a complete reorganization of the house – in the provision of new curtains, new linen, and new furniture in place of the shabby sticks which Meninsky had 'picked up' as bargains on the Market Square during the forced sales of the first depression. Within a few weeks she had transformed the dismal little place into an abode of lightness and delicate colour – she knew the right setting for her own sanguine beauty – which, if it were less magnificent than Lavinia's house, was certainly in better taste. She also saw that Janse's meals, which had been mere improvisations, were properly cooked and served, and dismissed the two 'boys' at whose mercy he had lived for years, astonishing them with a flow of abusive Kaffir obscenities such as they had never heard, or were ever likely to hear again, from the lips of a white woman, and which neither Janse nor Lena herself understood.

He took this terrific lustration with rapt submissiveness, delighted to find that anything in the new life could absorb and content her; for he had imagined, not unreasonably, that no sooner would she have arrived than she would be snatched away from him and plunged into the gay social life of Johannesburg, in which he had neither the qualifications nor the desire to follow her. He felt flattered and grateful and a trifle guilty at the way in which she clung to him.

'I don't want you to feel you're tied to me, Lena,' he told her. 'After all, I'm a dreary, quiet old bachelor, and nothing would give me greater pleasure than to know you were enjoying yourself, even if you were away from me.'

'I think you are talking nonsense, Janse,' she said. 'I like being with you. I'd far rather be with you than with anyone else. The people who fancy they're smart in Johannesburg don't entertain me. No doubt they're hospitable and kind and all that; but the only way the poor things can show it is by spending a lot of money, and I think that's just dull. Jimmy quite agrees with me. Of course, if the dreary old bachelor finds me a nuisance . . .'

'Now *you*'re talking nonsense, darling.'

'Well, thank heaven for that. Johannesburg people never talk nonsense: they only talk money. If I weren't happy, I should jolly soon tell you, Janse dear. I always speak the truth – or very nearly always. That's the fun of being with you. You see, *you* understand me.'

'Still, you're young and full of life, Lena. I don't think you ought to bury yourself. If you went more often to your Aunt Lavinia's ...'

'Janse, darling, I'll tell you a secret: I don't like Aunt Lavinia very much.'

'You mustn't forget she's been awfully kind to you, Lena. You ought to be grateful to her.'

'There you go again! Being grateful has nothing whatever to do with liking people. It's like falling in love. The people you fall in love with don't have to do anything but be themselves, or what you imagine they are. And I've never liked Aunt Lavinia – not even when I was a child with her at the Cape. Aunt Lavinia's a snob and a bore; and she's cold as ice inside.'

'My dear child!'

'She is, Janse. And I don't much like Uncle Piet, either. I know what Uncle Piet is: he's one of those people who look on. Don't you know what I mean? He likes to see other people letting themselves go and making fools of themselves. He stands by and smiles, and they think he's charming; but he's always apart from them; he won't risk giving an atom of himself. When I was in Paris last year I heard someone describe a man we knew as a "*faux bonhomme*"; and the minute I heard the words I thought: "Yes, that's Uncle Piet!" The only genuine people here, apart from yourself, are Mr. Meninsky, who's good as gold, and those old dears at Wonderfontein – particularly grandmamma – and Aunt Maria. I should never go near Uncle Piet's if it weren't for Jimmy.'

She did not often have to go to her Uncle Piet's house to find Jimmy. During his month in Johannesburg he spent most of his time at Janse's. He was there late and early. Whenever Janse came back from his work in the city he found him ensconced there; and Janse welcomed his presence – not only because it made Lena happy but also because he liked the boy for himself. He was so frank and clean and innocent; his nature, even compared with Lena's, seemed so uncomplicated. Each was the other's complement: when the two were together they were entirely self-sufficient. After all, Janse reflected, they had grown up together and shared the memories of a common childhood which the years in which they had been separated only served to make more precious.

It was true that, like Piet, he sometimes found himself an elderly outsider, unable to share their interests, to understand their allusions or even, at times, their language. But, unlike Piet, Janse did not resent growing old, and was not irritated by the contrast of their bright youth. There was not – and there never had been – the least shade of suspicion or jealousy in his nature; he had learnt, in his laborious and lonely life, a wide charity; and the fact that his own youth had been so unhappy and turbulent made him smile, without envy, on the happiness of others – a little wistfully, perhaps; but then, as Meninsky had always said, he was a born sentimentalist.

For consolation – if consolation were needed – he was certain of Lena's constant affection, which he counted far more highly than her dutiful recognition of what she owed him. In this, as in all her other acknowledged devotions, she was passionately steadfast. Even when her other idols, Maria and Jimmy, were present, Janse always felt he came first. This preference made him grateful and humble – and even, at times, smilingly embarrassed – but he could not deny that it was sweet.

The delicious Eden showed every sign of lasting, until, of a sudden, Lavinia introduced the apple of discord. One evening, when Jimmy and Lena were safely engaged in a tennis-party, at Piet's, she drove down in her smart victoria to visit Janse. It was the first time his sister-in-law had paid him such a compliment, and Janse found it hard to account for the honour of it. Not that he was distressed, as he would have been only a few years ago when the old wound was still raw: the Lavinia of today was very different from the Lavinia of his first love. She was Piet's Lavinia. Though the beauty which he had worshipped still persisted and was enhanced, through Piet's wealth, by a new elegance, he could contemplate it without the least renewal of emotion. He showed her over the little house with a naïve pride in the graces with which Lena's taste had transformed it.

'Yes, it's very nice, but it's very small, isn't it?' Lavinia said. 'As a matter of fact I slipped down here this evening to talk about you and Lena.'

'About Lena and *me*? What on earth do you mean, Lavinia?'

'Well, it's a delicate subject, Janse; yet I feel, and Piet feels,

487

too, that it's only fair to let you know that people are beginning to talk.'

'Johannesburg people never stop talking; that's nothing new. But how can their talk affect me so long as I don't hear it?'

Lavinia smiled. 'That's exactly what Piet and I were saying last night. You live so much in a world of your own, and you're so innocent, Janse. But Johannesburg isn't any longer a mining-camp where people can do exactly as they like. It's a civilized place, and civilized people have certain standards. Does it strike you as odd that people should raise their eyebrows and begin to ask questions when they see a bachelor like yourself living alone in a tiny isolated house with an attractive young woman like Lena? You can't go on doing that and expect not to hear any comments. Most people as not so innocent-minded as yourself. Of course, if you're going to marry her . . .'

'Marry Lena? You must be mad, Lavinia. Lena's only a child.'

'That's where you're wrong, Janse. She isn't. There's not a young man in Johannesburg who doesn't realize that she's an extremely desirable woman. Of course, if you don't mind creating a scandal, you can say that this isn't our business. . . .'

'No more it is, Lavinia.'

'And yet, when you come to put yourself in our place, you must really admit, I think, that it's not very nice for Piet and myself *and* the children to have anyone closely related to us talked of in this way. After all, Piet is now a very important man, and any family scandal of this kind must affect his position.'

'Scandal? Scandal? Lavinia, I don't see you have any right to use such a word.'

'You would, my dear Janse, if you knew what people were saying.'

'Well, what are they saying?'

Janse was white with anger.

'They say – and you hardly can blame them – that you're living with Lena.'

Janse laughed. 'Do you think I care a damn for such a foul-minded crew?'

'I don't suppose you do, or you wouldn't have done it.'

'Done what?'

'Kept this girl in the house alone with you. You may feel

488

quite innocent, Janse, and I'm sure you are . . .'

'That's kind of you, Lavinia!'

'. . . But we feel, Piet and I, that it's most unfair to Lena to spoil the child's name and ruin her chances by branding her with an unsavoury reputation. No doubt she realizes her position as little as you do; but people *will* talk, you can't stop them, and there it is.'

Janse was calmer now, though no less indignant.

'Do you seriously mean to say her reputation has suffered?'

'Really, you're too ridiculous, Janse. Of course it has. Piet was saying only last night that if this talk goes on it will be difficult for us to have Lena at the house or let Jimmy come here as he does. Even now Piet finds it difficult to explain when he's chaffed at the Rand Club.'

'You can tell him from me he needn't explain any more than I do.'

'That's all very well. If you were in Piet's position . . .'

'You don't like Lena, do you, Lavinia?'

'Whether I do or don't has nothing whatever to do with it. Of course I like Lena. I know she's wild and impulsive; but considering her origins what else could anyone expect? But she has a good heart, I think; and it isn't her fault that she excites every man who sets eyes on her. That's all the more reason, in fact, why you ought to consider her.'

'Consider her? She's dearer to me than anyone else in the world!'

'Well, of course, if you're ready to admit that, it only makes matters worse.'

'Oh, you don't understand what I mean.'

Janse limped to and fro in an agony of angry resentment. He turned on her abruptly:

'What do you want me to do, Lavinia?'

'Well, we thought, Piet and I . . .'

'You can leave Piet out of it. You're apparently the guardian of our morals.'

She flushed; the null, beautiful face became ugly. 'There's no need to be rude, Janse.'

'All right, then. Go on.'

'We thought, Piet and I,' Lavinia went on firmly, 'that the best way to stop any further scandal would be for Lena to live with us . . .'

'I don't think she'd do that.'

'. . . . or to have Maria to live with you here for a while and act as a chaperon. It might be a bit hard on your mother at first, of course; but Wonderfontein's not so very far away; she could drive over there every day. So long as she *sleeps* here. . . .'

Janse laughed at the emphasis, and the laugh, though bitter, helped to restore his lost temper.

'Well, you, as I've said, are the judge of these things, Lavinia,' he said. 'If Piet and you feel that Lena and I are disgracing the family, I'll speak to Maria about it – though that doesn't mean for a moment that I agree with you.'

Janse rose and limped to the door to show her out; he had no more to say. As he opened it Lena, flushed from her tennis-party, mounted the stoep. The sight of Lavinia surprised her.

'Hullo, Aunt Lavinia,' she said. 'What are you doing here? I left Jimmy looking for you.' Her keen glance passed from one to the other and quickly became aware of the afterswell of that stormy interview. 'Janse darling, your face is all red – and so is yours, Aunt Lavinia. I do hope you haven't been quarrelling.'

'I'm hot. He's been showing me over the house,' Lavinia said, 'and I think it's charming. Good-bye, Janse!'

She slipped away to the waiting victoria. Lena threw down her racket and gazed at Janse searchingly.

'I can see you're upset,' she said. 'What has that bitch been saying to you?'

Janse laughed, in spite of himself, at the unaccustomed violence of this lovely fury. He recognized in her eyes and on her lips an expression of fierce determination he had not seen since the day, years ago, when he had left her behind with Mrs. Wilson at the Devil's Kantoor and she had slipped through the bedroom window to join him under the wagon. He reminded Lena of this in the hope of evading her; but she saw through him at once.

'You'll have no peace till you tell me, darling,' she said, 'so you might just as well, first as last. Come along, Janse.'

She spoke as if he were a child; but he knew what she said was true. He gave in, and softened the story by making a joke of it. It was no joke to Lena.

'Well, wasn't I right to call her a bitch?' she said angrily. 'She and Uncle Piet are a pair; it's a good thing they're married. Those mean, horrible, hypocritical, middle-class minds! Oh, Janse, you poor, poor darling: how I wish I'd been here!'

'I'm glad you weren't.'

'Oh, but, Janse, what did you tell her?'

'I told her what you think, but much more politely than you would have done.'

'Is it possible ... I mean that they think and say things like that, Janse!'

'I suppose it is. Johannesburg only looks like a city; it's really still a dorp. In small towns that sort of thing is all people think of.'

She was silent for a long while. Then she suddenly said:

'Do you want to marry me, Janse? I mean – are they right when they think you're in love with me?'

'My child ... what a question!'

'Because, darling,' she went on impetuously, 'if you do love me, in that way, I mean, I suppose I ought really to marry you, and, if you want me, I will. I'd do anything, anything in the world for you; you know I would, Janse.'

For a moment he felt himself shaken; for loveliness stirred him; but the leaping fire died down swiftly; he suddenly felt very old. He took her hot hand and smiled at her, shaking his head.

'My sweet, you don't know what you're saying,' he said. 'I'm worn old man, more than double your age, and you have your whole life before you. If we were in love with each other, it wouldn't be right. And you're not in love with me, are you?'

She was silent again for a moment. Then she said:

'No, darling, I'm not. I love you dreadfully, but I'm not in love with you. You can't very well be in love with two people at once; and I am in love, most terribly in love, with Jimmy. Now you've made me tell you!'

'Well, well. .... And what about Jimmy?' Janse said gently.

'Oh, Jimmy's just as bad. He'd be worse if he could be. It's awful. I always thought being in love would be so happy. But it isn't. We're both of us miserable now that he's going away.'

'Do you think Aunt Lavinia knows anything about this, Lena?'

'I don't know. I believe she suspects. She watches us like a cat, Janse. I shouldn't wonder if that's what's made her so beastly. If there's been any talk, I bet she and Uncle Piet have been at the bottom of it.'

'I should hardly think that. All the same, there may be something in what she says. She thinks, for your sake – and that

491

means for her own as well – I ought to consider your delicat
reputation. There'd be no harm, after all, in asking Aunt Mari
to come here.'

'I should love Aunt Maria to come; but I hate looking as i
we were giving way to them and their nastiness. Oh, Janse dear
I'm so glad I've told you about Jimmy. It makes me feel hap
pier already. That's the beauty of having you: it's so marvellou
to be able to share things, and I've nobody else.'

Janse smiled – he was strangely happy, too – and kissed he
tenderly. They sat side by side, and Lena snuggled up to him a
the sky darkened, just as she used to do, long ago, when she wa
a child.

Next day he drove over to Wonderfontein and put the case t
Maria.

'How like Lavinia!' she said. 'Yet I think perhaps she is righ
Our dear sister-in-law is not lacking in wordly wisdom; and o
course I'll come and stay at Doornfontein as long as you like.'

It was providential. Janse thought, that she came. Lena wa
harder hit than he could have believed by Jimmy's departure
there was no mean in her nature between desolation an
ecstasy, and he shared her sufferings so deeply that he knew h
would have been of little use as a consoler compared wit
Maria, whose temperament was so much more equable tha
either of theirs.

He was surprised to hear that Jimmy had been ordered t
join the Mashonaland Police, not at Salisbury or Bulawayo, a
they had all expected, but at Mafeking on the Bechuanalan
border of the Transvaal. Cecil Rhodes' plans had been movin
rapidly. He had been granted his strip of land for the protectio
of the railway: his 'jumping-off place.'

CHAPTER FIVE

(1)

JAMESON visited Johannesburg, as Rhodes had promised, 'to see his brother Sam,' and saw a good many others, including Piet and the leading Reformers. They were beginning to get down to details now, and had even settled on an approximate date for the revolution, which was to take place at the end of December.

Their calculations were all based on simple arithmetic: on a certain day Johannesburg would rise, equipped with the ammunition, the three Maxims and the five thousand rifles which the head-storekeeper at de Beers was now smuggling into the city in coke-trucks and oil-drums (fitted with taps that actually dripped oil!) consigned to the Simmer and Jack Mine. To this armament would be added the thousand rifles already in private hands, and fifteen hundred more which Jameson's men would bring with them, if they were invited, in addition to their own. Nine thousand rifles in all would be available; and, if more were wanted, a surprise attack on Kruger's arsenal in the fort at Pretoria would supply them without any difficulty.

Piet was amazed at the change in Jameson, whom he had not seen since that evening in Kimberley when he had consented to throw up his practice and ride north with his bottle of colchicum to cure Lobengula's gout. The Doctor had altered little physically, though his skin was yellow with fever and his head was balder. He still appeared, on the surface, a little, nervous, middle-class Scotsman, with a quizzical, impish humour, a quick sarcastic turn of speech, and a flamboyant levity which the Reformers, who were serious men, found hard to understand.

It was the spirit of the man that had changed. During the last few years he had grown accustomed to living so dangerously – and withal so successfully – that no enterprise, however hazardous it might seem, could daunt him. He was, in fact, as Rhodes' almost infallible instinct had divined, a born adventurer, a romantic of the Stevensonian brand, who had escaped, to his own surprised and excited amusement, from the petty material preoccupations of a small-town doctor's life, into a sphere of action, with a continent for its background, in which no triumph was unattainable to a man of daring. All along the line, with the Matabele, with the Portuguese, with Adendorff's trekkers, he had gambled, staking his life again and again, and had won. Like Clive, his present idol, he could see himself building an Empire; yet, more fortunate than Clive, he knew that he had behind him the vision, the power, the unbounded wealth of the patron and friend who had made him – or at least set him free to become what he was. Life had proved, in the last few years, that Fortune favoured the Bold. He believed in his luck – above all in Rhodes' luck. His successful principle had been to act swiftly and, if necessary, to think afterwards. Up to now he had found that thinking was rarely necessary.

As he confided to Piet, an old friend of Kimberley days, he thought the Reformers cautious to an unconscionable degree, so anxious to cover themselves that he lost all patience with them. There was nothing of the adventurer about any of these damned Johannesburgers. They counted the cost of this superb gamble (if gamble it were) like a lot of bloody accountants preparing a balance-sheet.

'Well, they've a great deal to lose,' Piet told him. 'You can't exactly expect irresponsibility in the leaders of an industry worth a hundred million pounds.'

'They don't realize the importance of Time,' the Doctor declared. (It was as though Rhodes were speaking, Piet thought.) 'You can't go on hedging and havering in a business like this. You must take some responsibility. That's what they're afraid of. The only man of the whole damned lot with a shred of imagination is Lionel Phillips. Frankie Rhodes is all right because the old man's behind him and he'll do what he's told; but Frankie, after all, is only a regular soldier.'

'You'll have to be patient, Doctor.'

'Was patience one of Clive's virtues? Is Rhodes patient?'

'You also have to take count of local conditions,' Piet said. 'A few years ago, when the Reform agitation started, the gold-mining industry was going through an uncertain period and being handicapped by the lack of railways, the Baring's Bank crisis, and so forth. But the railway question is more or less settled now, and in spite of all sorts of irritations, such as the Dynamite Concession, the mines are prospering. People don't trouble to think about politics in good times, when money's abundant. It's when the shoe pinches that they squeal. If some major disturbance cut short this boom at its height . . .'

'Money, money! Johannesburg thinks about nothing but money! What has money to do with your rights? What has money to do with the Franchise?'

'If you want to know the truth, Doctor, I don't think the ordinary Johannesburger, the man in the street, cares a twopenny damn for the Franchise so long as his stomach is full. The big mine-owners certainly don't.'

'Then why the devil, Grafton, am I wasting my time in Johannesburg? Why am I keeping my fellows kicking their heels at Pitsani and Mafeking? Really it's time these chaps made up their minds. You can warn your friends that I'll throw up the whole damned business if they continue to sit on the fence. You can tell them, too, there may not be another chance. And I must have that undated letter of invitation, which Charles Leonard drafted, signed.'

He got his signed letter. When it had been given to him, one or two of the leaders took fright and wanted it back again; but Jameson, taking no risks, had already sent it to Capetown. He himself returned to Mafeking, where the Mashonaland Mounted Police were already in camp 'protecting' the railway strip. Men and arms and horses were also arriving from Kimberley. The Rhodesia Horse, a thousand strong, were called up for 'a camp of exercise' with a promise of extra pay should they be moved 'down-country'. More trained men were recruited from the Bechuanaland Police which, on the handing-over of the Protectorate to the Cape Government, were being disbanded. A strong, well-armed force lay kicking its heels on the Transvaal boundary at Mafeking and Pitsani Potlugo, while Jameson, that stormy petrel, flew hither and thither, from Bulawayo to Mafeking, from Mafeking to Kimberley, from Kimberley to the Cape and back again.

He had left Johannesburg in the belief that everything was settled – to the very date of the rising, which would take place on the twenty-eighth of December or, at latest, on January the fourth; he had fulfilled his undertakings – arms and ammunition were still being smuggled into the city. The Reformers, too, began to do their part, laying in supplies of provisions against a possible siege, drilling corps of volunteers in the mine-enclosures, forming depots for the issue of arms.

They even devised, with an infantile love of mystery, a telegraphic code to hoodwink the 'Government's innocent postal officials, in which the rising itself was referred to indiscriminately as a 'Directors'' or 'Shareholders' Meeting' or, at times, as the 'Sicheleland Flotation' or 'The Polo Tournament', Jameson's Intelligence Department was 'the Rand Produce and Trading Company', and its head, Dr. Wolff, 'the partner'. Jameson was sometimes 'The Veterinary Surgeon', sometimes 'the Contractor'; the Reformers were 'Our Foreign Supporters'; the Boers, 'Opposition Shareholders'; Rhodes' secretary, Harris, was 'Ichabod – or once, inexplicably, 'Godolphin' – but indeed, the whole code was so hopelessly and childishly involved that not even the men who used it could always be sure what their allies meant.

This code was used a great deal during that crucial December. With Jameson no longer there to hypnotize and inspire them, 'Our Foreign Supporters' were getting cold feet. They distrusted Jameson as deeply as Jameson distrusted them; they wanted assurances that somebody besides this volatile adventurer was in it'. Furthermore, it soon became clear that 'Our Foreign Subscribers' had begun to distrust the will of the rank and file to rise. There were racial divisions in this mixed population of Englishmen and Americans, of Germans and Dutchmen, of Afrikanders and Jews. The English suspected the 'foreigners' of a likelihood of 'dwelling at the post'; the foreigners suspected the English of an unavowed plan to bring the Transvaal under British domination. They havered, as Jameson would have said; they were afraid and unready. And the markets were still dizzily active. It was a crime to neglect such chances of making money.

The wires throbbed with an anxious, three-cornered correspondence of contradictory messages in code. Beit telegraphed to Phillips, urging 'immediate flotation'; Harris wired to Jameson that the 'company would be floated on the 28th at midnight', and warned the Foreign Subscribers, at the same time, that he could not give extension of refusal', as the Opposition Shareholders were also calling a meeting. Then Frankie Rhodes bombarded his brother in Capetown with messages declaring it was 'absolutely necessary to delay flotation'. Harris was 'beginning to see that our shareholders in the Matabele Concession were very different from those in the Sicheleland matter', and

Phillips told Beit: 'If foreign subscribers insist on floating, I anticipate complete failure.'

Why must the 'flotation' be postponed? Because the 'Polo Tournament' – they were getting rather mixed up – would clash with the Races. The Races had nothing to do with the code; it was even possible that some of the 'Foreign Subscribers' had horses running in them, and it was apparently easier to postpone the Rising than the Races. But there was another, and a less frivolous reason for the postponement: the question of the Flag; that symbolic bit of variously-coloured canvas which has stirred up bitter dissensions in South Africa from the time of the Voortrekkers until today. Somebody had put it about – one wondered who? – that the Reformers' acceptance of the Republican flag was lip-service, a means of keeping the mixed nationalities 'sweet'. As soon as Jameson came in – if he did come in – there would be no more nonsense: the Union Jack would be hoisted and the Majuba avenged.

If that were going to happen, the Americans, the Continentals, a large part of the Afrikanders said, Jameson had much better stay where he was. So far as they were concerned, the rising was not merely postponed but 'off'. They were Reformers, not agents of a foreign conspiracy. Before they accepted Rhodes' or Jameson's help, this point must be made clear. 'Charles Leonard says flotation not popular,' Harris wired, 'and England's bunting will be resisted by public.' But code-telegrams would not do (and what wonder!). Charles Leonard must go to Capetown and hear the old man's verdict from his own lips.

In any case, here was a breathing-space. The market made a new prodigious leap upward. But while Johannesburg made money, it buzzed with rumour and anxious debate. This secret conspiracy was surely the most widely advertised that had ever been hatched. Its details were discussed at streetcorners no less than in the bar of the Rand Club. Everyone knew that a rising had been planned for the third day after Christmas and then, unaccountably, postponed. Everyone knew the number of smuggled rifles and where they were stored. Everyone knew precisely how many men Jameson had on the border: approximately three times as many as were actually there. Everyone was pledged to secrecy – and nearly everyone blabbed as a matter of course. Even Janse, far removed as he was from the plot's inner circles, knew all about it. It was the 'flag question', oddly enough, that troubled him most.

In this, for the first time, he came into conflict with Meninsky. When he had aired his suspicions, Meninsky looked at him curiously.

'Why are you so dead set on that Vierkleur of yours, mate?'

'It's the flag I was born under, Meninsky.'

'Come to that, mate, *I* was born under the Russian eagle. I was a boy and not as good as a dog in Poland. My dad smuggled me over to London before I could speak a word of English. And there was the Union Jack! He showed it me flying on the Tower, when that old tramp came up London River – and I was a human being instead of a dog. Do you reckon I can ever forget what that meant to me, mate? The justice, the freedom? These people here don't know it; all these chaps from the continent don't know it – what's more they don't want it. But you'll never get me to go back on it, Janse, so long as I live. Not that I mean to fight for it, mind: fighting's not in my line, nor politics either. I'm a plain businessman; but if you ask my opinion this ruddy rising is going to be a fy-asco, in spite of all the talk. At the time when they closed the drifts they were ready for anything. Now it's different. Johannesburg won't rise till the market falls.'

'Well, it seems that Leonard's gone to the Cape to settle the matter with Rhodes.'

'Rhodes'll never go back on the Union Jack, mate. You can take that from me.'

'Leonard will be sending a secret message tomorrow morning one way or the other; so by the afternoon we should know.'

Meninsky laughed. 'Yes, this secret business amuses me. What's all this about rifles? Where are they?'

'There are some in the Wanderers' Ground.'

'Well, if you know that, I bet Oom Paul knows where the rest are – if there are any. People go about talking in this town as if they thought nobody but themselves understood a word of English. They're no better than a flock of ostriches with their heads in the sand. I don't mind betting Oom Paul and your brother are better up in the whole business than the ruddy Committee. Whatever happens, Pretoria won't be surprised.'

Pretoria, in fact, was watching Johannesburg more coolly and warily than Johannesburg watched Pretoria. As the reports

498

came in, Kruger's friends, and Adrian among them, were urging the old man to step in and take advantage of the confusion. He sat on his stoep and smoked and refused to make any move.

'I'll tell you a thing I learnt as a boy,' he said: 'you must give the tortoise time to put out its head before you catch hold of it.'

New rumours reached Johannesburg from the Cape: Rhodes had said that he regarded the flag as a relatively unimportant matter; Rhodes had said that, unless the flag were hoisted, he would wash his hands of the whole affair and call Jameson off. What was one to believe? Piet. Lena's 'looker-on', disliked the look of things, anyway. If the rising succeeded, he would like to be 'in it' up to his neck – for ever since his meeting with Adrian on the slopes of the Majuba he had feared as well as hated the Transvaal Government. If it should fail – as it now looked like failing – he would prefer not to be in Johannesburg at the time. As an old friend of Rhodes, he explained to the admiring Lavinia, he felt he might be of some use in clarifying the situation. It was his duty to his companions, he felt, to take a little run down to the Cape and see how things stood. He did not explain that it was the part of a prudent man to examine the landing-ground on either side of the fence before he decided on which side to come down.

(2)

At Wonderfontein – as perhaps nowhere else within easy reach of Johannesburg – the doubts and confusions that vexed the city had not even been heard of, much less discussed. It lay there, the old farm, or what remained of it, entirely untouched by the greed or the political passions of the surrounding multitude. John Grafton, advised by Adrian, had refused to add his name to the franchise-petition. He had never engaged himself in active politics, and, at his time of life, was not going to begin. All he asked was to be left to enjoy the remainder of his days in the peace that his unobtrusive labours had earned for him. Since the day when the outlying part of Wonderfontein had been declared a mine-field and pegged, he had neither set foot beyond the boundaries of his *mijnpacht* nor eyes on Johannesburg.

He would probably never have done so as long as he lived, had not Carel Strijdom, who, even when Maria had taken up her abode with Janse and Lena, continued to be a faithful and frequent visitor to Wonderfontein, invited him and Lisbet to take part in the celebrations which had been planned, that year, to commemorate Pretorius's victory over Dingaan at Blood River.

This was an invitation which he could hardly refuse with grace, for though there was still a number of elderly men who had fought under Pretorius, Lisbet and he were practically the only active survivors of the Blaauwkrans massacre. The gathering was, as Carel Strijdom urged, a solemn and symbolical occasion, a celebration in which not merely the Transvaal but Natal, the Free State and the Cape Colony would take part: a reminder of the essential unity of South Africa which had been consecrated by the blood of her pioneers. It was possible that Strijdom had an ulterior aim: the unique opportunity of accompanying Maria, who would certainly have to go with her parents, on a long journey made in highly emotional circumstances.

For a long time John Grafton fought against the suggestion. Though he appreciated the honour of having been invited, he was too old and too feeble, he said, to contemplate such a fatiguing excursion; he had made up his mind never more to leave Wonderfontein; though the farm was small and his duties were unexacting, the little there was would be bound to suffer if he left it in the hands of his 'boys'. Yet, as he reflected on Strijdom's invitation, and memories of his remote, adventurous youth crowded in on him with the astonishing detail which is the privilege of old age, he was seized by an increasing desire to revisit the scene in which, fifty-seven years ago, the most stirring events of his long life had been set. For days he could talk of nothing else: Lisbet saw his opposition was weakening; and in the end, to Strijdom's delight, he consented to go. After all, the journey to Natal, which had frightened him when he thought of it first in terms of wagon-transport, need not be fatiguing, nor his dreaded absence from Wonderfontein prolonged. The new line from Natal had just reached Johannesburg, and, as Strijdom assured him, the whole expedition should not last more than four days.

The journey was almost as exciting to Maria as to her parents. Though John Grafton never willingly spoke of the

500

Blauwkrans tragedy and the massacre of the Prinsloo family from which he and Lisbet had escaped, her mother had often told her the story of the Zulu attack, their hazardous flight and the heroic end of her cousin Jan Bothma. To Maria, Piet Retief and Gert Waritz and Andries Pretorius, with whom her mother had actually spoken, were already fabulous figures in a kind of private mythology, and this strange expedition to hallow the heroes' memory and bury their bones, had a quality not of this world which made her embark on it in an oddly excited and emotional mood.

It was a mood, perhaps, communicated to her mind by her parents. They, too, were excited. As they sat side by side in the train, holding hands, while the peaks and bastions of the Drakensberg rose behind them and the descent to the tumbled green hills of Natal began, Maria was more than ever aware of the tensity of their feelings.

'Look, Lisbet,' John Grafton said, 'it is just as when first we saw it. Do you remember how your father came to the edge of the Berg and looked down? He was an old man then, my love, but not so old as we are, and he did not know what awaited him. But I can see Oom Adrian standing there now, looking down – ay, and hear his voice. "Alas for the land," he said, "that has shadows on its borders. Alas for the land . . ." '

Lisbet shook her head: 'Yes, yes, John; well I remember it,' and Maria, listening and watching them both, was overwhelmed with a sudden compassion for these two who, so long ago, had loved and suffered and had now grown old. As she saw her father's eager face, his eyes made young by the light of memory, and her mother's age-wrinkled hand that clasped his as she sat beside him, she was moved to think how, fifty-seven years ago, as young lovers – even younger than herself – these two had gone over the same Drakensbergen hand in hand to meet whatever fate had in store for them, and how, by a miracle of Providence, they were still alive and still loved one another.

She was, indeed, so profoundly moved by the proximity of the old people's suppressed emotion and by her own reflections on the mysteriousness of life, that Strijdom found her remote and unresponsive; yet he was sufficiently sensitive to her feelings to respect her silence and leave her thoughts undisturbed. Whatever the nature of these might be (and he could not pretend to guess), they certainly gave Maria's beauty a tenderness which was lovely of itself, even though it were not for him.

Soon after dawn, after descending the flanks of the Biggarsberg and passing through Ladysmith, where more pilgrims from the Free State joined them, they dismounted from the train at Chieveley, a bare railway-siding, not more than ten miles from the Blaauwkrans river, where a collection of vehicles of every description, from wagons and coaches to cape-carts, awaited them on the veld. Once again Maria was touched by the fragile courtliness with which her father helped her mother to mount the mule-wagon to which they were allotted. In their flight from Blaauwkrans, as she remembered, Lisbet had ridden a horse, with her little brother Hendrik bleeding to death in her arms, and John Grafton had run beside them for six hours on end. This was the country through which they had fled in the light of that dreadful dawn. As she watched her father's face she could see the excitement with which his old eyes searched the landscape for any feature he could recognize; but to her, at least, it seemed a featureless country of low green hills and valleys scattered with mimosa through which many streams swollen with tawny water flowed.

Their course did not lack direction; many hundreds of wheels had scarred the track before theirs; but the going was not easy: during the two previous days and in the night, heavy rain had fallen; the mule-wagon floundered and slithered on through a wide track of churned and rutted mud in which several of the preceding coaches had sunk to their axles and been left abandoned.

It was a rough journey, she thought, for two old people to face; yet neither their courage nor their composure failed them. John Grafton's eyes still scanned the landscape with increasing excitement; he still clutched Lisbet's hand. After an hour or more of this slow, montonous progress, the wagon lurched out of a denser patch of acacia-scrub into a sort of clearing which dipped to the deep-cut banks of the river. Maria heard her father speak:

'It was here, Lisbet,' he said. 'It was here. Yes, this is the place.'

'Yes, this is the place, John,' her mother repeated quietly. Her hand tightened on his. 'God has shown us great mercy, my love.' She looked at him with a surpassing tenderness and

502

smiled with a smile so sweet and serene that Maria felt her heart breaking and turned her eyes away from them. When she looked again, their eyes, too, were closed. It seemed to her they were praying.

It was nearly midday when they reached the place of assembly between Moord Spruit and Blauwkrans, and dismounted. In an open space a white marquee had been pitched; but even that was not large enough to shelter the gathered multitude. Seven or eight hundred people were already assembled; there would have been hundreds more, Strijdom said, if the last day's deluge had not made many roads and spruits impassable. He took Lisbet's arm and led her and her husband into the tent. Maria walked behind them. There was no face that she knew to be seen, and yet she felt strangely at home among this anonymous crowd from whose presence there emanated a moving sense of community, almost of brotherhood, which warmed her heart and brought tears to her eyes.

'I am one of them,' she told herself. 'These people are my people.'

Carel Strijdom led John and Lisbet through the press to the platform where Maria recognized the bearded figure of General Joubert, who welcomed her father with a smile. There were a few other old folk on the platform, and a number of dignitaries who looked like Englishmen and whom she supposed, from what Carel had told her, to be the Ministerial party from Natal, and behind these, again, a group of predikants. Between the platform and the front row of the gathering stood a large box draped with funeral trappings, which the man who stood next to her informed her in Afrikaans contained all that was left of the remains of the Blauwkrans victims, which the committee had piously and laboriously collected from the graves that were scattered along that dreadful valley.

'My poor father and mother are among them,' he said; 'or at least that is what I am hoping. They had left me behind – I was seven years old – in Gert Maritz's camp.'

'My grandfather and grandmother, too,' Maria whispered, 'and my mother's cousin, Jan Bothma.' She felt a strange pride in telling him this.

'Jan Bothma? I have heard of him. It was he who rode through the Zulu impi and held them while the rest of his party escaped.'

'Only three. And one of them, a little boy, died on the way.'

'I think I have heard of that too. Look, then; over there in the corner are two coffins holding the bones of Retief and Maritz.'

'My Uncle Sarel was murdered by Dingaan along with Retief.'

'And an uncle of mine as well. We are all brothers and sisters here.'

The party on the platform had arisen. The whole congregation was singing the Sixty-eighth Psalm.

Let God arise and let his enemies be scattered; let them also that hate him flee before him.
As smoke is driven away, so drive them away: as wax melteth before the fire, so let the wicked perish at the presence of God.
But let the righteous be glad; let them rejoice before God; yea, let them exceedingly rejoice ...

Maria and the man beside her were singing the familiar words: a volume of triumphant sound rose from the crowded tent and from the multitude standing outside it in the fierce sun. Maria saw her father's lips moving. Far away on the platform, he looked very white and frail beside Joubert's strong bearded figure.

Sing unto God, ye kingdoms of the earth: oh sing praises unto the Lord; Selah:
Ascribe ye strength unto God; his excellency is over Israel and his strength is in the clouds.
O God, thou art terrible out of thy holy places: the God of Israel is he that giveth strength and power unto his people. Blessed be God!

One of the predikants gave an address. His name was Kestel; he was a Free Stater from Harrismith, Maria's neighbour told her. He reviewed the story of the Great Trek, a story she had heard told again and again; yet here, on this soil and in these surroundings, it seemed to her to take on a significance personal to herself. She began to feel the influence of those surroundings even more deeply when, the religious service over, the congregation fell into lines and the long cortege moved, eight or ten abreast, towards the site that had been chosen for the burial-place and the erection of the monument.

Andries Pretorius, the conqueror's son, and Martinus Oosthuizen led the procession; behind them came the wooden box full of Blauwkrans remains with their funeral drapings, and behind these, again, a spider on which were set the coffins of Maritz and Retief. Piet Joubert took his place immediately in the rear of these, a solitary chief-mourner. Eight hundred men and women and children followed him, bare-headed under the blistering sun. Maria thought of her parents.

'Poor things, they will be so worn and exhausted by this. The emotion, of itself ...'

She felt a touch on her arm and found Carel Strijdom beside her. She smiled and pressed his hand. They walked on together.

'He is kind and good and earnest,' she thought. 'I have used him badly; but today we are nearer to one another than ever before. Even so I must not mislead him or let my own feelings be misled. Emotion of this sort is infectious. I ought to resist it. One kind of feeling opens the way for others. I could easily persuade myself that these Voortrekkers whose bones they are burying are really important to me; but not all of them put together – Retief and Maritz and the rest – mean so much to me as my Richard, who was murdered just as helplessly at Bronkhorst Spruit as Retief and Uncle Sarel were murdered by Dingaan.'

The cortège had broken and now surrounded the plinth of the monument.

'Piet Joubert is going to speak,' Strijdom said. 'May God put words of peace on his lips.'

General Joubert spoke:

'Brothers, friends and countrymen,' he began. .... His strong voice trembled. It was impressive, Maria thought, to see this remarkable man, whom half the folk of the country regarded as their leader, so deeply moved. He was called 'Slim Piet' by his enemies, she remembered; yet she could not believe that the feeling he now betrayed was not genuine. He spoke, as the predikant, Kestel, had spoken before him, of the Blauwkrans massacre; of how ten thousand Zulus had swept on from the murder of Retief to ravage and pillage and burn the pitiful, innocent little encampments along the river.

505

'Ruthlessly were they murdered,' he cried, 'their bodies mutilated and left unburied to lie festering in the sun, to be eaten by birds of prey. Brothers and countrymen, we are here today to honour the memory of this terrible event, and we have reason to be thankful that we are enabled to stand peacefully on this hallowed spot which is now governed by a civilized and a Christian people. I do not believe,' he went on, 'in deifying individuals; but this is really a national monument, erected by a grateful posterity in remembrance of the sufferings of the men and women who met their death in what was then a wild and barbarous country. We, my brothers and countrymen, are entering into the fruits of their bitter labours and justifying their unshaken trust in all-ruling Providence. The honour that we and our English friends from Natal are paying to their memory today has a deeper significance. It leads me to hope that the bond of unity and peace between the different states of South Africa may be drawn closer and closer. A time is coming. I believe, when men, irrespective of their nationalities, may feel and become one people and reap, in peace and amity, the benefits conferred on posterity by these voortrekkers. I hope and trust that in this grave may be buried not only the remains of those who fell in that fight, but also all past bitterness, and that we may join together in concord and harmony for the unity of South Africa – our dear, our own, our common land.'

'He has said what I hoped he would say,' Carel Strijdom whispered. 'Now Robinson, the Prime Minister, will speak for Natal. But what is the use of that to these people? He will speak in English.'

Maria turned on him:

'Carel, Carel, what are you saying? One moment you are pleading for Unity, and the next you are taking offence because a born South African chooses to speak his own language! How can we ever have Unity when intelligent people like yourself are so narrow and obstinate? You make me feel hopeless and ashamed of you.'

'You are right, you are right, Maria. I know you are right. I'm ashamed of myself. But there is something deep down in me that rebels and protests in spite of my being ashamed. It's a feeling that can't be mastered by reason, only by the love that casteth out fear. Yes, fear is behind it. You can help me by loving me, Maria, if it were only a little!'

She shook her head helplessly. 'Even now you are not trying to listen to what the Prime Minister says.'

'Forgive me, my love . . .'

'And now it is going to rain. We must think of my poor old people. They have nothing to cover themselves with. Oh dear, it's beginning. Carel, what can we do?'

They could do nothing; for now the storm broke and the heavens opened. Rain fell in solid columns and sheets with the violence of a cloud-burst. In three minutes the whole assembly was drenched to the skin, and the space surrounding the monument became a trampled quagmire. Maria had only one thought: to find shelter for her parents; but the great marquee had already collapsed beneath the weight of falling water and they had more than a quarter of a mile to wade, ankle-deep through red mud, before they could reach the only available cover, a deserted farm which one of the Committee, a man named Labuscagne, had roughly furnished for the entertainment of his friends. There, wedged in a steaming mass of humanity, John Grafton and Lisbet waited patiently till Carel, his black clothes clinging to his body, arrived to tell them that the mule-wagon was ready to carry them to the railway-siding at Chieveley.

The journey back to the Rand through the night was a foretaste of purgatory. They sat shivering in their wet clothes, huddled closely together for the sake of each other's warmth. John Grafton suffered most. The stress and excitement of the day had exhausted his spirits, too highly keyed for endurance. His eyes were no longer bright with anticipation and interest. His face looked as grey as his hair, and his thin body quaked with fits of shivering. Carel Strijdom took off his skirted clerical coat and wrapped it round him; but nothing could replace the inner warmth that his old body lacked. When at last, on the following afternoon, they reached Wonderfontein, Lisbet put him straight to bed under heaped karosses and blankets. He lay there, as quiet as a child, without moving or speaking.

'There seems to be no more strength or will left in him,' Lisbet said. 'You must let Janse know, and he will tell Piet and Adrian how anxious I am; for I have never seen your father like this before. He won't look at me, Maria, nor will he answer me. He has turned his face to the wall.'

Maria hurried over to Doornfontein.

'Piet has gone to the Cape,' Janse said, 'but I think Adrian may be in Pretoria, so I'll send him a telegram. You must drive back with me now, Maria; we can't leave mother alone; and we will call for a doctor on the way. Max Mehliss is the man for us. I worked with him during the small-pox epidemic.'

They found Lisbet sitting beside John Grafton's bed.

'He does not answer me,' she said pitifully. 'I don't think he even knows me. But he has begun to talk to himself and seems, too, to be talking with people I have neither known nor heard of, with English names. Just now he was making a speech, as if he were in Parliament. "Sirs," he said, "I have walked here a hundred miles or more: I am sent here to protest by the people of Grafton Lovett. . . ." ' (*Grafton Lovett?* The name stabbed Maria's heart. What could he know of Grafton Lovett?) 'But now he has fallen quieter,' Lisbet said; 'I think he is too weak to talk. He has worn himself out. I almost think he is asleep. If he wakens he will be frightened: he has never had a doctor before in his life.'

The tall distinguished figure of Max Mehliss bent over him.

'Do not disturb yourself, Tante Lisbet,' he said in his guttural English. 'If he's asleep I shan't wake him; but I can tell by this rapid breathing that there is something amiss with his chest, and I must listen to find out what it is.'

He pressed a finger to John Grafton's wrist and counted the pulse. Then he laid his ear firmly against the thin chest and listened intently. Next, with gentle, powerful hands, he rolled the old man over and listened again with his ear to the back.

'I will not trouble your husband more, Tante Lisbet,' he said.

'It is the lungs, then?'

'Yes, it's pneumonia: a double pneumonia.'

'That is a bad thing, doctor?'

'A very grave thing for a man of his age. How old is he?'

'In his seventy-sixth year. We have been married fifty-six.'

'You have had a good share of life and happiness. That is to be seen from your face.'

'A life like most other lives, doctor, of joys and sorrows. But happy, yes. My husband is a good man, and our children, too, are good.'

'It is strange that a disease of this kind should have come in full summer. It is usually the result of exposure and strain.'

Maria told him of the pilgrimage to Blauwkrans, the drenching deluge, the shivering journey home.

'Ah, that accounts for everything,' Max Mehliss said. 'The fatigue, the excitement, the chill – all three together.'

'Must we lose him then, doctor?' Lisbet asked. 'Can nothing be done?'

'Very little, I am afraid. It's a lonely battle. They call this disease "the old man's friend". He's a tired old man, Tante, and he has come to the end of his days.'

Lisbet drew a deep sigh and set her lips firmly.

'It is strange,' she said. .... 'Fifty-seven years ago, at Blauwkrans, God spared his life, and now, again at Blauwkrans, He takes it. His will be done.'

They buried John Grafton a week later in the little family graveyard at Wonderfontein. Adrian and Janse carried the coffin between them – it was not very heavy – to the grave the two Kaffirs had dug, and Carel Strijdom read the burial service over it. When they returned to the house a messenger came from Meninsky with a telegram addressed to Janse which had arrived at the office during the ceremony.

IMPOSSIBLE TO LEAVE CAPETOWN, Janse read. TELL MOTHER MY HEART IS WITH YOU ALL STOP HAVE TAKEN OPPORTUNITY OF CONSULTING BEIT ABOUT WONDERFONTEIN 'MIJNPACT.' SUGGEST WOULD FACILITATE MATTERS IF YOU AND MARIA GAVE ME POWER OF ATTORNEY. AFRAID YOU MUST DEAL WITH ANDRIES AND ADRIAN BUT HOPE WILL BE REASONABLE. PIET.

Janse handed the telegram to Adrian who read it and frowned.

'What is it then, Janse?' Lisbet asked calmly.

'A message from Piet, mother. He says he cannot leave Capetown. "Tell mother my heart is with you all," he said.'

'Dear Piet . . .' Lisbet sighed.

(3)

From the day of the funeral at Wonderfontein – it was on Christmas Eve – the telegraph-machines at Capetown and Kimberley and Mafeking and Johannesburg were tapping out streams of conflicting code-messages in Morse:

Harris, Capetown, to Jameson, Pitsani:

YOU MUST NOT MOVE BEFORE SATURDAY NIGHT. WE ARE FEEL-ING CONFIDENT IT WILL TAKE PLACE SATURDAY NIGHT. DR. WOLFF LEFT FEELING OUR SUBSCRIBERS GREATLY IMPROVED.

Rhodes, Johannesburg, to Charter, Capetown:

IT IS ABSOLUTELY NECESSARY TO POSTPONE FLOTATION. CHARLES LEONARD LEFT LAST NIGHT FOR CAPETOWN.

Harris, Capetown, to Jameson, Pitsani:

CHARLES LEONARD WILL ARRIVE CAPETOWN SATURDAY MORN-ING; SO YOU MUST NOT MOVE UNTIL YOU HEAR FROM US AGAIN. TOO AWFUL. VERY SORRY.

Rhodes, Capetown, to F. Rhodes, Johannesburg:

JAMESON SAYS HE CANNOT GIVE EXTENSION OF REFUSAL FOR FLOTATION BEYOND DECEMBER AS TRANSVAAL BOERS' OPPOSITION SHAREHOLDERS HOLD MEETING ON LIMPOPO AT PITSANI.

Hays Hammond, Johannesburg, to Jameson, Pitsani:

WIRE JUST RECEIVED. EXPERTS REPORT DECIDEDLY ADVERSE. I ABSOLUTELY CONDEMN FURTHER DEVELOPMENTS AT PRESENT.

Harris, Capetown, to Jameson, Pitsani:

IT IS ALL RIGHT IF YOU WILL ONLY WAIT. HEANY COMES TO YOU BY SPECIAL TRAIN FROM F. RHODES TODAY KEEPING MARKET FIRM.

Jameson, Pitsani, to Wolff, Johannesburg:

MEET ME AS ARRANGED BEFORE YOU LEFT ON TUESDAY NIGHT, WHICH WILL ENABLE US TO DECIDE WHICH IS BEST DESTINATION. MAKE J. W. LEONARD SPEAK. MAKE CUTTING (of telegraph wires) TONIGHT WITHOUT FAIL. HAVE GREAT FAITH IN HAMMOND AND LAWLEY AND MINERS WITH LEE-METFORD RIFLES.

Heany, Kimberley, to Harris, Capetown:

SPECIAL ONLY READY 3 P.M. SHALL LOSE NO TIME. BE IN MAFE-KING THREE IN MORNING, AND IF LATE SHALL FOLLOW.

Jameson, Pitsani, to Harris, Capetown:

HAVE NO FURTHER NEWS OF HEANY. I REQUIRE TO KNOW. UNLESS I HEAR DEFINITELY TO THE CONTRARY, SHALL LEAVE

TONIGHT FOR THE TRANSVAAL. IT WILL BE ALL RIGHT. MY REASON IS THAT FINAL ARRANGEMENT WITH WRITERS OF LETTER WAS THAT, WITHOUT FURTHER REFERENCE TO THEM, IN CASE I SHOULD HEAR AT SOME FUTURE TIME THAT SUSPICIONS HAVE BEEN AROUSED AS TO THEIR INTENTIONS AMONG THE TRANSVAAL AUTHORITIES, I WAS TO START IMMEDIATELY TO PREVENT LOSS OF LIVES, AS LETTER STATES. WE ARE SIMPLY GOING TO PROTECT EVERYBODY WHILE THEY CHANGE THE PRESENT DISHONEST GOVERNMENT, AND TAKE VOTE FROM THE WHOLE COUNTRY AS TO FORM OF GOVERNMENT REQUIRED BY THE WHOLE.

High Commissioner, Capetown, to Resident Commissioner, Mafeking:

IT IS RUMOURED HERE THAT DR. JAMESON HAS ENTERED TRANSVAAL WITH ARMED FORCE. IS THIS SO? IF SO, SEND SPECIAL MESSENGER ON FAST HORSE DIRECTING HIM TO RETURN IMMEDIATELY. COPY OF THIS TELEGRAM SHOULD ALSO BE SENT TO OFFICERS WITH HIM, AND THEY SHOULD BE TOLD THAT THIS VIOLATION OF THE TERRITORY OF A FRIENDLY STATE IS REPUDIATED BY HER MAJESTY'S GOVERNMENT AND THAT THEY ARE RENDERING THEMSELVES LIABLE TO SEVERE PENALTIES.

Harris, Capetown, to Abe Bailey, Johannesburg:

THE VETERINARY SURGEON SAYS THE HORSES ARE NOW ALL RIGHT; HE STARTED WITH THEM LAST NIGHT; WILL REACH YOU ON WEDNESDAY; HE SAYS HE CAN BACK HIMSELF FOR SEVEN HUNDRED.

Rhodes, Capetown, to Jameson, Pitsani:

HEARTILY RECIPROCATE YOUR WISHES WITH REGARD TO PROTECTORATE, BUT THE COLONIAL OFFICE MACHINERY MOVES SLOWLY, AS YOU KNOW. WE ARE, HOWEVER, DOING OUR UTMOST TO GET IMMEDIATE TRANSFERENCE OF WHAT WE ARE JUSTLY ENTITLED TO. THINGS IN JOHANNESBURG I YET HOPE TO SEE AMICABLY SETTLED. AND A LITTLE PATIENCE AND COMMON SENSE ARE ONLY NECESSARY. ON NO ACCOUNT WHATEVER MUST YOU MOVE. I MOST STRONGLY OBJECT TO SUCH A COURSE.

The last of these telegrams was tapped out from Capetown over a dead wire. The line had been cut, by Jameson's orders, on Sunday evening, and the message never reached him.

511

Jimmy Grafton had been having the time of his life at Pitsani Potlugo. The military training came easy to him, after four years in the Cadet Corps at Eton with its manoeuvres in the Great Park and its annual fortnight in camp, and he was already a passable horseman, having been accustomed to riding every day in his boyhood and having spent his last Christmas holidays, a year ago, with a school-friend named Folville, who lived in High Leicestershire, and hunted five days a week with the Quorn or the Cottesmore. He was also an excellent shot with a rifle, and quickly mastered the use of the Lee-Metford which had lately been issued to the Mashonaland Police in place of their old Martinis.

There was nothing he would rather have been than a professional soldier, like his grandfather, James Haskard, and his Uncle Edward; and soldiering of this kind, in what, for all its newness, was a *corps d'élite,* yet unhampered by the traditions of a regular regiment and relying for its discipline on a spirit of *noblesse oblige,* was very much to his taste. He was South African born; and his sudden return, after five years' confinement in the humid greenness of Southern England, to the brilliant air and vast spaces of his native land filled his body with a freshet of vigour and his mind with a gay, adventurous exultation.

Everything had been in favour of his enjoying the best of two worlds. He was completely at home on the veld with his fellow-troopers, yet able, also, to mix without any feeling of inferiority with his officers, most of whom were English regulars of an unconventional type. He had come to Pitsani with a letter from Rhodes to Jameson and had been recommended by Jameson to his commanding officer, Harry White, who turned out to be a brother Etonian – a fortunate fact which promised him easy and early advancement. He was on the top of the world, and the more exalted because, as Lena had confessed to Janse, he was 'terribly in love'.

His separation from Lena was, in fact, the only fly in this precious ointment. Yet, though he thought and dreamed of her, the natural happiness of an uncomplicated disposition and the novelty of his exacting pursuits (the second-in-command, Inspector Bodle, an old Carabineer, kept his troopers well exercised) prevented him from brooding over her absence.

Though he hardly had time to answer them, the stream of letters, aglow with the intimate warmth of Lena's ardour and rich with her sweetness, which arrived by every mail from Mafeking, made him feel that he was never out of touch with her. Even physically she did not seem really remote. Pitsani was less than a hundred and eighty miles from Johannesburg, and his imagination could easily bridge that trivial distance. Moreover he was young, so young that the sense of the passage of time did not weigh on him; and so confident in her complete devotion and in his own that nothing on earth could conceivably threaten their love.

His older companions, who lacked this sublime exaltation, were less tolerant than Jimmy of their protracted stay at Pitsani. They were 'guarding the railway', their officers told them; but that was 'all my eye'. Against whom were they guarding it? The natives of Bechuanaland? These were harmless enough. Against the Boers? The Boers, as usual, were busy with politics. The Transvaal frontier had been marked out long ago, and there were no Boers within reach but the inhabitants of a few scattered farms. No, there was something behind this concentration, this intensive training, this watchfulness, this coming and going of highly-placed officers, including the Administrator, Dr. Jameson himself, and Sir John Willoughby, commanding officer of the Rhodesia Horse, whose arrival from Bulawayo, 'on leave for England,' had coincided with even more active preparations. What was it all about?

They had not long to wait before they knew. On Sunday afternoon, four days after Christmas, the Mashonaland Police paraded in marching order, three hundred and seventy-two strong, with all their artillery and transport and rations for twenty-four hours, and Jameson and Willoughby addressed them. Jimmy had only seen Dr. Jameson once before, on the day when he had presented his letter from Rhodes; but he knew also that 'the Doctor' was an old friend of his father's and had been, therefore, prepared to like him, though he found his manner perfunctory and not inviting. Even now, on the parade-ground, Jameson's presence was not impressive: Jimmy found it hard to believe that a small dark man with so little physical distinction could be an inspiring leader. But the Mashonaland Police, who had already served under him in more than one tight corner, were evidently of a different mind.

Jameson spoke colloquially, almost jauntily. They were going to Johannesburg, he said. (Johannesburg! Jimmy's heart leapt. Johannesburg, for him, meant Lena.) He took out the undated letter of invitation and read it in a clipped Edinburgh accent: 'Thousands of unarmed men and women and children of our race will be at the mercy of well-armed Boers!' That was why they were going. 'The odds are,' he said, 'that not a single shot will be fired; we shall probably get through without any fighting at all; but if we do have to fight, we must be prepared to go on fighting. At Malmani, a few hours' march from here, the Bechuanaland Border Police are going to join us. If it comes to a push, the Cape Mounted Rifles and the Natal Mounted Police will probably come in too. Now then, what do you say about it?'

The force broke into cheering, raising their hats on their rifles, and Jimmy cheered with them. A hard-bitten trooper on his left turned to him and said: 'I'm damned if I know what it's all about, this women-and-children business; but I know one thing well enough, and that is that we'll all of us follow the Doctor to hell!'

In the cool of the evening the force moved off for Malmani in column of march. The men rode in silence; there was no sound through the night but the squealing of distant jackals, the clink of accoutrements, and the measured, muffled tread of the horses' hooves on dry veld; yet there was a rhythm in this; the sound of the plodding hooves resolved itself into a steady beat; and every beat, Jimmy thought, brought him nearer to Johannesburg and to his meeting with Lena. It was a lulling sound, too, which encouraged drowsiness. At times he was nearly asleep, and then, starting awake, became aware of his shadowy companions moving beside him slumped in their saddles, and thought to himself: 'This march is different from any I have known before. This is not a mere exercise. We are riding to war. Though the Doctor tells us that not a shot will be fired, it's quite possible that within a few hours we may be fighting for our lives against men who want to kill us, men like Uncle Adrian. I have nothing against these Boers whom we are going to fight; the Boers I know have always been hospitable and friendly. I suppose I am going to fight, and kill them if I can, because, if I didn't, they would kill me, and I am a soldier. This will be my first engagement, the baptism of fire to which soldiers are supposed to look forward. I ought to be feeling tremendously heroic and excited. Well, I suppose I am excited, and also, to be quite honest, rather afraid: that's part of the excitement. And I ought to be proud and happy as well, because this is the work of a man: I am proving my manhood. There are dozens of fellows at Eton who would give their eyes to be in my shoes at this moment, making this night-ride over the veld to rescue "thousands of unarmed men and women and children of our race" – yes, that's what the Doctor said – "at the mercy of well-armed Boers." Women and children: that means mamma and the kids and Lena. . . .'

At five o'clock, in the dawn of Monday morning, the column reached its rendezvous and saw the Mafeking contingent, the Bechuanaland Border Police, approaching Malmani from the south-west. There seemed to be very few of them, not many more than a hundred rifles, Jimmy thought. One of their officers left the column and cantered over to meet them; the rising sun reddened his pleasant, high-coloured face. Jimmy had seen him before at Pitsani, and had been told his name: Charlie Coventry. He fell in with Colonel White and the two rode on side by side, talking and laughing. Jimmy could hear what Coventry said.

'Pretty good staff-work, Harry. I don't think we're half an hour out. Any news?'

'None that I know of. I suppose your fellows have cut the wires: at least I hope so. Heard anything more from the south?'

'Not a squeak. We had to go easy: too many curious eyes about in Mafeking. We didn't parade until half past seven, and then some of our time-expired troopers fell out. Insisted on knowing where we were going. I told them, of course. Even then there was a bit of a palaver and the Colonel had to explain to them. One chap wanted to know if he was going to fight for the Queen. However, most of 'em fell in again.'

'How many are you?'

'A hundred and twenty. Two Maxims and two seven-pounders.'

'That makes just on five hundred in all. It's none too many, Charlie. The Doctor promised Johannesburg fifteen hundred. However, I suppose it'll be all right.'

'Oh yes, it'll be all right. We've got a flying start. At this moment what I could do with is a nice cool whisky and soda.'

Jimmy wished he hadn't mentioned it. His own throat was parched with dust. The columns joined forces and rode on to

Malmani Oog, where the first dump of rations and forage had been laid, and off-saddled to let the horses roll, and ate their breakfast. By this time the High Commissioner's message had reached Mafeking, and the man 'on a fast horse' was riding after them ...

Though nothing as yet was definitely known in Johannesburg, the city was restless. Janse felt that communicated unrest in his isolated house at Doornfontein. They had none of them yet had time to recover from the solemn memory of his father's funeral and the poignancy of his mother's departure from the farm in which she had lived for fifty-five years. Lisbet had watched them dismantle the old house with a calm fortitude which, in itself, was harrowing, and was now established, a little lost soul, under Maria's care. Janse's heart ached for her in her lonely bewilderment; but that was all it could do for her. He felt singularly impotent and even, at times, in the way; so, although he had nothing to do, he walked down to the office, where he found Meninsky working at a desk in his shirt-sleeves and smoking a long cigar.

'Fourth this morning, Janse,' he said. 'Half a dollar a time. It'll ruin me, mate; but them's the only things that keeps my nerves together.'

'At this rate you'll ruin them, too, I should think. Any news?'

'Any news? That's what every man down in the street there is saying. The words'll be worn out by evening. Rumours are hatching out like blow-flies – them big glossy beggars, every colour under the sun – buzzing all over the Rand Club, they are, as if they were in a trap and couldn't get out. That's where most of them's bred. Must be something rotten buried under the bar, I reckon.'

'Nothing definite at all?'

'Not unless you call this definite. Abe Bailey's had a telegram signed "Godolphin", saying the Veterinary Surgeon started last night with the horses and can back himself for seven hundred."

'What does that mean?'

'Abe Bailey don't know, so how the hell should I?'

'There's generally something behind rumours, you know.'

'Not in Johannesburg, mate – and certainly not in the Rand

516

Club. Reformers! There's only one of the lot I'd give a damn for, and that's Lionel Phillips.'

'You say that because he's a Jew.'

'I say that because he's got more brains and courage than the lot lumped together. But I'm out of it, anyway, and none of your espree decorpse is going to drag me in. You keep out of it, too, Janse. Take your Uncle Isaac's advice. Where would you be this moment if I'd let you gamble in gold-shares?'

'Me? Gamble in gold-shares? Why, I pulled you out of the market by the scruff of your neck!'

'Oh Lord, the poor beggar's lost his sense of humour!'

'I can't see any jokes this afternoon,' Janse said.

'And I can't stop smoking Havanas. Half a dollar a time. Wicked, ain't it?'

'I'm going over to the club, Meninsky.'

'Then take a fly-switch with you and a bottle of orde-Cologne, and keep away from the bar.'

The decorous Rand Club roared like the Stock Exchange, with everybody in it sweating and talking at once. The usual inhibitions had been relaxed. The bar was crowded with members in shirt-sleeves, the air dense with tobacco-smoke. Janse filled his pipe in self-defence with Magaliesberg from one of the jars of tobacco the club provided. A tall, pale-faced man came in from the Goldfields' Office and was besieged by anxious questioners.

'Yes, it's true,' he said. 'It's all up, boys. Lawley's had a telegram from the Doctor: 'The contractor has started on the earthworks with seven hundred boys; hopes to reach terminus on Wednesday." That means he's jumped off in spite of everything.'

'Wednesday? That's the day after tomorrow. He must be moving quickly.'

'Seven hundred, d'you say? He'll never get through with as few as that.'

'That's not counting the Bechuanaland Police. They'll join him later.'

'What are they doing about it over there at the Goldfields?'

'Ask me another. What can they do? If he's started, he's started. He's let us down, that's all: he and Rhodes between them.'

'I'll never believe Rhodes has let us down. There must have been some mistake. Can't they get at Jameson, anyway?'

'They've sent out two fellows on bicycles by different routes. Phillips is taking the lead. I gather they're going to form a new Committee and send representatives to Pretoria to treat with Kruger. It's the only chance of saving Jameson's life: a big Committee, with every important name on it. They've opened a book for signatures at the Goldfields.'

'Can't they send out to meet him? What's the use of all these rifles, and all these chaps drilling?'

'That's all very well. We want them. We may have to defend Johannesburg and stand a siege. The best thing to do is to join the Reform Committee and sit tight. It's odds on that Kruger will come to terms if he sees we mean business. He's always climbed down up to now.'

'It looks to me like a devil of a mess. They ought to have stopped him.'

'They tried to. Damn it all, they sent Heany along in a special train!'

'You see the market tomorrow morning! This is going to shake it up.'

'Everything really depends on whether they know in Pretoria.'

'Well, all the wires have been cut.'

'I hope to God they have!'

Janse returned to the office to find Meninsky lighting another cigar.

'Number eight,' he said, with a wink. 'A quid's worth. I shall be bust.'

'Never mind, we're all bust, anyway,' Janse said. 'He's ridden in.'

Meninsky blew a cloud of smoke into the air.

'Can't they stop him?'

'They're trying to; but I don't think they will.'

'Nor do I. That's a wilful beggar, Jameson. I knew him in Kimberley. Seen him play poker. Kind of chap who won't know when he's beaten – and, even if he did know, wouldn't believe it, if he thought Cecil Rhodes was behind him. What's more, if Rhodes wasn't behind him, he wouldn't have started.'

'Rhodes isn't a fool.'

'No, Rhodes isn't a fool: he's much worse than that, mate, he's a genius. I've watched Cecil Rhodes from the first, in the days when your brother Piet was always rubbing him into me;

and I've always distrusted him, simply because I reckon he's too damn big for Nature. When anything gets up to that size, it's bound to bust sooner or later. Look at the Great Eastern. Look at them poor ruddy mammoths – dead in ice, every one of 'em. Look at Napoleon. Think of the power that beggar had! Power? Why, d'you know he made every Jew in Europe change his name? Well, that's what happens. A sudden lapse of judgment – and pop! there's the end of it.'

'I think Phillips is doing his best.'

'You bet he is. Little Lionel's all right. Not too big – the same as I told you. What's his line?'

'I heard in the club that the Goldfields is forming a big Committee, getting everyone of importance in Johannesburg to sign. The idea is to get good terms for Jameson if he's stopped.'

'Have they asked you to sign, mate?'

'I expect they will.'

Meninsky put his cigar on the floor and ground his heel into it.

'Now, look here, Janse,' he said. 'This is serious. Don't you sign nothing, for my sake as well as your own. Now mind, mate, no nonsense!'

Janse left him. On the office door-step he ran into the tall, pale-faced man who had brought news of Jameson's last telegram to the Rand Club.

'Hullo, Grafton,' he said. 'Have you signed up yet? The book's at the Goldfields.'

'What is it all about?'

'We've simply got to strengthen Phillips's hand. He's going with Abe Bailey and two others to see Kruger in Pretoria and put our case for the last time. It's now or never. If we show a united front, the Government will climb down. We've heard from Pretoria that the old man's really rattled this time.'

'What do you want me to sign?'

'All you have to do is to record your name as a member of the new big Reform Committee. It won't bind you to anything but a general support of our claims. You signed the monster petition, didn't you?'

'Yes.'

'Well, that's all it means. Phillips is going to ask for nothing more than what we demanded then. We don't want to fight; we're determined to stop any violence; but we must stick

519

together, and the more men of standing we have with us, the stronger our bargaining hand.'

'There's no question of any rising against the Republic?'

'Good Lord, no. I've told you it's all to be on the lines of the monster petition. This movement is one of good will and conciliation, not revolution. We stand for law and order. We want to get Jameson out of the country as soon as we can and settle everything peaceably. All we're going to ask for is a square deal under the Republic flag, and I believe we shall get it. You can't have any objection to that, Grafton.'

'No. I think that's the best thing to do.'

'Then for God's sake go to the Goldfields and sign the book, there's a good fellow.'

Janse went to the Goldfields to sign.

'Is there anything to pay?'

'No, no. This simply means you become a member of the new Reform Committee. It's your name we want, not your money.'

As he took up the pen that was handed to him, Janse remembered Meninsky's warning. 'What on earth am I doing?' he thought.

'I'm going to think this over,' he said.

'All right – but you needn't run off with my pen.'

Janse laughed, apologized, and handed it back. He was to thank his stars and Meninsky a week later when every single man who had signed that book at the Goldfields was arrested and packed off to jail in Pretoria.

Walking back to Doornfontein, he saw shopkeepers barricading their windows with planks. The *Star* had rushed out a special edition. He bought one and glanced at the headlines:

CROSSED THE BORDER
FORCES MAKING FOR JOHANNESBURG
CONFLICT LAMENTABLY IMMINENT
SUSPENSE AT AN END

The approaches to the Park Station were blocked by a crowd through which he found it impossible to make his way; so he allowed himself, partly out of curiosity, to be carried along with the concourse. Two mail-trains stood waiting in the station, one for the Cape, and another for Natal. Every seat in both of them was already filled, though they were not due to start for several hours. Most of the coaches were full of women and children; but one, crammed with Cornish miners, was surrounded by an angry, hooting crowd. Somebody had sprawled the words 'Cowards' Van' on the side of it. Hysterical women were running about with handfuls of white feathers. One had stuck a feather in Janse's button-hole before he knew what she was about. A railway official came shouting along the platform:

'No more tickets will be issued to men! No more tickets will be issued to men!'

Janse fought his way back to the station entrance. The crowd was still pouring in; there seemed no end to it. It was past ten o'clock when he reached his home. His mother had gone to bed, but Maria and Lena were waiting up for him, with anxious faces, pale against their mourning black.

'Well ...?' Maria said.

Janse handed the crumpled *Star* to her.

'It seems Jameson's crossed the border from Pitsani,' he said.

Lena gasped:

'Pitsani. But that's where Jimmy is,' she cried. 'Oh, Janse ... Janse!'

Maria put her arm round her.

Janse went out into the garden and looked at the stars through the motionless, plumey tops of the blue gums. The night was uncannily quiet – he could not think why, until of a sudden he realized that the usual background of sound – the thudding of the stamps in the batteries of the Central Rand – was absent. It was as though the heart of Johannesburg had stopped beating ...

Jameson's column advanced by forced marches. Jimmy Grafton had always prided himself on being pretty tough; but forty-eight hours in the saddle, with no chance of sleep, and never more than two hours of rest at a time, was more than he, or any of the others, had bargained for. The horses, too, were beginning to feel the strain. Though the dumps of food and forage along the road never failed, neither man nor beast had time to eat or digest; so the headlong pace of the cavalcade began to falter.

The flat landscape rolled by in a dreamlike monotony: not a bird, not a beast, not a tree not a human figure. The very farms

521

seemed deserted. That was all to the good; for surprise was the essence of success, and surprise seemed to be assured. Thanks to his letter from Rhodes (and possibly his Eton accent) Jimmy found himself transferred from his squadron to the Headquarters staff as an orderly, and rode within a few yards of Jameson, who quickly recognized him.

'You're Piet Grafton's boy, aren't you?' he said. 'How old are you? Under twenty? Well, you're starting the dangerous life early, my lad: You're a lucky young devil, isn't he, Willoughby?'

He laughed. Jimmy noticed that Jameson laughed and joked a great deal. He thought him charming, and now understood why the trooper on his left had said he would follow him to hell; for there was something extraordinarily gallant about this yellow-skinned, bald little fellow. He did not perceive, beneath Jameson's forced levity, a man whose nerves were strained to a cruel pitch and who was forcing himself to laugh.

During the morning, the messenger who had set out from Mafeking in pursuit of them rode up on a foam-flecked horse, and handed Jameson the High Commissioner's order recalling him. The Doctor glanced at it hurriedly.

'What's your name?' he asked.

'Sergeant White, sir.'

'Your name suits you, Sergeant. You look like a ghost.'

'I've ridden all night, sir, and covered eighty miles. I was stopped by the Boers at Malmani and held up for four hours.'

'The devil you were! D'you hear that, Willoughby? How many were there, Sergeant?'

'It was the Landdrost, Marais, sir, with four or five men.'

'Well, you'd better get some breakfast. Grafton, see that the Sergeant gets a good meal and has a fresh horse.'

The man stood firm at attention.

'I have orders to take back a reply to this message, sir.'

'What had we better say, Willoughby? It's just what I expected.'

'Better say the dispatch had been received and that we'll attend to it.'

'Very well. Do you hear what Sir John Willoughby says, Sergeant? Now go and get some food and a drink. We'll look after your horse.'

The bugle sounded 'Boot and Saddle'. The column moved forward again.

About noon a Boer messenger was brought in by two troopers of the advance-guard with another protest – this time from the Commandant of the Marico District.

'This headquarters is becoming a regular post-office,' Jameson said. 'Get some paper and a pencil – you'll find them in my saddle-bag, Grafton – and put down what I dictate. I've a doctor's fist, and nobody but a qualified chemist can read it. Are you ready?'

'Yes, sir.'

'Very well, then. What is the date? December the thirtieth. Put that down. Now begin:

'*Sir,*

'*I am in receipt of your protest of the above date, and have to inform you that I intend proceeding with my original plans, which have no hostile intentions against the people of the Transvaal; but we are here in reply to an invitation from the principal inhabitants of the Rand and to assist them in their demand for justice and . . . let me see . . . and the ordinary rights of every citizen of a civilized state.*
'*Yours faithfully. . . .*'

'Give it to me and I'll sign it. H'm, your writing's quite fairly legible. One up for Eton!'

He signed the letter and handed it to the Boer messenger.

They rode on in silence, with half-hour halts at the end of every twentieth mile for rations and rest and water for men and horses. They were no sooner out of the saddle, it seemed to Jimmy, than the bugle sounded for them to remount and ride on. He was so short of sleep that, from time to time, he found himself nodding in the saddle and ready to drop from it. The column moved on before him in its usual marching order; first a patrol of picked scouts, with the man who acted as guide; next the advance-guard, a troop with a Maxim; then the main body of mounted police with four Maxims, the artillery, and all the wheeled transport; and last the rear-guard, with the remaining machine-gun.

They were moving now through rather more populous country. In the distance they sighted numbers of Boers riding or driving wagons; but all the farms they passed appeared to have been recently abandoned, and there was no sign of armed opposition. Jimmy lost all count of time. He was too dazed to reckon how many hours they had been on the march. When they halted at night the men were too exhausted to eat, and lay sprawled on the veld, dog-tired, beside their horses. Lying there, half asleep, Jimmy heard Jameson talking to Willoughby:

'Man, d'you realize this is actually New Year's Eve? This is a great night in Scotland! There'll be crowds singing "Auld Lang Syne" in Prince's Street and Sauchiehall Street – and not one of them ever dreaming what's happening here.' He chuckled to himself. 'It's an odd world, Willoughby.'

A very odd world, Jimmy thought, in which the only thing that really mattered was sleep. He rolled over and closed his eyes, and wondered if he might be blessed with a dream of Lena.

At half past three, in the middle of the night, the sound of tramping feet woke him. One of the advance-guard had been wounded by a shot from a sniper and carried back. The rear-guard reported a party of sixty Boers a mile behind them. Two other, larger, detachments were shadowing both flanks, and a fourth was slowly retreating on Krugersdorp. Things were evidently growing warmer; so Willoughby ordered the column to saddle-up and stand to arms until daylight. It was clear that they no longer had the element of surprise in their favour; yet even when they moved on at dawn there was no attack. It would have been less nervous work if there had been one.

In the middle of the morning, the two dusty cyclists from Johannesburg appeared, with letters hidden in the pillars of their bicycles. Jameson eagerly read them aloud. The first was from Frankie Rhodes:

Dear Dr.,
    The rumour of massacre in Johannesburg that started you to our relief was not true. We are all right. Feeling intense. We have armed a lot of men. Shall be very glad to see you. We are not in possession of the town . . . ('Which town does the silly ass mean? Pretoria?') *We will send out some men to meet you. You are a fine fellow. Yours ever, F. R.*
    We will drink a glass along o' you. L. P.

'That's Phillips. He must have been thinking of New Year's Eve.'

He read the second: 'This is from Frankie, too.'

524

31st. 11.30 – Kruger has asked for some of us to go over and treat: armistice for 24 hours agreed to. My view is that they are in a funk at Pretoria, and they were wrong to agree from here. F. R.

Jameson questioned the riders. One was Dutch and the other English. They told him there had been no fighting as yet in Johannesburg and that the town was being policed by the Reform Committee. They had passed through a force of three hundred and fifty men under Potgieter, and five other commandos were expected to join him at Krugersdorp.

'That means a big force,' Jameson said. 'We had better push on and try to prevent their joining.'

He dictated another letter to Jimmy:

'As you imagine, we are well pleased by your letter. We have had some fighting . . . (Jimmy looked up inquiringly) . . . and hope to reach Johannesburg tonight; but of course it will be pleased to have 200 men meet us at Krugersdorp, as it will depend on the amount of fighting we have. Of course we shall greatly encourage the men, who are in great heart although a bit tired. Love to Sam, Phillips and rest.'

He turned to the messengers with a smile.

'Do you think you can get this back to Colonel Rhodes?'

'You bet we will, sir.'

'All right, then. Best of luck.'

The column moved forward again . . .

As soon as the first rumours of the raid reached Piet in Capetown on Sunday evening he hired a cab and drove out to Groote Schuur to see Cecil Rhodes. The white house looked as gracious and reassuringly peaceful as ever. Doves crooned in the trees; the great banks of hydrangeas fell away down the slope in a mist of soft blue. But Groote Schuur was strangely, intimidatingly quiet. When he rang the bell, nobody answered. In the distance Piet saw Rhodes' native servant, who knew him. He called him by name.

'I want to see the *inkos*', Tony,' he said, 'Go and tell him I'm waiting.'

The *inkos*' was locked in his bedroom, Tony said, and had given an order that he must not be disturbed.

525

Piet wandered over the house and almost fell into the arms of Rhodes' secretary, Milton.

'Thank goodness there's someone alive in this place,' he said. 'I want to see the old man.'

'You can't possibly see him. He won't see anybody.'

'I'm certain he would see me.'

'Not a ghost of a chance. He's ill.'

'Will you give him a message from me?'

'What sort of message?'

'Just say that I'm here and would like to see him, and that I'm very worried about these Johannesburg rumours. You see, my boy is with Jameson.'

'Well. . . . Yes: I'll do that if you like.'

After an interval that seemed endless, Milton returned.

'He won't see you; I told you he wouldn't,' he said. 'But as for Johannesburg, he told me to say: That it's all right.'

'All right? What does that mean?'

Milton shrugged his shoulders.

'That's what he told me to tell you.'

Piet drove back to Capetown, discomfited. The whole town was shut up, for it was Sunday; a crowd of coloured people listlessly paraded the streets. During a sleepless night he made up his mind. Next morning, by half past eight, he was waiting on his stockbroker's doorstep.

'Look here,' he said, 'do you know what's happening in Johannesburg?'

'No more than you, Mr. Grafton. I've been trying to get through to my partners. It looks to me as if the Exchange is closed.'

'I want you to sell some shares for me.'

'You won't find buyers in Johannesburg – nor here, for that matter.'

'Well, sell in London, in Paris, in New York. I want to unload.'

'I think you should wait a bit, if you'll take my advice.'

'Damn it, man, I don't want your advice. I'm giving you instructions. You can't sniff at the brokerage on a quarter of a million. Whether these rumours are true or false, Kaffirs are going to crash.'

'And a quarter of a million of sales will help them downward? I see. You know more about mines than I do. You may be right, if you're looking to take your pick at bargain-prices.

All right. Give me a list of what you want me to sell. Don't forget that the New Year's holiday may complicate matters.'

Piet gave him the list he had written out in his bedroom at the hotel. He sold only speculative counters; but he had been careful even in his speculations, and knew that every one of the shares he sold would be worth buying back at the bottom of the market. With any luck, he should stand to net half a million. He was glad he was not in Johannesburg, anyway; for if he had been there he would have been compelled to take sides, and he wasn't certain, as yet, which side would win. There was nothing to worry about. Whatever happened, old Janse would look after Lavinia and the children; and Jameson would see that young Jimmy came to no harm.

Still he could not be happy until he had seen Rhodes and questioned him. In the afternoon he drove out again to Groote Schuur and inquired if the Prime Minister was better. He was up the mountain, they told him, and had been there all day. Piet left a message to say he would call again after dinner. That was the time, as he knew, when Rhodes was always at his best and most talkative. A hint, at this moment, from the only man in Capetown who knew, might be worth a lot of money.

As he walked down the tree-shaded drive to the house, he saw two figures advancing to meet him. One was Rhodes' man, carrying a lantern, the other William Schreiner, the Attorney-General. Piet stood in their path.

'Hello, Schreiner, what are you doing here? Has Rhodes finished dinner?'

'I left him in the library; but I don't think you'd better try to see him, if that's what you're after.'

'Then it's true?'

'Yes, it's true. Jameson's ridden in. This is a tragedy, Grafton, a tragedy.'

'I'm an old friend of Rhodes's, you know, Schreiner; so you can speak to me frankly. Did he try to stop Jameson?'

'He thought he had stopped him; but Jameson had cut the wires. "Old Jameson's upset my applecart": that's what he says. When I told him he still ought to try to stop him, he went to pieces and simply refused to do anything. I don't think he's capable of action. The man's broken down – broken down. The most painful thing I ever saw in my life. If you're his friend and have any feelings, you'd very much better leave him alone.'

The rumours reached Adrian as he rode into Pretoria on New

Year's Day. He went straight to Paul Kruger's house. A crowd of angry Raad members were waiting and arguing volubly on the stoep, but Oom Paul was not there.

'The President's saddling his old white horse,' one said. 'He's out at the back; but if I were you I'd steer clear of him.'

'Then it's true?'

'Yes, they're moving on Krugersdorp. Potgieter's waiting for them there, and Cronjé will join him from Potchefstroom.'

'How many are there?'

'Eight hundred, they said at first; but I think there are less. Five hundred, perhaps.'

'They'll never get through, then.'

'No. But there'll be some fighting. Oom Paul wants to go to the front himself.'

'That must not be allowed.'

'*Allowed?* You say that of Paul Kruger?'

The old man stumped in, breathing heavily; his face was purple-black like a thundercloud.

'Ah, Grafton,' he said, 'this is good: you're the man I've been looking for. I want you to take a message to Piet Cronjé at Krugersdorp. These fellows here would like me to hang Jameson and shoot his *rooinekke*. They're wrong.'

'These men are rebels, President, and that is what rebels deserve,' an old man exclaimed.

'If we shot every rebel in this country, Oom Koos,' Kruger said sardonically, 'there'ld be no more foreigners left to pay the taxes, and you'd have to pay them yourself. Which is more valuable – a live horse or a dead one? It's no good making Jameson a martyr by shooting him and turning the English against us, when we can get all we want by holding him prisoner. Every man we can take alive is valuable. Let them pay for their heroes!' He turned to Adrian: 'That's what I want you to make clear to Piet Cronjé, nephew. Tell him from me that dead men are no use to me, but that every prisoner is worth his weight in gold. The leaders in Johannesburg now want to talk with me. With Jameson in jail I shall be able to talk more loudly. Now go quickly, and God be with you.'

It was late at night when Adrian reached Krugersdorp and delivered his message to Cronjé. All that afternoon there had been desultory fighting, which had included a futile charge by the raiders on the stony ridge that separated them from Krugersdorp. Willoughby had shelled the slope with his seven-and twelve-pounders, without doing much damage, and a following frontal attack on the position had failed.

'We could have killed many more,' Cronjé said, 'if we could afford to waste ammunition; but sixty rounds a man does not leave us much margin, and who knows when more may come up?'

'The fewer you kill the better,' Adrian insisted. 'The President wants you to surround them and force a surrender.'

'We can do that well enough,' Cronjé said. 'At first we thought there were over a thousand of them, but I doubt if there are half as many. More burghers are riding into Krugersdorp every hour, and if we can keep the *rooinekke* from advancing until we are strong enough, we shall have them in our pockets. They know by now that they cannot carry that ridge; so I think they will try to move to the south, and I shall not stop them. The best thing now is to give them a wakeful night. If you are going back to Pretoria, you can tell Oom Paul that I'm sure we have got them.'

'I shall not go back to Pretoria, Oom Piet,' Adrian said. 'I shall stay till the end. But what about Johannesburg?'

'The scouts say, not a man has left Johannesburg; and in any case our rear is well guarded. The Johannesburgers are better at talking and signing petitions than fighting. Only wait, and all will come right.'

Early that evening Major Villiers rode into Jameson's Headquarters to report that the country farther to the south was open. The whole force swung right, in the dusk, and climbed the Witwatersrand to establish itself, without opposition, among the mine-buildings of Luipaard's Vlei. From this point, another road led straight to Johannesburg. As they halted they heard what sounded like Maxim-fire straight ahead, on the outskirts of Krugersdorp.

'That's Frankie Rhodes,' Jameson said exultantly. 'He's moved out of Johannesburg and is attacking the Boers' rear. We'd better press on and join him.'

The weary column re-formed and rode on; but the firing in Krugersdorp had not come from Frank Rhodes. A commando of Boers had ridden in there at nightfall, and had fired their rifles in the air to celebrate their coming. Piet Cronjé had thrown these new arrivals into the fight at once. They were advancing in force along the coveted road. Flankers rode in, reporting that other bodies of men were converging from north, east and south. The raiders' fresh hopes had been dashed, and they were in no humour for fighting. Jameson decided to bivouac for the night.

It was a hellish night for them all, as Cronjé had promised Adrian that it would be. Jimmy Grafton, in spite of his tiredness, could not sleep a wink. The Boer snipers fired on them as they lay in the dark, creeping up to within a hundred yards of the bivouac. Though the outposts' Maxims occasionally silenced them, sweeping the front with a blind fire, stray sniping continued all night. Only two men were killed and two wounded, but the losses among the horses and mules were heavy and horrible. Jimmy began to think that war was not so romantic as he had been told.

Still Jameson, that little, yellow-faced bundle of nerves, was cheerful, and at dawn they advanced along the road to Johannesburg, continually resisted and sniped at from either flank.

'We're not more than twenty miles from Johannesburg now,' he said.

'Give us open ground, and we'll do it,' Willoughby answered. 'I don't like all those damned mining-dumps and head-gears: they give too much cover. It may be the longest way round, but we can move much more rapidly if we keep to the south.'

'Very good. You're the man in command.'

It was seven miles farther round; but the horses were better rested now, and the column moved at a fast trot over the open ground, under a sporadic dropping fire from either flank.

'We ought to get round them at this rate,' Jameson said cheerfully.

But the Boers, four hundred of them, moving on interior lines, were already in front of them, astride the road between them and their goal, on a stony ridge.

'Well, we've got to shell them out of it first, and then rush it,' Willoughby said cheerfully.

He brought up the guns and the ridge was shelled methodically. Then Charles Coventry lead the assault. It was an exhilarating and terrible sight, Jimmy thought, to see the line sweeping forward in extended order. Jameson watched the charge through his field glasses, while Jimmy stood beside him, eagerly listening to his rapid commentary as the attackers went on and on under a murderous selective fire.

'They've reached the top, they're over it,' Jameson cried.

'We're through ... we're through! My God, Charlie Coventry's hit, though, and so is Barry!'

The main body surged on up the slope behind the attackers, passing between the fallen horses and men on the ridge. They looked down on the other side and saw the deadly trap into which they had plunged with such reckless gallantry. Round their front, at their feet, lay a semi-circle of marshland with a brook running through it. At one point – and only one – a drift made the brook fordable; but this drift was commanded by a precipitous kopje on which the Boers were already posted. Even when the drift had been crossed – if it could be crossed – the road would be swept from either side from rocky slopes on which trenches had been dug and manned. They could not move forward, save at a terrible and incalculable cost. They could not move backward; for already superior forces were crowding in on the rear-guard. They could only stay where they were, and make what answer they could to the fire of an enemy whose position could only be guessed at from the white puffs of powder-smoke that dotted the hillsides. There was no cover; there could be no cover for them on that naked slope. The men and the horses were dead-beat, for they had marched a hundred and sixty-nine miles in eighty-six hours, and had fought more or less continuously without food during the last seventeen. The morning sun glared down on them as they lay on their empty bellies and fired at those malicious puffs of smoke which they could not disperse. At nine-fifteen somebody put up a white flag. Nobody knows to this day who raised it, and it seems hardly to matter ... .

The Jameson Raid was over. It had failed before ever it began; but before it failed, it had come within fourteen miles of its object: Johannesburg. The raiders had lost forty-eight men, killed and wounded. It seemed curious to Jimmy that he himself should have come through without so much as a scratch.

So Willoughby sent his offer of surrender through the drift, and Cronjé accepted it. Jameson and his officers waited for him to come over in a stone-walled cattle-kraal on the edge of the stream. He rode up, a harsh and sinister figure, Jimmy thought, and solemnly saluted.

'Dr. Jameson,' he said, 'I have the honour to meet you.'

For three days the crowds in the streets of Johannesburg had

531

been buoyed up with false hopes or tormented with vague anxieties. They had been crushed, too, by news of a railway disaster which had befallen one of the trains full of refugees on the way to Natal, with a loss of thirty women and children. They had been harangued from the windows of the Goldfields office, and had besieged it with cries of: 'Tell us the truth,' and 'Where is the Doctor?' and 'Have you deserted him?' They had heard, with anger, the news of the High Commissioner's injunction. When, late at night, they learnt the truth they had asked for from the lips of Frank Rhodes and James Leonard and Bailey, they broke into a tumult of rage against the Reformers. The crowd booed and hissed and swayed so uglily in the street outside the Goldfields that Janse, who had been waiting to hear the news, struggled through the press and made his way to Doornfontein.

When he reached the house, Maria and Lena were waiting up for him. Carel Strijdom was with them, looking terribly intense and pale. All three gazed at Janse anxiously; but only Lena spoke.

'Is it all right, Janse?'

'It's over. Jameson's surrendered.'

"But Jimmy?' Lena cried.

'We can't tell, my child. They've taken the prisoners and the wounded straight to Pretoria.'

'Then we must go to Pretoria, Janse, and find Uncle Adrian. I'm sure he will let me see him. Will you take me, Janse?'

'Tonight?'

'I must go tonight. He may be wounded, Janse.' ('He may be killed, my child,' Janse thought, and his heart went cold.) 'I can't stand any more,' she said. 'Do take me, Janse darling.'

Janse sighed and kissed her pale face.

'All right. I'll take you, little one. We'll put in the horses and drive to Pretoria at once.'

'Oh, Janse, how good you are to me!'

They went out together . . .

'Yes, Janse is good to her,' Carel Strijdom said.

'Janse is good to everyone,' Maria replied. 'Poor Janse's a saint if ever there was one on earth. The child is right, too, when she says she can't stand any more. She's suffered dreadfully. It's a terrible thing to be faced with such uncertainty when one is young and in love. You and I are old and hard, Carel.'

'You could never be hard, Maria.'

'Things like this make one hard and rather hopeless, Carel. The other day, when we came back from Blauwkrans, I felt a kind of new inspiration – I hardly know how to describe it. I felt, somehow, as if life had changed for me, as if I'd discovered something for which I'd been groping: a new ideal worth living for. The sky grew suddenly clearer.'

'I know, Maria, I know. I felt that with you.'

She smiled. 'I think you feel many things with me, Carel.'

'I want to feel everything with you. You know that, Maria.'

'And then comes this awful, brutal, careless folly, to smash up all our poor little new-born hopes. I don't want to be bitter. But if Mr. Rhodes has really done this, as they say, I think he must be the devil.'

'Satan's sin was the pride of power, and that is Rhodes's. Power has driven him mad. But you're right. This raid of Jameson's will not be forgotten in this generation, perhaps not in the next. It has put back the clock twenty years. And not only that. The dreadful thing about it all is that violence breeds more violence. Yet we know our ideals are right. We still must keep faith.'

'You have faith, after this? I think that is wonderful of you. Can't you give me a little share of it?'

'I have long since given you everything I possess, Maria; it's all there for the taking. If you could only forget the past – I mean the whole past – and begin again with me! We should both of us be far stronger together than we can be apart.'

He watched her harrowed face eagerly, but she did not answer. Her head was downcast and he could not see her eyes. But her hands moved slowly; he wondered what she was doing, till he saw she had slipped Cecil Rhodes' ring from her finger. It lay there in her outstretched palm, the flawed diamond sparking brilliantly as she offered it to him.

'Take this, Carel,' she said, 'and do what you like with it. I don't want to see it again.' She shuddered. 'There is blood on the hands that gave it me.'

Carel Strijdom took the ring from her palm. He went out on to the stoep and sent it spinning away to fall, unheard, in the undergrowth between the dark trees. When he returned to the lamp-lit room, Maria was still standing, a slender, black-clothed

533

figure, where he had left her; but her solemn face was now raised and her eyes met his.

'It is done,' he said, as he held out his arms to her, 'and now we begin again, my love.'

'Yes, now we begin again,' she said. 'One people . . . one land. . . .'

Janse roused the Kaffirs in their malodorous shack at the bottom of the garden, ordering them to fetch Meninsky's horse from the stable and 'put to' in the slap-up cape-cart. They obeyed him sluggishly and without curiosity: the ways of white men were unaccountable. Lena watched their slow-moving lantern-lights with impatience, but did not speak. Janse felt her restlessness; but he, also, was silent – not only distrusting his power of consoling or reassuring her, but also ruefully aware, as never before, of his own small importance in her life compared with Jimmy. When the cape-cart was ready and they mounted the driving-seat, he turned the horse's head westward.

'Where are you going?' Lena asked quickly. 'This isn't the way to Pretoria.'

'We must give your Aunt Lavinia the chance of coming with us.'

'Aunt Lavinia? Oh, Janse . . .'

'After all, she's his mother, Lena.'

She sighed. 'I suppose we must; but I wish we didn't have to.'

He left her outside Piet's house, while he knocked up Lavinia who was fast asleep.

'Of course I must come with you,' Lavinia said, 'but I do think you might have let me know earlier, Janse. This is most inconvenient. I don't even know what time it is.'

'Just on midnight. I only heard the news myself a short time ago.'

'Well, you'll have to wait. I must waken the governess and make all sorts of arrangements. What a pity Piet isn't here. If he hadn't felt it his duty to go to the Cape, they wouldn't have made such a hash of everything.'

She took more than half an hour to prepare herself for the journey. When she emerged at last and saw Lena's shadowy form, she made no attempt to conceal her displeasure.

'What's that child doing here?' she asked.

534

'It was she who insisted on going to Pretoria tonight. You now that Jimmy and she are in love with one another?'

'In love? She and Jimmy? I never heard such nonsense. iet would never permit it. They're just a couple of children.'

'Well, don't tell her that, for God's sake,' Janse said huredly, 'or she'll probably break down. She feels all this insely.'

Lavinia laughed. 'Oddly enough, so do I. But you may be sure don't want any scenes at this time of night.'

It was not a comfortable journey. Janse, wedged in between em, was conscious, all the time, of Lavinia's indignant hosity towards Lena. It was strange, he thought, how much more sily a silent dislike could make itself felt than a silent love. He new it was beyond his power to smooth over the differences etween such incompatibles – as well try to reconcile fire and e. So he left them alone.

They reached Pretoria at daybreak. On the outskirts, senies challenged them. The streets were lined with bivouacs of obilized burghers and detachments of the State Artillery. drian's name, as usual, proved itself a sufficient passport; but nse was by no means sure that Adrian himself would be as commodating as the sentries; he knew that mentioning Piet ould make his brother bristle, and drove on to the outspan, here he expected to find him, in a doubtful mood.

He had never, indeed, found Adrian so grim and unpromisg. When he saw Janse limping towards him, he did not even nile.

'What are you doing here?' he said roughly. 'Your damned hannesburgers have made a fine mess of things now.'

'I've brought over Lavinia and Lena,' Janse told him. 'I want ou to get them a pass to see Jimmy, Piet's boy.'

'Piet's boy? I know nothing about him. I thought he was in ngland.'

'He's a trooper in Jameson's Mashonaland Police. If he's ive, he's a prisoner.'

'Like father, like son! What have I to do with such aitors?'

'Piet's our brother, Adrian.'

'Piet's no brother of mine. I know more about Piet than you o. I spared his life fifteen years ago on the Majuba. If I had one my duty then he'd certainly have been shot – and a

535

damned good riddance! Why should I worry myself about his son?'

'Jimmy's a decent lad. There's no question of his being a traitor. As a soldier he has to obey his superiors' orders. We can't blame him for that. His poor mother doesn't even know if the boy's alive.'

'Well ... I'll do what I can,' Adrian said. 'Where's Piet himself?'

'At the Cape.'

Adrian laughed. 'He would be. You can trust our little brother to look after his skin.'

It should not have been difficult for a man in Adrian's position to obtain a permit to visit the Raiders' camp. Apart from Jameson and his officers, who were under strict guard, they had been treated with kindness and even with laxity. Even so, it took him the greater part of the day – during which Janse deposited the two women in a back room of the hotel before which, on the day of Loch's visit, Paul Kruger had been left marooned in his horseless carriage – to get what he wanted. Janse limped with him from office to office through the hot streets. All officials were wary and evasive. They still feared unreasonably, had they but known it – an attack from Johannesburg, and it was late afternoon before Janse received the three passes which the President himself had signed at Adrian's request.

'Now I have done what I can,' Adrian said. 'Don't ask me for more, Janse.'

'I shall ask for no more,' Janse said.

He tramped back to the hotel, collected Lavinia and Lena and drove them to the wired compound where the prisoners were lodged. They were kept waiting at the gate, in spite of their passes, until Janse recognized among the prison-guard the *Vee Boer*, Trichard, who had given him his liberty after the fight at Bronkhorst Spruit.

'It seems you are always mixed up with the English, nephew,' the old man said suspiciously; 'but since the President has signed your passes I will do what I can – though there's little time to spare: at sunset the gates will be closed.'

He turned away and was lost among the scattered groups of war-worn, dishevelled prisoners. As the dwindling moments passed, and still he did not return, Janse's heart grew sick with suspense. Supposing that, after all, the boy was not there, but

536

lay dead and hurriedly buried under the shadow of Doornkop? He dared not look at Lavinia or Lena, for he knew they must be suffering even more than himself.

Then, suddenly, he heard Lena's excited voice: 'He's there, Janse. . . . He's coming!' and lifted his eyes to see Jimmy's slim figure hurrying towards them in old Trichard's wake. 'What did I tell you, Janse?' she cried. 'I knew it. . . . I always knew that Jimmy was safe. Oh, Janse, how happy I am!'

Lavinia contemplated this enthusiasm with disapproval.

'We must send Piet a telegram as soon as we can,' she said. But her voice, too, was broken.

Janse left them there in Pretoria and drove slowly back over the veld towards Johannesburg. The night was so dark that nothing save the ruts of the wagon-tracks assured him of his course, and only the dips of the Six Mile Spruit and the Yokeskey River measured his progress. He welcomed the darkness no less than the solitude, for his mood, too, was darkened. The events of the last three weeks seemed to mark the end of one period in existence and the beginning of another; he had reached a spiritual as well as a bodily climacteric, and this obscure, solitary journey was in keeping with the solemnity of his thoughts, affording him the opportunity of mustering them and adjusting himself to a new condition of life.

First of all, he knew he had lost Lena. When these troublous times were over, she and Jimmy would probably marry. Her presence would no longer brighten his house at Doornfontein. Though he might see her often, their relationship must inevitably lose its intimacy. Again, Wonderfontein, where he had been born and lived as a child, was gone for ever, and the death of his father, though it had moved him with pity for his mother rather than sorrow, with awe rather than pain, reminded him that he himself had in all probability spent more than two-thirds of his life. Janse neither resented this discovery nor rebelled against it. Yet the prospect of a lonely old age to be spent among strangers in surroundings made melancholy by wistful reminders of past happiness was not welcome to him. And why, after all, he asked himself, should he accept it? Why should he stay on the Rand? There was one place in the world where, as he remembered it, a man could be happy in complete solitude. And that was the Low Country.

The Low Country. . . . Even now, as his thoughts returned to it, he was caught by a burning desire to seek sanctuary in that savage, lovely wilderness, to immerse himself once more in its primordial peace. Who could blame him for wishing to end his days in his spirit's home? But now, as he thought of the Low Veld, and saw himself, in imagination, at their old summer camp on the face of the Berg, looking down into the green recesses of Brunner's Spruit where the cataract thundered, and over the rolling thorn-savannahs to the sea-lit sky beyond the Lebombo Hills, the vision widened: he became aware not merely of that immediate landscape but of the whole mountain-chain of the Drakensberg outstretched over half a continent, from the Stormberg and the barren peaks of Basutoland to Groot Andries' Zoutpansberg. Within the range's gigantic ramparts he imagined the grass-plains of the Free State and Transvaal; beyond them, the green, tumbled hills of Natal; the Eastern Province from which his forbears had trekked, the two Karroos, and, pointing south to the pole, the Cape of Storms on which two oceans thundered. From the vantage-point of that speck on the crown of the High Veld which was his slow-moving cape-cart, Janse's inward eye covered the whole subcontinent lying vast and silent beneath the blackness of night.

He had never before envisaged South Africa as a whole; but now, as his lonely imagination brooded over its magnitude and variety, he was seized with an unfamiliar emotion of mingled awe and pride.

'This great land is my land,' he told himself, 'my possession, my birthright, and those who, like myself, are born of it are my brothers. There is no greater wealth or amplitude or beauty than this bestowed on any other men living on this earth. There is room and sustenance for a great nation within our boundaries, and yet we, a small sprinkling of two races born of the self-same stock, must forever be grudging and jealous and full of suspicion and ready to fly at each other's throats! Was there ever a folly more monstrous than this?' he asked himself. 'Was there ever a stupidity more unreasonable or more petty than this blind rejection of such a superb inheritance which it should be our pride to share and enjoy? And yet none of us is guiltless in this: even I, to my shame, am not guiltless. It is my duty, for what I am worth, to make amends.'

Janse suddenly pulled up his horse and left it to graze. In this moment of surprising conversion or revelation, he seemed to need an even completer solitude. He limped away from the track until he felt himself utterly isolated between the two dark immensities of earth and sky. There, obedient to a strange impulse, he fell to his knees and prayed silently to the God whom, since childhood, he had almost forgotten. He prayed that he might be given the power to fight against discord and prejudice, not only among others but in his own heart; time to justify the purposeless years that had passed by dedicating what remained of his life to the conscious fostering of peace and good will; faith and courage to master the discouragement, the scorn, the frustration with which he knew he would be faced.

Even though he was alone, he felt slightly embarrassed by this secret indulgence of an impulse so foreign to his nature as he knew it; yet, when he had disburdened his soul of its passionate content, he found himself strangely relieved and happy, and even confident, and went on his way with a lightened heart. For the first time in his life, and late in it, he knew he had found a vocation.

An hour later, still conscious of this serene exaltation, he climbed through the kloof to the brow of the Witwatersrand and looked down on the scattered lights of Johannesburg. It was here, he told himself, in this prodigious City of Gold – where not merely the wealth but the most vital energy and intelligence of the land were concentrated – that he would find the opportunity for justifying his new-born devotion, the field for the labour of love which would absorb the remainder of his life. It lay there, sprawled at his feet, this turbulent microcosm, its hopes and fears, its loves and hatreds, its degradations and splendours stilled by a deathlike sleep. And yet, as he gazed on it, he became aware that the city was not only alive but also awake. Since the time when he left it, twenty-four hours earlier, a change had come over it. Then, as he remembered, it had lain, as though stunned, in a mortal silence. Now, there came to his ears a far, sullen rumour, faint but persistent. The great batteries of the Central Rand were already at work. The heart of Johannesburg had begun to beat again.

BEST SELLING MAYFLOWER TITLES

All these books are available at your local bookshop or newsagent; or can be ordered direct from the publisher. Just tick the titles you want and fill in the form below.

Write to **Mayflower Cash Sales**, Kernick Rd. Industrial Site, Penryn, Cornwall.
Please send cheque or postal order value of the cover price
plus 9d. for postage and packing.

Name ....

Address ....

....

AN AMERICAN DREAM 5/-
Norman Mailer

Author of *The Naked and the Dead*

There is nothing insubstantial or fairylike
about *An American Dream*. It is a great
powerhouse of a novel; a masterpiece of brutal
realism; a blend of raw sex and tender love,
hate and brutality, Good and Evil, with all the
terrifying tension and pent-up violence of an
awakening volcano.

With *An American Dream* Mailer reaffirms
his towering stature as a novelist. Using the
framework of a first-rate detective story,
he has created much more—an epic of our own
time, a triumphant return to the greatness
which made *The Naked and the Dead* the
outstanding novel of World War II.

ALL QUIET ON THE WESTERN FRONT 5/-

Erich Maria Remarque

Erich Maria Remarque belongs to a family of
French extraction that emigrated into
Germany at the time of the French Revolution
and settled in the Rhineland. In 1914 at the
age of 18 he went straight from school into the
army and was sent to the Western Front.
During the course of the war his mother died
and all his friends were killed. At the end of
the war he found himself alone in the world.
He wrote his book, without taking previous
thought, about his own and his friends'
experiences in the war. It arose out of the
consideration that so many men of his
generation, who were yet still young,
nevertheless lived a friendless, embittered,
resigned life without knowing why.
All Quiet on the Western Front
sets out to describe three things: the war, the
fate of a generation and true comradeship.